W9-ASZ-148

TRANCE

TRANCE

CHRISTOPHER SORRENTINO

FARRAR, STRAUS AND GIROUX
New York

Farrar, Straus and Giroux
19 Union Square West, New York 10003

Distributed in Canada by Douglas & McIntyre Ltd.
Printed in the United States of America
First edition, 2005

Library of Congress Cataloging-in-Publication Data
Sorrentino, Christopher, 1963–
    Trance / Christopher Sorrentino.
        p.   cm.
    ISBN-13: 978-0-374-27864-9
    ISBN-10: 0-374-27864-4 (alk. paper)
    1. Hearst, Patricia, 1954—Fiction.   2. Symbionese Liberation Army—Fiction.
3. Los Angeles (Calif.)—Fiction.   4. Kidnapping victims—Fiction.   5. Guerrillas—
Fiction.   I. Title.

PS3569.O697T73 2005
813'.54—dc22   2004058333

www.fsgbooks.com

1   3   5   7   9   10   8   6   4   2

This book is for Violet

Distilled to their essence, revolutions
are acts of supreme creativity.

—"THE REVOLUTION IN MILITARY AFFAIRS
AND CONFLICT SHORT OF WAR,"
BY STEVEN METZ AND JAMES KIEVIT

PART ONE

In Darkness,
in the Deeps

. . . she or he who is NOT AFRAID and who actively seeks death out will find it NOT AT THEIR DOOR.

—NANCY LING PERRY, APRIL 4, 1974

Regard your soldiers as your children, and they will follow you into the deepest valleys; look upon them as your own beloved sons, and they will stand by you even unto death. —SUN TZU

Here's a red and white VW van, parked and baking in the sun on this clear and warm May day, and the young woman seated in the front passenger seat, the van's sole occupant, stirs uncomfortably, her clothes sticking to her, her scalp roasting under the towering Afro wig she wears. She is, she hopes, inconspicuous. She lifts her buttocks from the seat, rearranges herself, sits. She moves again, leaning across and over the stick shift to roll down the driver's side window, letting in a warm draft redolent of exhaust and cut grass and what she thinks may be roasting frankfurters. Her nonprescription eyeglasses begin to slip down her nose, and she removes them to blot the perspiration from her face with a Kleenex. When she again looks up, a small boy meets her eyes. He walks beside a woman, his mother she guesses, toward a Chevrolet sedan, struggling with an oversize paper bag that appears to contain some cheap and colorful reward for enduring, with a minimum of fuss and fidget, Mom's afternoon of shopping. They stare at each other, the boy's head following his gaze as he hurries to keep up with the woman—definitely his mother, the young woman sees now; the boy is her diminutive masculine echo in nearly every way—and then his arm is tugging the woman's, *Mama . . . Mom . . . look . . .* The young woman quickly replaces the eyeglasses and moves to the rear of the van, where she sits cross-legged on the metal floor and reaches for the paper: the funnies, "Dear Abby," the movie listings, and her stars for today, May 16, 1974.

The horoscope for Pisces is mysteriously oblique: "Rumor has it that others have a bonanza in the works, vast unearned rewards. Truth is some people work hard, get paid. Some loaf, don't use a lucky break."

She reads on, flipping the pages of the newspaper, dotting her index finger with saliva and turning the pages from the bottom, giving each a little shake as she separates it from the ones remaining so that it won't wrinkle up. And then there's a disturbance across the street. Its sounds at first have the lazy quality of shouts carrying across open distances, the slightly rude hollering of Sunday afternoon intramurals, and she pays no attention as she reads. But then she clearly hears Yolanda's biting tone: "Get the fuck off him, you motherfucker! Let him go!"

She cranes to see her comrade straddling the back and punching the head of a young black man who wrestles with General Teko in the parking lot of Mel's Sporting Goods, where Teko and Yolanda went to pick up a few things for the search-and-destroys. This is a strange sight, totally unexpected. And a little dispiriting; she had just wanted to go shopping, get out of the safe house for an afternoon, get a little fresh air. She cranes and stares, her jaw dropping. Three other men rush out of Mel's. Two of the men lift Yolanda off the young man's back, and she thrashes and curses, kicking at shins, trying to stomp on her captors' insteps. The young woman drops the newspaper and, feeling for it on the floor with her fingers as she begins to scramble toward the front seat, picks up a .30-caliber submachine gun. Bracing herself on the door frame, she points the submachine gun out the driver's window, wanting to hit the top of Mel's building across South Crenshaw. She wants bullets zipping over the heads of her comrades' attackers. She squeezes the trigger and the gun just jumps out of her grip, and she gasps, pulling her hands away. She sees the greenery planted on the center divider rocking, sees shards of concrete spinning through the air to land amid the traffic that glides down Crenshaw, oblivious, and hears her own gasping exclamation of surprise: they'd told her the gun wouldn't buck. Inhaling deeply, she picks up the gun again, aims, squeezes and holds the trigger. The thirty-round clip emptied, she picks up the M-1 carbine. At 850 rounds per minute, she's gotten their attention across the street. Teko and Yolanda break free, begin the dash across Crenshaw while their four assailants head for cover. She fires. She fires. She fires. She knows this weapon, can strip it and reassemble it blindfolded. She hears glass breaking, the sound slapping back at her across the distance, a small, contained noise, like something carefully controlled, ultimately disappointing. The doors open and she slips to the rear as Teko and Yolanda jump aboard.

There's pride in her voice as she asks: "How'd I do?"

"The fuck took you so long?" says Teko.

A day shy of a week ago Cinque had them split into teams for the southward migration, and these three had driven the length of the state, Highway 99, breathed deep the wet smell of soil and manure in the night, stared into predawn tule fog near Fresno. It hung outside the van windows, thick five-and-ten Halloween cobwebbing hanging sinisterly still, inscrutable, and they crawled through it. Yolanda hunched forward over the wheel, her long face a skull mask of tension, and Teko reached over to wipe the condensation from the inside of the windshield with his jacket sleeve. Near Bakersfield Yolanda had at last pulled off and crawled into the back, telling her to drive. Ass numb, fingertips bone tired on the wheel, she'd merged with I-5 at Wheeler Ridge and then pushed the van onto the Grapevine for the long uphill crawl (Teko sputtering angrily about her driving) and then the stunning rush of the drop into Los Angeles County; how heartening to cross the threshold of another world after the scary hiatus of being in between. The roads acquired names, Golden State Freeway, Hollywood Freeway, Harbor Freeway, each a sort of vivid promise.

They rendezvoused with the others at a nondescript tract of patchy grass and few trees. Still, walking and stretching in the warming sun of late morning, they were grateful for the birds and insects and barking dogs of spring. She and Cujo held hands, squeezing, squeezing each other's palms, kneading messages to each other to be read deep in the flesh. They had time for this indulgence as the team leaders met in Cinque's van, the red-and-white VW with the matching curtains. They thought about buying churros from a man selling them from a pushcart, the warm sweet smell inhabiting the still air, discussing this, but Gelina reminded them that Zoya would make them pool and redivide the money again even after this purchase, so they laughed and said forget it.

They said, "Oh, that's right, Christ, forget it."

"Oh my God, never mind then, I forgot."

And laughed, Zoya eyeing them suspiciously.

She's off-balance; her wig is slipping; she slides around on the bare metal floor in the back of the van, bumping and banging into everything and thinking that one crappy carpet remnant would make a world of difference back here. Teko is driving very fast, weaving in and out of traffic, turning frequently. She sees that they are driving through a neighborhood of low bungalows right now, where the short driveways have only two thin strips of paving on either side, for the tires to ride on, with unloved grass sprouting in between. Tacky. Strange. She thinks.

Yolanda says, "So would you mind telling me what the hell happened back there, Teko?"

"Fucking junior pig. I only wish I'd blown his motherfucking head off," says Teko.

"OK. But this is not what I asked."

"Because that is the absolute worst. You know? The absolute worst. Here is a beautiful strong young brother doing the dirty work of the Man."

"Mm-hm. But, so tell me."

"This brother from a heritage of chains, three hundred motherfucking years of the Man dangling chains off him, and *he* tries to chain *me* up like a—like a—" He raises and shakes his wrist, the cuffs there dancing.

"Like a three-speed, Drew."

There is a silence. Without looking, she knows Yolanda sits with her arms folded.

After a moment Teko says, "Where the fuck am I going anyway?"

"Well, you sure got me there. Let me have a little look."

"Well you sure don't sound, geez! What. You on the rag? Or what?"

"Ruthellen." Yolanda twists her neck to read a street sign as they pass. "No, I'm not *on the rag*, Drew. The hell happened back there?"

"Ruth . . . Ellen." He pronounces the name as if he could do something with this.

"What happened?"

"You know, what we need is we need to get rid of this fucking van."

Then Teko brakes abruptly as he encounters a line of waiting traffic at the top of a rise.

"Shit," and he's turned around to see about backing up.

"Well, you want to get rid of this van how about this red car parking right here?"

"Right now?"

"When's better?"

But Teko's shifted into reverse and has begun moving when he notices a car approaching from the bottom of the hill.

"There's that little fucking junior pig again!"

"You're kidding me. Well, maybe you *had* better waste him." Yolanda looks at him out of the corner of her eye. There is more than a trace of sarcasm in her voice.

"Ah, as leader of this fire team I personally oversee expropriation and commandeering of goods and matériel." Teko wags a finger at the red car, a Pontiac LeMans.

"Uh-huh," says Yolanda.

Ignoring Yolanda, Teko addresses her for the first time since the ride began. He says, "Take the carbine," and points to the other car, the one that climbs toward them.

There's a *High Noon* aspect to this that doesn't escape her. She's holding the rifle before her—"at port arms," it'll later be described—as she approaches the car below. She's made strangely happy by the mere sensation of walking downhill; it's an old elation, unquestioned, its source a mystery. She feels tall; maybe that's it. The distant car is her strange, thrumming opponent; she doesn't look at the man inside, but at the face of the car: the headlight eyes and radiator grille grimace. As she advances, she thinks she will aim dead center of the windshield and wonders how many rounds are left in the banana clip. Behind her, she hears Teko's goofy greeting: "Hi! We'll be needing your car *right now* if you don't mind. I *don't* want to have to kill you!" She takes another step and then another. She slips her finger inside the trigger guard and raises the gun to sight down its length. Within the car there's an abrupt flurry of motion as the occupant throws his arm over the seat back, looking to the rear as he rolls back and out of sight. She returns to the van, but Yolanda calls her to the Pontiac.

"This is Arthur, and, Ruby? Ruby. Arthur and Ruby are letting us have their car for now." She indicates the LeMans. "Would you please tell them who *you* are?"

She smiles, broadly, as she's been told, and removes the eyeglasses. Neither crude disguise nor subsistence rations nor the rigors of combat training have altered a face everyone has come to know.

Speaking slowly and clearly, she says, "I'm Tania Galton."

As they begin to drive and she feels her heart slow she indulges the old luxury of feeling annoyed with her comrades.

"So anyway. What happened, General Teko?" asks Yolanda.

"Nothing. Well. I saw something, a bandolier. I thought we could maybe use it."

"Jesus Christ, that was stupid."

"Oh, shut up."

"What did it cost, two big bucks?"

"Jeez, will you just. Come on, Diane." He pounds the steering wheel with the heel of his hand.

"Yo-lahn-dah."

They go on, a soft-shoe demonstration of marital antagonism. Tania wonders if this kind of life intensifies conjugal discord or just frees it to seek its regular expression. She wonders if there was ever a little off-campus apartment for Mr. and Mrs. Andrew Shepard of Bloomington, IN, with jug wine on the counter, Ritz crackers and a hunk of Kraft on the cutting board, and a Mr. Coffee hissing and spitting brown liquid into a steamy carafe, a place where they lived politely, planning their evenings around the listings in the *TV Guide*, while Teko earned his master's in urban education. She sees the clean shower stall, the carpeted staircase, the burnt-orange Creuset saucepan simmering with Campbell's soup atop the range centered in the island overlooking the living room. A little off-campus nest full of the twigs and string of stifling ambitions. All that clutter coming between the hairy little grad student and his tall wife with the bland athletic good looks and the slightly off-center face, between their hostility. Now it flows like lava, burning clean.

Under her annoyance, Tania admires them. She thinks of Eric Stump, her lover since she was sixteen, her fiancé for some months, and now the deserted cuckold. He was like a radio receiver eternally on and tuned to receive garbled flashes of superior intelligence from distant reaches of the galaxy. Her job had been to monitor the airwaves for sudden bursts of communication that would inevitably be followed by cryptic silences. She imagines the Shepards into a past that resembles her own because it's easier that way to imagine their path out of the familiar. Though little could compare with the sudden violent rupture that had removed her from Eric. Still, she can see the need for its having happened now. She might never have gotten around to it otherwise, because what's there to hassle about when you can watch *The Magician* at eight o'clock? How can you admit you hate being with someone when you've gone and bought an ADT system to remain locked safely alone with him? When you've had your formal engagement photograph taken, standing posed beneath a portrait of your long-suffering grandmother Millicent?

Once the clutter started rolling in, it was almost impossible to stop it: silver and china and crystal, all at her disposal for a light supper on the TV trays, eaten in silence while Bill Bixby sped around in his Corvette, pulling knotted scarves out of his sleeve.

And even as she picked out her formal Royal Green Darby Panel, Hutschenreuther cobalt blue, and Herend VBOH china patterns, her Towle Old Master silver, her thumbcut Powerscourt crystal by Waterford, she was beginning to think of those things as objects to be set between her and Eric.

She fingers the ugly stone monkey that hangs from her neck. Cujo gave it to her and as far as she's concerned it's the only gift she need ever receive again.

Her parents have released photos of her receiving her first Holy Communion. A photo of her and Eric, taken to commemorate the announcement of their engagement, in which their faces are imprinted with their forced enthusiasm. A pensive *16* magazine shot showing her with knees drawn up to her chest, hands folded across her knees, cheek resting on her hands, eyes staring off to one side— just an ordinary girl with her head full of confusing fun choices.

Her mother had gone to town, to the press actually, describing the pearl-handled fruit knives and forks she'd given her as an engagement present.

They would offer this, the weight of a life of well-intentioned privilege, in evidence against the bewigged specter in the bank captured on dozens of pictures shot by two Mosler Photoguard cameras firing away at four frames per second; against the guerrilla girl, legs astride, hugging the M-1 to her hip before the seven-headed Naga symbol (Xeroxed flyers made from this Polaroid have shown up all over Sproul Plaza, declaring WE LOVE YOU TANIA); against the voice referring to her parents as "pigs"; against all the overwhelming documentation that Tania had devoured Alice, that the girl had simply become divorced from her own self.

"Stop. Stop. Stop. Slow down," says Yolanda.
   "Well, which one? I mean. Man."
   "Slow *down*. We need to find another car."
   "Already? Like, two blocks, this car."
   "Yes, already."
   "Try and, you know. Where I'm coming from, here."
   "Over there."
Two men are unloading a lawn mower from a blue Nova wagon when Teko pulls the LeMans up and jumps out, carrying the submachine gun.
   "We're the SLA. We need your car right now. This is not an expropriation; we're just borrowing it. I mean, you'll get it back, man."
   "Just put our stuff in the car, Teko," says Yolanda. "Stop talking now."
   "Sure," says one of the men. "Long as you need it."
   "You can, ah," says Teko, "keep the lawn mower." And the men move it off the back of the wagon, double time.
   She's about to get in when Yolanda reminds her, nodding in the direction of the two men. "Tania?"
   "Oh. Yeah." After straightening her wig, she removes her eyeglasses and smiles at the men. The younger one smiles back.

It's now 4:33 p.m. Yolanda turns the dashboard radio dial searching for news reports, while Teko drives. At this hour, helicopters hover in position over the freeways that enlace the city, delivering traffic reports to the drivers anchored below. The unfamiliar road names, and the conditions on each, are enumerated over the radio. There's no word yet of a manhunt, or the incident at Mel's.
   They stop at a shopping center called Town & Country Village. Tania enjoys these oases, the hand-painted signs in the supermarket windows, the faded placard outside the restaurant and cocktail lounge listing the specials. This one has a slightly rough-hewn theme, the storefronts framed in wood stained a dark brown. A boy in a blue apron retrieves the shopping carts scattered throughout the parking lot. He links them in a long unwieldy train and pushes them toward the entrance of the supermarket. A lot of crashing noise accompa-

nies the task. It looks like not such a bad job. Tania's only job, ever, was working at Capwell's, in Oakland, clerking in the stationery department for two and a quarter an hour.

But her scalp is starting to itch like hell, and she is nearly overcome with anxiety when she realizes that Teko and Yolanda are discussing switching cars once again. Teko parks and they all get out of the Nova, Teko carrying the submachine gun concealed in a plastic shopping bag from Mel's, which says brightly in red script Thank You For Your Patronage! with some sort of exploding curlicues or whatever all around the words. A festive-looking bag. They stroll around the shopping center periphery, listening to the thin strains of the Muzak, "Raindrops Keep Fallin' on My Head," which Tania has heard so often in such places she believes it must act as a subliminal inducement to shop. As this gives way to "Moon River," an old pickup with a camper top pulls into a spot, and a man, youngish, in faded denim, with long hair, gets out and walks around to open the passenger door for a little boy. The boy wears a sateen windbreaker with appliqué patches shaped like baseballs. She thinks it's called a varsity jacket. She's fascinated with the little boy's jacket. It's new and clean and looks like the largesse of Grandma or Grandpa, or so she guesses.

Teko asks Yolanda, "How about that hippie's camper?"

"How 'bout it?"

"Fill the bill?"

"Go for it, Teko."

"You think?"

"Go go go go *go*."

"I'll talk to him, see what he says."

The man has squatted to tie his son's sneakers. Tania hears the boy's high little voice carrying across the lot—it demands: "Tight! Tight!"—while the man squats, pulling the laces tighter, unaware of the presence of danger and revolution as Teko comes near, swinging the bag with the submachine gun nestled in it beside thermal underwear and socks and a flannel shirt. It unfolds like a two-reel silent: Teko hails the man, and they talk, friendly enough; Teko, speaking, gestures toward the camper, and the man startles, a little flurry of the arms and upper body; Teko lifts the muzzle of the gun out of the bag; the man leaps to his feet and grabs his son and dashes around the camper; Teko shuffles back and forth near the front fender, trying to keep the man in sight. When the man breaks away, Teko tears the submachine gun out of the bag and rushes after him.

"Oh, shit," says Yolanda. Teko screams, gesturing with the gun, at the man, who is crumpled against the hood of a car, his arms draped over his head, moaning. Teko turns to Yolanda and hefts the gun, as if he were testing its weight.

"Should I off him?"

"Don't, Teko."

The man moans, "No, no."

"Shut up! Should I just fucking off him right now?"

"Teko, you'll bring the pigs down on us!" says Tania.

"No, no."

"*Shut! up!* Who asked *you?*"

"Teko, she's right, we better go now!"

"OK. OK. OK. Listen, you hippie dipshit. You listening? Listen! You tell anyone about this and we will be *on* you like *white* on fucking *rice!* We will cut off your balls! You hear? We will tear out your fingernails! You hear? We will take that kid of yours and roast him on a fucking spit! You hear?"

"No, no."

"Do you *hear* me?" Teko holds the gun close to the man's ear and fires into the air. He backs away. Yolanda and Tania are already running for the Nova; the gunfire releases them to their fear. "Close to You" is playing on the Muzak. The ice-cream families of America keep coming out of the shoppes, unawares, poised and carefree.

"I can't necessarily agree with these tactics, Teko."

"That's why you're not a general."

"Don't even start."

"You might not want to admit it, but: it's true."

Yolanda is driving now. Tania is beginning to get hungry. It's six, and the top-of-the-hour newscasts are reporting the incident at Mel's and the Southern California manhunt for "suspected SLA members, possibly including kidnapped heiress Alice Galton." Who is being sought for questioning in connection with the San Francisco bank robbery last month in which she was an apparently willing participant, in which innocent family men were gunned down; who has turned her back on her loving family and devoted fiancé; who has adopted the name Tania. Is she, as U.S. Attorney General William Saxbe claims, "nothing more than a common criminal"? Is she the mindless, programmed victim of brainwashing? Or is it more likely that she may have been coerced and is just waiting for the opportunity to send us all a message of reassurance?

There's a hearty laugh in the Nova.

In any case, it is a mystery for the public and law enforcement officials alike. In any case, it is clear she is not what she once was.

The mood in the car turns sour again when the announcer reports that Teko had been caught stealing a pair of sweat socks.

"It wasn't sweat socks. And I didn't steal it."

WILLIE WOLFE
Cujo

The exact meaning of those sprawling urban stucco barrens evaded him. Not that he'd been looking for it. But what did it all mean, the ugliness they'd wrapped themselves in, the beaten cars and shabby houses and dingy streets? He saw boys on the corner carrying golf clubs, black boys, a little younger than he was, never been near a golf course in their lives. He saw two men drive up to a house and furtively unload unopened cases of Viva paper towels and bring them inside, then come out on the tiny porch laughing when the chore was done. He saw two used condoms in the gutter and a third that had been inflated and a stylized girl's face drawn on it with lipstick. It was like observing something a million miles or years distant.

Tania said that what they needed was to break out the Polaroid Pronto and take plenty of clear, crisp SX-70 pictures. Why? So he could look twice at everything, once to live it and again to try to understand, she said.

Typically for her, it was just apolitical enough to make perfect sense while seeming like a non sequitur.

You took the picture, you listened to the motor whine as it ejected the print, and then you held it by the one-inch border at the bottom, shaking it to get it to develop faster. She'd demonstrated, waving dry a snapshot of a grinning Cujo who looked just a little too much like Willie Wolfe, the all-American boy.

It was also apolitical enough to enrage Cinque, who only liked to use the camera these days to take heroic pictures of their army, the seven-headed Naga banner pinned to the wall behind them.

General Gelina cut his hair that afternoon. Gelina breached security to remove the surveillance drapes from the window over the sink and let a little daylight in. A towel was draped over his shoulders, and he sat cross-legged on the kitchen floor, watching his damp hair fall to the cracked linoleum.

It was quiet that day, with Teko, Yolanda, and Tania gone. He wanted to talk about Tania but didn't know how to go about it. He shifted restlessly. There were other things to talk about, but he didn't want to talk about them. The arrow of his consciousness flew directly to her.

Gelina understood, he thought. He and she and Tania were what he once would have thought of as "friends," though the bourgeois connotations of the term could be quite simply mind-boggling, as could be the bourgeois connotations of almost anything. He had never realized how hard it was just to live.

Anyway, Gelina was a comrade, a very sympathetic and intuitive comrade, and as she snipped his hair, cutting away the remains of the bright red dye job that had so bothered Tania, guiding his head into position with gently prodding fingers, she gradually brought the conversation around to where he wanted it.

"I think your comrades will appreciate your new look," she said.

"One comrade," said Cujo.

From behind him he could hear Gelina sharply expelling breath through her nose, an understanding laugh.

"Sometimes a pretty effective costume isn't what you'd call the most suitable," she said, holding out a clipped lock of dyed hair for their scrutiny. "In acting, you learn how to get past it, get outside the sense of yourself to play a role you couldn't ordinarily identify with."

"As a guerrilla I could definitely appreciate the costume." Cujo nodded as Gelina paused, scissors upraised, allowing him his gesture. "But as a man . . ." Cujo let the sentence hang.

Gelina began cutting hair again. "Hasn't anyone been feeling comradely toward you lately?" She sounded amused.

"Well . . ."

"Sometimes some people feel more comradely than others," she continued. "I see you gave Tania that little stone monkey face, the whatchamacallit. It's *cute.*"

Cujo blushed. "The Olmec monkey. It's Mexican."

And Gelina very exaggeratedly put her hand to one side of her mouth, as if to shield her speech from eavesdroppers, and said in a stage whisper, "Sometimes when the heart speaks, you gotta listen. The bourgeois aren't wrong about *everything*, you know."

Cujo nodded.

"Some people shouldn't talk," she said.

"Like Gabi and Zoya and all their dykey dramatics. I mean, come on, what, is this a soap opera?" she said.

"Like you-know-who and you-know-who whose last name rhymes with Shepard, give me a break. It's like *The Honeymooners*. You remember *The Honeymooners?*" she said.

Cujo agreed. "Yeah, Tania was saying, like, this is a big problem."

"Oh, I can see how it would be for her. I really relate. I'm so glad I'm not on their team. Anyway."

Gelina dipped a comb in a basin of water and ran it through Cujo's freshly cut hair. Gradually, over the last few weeks, the awkward postadolescent had repossessed him. First he'd ditched the beret, then the wispy experiments with Ché-like facial hair. Now he sat, slunched forward, clean-cut and shorn, a silly smirk on his smooth face.

"All finished, hon."

After the haircut Cin called Gelina to bed, and Cujo stayed sitting on the kitchen floor because he didn't feel like watching them fuck. He felt lonely and blue and wanted Tania to come home so he could surprise her with his new hair. He dozed off.

It was about six o'clock in the evening when there came a knock at the door of the house on Eighty-fourth Street. A pretty odd thing to be happening at a secret hideout, thought Cujo, as he came awake. The phrase, *secret hideout*, just appeared in his thoughts from out of the past, the days when he was Willie Wolfe; from out of backyard stands of elms and sycamores and maples and other craggy trees of the Northeast, kids in striped tees and jeans and U.S. Keds scrabbling through, heading for some crude structure of plywood and two-by-fours, secret doings under the high armadas of furrowed cumulus drifting through a honed October sky and the wind shaking leaves from the trees, the explorations of that after-school wilderness ca 1963 fueled by Tang and Twinkies, Ovaltine and Oreos, ammonium nitrate and fuel oil.

Wait a second. Huh? He was still waking up.

Ammonium nitrate and fuel oil were well-known as primary components of homemade explosives. The thought excited him, the thought of a *bomb factory*, another piquant phrase.

A knocking, an insistent knocking on the door in this tough neighborhood, where it paid to be what was the word? Reticent. Circumspect. His lips formed the name: Tania.

More of a thudding, now, the ham of an impatient fist striking the door: not Tania.

Back when Cujo was Willie Wolfe, when he was falling out of trees and kissing Amy Alderson on her sun porch and serving as sports editor for the *Mount Hermon Clarion* and swimming varsity, his dad, Skip, was the one who strode to the door in response to the chimes, brimming with authority. Young Willie had watched this banal act about a thousand times, slumped on the sofa or wherever he happened to be when it came to pass that Sally Brooks arrived to collect for the Shriners or Santo the gardener needed to get into the basement or little Kerry Sherman came around with her Girl Scout cookies and had never thought twice about it. And now here he was, Cassandra's "my brother the Communist," and was he supposed to draw his gun and take cover or answer the knock?

But it was a *safe house* and he was *not* Cassandra's weird little brother anymore; now he was a revolutionary, committed, divested of emotional baggage and material wealth. But as soon as Cujo began thinking of his dad, his family, the jig was up; he was a basket case, meditating deeply on a loss that was politically incorrect to mourn and that marked a definite reduction of himself.

Cinque came in from the other room, sleepy, stiff-legged and bare-chested. Hitching his pants, he stuck a revolver in the waistband, undid the locks, and opened the door. Just like that. And Cujo watched, mouth agape.

It was Prophet Jones, come to call, six foot five and solid as a cannonball. Prophet Jones had first shown up late on the first night to check out his new tenants, scrutinize them in the wavering candlelight that illuminated the doleful space of the two rooms. He'd reminded them to lay low. Prophet Jones thought Fahizah might not have taken very seriously his earlier suggestion to that effect, made when she'd rented the place from him. He scolded them and criticized and looked from face to face, but mostly he stood looking down at Cinque while he did it. Cujo was in awe. Prophet Jones dressed down the Field Marshal as if he'd been just *anybody*. But he knew Cin was bound to respect him. It was the mutual respect that was only natural between a brother and a freedom fighter. Prophet Jones talked, and they all listened. Cujo loved that cadence; it jangled him right down to the white of his bones, set the marrow vibrating. Fungg-kayy! He loved the man's name. He loved Fahizah's story of the Malcolm and Huey posters on his walls, of his poised nonchalance when, in an effort to prove that she was indeed a general in the SLA, she'd pulled her submachine gun out of the Ralph's shopping bag she was carrying.

Oh, how he couldn't wait to be a real urban guerrilla! Oh, how he couldn't wait to be black!

NIGHT IS FALLING. THE Nova is beginning to feel like bad luck rolling. Tania is still hungry, and all that neon against the darkening sky puts an edge on her appetite. Signs that rotate and light up in sequence, that point the way to satiety. A green arrow appears, and they turn. A circle shines yellow, and they speed up. Soon they are working through the cul-de-sacs again, the turn signal clicking and the brakes sighing softly, marking time.

"This car, it's starting to feel a little, I don't know."

"I'm hip."

"Dangerous, especially after the whole thing back at the shopping center."

"Well," says Teko, "I'm aware of that."

"You always have to be, I don't know, demonstrative that way."

"Well. What do they say? Desperate times."

"First the socks, then this gun thing."

"It wasn't socks. It was a bandolier."

Entering a small, unheralded city called Lynwood, they turn onto Pendleton Avenue and drive slowly for about two blocks before Yolanda pauses beside a parked Ford Econoline van that has a FOR

SALE sign taped in the back window, listing a phone number and an Elm Avenue address. As it happens, the address is directly adjacent to where the van is parked. Yolanda gets out of the Nova.

Dan Russell contours himself to accommodate the shifting shape-lessness of the beanbag chair, his right hand inside a Claude Osteen model MacGregor fielder's glove. The fingers of his left hand rest idly on the thongs that will allow him to fine-tune the glove's Adjusta-Wrist. Tomorrow's the big game. He takes the glove off and balances it on his lap, gazing into the dark oiled pocket. The weight of the glove on his crotch begins to give him an erection, and he puts the glove aside and prods himself through his jeans as he stiff-ens. Then he begins to think about Geraldine. Now, Dan Russell is not supposed to masturbate before he pitches. Coach has made this abundantly clear, using a number of creative and evocative euphemisms, the most memorable of which makes reference to "keeping the pearl jam in the jar." Also, Dan is motivated to stop by his grave misgivings about masturbating while he thinks about the transvestite alter ego of a stocky black man. Yet his fingers undo the snap at the waistband of his Wranglers. He thinks: Geraldine is not a woman; she is Flip Wilson in drag. He works out a compromise: If he must jerk off, he will substitute for Geraldine in his thoughts Mary Ellen Walton: wholly female, about his age, warmhearted, levelheaded, white like him, enduring the Great Depression back in the forties or whenever with John Boy and the rest, and, if he didn't mention it yet, someone who is both *white* and a *girl*.

These two characters compete against each other on TV Thursday nights. Which happens to be tonight.

But then Geraldine sashays back into his mind, wearing a saucy double knit skirt and bright rayon blouse. Dan Russell puts one hand on her arm, another around her waist. "Don't you touch me!" protests Geraldine. "You don't know me that well!" He silences her with a vi-olent kiss on her big black lips. He pulses involuntarily under his cot-ton briefs and then frantically pulls his dick out of his pants. This is not anything anyone has to know about: not the jerking-off part, cer-tainly not the Geraldine part. In his mind he is twisting one of Geraldine's arms behind her back, yanking the skirt up and the panties down. The sudden idea of Geraldine with dick and balls makes his own dick throb with excitement. Then his brother starts in hammering on the door.

"Huhhyeah?"

"Open up, shithead."

"Huhhwhat is it?"

"Stop beating off in there."

"Fuuuck yooooooou." Dan Russell leaps up and, with pants around his ankles, shuffles across the shag carpet to make sure the door is locked. He gets a shock when he touches the knob.

"Trying to stick it in the keyhole?"

"Fuck you."

"It'd fit in there too, I bet."

"Up yours."

"Yeah bet you'd like it you homo."

"Fuck you! What the hell you want anyway?"

"Open up and I'll tell you. Someone's here to see you."

"Someone? Who?"

"Open up. A lady."

"A lady? Who?"

"Open up. She's got big knockers."

Dan stuffs his penis back into his pants and slowly zips up. He gives himself a couple of flicks with his index finger to make his hard go down and then opens the door. His brother is leaning against the door frame. He crosses his eyes at the sight of Dan, then blocks his path.

"Where is she?" Dan says, by which he means get out of the way.

"Maybe she left already, dickbreath."

"Fuck you. Where's she?"

"She's up front. She goes, I saw a sign, stud for hire. Hope he's not shooting it all into an old sock with red stripes that his mom goes in front of everybody, how *ever* did you get this *soooo dirty*, Dan?"

Dan pushes his brother out of the way. "Shut up."

"She goes, I'm here for some of that hot Dan Russell action."

"Wouldn't surprise me." Dan muscles past and begins down the hall.

"Keep believing it, shitforbrains," says his brother.

He's a good-looking boy, well built, with hair he constantly is pushing out of his eyes. His mother had stood there holding a semen-encrusted sweat sock, a look of genuine concern on her face, as if his foot were discharging some sort of toxic secretion.

At the end of the hall, Dan sees her silhouetted in the doorway. She does have big knockers, and roundish hips, and long, straight legs that he imagines wrapped around his back, and a kind of pretty OK face. He pushes the hair out of his eyes.

"Hi," he says. "You wanted to see me?"

"Well, I think you're the person I want to see." She smiles. "Are you the man with the van for sale?"

Something about the way she calls him a man just makes his day.

"Yes," he says, deliberately deepening his voice. "Are you interested?"

"I'm *very* interested!" The woman smiles.

"Well, I'd be happy to show it to you." He crosses his arms, turning the palms of his hands so that his biceps swell. "I'm Dan, by the way." He smiles. They stand for a moment.

"Well, I'd love to see it."

Dan makes this kind of what-a-doofus-I-am facial expression and reaches over to grab the keys off a hook. They walk out together, and he has trouble coming up with anything else to say. He's relieved the van is there to talk about.

"It's not like there's anything wrong with it or anything. I just need something more in the line of an economy car what with gas costing what it does these days." He shrugs.

"I know, isn't it awful?" the woman agrees. "If I didn't have all this stuff and people and things I need to carry around."

"Well," says Dan. "It's a very *comfortable* van," and he begins doing a walkaround to point out the features and open the sliding panel door and, not incidentally, show her the back, carpeted in thick shag.

But she says: "I'm sorry, I'm in a bit of a hurry. I'd like to just test-drive it. I'm sure all the, you know, is just fine."

Faintly disappointed, Dan hands her the keys, taking advantage of the opportunity to cast a glance at her tits. He climbs into the passenger seat. The woman gets in, settles herself behind the wheel, and looks around.

"What a nice, comfortable van," she says.

"You must take great care of it," she says.

"Roomy," she says.

"Starts right up," she says, putting the key in the ignition and turning it.

"I, uh, had it tuned," Dan says. She turns to him and smiles, throwing the van into gear. It's a funny smile, tight; it makes her eyes crinkle up. Her right eye is noticeably bigger than her left eye. She has regular features, drearily pretty. A weak chin. He imagines her naked on the carpet in the back.

"It's real reliable," Dan says. "I mean, sometimes I think I must be crazy for getting rid of it. It's real handy. I mean, I use it for the team, to take equipment, stuff like that."

"Team," says the woman, considering the word. She looks at him again. "I should have known you were an athlete. You have the build."

Dan blushes. "Baseball," he says. "I pitch." He considers the possibility that now might not be a bad time to point out the luxuriously carpeted back. The van is turning right, and he leans toward her involuntarily and smiles at her, and sensing his smile, she smiles back, without looking away from the road.

She says, "I was wondering."

She says, "I have some friends who brought me here, and I was wondering."

She says, "Would it be OK if they came along on the drive? They're right over there."

Dan looks and sees two people, a man and a girl, standing in the road. They wave. "Sure," he says. "It's OK with me." He feels slightly stung by the request. But the girl in the road is sort of cute he guesses. The van pulls to a stop and he turns to unlock the sliding panel door behind him. But then his own door is opening and he's a little confused and he looks around to see the man standing just outside, staring up at him. "Get in the back," the man says. He gestures with the machine gun he's carrying.

The machine gun he's carrying.

Dan moves into the back, not quite sure what to do with his hands. At any rate, he can't shift from the passenger seat to the floor in the rear with his hands above his head, so he takes his chances, moving to the back the way he normally would and then quickly sitting cross-legged, resting his hands on his knees. Hope that's OK. It must be, because the girl and the man get in and then the man just closes the panel door and doesn't kill him or anything.

"We're the SLA, and we need your vehicle," says the man.

Dan wants to ask what the SLA is but figures it'd be better if he didn't.

"You don't do anything stupid, you don't get hurt," explains the man.

"That's fine with me," says Dan. "Just as long as I don't get shot."

The man and the girl laugh, and the man, who's squatting on the wheel cover, reaches out and pats his shoulder. The lurching of the van nearly sends him sprawling.

"Watch it, Yolanda," he says to the woman. There is a faint, derisive sound from the front seat. The man ignores this and turns to Dan, gesturing toward the girl beside him. "You know who this is?"

Dan shakes his head.

"Tania. Tania Galton."

Dan nods now and as he does he feels himself sighing involuntarily, like, *huuuhhhhh.* His recognition of at least one of the many things that all of a sudden seem to be happening to him yield this hugely physical expression of release, as he feels himself freed from at least some of his confusion. He fairly rocks as he nods, and the sighing comes from deep inside. The man and Tania are smiling and laughing, and at the sight of this Dan can't help smiling and laughing too. In fact, he's basically crying over his luck in encountering smiling faces here and now.

"Wow," he says. "Wow."

"You know what?" says the man. "We need to stop and get a fucking hacksaw." He holds up his wrist to display the dangling handcuff. And they all laugh some more.

PROPHET JONES

When he drove up he saw the two gals lying out on the grass he won't bother to call a lawn because he may be a cheat but he's no liar. It was the hard-looking one, Zoe or some such, and the fat old lady–looking one. The radio basically giving out a grave invitation to escape and they are not getting gone, they are sunbathing. He got out of his car and took their arms—some protest here, which he smirkled at a bit—and brought them to the door.

"What you doing on that lawn? I told you white folks got to stay out of sight around here."

"It's cool," said DeFreeze.

"It's *cool*. You listening to the news?"

"I say it's cool, it's cool," said DeFreeze. "We reconnoited the perimeter."

Prophet Jones stared at the man for a moment, his head moving with the slightest trace of a poor-fool shake.

"Where's the radio at?"

"Ain't no *radio*," said DeFreeze.

"Come on here," said Prophet Jones, and he waited while DeFreeze got himself a T-shirt, and then the two of them walked to Prophet Jones's car, parked at the curb. Which was good because the smell coming from the house was like pussy and okra and old piss and was upsetting to the stomach. DeFreeze climbed in the passenger side. Prophet Jones walked around the car slowly, looking at the yard, the jalopies crowding the driveway, back at the house and the cell of white faces clustered in the open door. He waved slightly, a dismissive gesture, and the cell withdrew inside and the door closed. After a moment's hesitation he smoothly folded his large body and inserted it in the space of the open door, which he shut behind him.

Inside he gave the ignition key a half turn, and the radio came to life. Top of the hour, drive time, the news on every station the same: SLA in L.A., committing the daring daylight robbery of an Inglewood sporting goods store. Witnesses reported being fired upon by a young Caucasian woman, whose identity authorities were working to establish. The suspect vehicle, a VW van, had been recovered nearby. Prophet Jones folded his arms across the steering wheel and laid his face on them, peeping over to see how Field Marshal Cinque Mtume, the dumb motherfucker, reacted. His eyes widened, his lips ovaled, a comic *wooooo-eee* face. But there was nothing funny going on.

"The fuck they doing a holdup for?"

"Say your boy stole some *socks*." Prophet Jones felt a deep pleasure resonating within as he emphasized the word *socks*. His dislike of the Field Marshal was intense at that moment. The word on Donald DeFreeze was that he was a common police informer, a weak man, a cuckold, a chump.

"Say what? Socks?"

"What they say." Prophet Jones shrugged.

"Damn. We got to get out of here."

"I advise it."

"Not what I wanted to do."

"Don't matter what you *wanted*, Jim."

"Damn. This plays havoc with our strategy."

And who the fuck this fucking mutt think he fucking is, Bernard fucking Montgomery? Prophet Jones raised his head to look square at the Field Marshal. Why'd he bother coming here, is the major question. Because he didn't want the house shot up: it's not much, but it's what he got. DeFreeze was processing the data, drumming nervously on his knees with his open palms, looking straight ahead through the windshield. As the warm evening drew near, the neighborhood settled into its torpid routine. Boys appeared on the streets, in growing numbers, in pairs and trios and half dozens, drawn like a magnet to the corners on the broad intersection at Vermont.

"You better go, Sin-Q Em-toom-ay." Prophet Jones stretched the name beyond ridiculous. "Better go rally your troops."

"Where I'm gonna go?"

"I don't know. Go back to Frisco. Go back to your wife. She still around here, ain't she?"

When DeFreeze turned to him, Prophet Jones could see that the man had been overwhelmed as if by a sudden shadow that covered the continuous succession of postures that substituted for his personality. He modeled a curious little boy expression on his face.

"How you know my wife?" he asked.

"I just hear about her."

"What you hear?" DeFreeze twisted in the car seat, the vinyl squeaking.

"This and that." Prophet Jones was leery of this particular avenue.

DeFreeze balled his fists up and slammed them into his thighs. "Damn," he said. "The little stories just keep coming on me. I hear and I close up my ears and they just keep coming."

Motherfucker was freaking out on him. "Damn, nigger, you got no time for this. Got to get out of here right now."

And what Prophet Jones definitely did not want to be was sitting inside his personal vehicle with Donald DeFreeze when the Man rolled up with his gotcha grin.

DeFreeze went right ahead. "Try to turn my back to it, put faith in her, but even now the little stories make their way here."

"It's bad. I know it. We all know the story. You not alone. They all the same. But you got to get going. Go get your shit together and find someplace else to be."

He thought of the lockup downtown and how little it would take for the Man to offer him deluxe accommodations therein. Plus all the Man had to do was break a fucking window and that house was a what you call shambles.

"They ain't all the same," insisted DeFreeze, suddenly argumentative.

"What? Who?"

"I want you to know I got some really beautiful, aware comrades right in here. They are helping me put all this motherfucking shit behind me." DeFreeze's voice rose in pitch and volume and he tilted his head back. "I am truly blessed. My God has said unto me that I sinned and I must pay. But in his forgiveness my evil has perished and I am come unto the meek to offer them deliverance."

What the fuck. Prophet Jones was not bargaining for anyone to be shoving a cross up his ass. Just took him on in here so he could hear the radio, and all the sudden he's Reverend Ike. He reached past DeFreeze and unlatched the door, giving it a little push. Like, hint hint. The Field Marshal put one foot on the sidewalk but kept the rest of his body in the car. Prophet Jones exhaled sharply, opened his own door, and came around to the passenger side, where he fully opened DeFreeze's door and gestured up at the house.

"Listen, DeFreeze. Go in there, get everbody together, put they guns, they C-rats, all they shit in they ditty bag, get going. They find you, you won't be *delivering* a motherfucking pizza, you hear? Get out. Get on out."

Hacksaw 1

McLellan's Home Decorating Center extends deep into its low building, long narrow dark aisles formed from ceiling-high shelves leading like tunnels to the back of the store, where the overhead fluorescents are shut off and the parched dust of provident thrift has settled on every anciently untouched surface. The store smells of old cardboard and potting soil and it has the empty silence of a place that has only just stopped making noise. Toward the front, the remaining fluorescents flicker, and there's also a large blue-lit device that first lures and then eliminates flying insects, sizzling them disconcertingly. Hoes and mops and nets and pickaxes and push brooms and rakes and scythes and shovels and window poles and window screens lean against the walls, and there are bins holding nails and screws and bolts and nuts, and stacks of paint cans, and canvas dropcloths folded heavily on low shelves, and terra-cotta flower pots and planters and window boxes of all sizes stacked on the floor, and the walls lined with perforated Masonite panels for paintbrushes and rolls of tape and sanding blocks and tape measures and work gloves to hang from, and the man at the counter is obscured behind the revolving display of shiny key blanks. Yolanda approaches the man, who is entering figures in a little notebook.

"May I buy a hacksaw, please?"

The man looks at her. He raises his nose and shakes his head slightly to signify incomprehension.

"A hacksaw. Hacksaw." Yolanda mimes the act of sawing. She almost mimes the act of sawing off a handcuff but catches herself.

The man turns to look at the tools hanging behind him. He takes down a small crosscut saw.

"Yes, but . . . no. A saw, but different."

He replaces the crosscut saw and removes a circular saw blade from a hook.

"*Hack*saw. Hacksaw?"

"We closed."

"But—"

"Closed." He reaches behind him to snap off another row of fluorescents.

Dan Russell wants to know: "When you start these house-to-house things, what do you do? Just burst in with guns and all?"

"No, we'll knock on the doors and announce ourselves and explain that we need the People's help, so can we please billet some of our troops here or at least spend the night?, blah blah blah," says Teko.

"Well what if they say, sorry no thanks?"

"We'll move on to the next house."

"What if they call the police?"

"They *won't*, Dan," says Yolanda. "The People know we're doing it for their sake."

"Um," says Dan, "am I the People?"

Hacksaw 2

Yolanda reaches for the door at Klein Bros. Ace Hardware and is surprised when it opens automatically. Inside the place is bright and air-conditioned and playing "I Shot the Sheriff" from speakers stuck in the dropped ceiling so that the song follows her around. A teenage girl is mopping beyond a barrier of yellow WET FLOOR signs and a young man wearing a red blazer and carrying a clipboard emerges from a tiny office like a tollbooth set in the corner.

He asks the girl: "Can I see myself in it?"

"It's good and shiny."

"Can I eat off it?"

"It's pretty clean."

"Can I perform surgery on it?"

"It's real clean."

He spies Yolanda and disappears into the tollbooth. A moment later his voice interrupts Clapton's backup singers. "Chaz help the lady in Window Treatments."

A big pimply boy wearing a short-sleeve shirt and a clip-on bow tie under a shiny green vest approaches Yolanda. His name tag announces him as Chaz. "Help you, ma'am?"

"Oh. Hello."

"Looking for something nice for your windows today."

"No. Actually."

But there are no further queries forthcoming from the boy, whose expression is as blank as a bowl of dough, and the journey from window treatments to hacksaws seems longer and more savage than she would have imagined.

"A saw," she says.

"A saw. Oh"—and an eager look that hints at his contempt settles

on his face—"you're totally in the wrong place. That's over there."
And he jabs at the air with his forefinger before turning away.
Yolanda begins walking to the other side of the store, where another
teenage boy in a similar outfit is waiting. This boy is named
Douglas.

Clapton sings, ". . . *Every day the bucket goes to the well . . .*"

"Help you find what you're looking for today," the boy breathes.

"Hacksaw," she says.

"Hacksaw! You sure you need a hacksaw? Most people, I find,
they're like, 'I need a hacksaw' and whatnot when really they need
something else."

"I think I need a hacksaw."

"Do me a favor. What are you exactly trying to cut? It makes a
difference."

". . . *yes, one day the bottom will drop out . . .*"

"Pipe."

"Well what kind? Cast-iron pipe? Galvanized steel? Copper?
Plastic PVC? It makes a difference, believe me."

"Um. I don't know. Pipe."

"Inside or out? I know you're wondering, 'Why's the guy asking
so many questions?' And you know, I'm not trying to denigrate the
valuable addition of a hacksaw to anyone's home toolbox. But let's
make sure we're using the right tool for the right job, right? And after we figure out what that is, if you still want a hacksaw, we'll set
you up with a hacksaw."

"What was the question?"

"Inside or out?"

"Inside."

"Right. So. It's probably not cast-iron then, so what you probably
want is not a hacksaw at all but a pipe cutter."

"You know. I should probably ask my husband. He knows."

"He out in the car?" Douglas looks over her shoulder, very enthusiastic about extending the conversation.

"No. No. No, he isn't. He's home. With the baby. I'll have to
come back tomorrow."

Dan Russell wants to know: "If you take over the country—"

"*When*, Dan," stresses Teko.

"—what happens to a guy like my grampa? He's pretty like, you know, Nixon's the One. But he's a good old guy I think. He volunteers and stuff. Is it OK if he's like, all the same to you I'll be voting for Governor Reagan?"

"*That* asshole," says Teko.

"We take over, your granddad will see why Nixon's *not* the one," says Yolanda.

"What about Reagan?" asks Dan.

Hacksaw 3

Avery Trust-Rite Lumber & Hardware looks the way a workingman's saloon does when the weary day flowers with night; several men in coveralls and carpenter's pants line up on the customer's side of the counter, bullshitting with the man behind, who actually paces its length on duckboards like a bartender, and why not?—a day spent on his feet, back and forth, crouching down, reaching up, cutting keys and mixing gallons of paint and smashing flower pots with a mallet to be mixed in with sacks of fragrant soil. The place stops dead when Yolanda walks in. She smiles, and they return amused looks. One man tips a Dodgers cap.

"Lady needs some help, Ed," says the man in the Dodgers cap, and the other men on the customer's side of the counter laugh.

Ed leans across the counter tiredly; thank God he's not going along with the joke: "Help you, miss?"

"Yes, I need a hacksaw."

Ed is starting to ask her if she just needs a blade or if she needs the whole thing when the men explode:

"—*hack*saw? Oh, ho-ho-ho—"

"—*she* need with a hacksaw?—"

"—Whoa. Whoa. Lady gotta be *careful*—"

"—oh, ho-ho-ho-ho-ho-ho-ho-ho—"

"—wouldn't want to be *her* old man. Lady with a hacksaw—"

"—damn, god damn—"

"Miss?"

"The whole thing, please. The blade and the handle part."

"I'mon tell you, I don't know if you ought to *sell her* a *hacksaw*, Eddie."

"Maybe one of those chamois cloths."

"A nice feather duster."

"Can of silver polish."

"Oh, ho-ho-ho-ho-ho-ho-ho-ho."

"But a *hack*saw—"

Ed shrugs. "Lady's free white and twenty-one, and she can do as she pleases."

"Now, who here's wanting a hacksaw?"

Everyone turns to see a uniformed L.A. County deputy sheriff, carrying a roller tray, two rollers, a dropcloth, and a gallon of standard white, emerge from one of the aisles. He puts the stuff on the counter and stares straight at Yolanda.

"Lady right there," says the man in the cap.

The deputy looks at her appraisingly, a slight smile on his face, drumming his fingers on the counter with an even rhythm. Yolanda knows the other men are with him on this. No way any of this is in fun anymore.

"Mind if I ask any special reason why you're needing a hacksaw at"—and here he very pointedly gazes at his wristwatch—"eight forty-five at night?"

All of the men wait patiently for her answer. She smiles and tosses her head.

"My husband just escaped from custody, and we need to saw his handcuffs off."

Amid the laughter Ed takes her money and bags the saw. As Yolanda is leaving, she hears one of the men sum up: "She ought to take that and saw the balls off herself 'cause she has got some pair down there."

Dan Russell wants to know: "Well I mean I just don't understand why you robbed the bank in San Francisco if you're these revolutionary army people and all." He is on his knees behind the bucket seats in the front of the van, working away with the saw at the handcuff on Teko's wrist.

"Well," says Teko, somewhat nervously watching Dan at work, "running a revolution is pretty expensive business. You'd be surprised. You need vehicles—"

"But, I mean, I thought you stole the vehicles." Dan shrugs and gestures to take in the van.

"This is a definite exception in the case of an emergency. I mean, ideally we purchase the vehicles legitimately. So called. Try and keep a low profile." Teko winks. "Anyway. You need matériel. You need ordnance. Arms, ammunition, tools—"

"Sweat socks," says Yolanda.

"Oh, I just. OK. Attention please: It was not sweat socks. It was a bandolier."

"Yeah yeah."

"Dan, let's not get sidetracked here in the details, the minutiae of revolutionary struggle. I want to make one thing perfectly clear: We aren't crooks. We've declared war on the fascist United States government, and the bank job was an expropriation of enemy funds in order to meet our simple revolutionary needs."

"Oh," says Dan.

DONALD DEFREEZE
General Field Marshal Cinque Mtume

He walked that patch of grass leading to the shack looking around as if the whole world had changed its constitution, had undiscernibly come apart and then reassembled itself along slightly askew lines. The truth hid in the shadows angling from the objects all around. There were signs to which an instinctive hustler was sensitive: the marked card, the bill protruding conspicuously from the unattended wallet, the calm quiet before a bust. Then again, maybe it was just sitting in the car with that bald motherfucker Prophet Jones. Dude always got his nerves all blanged up.

It was a hostile place into which he'd been born, in whose light he now floated between the darkness at either end. He knew the darkness into which he'd exit differed from where he'd come in because it would be corrupted by his regret. The idea was to regret nothing: neither Gloria nor her children he'd accepted as his own nor the one or two he'd actually fathered with her.

There'd been a sense of receding since Tania's annunciation; it was a tough act to follow. As he'd worked his way through his own early enthusiasm, that of his followers, and come to recognize that his army was already with him in its entirety; that he'd come up empty foraging for members even amid the Berkeley Left; that he hadn't convinced political recruits so much as entranced true believers; that he'd done less to shape his enlistees into an army than they'd done to elevate him to its leadership, as he had come to see these things clearly, he'd also seen that his most incandescent vision had been realized as political theater rather than as a terrorist act. Its ruling-class victim had renounced her victimhood, disavowing the very self that had been victimized and thereby annulling the crime that millions had been convinced took place. Thus the SLA's greatest success—the abduction and conversion of Alice Daniels Galton—a success that had brought it fame and notoriety and the power to make extortion-ate demands also clearly marked its limitations as well, for if Alice Daniels Galton was human enough to disappear into a new identity as one of the People, what did that say about the "fascist insect"? If the victim's declaration that her ravishers were in fact heroes led to the People's repudiation of her, what did that say about the People?

That it was the wrong time, place, ideology, and army everybody already knew. He'd sensed it since he saw a hundred doors in pre-carious dingbat apartment buildings and crappy bungalows close again and again on his primitive importuning, the gestures and ca-dence he'd learned in Buffalo from Reverend Borrows twinned with retread political oratory. The fearless Left covered its soft white ass, oh so politely. But while before there was always some residual feel-ing of hope, now, on at least one level, Cin knew he was totally fucked. Send the man out to procure field supplies using the local currency, easiest fucking thing in the world—oh what the fuck say he got sent to *go shopping*—and he tries to take some motherfucking *socks* off them. He walked back to the shack through the subtle un-familiarity of the world, thinking about how losers seemed always to be packing up, how he'd been packing his bag up since the day he left Cleveland.

"I don't like him," said Zoya as soon as he came through the door. Out with the opinion, right up in his face, like she'd been doing from Day One. "I get a bad feeling."

He ignored her. Whatever the others might have had to say to her about this they'd probably already said, because they stayed quiet.

"Uh-uh," she repeated, "don't like him."

"Well," said Cinque, finally, "you won't have to see him no more. We're booking on out of here."

The shape the predictable protest took was: What about Teko, Yolanda, and Tania?, but Cin could tell it was inertia speaking, the tedium of unscattering everything that lay strewn around the house, stuffing it into duffel bags and grocery sacks; of bugging out of another safe house without even leaving behind one of the successively less grandiose valedictory gestures—e.g., the incendiary bomb at Sutherland Court (to "melt away any fingerprints," Fahizah had said), the cache of papers they'd placed in the tub and then pissed on at Golden Gate Avenue—that had accompanied each previous evacuation, and his five troops had begun complying with the general order even before their objections ceased, as he fell into a meditative mood and fetched his bottle of plum wine to sit leaning against the wall, drinking and smoking.

Even as the chrysalis had cracked and Tania had entered dripping into their presence—taping her declaration of herself while posing for the photograph that seconded that declaration more persuasively than any words she'd spoken, the picture depicting her before the Naga banner, armed and ready for just about anything—Cin had felt the end drawing near. He painstakingly crafted what amounted to goodbyes to them all—to Victor, Damon, Sherry, Sherlyne, Dawn, DeDe, and, by implication, Gloria—to be tacked onto the end of that tape (after Fahizah's curiously cultish anointment of him as a revolutionary messiah, which had swiftly and decisively destroyed any remaining credibility the SLA had with the Left), along with a couple of death warrants that he'd issued more in the spirit of rhetorical What the Hell than in true seriousness. There was just this strange foreboding that he would not be allowed to live through this. He saw himself dying in fire and smoke.

They packed up and then Fahizah and Cujo went to warm up the vehicles and for an instant, before he heard the engines turning over, he sensed, from some strange deep part of himself that was in touch with the darkness of childhood nightmare, hopeless encirclement, that waiting for him were highly efficient shock troops with rifles and tear gas and Nixon's the One bumper stickers and flagstone backyard patios and weekend ticket plans at Dodger Stadium and color TV and a thousand other things that made him wince, waiting and snacking and sipping and chatting in their idleness and not even taking the whole thing seriously.

33

He wanted to go.

He wanted to wait.

He wanted someone to tell him what to do.

He wanted someone to come up and say, It's OK.

Instead his sullenness generated a zone around him into which no one crossed. The evening brought a darkness to the two rooms that had the glow of his cigarettes at its center. He lit them, each one from the last, then absently field-stripped the butts. Fahizah and Cujo went and shut off the motor again after a while. Inside, it was implicit that silence was part of the bargain. Outside, the voices of young men, a shouting-out into the spring evening. It was like that feeling after a bad argument with Gloria, when he was crushed and empty, sitting there as depleted as after sex, while the world kept moving right outside the windows and you just couldn't believe it was still going on, that anything still bothered.

"ORDERS, EVERYONE?"

Yolanda and Teko are smiling! And before Tania has a chance to really think about it, she realizes that they're happy simply to be here at the Century Drive-In! Workers of the world, unite—and let's go to the movies! Though that would not, strictly speaking, constitute a Maoist aphorism. And of course *she* is not a member of the proletariat. And while the folks all around them enjoying *The New Centurions* from the comfy depths of their bucket seats may be the lumpen of the westward dream, they are also the bourgeois, putatively enfranchised, silent majority, and they surely are getting a different charge from this cops 'n' robbers melodrama than the SLA Three, who, though the major reason they're here is to rendezvous with the others, are enjoying the rare opportunity to study enemy propaganda that their being here allows.

"Shoot 'em, kill the pigs!" urges Teko.

Forget she said anything.

Teko: Cheeseburger, Fries, Coke
Yolanda: Chicken 'n' a Basket, Fries, Tab
Tania: Hamburger, Onion Rings, 7-Up
Civilian Prisoner of War: Hamburger, Fries, Coke

A knit cotton blanket speaks from the back of the van, requesting extra ketchup. It's the prisoner under there.

Old grizzled cop George C. Scott is showing the ropes to idealistic rookie Stacy Keach. Tania has heard that Stacy Keach overcame the obstacle of a harelip to become an actor. And what a beautiful and mellifluous voice he has! Like Orson Welles. She thinks instantly of the famous movie.

(As a countercultural document, the SLA finds *Citizen Kane* virtually useless. For one thing, its criticisms of the media are outmoded, made obsolete by the emergence of television as the major information source for most people. But mostly, there's a problem with its reductionist preoccupation with Kane's megalomaniacal villainy and its definition of that villainy as merely the greatest flaw in his heroic makeup, which render the film romantic propaganda for the fascist establishment. Even now it's said that Hank Galton's forced exposure to the "underprivileged" has changed him; it's said that he and the notoriously right-leaning *San Francisco Examiner* are beginning to address the concerns of "the people" and to run "hard-hitting" investigative pieces that "expose" things, lack of hot water and potholes and unsanitary conditions in the Western Addition and such. Tania's not sure who it is who's said these things. The *Examiner*, she thinks.
Alice has never seen *Citizen Kane*. Tania isn't even curious.)

Tania wanders through the rows of parked automobiles, seconded by the enormous image of Stacy Keach, which itself approaches a parked car, intending to warn its occupants to leave the scene of some impending carnage. Little does he know. The helpful rookie leans toward the passenger window to address the lovey-dovey couple and encounters a young woman with a shotgun laid across her lap, pointed directly at him. Shock, surprise. She pulls the trigger, sending Keach flying. Tania hears Teko cheering from the van.

Right around when Tania heads back to report that she hasn't seen any sign of the others and that their signal—a big paper cup set upside down on the speaker stanchion—is clearly visible, Keach is being dumped by his wife, who can't really take it anymore: it's hard being a cop's wife; it's all the worrying, the late hours. It's the not knowing.

As if you ever do.

CINQUE

Later he heard the voice of a child in the street, a strong little voice forming sentences of pealing innocence. It was 11:50. Reverend Borrows: "There are two kinds of people in this world. The kind who auto-MATically look at the clock when they hear a child outside after dark, and *those who do not.*" He'd been sixteen when Borrows laid that on him, about to get caught robbing parking meters and sent up to the reformatory at Elmira. He got to his feet, stiff and cramped. He watched the shadows of the others as they followed suit, except Cujo, who seemed to have fallen asleep.

"All right, comrades," he said. "Let's get on out of here."

Fahizah spoke, her voice coming from near the kitchen. "We have just enough time to get to the rendezvous, I think."

"Rendezvous?" said Cinque.

"We were supposed to meet up at the last show at the Century Drive-In." She added: "Um. You picked it."

"Well, why the hell didn't you mention it before now?"

"Well, I. I thought, it seemed like you, like you wanted, I don't know."

"You don't know?" demanded the Field Marshal.

"Like you wanted us to be quiet, like you needed to think things over."

Because of a painful corn that had formed on the ball of his left foot, what Cinque had thought over was this: Reverend Borrows liked to treat the smallest cuts with iodine that hurt so bad it felt like you were trying to scare the dirt out. It was a pleasure to him to treat wounds, to sit with his teenage boarder with surgical tape and a blue box of cotton and little brown bottles of stinging ointment between them, disinfecting and bandaging up his cuts and scrapes. Cinque had let him do it too.

It was information of a kind, neither more nor less important than anything else he might think about. Always expecting him to have like these *great thoughts*, damn.

Reverend Borrows's daughter was Harriet. If Borrows had let him marry her when he got out of Elmira, everything would be different now. OK, she was only fourteen. But with the reverend's permission he would have waited around, learned a steady trade, gotten work. Instead he floated to Newark, swum into the waiting maw of Gloria Thomas, twenty-three, drop-dead gorgeous, mother of three.

"Too dangerous. We'll check out the drops tomorrow. What we need tonight is to get out of here and find a place to stay."

Was there a hint of discontent in the ranks as they filed out the door in quiet pairs, himself and Gelina, Cujo and Fahizah, Gabi and Zoya? Well?

Patricia/Mizmoon Soltysik
Zoya

Once a senior class treasurer . . . She divided and redivided the money, enjoyed seeing it split into equal parts. No "more or less." Her best work was done at a desk, in bright light. She liked thinking and plotting. She liked the look of an idea as it took shape on paper. She liked the look of a number in a box or a circle. She wished she had a typewriter. She enjoyed working with reams of paper, generating drifts of ideas from out of nothing. The sheer accumulation, as the stack of papers mounted, as collections of receipts grew fat in a stained number ten envelope imprinted with the address of the Berkeley Public Library. Where she worked for a while and helped organize fellow workers in a labor dispute. This was something she would put on a résumé one day, after the revolution, at the very bottom so that people could see what a long way she'd come.

At the library it had been thought that she had difficulty communicating with older workers. She categorically disagreed.

The dispute had ended up with the library's remaining a nonunion shop. Still, she reminded herself, significant advances had been made.

Leaving stuff like that behind—the receipts, the notes, the drafts, the lists, the correspondence—*killed* her, not just because the others pointed out that their movements could be tracked exactly if such a rich trove of evidence were to fall into the wrong hands (she had to admit that she didn't care, instinctively disliked the idea of vanishing off the face of the earth) but because it was a comfort and a relief to watch evidence of herself add up on the record. White drifts of her self, piling up on a tabletop on either side of the blue Smith-Corona

37

portable. She wished for personalized checks, for a business card she could give out. Checks were better; they came back. She wrote graffiti on the walls of the safe houses instead.

And now maybe this was not what she wanted. She had grown used to things not being precisely as she wanted them; that was no longer her life's objective, so it wasn't where the problem was located. The problem was not quite knowing what the objective was. Zoya knew armed struggle was not about to happen down here. These people were in love with their Chevrolets and Smoky Joes: so what? They would come around. That wasn't the problem. Inevitably her mind returned to Gabi. She couldn't help thinking that Gabi had manipulated her into a situation where the ultimate point was for her to be with Gabi. This was unacceptable, and the word she used to describe it in her thoughts was *travesty*, a *travesty* of her beliefs. At the same time, she just had to look at Gabi—shlumpy in her fatigues, apart from the others—to feel an unwelcome wave of guilty feelings wash over her. It was like trying to abandon a kitten and hearing it calling for you from the back alley. Gabi cried from the physical effort of her training. She lumbered through drills, bulky and awkward, and Zoya wished she would just stop. Gabi stubbornly made it plain that her ideological commitment was less than 100 percent, and the fact of her actually having lived among the third world poor to whom her father ministered made everyone suspicious, including, Zoya realized, herself. Gabi had settled in as the butt of the cadre's jokes. Cin gave her a horrible time. She'd seen her unmet sexual needs become the topic of an evening's discussion more than once, and Zoya resented the implication that *she* was the one obliged to satisfy them. The whole focus of Zoya's involvement in the group now was to keep Gabi from having a negative net effect on operations. Hand-holder. Babysitter. She jollied her and walked with her. Explained why they weren't on the same team.

Today they'd sat on the lawn, and Gabi had cried while she accused Zoya of not thinking to suggest to Cinque that the two of them carry out the errands Teko, Yolanda, and Tania had been sent to complete. Of just plain *not thinking*. Gabi shook her head, burdened with the inexpressible complexity of her emotions. But they knew each other so well now that Zoya no longer wished to see to a deeper level of Gabi's character: Gabi was now as much an agglomeration of annoying habits as any stranger, except that she was stupefyingly predictable to boot. When Gabi cried, Zoya always had to fight the impulse to laugh. It was the cruelest thing she'd ever recognized in herself. It was like watching a clown weeping clown tears in clown clothes. Gabi blubbered and snuffled on that retarded Compton lawn and Zoya wanted alternately to laugh out loud and to crush her ex-lover's skull.

Now she started heading off to her own van, with her own team of Cujo and Fahizah. Gabi reached out and held her by her sleeve.

"Mizmoon," she said, "happy birthday." She held up her wristwatch to show that it was past midnight. May 17: Zoya was twenty-four.

"Damn, don't call me that."

"That's your *name*. You *chose* it."

"I *choose* Zoya."

"We need to talk."

You need, thought Zoya, but she looked directly into Gabi's eyes and raised her chin to indicate that she was listening.

"There's something wrong here."

"What do you mean, something wrong?"

"The way we sat. For hours, Trish."

Zoya cringed. Especially don't call her Trish. She would choose her names from now on, as often as necessary, swapping whenever one became freighted with outcast meaning.

"So?"

"The police are supposedly coming, and we sit for hours without a word of protest."

"Protesting what?"

"The just sitting there."

"Cinque had to work it out."

"And no one's allowed to talk while he does it? That's bullshit, Trish."

They were whispering in the din of the complaining engines.

"What's your point? My team's leaving."

"Team. You know what this is turning into?"

"What is this turning into?"

"This is turning into like one of those whatchamacallits I read about in *Time* last year. Cults."

"Like people in hoods and altars? Drinking blood? You insult me. You insult our hard work, our comrades." Then, bitterly: "*Time*."

"No," said Gabi, falteringly. "Like the Hare Krishnas. The Moonies."

Utopian hucksters, dealing in a new variant on the familiar people's opiate, with daily sales quotas. Their kind would be put against the wall. A look of disgust crossed Zoya's face: a slight curl of the lip, the subtlest suggestion of a rolled eyeball. She sensed the presence of the expression and exaggerated it in case Gabi had missed it.

"'Any comrade may leave the guerrilla forces if she or he feels that they no longer feel the courage or faith in the People and the struggle that we wage.'" Zoya quoted from memory.

Gabi walked off.

It was snug in the little apartment on Parker Street where Zoya wrote the Codes of War with Cinque the previous March. It was a rainy spring, and they worked in the kitchen, with the oven door open to warm the room. In the persistent damp, paperback book covers curled back upon themselves and photographs she'd pinned to the walls rolled up tight as scrolls. They had a series of running jokes about the oven, the oven door. Very funny at the time. Delirious. Everything had a heightened sense of meaning in that brief interlude of revolutionary domesticity. Cin was handy. The circular fluorescent buzzed annoyingly; he went to the hardware store and brought back mysteriously useful items in a brown paper bag, replaced the fixture with an incandescent. Soon they sat in the white silence of a GE Soft White bulb, hunting and pecking, holding the world at arm's length while it waited for their embrace.

TANIA CAN'T STAND BEING with these people, she realizes. While Teko and Yolanda argue about whether they ought to leave now or remain through the second feature just in case, she stretches out in the back next to the blanket. The van smells like warm ketchup. The blanket seems to shiver or tremble from time to time. She pats the blanket on the head. "It's OK," she says. "You'll be OK."

Despite the engaging subject matter of the film, Teko is in favor of leaving. Yolanda is opposed. The details of the argument are sheer static, a kind of buzzing in the front, and Tania ignores them, patting the blanket with Dan Russell under it at regular intervals, as if she were stirring a pot. At one o'clock the movie ends, and dozens of cars start up and switch on their headlights. Teko and Yolanda argue about whether they should leave right away or wait until the numbers of cars jockeying to join the long line have thinned. Teko wants to get started right away; Yolanda wants to wait awhile. The van sits motionless as they gesticulate and whisper fiercely in the front, occasionally bathed in the headlights of the cars outside that slowly turn, gravel crunching beneath their tires. Moths spin in the dusty shafts of moving light.

At last they join the queue and after a while merge with the traffic on the road.

"We need to get some sleep. We've got a big day tomorrow," says Teko.

"Can we just kind of scoot by the house? I mean, just to see."

"See what? They've gone. Gotta be."

"Well they didn't—when they never showed up at the drive-in I was thinking maybe somehow they haven't heard about the whole thing, our problem today."

(Another fight brewing, Tania thinks.)

"That's absurd. And you have any idea what the risk is?"

"This is the guy who fires off three rounds in a shopping mall talking to me about risk."

"It's against all the rules of urban guerrilla warfare."

"This is the guy who shoplifts a pair of socks talking to me about rules."

"*GOD* damn it, it was *NOT* a pair of socks it was a *FUCKING* bandolier, *do you have* it *FUCKING* straight?" The heel of his hand smacking the dashboard on each emphasized word. Yolanda, who has been driving very slowly in the right lane, pulls over to the side of the road and begins to cry, enormous choking sobs.

"Well can you just get a grip. I mean, until we're somewhere else? Ow, I hurt my hand."

"Where else? *Where*? Bandolier, socks—who cares? You did it, you stupid bastard. You had to go and take it, and now we're here, going in stupid circles nowhere. I feel lost, I feel totally lost and alone and stupid, stupid, *stupid*! for listening to anything you ever say."

"Let me tell you something."

"Don't tell me anything."

"Let me just tell you this, OK?"

41

"*Don't! Don't tell me anything!*" Yolanda opens her door and is out of the van.

"Oh shit. This isn't good. OK. We'll be back. Sit tight." And Teko leaves.

Tania and Dan Russell are alone in the van. Outside, the scanty traffic speeds down the road, each car making its own clean, distinct noise as it passes, the sound of things going smoothly for someone else.

"You OK?" Tania asks the blanket.

"I'm OK," says the voice of Dan Russell.

"Don't be scared," suggests Tania. "You'll be OK."

"I'm not scared," answers Dan.

"I was scared," says Tania. "I was really fucking freaked out. Man. They came through the door and they knocked me down and tied my arms and carried me out kicking and screaming. They hit me in the face and threw me into the trunk of a car. I thought I was gonna die."

"Well. You've all been pretty nice to me."

"We don't want. See, look: they *had* to scare me. I mean, my head was *so* screwed up before you wouldn't believe it. Plus, you know, they were planning for me to be with them, to learn with them, for a while. While with you we just need to have you with us for a little bit because of the van and all."

"Would you be being mean to me if I were going to be staying for a while?"

Tania smiles through the dark at the blanket. "No," she says.

They are quiet for maybe thirty seconds, and Tania watches Teko and Yolanda standing outside on the shoulder of the road. They're not arguing now; they're talking, working it out, and she suddenly feels both tremendous loneliness without the others, without Cujo particularly, and unexpected warmth for the two of them.

Dan Russell asks, "When did you decide to go with, join their army deal? Was there a plan with a deadline or something, or did it just like happen?"

Tania shrugs. "I just started listening and learning from like the day I was taken away, and I started changing my views about things. It was a real *process*, the way *I* see it, though I guess it seems like a real sudden change. But first it seemed like my dad wasn't trying real hard to get me back, so I start wondering why isn't he interested in complying with the spirit of the ransom demands, blah blah blah. I mean, he's cheaping out in this kind of totally obvious way when, you know, my family's got more money than God: let's face it. So they helped me, my comrades, they helped me see that these are all signs of like a hidden agenda, that there's serious pressure coming from somewhere to keep me from coming home because they don't want to be seen as giving in to the SLA demands."

"They who?"

"The pigs," answers Tania.

"Oh," says Dan.

"Because they're really, you know, the *People*'s demands. And so they gave me all sorts of shit to read and talk about. We do a lot of studying you know. This was like George Jackson and Malcolm and *Soul on Ice*. Blew me away."

"Oh," says Dan.

"And plus it was getting pretty obvious that the FBI and police are going to be gunning for me, what with all the statements flying around the press where they're just assuming that I haven't been even really *kidnapped*, even, like it's just this *ruse*, and the pigs are grilling Eric—you know who that is?"

"Your fiancé?"

"*Ex*. Who had totally nothing to do with it, which I didn't either I might add. Anyways, and then my mom accepts her being reappointed by Reagan to the UC Regents, which is this totally bogus inflammatory thing and in such bad faith under the circumstances I just basically thank the reasonableness and patience of the SLA for not killing me right on the spot."

Dan nods judiciously.

Outside, Teko and Yolanda have walked a little ways, hand in hand, and appear to be talking calmly. Tania sighs. Then she pats the blanket, which asks anyway why are the three of them on the run. And she sighs again and tells about Mel's, and about how she fired on the store, and about all this driving around, and car switching, and how it was they decided on Dan's van, and then about Mel's again: the shots, the gun jumping away, how it was the first time she'd fired using live ammunition, and Dan asks her how it felt.

"It was a good feeling," says Tania emphatically. "It was a good feeling to see my comrades come running across the street."

He just meant the actual what do you call physical act of the shooting. How did it feel to shoot the gun?

The doors open, and Teko and Yolanda get in.

"We're going to drive by Eighty-fourth," says Teko. "Everybody stay down back there."

The house on Eighty-fourth appears, sitting dark as they approach it. Not that there was any electricity to begin with. But the other cars have gone from the driveway and are not parked anywhere on the street, and the heavy surveillance drapes have been removed from the front windows. Teko sits behind the wheel staring rigidly ahead, proceeding at a steady 25 mph, while Yolanda and Tania both study the empty house as openly as they dare when they pass. Teko rounds the next corner with deliberate care, signaling ahead of time and decelerating into the turn. Then he gives the van gas, gradually bringing its speed up, heading for the anonymous arteries.

CAMILLA HALL
Gabi

What could be a more trusted component of American sensory experience than the feel of getting into a car for a long trip, the familiar abbreviation of the body as it settles into its seat? Gabi could have closed her eyes and imagined that she was heading just about anyplace as they set out into the ghetto night of Los Angeles. A little more than a year before she'd driven west from her parents' in Illinois to reunite and reconcile with Mizmoon, who'd flown to Denver to meet her. Life aboveground was so near at hand. Even today she could feel the familiarity of the enveloping seat during that trip, her car clean from its months inside her parents' garage, and well tuned, and an air freshener in the shape of a pine tree dangling from the rearview—her father's idea—emitting its overpowering aroma. Taking turns at the wheel, driving back to the Coast, they read aloud to each other from magazines with campy quizzes and grave stories about failed marriages. They stopped, got out, stretched, and walked around. Fill 'er up, ladies? Her plain round face behind its eyeglasses was anonymity itself. Her most political act was the writing of faintly erotic lesbian poems. And Mizmoon, flying into Stapleton, opening little cellophane packages of peanuts and counting out money to buy headphones from a smiling woman in a pillbox hat, she herself must have looked more like a stewardess than a radical.

And now this. She shook her head (Cin's eyes darting toward the rearview, to glare at her reflection, alert as ever for any sign of insubordination). One day Mizmoon had been talking about composting, the next about armed revolution. Was it that facile a set of alternatives? Had there been no sense of a complete overturning of one's life, much less of a wholesale exchange of personalities, when she'd taken up arms? And Gabi just felt dumb, reciting for Mizmoon ("*Zoya*, damn it!"): *I will cradle you/In my woman hips/Kiss you/With my woman lips.* "Stupid little boudoir poems," was what Mizmoon called them now. OK. All right. Gabi would follow her in good faith. She accepted that this was the love she just had to follow, wherever it led, even as it forsook her, turned on her, spit on her.

Oh, what was she doing here?

"What you having a conversation with your own self back there about, Comrade Gabi?" Cinque sounded mellow enough. He tilted back a pint bottle of blackberry brandy as he drove, his left hand laid atop the steering wheel.

She responded forthrightly. "I was just thinking it was funny, how we've come so far together in such a short time. This is never what I'd have imagined for myself just a year ago, but here we are."

"Funny?"

Cinque still sounded even-toned, but in Gelina's quick response Gabi read that she'd provoked him somehow:

"I think she means it like we came together so well that it's hard to believe it's only been, what, eight months?"

"Well, that's not 'funny.' That's a vision. On behalf the People."

"I don't mean ha-ha funny—"

"Watch you say, *bitch*. Enough trouble without you calling the SLA *funny*. *You* be the only thing *funny* here. Not *funny* we separated from our comrades, who may've fallen into enemy hands. Not *funny* we out in the open right now. Damn."

"I don't think she meant it that way, Cin." But Cinque shook Gelina's hand off his right arm, raising the pint bottle to his mouth.

"Then she ought to watch she says."

Gabi sighed; she was done talking. She was very tired anyway. Leaning her head against the cold window, she looked out at the dark houses they passed. Inside each was a blossom of life as complex as a flower, beautiful and strange and triumphant for as long as it continued. Her father had taught her that anyone else's life was unimaginable, that you needed patience, that it was the utmost arrogance to draw assumptions from the disheveled flesh that encased the spirit. Flowers she had taught herself about, drawing and painting them in compulsive detail from a bee's-eye view, in order to learn something about beauty's working parts. She looked at Cin, recalling "A new commandment give I unto you, that ye love one another," the divine injunction that had brought her family first to Africa, and then to South America. What she'd seen there had roused the gentleness in her. She was the most surprised of anyone to find herself holding a gun in her hands. She imagined herself explaining her life to her father, sitting opposite him before a fireplace, describing how similar her work was to his. They each had mugs full of some hot comfort, and her father nodded, nodded, though his eyes displayed the faltering of his understanding. Gabi slept.

ANGELA DEANGELIS ATWOOD
General Gelina

Make memory into a postcard and mail it off and it doesn't come back to get you.

Postcard one shows a high ranch house in North Haledon, NJ. A picture window to one side of the front door looks out on the house's twin, opposite. A pair of knotted-together sneakers swings from the power line overhead: the modern-day equivalent of heads on pikes, a form of expression imported from the nightmare crater of Paterson, scant blocks distant. But it loses something in translation. Here it signals boyish exuberance, the Norman Rockwell touch.

Today the driveway is full of cars. There are balloons taped to the English plane tree that shades the front yard. A hand-printed sign that says "Denise & Barry," with two entwined hearts, is stapled to the trunk. More hand-printed signs, arrows, guide arrivals around the house to the backyard, from which music can be heard, the sound of a Fender Rhodes keyboard that bangs out "Happy Together" from the muzzy depths of its sonic register.

It's Angel's sister's wedding. Angel's home from the land of the nuts. You seen Angel? What a mouth she's got on her. Beautiful wedding, yeah, but so what's up with Angel?

Gelina is stewing in her polyester floral sheath, counting the covered dishes being brought out from the kitchen, where the caterer is working, and laid on the white tablecloths clamped to the three long folding tables near the pool. She catches one of the waiters staring at her unshaved legs, and she gives him the finger.

She's got a real fuckin attitude today.

You know how many people all this shit could feed? She gestures toward the table, laden with trays and tureens and platters and chafing dishes abubble over cans of flaming Sterno. You know how many people are dying so you can eat this shit? Gestures with a lit cigarette, ash tumbling into some macaroni salad. Plus she's just a little pissed off she's not maid of honor.

Take it easy, Angel.

That's *Angela*.

Her sister: Cries. Cries and cries, how could you?

Her father: You know this is your sister's day, blah blah blah.

Her sister's privileged status notwithstanding, Gelina has no intention of just silently taking it. Soon she and her father are toe to toe, arguing intensely. There is a dusky blush to his face as he attempts to preserve decorum. The last time most of these people, the guests, were together was at her mother's wake. They look on through their crushed recollection of the saintly young daughter in mourning. She ruins the day.

You've ruined my special day, says Denise.

How dare you lecture me . . . as long as you're in my house . . . She doesn't need to hear the end of a single one of these sentences.

The next day she calls Pan Am to change her ticket. She takes a New Jersey Transit bus to the airport and pointedly stuffs the bridesmaid's dress in the garbage as she walks to the corner.

Postcard two shows the Great Electric Underground. A fake "mod" cocktail lounge on the ground floor of the B of A building, a place for horny businessmen and their pet toupees. About the hippest spot you'll ever find in a building named after a huge commercial bank. A month after participating in the assassination of the Oakland superintendent of schools, Gelina is finally ready to quit her day job.

Susan Rorvik, a friend she met while in the cast of a Company Theater production of *Hedda Gabler*, is quitting with her. She was Thea, Susan Hedda. They both are sick of being exploited in order to earn money, and neither of them is willing any longer to work for

47

"agents of the ruling class," as their five-page parting letter describes their employers, much less in the revealing dresses that accompany the job's compulsory flirtatiousness. They quit flamboyantly, dropping copies of the letter on the tables of their customers. Who look up in sleepy confusion, seeking the source of these unwanted gifts. Whatzis? Before leaving, Gelina turns around to survey the room. A bunch of affluent white men working on an afternoon buzz amid the weekday torpor of the gray holiday season. Composed. Serene, even. She raises a fist.

"Death to the fascist insect that preys upon the life of the People!"

Hey—'sChristmastime. Take it easy. A self-congratulatory laugh circulates softly throughout the carpeted room, like a shared secret, or the punch line to a dirty joke at her expense.

She and Susan send copies of the letter to KPFA and to the *Bay Guardian*. The one never airs it and the other never prints it. Angela moves in with her friends from Indiana, Drew and Diane Shepard, to cut costs and prepare for life underground. She stays in their closet-size spare bedroom, listening every night as they fight. She and Susan fall out of touch.

Cin was funny today, Gelina thought. She watched him, wondering what could be bothering him, as he sort of pitched and yawed behind the steering wheel, peering out into the night as if they were surrounded by a thick fog, turning to see that the other van still followed them, sighing and muttering inaudibly to himself. She sensed an approaching decision, a big one, judging from his behavior. Actually, she'd spent most of her life thinking about what could be bothering men, what it was that would please them. She wanted to hate her father, but as much as she tried to politicize all the "discoveries" she'd made about her banal upbringing, he was just another dumb daddy aching for the little girl he'd loved. The agitator's role didn't come naturally. She was a born conciliator, felt the memory of her sister's wedding as a bayonet.

And deep down she did think it was a special day. That's what she'd tell Denise when she saw her again, after.

She was basically a stuffed animal–type person.

Memory is a bayonet. *Mail it to some distant isle / with palm trees and a beach / where your daily troubles all will be / safely out of reach.*

. . .

Postcard three: Gelina's body goes unclaimed for days. Her ex-husband finally signs the necessary paperwork to have it shipped for burial.

Cin had a penciled list of addresses he consulted now and again, but apparently something at each of those locations disturbed him, because although he would slow the van as he approached them, he never stopped except once, on which occasion he'd gotten out and stood for a while on the dark lawn before a small house, the wind ruffling his jacket, before climbing back into the idling van, shaking his head. Something about this man today: not talking. Gelina held her wrist to the window to read her watch under the passing street-lights. Close to 3 a.m. There was zero traffic out at this hour, and the unmuffled engines made a lot of noise. Cin signaled a turn and headed the van toward Slauson, a big road where they wouldn't seem as conspicuous as they did crawling through residential streets. Behind Gelina, Gabi was sleeping, mouth agape and with her cheek pressed unattractively against the window. The only people she liked to watch sleeping were children. Through the rear window she saw the other van turn onto the avenue and begin to follow a few lengths behind. They rolled through a landscape of raw cinder-block meanness, past empty service stations, liquor stores, pawnshops, and check-cashing places. A used car lot sat behind a chain-link fence topped with barbed wire and multicolored plastic bunting that flapped noisily in the warm breeze. A patrol car heading in the opposite direction cruised toward them. Cin stared straight ahead, the muscles in his jaw bulging. Gelina tried to look unconcerned and happy. The two cops in the cruiser slid jaded eyes over them in the instant in which the two vehicles passed each other and decided it wasn't worth the trouble, apparently making the same decision about the van containing Cujo, Zoya, and Fahizah.

TANIA HAS BEGUN TO drop off to sleep when Teko speaks sharply to her, telling her to check her weapon to make sure there isn't a round in the chamber. She knows there isn't, but recognizing that this is to be a command performance for their captive, she chambers a round, and she's pleased that he watches avidly as she then easily ejects the bullet, removes the clip from the weapon to reinsert the cartridge, and then rams the clip home. She handles the rifle with the little showy flourishes that her familiarity with it will allow. All its working parts engage with satisfying clicks and snaps.

"You know," says Tania, offhandedly, "I heard a lot of bullshit about that bank robbery."

"Did you?" asks Dan, politely.

"It was totally, I don't know. Much ado about nothing."

"Well, I mean. I guess people were interested that you seemed to be doing something like a bank robbery. I mean after being kidnapped and stuff."

"But not that. Stuff about me being like tied to my gun so I couldn't put it down and go, Help, help, save me. About the others pointing their guns at me. I mean, what is that? I'm so obviously a committed, you know, guerrilla."

"Well, I guess since you got kidnapped people thought maybe you wouldn't want to, um, rob the bank with your, you know, kidnappers."

"Tell people that I said I did the bank robbery out of my own free will."

"Tell the press," emphasizes Teko.

"OK," says Dan.

You can mount these hills, climb toward the stars hanging high in the dark. The canyon roads remind Tania of the coast-bound highways back home, 84 and 92. The winding drives to those foggy, rocky beaches. Teko is hunched over the wheel to take the unfamiliar turns, giving the impression of great physical exertion. 92 she could drive in her sleep, she thinks, and she closes her eyes to greet the phosphene memory of the Denny's and Charley Brown's signs that lit the way until the road narrowed where it had been blasted out of the hillsides to form a high, perilous terrace over the coastal valleys of bush lupine and redwood. She thinks of 280, "The World's Most Beautiful Freeway." Sometimes, heading to Eric's apartment after school, when they'd first begun dating, she would downshift on the tight curve of the Sand Hill Road exit ramp, avoiding any contact between her foot and the brake pedal while she cycled through the gearbox as the car climbed to the end of the ramp. Eric had an apartment down the Peninsula in Menlo Park, a cute IMMAC. 1BR, rumpled and full of books and papers, somehow looking collegiate and manly instead of monkish and bookwormy. He was brilliant and handsome and perfect. She was sixteen.

Her parents called him Toothbrush for the mustache; it was the most beautiful mustache in the world. They thought he was poor and after her money, though he was the son of a Palo Alto stockbroker; she would have given him everything or lived with him in a tent. They thought he was a weakling (her mother asked, "Where did all the real men go?") when he was actually a champion all-around athlete; she saw him as an Adonis. They thought he was effete, an irrelevant aesthete, though he'd been trained in physics; to her he was a practical man of action. They thought he was a radical, a bomb thrower, though he was a McGovern liberal; together they'd change the world.

Then she got tired of proving the point. She sat and watched as he twirled the dial and then fell into silence to begin his indiscriminate TV watching. Every night the same. She heated up food in cans and pouches and poured it onto plates and bowls. Then she talked on the phone, or studied, and watched him watching TV. Every night he would bask in the television's cold shifting light that lent him the pallid aspect of a corpse. And then one night.

She entered the kitchen, and the doorbell rang. The doorbell rang, and Eric headed for the door. Eric headed for the door and slid it open.

Oh, she thought. This is pretty weird. "Put the chain on," she said. Eric responded with the slightest dismissive shrug.

Slid it open to confront a girl who said there'd been an accident.

Alice thought that she meant she'd hit her MG and became pissed off.

She said there's been an accident; can she use the phone? She backed up and hit a car. She pointed down at the ground, to indicate the parking garage beneath.

There was a strange vibe coming from this girl, emotion shredding that voice on the doorstep, a wayward pitch that marked a seeming contradiction between what this girl was saying and what she meant, and what she was doing and what she would prefer to be doing, and this agitation was beyond that warranted by a low-speed fender bender.

She pointed at the ground to indicate the parking garage downstairs. Eric glanced down the hall at the telephone, a green wall model, peering at it as if to see if it was capable of being used by a stranger seeking help on a winter's evening. When he looked down the hall, he looked right through Alice. It's her last memory of him.

The girl outside shifted her weight, Eric turned back after checking out the phone, and from deep inside Alice actual expressions from the xenophobic nightmare of her mother's phrasebook began rising up, free-floating, to seek their application in this circumstance: *drop out, druggie, going to hell in a handbasket, hippie, take some responsibility, nigger lover, have they no shame, undesirable elements*, each sounding fluent and expressive to her though she felt no anger, only the pull, from the next room, of the neglected television making her impatient with this interlude.

And then the door was shoved open entirely, and the two men came in, with guns.

She tries to imagine, for the hundredth time, Eric aiming a rifle at a living target.

There was a time when Alice thought it was possible that a poem or a song could save every faltering affair in the universe; there was a time when Alice thought she would use it, as she might an incantation, on a night when the TV finally ran out of things to say.

Tania wryly quotes to herself: *Death to the Fascist Insect that Preys upon the Life of the People!*

NANCY LING PERRY
Fahizah

Fahizah noticed in the rearview that the instant after passing them, the pigs swung into a wide arc to make a U-turn and began following them from about twenty yards behind. It was a quiet and ominously piglike move, and she was sure the pigs' eyes glowed red at the moment they'd targeted them, like pig androids in a pig killing machine. Fahizah checked her speedometer to make sure she was within the limit, whatever the hell that was around here. Thirty? Eighty-seven? Quarter past three? Huh? She was actually going about forty-two. Holy shit. She realized that she was sort of near Whittier College. The memories came seeping back into her pounded consciousness. Not a happy year, the one she spent there, but it presented her now with a golden opportunity to exercise classic revolutionary deceit: She was on her way to Whittier College, OK, pig? Go ahead and call Pig Central and find out if what she said wasn't true. She could tell all about the local landmarks: the library, the college theater, the fire-breathing stanwixauropodinoose . . . and . . . and . . . they better believe her, man. The cruiser followed them, flat and menacing. She would shoot their pig faces off. She would steal their pig badges and pig guns from their faceless pig corpses. She thought: Fahizah: the name means one who is victorious. Was her mouth moving? She raised a hand from the steering wheel to touch her lips and found them muttering, in silence, independent of her thoughts, whatever the hell they were.

Cujo turned around again to look at the cops.

"Will you stop?" said Zoya. "You're just giving them a reason."

"Pigs don't need a reason," said Cujo. "They're pigs." He and Fahizah giggled. Zoya looked annoyed.

"Just stop looking back there."

"I smell *bacon*," said Cujo, singsong. He raised his nose and sniffed noisily.

Fahizah looked into the rearview, thinking: There is no flight to freedom except that of an armed projectile. She kept the van at a steady forty, the engine quietly speaking to her, *fine fine fine you're doing fine fine fine*, the message traveling from the gas pedal to her foot and up through her spinal cord, as she signaled and eased into the right lane to give the pigs a chance to pass them, to disengage. A fighting chance. To the rear, the cruiser shifted along with them. She thought it might take off any second now. She thought she'd read something about that, flying pigmobiles. Pigs with wings. Heh. They would fly overhead to release the death gas on them, cause them to crash their cars. Then take their bodies to the Dissection Center. Display their brains in some pig trophy case that toured Amerikkka to dissuade the People from attempting to challenge fascist power. They would hook the brains up to a pig Mind Control device that would have them spouting pigisms in their own voices. That was probably something to worry about maybe.

"I say if they pull us over that we just kill them, ask questions later," said Zoya. That suited Fahizah just fine. She patted her personal sidearm, a revolver, snug in its shoulder holster, thinking: The only way to destroy fear is to destroy the makers of fear.

They continued east on Slauson for another half mile or so. Ahead of them, Cinque kept a steady course. Suddenly he signaled left. The van's brake lights flared as it slowed and turned into a small street leading back into the bungalow maze. Fahizah noted its name as she passed: *Ascot.* Like a man in a whadayacallit smoking jacket. Like a man in a smoking jacket holding a whadayacallit snifter. Like a man in a smoking jacket holding a snifter taking a cigar from a whadayacallit humidor. Like a man in a smoking jacket holding a snifter taking a cigar from a humidor. Yeah. That's what it was like.

"Nobody look!" warned Zoya.

Fahizah said, affecting a British accent: "Would you care for a cigar?" Zoya stared.

Why the hell would anyone *look*, man? Fahizah would *feel* her way back to her comrades. She had reversed the polarity of the Fascist Government transponder that had been subcutaneously implanted, and now she could home in on her comrades at any distance on Earth as well as Zibiriliax; she'd tested it.

Still, she tried to suppress the desolation of the thought: *We're totally alone.*

They drove on, perhaps two miles, until they approached the dry bed of the Los Angeles River and the overpass that crossed the Long Beach Freeway. There the cruiser that shadowed them abruptly turned off to follow a course parallel to the highway. When their pursuers disappeared from sight, Fahizah pulled over, bringing the van to a stop amid the low industrial buildings.

"Now what?" said Cujo.

"We go back and rendezvous," said Fahizah.

"Where'd those guys turn off?" said Cujo.

As Fahizah opened her mouth, Zoya answered: "Ascot."

Such a display of diligence should have pleased General Fahizah. It pissed her off instead, as she was forced to add lamely, feeling the weakness of the imprecision, "It was kind of near Central." Abruptly she opened the door and got out to stretch her legs. She felt drained and let down all of a sudden. Her mind felt flat and ordinary.

The street outside was quiet, with only a faded wash of noise from the nearby freeway. She was tired, and her eyes ached. She stared morosely across the street at the unappealing landscape, considering her last meal, a congenitally nasty farrago of canned spinach, okra, and mackerel. An ember of discomfort burned at the center of her stomach. She wanted a cheeseburger from the Zim's restaurant on Nineteenth and Taraval, with french fries and an icy glass of Coca-Cola that burned the back of the throat as it went down.

She felt like nothing, a nobody from nowhere.

Inside the van, Cujo was absorbed in picking his nose. Zoya climbed out to stand beside Fahizah.

"That got kind of scary," she confessed.

"Oh, man. I need, like, a fucking break. That wore me out," said Fahizah.

"You want me to drive?"

Fahizah nodded. She leaned against the van and put a hand to her face, sensing some stifled impulse behind her eyes, the snots and tears that never came—never! She felt so sorry for herself she decided to fake it, a little, drawing in big gulps of air and shaking with a simulated passion that was totally counter to the crawl-in-a-hole thing she was feeling. Anyway, it was the wrong audience. Zoya just stood and watched. She'd spent the day with crying Gabi, Fahizah remembered. Gabi cried, Yolanda cried, Teko cried, Gelina didn't cry much but you knew she would if it came down to it. Tania didn't cry. An interesting thought. She pitied her, stuck somewhere with Teko and Yolanda; what a pair of royal pains in the ass they could be. If anything could make her cry, it would be getting caught with the two of them at a fork in the road; the arguing would go on forever. This made Fahizah smile. She lifted her dry face from her cupped hand and reached up to clap Zoya on the shoulder, then walked around to get in on the passenger side.

Zoya drove back to Ascot slightly above the limit. The cops were either after them or they weren't, they figured. A certain jaunty fatalism seemed called for. They zipped down the dark street, and Cin's van flashed its lights at them as they passed. Zoya slowed and parked at the corner (next to a fire hydrant, Fahizah noted. But she didn't say anything) and the three of them walked back for a brief, excitedly whispered reunion with the others.

Cin suggested that now would be as good a time as any to institute the search-and-destroys, so they re-formed their caravan of two and began slowly driving through the neighborhood in search of a welcoming sign. It wasn't long before they spotted the lights inside the stucco house at 1466 East Fifty-fourth Street.

Awakening in the 6:30 gray, Yolanda asks what time it is. All four of them are lying on the carpeting in the back of the van, and Tania wakes up confused and exhausted. When she opens her eyes, she sees Dan Russell is out from under the blanket and gazing at her, and his smile is a pretty nice how do you do first thing. Her hand reaches for the monkey.

Teko suggests hijacking a car, striding purposefully toward one stopped at a red light and ousting its fucking occupants at gunpoint. Yolanda intimates, though she does not come right out and say, that to allow Dan to return home while nearly simultaneously making their presence known to yet another, almost certainly more hostile party would undo all the hard work of the last twelve hours. She would prefer that she and Tania first pose as attractive hitchhikers (she guarantees that a typical sexist will bumble along) and then, after securing a ride, kidnap their benefactor, who'll be in no position to alert the pigs. Yolanda's will prevails, and Tania now hurriedly prepares to commit at least one more capital offense, as well as miscellaneous lesser felonies, adjusting her wig and pulling her shoes on. Yolanda gives her a revolver, which she tucks into her waistband, but Teko tells her that her blouse doesn't cover it completely. She tries closing her jacket over it, but that leaves a curious bulge. Finally she places it in her waistband at the small of her back, then tries drawing it a couple of times. It appears in her hand smoothly enough, though Yolanda assures her, "I'll draw first." They leave.

"Dan," says Teko, "there's something I've been meaning to mention long as we're alone for a couple of minutes."

"Uh, OK."

"We just want to let you know we think you're really great. A big help, with the handcuffs and all. And when I think: some people would make a real big stink out of getting abducted. I remember I was a kid, around your age, something interrupted my plans I went apeshit, big time. But you've been aces: driving around, lousy fucking night's sleep, wondering what was gonna happen."

"Well, you've been real great too. All of you."

"Well, good. Anyway. I just was thinking, Yolanda and me and Tania too, that if you wanted to lead a youth unit of the SLA, I think you'd be perfect. You're just the sort of young person we're looking for."

"Well, um. I don't know what to say except that well, I'm flattered, first, but even though I can see your point?"

"Mmm?"

"Even though I can see your point of view politics really isn't my thing? You know? No offense."

"No, no. I understand. Just the same, if you change your mind."

"Oh, sure."

"We know where to find you."

"Oh, sure."

"We know where you live, OK." Teko makes a little gun out of his thumb and forefinger and aims it at Dan, bringing down the hammer of his thumb. He grins. Then Yolanda and Tania drive up in a new Lincoln Continental. A man is sitting in the backseat, looking like a frightened bird.

"Well, Dan. You take care, now."

"You too. Good luck."

"Need any gas money to get back home?"

"Um, I'm all right."

"'Kay. Let me have that blanket we used on you, will you? Just wrap the rifles up in it. Yeah. And give us about a half an hour, OK? Count to a million."

"Jeez," says Dan, a little affronted, "I won't tell anybody."

"I know you won't. Bye, Dan."

"Bye!" Dan waves out the window at Tania and Yolanda as Teko gets out of the van, carrying the bundled rifles, shopping bags, and other gear.

"You're gonna have to scunch down, mister," says Teko, getting into the backseat. "Hang on a sec. Did you check him out?"

Yolanda shrugs, and Tania shakes her head.

"Christ, for all you know the guy could be a pig." Teko goes through the man's pockets, finding a wallet. "Ray Fraley. What's your line, Ray Fraley?"

"I'm a, I'm a contractor."

"Like, buildings? Excellent. Useful, productive. Do you build good buildings?"

"I. Yes. I mean. How do you mean?"

Teko shakes his head. "Man, I'm not trying to trip you up with bullshit doublespeak. Do you build *good* buildings or do you build *bad* buildings?"

"Yes, they're good, I'm proud of them."

"Good. Good. OK, now, I'm hereby expropriating this here two hundred fifty dollars in your wallet in the name of the Symbionese Liberation Army. It will be put to good use. Now, scunch down. We're going to put this blanket over you for your own protection. Don't do anything weird or flaky or we'll shoot you and you'll be dead and that's just not gonna be a good thing. OK?"

"OK."

Teko drops the blanket over the man sprawled uncomfortably across the floor in the back of the car. He notices that the blanket is trembling; his mind articulates the phrase *shaking like a leaf*, which reminds him, inexplicably, of his mother. He asks the shaking blanket: "Are you OK under there? You don't have a bad heart or anything, do you?"

The blanket shakes some more.

"I mean, we really don't want you to get sick on us or anything. I'm asking are you OK?"

"I'm OK."

"That's good. 'Cause you're just shit out of luck if you have a heart attack. I just need you to know that."

1466 East Fifty-fourth Street

Sheila Mears wanted the lights down low while they sat quiet and listened to music in the front room, but she didn't want Charles Gates getting the wrong idea. She could tell from the look on his face all night that he figured he was the wolf in the chicken coop with them all, and when the card game stopped and the wine kept coming she just knew, she read in his face that taking your pick look she's seen before. And she didn't feel like it, she knew Lillian didn't if what she said was to be believed (which it wasn't always), and she didn't either think it was correct for a girl of Crystal's age of seventeen years, not that she was all that innocent, but you know.

And her own kids would be getting up pretty soon now for school; she didn't want all that going on while they trying to get to the corn-flakes.

She'd gotten up to go into the kitchen to get another nerve pill when there was a knock at the door. This wasn't that unusual. People knew Sheila and Lillian liked to stay up and have company. Nothing duller than a quiet house. Her mother kept a quiet house. But four in the morning: kind of late. Other hand, here come the cavalry is how you want to look at it in regards to Charles Gates and his wolf-looking face. She opened the door. Lillian joined her at the entryway. Outside a good-looking stranger was standing at ease on the porch like the most natural thing.

"Hello, sisters," he said. "My name is Cinque."

"Sin Q?" repeated Lillian, giggling.

"Yes, sister. I need your help. I saw your lights. The police are looking for my friends and I, and we need a place to stay for several hours."

He spoke formally; he was reaching. Sheila was impressed and amused at the same time.

"Why I'd want to hide you from the police?"

Cinque smiled. He was a fine-looking man. "We're the SLA. Freedom fighters fighting on behalf of all the People. Maybe," he added, "you've heard of us."

"What's going on out there?" yelled Crystal, who'd been left alone with Charles Gates in the front room.

"Well, I don't know," said Sheila.

"There'll be no trouble, I promise you." He reached into his pocket and pulled out five twenties, which he fanned out so that Sheila and Lillian could see them all. They looked real. Sheila and Lillian put their heads together for a little chat.

"What we got in here," said Lillian, phrasing the decisive argu-ment, "they could take worth a hundred dollars?"

Charles Gates was drafted to help tote in supplies. Soon Sheila was surprised to see all manner of arms and ammunition coming in the front door and being carried through the house to the kitchen, along with suitcases, footlockers, and cardboard cartons. Plus white people. Sheila never had a white person in her house before. They come to the door to sell her Jesus. They read her meters and delivered her mail. But never inside. She kept waiting for another black face, as four white women and a white man came through the door, all partly hidden behind whatever they carried.

"Thank you, sister. You are helping the cause of freedom." The fact that Cinque uttered this while holding a sloshing gasoline can put a vague fear in Sheila's insides. The others followed suit as if cued, mechanically thanking Sheila.

"What about me?" said Lillian, jokingly.

They all dutifuly extended thanks to Lillian, who burst out laughing, breaking the tiniest of holes in the white ice. Cinque then explained that they needed to hide the vans somewhere. Charles Gates knew just the place. He said he'd take Cinque.

Outside, Charles Gates said, "You the ones took Alice Galton."

"We have liberated her mind of fascist oppression," said Cinque, still grandiloquent.

"Where she at?"

"She is with a combat unit, brother, on special assignment. And that is all I'm at liberty to say at present."

The sky began to grow light. Darkness would never touch this home again. Lillian, Sheila, and Crystal remained in the front room while their guests occupied themselves in the kitchen.

"You see all that? What you get us into?"

"Me? You the one said let's take the hundred dollars."

"Damn, I didn't know they was a whole army and shit."

The front door opened, and Charles Gates and Cinque entered.

"Cinque say they need a place to stay about two weeks," reported Charles Gates.

Sheila snapped her fingers; there was a place for rent around the corner, on Compton. Oh yeah, said Charles Gates, lightly striking himself in the forehead. And we was right there, too. They went out again.

"Hi." It was two of the white girls, the teensy one and the pretty one. They didn't know what to say but wanted to say something. This was white gratitude toward blacks: the idea was you were supposed to divine it from their sheer dumb presence. Lillian asked them why they were on the move.

"Long story short, pigs foun' us," said the teensy one. "Dey lucky we all left fo' dey got there."

Sheila wrinkled up her nose as if she had smelled a mouse lying dead behind the baseboard.

"I believe it," said Lillian amiably. "You look like you ready for them."

Gradually the kitchen emptied, and the hall filled with milling SLA members again, peering in at their black benefactors with that mutely abject appreciation. Sheila felt uncomfortable. And she wanted to see what was going on in her kitchen.

"Why don't you all sit down and I will see what is going on in my kitchen," she said. She prided herself on being a very direct person. The SLA obediently traded places with the black women.

Sheila had some trouble with the kitchen. One thing, she spent about an hour the day before cleaning it all up with Fantastik and Mop & Glo and all that. The real official cleanup for killing things that can't be seen with your naked eye. And now there was a bunch of dirty ass shit in here, and stacked on her dinette too. Like who hasn't got sense enough to stack crates of bullets on the floor, thank you.

Lillian knew her roommate was a fussy person. She saw the look on her face.

"Sheila, girl, it's just for today. They call up about Compton Avenue and they gone."

"Yeah, they in here now, though."

"Sheila, the man just paid the rent."

"Girl can't add."

"Your half the rent."

"Can't buy peace of mind."

"Buy a whole lot of other stuff," said Lillian.

Charles Gates banged on the glass of the kitchen door with his fist and the three women jumped.

"Here's Cinque," announced Charles Gates. "He likes the place. He thinks it's fine. He's calling up today." He sounded breathless, excited. He added, "I'm skipping work today, helping Cinque out."

"Who cares?" said Sheila sulkily. Someone was honking in the driveway.

"That's my ride," said Charles Gates, beaming. "I'm telling them to go on without me."

"How they know you suppose to be here? Cocky turkey."

. . .

"Charles, what?"

"You never guess who's in here. Cinque, that's who. The Symbionese Liberation Army who took Alice Galton. They got guns and they got bombs. You want to see him? They just show up, middle of the night, blam, out of nowhere. I'm, like, wooo. This is different. I'm staying. I'm helping Cinque today. You want to see him?"

The other man looked at his watch. "I gotta open today," he said, apologetically. "Maybe I'll come see him tonight."

LETTER TO THE PEOPLE
May 18, 1974
Women's Bathroom
Hollywood Station, Vine Street

It's an odd note that Tania duplicates in her Palmer script on sheets of blank notepaper she finds in Ray Fraley's glove compartment, taking whispered dictation from Teko and Yolanda. The brief message will be deposited at several prearranged dead drops around South Central Los Angeles. What it means is that tomorrow another communication will be left in the restroom at the bus station. If conditions are favorable, there may actually be a physical reunion there between the divided forces of the SLA.

They stop at a drugstore off Hollywood Boulevard to buy Scotch tape before getting on the freeway and heading back toward Inglewood. On one occasion Yolanda believes she sees Dan Russell's van up ahead in the number two lane, and she slows so abruptly that Teko slides off the backseat, landing with his knees on Ray Fraley's back. Teko curses and snarls but Ray Fraley gives only a sharp inhalation, because he is afraid to cry out.

1466 East Fifty-fourth Street

Sheila's kids came into the kitchen for breakfast.

"I'm hungry," said Timmy, the eleven-year-old.

"I'm hungry," said Tony, the eight-year-old.

But there were all these boxes, bullets and the like, stacked up in front of the cabinet where she kept cereal, and she wasn't about to touch them.

Who're these white people? What's all this stuff? It was a different kind of morning, just say. She put glasses of milk in front of the kids.

"Yuck!" said Timmy.

"I want Lucky Charms!" said Tony.

"We don't have no Lucky Charms, you know that," said Sheila. She got up the courage to take the boxes of cartridges and gingerly move them to another spot. They were heavy. She opened the cabinet. No cereal. In the other room, Cinque was handing Crystal a twenty and sending her to Sam's to buy beer, bread, cold cuts, and cigarettes, and Sheila asked her nice to buy some cereal and milk. Crystal shot her some look; probably she was counting on keeping the change. Sheila wasn't going to hold her breath, just say.

Dead Drop 1
UNITED STATES POST OFFICE, COMPTON STATION

He says, Are you telling me these trucks stayed right here? and I said, Yes, *sir*. And he looks at me funny and says, They're dirty, these trucks, because they are parked on this street all night. At first, you know, I think he is joking. But still I'm looking him right in the face because it's near impossible to tell. He's a real cold fish. Cold fish eyes. By and by I'm like: he means it.

So what I said?, I said to him, We ain't got the keys, sir. And he says: What? What did you say?

Yeah, like that. I tell him, We'd like to keep 'em looking clean too, sir, but we ain't got the keys to the trucks. The carriers come back and park them where they like. Been doing it that way a long time, I guess.

Well I, well you know, you know what I heard was. What I heard was that they sent him over here from Century City 'cause he's re-weighing all the damn flats up there. Says he knows the mailroom boys in all the office buildings are fudging on the first class rates. Every now and then he finds one that's under by ten cents or so and he sends a bunch of 'em right back. Lawyers going bananas in their fancy offices. You know how they like to send out their flats.

Say, now what's that gal up to?

You lose something under there, miss?

Damnedest things people do.

Sure be happy to help you find it. No questions asked.

Well, she's got her mind fixed on something. Not that I'm ever sorry to see a lady in that position. Anyways, that's why I'm heading out to the hardware, get these here keys copied. Bet you lot of people get their mail late today, I'll tell you.

Tania stands and readjusts her wig and casts a quick glance around her. The man and his companion, both wearing uniforms that seem somehow even more drab, even less convincing an assertion of authority, than those worn by ordinary letter carriers, watch her abstractedly while they talk. She is a sort of oddity here in Compton. The drop is under one of the drive-up mailboxes behind the post office building; the Lincoln waits around the corner. Tania is unarmed and feels exposed here without the others. As she hustles back, more anxious about getting to the car than she is concerned about the LETTER TO THE PEOPLE's surviving the curiosity of the two postal employees, she catches a sidelong glimpse of her own photograph, hanging among the wanted posters.

1466 East Fifty-fourth Street

Sure enough, there was no breakfast in the bag Crystal lugged back. Sheila hoped it was nice and heavy. Cinque cracked open one of the quarts of Colt .45 and lit a cigarette while Crystal carried the remaining stuff into the kitchen, where the fat white one right away started making sandwiches. She was pretty nice, the only one didn't creep around like she was in a museum of black people or something. Sheila asked for two sandwiches for Timmy and Tony right away, then called them in from the front room, where they were watching cartoons with the white man. The kids ate a sandwich and Charles Gates had one and Crystal too and the pile of sandwiches for Cinque and the white people looked pretty skinny, but the fat one didn't seem to mind too much. Sheila took another nerve pill.

Charles Gates took his sandwich into the front room, where he stood eating it, looking on as Cinque and the white dude watched the street through the windows. Cinque spoke to him without turning around.

"You think you could find us a cheap van or station wagon? Just buy it from whoever?"

"Well, I could look around."

"Just need to run, that's all." Cinque reached into his pocket and pulled out a wad of cash. He counted out ten twenties, two fifties, and two hundreds.

Charles Gates suddenly had this great entrepreneurial idea: He'd call around to friends on behalf of the SLA, offering fifty dollars for the afternoon's use of their car, and then offer copious apologies when the SLA disappeared with it. It was such a sweet idea he started right away, walking to the pay phone down at Sam's. Hey, man, I said it's for the SLA! No takers, though, and they all gave him shit about it. Think I'm lying? He walked back to the house, fingering the cash in his pocket, to tell Cinque he'd try again later. He'd hold on to the money, right, just in case he had to make a deal quick.

Dead Drop 2
MABE'S, NORMANDIE AVENUE

Mmmmm-hmm. So I say, I'm a tell you what you need to do, girl. You better watch your mouth. Mmmmm-hmm. 'Cause I don't want to hear that. 'Cause that's some feeb excuses. 'Cause that's *bull*. I never had no problems getting in the movies. I hand them they money and they say, Come on *in*, Sharifa, same as everbody else. And she say, she say, Why you don't believe me? See my ticket? Show me some raggedy-ass stub she be picking up off the ground somewheres. This here girl a genius of deception, I tell you. Mmmmm-hmm. And she goes, they say I dressed in-appropriate. And I say of course you are dressed in-appropriate*ly*. You dressed in-appropriate*ly* in here. You dressed in-appropriate*ly* when you be going down to the church. You dressed in-appropriate*ly* when you lying on your sofa at your house. You are a in-appropriate person by in large, you knowm saying? That's why my momma tell me not to book around with you when we kids. That's why you pregnant when you eighteen, fool. Mmmmm-hmm. That's why you gots *four* kids and *no* money. Mmmmm-hmm. But they let anybody in the movies. They let Woolsy in and he a screamer. They let gang kids in and they be ripping on the seats with they knives. And I give you five dollars to be taking my kids to the matinee, and I want to know where it's at and what you did with them when they wasn't at the movies like I said. I'm sorry, I just saying the truth 'cause God don't like a liar and God don't like ugly. That's what I tell her.

Honey, what can I get you?

Just coffee? Honey, you look hungry!

All right, all right, just axing 'cause you look like you need a real meal. In there. Uh-huh.

Damn, they got a what you call, Hamburger Hamlet, right up near the Forum if she only want to eat where the white people at.

Well, if she just need to take a pee, I let her. Not like some cheap white restaurant lady.

In the ladies' room Yolanda raises her shirt and untapes the note from her abdomen. Stiffly, she lowers herself to her knees to peer under the sink and, feeling satisfied that conditions are OK under there (on the basis of criteria she invents on the spot), she tapes the message to the underside of the basin. She rises and dusts off her knees and then leaves the room. She places a quarter next to the steaming cup of coffee and is about to walk out, but then she stops, fixing the coffee with sugar and plenty of milk to cool it. She drinks it down quickly, feeling upon her the eyes of the counter woman and her single customer. She tells herself that she feels closer to these people every day. She is trying hard to love them.

Meanwhile . . .

It is 8:55 and a police sergeant lifts a bullhorn to his lips.

"To those inside the house at Eight thirty-three West Eighty-fourth Street, this is the Los Angeles Police Department. We want you to come out of the front door with your hands up. We want you to come out immediately. You will not be harmed." He lowers the bullhorn and looks at the device while he awaits a response, as if he expected to see smoke curling from it. One hundred twenty-five cops and federal agents are here, ready for a siege, ready to see blood rain from the poor shack they surround and fix their attention on, 125 law officers wearing jumpsuits and flak jackets, laid across rooftops with powerful scoped rifles trained on Prophet Jones's hovel, concealed in the shrubbery with M-16s and tear gas canisters, crouched behind unmarked cars, all squired by dozens of members of the press, who stand back across the street with notepads and doughnuts and cardboard cups of tepid coffee. Their attention is beginning to wander. The LAPD commander on the scene notes this and imposes himself on the FBI supervisor, calling for immediate action. The agent agrees.

There is a ritual uneventfulness to what follows, the way that brutal and violent games intersperse bursts of outraged fury with prolonged and decorous procedural maneuvers. Four FBI men break from cover to dash toward the house, two covering with M-16s as the others fire Flite-Rite rockets bearing CS tear gas through the front windows of the building. Then all four men disappear again, to rejoin the waiting.

Five minutes later another team of four agents storms the house, breaking down the door and rushing in with rifles. The remaining lawmen and the press wait.

Then one of the agents emerges from the house, his gun put up, and removes his gas mask. He is supposed to be indignant—he says, "Shit!"—but he's actually relieved to live another day.

Dead Drop 3
CRENSHAW ACRES SHOPPING CENTRE, INGLEWOOD

So I'm out here with my staple gun and my flyers, going around and hoping for the best. They do run away sometimes and you just have to face that and I said to Ralph last night just before bed when I'd gone outside and called for her for a little while with no luck that

67

you just have to face it. Cats aren't the most domesticated of creatures, you know? It is the essence of their appeal if you ask me. They were in the wilds aeons after dogs had already made themselves right at home among man, because I suppose dogs had more of a function in a hunter-gathery kind of culture like they liked back then. Then of course people started growing things and storing grain and before you know it you have mice and rats getting into the grain and that's just not good at all for the good people of the Fertile Crescent or wherever it was and so cats sort of insinuated themselves and the people looked the other way and then the next thing you know they're carving these big statues of them and praying to them! And from there you get the common house cat that we all know. But common as they are, you become oh so attached to them. The last one I had, it was all over at seven, kidney problems, that's how the males go. I'll never have another male again; it breaks your heart. But we moved recently, not too very far from where we were, I suppose she may have gotten confused. Somebody over there is probably feeding her, and I'll be heading over there with my flyers and my staple gun, and then I'll be off to the Humane Society to check the binders and see if anyone's reported finding her. There's always a little hope.

Young man, do you need to get in here? I don't mean to be blocking your path but as I'm telling this young lady here I want to cover this bulletin board nicely because—oh, excuse me!

Some people just aren't very nice these days. Well, I don't let it bother me, though I do hope that it's a nice sort of person who spots her. I've heard terrible stories about vivisectionists, do you know, who slice open living animals for science—science they call it!— they roam around looking for lost pets to take to USC for secret experiments. It's too horrible to even think about! So I won't.

Yes, young man, I can, and I would. I'm just not so spry as a strong young fellow like you . . . oh, you look perfectly healthy to me, young man, your knee may have been injured once upon a time but I'm sure it's healed completely, the young are lucky that way, but please do not push past me, I told you that I will move out of your way just as I did before, you have only to ask.

It gets worse and worse. It really does.

This is General Teko's most daring move yet. The drop is on the community bulletin board of the Crenshaw Acres Shopping

Centre—directly across from Mel's Sporting Goods! It was while scouting out this drop, during their first day in L.A., that Teko had spotted Mel's and made a mental note to return for supplies. There is some bright yellow police tape demarcating the crime scene in front of the store and plywood covering the plate glass panes that Tania's bullets shattered. Otherwise things look pretty peaceful. The old biddy is staring daggers at him but looks away when he meets her eyes. He wonders whether she noted the relative incongruity of the LETTER TO THE PEOPLE amid the ads for dance lessons and used cars or if his photograph has been broadcast locally. The radio has already aired news reports that the police have surrounded a "bungalow in the ghetto area of Compton." And here he is back at the scene of the skirmish. He looks at his watch. About five to nine.

1466 East Fifty-fourth Street

Some girls came to see Crystal. They wanted to know if she wanted her hair cornrowed. She was wearing it in a sort of sloppy natural and she and her two friends went in the bathroom and studied their hair in the mirror. One thing they knew was that it was one hot-ass day. They wanted their hair out of the way if this was how summer was going to be. Casually, one of the girls asked Crystal who were all the white people in the house.

"They the SLA," said Crystal authoritatively. She poked out her lips and opened her eyes big. It was her mirror face.

"The *who*?" said one friend.

Cinque stopped in the hall and poked his head in the bathroom door.

"How you sisters doing?"

One girl, Cathy, rolled her eyes. The other, Rondella, asked him: "Who's the SLA?"

They were going to start a revolution and get the police. Not necessarily in that order. They were recruiting too. Interested? The girls shook their heads.

Crystal decided not to get cornrows because Rondella, who was good at it, wanted three dollars. She walked out with the two girls when they left the house. While they stood on the shaded porch, two of the white girls came out. One carried a rifle, and the other had her pistol out and was cleaning it. Cathy and Rondella were bugging out. They went off to tell people what they'd seen at Sheila Mears's house.

T HE VOICE SAYS, "THERE'S a real scientific reason for this. The reason that you so often see dogs in older photographs with pipes and cigars and cigarettes in their mouth is because photographers found that they were extremely sensitive to nicotine, the dogs were."

The radio host says, "Sensitive? As in, they responded to it as they might have to a drug?"

"What a load of crap," criticizes Teko.

The Lincoln pulls up beside a newspaper vending machine, and Yolanda, who has been sprawled across the seat to avoid stepping on Ray Fraley, emerges to buy a copy of the *Los Angeles Times*. The fugitives are looking to buy a car.

"Yes. Exactly. Photographers found that it was extremely helpful in terms of getting the dog to stand still and in place during the somewhat lengthy process of exposing the plate. So it became a common thing."

"And there was no comic intent? No sense of here, just for laughs let's dress this dog in a top hat with a cigar?"

"So why," says Teko, "didn't they just mix some tobacco in with their food?"

Yolanda runs her finger down the column. BUICK '69 EL'TRA; CHRYSLER, '68—NEWPORT; FORD GALAXIE 500 '69; PONTIAC CATALINA '62.

"Too big," says Teko. "Too much money. Check the foreign cars."

"And yet frequently," says the interviewer, "you do see these animals wearing human clothes in photographs of the time."

"Yes, but there was no true scientific reason behind it, as with the tobacco items."

DATSUN '72; TOYOTA, '71, CORONA; VOLKSWAGEN '68 BUG.

Teko: "Anyways, how would they get enough nicotine to actually be, like, *drugged*, just from having an unlit cigar in their mouth?" No one answers him. "What a load of crap," he concludes.

"Now we'll be accepting some questions from our listeners at home."

Teko stops again. Yolanda takes a handful of dimes and goes to make some calls from a pay phone. The three occupants of the car sit without speaking.

"Hello? My young cat is very active and seems to want to be played with, but the thing is whenever I try to invent a game for her, she just stalks away. What's wrong?"

Yolanda makes a thumbs-up as she walks back from the pay phone. Leaning in the driver's side window, she points to a circled ad for a '63 Corvair offered for three hundred dollars. She then points to an address written in the upper margin of the page. All this silent business is so that Ray Fraley has no way of identifying the make and model car they buy. Teko nods.

"Am I on?" asks a man. "What I wanted to say is it seems to me that everyone knows about dogs, but nobody knows about horses. What I mean is that practically everybody can tell the difference between a poodle and a bulldog, but nobody knows the difference between, say, a quarter horse and an Arabian. Why?"

"I honestly don't know, but I certainly agree with you. And the strange thing is that horses are such a big thing, quote unquote, today."

1466 East Fifty-fourth Street

Jimmy Reddy knew Lillian Maybry liked her greens, so he picked some fresh that morning before the sun got too hot to be standing around like a old fool and made up a brown paper bag for her. He carried it over. Hot already, with one of them warm winds that put a angry in you.

Lillian was a nice girl and easy to look at. Something funny, though. The house seemed to be full of guns and white folks.

"Where's Lillian at?" he asked a young white man who sat in the front room. The white man shrugged, so he carried his bag into the kitchen and set it down. A fat white girl came up and upped herself on tiptoe to peep in the bag, nice as you please.

"Hi," she said. "Did you *just pick* those? They look *fantastic.*"

"Got 'em out my garden," he said.

"How do you *make* them?" she asked.

"You just, you boil 'em, or you can fry 'em up in a little oil, you know, till they get wilty." He sort of backed out of the kitchen. That girl was wearing a gun.

The old man found Lillian in her bedroom, fully dressed but looking kind of groggy on the edge of the bed.

"Brought you some collard greens," he said.

"That's nice," said Lillian. "Thank you."

"What's going on around here?" he asked. "Sort of funny-looking."

"Oh, hi."

Jimmy looked toward the open door and saw the fat girl again with a hard-looking white girl, hard-looking. She had a gun too.

"Is Lillian feeling OK?" asked the fat girl.

"Ask her yourself," said Jimmy. "I got to go."

Yolanda clears her throat.

"Yo deseo la compra el azul coche que usted coloca el anuncio en el Tiempo de Los Angeles."

"No entiendo." The small woman stands on her doorsill, arms folded.

"¿El coche usted desea venta?" Yolanda tries again.

"¿Mi car? ¿Usted quiere intentarlo? You drive it?"

"Um. No una cosa importante. Aqui dinero suficiente y la coloco en manos de usted."

The woman shakes her head and reaches to close the door on her visitor. "No entiendo."

Yolanda: "¡Puse el dinero a usted para el azul del coche!"

"OK. ¿Usted quiere pagarme y tomar mi car *ahora*? Right now?"

"Sí. Um, yo quiero pagarme y tomar el car. Coche."

The woman shakes her head at the dual idiocy of this Anglo lady's Spanish and her willingness to purchase the car sight unseen.

"Trescientos. Three hundred dollars."

"Esto es dinero requerida."

"¿Huh?"

"La suma requerida está aquí."

"OK. OK." The woman can't help laughing now. She has the cash in her hands and holds it close to the bosom of her tired house-dress, gathering it in as she laughs.

"Me deseo hago los papeles necesarios al gobierno. ¿Todo a la derecha?"

"No entiendo. No entiendo." The woman laughs and laughs.

"Hago los papeles al gobierno. OK?"

She laughs: "Bueno, bueno. OK. No cuido."

Rᴀʏ ꜰʀᴀʟᴇʏ ʜᴀꜱ ᴀɴ IRA, which he pronounces like the male given name. Lest it be confused with the terrorist army, ha-ha. He has a certificate of deposit, and a mutual fund, and a savings passbook he wants to bring in to have the interest registered. He has term life insurance through his company and whole life through Irving Kreitzberg, CLU over in West Hollywood. He has a death, disability, and dismemberment policy, which pays incrementally greater amounts for the loss of a single finger, a hand, an entire arm, and so on, and does he really want to think about this now? He has Blue Cross, which provides for a semiprivate hospital room. He has a house that last belonged to Ted Bessell. From *That Girl*. Or was it Dick Sargent? Dick York? It was a colorless male lead. He sees the face and hears the laugh track smothering the unfunny lines. Bob Crane? Bob Cummings, ring a bell? Bob Montgomery? That would be Elizabeth's dad. She starred with Dick York—or was it Sargent?—in that show. But whoever it was who'd walked the halls of his house, burned meat in the barbecue pit, and pissed in the toilets, he just can't remember at this particular moment. Anyway, these are the assets he has counted on being able to marshal against the onslaught of the world. They had looked formidable, solid, marking him as a proper-tied man, a man of means, of a certain impermeability. And now?

Bob Cummings had been Robert in the movies. Ray Fraley had watched his movies at the Fox, in Detroit, when he was a boy. Not a pot to piss in then. If he'd had a way then to articulate his desires, they would have come out: IRA, life insurance, mortgage, etc. It is these financial instruments that give form to his dreams. His dreams wrap themselves in their legal names.

Impermeabile means raincoat in Italian. Ducking into Renascente on a rainy February day, "Vorrei un impermeabile." Feeling like Gregory Peck, picturing himself in the future, telling the anecdote of this needful Roman purchase, the rain angling out of a slate sky onto the very history of Western civilization.

But it wasn't Robert Cummings stalking those drafty halls he now owned. Bob Cummings hadn't sat on his patio or poured an old-fashioned at his wet bar. Who?

And what else? He has a very exciting oral-genital relationship with a married middle-aged secretary in his office named Maureen. He has a teenage daughter with a canopy bed. An ex-wife whose wedding he will attend because they are "good friends." When he pictures her mentally, he sees a figure sitting propped up in bed, wearing sunglasses, a hundred-millimeter filter cigarette burning in an ashtray at her bedside right next to her sweating tumbler. That aggrieved noontide voice.

This car purrs just like a kitten.

1466 East Fifty-fourth Street

This is the talk of the neighborhood. Over the fence while you hanging the wash and whatnot: Y'all hear what's up at Sheila's? What they coming in all bold like that unless they wanting people to know. Because they don't know how dull it can get around here. They are the number one topic, mmmmm-hmm. They gonna kill the cops. They gonna start a revolution. Revolution? What we need a revolution for? Just open a supermarket around here we don't be going to Sam's for every damn thing. Ha-ha-ha.

Meanwhile . . .

At 1220 hours Metro Squad Castle-Bravo Six on routine patrol did observe two unattended vehicles at location rear of One Four Five One East Fifty-third Street matching APB descriptions on vehicles sought in Eight Three Three West Eighty-fourth Street incident. Per bulletin, dispatch informed but no further action taken.

E N ROUTE TO GRIFFITH PARK, the suitably remote location where they plan to release Ray Fraley with a stern warning and switch to the Corvair, Yolanda, following in the new car, misses the exit. Tania, who drives the Lincoln, watches helplessly in the rearview as the little blue car continues on the freeway, heading toward beautiful downtown Burbank. *That* was stupid. Teko curses.

Once in the vast park, is she a little surprised to find herself on Crystal Springs Road? She'd graduated from Crystal Springs School for Girls, where she'd met and commenced the seduction of Eric Stump.

She sees it now as an act of bourgeois self-annihilation. I mean, wanting to be a *housewife* at age sixteen?

But anyway, Crystal Springs, the reservoir itself, had been a long streak of glittering mercury in the sun that slanted over the coastal ranges, another of the Bay Area's limitless ornamentations, fenced off from the public and viewed mainly from the viaducts she drove her MG across.

Teko leans close. He whispers, "We have to waste this guy. Yolanda's not showing up."

Tania's eyes fill with tears.

"We'll leave his body in the bushes. Nobody'll find it for days. Now, you knock it the fuck off. The last thing I need is any of your rich bitch bullshit. Just shut up and do as you're ordered."

"We could wait a little longer. Please. Just a little while longer."

They wait. The radio reports again on the useless raid on Eighty-fourth Street. The garbage-strewn house has been found to be unoccupied. Teko sneers. Tania reaches out to change the station, slaps away Teko's hand when he moves to restrain her. It is an unpremeditated, unprecedented act, and they stare at each other in silent hiatus before Tania turns the knob, seeking music.

In the back, Ray Fraley hears the famous voice singing the grinding dirge: "*If I ever get out of here, thought of giving it all away.*" He says to himself, Oh Yes God Please.

Whispering again: "Fucking have to off him. It's him or us."

"Just wait. She'll come."

"You do what I tell you, or I swear it'll be both of you rotting in the bushes."

Tania has basically made up her mind that she isn't going to allow Ray Fraley to be killed just because Yolanda can't read road signs, or follow big white cars, or whatever her problem is. She works to convince herself that this mutinous plan is worth it on the basis of what seems like the distant memory of Ray Fraley's not-so-bad smile as he leaned out of his car window to talk to two apparent hitchhikers in the early morning. The bright, mildly lecherous smile of a man taking time out of his busy day.

"We wait five more minutes."

"I'm not fucking *bargaining* with you, Tania."

"Five minutes, then you can kill him."

"The fuck? Quiet the hell down, will you?"

"Just not yet. Don't kill him yet. OK?"

"Just, like, shh! Shhhhh! Come *on*."

Tania finds it easier to talk to Teko like this when she's alone with him. Together he and Yolanda just wear her down. But separately they're both little nothings. In the old days she wouldn't have given either of them the time of day. She is amazed at how easily that old sense of class privilege resurfaces. On the other hand, she's a little proud of how well she's adapted; this is the very first time in her life she has had to associate, for a sustained period, with people she hasn't chosen.

"OK. OK. I'm ready to move on to plan B." Teko is holding a revolver and gesturing with his head toward the huddled prisoner in the back. He nervously cocks and uncocks the weapon's hammer, the barrel aimed carelessly at his own femoral artery.

"Are you sure you want to do it in the car? Pretty messy."

"Well, I guess not. But where'm I supposed to?"

"I don't know. It's your plan."

"Well, I can't just shoot him in plain sight."

"Well, we can't just go driving around with a bloody body in the back." Tania slackens her face to demonstrate the stupidity of this prospect.

"You're shouting again."

"I'm not. I'm not shouting. This is talking."

"Well, whisper."

"I'm so sick of whispering. I don't have a whispering voice. Some people were born to go mousing around whispering their whole lives and I'm not one of them. I'm so sick of whispering I could scream."

"Don't scream."

"I'm not screaming. I'm not shouting. I'm just sitting here talking. You're the one who puts us in these situations where we have to be going around talking in these little like whispery voices. Talk about something else and we don't have to whisper. Just, like, change the subject."

"You're *crazy*. You'll never be an urban guerrilla. You just don't understand that this sort of work calls for instantaneous reactions to rapidly unfolding developments."

"OK. Sure. I don't understand. Let's just shoot the guy. Mr. Fraley, will you please sit up?"

"Stop! Shouting!" screams Teko. "Fraley, you just lie there, man! Don't listen to her! She is *fucking* around with us."

The blanket is trembling. Nearly twenty-four hours of trembling blankets. Something about this upholstered fear that makes it more palpable, more pitiable; something about it that marks the total destitution of these seized and interrupted lives. She is moved beyond words by these frightened people hidden away under blankets; she is furious that Teko sees them merely as markers at arc's end of a gesture he is determined to complete.

Teko is red-faced, and he is shaking with anger. He raises the gun and presses it to her collarbone.

"You"—he taps the gun against her—"fucking"—tap—"watch it"—tap.

Then there is motion in blue heading up the road and through the parking lot. It's the Corvair, with a harried-looking Yolanda behind the wheel. She pulls up beside the Lincoln, yanks the emergency brake.

"Sorry I'm so late," she says.

1466 East Fifty-fourth Street

Everybody began falling by to see the SLA. Cinque sent Crystal out to get some Boone's Farm, and Sheila watched uneasily as he slugged that down while describing the SLA's goals, showing off his quick-draw technique with his Chief's Special, and occasionally seeming to drop off to sleep in mid-sentence. The white man kept watch out the front windows. Charles Gates went up to Cinque and whispered something in his ear. Sheila rolled her eyes. Mr. Big Secret. Man so full of it he can't see straight. Cinque nodded, and Charles Gates left.

Charles Gates was booking on out of there with that easy five hundred. Never to return, baby.

Sheila went to stand behind Willie and look out her own front window, thank you. This was a day of wonders for sure: another white man, wearing a coat and tie, was outside talking to Charles Gates, pointing and gesturing at her house. He looked familiar, and then his friend or what you call colleague with the little camera comes up, and she sees the camera has on it "KNXT MiniCam Unit."

She heard Cinque ask, "Where's the station wagon?"

"I don't know. When did you send that kid?" asked the hard-looking one.

"While ago, now."

"With the money."

"What you want me to do?"

"Bye-bye."

"Well, what you want?"

Sheila was tireder than she could ever remember. Up all night and then this whole day being what her grandma would have called a tribulation. Cartons and boxes seemed to be piled in every corner of her home now, and she picked her way past, heading for her bedroom, where she found that white boy stretched out on her own bed. She put her hands on her hips. Not a word. Just one look was all it took. He leaped up as if she'd stuck him with a hatpin and was gone. She closed the door behind him.

. . .

When Timmy got home from school he didn't see his mother but he did see all those white people and their guns were still there. The man told him to Sit Down and Shut Up and he went out the back. Mr. Reddy was out there and he told him to go to his grandma. "Go get your grandma," said Mr. Reddy.

Even after five o'clock, the main parking lot is jammed and a long line forms outside the gates of the happiest place on earth, Disneyland. Curled in exhaustion on the backseat of the Corvair, Tania senses a distant agitation, in the noise and aromas, in the quality of the light that falls upon this former citrus orchard. It is a place as peculiarly essential as can be. For millions it is an introduction to crowds and their logic. It is rules and order in carefree guise. It is a walk inside a giant rendering of the sugar coating that swathes American life, an exhibit like the Smithsonian's enormous and anatomically precise organs. But who sees it that way? A million kids with stomachaches? Parents in ridiculous tourist garb, popping off flashcubes like confections of frosted light, the fathers encumbered with Nikons and Pentaxes, the mothers easily swinging Instamatics from their wrist straps? These people waiting to buy sugar water, spun sugar, sugar baked in the familiar forms of nutritious items? Those who stand in line to sit in moving chairs? It is the greatest fun of all, to ennoble all of a culture's half-forsaken myths and shibboleths by reducing them to cliché and sanitizing them. Yet even among clichés there are those that aren't permitted here, they're so ambiguously evocative or of such unpalatably grizzled mien. Everything here looks as clean and disposable as a Dixie cup.

E.g., the motels across Katella Avenue. This is the epicenter of a kind of beauty, the wild optimism of transience. These postatomic permacrete structures stand in mute astonishment at their survival into the 1970s. There are the Little Boy Blue Motel, the Magic Carpet Motel, the Magic Lamp Motel, the Samoa Motel, the Space Age Inn, and a dozen others, each asserting itself through its towering sign, its brummagem modernism, its paradoxical insistence on the eternal half-life of fads.

Yolanda worked here, at Disneyland, one summer, having traveled to the Coast from Indiana. Tania tries to picture the grim revolutionary as a rube fresh from the Midwest, an eight-hour smile on her face throughout her shift, her uniform soiled and smelling of grease.

Teko pulls into the broad driveway of the Cosmic Age Lodge, which sits unobtrusively enough in the harsh light of late afternoon. Driving the Corvair slowly through the half-empty lot, he circles the structure, choosing a spot in the rear with plenty of vacant spaces on either side of it. As Yolanda and Teko instruct her to remain hidden in the backseat while they register, Tania worries for a moment that the little blue wreck will be mistaken for abandoned in its purposeful isolation. Set apart from the sturdy late-model Buicks and Mercurys that muscle up to the building, their car has that telltale bent and faded look of automotive worthlessness.

And it doesn't escape her that now she's the one stowed away under that blanket.

Meanwhile . . .

The law couldn't believe its good fortune. Los Angeles ASAC Haff had been informed not only that the SLA vans had been located, but that someone had phoned to report that she had seen the SLA and to provide their address, while another caller had reported "white girls" sneaking around backyards—and all in the same immediate vicinity.

Now Haff leaned back in a chair and stared at the water-stained dropped ceiling in the office of the tow truck business where the field command post had been established. When the op had begun taking shape, he'd headed here from his office. Tips had continued to come in. When he arrived, he was briefed by an agent supervisor: "The switchboard's like a Christmas tree." Haff liked that one; it was the sort of malapropism that made his day.

But the LAPD was up his ass. They were just being outrageously aggressive. So Haff quietly made arrangements to minimize the Bureau's role. Rather than leave the locals holding the whole bag, though, he thought he'd grant them one small favor, just for the sake of auld lang syne, their mutually beneficial relationship, and all the usual horseshit. He picked up the phone and dialed.

He said, "I'd like to speak to Commander Montag, please." Randy Montag was the LAPD's public relations liaison. Haff called him the Shadow because of his ability to cloud men's minds.

Haff waited a few moments, drumming his fingers on the metal desk, and then said, "Randy. Gary Haff at the Bureau. We have an operation coming down that'll require your fine hand. Oh, yeah. Lucy, you gotta lotta splainin to do."

He laughed. "Oh, because it's all yours, my friend. The federal government is just going to be pitching in and directing traffic." He tilted his head back and laughed again. "Literally."

1466 East Fifty-fourth Street

Cinque handed Crystal another twenty; he was running low on cigarettes. Crystal took the money and headed up the alley toward Sam's one more time. That was funny; there was cops all over the place.

The man behind the counter smiled at her. "You busy today," he observed. "Gonna wear a groove between here and your place."

She shrugged. She was pretty sensitive to what she perceived as criticism at her age. She handed him the twenty, and he exhaled sharply. "Y'all know I need to keep some change for other folks, don't you?" he said, giving it back.

Sullenly she reached into her pocket and dug out a couple of singles and handed them to the man, keeping her hand extended for the change.

"Y'all want a receipt with that?" he asked sarcastically. She turned and left without answering.

As she turned down the alley she saw a white man sliding up to her sideways and she stopped and sighed. It was predictable on the level of cop bullshit. He took her aside, plunked her right out of her real life and into the realm of his convenience. Name and who you going to see, all that. Then he said she had to turn around. No one going through here. This was new. Why? Because he said so. He got a little look on his face, just this angry smile like he was going to cross that line they sometimes did where they start taking little liberties if you don't start doing what they wanted so she dropped it and turned around. Before she entered Sam's to return the cigarettes she remembered to put a big smile on her face.

Y OLANDA RETURNS TO THE car to retrieve her purse and tersely whispers the room number to the hidden Tania. Tania waits another five minutes and enters the motel at 5:30 to join the others.

The brightly lit public areas of the Cosmic Age are unusual, with panels depicting odd geometric patterns affixed to the walls and staircases, and hanging lanterns offering a not altogether incongruous hint of tropical Orientalia. Sunlight streams blindingly through the tall windows that vertically band the building, and two clerks working the front desk squint across the counter at their guests. At this hour the lobby is becoming busy, as tired vacationers return to their rooms after an afternoon at the theme park. Blending easily with them, Tania ascends a staircase of molded cement steps mounted on an angled steel track.

The interior of the room is pure American Motel: beds, night tables, credenza with color television, picture of ships at sea bolted to the wall. Yolanda is keeping the heavy drapes closed. She lies faceup on one of the double beds, and when Tania enters, she informs the ceiling that Teko is checking the perimeter. Tania switches on the TV.

Tania likes to adjust the color, the tint and the hue. She likes a bright, vivid picture, with unreal shades. To her, that's the point of color television. It drove Eric Stump nuts.

She suddenly realizes that she hasn't seen television since the night she was kidnapped. The whole country that she's planning to take over is right here in this box, and she hasn't even had time to notice how much she's missed it, the detergents and the new Chevys and the powdered soups that come in an envelope, awaiting boiling water. There are Kenner nail salons, SST Smash-Up Derby cars, training schools that provide free tools upon graduation from their certificate programs. The double knits, the K-Tel records, the lonely Maytag repairman. Even Yolanda raises her head from the synthetic counterpane to watch.

And then there's nothing more American than this, a preemption of the regularly scheduled broadcast for a special report. Uniformed men with guns outside a flimsy house. The only question is why is this so special after a television lifetime of Vietnam?

It's the most ordinary of Southern California houses; Tania must have seen a thousand of them in just the last two days.

And they are saying, "SLA."

And they are saying, "Kidnapped newspaper heiress Alice Galton."

And they are saying, "Surrounded by police and FBI agents."

Teko comes in, all excited, though for a brief instant he considers becoming pissed off that Tania and Yolanda have found the news on their own, that he was not the first to watch television. But he settles in, sitting at the foot of the bed Yolanda lies on. "It's live," he says.

1466 East Fifty-fourth Street

Della Hurd didn't believe the boy's story because his imagination was alive with bedevilment and he was a handful. But there was a look on his face like she doesn't know what and that old fool Jimmy was standing by the fence with a waiting face. So she went in the back and checked the oven and the range and she shut her back door and turned the lock, all with profound misgivings. At her age there was less time to be wasting.

"I seen some strange things over there myself, Della," said Jimmy. She waved her hand at him to shut him up.

"Lillian was there looking pretty sick."

Lillian was like living with a auto wreck as far as Della Hurd was concerned.

"Place was a mess."

What she just said?

"Full of white people and lots of guns."

Della Hurd put her hand on Timmy's shoulder and told him to stay with Mr. Reddy. Then she got on her horse and got over there.

It was worse than she expected. House looked like a army base except with beer bottles and half-eaten sandwiches all over. Ignoring the white people, she went to Sheila's room and found her lying insensible on the bed. She went to that Lillian's room and found her barely more responsive.

"Is everybody here drunk?" Della Hurd asked herself.

In the kitchen she found Cinque and some girl, catching the tail end of the same tired rap his daddy had laid down.

"I am *ready* to die," he said, swigging from a bottle of plum wine, "but I'm gonna take a lot of motherfucking pigs with me. You got a smoke, baby?"

Della Hurd went up to the girl, a teenager she knew from around, and told her to get herself home. Then she turned on Cinque.

"What the hell you doing here? Get yourself out of this place right now and all your friends with you. This is my daughter's home and my grandsons'. And you are not welcome to come in here and start making trouble."

"Elder sister, your daughter has generously—"

"Don't older sister me."

"Don't you think that black people need to stick together?"

She stopped talking to him and went back into Sheila's room. She gathered between her thumb and forefinger some flesh from behind Sheila's knee and gave it a twist. Sheila screamed.

"Get up, you. If I don't get nobody else to listen to me I'm going to get you. We're getting out of here right now."

She helped Sheila off the bed.

Her daughter asked, "What about Lillian?"

"Not enough hours in the day to worry about Lillian," said Della Hurd, and as she said it she looked at her watch. Just about 5:30.

As they walked out the door together, two of the white girls looked up.

"Oh, nice to meet you!" said one, brightly.

"Bye-bye!" said the other.

They think she's in there. Tania sits on the floor at the foot of one of the beds, staring up at the spectacle efflorescent on the television screen.

OCCUPANTS OF ONE FOUR SIX SIX EAST FIVE FOUR STREET: THIS IS THE LOS ANGELES POLICE DEPART-MENT SPEAKING. COME OUT WITH YOUR HANDS UP. COMPLY IMMEDIATELY AND YOU WILL NOT BE HARMED.

The police have made numerous surrender demands. At this point the SLA has to be aware that it is surrounded. The choice is theirs whether to surrender or engage the police in a shoot-out.

PEOPLE IN THE YELLOW FRAME HOUSE WITH THE STONE PORCH. ADDRESS ONE FOUR SIX SIX EAST FIVE FOUR STREET. THIS IS THE LOS ANGELES PO-LICE DEPARTMENT SPEAKING. COME OUT WITH YOUR HANDS UP. COMPLY IMMEDIATELY AND YOU WILL NOT BE HARMED.

She thinks, Stone porch?

ALL PEOPLE IN ONE FOUR SIX SIX EAST FIVE FOUR STREET: COME OUT WITH YOUR HANDS UP.

She watches as an entire family, a woman carrying one child and pushing two others ahead while a third child and an adult man bring up the rear, heads for safety, skirting a SWAT cop in a gas mask who is assuming an awkward combat stance, covering someone with his M-16.

YOU WILL NOT BE HARMED.

A window covered up with a flattened cardboard box that says VIVA. As in paper towels.

Is she in there?

COMPLY IMMEDIATELY AND YOU WILL NOT BE HARMED.

From inside the house there come heavy bumping sounds, like furniture being pushed against the doors.

We are not sure but Alice Galton, the kidnapped newspaper heiress who is wanted for questioning in a San Francisco bank robbery, may be in there with her SLA comrades, repeat may.

She knows that they think she's in there. The surrender demands continue to come; she waits for her name to be called. Her name uttered through a bullhorn, what an idea.

There's a whoosh as the Flite-Rites are launched. The front windows shatter. The first sounds of automatic rifle fire come from the house. The police response is immediate.

"That's Cin's weapon!" says Teko, with dubious accuracy.

WE NEED ALL THE GAS THAT YOU CAN ROUND UP FROM PARKER CENTER OR ANY GEOGRAPHICAL DIVISION AND WE NEED IT DOWN HERE CODE, AH, THREE, FAST AS YOU CAN GET IT DOWN. IN ADDITION TO THAT WE NEED ALL THE AMMO THAT WE'VE GOT IN THE SAFE. WE'RE TAKING AUTOMATIC FIRE FRONT AND BACK FROM THIS LOCATION; THEY'RE MUCH BETTER ARMED THAN WE ARE.

Police are saying the fugitives are better armed than they are.

holding the Negro residents of the house hostage.
    Teko: "Bullshit! Fascist bullshit!"

here in the newsroom we have a noted expert

We have been informed that more than three hundred police and FBI agents are participating in this operation, an awesome amount of firepower marshaled against the radical sect the SLA.

who is here to tell us about the SLA and their strange beliefs.

Reporters and police both fall back, fall back in a wave broadcast in a series of shaky images by the MiniCam Unit of KNXT-TV.

The dry wind sends the CS gas coming back. Searing and choking.

FALL BACK, GET BACK.

Doughnuts and crushed paper cups on the street from the reporters, down there where their feet had been.

The police have made more than a dozen surrender announcements, folks. They have given the radical members of the Symbionese Liberation Army ample chance to drop their weapons and surrender.

have brought this fusillade of death upon themselves.

unsubstantiated reports that there are hostages inside.
"Bullshit! Damn it!"

A SWAT cop on a neighboring roof edges over to peer into the kitchen window at 1466 and is fired upon. He throws himself backward and rests, breathing heavily, on the shake roof.

THIS IS SKY ONE WE HAVE POSSIBLE WOUNDED TEAM MEMBER ON ADJACENT ROOFTOP REPEAT POSSIBLE WOUNDED REQUEST IDENTIFY AND STATUS TEAM TWO MEMBER OVER.

The camera jumps and turns. It pans past the long, low fieldstone wall surrounding this bungalow.

speculated the SLA may have picked this house because of its natural defensive barrier in anticipation of just such a siege as this.

Then with the sound of sustained gunfire the camera lens is suddenly pointed at the pavement; it jogs wildly before someone turns it upright to aim it again toward the horizon. Teko reaches forward and changes the channel.

tells us that groups such as the SLA often have a strongly suicidal bent.

MOVE 'EM BACK. MOVE 'EM BACK.

I'm told the gas is launched through the window in canisters where it explodes, a nonlethal explosion inside that's of sufficient force to release the gas and, hopefully, to subdue

Unknown whether the SLA is equipped with gas masks. They are, in any case, very heavily armed.

Three cops slam a group of boys to the ground when, curious, they stray within an unstated "inner perimeter." The boys have come from one of the neighboring houses, maybe. One, who complains about the rough treatment, gets his lumps right away, an indiscreet knee to the kidney. There is a boo from the surrounding crowd, and the cops redouble their zealous effort to push its members back.

The cops are interested in mopping this up fast. They don't want to be here after dark.

—Is this Watts? says one reporter. Watts, damn it? Someone said Compton and I want to know is it Watts?
—The fuck do you care? You need a dateline for TV?
—What's a dateline?

The SLA's trail was picked up by the police department and the Federal Bureau of Investigation after the robbery yesterday of a Los Angeles sporting goods store. A member of the SLA is reported to have stolen a pair of sweat socks and when store employees confronted him with the theft they were fired upon by a young woman who may have been missing heiress Alice Galton.

"It wasn't socks," says Teko.

—When's the last time you were here, buddy?
—Nine years ago, just like you.

—Get this, get this. Get over here with the minicam, damn it. Look at those holes, those are bullet holes, damn it. Zoom in on them. Zoom in.

· · ·

The press moves back to yet another redoubt, the police are pushing them back, they're pushing back the blacks, they're pushing everybody back, in helmets and joyless eyes sheathed behind aviator sunglasses and ugly batons held at port arms.

—Watts, not Compton. Watts. What's the fucking difference?
—Yeah, but there are white people in there . . .

The ghetto the ghetto this ghetto area is taking some of the heaviest damage it's seen since the Watts riots, ah, nine years ago, Watts riots. Very heavy fire now. We are moving for cover.
THERE'S ONE DOWN AND ONE'S FIRING, HE CAME OUT AND WENT BACK IN, POSSIBLY HIT. HE'S STILL FIRING. THREE FEMALES ARE SHOOTING.

They think she's in there.

Police believe newspaper heiress Alice Galton is in the house with her former captors, the people she's come to identify as her comrades

she now wishes to be known by the name of Tania

will the strange saga of heiress Alice Galton come to an end here in the Los Angeles ghetto?

They think she's in there. And they don't care. Never did. Cinque was right all along: She is a sacrifice, she is a traitor to her class, she is a common criminal. Whatever justifies the rabid fury of this assault is what she is. Alice Daniels Galton, her old name rides on waves of ions and electrons, bouncing off lofty satellites and trundling under the sea in stout cables, carried the world over, flying across the oceans and vaulting distant mountains, uttered with alien accent and inflection. Is she dead? Is she dead at last? Is the ungrateful bitch dead?

Some might say that she's getting what she's got coming.
THIS IS SWAT TEAM TWO, REPEAT TEAM TWO. REQUEST PERMISSION DEPLOY FIVE FIVE FIVE INTO LOCATION REAR, REPEAT, REQUEST PERMISSION TO DEPLOY FEDERAL FIVE FIVE FIVE GAS INTO LOCATION REAR, OVER.

Smoke. Fire. Fire. She sees fire. She looks quickly at Teko and Yolanda to see if they see what she sees. Sheets of flame rising from the windows and up to the roof. Teko is shaking. Fire is terror.

"They've fired incendiaries! Those fucking—" and he loses language suddenly, a regression to animal wrath, guttural horror.

COME ON OUT. THE HOUSE IS ON FIRE. YOU WILL NOT BE HARMED.

But the guns are still firing from within the house. Yolanda cheers, a sort of throttled scream. She hugs a pillow to herself. Teko pounds on the bed with both his fists, his glasses falling off.

"I wish I were there with them," he says. "I wish I were there with them. I wish I were there with them."

Tania stares at the black smoke and fire. The rear of the house is a wall of searing, kinetic color.

Suddenly a woman comes out of the house and is dragged on her belly and handcuffed after a brief struggle.

What's this! A Negro just came out of the house! A Negro woman has just emerged from the burning house! It's not we don't She may have been one of the Negro hostages. The police are taking her to safety now.

The police report later describes how an officer places "his foot firmly but lightly on her back to stop her voluntary and involuntary movement."

The militant radical SLA members, who seek to violently overthrow the government of the United States, are still firing upon the police. The gunfire is coming at a less constant rate now.

this onetime law-abiding girl who now calls her parents . . . PIGS!
COME OUT, YOU WILL NOT BE HARMED. THE HOUSE IS ON FIRE. IT'S ALL OVER. THROW YOUR GUNS OUT THE WINDOW. YOU WILL NOT BE HARMED.
All are probably dead or dying in there. Hard to believe that anyone could survive such a fiery inferno. Only time will tell if missing heiress Alice Galton is among the dead.

Yolanda rationalizes, "It would serve no purpose to go there . . . we'd only be killed." But Tania knows that they all are equally immobilized by nauseating fear as they look at the blaze and the greasy smoke.

The police are working against a background of bordello colors: twilit lavender with the peach and melon tones of the fading May sun and the uncanny flux of light and shade from the fire and smoke.

Getting ready for the final assault. Cops moving 'em back hard. Can't say but maybe. Maybe an explosion in the offing. Gas mains and whatnot. Moving back. The bravely professional members of the LAPD doing one hell of a job here today!

Children pressed tight against the walls of the surrounding houses, sightseeing in their own neighborhood. Overhead a helicopter drones. The children stare, openmouthed; the camera zooms in on their faces briefly.

Snipers ready ready on the roofs in case some of the SLA try to make an escape.

Every vision of hell from her Janson's is conjured up. Tania wishes she could tell Cujo. She wishes she'd paid more attention when she stood jadedly before the Breughels and Goyas of Europe.

The sound of windows bursting, exploding from the heat. It is a molten thing in the shape of a house that glows there on the TV screen.

What was a house just a few minutes ago is now a funeral pyre for the Symbionese Liberation Army and their twisted beliefs.

proving that those who live by the sword

Whatever else happens the police and FBI have established an unbreakable cordon surrounding this area no one will get in or out!

Tania fingers the stone monkey around her neck. Everything, ending. Everything over.

KEEP BACK FOR THE FIRE DEPARTMENT, THEY
WANT TO MOVE THAT APPARATUS IN. THEY HAVE
SOME THEY HAVE SOME.
Fire trucks moving in, containing the fire damage before it spreads to other houses
SOME RESCUE EQUIPMENT SMOKE INHALATION
AND THAT SORT.

They killed them. They killed him. They killed her. She crawls on
hands and knees to the bathroom, closes the door with her shoulder,
and then wedges her upper body in the space between the tub and
the toilet, feeling the cool of the porcelain and tile against her skin
and through her thin shirt. She reaches up to reassure herself: The
monkey is still there. She will never see Cujo again. They've taken
him. She will not know this grief again until she repudiates him in
open court. But that is twenty-one months away. What's in her mind
now is what's always in the mind of the shattered   to identify
what provides solace   but   there's none here. There's nothing. He's gone, all gone. Her world is rising black into a darkening
sky thirty miles to the northwest. She reaches for the monkey and
fingers it. Hope and love leave the earth and rise in rolling dark
clouds. Oh God please let his monkey burn with him don't let them
have it.

Yolanda starts banging on the door.

"Come out here, Tania!" she says peevishly. "You're not being
very respectful of our fallen comrades!"

Tania rises and opens the bathroom door and then strides
through the room, opens the door, and steps outside, ignoring
Teko's stern admonition. They will cast this in revolutionary terms.
Let them cast it in revolutionary terms, this is her loss not the
People's, This is my loss *I will not share it.* I hold on to it. I'm hold-
ing on.

Outside in the parking lot she sees that the walls of the Cosmic Age
glow an eerie blue against the twilight: both she and Cujo are in
glowing houses, and she has to smile. The solitary trace of their
bond, of this catastrophe, that the gathering darkness accommo-
dates is in the coincidence, and, sensing that the charity of signs and
omens will be scarce in the days to come, she clings to it tightly.

Threnody

Threnody (1)

SING OF GRIEF. GRAB the collar of the old shirt you loved and pull until it tears. You didn't know your own strength. This is the outward part, the rending of garments as they say. Sit in your chair holding that strip of shirt in your hand, one end still attached to an actual article of clothing you actually wear. Your hand ringing, with a sensation between discomfort and pain, from the effort. That you barely notice. That's shock.

Then to focus on the smallest of your chores, break it down to atomized movement, elemental gestures as ritualized as ballet. To scrub, to sweep, to put away. It's a good thing that things go askew by themselves, or rather, that it seems to happen pretty regularly in the course of events; at any rate, that things make themselves available to be straightened by you. Otherwise your fingers would dart out at nothing at all. To file things away, to stack papers evenly, to search for the wrong amount in the checkbook register, tapping the point of your pencil on your scratch pad: you hate being off by any amount. And: mystery novels. And: loaves of banana bread, the sink filled each day with soiled mixing bowls and rubber spatulas. And: God knows what else. You fill time.

But grief requires the daily subterfuge among the unknowing. You take refuge in their callousness, their total lack of caring. Public sympathy is something to recoil from. So you maintain a certain whatever it is you maintain that marks you as normal, as living in a healthy continuum of good-mornings and good-nights and everything in between, world without end. As if you hear a jaunty theme when you bend to get the paper off the front step. You fill the car up—and they don't know. You buy a paperback, a travel iron—and they don't know. There's a virtuousness to this kind of imposture. Your lack of affect is a mighty effort.

It's as if you felt you could hold in reserve your honesty, the honesty of your grief, a new candor that will be pure and indiscriminate and cruel. When this old world starts getting you down, you can unsheathe it, the true edge of your pain. You feel as if you've refrained from such honesty until now out of fear. But what could they do to you that could compare with this? It's almost as if the real life of your candor can begin, the life that has been kept secret until some outcrop of your being was demolished.

So—now that you know how you're feeling, what are you going to do about it? You don't have much time. You're a little surprised, though not in an angry way, that you're still doing what people tell you; that the telephone receiver is in your hand and you're placidly whistling along with the Muzak, waiting for an operator to take your charge card number and sell you an airplane ticket.

You will not ask for a discount.

You will not make a fuss.

It's just another day of whatever's left of your life, which as far as you can tell isn't saying much. You have a body to identify. The hand smarts. And you liked that shirt too.

Well, you're off the plane now. That paperback's in your jacket pocket; the travel iron's tucked away in your luggage. And here they come with their cameras. Here they come, and you wonder why they bother to make it look so orderly in the newspapers, so absolutely stately, why they sit them behind walnut desks on TV and hand them papers to grip while evocative graphics flash over their shoulders; why do they bother when what it is is a sweaty man holding a small tape recorder aloft, when it's a tall woman lunging with the epée of her microphone to the forefront of the cluster that surrounds you, now, as you walk; when it's the shouted questions the cluster directs at its nucleus?

"Have you seen the body?"

"Have you been in touch with the other parents?"

"We understand those bodies are burned beyond recognition!"

"Do you think this is just deserts for the Hibernia bank robbery?"

"Do you plan to sue the police?"

"Who taught your child to want to overthrow the government?";

—can you react for us, please, can you drop the unwavering pose of dignified solemnity, can you give us something raw, the way bone answers the knife that opens the flesh, something we can show people? Something we can use to sell cars, and the deodorant soaps that make our elevators friendlier places, and piping food in trays that's as good as having a loving family? Can you?

Threnody (II)

Would you have guessed, Mr. Galton, that burned corpses possessed so many specific traits? Would you ever have suspected the need to catalog them?

But then, some of these traits exist only in the realm of perception. They are not, in other words, the traits of burned corpses at all, but the peculiarities of your own imagination as it struggles to compare new horror with what's already known to it.

Well, for example: upon being ushered into the autopsy room for your "VIP tour," didn't you think, Mr. Galton, that the SLA corpse that lay on its side partially covered by a green sheet looked like a roast tucked sweetly into a hospital bed? Until you drew closer, at least, and could see the lungs and the heart through the cavity formed when the back, rear rib cage, and spinal column had burned away?

What made you want to see these things?

Well, but what about those traits that *can* be explained scientifically? Those lungs, that heart, for example. Were you surprised to learn that this is typical, that even the most badly burned corpses routinely present with organs that are more or less intact? That the fluid level in the organs and body cavities prevents total incineration?

Not that you could use those organs for transplants, or anything. Even if they hadn't been cooked through as thoroughly as if they'd been baked in a clay pot, there is the matter of the carbon monoxide, which generally is to be found in the blood and tissues. CO saturation is in fact one of the first things to look for in the bodies of burn victims.

The quest for scientific knowledge justifies itself, doesn't it?

More science: Did you consider the materials in your own sports jacket and shirt, the iridescent weave of your necktie, did you feel these things between your fingers, when you learned that ignition generally starts with the victim's clothing? When the bits of shiny crystalline matter running from just below the neck and spreading around the gaping crevasse that had been burned into the body were pointed out to you? That was what remained of the victim's shirt. The new synthetics go right up. Stick like napalm.

Not that cotton is much better. Whatever you do, Mr. Galton, avoid cotton pajamas.

How about the zeal with which the pathologist and the two technicians who wandered in during the course of your "VIP tour" competed to explain the so-called multiple wick effect? Was there something healthy and American about this competition in how best to describe a theory that posits that only those body parts covered by clothing will burn?

With their high-spirited verbal jousting, they truly brought the subject to life!

The idea is that separate articles of clothing act as multiple wicks when the subcutaneous layer of body fat liquefies and soaks into them.

This is supposed to encourage burning over a long period, which explains the very severe combustions that occur at relatively low temperatures—like, for instance, when one falls asleep while smoking.

The clothes maintain the fire, and the victim burns to a crisp.

Here the pathologist had reached out and rapped on the friable flesh of the corpse. Remember?

Did you both want and not want to look? Did you find that the wretched tissue was so removed from the condition of human flesh that the dread had been incinerated along with all traces of the young woman it had been? Did you wonder which one it was?

Did you recall the infant your daughter once had been when you gazed upon the body drawn tight into the fetal position, its arms and legs pulled close to the torso? And what exactly did you think it was that you were observing, Mr. Galton?

No, Mr. Galton. Not rigor mortis—but *good try*.

Because of the characteristic resemblance to a boxer crouched and guarding his midsection, this is known as the "pugilistic pose." It too is typical of burned bodies; the sustained exposure to the heat of a fire causes the major flexor muscles of the limbs to contract, drawing them toward the body.

Were you very surprised to hear Dickens and *Bleak House* cited in a Los Angeles County autopsy room? Were you? And did you wonder, briefly, if a strangely inappropriate attempt was being made to impress you? Were you, in any case, relieved to learn that science has shown that there cannot possibly be such a thing as spontaneous human combustion since the temperatures necessary cannot occur spontaneously or without an evident source of fuel? You may rest assured.

And had you been wondering about the frequency of accidental or incidental cremation? Was it news to you that the burning of a body doesn't usually result in cremation, which technically is the body's actual reduction to ash and bone fragments, about six or so pounds of them? It is amazing, is it not, that despite an experienced pathologist's occupational encounters with many bodies over the course of a long and satisfying career usually none of them has met with the sort of sustained exposure to a steady, high temperature necessary to produce total incineration.

And what did you think an *anthropologist* might have to do with something like this? Not exactly Margaret Mead's beat, is it?

Did it enliven your existence to learn that in cases involving large numbers of severely burned fatalities, a forensic anthropologist is sometimes called in to assist in the body recovery process? This assistance is especially helpful in identifying so-called commingled remains in situ so as to preserve the scene.

The forensic anthropologist also aids in distinguishing human remains from those of livestock or other animals. Pretty tricky business.

Were you impressed by the number of different specialties and subspecialties of forensic science that might be consulted in a case like this?

In this case, however, the only specialist whose aid was required was the forensic odontologist. You remember, Mr. Galton, the request to have Miss Galton's dental records flown down.

. . .

99

Do you understand now why science sharply discounts the possibility of what people like to refer to as *natural causes*? It is nearly always more useful to assume that the term is being employed in a given case as a euphemism, a sort of palliative for the sake of the bereaved.

What is important to remember is that forensic pathology illustrates the intertwined relationship between science and religion most explicitly. Each shares a sort of faith in that which unfolds only in death.

People generally die from unseen things, and for the scientist to believe in them, in these hidden manners of death, in the ways in which a body holds back the secret knowledge of its defilement, is a kind of faith. There are always things that go unseen.

Thus it is a good idea to clamp off the airway of a corpse and therefrom recover unconsumed accelerant.

Also always a good idea to dissect the airway and search for soot to determine if the decedent was alive and breathing during the fire.

Another good idea to check the percentage and degree of body burns in search of inconsistencies.

To check hemoglobin levels, that is a good idea.

Cyanide levels too.

It is always, always, *always* a good idea to check female corpses for gravidity.

A good idea to check for signs of trauma.

A good idea to bear in mind that the bodies of murder victims are often burned to disguise the crime, or aspects of the crime, such as sexual assault.

To x-ray the corpse or corpses to look for metal and such, as in bullets.

It is a kind of faith; there are always things that go unseen. The other kind of faith is for the graveside, to succor the horror of those goodbyes keened beneath the unbroken sky that drapes the rolling chill of an American cemetery, huge and groomed and implacable.

Thank you, Mr. Galton.

PART TWO

The Locust v.
The Elephant

I keep asking you why you had to leave your country,
and all you talk about is things that happened to you
there.

—U.S. IMMIGRATION JUDGE TO ASYLUM SEEKER,
AS REPORTED BY AMNESTY INTERNATIONAL

Wᴴᴬᵀ ᵀᴴᴱʸ ʀᴱᶜᴱᴵᵛᴱᴰ ᴵᴺ Los Angeles were negative updates. Before each other set of SLA parents was told of the positive identification of its dead child, Hank and Lydia were first informed that the remains had been determined not to have been Alice's. Whether this protocol had been formally established ahead of time or had just spontaneously evolved, Hank couldn't say. It was a strange manifestation of privilege. The report would come, and afterward Lydia would raise her magazine like a mask, replacing her features with those of the cover girl.

It was while all the parents waited for them to run out of corpses to identify that Hank had taken time out to educate himself in the fundamental principles of violent death. He thought he was being brave. He thought there was some convertible value to the stoicism with which he would carry around the knowledge of death by fire, the specific appalling nature of wound ballistics, of kinetic energy and temporary cavity formation, contact wounds and shock waves and secondary projectiles. He thought of preparation for the worst as an amulet against unwelcome feeling. Above all, that.

Helene had come with them. They couldn't find someone to stay with her at the house on such short notice; it was as stupid as that, just like for a regular family.

She wore one of Alice's jackets. She was the little sister. She folded her hands and stared into space while her parents spoke to the press, submitting to the inconvenience the way she might have if her parents had run into a chatty acquaintance on the street. At one point, sitting on the edge of her bed the first evening, Friday, she began to sob. She felt the muscles of her face pulling at her and knew how ugly she must be. Lydia descended on her like an infuriated bird. "You stop that. I don't need this. Just stop it, stop it right now. I don't need it. Stop now."

Most of the restaurants they'd known as a family were gone. Now Hank was familiar with L.A. as the sort of girdled entity that business trips held within them, endlessly replicable, but all that was left of the city where they'd made their home for several years was a faint trace; the time they'd spent here was carried whole in the briefest cat's-paw of breeze that came down off the hills, holding the scent of years; it was here now, but it was not the smell of the present. Then it was gone.

So they sat in a strange restaurant, dark and womblike, its sounds absorbed by the padding that seemed to cover all its surfaces, and ate bacon cheeseburgers on kaiser rolls with fries and Cokes. And everywhere they went, they watched television. There was only one story and they were in it.

They chartered a plane, flew back. What was the point in staying? Alice Galton was not among these insulted bodies. Alice was alive!

They experienced the trip itself as any family might have: Hank resisted buying the expensive airport food. Helene wanted a T-shirt. Lydia bought a magazine and a Vicks inhaler at a newsstand.

In the VIP lounge they were the most famous among the famous. Lydia sat in a corner, far from other people, alone in the contagion of her shame. Her daughter was an armed and dangerous fugitive, charged with nineteen criminal counts.

In Hillsborough, Hank Galton watched the rain, a mist of fine droplets that condensed on the eaves overhanging the leaded glass windows of the study to hang there before falling in stuttered drops to the gravel that ringed the house. There was a damp chill that seeped through the house's bones and into his, a dank humidity that curled papers and started mildew growing on the soles of unloved shoes in the neglected depths of the closets. He sat at his desk, a large neat rectangle of wood glimpsed from beneath a quarter inch of polyurethane, and watched through the mullioned panes: the rain coming off the roof, the wide gravel belt, the lawn sloping gently toward the wooded hills beyond and the vast gray threat above. Within the past hour the house had filled again after having sat empty for two days, the reporters once again stood outside under the canopy that had been erected for them, the FBI agents camped in the library with their papers sprawled across the old refectory table, but this room retained the forlorn stillness of its vacancy, and Hank settled into it as if he'd sought it out. He smoked and watched, the garlands of smoke oddly holding their shape, compact and sinuous, in the damp, still air, twisting slowly before dissipating.

After a while he stood and moved toward a small armoire. He removed a powder blue cardigan from it and studied the slack flesh of his face in the mirror as he buttoned up. It was a pleasant face, with bland good looks corrupted by heavy black-framed eyeglasses and a weak chin. He shrugged the sweater into place and left the room.

Outside the study, the house had opened itself up to life; through the windows the gray sky spilled a brightened shade of itself. Through a door he saw a maid running a vacuum cleaner, its distant roar rising and falling in ostinato as her hips and shoulders swayed, working the device back and forth over the rug beneath her feet. The bags the driver had carried in were gone from the entryway. Hank thought of all this as a kind of progress, a continuation, a retrieval of life. But when he climbed the stairs, the shadows descended over his body as he rose toward the darkened landing, where the only light came from the windows at each end of the long hall. The damp lived here. All the doors were closed except for that of a bathroom, in which something rhythmically dripped. He approached his wife's bedroom and knocked at the door, his head inclined to listen for a response. When it came he opened the door carefully, and the light from the room escaped to lie across the dim hall.

Inside Lydia was half reclined on the bed, her head and torso propped up with pillows. She held a paperback in her hand that Hank dimly recognized from the airplane, her index finger holding the pages apart at her place. The room's light came from a rose-shaded lamp that sat on the bedside table adjacent to an open box of chocolates, which gleamed dully in the pink glow.

She looked across the room at him from behind the hard surface of her eyes, hooded and cold below the lacquered ornament of her hair.

"What is it, Hank."

"I just wanted. The news, alone, it's."

"What news? We have no news that I'm aware of."

"Lydia. We've had the best news."

"What we have means only that nothing's changed. Nothing's changed at all."

"But she's *alive*, Lydia."

Lydia began to make strange jerking motions with her head and neck, her lips moving, some sort of prearticulation that anticipated her toxic disdain. It came.

"*Alive*? Alive in that filth, again?"

Hank was unsure what she meant by "again."

"With those cuckoos, driving around, with guns? Shooting at people, kidnapping them."

Hank began to wring his hands.

"It almost," said Lydia, looking through the window into the distance, as if deriving her opinion from the churning sky. "It almost would be *better*," she said, "*better* if—"

"No, it wouldn't," said Hank.

"Don't interrupt me. Yes, better."

"No."

"Yes, yes."

"No, it wouldn't be better. Do you think the other parents feel better? The other parents would give—"

"Who cares about them and their low-class hoodlum children?" Her hand came up and then the book left it to fly across the room. It landed on a wing chair and bounced softly to the floor.

"You lost your place," said Hank.

Lydia was crying and Hank walked over and sat at the foot of the bed, not exactly beside her. He reached out and put his hand on one stockinged foot. It felt strange, sharp and armored, through the gauzy fabric of her panty hose.

"Well, the important thing," he said, "the important thing." He patted the thorny foot.

"What about our *family*?" she said, furious. "What about our *honor*?"

Hank stared at her foot. Some people's feet had personalities all their own.

"What about *me*? I don't understand how it is I'm supposed to get through all this. What am I to tell people?"

Alice had a room here. Things hung in the closet still, ready for her to return home any time she wanted. A tennis shoe peeked out from under the dust ruffle that skirted the box spring. This was normal, wasn't it? People behaved as if he'd received lessons of some sort on how to live, as if he didn't put old letters in a shoebox like all the rest of them. His daughter's clothes still hung in the closet; her dusty photos, framed moments that were famous to her, sat silent on the shelf. All ready, anytime she wanted. All his life Hank had been confident of an answering echo, the sonar of conviviality. To speak was to receive a reply. And suddenly this. They knew she was alive only because they'd sifted through bone and ash. There was no reassuring phone call from her, only photographs of her jaws and teeth flown specially to Los Angeles.

THREE NIGHTS AT THE Cosmic Age. Every minute, all thirty-seven hundred of them, meaningless, each a sort of obstacle to be overcome by the habit of being. First you put one foot down. Then you put the other in front of it. Repeat. It gets Tania to the bathroom, back to the bed. Her job is to stay in the room. Just another face in an upstairs window, she parts the drapes to survey the parking lot, the cars rolling in and out. Vacationers, deliberately insulated from the news, arrive wide-eyed, like refugees from the road, the desert's affectless severity. The only news that matters is Here We Are. The plates say America's Dairyland and First in Flight and Garden State and Great Lakes and Keystone State and Land of Enchantment and Live Free or Die and Show-Me State and Sportsman's Paradise. It infuriates her. She wants them hiding, with her. She wants them to fear the state's unchecked power. She wants them as angry and terrified as she is. But they aren't even conscious.

Teko comes into the room and tosses on the bed a newspaper that has been clearly marked in the upper right corner "204." Their room is 226. Tania says nothing about his inability to resist petty thievery even under these circumstances, even given what happened the—but never mind. There is a story about her parents on the front page. They have returned home. They are relieved but concerned. Grim work continues for the coroner.

"It's always about you, isn't it?" Teko says. "It's not that they're dead; it's that you're *not* dead."

"Sorry," she says.

The good news is that she's now third-in-command.

And after Disneyland, what? Yolanda went out and got new disguises, and now they crowd into the bathroom to make themselves over quickly. Teko goes to settle the bill, and she and Yolanda exit through the rear. In a little while someone else's family will shape itself to the rhythms of room 226. Maybe the one in that car with the license plate that says Je Me Souviens. They cross the broiling lot to where the Corvair sits neatly parked between painted lines. Yolanda wears a gray wig and hangs on to Tania, as if for support. They walk slowly.

The road swallows them, Monday morning's lackadaisical rush pulls the Corvair forward in fits and starts. A shadow fills the car, and from her vantage—lying on the floor, in back—Tania sees the cab of an enormous truck that's drawn abreast of them, a plump tanned forearm resting on the door frame. Yolanda turns to look down at her, speaks abnormally loudly in her old lady voice.

"Did you find it, dear?" Then she growls: "Get up! Damn it, get up!"

Tania sits up and pretends to hand something to her. There is no need any longer even to figure out these deceptions. Passing on the right, the truck cuts them off.

The bad news is that Cujo is dead and nothing matters.

Teko finds the Golden State Freeway, but it soon becomes apparent that they're heading in the wrong direction, south.

"Orange County," he says, grimly.

"Teko, Anaheim *is* Orange County," says Yolanda.

"I mean, like, the *real* Orange County." He sings, "*Folk down there, really don't care, really don't care, don't care, really don't.*"

Tania is impressed.

Over the hills, where the spirits fly, is Costa Mesa, which seems like a perfectly good reason to leave the freeway. They roll down a straight road with the green Pacific at its end and the Catalina Islands on horizon's edge. Finding a motel is not a problem; there are plenty of them, their signs looming over the road, practically extending into the lanes, competing to offer amenities. Teko picks one that promises LO WKLY RATES and KCHTTES. Tania lies down on the floor of the Corvair under a Cosmic Age bath towel.

It's thirty dollars a week for a single and another ten for each additional adult. As she sneaks her into the room, Yolanda tells Tania that her presence has to remain a secret because Teko thinks that a man and two women traveling together will arouse too much suspicion, but Tania knows it's the ten dollars.

She has to hide in the closet for the duration of each of Teko and Yolanda's frequent outings.

She has to hide in the closet when the clerk comes to explain the two-burner range.

She has to hide in the closet when the maid comes to clean up.

She has to hide in the closet when the manager drops by to ask a question.

She has to hide in the closet when there are footsteps on the walkway.

"You are a fucking ungrateful bitch. Think about what our comrades went through and you're complaining about being crammed into, quote unquote, the closet. Don't you think *Cujo* would give anything to be 'crammed into' a closet right now?"

"Yeah, you think *Cujo* would be complaining? Huh?"

This is enough to bring forth instant capitulation. Tania sighs heavily and turns toward the closet, or places her hand on the knob, or squats to insert herself, or whatever action's most appropriate depending on her proximity to the fucking closet.

"The pigs killed Cujo like an *animal.*"

"An *animal.*"

"But I bet he didn't complain."

"He was a devoted soldier."

"I recognized the sound of his rifle firing to the last."

"I bet *Cujo'd* be *real disappointed* in *you.*"

She's inside, closing herself into the muffled darkness.

She sits in the dark of the closet on the plywood floor, crying silently, the hems of Yolanda's dresses draped over her shoulders, feeling the tears running down her cheeks, first the hot rolling droplets and then the cold tracks, to pool at her jawline and fall. It feels sometimes as if she's spent her life crying without making a sound, has acquired a dubious expertise.

· · ·

Teko returns one afternoon with a gallon jug of Gallo Hearty Burgundy. He fills the ice bucket from the machine and, with two hands holding the jug, pours drinks over ice for all three of them. Three rounds later, it is apparent that this libation flagrantly violates the letter of the SLA Code of War that stipulates, "ONCE TRUE REVOLUTIONARIES HAVE SERIOUSLY UNDERTAKEN REVOLUTIONARY ARMS STRUGGLE, MARIJUANA AND ALCOHOL ARE NOT USED FOR RECREATIONAL PUR-POSES OR TO DILUTE OR BLUR THE CONSCIOUSNESS OF REALITY, BUT VERY SMALL AMOUNTS FOR MEDIC-INAL PURPOSES TO CALM NERVES UNDER TIMES OF TENSION, NOT TO DISTORT REALITY."

A glass of iced burgundy on the bedside table. Tania watches the Watergate impeachment hearings. By Thursday she is pretty much ignoring her standing orders to conceal herself in the closet when she is alone. Sometimes when the others enter the room, they find her leaning in the closet door, eyes on the TV, a cigarette burning across the room in the ashtray near the bed—not even trying, really, to fool them.

"What are you doing?"

"Watching this."

"That's not what I mean."

"What do you mean then?"

"What do you think you're doing?"

"Watching this."

"Is that what you're supposed to be doing?"

"I don't know."

"What are you supposed to be doing?"

"Waiting."

"Waiting where?"

She giggles.

"You think it's funny, hah? Maybe you'll think this is funny too."

Teko crosses the room, rapidly closing the space between them. Tania is caught between panic and apathy. So she tosses her wine at him. He freezes. There is the sound of the ice cubes hitting the carpeted floor. The expression on his face indicates his attempt to scale new heights of rage. Without a word she disappears into the closet and closes the door behind her. She stays there for the remainder of the night.

It's Nixon's viscid gift that his presence haunts these hearings, clammily, despite his physical absence, his attempts to appear above the fray. Even Yolanda is made uneasy by the transcripts the White House has newly released in an effort "to put Watergate behind us," the ones in which their profane, bigoted, scheming president vents his paranoia. Despite her generally inflationary use of terms like *pig* and *fascist*, the revelation of Nixon's true character surprises her.

"You met him?" she asks Tania.

"I don't know."

"How could you not know?" asks Teko, fixing an iced burgundy in the kitchenette.

"I just don't know."

"Oh, I can believe it," says Yolanda. They're both on one of the beds, leaning up against the headboard, watching television. Yolanda reaches out with her leg and seizes Tania's foot between two long prehensile toes, giving it a little shake of solidarity. "They're all alike. How could you tell the difference?"

"Quit it." Tania giggles.

"Screw *this*," says Teko vaguely. He drops into a chair, placing the wine before him.

"But what was he like?" asks Yolanda.

"I don't remember."

"First you don't know. Now you don't remember." Teko is pointing at her.

"I don't," says Tania. It dawns on her, too late, that she's been drawn into a trap.

But tonight for once Yolanda doesn't feel like joining Teko in batting her around. "I don't see what difference it could possibly make," she says to Teko as she hoists herself up and then weaves her way to the kitchenette to refill her glass.

"It makes a *big* fucking difference," says Teko. "As if her family and Nixon aren't asshole buddies."

"Like, what, Teko?" Yolanda drops ice into her glass, "Like she infiltrated the group? Come on. We *kidnapped* her, remember?

Anybody home?" She pauses beside Teko and pantomimes tapping on his head with her knuckles. He recoils angrily, but does nothing more.

"Who'dja think you were kidnapping, chrissake? Angela Davis?"

"*We* had nothing to do with that operation," says Teko.

"Pick, pick, pick," says Yolanda.

"We had nothing to do with it, Tania." Teko rises, gesturing earnestly.

"Are you *apologizing* to me?" Tania asks in wonderment.

"Sounds like he's copping a plea to me," says Yolanda.

"That's enough out of you," says Teko. Without warning he swats Yolanda's drink out of her hand and then slaps her across the face. She stares, for a moment, at her hand, dripping with wine, and at the spreading stain on the carpet, and worries about inconsequential things, permanent marks and stains, the feelings that suddenly lance her from out of the midwestern early sixties. Sometimes she can smell the ammonia and Pine-Sol, see the gleam of the dark wood. This, dripping from her hand, is an insult to order. Such decadent worries, how dare she? She lunges for Teko, her indignation suddenly having taken shape, trying to stick her thumb into his eye. She misses, jamming it against the bridge of his nose, and each seizes up, Teko with his hands to his face and Yolanda with her wrist cradled against her chest.

Tania notices, not for the first time, how absurd ice cubes look lying against the beige carpet.

"I think, actually," she says, "that I met President Eisenhower."

Tania has lived in three closets since February. This is the worst yet, because she shares it with the clothes. In other words, she doesn't feel as if it's hers. She considers telling this to Teko and Yolanda, suggesting that maybe they could fold their clothes, or some of their clothes, and keep them in the bureau drawers, and then the closet could be hers alone, and she wouldn't say a thing about spending all the time in it they wanted her to. She is vaguely jealous of the clothes, she realizes, realizing also how strange this all is. She has become an expert at living in closets, has developed unambiguous preferences (e.g., length is infinitely more desirable than width), has slept in them and eaten in them and read books in them and been raped in them and recorded messages to the People in them.

This, just generally, is not the life she was raised to live. Here is a seizure of a kind of exquisite loneliness, a sudden shuddering. She wants to pick up the phone. She wants to go out for drinks. She wants the free fresh wind in her hair. She has always thought of herself as a simple person, but as her life has repeatedly cycled into the simplest of patterns—waiting, in an unadorned space—she has found that she is much more complex than she'd thought, both stronger and weaker, smarter and dumber, surprisingly void of sentimentality, abruptly affectless in grief after two days of crying herself blind.

She also holds dueling loyalties in her mind. Lately she's been thinking a lot about her old friend Trish Tobin. Trish's parents happened to own the Hibernia Bank, whose Sunset branch the SLA robbed in April, both to "expropriate" the very money that was paying for this motel room and to provide an appropriately public venue for Tania's own coming out. She and Trish had a lot of fun together and she wanted to send her a postcard after the robbery, just to let her know it was nothing personal.

But no postcards. No phone calls. No nothing. And without Cujo she suddenly is a very *lonely* guerrilla. She misses Gelina and Fahizah. Gabi too, kind of. But Zoya and especially Cinque she's pretty glad are dead. What she admits to herself once in a while is that if she were given a choice, she would add Teko, Yolanda, and herself to that pile of smoking corpses, in that order.

Tania blinks in the scrubbed light. The sun tingles on her bare arms. It is the morning of May 27, Memorial Day, and she is standing outdoors for the first time since the previous Monday.

During their week inside Yolanda grew embarrassed enough to start carrying their empty gallon jugs of wine—they finished five—out to the Dumpster herself, so that the maid wouldn't see (Teko ridiculed her bourgeois propriety). But what else was there to do in there?

Well, Teko, at least, had been planning, setting down on paper tentative plans for a more or less triumphant (as he saw it) return to the Bay Area. He worked with road maps and local traffic reports and his own rash ignorance. First he wanted to drive straight up the coast on Highway 1; next was a plan to head out past Palm Springs for a few days' bivouac in Joshua Tree, and then up, through the

Mojave, through anciently dry lakes, through the country of dead roads and ghost towns, right under the very nose of the enemy (Marine Corps Base, Twentynine Palms; Fort Irwin; Edwards Air Force Base; Naval Weapons Center, China Lake), the sound of whose exploding ordnance crackled through the calm arid sky beyond razor-topped fences.

"Drive that lemon into the desert?" asks Yolanda. "Are you nuts?"

"You picked it."

"I wasn't planning on joining the Donner Party."

Finally Teko reluctantly suggested "the obvious one": straight up via the seam of the state, Interstate 5. But they would have to wait until the holiday itself, when the roads would be jammed and the three travelers would be able to slip through checkpoints and roadblocks relatively inconspicuously.

In the parking lot, Tania hefts a duffel bag containing the submachine gun, the carbine, the shotgun, the ammo belts, the sheathed knives, and some loose ammunition and puts it in the Corvair's tiny trunk. Teko's hand is in his jeans as he adjusts himself, preparatory to settling behind the wheel. Yolanda places a bag of snacks on the floor of the car, then pulls her dark dress away from where it is stickily clinging to her chest.

"God damn it," she says, "it's too hot to wear synthetics. They don't breathe."

"So go change," says Teko. "Anyway, you don't even look like you're on vacation."

Memorial Day, to remember the fallen. For their purposes, though, it is Day Eleven, Year One.

"Crunch! Crunch!" goes a Granny Goose Sour Cream 'n' Onion Potato Chip, crisply delivering its valedictory inside Teko's mouth. Tania briefly wonders who will fry the potato chips when the revolution comes. Potato chips were invented by a black man, Cujo had once told her.

"But do you think he got the credit?"

A question to ponder in the closeted dark.

Rising out of the basin, the outlying beach the dun edge of ocean's glimmering, the end of America, the memory of a dream; dropping again into fertile bleakness, flat and fruitful and rolling toward the horizon through the Central Valley, miles of cultivated moonscape punctuated by giant elevated signs to announce flamboyantly fulfillment of the more subdued blue pledges of FOOD PHONE GAS LODGING, markers proclaiming the famous names that outshine the little towns that host them, farm towns whose fortunes are entwined with the road's, the land that was their reason all but irrelevant now, a mere furrowed moment in the dust and glare and insect spatter of freeway mph, hypnotic and droning; on the radio here shitkicker music, or religious zealots barking sulfurous and contagious fear out over these unspoiled plains of almonds, cauliflower, grapes, lettuce, onions, peaches, soybeans, watermelon; with miles of freight lined on the distant rails, hauling cargo from one end of human endeavor to the other; BRIDGE, and you look to see what torrent rushes by beneath as you pass, and it's just a dry gulch, a wash, an arroyo, such words occurring lightly to the native-born Californian, painting ideas you hold close about the land (and here you're with these outlanders, tourists really, guns and ambition notwithstanding); lemonade springs and rock candy mountains: the car burns at its steady fifty-five, which saves gas and lives in that order, every now and then a policeman in his black-and-white drawing parallel to peer in from behind the tinted aviators and from under the hat that conceals the Human Face of the Law. Stop. Gas. Snacks. You'd like a movie magazine or a *National Enquirer. You just want to know what's up with Jackie O, you little twat*, is the unvarnished opinion ventured from the driver's seat, and you know you could shove another brick of envious rage up his ass by mentioning that you've *met* the bitch, yes actually personally *MET* the *FUCKING BITCH*. Pacheco Pass and onto 152, sunlight spread across the windshield, imbuing the crushed insects with a delicate glow plus dangerously obscuring the view; you pass through Gilroy where there's a kinda cute 'n' kitschy little restaurant/hotel/gift shop, Casa de Fruta: Everything is "Casa de" something—Casa de *Coffee*, Casa de *Gifts*, Casa de *Wine*, Casa de *Sweets*, get it?—mercifully zipping straight through to hook up with 101.

Here, as you approach San Jose, where the old orchards have been turned under the earth, new housing rises, and the places in which its residents will labor appear, equally new, monuments to the city's ambition to sow itself beyond its boundaries, the orphan seeds of such civic aspiration sprouting right up to the very edge of the road, lighted and empty, solitary cars in the enormous lots, lining the freeway for miles, all the way north this replication of an epic and futile vanity, in a night that smells like rain. Home again.

Housewives sent things over, casseroles and vats of chili. Succor all with food. It was an expression of sympathy that had more force than words. Send enough food to construct a golem, another Alice; enough food to represent every single meal she'd eaten. Hank was touched, though Lydia found it mildly distasteful that fried chicken, urns of coffee, and macaroni salads were turning up, unbidden, on her doorstep, left like floral offerings ("In the middle of the night!"). She said, finally, that she thought it was *funereal*. The alien food would have to remain outside the house, like some kind of stray dog. She had a folding buffet table brought up from the cellar and placed on the lawn and directed that the spread be laid out daily for the reporters and for anybody else who wanted it. FBI men in shirtsleeves and TV reporters with their microphones stuffed in the pockets of their blazers lingered together in the sun over paper plates of chow. Pour out a half-drunk cup of coffee on the lawn at your peril, gentlemen. Genuine Zoysia grass. The lady of the house is ever vigilant.

Lydia was the one wearing black.

"How do they get onto the grounds?" she wanted to know. She meant the food, the people who brought the food.

Grounds. Lydia forcefully insisted that it was merely a six-bedroom house, the sort of home anyone with a large family might own, but if it suited her to speak of "the grounds," she wouldn't hesitate.

Every day, black.

Family snaps. Distribute pictures to the press but the press did them no justice. This was where Hank felt what the other parents felt, what Lydia denied them. The press turned it all into something else, something Hallmark. Here was a picture of her First Communion. A picture of her seated in a tiny bloated airplane at an amusement park, just tucked in like someone going on a long and mysterious journey, her unreadable look fixing the camera. Here she was with Stump, with her grandmother, in Europe, up at Wyntoon. And the press said tiny hopeful. The press said aglow with. The press said happier times. The press said no hint of. A bad translation, but why would you bother. To what end could the nuance be applied?

The story—such as it was—was as simple as "she went through a screaming period." Screamed her displeasure at everything. Just seemed to scream until he'd felt it necessary to approach her on his knees, to embrace her softly, gather her into his arms, and whisper requests that she just stop. The story was how do you please a little girl who demands juice but throws across the room the cup you've filled and kept cool in the fridge, anticipating her return from an afternoon's adventures? The story was she stepped off the sidewalk once, turning back to give him a look of hopeful noncompliance before he lurched forward, arms and legs working automatically, his mouth saying no. The story was she sat on his lap while he read to her and he got an innocent erection. The story was she never really liked having her hair washed. The story was what would all these wise second-guessers say if their own daughters took up with an Eric Stump? *No? Stay home?* The story was the same for everyone: There were the sixties, here were the seventies, and it had seemed so certain that the whole thing was going to blow over, leaving them untouched.

GRANDCHILDREN PLAY IN THE backyard. Shouts and tumult, tears and anger, amid the long shadows. Occasionally an adult will break from one of the groups clustered on the redwood deck to descend to the swing set, jaunty, ice tinkling in a glass, offering assistance or arbitration, an apparition of middle age materializing among the weepy kids.

Susan Rorvik's mother watches with a sort of cringing posture that all but says, Where are *my* grandchildren? A cigarette burning constantly between the first two fingers of her right hand. Though it would be a comfort to Susan if this were her major concern. Her mother browbeat her and her cousin Roger to show up here in Palo Alto for this family reunion, to demonstrate to the world at large, or to the relatives at least, that they were living, healthy, not particularly treasonable members of the clan. Because although Susan had been gratified, enchanted, even, by the minor celebrity brought about by her recent appearance on the evening news, she hadn't anticipated the possibility that these exact same broadcasts might have reached the members of her own extended family. Her mother set about to disabuse her of her ignorance: She may be more well-known than the average weirdo on Telegraph Avenue, but in this South Bay backyard she is nothing less than a superstar! She wants an existence in Berkeley separate and distinct from the rest of her life? Particularly the life that she enjoyed (which is the only word for it you have to admit) until she'd "run off" to Isla Vista? She wants to say what she says and do what she does in the service of her ideals as a so-called independent adult, but she wants it all to be completely irrelevant, forgotten, when she saunters into the bosom of her family? Well, guess again.

Susan's offered no rebuttal to her mother's viewpoint or advice or whatever it had been intended to be, which was delivered to her via two telephone calls and one of her mother's famous letters. She's been too exhausted, having left a nice, quiet, but poorly paying job working at a bookstore to wait tables at the Plate of Brasse, a restaurant located in the Sir Francis Drake Hotel, where the doormen wear shoddy-looking Beefeater uniforms.

The reunion is not huge. Dad's three siblings, the spouses, children, grandchildren. A few cousins who remain scattered throughout the upper Midwest, technical relations. A handful of neighbors. All at Uncle Jerry's.

Her father stands by the barbecue grill with Roger. He holds long, sturdy tools and wears an apron, and Roger's hands are covered by two insulated mitts that extend to just below his elbows. They look as if what they're doing is forging chicken and spareribs, reaching into a furnace for the product of heavy industry instead of for dinner. But, as is normal, they appear absolutely united in this task, as close as father and son. Outwardly, it's been the most normal of afternoons. Only her mother, still aggrieved, her hands busy with her drink and her smoke, seems to pierce the placid surface of things.

And Uncle Jerry. Susan goes inside the house to pee and when she comes out through the kitchen door to make her way to the broad backyard, there he is, waiting in the shadows by the side of the house. A long garden hose is coiled loosely on the grass beside a small inflatable pool. A single plastic flip-flop floats in the center of the pool. Susan is startled at first, wonders what Jerry wants. There's something in the dewy glint of his eyes, their steady, intent gaze. The drink in Uncle Jerry's hand definitely is not his first, and it is dark, dark; lots of booze in there, she's mixed enough drinks in her vocational lifetime to know.

"I've been meaning to look you up," he says. "How've you been? How's the acting?"

Susan shrugs noncommittally.

"Practically neighbors all this time too."

"I guess I don't get down here much."

"Not much excitement down here in Palo Alto. Not like Berkeley. No revolution here."

"Not really one where I am, either, Uncle Jerry. I'm working as a waitress."

Uncle Jerry shakes his glass, rattling the ice cubes. "D'ja know. Ho Chi Minh worked as a pastry chef in London. Malcolm X waited tables at the famous Parker House hotel, home of the famous Parker House rolls. Trotsky was a bookkeeper. Mao Tse-tung was a library assistant. Everybody has to start someplace." He rocks on his heels and grins.

"Why, Uncle Jerry. These are not facts I would've expected you to have right at the tip of your fingers."

"I have lots of facts at the tips of my fingers. Signal processing, pattern recognition and picture processing, solid-state fabrication technologies, computer-aided design, computer architecture, logic design. All the aspects of the future I'm currently working toward in my humdrum technical way. Enough facts about this type of thing to put you right out. But I'm not entirely out of the touch with all the old ideas and sympathies."

Old ideas and sympathies? Uncle Jerry? Jerry, aka Lucky Jerry; skipped the war and went to work for Hewlett-Packard in the late forties, laboring in the old Redwood Building. HP's future had been so iffy that the structure was designed so that it could be converted into a supermarket in the event that the company folded. But when HP went public in the fifties Uncle Jerry received a stock grant and options, and he was on the road to the riches he has on conservative display here. Susan's mother appears.

"There you are."

"Hello, Rose," says Uncle Jerry.

"Do you mind if I borrow my daughter?"

"G'right ahead."

Susan is steered in the direction of the deck.

"He's certainly feeling good," whispers her mom. "Why were you two lurking under the eaves like that?"

"Just talking, Mom."

On the deck Roger listens politely to a man railing about the flight paths that bring airliners directly over Palo Alto. He's building up the record, making sound recordings from his lawn. Circulating petitions. He's ready to fight them on this.

Her mother parks her in front of her Aunt Nancy.

"Susan. Your mother tells me you're working at the Drake."

"I'm in the restaurant."

"That is so nice. Are you developing an interest. In restaurants, food service, whatever?"

"Not particularly."

"And how is your young man? Are you planning on taking the plunge? Or are you going to keep letting him get the milk for free?"

Susan had grown up in Palmdale. Defense industry town. She'd always been drawn to performing, was aware that what she most sought was the love and approval of her audience, that what she most enjoyed was to manipulate them into admiring not merely her skill but her virtue as well. A kind of flashy extrinsic goodness—a quality, in short, of likability—was draped over these performances, inherently immature, a quality Susan herself found just cloying enough to miss being charm, though it was the sort of quality that was treasured in Palmdale. It also was the sort of quality that could carry you pretty far away from Palmdale, and it carried her across the desert and over the mountains and up the coast to UCSB, a school that filled her parents with vaguely defined misgivings. Who knew what you might undergo in such a place? As far as Susan was concerned, the point was to undergo something. So she sat in a trash can in a storefront theater in Goleta, doing *Endgame* in front of eighteen people, even as the drama department was staging its sold-out *Witness for the Prosecution*. Before audiences of farm workers, she performed guerrilla theater with a group modeled after El Teatro Campesino. Marched and sang. Raised her fist. Grew her hair.

She graduated and with Jeff Wolfritz, the man getting it for free, moved to a commune near Monterey, which she found a fundamentally disagreeable experience and thus not worth the fury of their parents' combined disapproval. A letter from her mother during this period:

August 12, 1970

Dear Susan,

I hope this finds you well. I am doing fine myself and your father feels much better, the doctor believes that it is just a muscle strain and has prescribed some cortisone that helps a good deal. Quite a scare, though. Thank you for getting back to us on that, I know telephoning is a little hard from where you are.

I have enclosed a clipping from the Sunday paper, which tells about a religious sect near here. I am sorry to admit that when I read it the first thing I thought of was you! You know your father and I both trust your judgement and we understand this is a time of many changes in a young person's life. But I think you will agree that the best decisions are made from all available information. I am trying my best not to see things as if you are "turning your back" on your family and the things that we value. I know that you are a level headed young woman and you have never really disappointed me as long as I have known you. Don't forget, though, that sometimes things done for the sake of novelty affect your life long after the novelty wears off! Jeff is a smart young man with a real future and you know what I think of your abilities and your father and I think that the best way for the two of you to work things out is if you just get back on track and start moving forward. "Dropping out" is NOT the answer.

All our love to you, honey, and tell Jeff your father and I send our best regards.
Love,
Mom

Such documents were enough to drive Susan up the wall, but a steady stream of these low-key implicative jeremiads, reinforced by periodic telephone calls (as her mother very well knew, phoning wasn't difficult at all), helped to hasten her and Jeff's departure from Monterey and move to L.A., where, looking for stage work while dealing with an unfamiliar city that she had, despite herself, romanticized, she encountered the sensation of superfluousness that gradually overcame people who were uninvolved in the Industry, while suffering the same rejection as any other aspirant actress. Beckett was no help. "We lose our hair, our teeth! Our bloom, our ideals."

Then Guy Mock stepped in to relieve the boredom. Just about the only thing you could always count on him for. Jeff had decided that it might be more fun to write about sports than to pursue the graduate economics work his degree had prepared him for, and he'd begun corresponding with Guy, a "radical sportswriter" dedicated to looking at sports within the larger context of social and political conflict, or something. Anyway, he pissed a lot of people off, and that was good enough for Jeff. When the three finally met in L.A., it was love at first sight, at least as far as Jeff was concerned. Guy was an intense, wiry, nervous man with the constant predatory gaze of an owl and a receding hairline, and he sat across the table at the downtown cafeteria where they met, his eyes boring holes into Jeff and Susan from below the shiny crown of his head, speaking nonstop about athletes and athletics and investing it all with a kind of metaphorical lyricism and a political urgency, turning his drill-like eyes first on Jeff and then on Susan with a slight and somewhat bird-like motion of his head, while saying something like "Sixteen out of nineteen black athletes at Cal felt that racism was rampant in the athletic department, and all nineteen were totally pissed off about their experiences." It lit up something strange inside her. She wanted to believe that the world was a bigger, more beautiful, more overwhelmingly exciting place than it had seemed in either Palmdale or Isla Vista or Monterey. She'd sat in garbage cans in front of strangers who'd paid to see her do it, but that had, perhaps unsurprisingly, made her feel small, ugly, and enervated. She'd performed "actos" before migrant workers, reenacting their daily struggle and exploitation, but they'd been unmoved. But Guy Mock, simply by sitting there talking about the tyranny of track and field coaches at the university level, made her realize the quotidian stage on which her boredom played itself out, the fact that the atlas of her days had been mapped out for her by people and institutions interested mainly in consolidating power.

When they were done eating, Guy took out a Pentax to photograph the shimmering Jell-O desserts; trembling, translucent parfaits buried under pompadours of Reddi-wip, ignoring the mild objections of the manager, who was not used to seeing his food paid such close and permanent attention, who perhaps thought Guy was an inspector. Of some sort.

On August 21, 1971, George Jackson, celebrated convict author of *Soledad Brother*, was killed in a supposed "escape attempt" at San Quentin, a death that helped ice the mood in Berkeley and among the Left in general. It was into this climate of frigid and bitter suspicion, paranoia, and anger that Susan and Jeff relocated from L.A. in early September, spending some chaotic time in Guy and Randi Mock's Oakland apartment, a period that Susan recalled with cancerous distaste. Guy and Jeff would sit around drinking beer and talking, occasionally in the company of another of Guy's proselytes, stacking empty cans of Coors and Olympia until they stretched toward the ceiling, and when it became patently obvious that Susan had no intention of feeding them, the proselyte would leave or the pair or three of them would rise and shuffle irritably out the door, leaving her with their mess. She was so mad at Jeff that by the time they found their own apartment she was ready to throw him out of it.

And here's Uncle Jerry again, a fresh drink in his hand.

"Nancy, I don't know what's worse. Your crass vulgarity or your stupid mixed metaphors."

"Oh, Jerry!" Aunt Nancy pretends to laugh.

Jerry takes Susan by the elbow.

"So what *are* you doing up there in San Fran? There's talk, you know. I happened to miss the notorious newscast, but you can believe me that plenty of people were more than happy to fill me in. The general picture that seems to be emerging is of you waving a gun around and laying an eternal curse on the powers that be."

He rattles the cubes.

"Oh, I didn't."

"Well, I thought certain of my informants may have taken license."

"What it was, I was very upset about a friend of mine who got killed."

"The Atwood girl. General Gelina. I heard."

The audition was for a role in *Hedda Gabler*. The place was like an oven. Susan wanted to ask someone to open a window, or a door, but figured that'd be just the thing to scotch the audition for her. She was mad because she'd had a quarrel with a woman in the small faltering dramatic reading group she'd formed. Why—the untalented but aggressively well-read woman had wanted to know—did Susan want to try out for a role in that sexist play about an unresponsive and frigid bitch, a play that clearly was the neurotic old Norwegian's castration fantasy? Sure, the character was a strong woman, quote unquote, but depicted in all the ways that reassure male chauvinist pigs that a woman's strength is a manifestation of psychosis and, above all, ultimately enfeebling sexual dysfunction. Why, Susan? Aren't you *aware*, Susan? Et cetera. Susan wrapped her arms around herself in the sticky heat of the small theater. All the other actors and actresses seemed to know one another, and they greeted one another with a warm effusiveness that both struck her as phony and made her feel lonely.

There was this girl who sat slouched in a folding chair in such a way that made Susan think, at first, that she was pregnant. Something about the way her interlaced hands lay on her belly, the way she had positioned her feet on the floor. Their eyes met, and for a moment they gazed at each other. The momentary nature of the gaze abraded the disaffection Susan felt. She wanted to sustain a gaze like that. No reason not to. No reason in the world. She rose from the chair and shuffled over.

"Murder in here, huh?"

"Yeah, you said it. Beats Indiana, though. Like living in a kiln four months out of the year."

Indiana? The accent was pure Northeast; she guessed Philly or New York. They chatted for a while. New Jersey was the actual answer. And she wasn't pregnant.

Each auditioned. Susan was only slightly disappointed to discover that her new friend appeared to have little talent. But there was a kind of ineffable presence to her, some essential kernel of femininity that seemed at home on display. When the casting decisions were announced, Susan had scored the plum, Hedda, but Angela Atwood seemed a perfectly natural Thea.

"Neat," said Angela.

"Yes," said Susan with relief. "Neat."

Susan had loved Angela. They'd enjoyed a friendship that was conspiratorial, flirtatious, confidential, inspirational, competitive, and tinted with the kind of maturity that presaged the open hopefulness that Susan thought should define her adult life. Until Angela abruptly went underground, she and Susan rang all the changes together.

It was Hedda who handled the guns in the play.

For a while they'd labored together, cocktail-waitressing at a den for Financial District pashas. Strictly grab-ass and glazed eyes studying your mandatory décolletage. The job was all about tits, finally, completely unfunny jokes about rising moons, full moons, ever land a man on those moons?; about Just lean on over and squeeze some fresh into my drink, about I see you're having a double too, about Gimme some milk but hey, I'll just drink it right out of the container. Hard to believe that these paragons of establishment success contrived to devote inordinately large portions of their theoretically spare leisure time to inebriation and the brutally undisguised admiration of the suggestively draped bumps on their chests. Susan's weren't even especially big. She and Angela could bore even hard-core feminists silly sitting there enumerating a day's random humiliations; it would be suggested that they just quit, but that seemed, they thought, to miss the point.

Instead they organized, trying to interest their coworkers in a union. The unanimous indifference was dismal enough to prompt them to take the advice and quit. Angela proposed a "dramatic reading" of the five-page parting letter they cowrote to denounce their working conditions, their employers, and the apathy of their coworkers. They'd never really had their audience, though. Instead of upsetting people, making them flinch, they'd just provided them with another funny little Guess What Happened Today. Before they left, Angela had turned around and shouted something odd: "Death to the fascist insect that preys upon the life of the People!" Susan thought it sounded familiar though it wasn't until after Angela had vanished into the underground that she remembered first hearing it after Marcus Foster had been shot; this "Symbionese" group had incorporated it into a communiqué justifying the November attack, which had killed Foster and wounded his deputy, Robert Blackburn. It also said, "Let the voice of their guns express the words of freedom," a line Hedda Gabler might have delivered had Ibsen not restrained her.

So Angela became General Gelina, and Susan got herself another job.

"Well," Uncle Jerry is saying, "lots of interesting events unfold when somebody gets wind of a friend's demise. Maybe particularly if they feel like they were standing on the sidelines? Look at the death of Patroclus. Just don't let your wrath get the better of you."

"All I did was I offered moral support. A way of publicly stating, Do we wait till the police kill the rest of them or do we provide principled assistance now?"

"Principled assistance." He utters the phrase as if he were pronouncing the name of a particularly interesting little wine.

Here comes Mom again.

"Susan, would you help me in the kitchen for a sec?"

On the long butcher-block island are stacks of dirty plates and glasses, the remains of a glazed ham on a platter, and half-empty serving dishes of macaroni salad, coleslaw, and string bean, onion, and bacon casserole.

"*What* are you two talking so intently about now?"

"Mom, he's doing the talking. You said it yourself, he's a little drunk."

"He's a *big* drunk. But that's beside the point. He's just trying to amuse himself."

"So?"

"I don't want him amusing himself at our expense. Everybody here thinks they know all about you, thanks to your star turn on the six o'clock news. Whatever you do, don't give him any ammunition." She lifts the lid of a covered dish and puts her cigarette out in something with bright paprika sprinkled over it. Aunt Nancy comes in with her granddaughter, who is crying.

"I think what we need is a Band-Aid," she says.

"And then how about some chocolate ice cream?" asks Rose, bending and placing her hands on her knees to address the child.

Where are my grandchildren?

126

Outside, her father calls her over. "You eat?"

"Not yet, Dad."

"Lose any more weight, I'll have to give you a brick to carry, keep you from blowing away."

Actually, Susan is feeling bloated; her period has been crawling in her direction for like two weeks, it feels like. But she accepts a plate from her father and holds it out for him to pile chicken and ribs on it. A cousin walks by, holding a weeping two-year-old awkwardly in her arms, saying, "No no no no no no." The kids are dropping like flies. The strap of the cousin's pocketbook slips off her shoulder, and her father rushes to help.

Fresh drink in Uncle Jerry's hand.

"Have to admit, when you were growing up I never pegged you as the type who'd go in for radicalism. But then, I bet you never thought your filthy rich uncle in Shallow Alto would turn out to be an old lefty. Thing is, usually what you figure you know about someone is what the person decides you ought to know. But you'd be familiar with that."

"Me?"

"Not you personally, necessarily. Your generation. The ones who distill entire schools of philosophy into what you can fit on a T-shirt or a bumper sticker. I see them whizzing around here. Sloganeering. One flat smart-ass sentence fragment, then another, and another, and another."

Here we go. Not only does he want to put on his old Mao jacket and get into the act, but the real problem is with her generation.

"No depth, no meaning. A pretty kind of symmetry. Nincompoop aphorisms, zipping past on the bumper of an old beater, telling me everything they figure I need to know about them and about everything else for all time. Or until they junk the car."

"Well hey. Dad there is wearing a WIN button." She gestures behind her.

"He *is*?" Uncle Jerry rears back and laughs. "My God. Well, your father has always wanted to do his part, God love him. I'm fairly certain Howard wouldn't try to foist an unwelcome point of view on anybody. Of course all that damned button is going to get him is a hole in his lapel."

What it must have been like growing up with this sententious prick. Her father's told her tales of an awkward and myopic boy, not nearly as popular as the athletic younger brother who served good-naturedly as a friend pimp, lay analyst, and punching bag.

"Because the WIN button has a purely talismanic function. It's a direct conduit to, communion with, the wishful thinking, the cerebral processes of, the power elite. That's why there's only one damned word on it, Christ's sake. They'd like for us to know that they too want inflation to disappear. A bolt from Olympus. After ten years of Vietnam, at last here's an enemy we all can root against."

"I don't actually think about it all that much."

"Personally I'd be disappointed if you did. Pocketbook issues are for people like your father and me, who supposedly remember when everything was hunky-dory. Yes, when we were growing up, all the mothers would wheel us around in our carriages, going from the butcher to the baker and so on and exclaiming to one another the whole time, 'My goodness! Everything costs exactly the right amount!'"

At this Susan laughs, and Jerry takes a slug of his drink and then rattles the ice cubes in his glass.

"Besides," he continues, "you have a different enemy to root against."

"Who?"

"People like your dad and me. Look at this place. What do I represent, strictly objectively? Funny thing, you *think* you know all about the sort of man who owns a place like this. If you *really* knew about it, you'd blow the whole town up tomorrow."

One day, after Angela had disappeared, an FBI agent came to Susan's apartment to talk to her. She spoke to him long enough to let him know what she thought of him and then shut the door, vaguely aware that in her attempt to sound confident she had come off sounding more like a bratty kid. She stood by the door for ten minutes, convinced the knock would come again. But when she worked up the courage to open the door, no one waited on the threshold.

In February she and Jeff were watching *Newsroom* one evening when Angela was identified as a member of the group that had taken an heiress from her off-campus apartment, the SLA. Susan was a little surprised to hear it. She *hated* those bastards, not just for the stupidity of the Foster murder, but because they'd allowed millions to put a finger, once again, on what it was that bugged them, really pissed them off, about Berkeley. Why, it was a drug-saturated cesspool of free love and women's lib and black militancy and miscegenation and homosexuality and Communist thought, that's what. Commentators thundered away. It was the Day of the Commentator. Oh, they loved to thunder, Old Testament voices booming from under shaped haircuts and poly-blend suits. Every opportunity was taken to use the past as a bludgeon, as an indictment against the present. And tourists had started coming over, coming down from the hills, from Piedmont, Walnut Creek, Orinda, straights milling around like drunks in North Beach, boorish and judgmental, snapping photographs of houses and storefronts and making everybody uptight.

Then one night Susan arrived home at about five-thirty. Jeff was working that day, housepainting, and wouldn't be home until later. She dropped her keys in the wooden bowl by the front door, got herself something cold to drink, and turned on the old Philco console set she and Jeff had found on the street and humped three blocks to the apartment. The picture was banded top and bottom by thick horizontal stripes of black that seemed to grow wider by the day, distorting the picture with a flattening, fun house mirror effect. Everyone was short. Everyone was stocky. When you were high it was very amusing. When you weren't high it was like watching TV with a persistently lousy picture. The jingle for a furniture store sang, "Dublin, Berkeley, San Lorenzo, Cupertino, San Jose," enumerating the store's outlets. She moved around the apartment, puttering, gathering up the mail, her unbalanced checkbook. She had nothing planned that night.

The room didn't feel quite right, the bright paced cadence of sound and controlled shifting of light that she expected from TV wasn't happening. This awareness came to her on a hypothalamic level, unease seeping into consciousness as a kind of itch. She shifted in her chair, looked out the window. She confirmed that her checkbook made no sense to her. She turned to the TV and was profoundly disturbed by what she saw.

The picture was grainy and slipped in and out of focus. It was so unsteady that Susan felt the presence of the cameraman. What the camera showed also told the story of his limitations, his human inability to do everything right.

Stories of the boundaries of craft are necessarily ruinous and unsettling.

The camera showed a frame bungalow—a poor house, ordinary in its poverty—as purple, deep-shadowed twilight began to fall. Something so homemade to it; formally it reminded her of a pornographic film. She couldn't take her eyes off it.

A voice through a bullhorn: *"Ocupiss uh fourtee sixeesix ee fifty fourstree: this izza luzangeles plice,"* is what she heard. The cameraman, her unseen protagonist, abruptly thumbed the zoom, and the frame now embraced a much larger area, an area occupied by squad cars and uniformed cops and soulless, armored creatures, carrying automatic rifles, who surrounded the bungalow. The same purple, deep-shadowed uneventfulness. In her limited experience with pornography, Susan had been impressed by its insistence upon the staging of a scene. Deliberate, leisurely, eschewing montage to allow tension to flirt with tedium. Still purple twilight with shadows and people. The picture bobbled a little, as if the cameraman were impatient with the pace of the story. She reached out and flipped the channel to KRON, KPIX, KGO. It was everywhere. Another bull-horned announcement, the deep basso thrum of a helicopter passing over the scene. Pornography, with its endlessly flimsy pretexts.

"Cupply emerdiately add you woonahbe hahmed."

The pretexts under which the "true" action commences. Now, what *was* this that she was watching?

Abruptly, a mediating voice broke in. "For those of you who are just joining us," it explained.

It was the worst news: Angela had been trapped. Caught shoplifting in L.A., members of the SLA had abandoned their car, leaving behind a parking ticket that had helped the police trace their whereabouts. "And now, death rains down on them from all sides, over a pair of stolen sweat socks!"

Socks?

She watched with a sense of inevitability. The moment at which the camera lens had changed its focal length to alter the banal street scene, to take in the spectacle of the potential siege that beset it, Susan knew how it was going to end. TV and Vietnam had taught her that much.

She learned a thing or two about "false consciousness" that evening. Her horror at the televised firefights from Vietnam had been contrived and casual, her disgust less debilitating than a stubbed toe. But the sense of dread that filled her watching the black smoke pour out of the blazing house once the cops were done with it; the lifelessness, or, rather, the sense of the recent elimination of life, that emanated from the place as, crackling, its ceiling collapsed and its walls crumpled; the open glee of the reporters; the knowledge that Angela was gone, leaving a charred log they could pin their judgmental misconceptions on: It all had her shivering as if with fever and retching.

What impressed her, later, was the clarity with which she received the message, for the first time in her life, that when terrible events occur unexpectedly, even a forcefully lucid awareness of the chain of their causation does not rob those events of the power to astonish. The guns, the armored men, the breathless reporters, the scene's redolence of inevitability: Even in their contribution to the swelling anticipation, none of those things matched the flight of the first bullet, its seeming spontaneity despite all the evidence that the machine of the state had ordained its firing.

Now Angela's in the ground and Susan has been dreaming every night of pets in danger; of children she knows with certainty are her own slipping out of her grasp and falling; of her father alone, his heart failing, his delicate aging body breaking—dreams of perfect anxiety that fill her nights. She would have thought she'd thrash in the bed under the influence of such dreams, but she lies still, feels in her tight chest and beating heart and irregular breaths as she comes awake in the predawn a sense of surfacing from beneath the weight of dark water. She lies beside Jeff, knowing that sleep is finished for the night, that the day begins now, begins here. Now, what do you do? Proximity alone doesn't place you at the epicenter of "struggle."

On May 31 the Weather Underground bombed the attorney general's office in L.A., for "our brothers and sisters" of the SLA. The unacceptable group had finally gained some limited entree among the Left. Encouraged, Susan threw herself into organizing a memorial rally for the group, to be held at Ho Chi Minh Park on June 2.

"I think that would be kind of an extreme reaction, Jerry."

"Well, as I said, you don't spend much time in Palo Alto."

"Even if I did."

"Oh, really?" Jerry smiles, rattles his cubes. "Well, all right, Miss

Principled Assistance." He smiles, frowns. "Look, the people to whom you're providing this *principled assistance* are responsible for some spectacularly stupid rhetoric. And you weren't far behind them the other day, I have to say."

"Oh, really?"

"This is not a strictly literary assessment. I mean their behavior, I mean their ideology and politics, I mean the whole chimichanga."

"Well, what about the behavior of the pigs?" spits Susan.

"Pigs?" Jerry rattles the cubes. "Go on."

"I'm waiting tables," Susan says, finally. "That's the day job. Just, you know, taking people's orders, making sure the kitchen gets it right."

"You're going to tell me you're a waitress." Uncle Jerry's tone is nasty all of a sudden.

"The tips are great," says Susan, and turns away.

Her father is laughing with someone, trying to remember the words to the Fargo Central High School anthem. As she comes near, he reaches out, without looking at her, taking her gently by the arm, drawing her into the conversation. When he has her close, he turns to her.

"The football team was called the Midgets, Susan. The Midgets!"

His face is happy, as if he were sharing a joyous surprise. Who wouldn't be happy about this? Rooted for a team called the Midgets. She's heard it all before, eaten it up. Summers at Camp Cormorant. Headed downtown to N.P. Avenue on Friday nights and tried to talk to girls. Joined the navy and flew gull-winged Corsairs in the PTO. Nobody complained about those flight paths. Hadn't everything been hunky-dory? Come back home, move to the Golden State, raise a family, teach high school English, coach sports. It's not like Uncle Jerry: the dilapidated leftism, the showy contempt for the trappings of his military contract millions, even the bookish allusions. It's clear to Susan that Jerry is not what he wants to be, that he feels trapped in his own life, that he is not "advising" her so much as urging her to take notice of him.

Yet from the curdled political outlook that led her father to vote—enthusiastically, and twice—for Nixon, to mutate from a New Deal Democrat into the sort of man who casts a ballot in the spirit of retribution, from the disconnected fear and anxiety that have netted her mother a set of annoying habits, a penchant for imagining the worst, and an open prescription for Miltown, from all these things she can see that somewhere down the line everything went to shit for them too. They were still the same people, fair and loving, nothing had changed to turn them into monsters, but they radiated disappointment, this sense that somehow American life was basically just a bust. It makes her sad for her father, all of a sudden. Sad for him that he knows something, has intuitively fathomed it even from way out in that scrubbed high desert country, knows the same thing that she knows and can't quite figure out what to do about it. Votes for Nixon and buys a porch light that responds to shadowy movement, out there in the dark, snapping on abruptly.

And she's figured out what to do about it?

They're not a kissy-kissy family. They do not effusively express their affection for one another. Deep Scandinavian reserve, tempered on the bitter plains of America's hinterlands. But Susan seizes her father now, throws her arms around him, kisses him again and again.

Someone cornily applauds. Someone cornily says, "Hear, hear!"

"I love you, Dad," she says.

"Well," he says, his face lit with a kind of bashful pleasure, "that's just fine."

Ho Chi Minh Park, June 2, 1974:

"Keep fighting! *I'm* with you! *We're* with you!"

Susan saw flashbulbs popping, the Mickey Mouse–eared profile of spring-loaded Bolexes fitted with four-hundred-foot magazines and the bosomy swelling of Canon Scoopic 16s, cameras panning across the hirsute crowd, the short-sleeved, short-haired men who operated these devices looking as incongruous as nature photographers amid a flock of agitated exotic birds.

She felt the thrill of fame.

Roger shakes her awake; they're parked outside her apartment building. She thanks her cousin and turns away to climb the outside staircase to her apartment, groping in her handbag for her keys. She sees the package leaning against her door. It's a book in a brown paper bag, *The Art of the Stage*. She's pleased with its familiarity, and then she opens it and sees Angela's equally familiar writing, the name *Angel DeAngelis* (a little halo over the first *g*) and a Bloomington, Indiana, address. A slip of paper falls from between the book's pages.

Are you with us?

Meet me in the park tomorrow.

"Oh, yes," says Susan.

Guy mock has a way of bouncing into a room like Tigger. That's
whom Randi thought of once, trying to compare the man's energy
to someone or something, an effortless flash of similitude that her
brain awarded her, another small fraction of the distance toward understanding this person she'd been dealing with since, oh, 1963. It
was, yes, Kennedy was president.

She'd told him this and he said that the man who did Tigger's
voice was a fascist.

He said, "You have to watch out for that voice because it's all over
the place in disguise."

Randi thought about that one, about watching out for a disguised
voice.

"Would you need special equipment, Guy, or what?"

A dismissive wave. "It's Cap'n Crunch, it's Toucan Sam, it's the
Pillsbury Doughboy, and for all I know it could be the little guy in
the rowboat stranded in the middle of the toilet bowl, or Armstrong
on the moon with his giant step and his baby step unless you actually believe they managed to shoot something with that kind of a
payload into space, which is a physical impossibility. But he is a total fascist, and a stool pigeon to boot. An undercover informer."

Randi wondered if there was any other kind of informer.

"He lulls people into this total lack of suspicion, granting command performances. Doing the nostalgic breakfast voices of these
sugary cereals that set off some pinball array of lights in your brain."

The voices of cereals? And what about the man in the toilet?
thought Randi. But she hadn't said anything.

Now he bounces into a room, specifically a kitchen, filled with
cardboard boxes, each bearing a label of woolly specificity,
"KITCHEN STUFF." Three of them are open on the floor, is-
landed away from the greater stack amid snarls of paper tape and

crumpled pages from *The New York Times*. These were where the skillet and spatula and silverware and plates and cups and coffeepot and salt and pepper shakers came from.

Guy and Randi have just moved back from New York, where they went to live after Guy had gotten shit-canned by Oberlin. For a while Oberlin could quasi-deal with a so-called radical director of athletics, but when Guy opened that big mouth of his to attack Bear Bryant, the shit really hit the fan.

Picture, like, a million angry alumni chanting imprecations from a hilltop.

It took a while, but the new president and the trustees finally sidled up to Guy with an offer to buy out the two years remaining on his contract. Second time that had happened. The first had been up at the University of Washington, where they paid him off without his having worked a single day. So they moved to New York. A little apartment on West Ninetieth with exposed brick walls and upstairs neighbors who had a washing machine that made the windows rattle in their frames when it hit the spin cycle. You could hear the machine moving across the floor overhead until it reached some apparently impassable groove in the wide pine boards and then the windows started moving, shuddering with a vehemence that made Randi think of earthquakes, of seismograph needles going berserk, every time. And they washed a *lot* of clothes upstairs.

But let's face it, you can blame the shaky windows and the flaky brick walls all you want, plus the parking problems because like a pair of dopes they brought the car with them to the city and then like a singular dope Guy refused to get rid of it—but let's face it, Randi is not a New York person. Nothing against the place at all. It is unique and vital and stylish and blabitty blah blah blah. Whatever it's necessary to say to keep hysterical N.Y.C. partisans from flying at her face like birds with talons or whatever. They can get pretty weird with the whole Manhattan fetish thing. Even here you run into ex–New Yorkers of fierce loyalty who always refer to themselves as *expatriates* for some dimly romantic reason. And all you have to do is mention California, and they're on you; it's like you issued an invitation to your own autopsy. Your life is stupid, your motives are stupid, and the very thing that maybe ought to redeem you, the moving to New York, is the stupidest thing of all plus makes you totally unwelcome. She couldn't figure it out. Say you're from Detroit and they love you to death, pat you on the head, and give you ice cream.

"So say you're from Detroit," said Guy.

"What's for breakfast?" says Guy.

"I had some eggs."

Guy's eyes are roving, looking around for an alternative. They come to rest on a box of All-Bran atop the fridge. Direct connection between Guy and this dowdy box of fiber. It was amazing to watch, a joy for Randi to behold. Whatever else he is, the man is in touch with himself and his needs; he is a conduit to some future time when hypochondria is bred into the genome. Imagine living with an evolutionary link. Better start having some kids.

When they left New York, they kept the apartment because they were so flush with the spoils of controversy that Randi didn't feel like arguing with Guy over the crummy $250 a month, though she definitely could have seen it going toward something more substantial. But Guy started in, pulling dubiously accented French phrases like *pied-à-terre* on her like concealed weapons, and she just tuned out: like, OK, zzzzzzz—*nap time!* When Guy went to work on you, it was like *Last Year at Marienbad* forever. And if he wanted it, so what? He was the one who'd gone to all the trouble of getting fired. He'd even gotten Spiro Agnew pissed off at him. ("Yeah, look what that got him," said Guy.) They piled their effects into boxes and labeled the boxes and piled the boxes into a U-Haul trailer and attached the trailer to their car and got some maps from AAA and some film for the camera and headed cross-country in a variation on a hardy American theme, hoping against hope that in years to come, as nostalgia became their dominant style of utterance, they would have completely forgotten that they spent a big chunk of the time creeping down the highway, bickering, afflicted with indigestion.

They came back to the East Bay. No place like it in the world. Randi loves the endless spring you earned after the months of rain, the soft summer nights when the other side of the bay is covered with fog and yecch. She likes the street people and the campus nearby. And they have friends here, which had been hard to swing elsewhere.

But Guy is already getting restless. He was definitely a person who needed something to do. Her, you give her some potting soil and the new Ross MacDonald, and she could disappear for about maybe three days. Some fresh lemons to squeeze into lemonade, a jug to fill with teabags and water and stick in the sun for a day. Give her a broom and a porch covered with sand and dried mud. She can pass months like this, marking time by the diurnal succession of events, flowerings, ripenings, gatherings, emptyings, endings.

Guy takes one look at the boxes on the floor, rinses out a water glass in the sink, and fills that with the All-Bran. He eats standing over the sink. He, what is the right way, he bolts his food. Not every time but when it's useful to him. She knows he has some big plans because he doesn't want to sit down with her and hold forth for an hour.

"What are you doing today?" she ventures.

"Susan and Jeff's."

"The barbecue!" says Randi, as if it were the solution to an enduring mystery, Professor Plum in the library with the candlestick. Susan Rorvik and Jeff Wolfritz had taken custody of their big barbecue grill when they'd left for Ohio, and they never had replaced it.

"Something's on the fire, all right." Spooning bran into his mouth, Guy hunches and unhunches his shoulders a few times, which Randi takes to be a form of laughter. Whatever. She is into her day now. She will begin penciling out a list soon. Tops on it is getting the KITCHEN STUFF unpacked and into cupboards and drawers because when your personal things are inaccessible it means you are dwelling in a state that is akin to death. It's a long June day and she wants its Alpha and its Omega down on a piece of scrap paper where she can keep an eye on them. She sees herself in the backyard as evening falls, drinking something cold at the round table, amid the petitioning of the crickets, the bougainvillea darkening in the failing light. California.

Guy finishes up and puts his glass and spoon in the sink. It's time to head out. He goes into the spare bedroom and gathers up some things he thinks he might need: a portable cassette tape recorder, a yellow legal pad, a copy of *The Athletic Revolution*, some pens. He puts these things in his shoulder bag and then pauses. The tape recorder would probably scare them off. He removes it. Now, a gift. As in other times of uncertainty, he refers to the movies. In which one bears evocative gifts when visiting prisoners or fugitives or soldiers far from home, chocolate bars and cigarettes. Always, the guy called Brooklyn (played by William Bendix) asks, "How the Bums doin'?" The emissary is maybe played by Robert Montgomery: "Two games behind the Cardinals last I heard, Flatbush." Then Bendix gets shot by the Japs.

He gets shot. Guy thinks of the footage. He watched it in a dingy bar up near Columbia, that little house burning for the cameras. Very weird, staring at the palms hard-edged against the flames and red smoke, the lives of those people roaring into that distant sky, while with one hand he searched around in a jar for a pickled egg in this place that felt as old as thankless endeavor itself. Strictly drunks, no students. It was the sort of place where his brother, Ernest, would have taken up residence.

A guy sitting next to him at the bar, said he was a vet, pointed at the screen. "Search-and-destroy. *That* is a fucking search-and-destroy op, just like Vietnam. Fucking *textbook*." OK, so this was not just any old bunch of kids standing up for their rights. They armed themselves and wrote inflammatory communiqués and shot progressive public school administrators and kidnapped people and robbed banks and shot innocent bystanders. He understood the pull of the suggestion that they'd "asked for it." And he further understood that police logic found its source at a strange and alien fountainhead. But the point was that something seemed wrong about this. The point was that pinning down the SLA in a house and setting it on fire seemed pretty extreme.

Susan had said: "She particularly, Guy, is very scared and plus very sad because of, you know, Willie, and they are all freaked out, but they're doing pretty well under the circumstances, though I think she's kind of paranoid because she's thinking she'll be singled out. Like, shot on sight. And I wouldn't say that she thinks that's the worst thing that could happen to her right now either. But I think what they really need is to get the hell out of California for a while."

Jesus, now how is he going to break this to Randi?

But what a fucking *gas*!

Cigarettes and chocolate bars he figures they can manage all by themselves. So far their ordeal hasn't required this kind of denial of the flesh. He is amused to think of revolutionaries, down from the hills, pausing at roadside restaurants to order their food from tasseled menus the size and shape of Monopoly boards. He's been to those places on I-5 and 101 and 99. You could try to apply your survival skills to the wilderness, to gather mushrooms and roots, but in the approximate center of the Golden State, cleared and furrowed and planted with the world's bounty, the big difficulty was to find a decent place with free refills. He moves back into the kitchen carrying the shoulder bag. The back door is open, and he sees Randi half inside the storage shed in the yard. Sitting on the counter is yesterday's loaf of zucchini bread, about a third of it gone. He shoves it into a brown paper bag and carries it to the car.

Guy has a fantastic idea in mind that's arrived so fully formed that he can't help thinking that he subconsciously conceived it sitting in Morningside Heights on that barstool beside the drunken vet and then filed it away for it to reappear at the proper time, which presented itself when his old pal Susan Rorvik called to tell him that she'd been contacted by Yolanda of the SLA. That had been a shocker; after Susan had organized the rally at Ho Chi Minh Park, Guy just assumed she'd be under surveillance by the Pigs. He can't believe the SLA has taken the risk of contacting her. Still, maybe that's a measure of their desperation. The SLA was unloved within the Movement, that's for sure. At best they were considered a joke; at worst they were suspected of being a front for the CIA. Now that they've been martyred—and gotten plenty of press in the process—opinion seems to be shifting. Here's where Guy figures he can help out. What he wants to do is to write a book-length treatment of the SLA experience: their ideas, their goals, their viewpoint, basically their side of the whole fucking story. Sure, there'll have to be a certain emphasis on Tania, but every show has its star, and he figures if he presents it to the fugitives as a saga about their carrying on in the face of adversity, while pitching it to publishers as the Insider Story of the Missing Heiress, things will work out fine. They have to. Guy's feeling a certain in-betweenness regarding his life these days that he's getting a little tired of, and after years of having taken for granted his ability to wander into situations where he's grossly out of place, wander in and deliver congressional testimony or wangle a faculty appointment or an editorship or swing a book deal, he's still shaken by his sudden dismissal from Oberlin.

In a weird way, Guy's ideas about sports had been greeted with even more hostility than the SLA's manifestos. He'd challenged some very entrenched notions about masculinity, about strength, about triumph, and he'd done it precisely at a time when thousands of young men were thinking twice about wearing uniforms and taking orders. From Guy's suggestion that it was unnecessary to listen to people like Bear Bryant or Bobby Knight, that there was something illegitimate about their absolute authority, it could logically be inferred that it was equally unnecessary to listen to Richard Nixon and Henry Kissinger. Of course the draft was finished. And the war was over too. But these were moves that had been made under a dread aura of concession, rather than in the spirit of progress.

Guy had no idea of what a lightning rod he'd become. While he could describe with admirable eloquence the sort of wrongdoing that went on every Saturday afternoon in the name of sport, he had been against the war because it was stupid and murderous, not because he had any per se objection to the way in which soldiers were trained. But the paranoid brain sees things in terms of metaphor: Guy thought that athletes were more important than gate receipts and Howard Cosell; ergo he was putting across a clandestine vilification of our South Asia policy. The man was unfixably askew from bedrock American principles. He was an "enemy of sport," Agnew said. He could just as easily have said "our enemy."

Ah, who cares about Spiro Agnew? Nobody cares about Spiro Agnew.

The thing is that when Guy had first heard about the Oberlin job, he'd been enchanted, thought of the place in terms of woodwinds, of simply dressed cellists with lank hair and calloused fingers, of listening to music in an amphitheater on a star-stung night. The stridor, the white roar of the arena, was far from his mind. He was tricked. The search committee flew him out. He opened his mouth, and the usual sounds came out. He didn't try to fool anybody; he told them he would hire women and blacks. He told them that he would attempt to make the ecumenical style of the place fit his principles, not the other way around. In his mind he saw himself sitting under the stars on a soft midwestern evening, listening to music.

Anyway, he was hired. Oberlin had built a nice new sports complex. And he and Randi stayed up late the night before school began, hanging a curtain across the men's locker room, since the architects had forgotten to put in a separate one for women: oops. He hired Linda Huey to coach women's track and promised her a budget equal to that of the men's team (faint stirrings of disquiet among the trustees). He hired Tommie Smith to coach men's track. He saw a gold medalist who had a sympathetic way with young athletes; they saw the black fist hanging in the Mexico City sky, hanging forever in commemoration of a shame this sort of victory simply couldn't address, the fist that still sent ripples of unease trembling across the dark fields of the Republic. After the billeting of this seditionist, the hiring of "fellow Negroes" (as one paper put it) Cass Jackson and Patrick Penn went almost unnoticed. Almost.

This is the college that began admitting women and blacks in the 1830s?

But nay, this is sport, in the name of which Stanley Royster is kicked off the Cal track team for becoming involved in black politics on campus. In the name of which Sylvester Hodges is prohibited from competing at the NCAA championship wrestling tournament because of the unpardonable offense of wearing a mustache. Rah.

He should have known better.

They pushed on. There was a peculiar sense not of siege exactly but of hollow impermanence. It colored every decision they made. Neighbors who wouldn't have voluntarily suffered their presence judged them to be "distant." They marked their calendars for the days when out-of-town friends passed through, Guy and Randi did, marked those square-inch boxes in the brightest red ink. They bought a Bell & Howell projector at a garage sale and found a mail-order place where they could obtain prints of ancient two-reel comedies, so they could avoid watching "moron TV."

Also, less cozily, out of sheer boredom, Guy began an affair with a town girl named Erica Dyson. Very uncharacteristic, that whole thing. She seemed to think she was pregnant all the time. Randi found out when Guy began a somewhat recklessly recurrent and increasingly compulsive line of inquiry with her regarding the (a) nature and (b) frequency of ovulation. She asked why one day (she knew she shouldn't, but), Guy answered her with habitual candor, and she went crazy and smashed all the dishes. Period. This is how American marriages stay together out here where the wind has a different sound and smell depending on which direction it's coming from and that's the big news of the day. To be honest, Guy was a little more concerned about Erica Dyson than he was about Randi. He pictured her parking her Duster across the tracks at some rural crossing where a freight train traveling at 80 mph would shower both her and the Plymouth into two adjacent fields, over two county lines, into the bailiwick of public inquiry. And the bundle, the potential heir whose likely imaginary presence her hand nervously traced across her detumescent abdomen: What if?

So Guy went to Allen Memorial Hospital that winter evening to get stitches for the cut above his eye that a jagged piece of Corning Ware had inflicted; and he sat in the waiting room of the new wing while he waited to be fixed up, holding an old copy of the *Reader's Digest* and turning its pages, composing the unbelievable lies he would tell successively to the nurse, the intern, the attending physician, and finally, later, Erica Dyson, wondering idly how many solid citizens of Lorain County belted their spouses, or slept around, or cheated on their income taxes, or took two newspapers out of the dispenser on Main Street when they'd paid for only one, and as he did these things, he knew that he was approaching the end of his midwestern sojourn, that the ingredients of his real life were being gathered up and prepared for him somewhere out there in the great meanwhile.

A pale boy, a sheen like dewy spider's webbing the only suggestion of hair on the sides and back of his skull, sat opposite Guy sandwiched between two morbidly obese women. Guy decided that they were his aunts. The boy was the living embodiment of the sort of characterless object that the popular culture had positioned as the representative face of American Boyhood when Guy had been growing up. The boy cradled his right forearm in his left; could it actually be that he had fallen from a tree? The aunts had looked up from the twin pies they were placing to cool on adjacent windowsills and seen the boy topple from the branches of an apple tree, the very one from which they'd gained the fruit to bake the pies, and rushed out, each drying her damp hands on her apron. The two of them, Guy and the boy, stared in frank and open astonishment at each other. The hair, the mustache, the staring eyes, which under the very best of circumstances made Guy look faintly rabid: Even by 1973 Guy was a curiosity. And the boy's fish belly looks we've already rehearsed. Finally, the boy reached up to tug on the nearest broad sleeve.

"Mama . . . Mom . . . look, it's the hippie who's doing it with Erica Dyson!"

Whatever the pretext, they soon were moving. The university handed him his hat and forty grand. They clumped through the empty rooms, their voices reverberating. They didn't toast any good times they might have had there. They left things behind, bags of discards and a forwarding address—his parents' home, a failing motel in Las Vegas—and headed for NYC, an ill-defined trip. Home of eight major professional sports franchises and focus of a world's derivative gaze. Unfortunately, Guy and his Institute for the Study of Sport and Society did not quite fit in with the steak-and-Löwenbräu ethos of Toots Shor's. Randi wilted like the houseplants that hung over the rattling radiators. They headed back to the California coast.

Now, a scant two weeks later, Guy is tooling through the streets of Berkeley, the offering of a substantial portion of an excellent zucchini bread seated beside him, the high splenetic clatter of the Bug echoing against the houses on either side of the street. He skirts the campus now, onto Hearst Avenue, and then, spotting the snarl of worshipful traffic outside the church ahead, turns quickly north, heading up into the hills and the stilted apartment buildings that loom above their open carports like the cut-rate imitations of the good life that they are. The real luxury is found on the serpentine turns that this street, Euclid, takes as it approaches its beau ideal— remote and faintly forbidding inaccessibility—farther on.

He passes a wall on which someone has sprayed THE SLA LIVES. Is it an affirmation of the remaining entity or a memorial to the six who were lost?

On the other hand, he's afraid he's going to make something of a bad first impression. Not that this is anything new to Guy. But he's really got to take a shit; the All-Bran has just scoured him out. You hear about people who decline to shit in other people's houses; Guy is not one of them. Guy will eliminate whenever he feels the interior clamor. He will eat that last pork chop. He will tell you if you've gained weight. He will ask how much you make or what you paid for your house. He will provide an honest opinion of your attire. None of which constitutes the violation of a taboo, strictly speaking, but each has a tendency to make people feel uncomfortable; hence the famous "difficulty" for which Guy is renowned.

The Bayview Apartments. Casa Euclid. The Trollmont. The

Oaklander. Grizzly Peak Residences. Albany Terrace Arms. He pulls in a couple of doors down from the building where Susan and Jeff are feeding the fish of a vacationing acquaintance. The late-morning air is still and very warm in the sun. He parks facing up the hill and sits for a moment, trying to remember which way he is supposed to turn the wheels; with his VW, it's not merely for the sake of appearance. He decides he is supposed to turn them facing out into the roadway and works the wheel, audibly grunting. Then he gets out, and, after putting on the shoulder bag, carries the loaf of zucchini bread under his arm as he walks up the street's oil-spattered margin.

He's pretty excited about this.

Guy enters his destination via a dank and shadowy grotto where a rank of mailboxes is embedded in a stucco wall, and gratefully crosses into a sunny central courtyard around which the complex forms an open rectangle, bordered on its open side by spare greenery that separates it from its nearly identical neighbor. On this level are the carports, most of which are empty of cars this pretty Sunday but full of other things: beach toys and cross-country skis and cardboard cartons and stacks of newspapers and barbecue grills and cans of motor oil. Above the carports are the apartments, inscrutable behind the identical hollow-core doors and curtained windows that line the tier. He pauses on the uneven ground, looking for number eleven, then heads for a set of stairs that gives every appearance of having been an afterthought.

He knocks, employing the ridiculously lively shave-and-a-haircut theme. After a silent interval he adds the two bits. More silence. He turns and, leaning on the wrought-iron railing, looks down upon the courtyard. A Ford Pinto pulls into one of the carports, and a middle-aged woman emerges in a pants suit an acute shade of green, keys dangling from her hand, and stares curiously up at Guy.

"He's away," she calls, shielding her eyes with the hand holding the keys.

"Pardon me?" answers Guy, raising a cupped hand to his ear.

"I say, he must have gone away." The woman has begun to mount the stairs. "His car's been gone for the past few days anyways." She points at one of the empty carports.

"I'm. Oh. Well." Guy has no idea what to say. He feels out of his depth, a vertiginous sensation that precedes what he knows will be an inept improvisation. He reaches for his shoulder bag. "Maybe I'll just leave him a note." He nods, smiling with tight lips at the woman. Who snorts.

"*If* he knows how to *read*." With that, she fits the key into the lock and lets herself into her apartment.

Guy removes the yellow pad and a pen from the shoulder bag. He gently lays the zucchini bread at his feet. What's he supposed to write? Yabba-dabba-doo? Death to the Fascist Insect? Well, you know, we all want to change the world? He looks up and, unsurprisingly, sees the curtain move at the window beside Miss High-Wattage Green's door. A good bet that his note will be inspected. He writes: "Was here Sun AM. Will try again. G." He tucks it under the door, leaving half an inch or so exposed so that the woman doesn't kill herself clawing it out from under there.

Back in the Bug he begins rhythmically contracting his sphincter, trying to stave off the inevitable. Plus give himself more sexual stamina and longer and more satisfying orgasms, to look at it in the long term. Primarily, though, he's trying to keep the shit up the chute. Usually he can manage to make himself forget about it, but he can tell that today he is on the verge of a rude and unpleasant experience, and he is about to turn the key in the ignition and head back to Oakland when he sees the distinctive tail of the Pinto, like the thalidomide nightmare of European design sensibility, emerge from the driveway as the green woman turns sharply and takes off up the hill. He's out of the car for one more try.

His note appears to be missing. He knocks. He knocks again, louder. He places his hand on the doorknob. He is feeling nakedly conspicuous and out of place here in this quiet apartment complex. He may as well act as if he belonged here, what the fuck. Besides, he has to get to a toilet right away.

The door opens when he turns the knob. Inside, a smell like that of a pet shop, vaguely aquatic. He spies the enormous aquarium that sits in a corner of the living room. The fish rise, fall, and dart in its soft glow, and he is drawn to them, comes near and watches the neon tetras and the angelfish and whatever else there are in there moving in loose and graceful formation inside the box of lighted water. He spots a toggle on the light ballast that fits over the aquarium's top, and when he switches it, the aquarium becomes, under the scrutiny of a black light, a lunar landscape, the neon tetras a liquid metal as if forged from the sultry waters of their origin, luminous and mercurial, dancing above the brilliant and depthless gravel in the ultraviolet cartoon of his gaze.

Then he feels it, a hollow clunk accompanying the metallic shock of the thing's making contact with the back of his skull, and a strange sensation of being probed, as if he were first to be examined by the instrument of his destruction, and also there is the oddly light grip on his shoulder as he is guided, backward, out of the living room and into the kitchen. He moves stiffly and takes tiny steps, feeling the terrain change from shag carpeting to linoleum. He is placed standing amid the cupboards before a small, round dinette table set in front of a sliding glass door, crudely curtained with floral bed sheets, that leads to a tiny balcony. On the dinette table is an army surplus gas mask bag, open, from which the butt end of a revolver and a pack of Tareytons protrude. A spiral-bound notebook lies open next to the bag, a capped Bic inserted in the twisted wire spine.

The butt end of a revolver, protruding, nearby.

A male voice, several feet away: "Well, did you check his bag?"

A woman, closer: "No." Guy notices that the object against his head moves ever so slightly when she speaks.

"Well, you know. I think I've mentioned before. Real, real important."

"I'm sorry." The voice is tiny.

"Sorry doesn't cut it."

Butt end, just a quick grab away.

But there is the sound of a chair scraping across the floor, and footsteps, and Guy's shoulder bag is roughly taken from him, and the bag of zucchini bread too.

If there is a gun in the gas mask bag, then this thing against his head definitely is a gun. Because otherwise they'd use the one in the bag. Right?

The man asks, "What's this?" A small hairy hand holds the bread up in front of his face.

Guy responds: "Zucchini bread."

"You a fucking baker, man?"

"I thought you might want something homemade."

"I might?"

"All of you."

"All of us. Shit." The man chuckles.

"Who do you think 'us' is?" The woman presses the gun into his occiput. Guy thinks he is going to shit in his pants.

"I'm Guy Mock. Check the shoulder bag."

"Did I ask who you were?"

"Well. But I think you're expecting me."

From outside there comes the hollow sound, surprisingly loud, of people ascending the staircase. Quick steps, which seem to jar the flimsy building to its very core, move down the walkway and pause outside the door. In the silence it's as if the room itself had been drawn in with their held breaths, all the isolating span removed from the space the three of them and the gun and Guy's tortured gut share. The only sound is the aquarium's humming filter. Then the sound of a key being shaken loose from the others on a ring and then inserted in the lock. The door opens, and Susan Rorvik enters, followed by an older woman, with graying hair and eyeglasses. For an instant Guy wonders why Susan has brought her mother here with her, and how nice, how weird, up from Twentynine Palms, or what is it, Palmdale?, some desert spot, an oasis of aluminum siding and thirsty imported turf, military bases of unknown purpose— covert training of desert assassins, testing of nerve gases that curdle the minutest aspects of human anatomy, dissection of alien visitors—hello, good to see you, glad to know you, ha-ha-ho. Then, as Susan gasps, "Guy!" the other woman removes the wig and the glasses, and Guy stares into the face of Diane Shepard, who is looking past his shoulder.

"God fucking damn it, Teko, that's Guy Mock. You want her to blow his head off?"

For the first time in about, oh, six lifetimes, a few shrill eternities in the lake of fire, an extended cosmic interval in which that famous solitary ant has carted off the greater part of the Gobi, the Sahara, the Gibbon, one grain at a time, the gun moves off his skull, and Guy turns, pivots carefully with no unnecessary movement of his extremities, to face Tania.

"I'm, like, really sorry," she says. She blushes.

They sit in the living room, Guy cross-legged on the floor between Susan and Jeff Wolfritz, who has joined them in the apartment sometime during the bathroom interval that restores tranquil immaculacy to Guy's GI system, with the SLA three lining the couch in the deadeye sepia pose of a nineteenth-century family group. The fish in the tank dive, dart, and coast. For his pitch, Guy settles into the lotus position. An affectation, to be sure, intended to imbue his physical aspect with the wisdom that his staring eyes and receding hairline combine to deny. And that he does, after all, possess to a measurable degree. Plus it stretches out the ligaments in his hips, allowing for deeper and more thrillingly pleasurable penetration during intercourse.

First, though, he has some principled questions.

What about the assassination of Marcus Foster, the Oakland superintendent of schools, who was universally perceived as a progressive influence and whose killing was angrily denounced by the black community and the Left alike?

"Neither of us was in the SLA then."

"We read about it in the newspapers."

"I was just an average Berkeley housewife then."

But did you agree with the Foster killing?

Here Teko lays out a sinuously convoluted rationale, in which he seems to have complete faith, concerning (1) the fascist Law Enforcement Assistance Administration, (2) the imminent implementation of a program in which "bio-dossiers" would have been maintained on all students attending the Oakland public schools, (3) fascist police agents patrolling the halls with shotguns and attack dogs, (4) fascist concentration camps for so-called troublemakers, and (5) Foster's complicity in all of the above. Plus the program was to be implemented under the direction of a "former police sergeant."

Guy thinks it's funny; an entirely new subset of clichés was coming of age. He hadn't realized that the SLA took its rhetoric *literally*.

Anyway, after the assassination, Teko and Yolanda bought up all the copies of the *Oakland Tribune* they could find: to send to friends.

"But then the community reaction was so overwhelmingly negative," complains Yolanda bitterly.

"Not that the People *really* liked Foster," says Teko.

"He was just a fucking fascist," says Tania.

"They *made believe* they liked him because they knew the pigs would come down on them if they talked about him the way they really felt."

It might have been a better idea, the harijan army agrees, to start slow, with confrontational graffiti and broken windows, before moving up to shotgunning Foster and his fascist lieutenant, Blackburn.

Guy thinks, *fascist fascist fascist fascist fascist.*

OK, then, what about the Hibernia Bank robbery? What was the necessity of shooting two bystanders? Hadn't you already obtained your objective of "expropriating" funds?

"It became imperative to obtain resources by any means necessary," says Yolanda.

"It was totally compulsory. We were forced into it since being underground had totally depleted our funds."

"We like couldn't work," explains Tania.

But what about the shootings?

"Oh, everybody was real shaken up by that," says Teko.

"It was an overreaction. I don't see that ever happening again."

"In combat you have to make these decisions on a split-second basis."

"They were *told,* the two men, they were *told* to lie on the floor like everybody else. They ran instead. And were fired upon."

That was their *split-second decision.*

"Exactly."

"We should have put something out explaining the mistake and saying we were sorry. It's important for revolutionaries to do that."

"A serious blemish on an operation that was otherwise extremely well done," says Teko.

Guy had expected something more from these bright people— the pep chairman and straight A student, the social chair of Chi Omega, and the art history major whose society wedding had been scheduled to take place this very month—more than for the three of them to sit here answering his questions with all the earnest insincerity of entry-level job applicants. They so wanted to provide the "right" answers. They were so convinced that there *were* right answers, and that he was looking for them. Now the big one:

How about the kidnapping?

"Which one?" More laughter.

"Well, that's just it. You're laughing. But there's something," Guy says, "about taking people by force, making them come with you under duress."

Teko and Yolanda look back at him brightly, attentively, though there's something about them that gives the impression that they're bracing for a body blow. Guy turns his eyes on Tania. She recedes into the couch, as if she were embroidered on its surface, an anchored superficiality. Her own eyes are steady, and looking at nothing.

"It's just, it's everything freedom isn't, whatever the 'reason' may happen to be. I guess you could argue for the political necessity of Foster's assassination; you could even make a case for shooting those people at the bank, if you really really had to. But there's something about taking over a person's life and making it something other than their own."

"Oh, Dan Russell loved every minute he was with us," says Yolanda. "I could tell."

Guy says, "I'm not talking about god damn Dan Russell, and you know it." He surprises himself with his sudden change of tone.

"What are you talking about?" Yolanda's face is rigid, lean with anger, and she sits straight up. Mean, Guy thinks. Mean woman.

In the end, Guy leaves, exhausted, without having made a single commitment to these people. Susan walks him to the door, holding his forearm, gripping it as they step out onto the walkway, gripping the arm as they move down the stairs and into the courtyard. She is leaning in, pitching for his aid. She is saying Angela: Angela this, Angela that, invoking—not entirely fairly, Guy thinks—the name of her dead friend. Ultimately, hers is not an appeal to his politics. Guy tries to imagine what it must feel like: to catch fire, and burn. He finally takes hold of the hand hanging on to him, holds it gently in his as a prelude to dropping it and walking away.

He is excited and troubled. The SLA sat there stripped naked—figuratively, anyway—bereft of comrades, friends, lovers, an operative sense of purpose, and all because they didn't show up. What's more, they lost the revolution. We can't forget that they lost the war, even if not many people happened to notice it, that's what it was to them—the Naga banner their battle flag, "Death to the Fascist Insect" their rebel yell—and in the end they were massacred by the state for having waged it, massacred in an act of lawlessness under color of authority. As General Teko carefully pointed out, most of the people in that house had not been charged with any crime before being surrounded; they were as innocent as the day they were born, were, in effect, martyrs to the cause, although they *were* at war with fascist Amerikkka (which word Guy noticed Teko had found a distinct way to pronounce), and Guy stayed with Teko despite this minor sophistry, thought he was *right on*, but then Teko had gone into some strange obsessive rap about Gigantic Black Penises and White Cunts and Bourgeois Fear while Yolanda and Tania accompanied him with this fake black churchy thing ("Tell it!" "Uhnh-huhnh!"), so Guy had carefully sorted through his memories until he located one of a breathtakingly cold swim he'd taken in Lake Tahoe one morning in early summer, of devouring the contents of a picnic basket after having emerged shivering from the jeweled water, one of many pointless reminiscences that spangle his consciousness, and it tided him over until Teko quit with all the dick talk.

So. They are these defeated people, crumpled up like old Dixie cups someone pissed in before deciding to toss them, fucked up with grief and regret. Right? No, they are giving him shit: "What kind of car is it you drive?" "Who'd you say it was that published your book?" "How big of an advance would a book like this be likely to get?" "Where will we be staying?" These American revolutionaries are interested in the amenities.

The afternoon has had an unusual effect on him. In having sat in a shabby North Berkeley apartment across from the fugitive heiress, the girl whose absence has been the strange floating turd in the punchbowl of jeunesse dorée, Guy feels that he has experienced the sense of wonder you might undergo in opening up an oyster and finding a pearl. So Guy decides he is going to be expansive about it. So they've fucked everything up, and they're mostly wrong, and every exchange they shared with him wobbled at the edge of argument. So the Shepards take a scattershot approach to assigning blame, at times conveniently impugning the dead. So there is not even a single focused reason that will serve to clarify his own motives. He sees a group of people. He sees a narrative. He sees himself having lunch with an editor.

He's not exactly sure how he's going to swing it. At least a couple of round trips are in store for someone, and there are the void distances of the interstate, where every caged body becomes an all too obvious ornamentation of the scrub 'n' sky landscape, where smokies in their cruisers lie in wait for miscreants, parked in the scant shade at the side of the road to avoid sunshine so hot it splits rocks and the sand-blasted bones of dead mammals. How obvious is the most famous girl in America? He'll Clark Kent her: glasses and a bun.

The wind is high, bending the tops of the trees, when Randi decides to call it quits for the afternoon. Guy's been out all day, and she managed to clear chunks of cement, probably left over from the construction of that damned patio that seems designed to unambiguously demarcate the limits of one's outdoor enjoyment, from out of her garden patch, to add fresh soil and fertilizer, and to stake and trellis her tomato seedlings, though it's probably a little late to be dealing with tomatoes. But she can see and taste them—ripe as blisters, their buttery tang, late summer's bounty—and it keeps her working through the afternoon. The boxes of KITCHEN STUFF have yet to be unpacked, but it just seemed like one of those days when staying indoors was like asking for an engraved invitation to a total comedown later on, a malignantly gloomy mood from which she would have demanded to be coaxed by Guy, if she could get him to sit in one place. She has been working without gloves, and the dirt has been driven up under her fingernails and embedded in the creases of her hands, inlaid streaks of black, and she admires her hands in the bright kitchen light before scrubbing them in the deep porcelain basin, admires them because dirty hands give shape to another moment in the day's orderly progression, from clean to dirty to clean again, the dirt spinning down the drain.

She puts on a sweatshirt and goes back outdoors to muscle the patio furniture onto that concrete pad; she swears to God it looks as if you could land a helicopter here if you wanted to. The wind, with its hint of someplace else's chill gale. She listens for the unmistakable sound of a VW Bug. Tonight she'll put out the citronella candles, and they'll relax outside.

HANK WALKED SLOWLY DOWN Burlingame Avenue, a penciled list in the breast pocket of his shirt. The day was bright and clear. He could hear the whistle of a Southern Pacific train behind him as it moved through the station without stopping.

Today was the housekeeper's day off and he'd driven downtown in the station wagon, yes, taking matters into his own hands, as Lydia had said with a sneer. He enjoyed doing the marketing. The Safeway was laid out to be enjoyed, bright and wide and colorful. He enjoyed the checkout counter, had a favorite among the clerks, Roy, whom he'd gotten to know slightly over the years, probably better than he knew certain of his colleagues. Was this embarrassing? Interesting? Signs of some sort of "common man" "hangup," as Lydia frequently suggested? Roy had been a bookbinder, high-quality precision craftwork that had given him a bleeding ulcer and a bald head at the age of thirty-one. So he'd quit and was now being paid something like four-fifty an hour to ring up groceries, to snap open brown paper bags and pack them up. Hard to imagine, on a busy Sunday afternoon, that this was less nerve-wracking than binding books.

Roy seemed to be off today, though, so Hank had steered the cart into the line forming before Delia's register. Delia's father had bought her a new car when hers "hydroplaned" on a slippery road. He'd provided the down payment for a little Milpitas cottage after her apartment had been broken into. He'd sent her to Santa Clara University for two and a half years before she decided that what she really really wanted to do was not go to Santa Clara University. Delia freely confessed her dependence on her old man. She looked maybe Italian or Greek; Hank pictured her father as a stern but indulgent type with hairy arms, but who could know? They'd never gotten on a last-name basis. The clerks were stripped of their surnames as part of the wave of epidemic casualness. Delia was lean and tan and had a big booming voice she used, raising a bunch of carrots or a canister of breadcrumbs high over her head to call for a price, bringing an assistant manager running over, keys jangling on the Key-Bak clipped to his waistband. So how is it, Hank thought, that you're here? How did your dad manage to keep you? How come you're ringing up groceries instead of carrying a rifle through your days?

"How you doing, Mr. Galton?"

Of course she knew him, famous fellow that he was. In the news more during the past four months than he'd been over the course of his entire life. Though he had not yet acquired the foul appetite for press conferences that possessed, say, his future son-in-law, if Stump was in fact still that. The contempt Stump had for what he thought of as the family's stale decorum! Whatever it was the family had decided upon, had been bred, to say, Stump could be counted on to say the opposite. Fine, OK. But this wasn't around the dining table. This wasn't someplace where Stump looked stupidly out of place, like the Burlingame Country Club, where dozens of eligible young girls entertained boyfriends who—who were not Eric Stump. Someplace where Eric Stump opened his yap and a knowledgeable person of experience, a Mickey Tobin, simply settled back with his drink and enjoyed the show. Someplace where Stump, ever dedicated to the prospect of his intellect as a burnished display (Hank didn't claim much of one, but he assumed that intellect should be like money: concealed yet present at all times), simply tired himself out from talking. This was in front of the reporters to whom none of it mattered. To them, Stump was one of the magical people dwelling in the tragedy-touched world of the rich and famous. Standing each day before the clustered microphones outside the house, Stump faced an inexhaustible audience expecting an illimitable story. And brother, when the big time came calling, he was ready. All his crap about philosophy, all his barely sheathed contempt for "the media," and he got weak in the knees at the idea of telling his story for publication, just like every housewife and longshoreman and shopkeeper Hank had interviewed when he started out as a cub with the old *San Francisco Call* back in 1940. Starstruck, his skin ready to receive the glow that constant, passionate scrutiny imparted to it. He'd helped with her homework touched her eaten the last meal she prepared seen the panties in which she was carried away "half naked" watched TV with her listened to her desires and goals. They smoked pot they made love and yes they'd had a very in-

teresting discussion, with friends, about politics just a day or so before it happened. But basically she just wanted a dog and a station
wagon. Yes, Stump warmed to his role as the interpreter of every
mysterious and occluded young mind occupying every messy rear
bedroom in every house.

"Thirty-seven forty, please, Mr. Galton."

Fishing in his pocketful of anonymous cash. Which is of course
exactly what it had never been.

The grocery bags were stowed now in the back of the wagon,
which he'd parked in the shade of a tree growing at the edge of the
municipal lot. Hank walked slowly, in a light breeze, slightly unsteady on his feet. These old suburban downtowns, bleached in sunshine. A tavern, a delicatessen, a store selling uniforms. A Chinese
restaurant, nothing sadder by daylight, the characters forming its
name, its true Chinese name, carved in red-painted wood and crawling down the bright stucco wall. Might say "Fuck You, White
Devil" for all Hank knew. The only Chinese person Hank knew was
Sam Yee, to whom he brought his shirts.

Feeling slightly unsteady, trying to take a true look at these things.
It was like touring a place you were about to leave permanently.

But all he was doing was running errands. Nothing suspicious
about that, correct? If someone was to leap out of a doorway and
confront him, confront him with the subject of his culpability, holding a microphone or a protest sign or a hand grenade (they seemed
equally likely possibilities), his list was as innocent as Christ. Now
see here: he wanted to buy some stamps, and a package of Aquafilters, and a pound of spiced ham, and a magazine for Helene. Lydia
laughed sharply. She thought it was ridiculous. She wondered what
would bring this playacting to an end. Going downtown in a brown
station wagon like a fool. And then, if he really wanted to, he could
come home and stack cans in the pantry.

But that was what he wanted. Affix a clean piece of scrap paper to
the fridge with a magnet and begin the list all over again. If you just
kept buying groceries the household would continue forever.

Groceries. There hadn't been enough money to satisfy the SLA's
ransom demand that he personally feed the state's poor. Not that
they'd believed him. He had a hard enough time explaining to the
immediate family, let alone to the fanatics holding his daughter,

the elaborately interwoven relationships among the old man's heirs, the Galton Corporation, the Galton Foundation, and the Galton Family Trust. In effect, Hank was the paid employee of his father's money, not its possessor. The bottom line was that he was worth about two million bucks, about a half million of it available in cash, which he'd duly forked over to the food relief effort, a program dubbed People in Need. For the remainder of what would be required, he'd had to appeal to the corporation, which, acting through the trustees, had given him a total of four million dollars to work with. He and the other five family members on the board had recused themselves from the vote. Though he was glad not to have been there, tired of hearing the value of his daughter's life weighed. They came out with the four million figure and he said fine. Sounds good. What the hell did he know? Not only did he have no idea how much it would cost, he had no idea what "it" was; in one tape Alice said that the SLA would accept a "good-faith gesture," that "whatever you come up with is basically OK." What he'd god damned come up with was one-quarter of his net worth. But later in the tape Cinque, to whose voice Hank had begun to react with nauseous loathing, had endeavored to clarify the matter by defining a "good-faith gesture" as a "sincere effort." Thank you so very much. Sincere effort further stipulated to mean seventy dollars' worth of "top-quality fresh meats, dairy products and produce," handed over to anyone who turned up to ask for it, regardless of need.

Oh, that was a *good* tape, the February 19 tape, a fine tape. They could seal that one in a capsule and blast it into space with a Snoopy doll and copies of *Jonathan Livingston Seagull* and *Sergeant Pepper's Lonelyhearts Club Band*. (How had he learned of these things?) Wherever it turned up, whatever bat-eared, green-blooded creature hauled it out of the icy void to discover something about the human race in the twentieth century, that tape would impart with complete accuracy an allusive record of all the ingratitude, the venality, the envy, the hypocritical greed, the ineducable recalcitrance, the superficiality, and above all the cavalier disregard for fact that, as far as he was concerned, distinguished the new generation from the preceding one. What ate him up was that he listened to the—you should pardon the expression—substance of what Cinque said and found himself trying hard to give a damn. Many of the things he'd always been secure from had been brought to his attention, and he wanted to sympathize. But that this repellent shit, Cinque, had appointed himself Official Spokesman just turned him off so completely that he had trouble doing so.

On the February 19 tape, Cinque berated him, provided a comically inaccurate list of "his" assets, demanded an additional four million bucks, demanded that the food program be handed over to the prickly Western Addition Project Area Committee, and then built to one of the trademark crescendos Hank had become accustomed to:

> You do, indeed, know me. You have always known me. I'm that nigger you have hunted and feared night and day. I'm that nigger you have killed hundreds of my people in a vain hope of finding. I'm that nigger that is no longer just hunted, robbed and murdered. I'm the nigger that hunts you now!
>
> Yes, you know me. You know me, I'm the wetback. You know me, I'm the gook, the broad, the servant, the spik.
>
> Yes, indeed, you know us all and we know you—the oppressor, murderer and robber. And you have hunted and robbed and exploited us all. Now we are the hunters that will give you no rest. And we will not compromise the freedom of our children.
>
> DEATH TO THE FASCIST INSECT THAT *PREYS* UPON THE LIFE OF THE PEOPLE!

That first distribution. A bucket of blood, as his father might have said. Angry crowds overran the distribution sites; men climbed aboard the trucks to stand in their beds, on their roofs, heaving frozen chickens into the throng. Imagine checking into the hospital with that as your chief complaint. Frozen broiler to the head. Roving gangs robbed recipients of their grocery bags. A Black Muslim bakery overseeing the distribution in Oakland billed the program for $154,000, claiming that it had provided that much of its own food to replace stolen and looted stock. "Volunteers" showed up at the warehouses, offered to drive laden trucks to the distribution centers, and then vanished, trucks, food, and all. Leaving Hank wondering: What do you do with two tons of canned Virginia hams? Security guards hired to protect the warehouses started looting from them as well. Reporters on the evening news took a gleeful interest in unpacking the groceries from random sacks provided by disgruntled recipients (no shortage of these deadbeats), displaying for their viewers weirdly juxtaposed food items: a can of tomato juice, a box of pancake mix, a head of lettuce. A jar of peanut butter, a sack of flour, a box of rice. Crackers, celery, and powdered milk.

"Hard to imagine serving a dinner made from these items to your family."

He'd spoken long distance to his brother Walt.

"You know what they say, Hank," Walt said in his light lazy drawl.

"Hmm?"

"Build a man a fire, and he's warm for one night." Walt paused, and Hank anticipated a punch line, picturing Walt's smile.

"Yeah?"

"Set a man on fire, and he's warm for the rest of his life."

Lydia had liked that one. It put her in mind of Reagan's comment, delivered at a Washington luncheon. "It's just too bad," the governor had said, "we can't have an epidemic of botulism."

He wanted the Aquafilters, to be sure, but it was a joy and a satisfaction to enter the Smoke Shop (Lydia's bark of a laugh), Isidore at the ancient register in his ridiculous toupee. Long, narrow store, much of the floor space occupied by unsold newspapers, tied and bundled for return. Buzzy fluorescents. Behind the counter hundreds of brands of cigarettes were ranked along the wall, and in display cases there were pipe tobacco blends, cigars, cigar cases, cigar cutters, humidors, tobacco pouches, lighters, cigarette cases, pipes of briar and meerschaum, cigarette holders of ebony, of bone, of tortoiseshell, crystal and alabaster ashtrays, and a small hand-lettered sign:

OWING TO THE POTENTIAL FOR
MISUSE WE NO LONGER CARRY
ROLLING MACHINES OR CIGARETTE
PAPERS. THE MANAGEMENT REGRETS
ANY INCONVENIENCE.

"Get a load of this bullshit," said Isidore. Hank turned to face him.

"Seriously," said Isidore, who appeared to be reading a trade magazine of some sort. "Have a look." He passed the magazine over the register. Of course he'd have a look. He was taking his own advice and filling his days. The Aquafilters, the spiced ham, the stamps, the whatever else was written on that validating piece of paper in his pocket: They could wait another minute.

What Isidore wanted him to look at was a display ad, for "SPIRIT OF '76" cigarettes. The pack depicted Archibald Willard's three familiar figures, silhouetted against a red, white, and blue background. Twenty Class "A" Cigarettes. Limited-time availability; participating retailers would receive special countertop displays. He passed the magazine back. This was not something for which he had a witty aperçu at the ready. For some reason this had struck Isidore as being a cut above, even shabbier than, the usual level of gross vulgarity. Or perhaps he thought Hank was class, would respond. Or maybe he was just an old man who ran a smoke shop and thought the Bicentennial, still two years away, was bullshit. Hank was leaning in that direction himself. Bicentennial this and Bicentennial that. Flags and banners all over. All it took was an anniversary to make everybody forget a decade's worth of troubles. Would that an ailing marriage could be cured that easily.

He felt suddenly woozy and sat inelegantly on one of the stacks of newspapers.

"You OK?"

"I just need some Aquafilters."

Isidore reached behind him and picked a package off a hook.

"Gotta watch that sun," he said. "I like to stay inside the store. Nice and cool."

"Can't stay inside forever."

"You could try."

"Believe me," said Hank, rising and digging in his pocket for money.

"Buy a Coke," said Isidore.

"Oh, I don't need a Coke," said Hank, "but I do need a magazine." He moved over to the rack and selected the one Helene wanted.

"*Seventeen*," said Isidore, beginning to depress the keys on the old register. "For your daughter?"

"Yes."

"Huh," said Isidore.

. . .

Sunwashed walls. Dead time of midday, cars here and there poked askew into the diagonal spots, waves of heat rising from their hoods and ruffling the still air. Hank stood under the shelter of an awning and in the mirror-bright window he saw an old man holding a paper bag. He knew if he lifted his left arm, the old man would lift his right, like something out of the Marx Brothers. Freedonia, Symbionia, one was a comic reflection of the other. If only his daughter had been abducted by Harpo and Chico, to be brought to Groucho's lecherous burrow. He began to laugh when, casting about for the proper counterpart for the superfluous Zeppo, he settled instinctively upon Stump.

M RS. MOCK CARRIED, WITH a little difficulty, the flat of zinnias to the patio area behind the owner's unit. There was a sliding glass door that she could push open with her foot, but she had forgotten first to open the screen, and after standing there indecisively for a few moments, staring out into the unsparing sunlight and allowing the centrally conditioned air of the owner's unit to escape into the desert, she set the flat down on the glass dinette table to open the screen and then returned for it, to carry it without further incident onto the patio area where her small garden plot was located. There. In the hot, dry air she felt her skin clench up immediately and classified the feeling as bracing. She could hear the sound of water slapping concrete and knew that Mr. Mock was indulging in one of his peculiarly meaningless morning rituals, the hosing down of the deck surrounding the heated swimming pool. As eggs fried, coffee brewed, and morning papers unfurled across the Las Vegas region, at least for those who lived and worked here and maintained normal schedules, as Mrs. Mock chivied her lovely, soft-spoken, unutterably stupid housekeeping staff into action, Mr. Mock could be found tightening lightbulbs in the breezeway, or testing the ballpoint pens at the front desk in the office, or hosing down the deck surrounding the heated swimming pool, whose otherwise still waters gurgled occasionally as they incorporated hose water runoff. Mrs. Mock affixed pads to her knees and donned work gloves, preparing to transplant the zinnias to her mostly luckless garden plot. The zinnias were in fact replacing an earlier, failed attempt at cultivating some rather temperamental ageratum. As she fitted the last surprisingly flexible and pain-free finger into a glove, the Trimline phone rang in the living room. The sound of the hose ceased immediately.

She heard, "Telephone!"

At least she wasn't on her knees yet.

She'd chosen a tropical theme for the designer living room, uncomfortable with the locally dominant southwestern look. She pretended to herself that she had been motivated by boredom with the latter style's austerity, but it was actually fear of its sterility, an eroded look that seemed an unpersuasive attempt to prepare her for her death. Anyway, she liked things that grew, not things that blew away or were bleached and scoured down to nothing in swirling storms of sand.

She thought of *Beau Geste*; what a fine picture that was.

So a living room in cool blues and greens, with rattan and cane furniture covered with floral patterned fabrics, and plenty of plants, and a big aquarium that had been full of tropical fish, until they died. The room sat cool and still behind the walls of glass that divided it from the desert, like the diorama of a remote ecology. It had been her idea, her decision, 100 percent. Mr. Mock didn't care. He walked about the room, sat down in its chairs, drank bourbon highballs and watched television and read his newspaper in it. He himself looked somewhat out of place, dressed in the blown-out clothing of a backpacker on an extended journey. The heavy, dark garments that had constituted his East Coast wardrobe lined the walk-in closet, useless. If he insisted on going around like a vagrant or a hobo in cut-off chinos and a frayed old dress shirt with the tail hanging out, that was none of her concern.

She had a picture in her mind of Mr. Dick Taranutz, who lived across the highway with his adorable if somewhat strident second wife Minnie and who wore crisp khakis and a fresh polo shirt even when washing his Cadillac. He'd stop the hose to wave across the lanes of traffic when he saw her. When he dressed to take Minnie out to dinner, he looked like something that stepped from the pages of a storybook. *That* was what she meant by active maturity.

She passed the color console on which sat framed portraits of Guy and Ernest. She sensed that this was one of her boys calling. Which troublemaker would it be? She was a pleasant, handsome woman in her mid-sixties who sometimes caught herself trying on the word *widow* as a term of self-description. She enjoyed dancing and dining out. A night at the pictures was always appreciated. She kept herself as busy as she could under the circumstances, but she couldn't help feeling sometimes as if there were a millstone tied around her neck. There were evenings when she would look across the Key lime tiles that divided the all-electric kitchen from the designer living room and see the ill-clad figure sitting in the shifting light of the television, hear the faint clink of ice cubes, and grow full with despair.

"Ma."

"Why, Guy. What a nice surprise to hear from you."

"I know it's been a while."

"Oh, don't you worry. We're out so much I often wonder if we don't miss more calls than we receive."

"All right."

"I was even thinking that maybe we should get ourselves an answering machine."

"That might be good, yeah. We have one at the institute."

"Oh, your institute. And how is that going?" She wanted to sound interested because Guy was very protective of his peculiar interests, bullying and evangelical. She did not like being bullied by Guy.

"It's going fine, Ma."

"I'm so glad. I think it's good that you have that, to occupy you between jobs."

There was a slight pause. "The institute's enough of a job, as it is."

"Oh, I'm sure it keeps you very busy."

"It does. You'd be surprised."

"Not at all. I do wonder, though." She trailed off.

"Yes?"

"Have you given some thought to a more conventional job?"

"Conventional jobs seem to take a dislike to me, Ma. It's not like I haven't tried."

"Oh, well. You may be right. I certainly don't want to argue with you."

"Right now I'm really just trying to concentrate on the institute."

"Hmm. Well, honestly, I just don't see how a bunch of ex-athletes sitting around hammering away at a typewriter are going to convince anyone of anything."

"It's not you we're trying to convince, Ma."

"Well, if not me, then who? I certainly count myself among those who believe football players should spend their time outdoors knocking one another down, not cramped in a closet with their big hands all over a little Italian typewriter. I say let the football players play football. Nobody forces them to do it. And it's been shown to build character."

Her son's controlled annoyance was tangible across the miles separating them. She had a picture in her mind of Guy holding the receiver away from his head and staring at it scornfully. It grieved her that he scorned her opinions. She decided she would continue to put her best foot forward with her younger son.

"Guy?" she said. Her voice sounded sharper than she'd intended.

"Yeah, Ma."

"Are you there?"

"*Yes*, Ma."

"So how is your lovely friend?" Mrs. Mock couldn't bring herself, for some reason, to call a grown woman Randi.

"Randi's fine. She's laying out a garden."

"It's a little late for annuals, wouldn't you say?" Mrs. Mock felt a twinge of guilt, given her own procrastination in the garden this year. But she *had* sent some perfectly wonderful heirloom seeds to Guy's lady friend when she'd heard that the two of them were returning to California and it grieved her that the woman was going to plant them for naught.

"She's actually not planting the flowers, Ma. She's trying for tomatoes."

"*Tomatoes!*" Mrs. Mock didn't quite know how to respond to that. The two fell silent, and the line was filled with the ghostly whistling sounds of all the blasted land that lay vacantly between them.

"Mom, listen."

"Yes, dear."

"I need you and Dad to do me a favor."

"What kind of favor, dear?"

"I need to borrow your car for a few days."

"I don't think your father is going to want to part with his car for a few days."

She certainly didn't. Mr. Mock was a man who disliked the slightest deviation from his routine. Just getting him to agree to a new brand of hand soap was an ordeal.

"He wouldn't have to. I was hoping that the two of you would come with me."

She laughed.

"Do you know how long it's been since I've gotten your father to go anyplace?"

"Well, see, it's a good idea then."

"Who will run the motel?"

"Dad told me the thing practically runs itself."

"What your father means is that I run it, dear."

"Can't you get someone to take care of it for you?"

He could be so insistent. They both—in fact, they *all* could be. Each concession wearing her down a little further. Look up *nub* in the dictionary, and there she was. *Where are we going? For how long? What was wrong with* his *car?* She would ask, but she had the distinct feeling that she wouldn't receive satisfactory answers to these questions.

"Where would we be going?"

"East."

"Nearly everything is east of here, dear."

"We need to drive to our place in New York."

"You and your young lady."

"Randi. *Randi.* But no. Not with her."

"I'm afraid I don't understand at all. What happened to *your* car? Why can't *you* take *your own* car to New York?"

"I really can't discuss it over the telephone."

"Then, dear, you shouldn't have *called* to *discuss* it."

"If you could just say yes, it would be so much easier for me to fill you in later on."

"And how on earth could I possibly say yes for your father?"

"Believe me, it'd be great for him. He'd love it. You'd *both* love it."

"Love what?"

"I can't discuss it."

Then the door opened, and Mr. Mock entered the owner's unit, his beaten Hathaway shirtfront soaked with water and clinging to him. When he peered over at her, Mrs. Mock instantly felt as if she'd been discovered doing something that she shouldn't. She was having a frustrating and, she hated to admit it but, unwanted conversation with her son and being made to feel as if it were the wrong thing to be doing and she was simply tired of being beset by bullies. She handed the phone off to Mr. Mock.

"Here," she said, "it's for you."

From the designer living room she watched as he studied the phone for a moment before lifting it to his ear. See the Designer Color, to match any household decor? (The Moss Green tone matched the refrigerator and dishwasher, but all three were, in Mrs. Mock's mind, unsatisfactory compromises.) See how the dial is Built Into the receiver, so that you can make calls more easily? See the lighted dial, allowing you to place a call in Total Darkness if the mood strikes you? See the long Tangle-Resistant Cord, so that you can effortlessly go about your business while enjoying a conversation? See the Contoured Design that rests easily in the hand and against the planes of the face? The Trimline. Mr. Mock finally laid the device against his skull.

"Dad."

"Guy."

"Dad, remember telling us about the war when we were kids?"

"I remember telling you. Ernest wasn't listening to me much anymore by then."

"He was older."

"The firstborn."

"It must have been rough on him."

"Those were the best years of our lives we spent over there."

"So I've heard."

"What about the war?"

"Remember telling me how sometimes you just had to do something someone asked of you, do it without question?"

"Or else you'd end up in the brig."

"But there was a reason, a principle behind the idea."

"I guess. Mostly you just didn't want to end up in the brig. All the nuts were in there."

"Dad, I need to ask you to do something for me, and I need you not to ask any questions. It's a matter of life and death."

"What did your mother say?"

"We can't expect Mom to understand matters of life and death."

"Why not? She's a mature woman."

"She's a wonderful mother. Ernest and I agree. I've no doubt she's been a loyal and resourceful wife. Sterling reports from the PTA and such. A model citizen. But life and death?"

"Guy, your mother's a senior citizen."

"Well, I don't blame Mom. But she wasn't real receptive."

"I'm glad you don't blame her. What'd you ask her to do? What are you asking me to do?"

"I need you to take a trip with us."

"Well, I don't know that I can take a trip. I'd really have to check."

"You know what you're doing. You're running around changing the bed sheets in that motel. Get that guy across the street to look after it for you. Taranutz."

"Ha. I am not the one convinced of the infallibility of Dick Taranutz."

"Still. I would suggest this trip. Whatever your final decision is, and I will respect that decision, I ask that you consider the benefits of a little change of pace, plus also these life and death aspects I mentioned. Not to put pressure, but because it really is a matter of life and death."

"Whose?"

"Pardon?"

"Whose life and whose death?"

"Well that, that I don't really feel comfortable discussing over the phone. Which I hope you understand. But I can tell you that Randi and I need your help driving a very important person from here, the Bay Area, to the East Coast."

"Randi's coming?" Mr. Mock's face lit up. He liked Randi. In the designer living room, at the sound of the inappropriately mannish, she thought, name, Mrs. Mock wrinkled her nose.

G‍UY IS A DERVISH today. The phone, the car, the knocking on doors, the typewriter, the tape recorder: All this industry should have him flat on his back moaning for ice and Darvon and a deep-tissue massage of the variety that tends, in his experience, to lead to intercourse and the sort of acute, spirit-wringing orgasm he would feel compelled to note in a journal, if only he kept a journal. Instead, manic, he smokes a joint, feeling the air around him in the kitchen.

It presses in on him, weighty. Vibes in here. There'd been an argument, of course. Here I am just getting it together here and you want me to head back to New York indefinitely? And so on. Randi is usually pretty pliant but he senses that in this case he's run up against the limits of her patience.

It still isn't exactly a question of will-she-or-won't-she, but he'll have to find a way to "make it up to" her. As he's promised so many times.

In the meantime, though, he is on this energy jag that he finds just exhilarating. Just to have been able to put an end to the "discussion" with Randi—she remained unsatisfied, he could tell, as he backed out of the room, hands raised in the air as if she were an armed bandit—just to have managed that was a minor accomplishment of a kind.

Oh, the methodically thrown plates that had zipped across the room the day that shouted name, Erica Dyson, had hovered, charging the air between them, becoming taboo evermore. Shards of china progressively filled the checkerboard spaces of the kitchen linoleum, skidding across them, coming to rest in the corners. When finally one had ricocheted, breaking the rhythm, to strike him just above the left eye, there had been instead of pain the feeling of awakening from a dream.

In and out, in and out, all day long. Armful of maps from AAA. Granola and some twiggy stuff for trail mix. Wigs from Wig City over in Oak Town.

The telephone's on his desk in the spare room. His squat little buddy, the phone. Calls like potato chips, just one and you're committed to a spate of them, helpless. Guy likes the phone. Invasive, irresistible, anonymous, it amplifies his core personality in all sorts of interesting ways. As a teenager he'd pick out girls he liked from his high school class and telephone their homes, basically tripping on the fact that he was making a disruptive noise *right where they lived*, causing all the wholesome activities there to stop, their dads rumbling up out of their easy chairs, grunting with the effort, to pick up the phone as their pretty blossoming daughters waited to see what news or worshiper's adoration the call might yield. Guy would hang up. He wasn't a heavy breather. It had nothing to do with sex at all. Sex was another thing; the fine art of masturbation he had honed to perfection was another story. Offered up lessons in technique in the school cafeteria before a captive audience of late bloomers and textbook cases of latency, pimpled pusses registering both faint disgust and budding interest. But the calls had been about sheer manipulation.

The plan has come to him in bits and pieces. His friend Gary Kearse will be arriving soon to take Yolanda first. Guy doesn't describe it this way, but it will be a dry run to see how things go before Tania goes across. When that happens he personally intends to escort her, posing as her husband; along with his real parents, posing as his fake parents (an interesting concept). Why not just send her with his parents? He can't fully justify his desire to accompany her. Definitely the sheer star appeal of Tania is a factor. Also the fact that conceivably he can swing the credit for recovering her if she takes it into her head to walk into a state police barracks somewhere and turn herself in. Also he figures that once he's in New York maybe he can reach for a few strings, sit down with his connections at some of the hipper publishing houses to discuss the Book Project. Also there's the sense that he's serving something bigger and more important than himself, though to be honest he is not exactly persuaded of the merit of the SLA's politics. That doesn't particularly matter to him, though. Fame, money, and high principles definitely figured into the scheme in that precise order. Also sex, in there somewhere. Sprinkled over everything else, say. He admits (to himself) that he has toyed with the idea of seducing Tania on the road, a visualization of himself as Humbert Humbert. There is a strange reckless something about the girl that tells him she's game for just about anything and that this sort of willing enthusiasm is still exhilaratingly fresh for her. Anyway, it'll be him, Tania, and his parents, the very image of propriety barreling down the highway in a two-ton boat. Dad of course will be let down when Randi doesn't turn up for the trip (if all goes according to plan, after Randi's done boiling over and Guy has a chance to sit down with her and discuss details, she will be leaving in the Bug ahead of time to open the apartment and find a suitably remote hideaway for the summer), but Guy hopes that Tania will prove a sufficient surrogate. So to speak.

Teko, Guy's decided, is going to have to stay here in the Bay Area and wait for Guy to return for him, a little payback for the gun-to-the-head incident that otherwise he's completely forgotten about.

Now Guy is in a chair, listening to KPFA. Susan has called to say that through friends (friends or "friends"?, Guy wondered. The occulted language sometimes got confusing), she arranged for the delivery of a tape to KPFK, KPFA's sister station in L.A. The tape contains a lengthy eulogy to the SLA dead recorded by the three survivors. KPFK broadcast the tape immediately after having been tipped off to its presence under a bunch of crap in an alley behind the station.

Guy loves the cloak-and-dagger stuff.

Commercial radio is already broadcasting parts of the tape, but left-leaning Pacifica stations like KPFA and KPFK will air the thing in its entirety.

Guy is aware that Susan is still trying to sell him on the SLA. He admits to himself that despite all his activity and plans, the way that he responds to the tape is going to make a difference, if only in terms of his personal feelings. Things will continue to happen anyway, since he's already set them in motion, a certain precipitousness for which he is renowned. Repent at leisure, ha-ha. Anyway, he wants to believe, at least, that Tania means what she says. Why will a scripted tape convince him? He doesn't know. In a way, it's pretty pathetic. He managed to sit and look into the girl's eyes, and he had his doubts, but a radio broadcast will tip the balance in one direction or another.

He leans back in his chair. It's a thrift shop find, a high-backed dark Naugahyde executive swivel chair that looks as if it would be at home in the corner office of a Hayward law firm. The announcer comes on and does some horsing around. KPFA can get a little smart-alecky, Guy thinks. It often sounds to him like a group of students who have taken over the high school PA. But that's the Movement for you. Willie Wolfe had probably segued directly from toilet-papering houses on Halloween to pointing guns at savings bank depositors, and Angela Atwood, Pat Soltysik, and Nancy Ling Perry must have been more familiar with their driver's ed manual than with the *Minimanual of the Urban Guerrilla*. Is he being glib? Yes, he is being glib.

Then Teko begins. "To those who would bear the hopes and future of our people, let the voice of their guns express the words of freedom." Guy hates to admit it, but he is growing drowsy as General

Field Marshal Teko rails on, sending greetings to obscure or fictitious groups, to "the Anti-Aircraft Forces of the SLA," to fellow travelers wherever (and whenever) they may find themselves, asserting, curiously, that the SLA fled San Francisco because it is "surrounded by water," complaining about having been accused of stealing a "forty-nine cents pair of socks" at Mel's Sporting Goods. "The People found this very difficult to believe when it was pointed out that we had already purchased over thirty dollars' worth of heavy wool socks and other items." Listening to Teko argue these points to death, Guy anticipates the long cross-country drive in his company with dismay.

Guy sits up straight, wide awake, when Teko makes the cogent point, the only point requiring relevance, really, that in their annihilating overreaction to the SLA, the "authorities" (a concept that seems to manage better in the abstract) had bared a fundamental contempt for the "People" (ditto). But Guy slumps again when Teko phases into the cant of affected mistrust, to rant about "white, sickeningly liberal, paranoid conspiracy freaks and spaced-out counterculture dope fiends," zooming in on the prospect of his own paranoia as he disavows wacky rumors about Cinque's "having been programmed and electrodes implanted in his brain" (this, Guy knows, is in reaction to the published opinion of local conspiracy oracle Mae Brussell, who is never happier than when she can declare that someone has been brainwashed), followed by Teko's familiar gleeful repudiation of the idea of white cunts "enslaved by gigantic black penises." (Guy idly wonders how big Teko's dick is.) Teko finishes up on a triumphally bum note with a little name-dropping. "As our dear comrade Ho Chi Minh once wrote from an imperialist prison, 'Today the locust fights the elephant, but tomorrow the elephant will be disemboweled.'"

By contrast, Yolanda's segment is short and sweet. There is the usual agitprop stuff, as she talks about "fifty or one hundred or five hundred irate niggers"—leaving her mouth, the word sounds as stiff and uncomfortable as a new and ill-fitting garment—"firing from their houses, alleyways, treetops and walls, with a straight and fearless shot, to bring down the helicopter, the SWAT squad, the LAPD, the FBI." As with Teko, though, even her rhetorical incapacity fails to diminish what Guy sees as the pointed truth in this haystack of mumbo jumbo. "There's been a lot of talk about wasted lives, refer-ring to the six dead bodies of our comrades and to Tania, Teko, and myself. There are no editorials written for the wasted lives of our brothers and sisters gunned down in the streets and prisons."

So far the eulogy's been short on tribute and long on exhortation. A belief system, not a group of dead comrades, is being memorial-ized. But now the moment Guy has been waiting for.

Hers is a small voice, precise though somewhat enervated, a voice that has been so carefully cultivated to enclose a sense of prerogative that even now, more than four months after having been excised from an orderly life, it still conveys her unreserved faith that her ex-pectations will in the end be met. But shortly Guy can hear in the voice the sort of anguish that wracks and diminishes the speaker. Just as he is flashing *She loved one of them*, Tania says, "Cujo was the gentlest, most beautiful man I've ever known."

How could he not have known? Susan had mentioned something about being sad about Willie, but at that point Guy still needed a scorecard to keep track of the names of the players. He supposes that he figured that the black guy was the one named Willie, don't ask why. Guy considers this a serious lapse on his part. The voice has the quality of an open sore. While her elegy draws upon the same jargon used by Teko and Yolanda, Tania circles again and again to Cujo. The things lovers tend to do.

Guy suddenly remembers a longish letter he wrote to his big brother, Ernest, making plain his love for a young woman whose name he claims, falsely, he can't even remember now. What was he, eighteen? It was a letter he'd wanted to write because he felt that the force of his love demanded not merely its revelation at every oppor-tunity but an accompanying detailed validation as well. He had la-bored—a letter filled to the margins with encomia and which went so far as to attribute to this girl opinions she had never held and sagacious quotations she had never uttered. *That* girl was *alive*, though. He had been writing of someone who eventually just walked out of his life, leaving him spangled in the sun of a morning long dead, chopped to half of what he'd been.

Come and get these memories, Guy snickers.

All wrapped up in Teko's world-in-flames rhetoric, Tania's naked mourning somehow seems even more poignant than it might have otherwise, as if she were struggling to express herself through tone of voice, through emphasis and cadence, alone. Now slow. Now monotone. Now barely audible. Cujo, Cujo, Cujo. It's very difficult to listen to this oration and not be convinced that Tania means what she's saying. Even if the cause was something she embraced half-heartedly, the love of Cujo justified any level of involvement. Cujo's own involvement was total, ultimately a self-disappearing act. Guy wonders: Did Cujo imagine his death? But of course: all SLA rhetoric is steeped in the language of suicidal devotion to the ideals and goals of the SLA. Those ideals and goals are less precisely stated than the penalties for having trespassed against them. The goal is to defeat the pig, to kill the fascist insect. Guy sits listening to the tape broadcast over foundation-supported noncommercial radio, turning over in his mind the ways he can apply it to the authorized story he'll try to peddle to Macmillan or Viking or Doubleday, and he knows that Teko, and certainly Yolanda, are aware that the fascist insect will never die, but that they already have attained something even better: They're handling the biggest star in America. FROM HEIRESS TO TERRORIST. It almost rhymes.

The way she keeps coming back to the subject that haunts her. It just wipes him out.

Cujo was the gentlest.

Cujo taught the truth.

I loved Cujo.

Cujo was beautiful.

Cujo's name meant something beautiful.

Cujo's *life* meant something beautiful.

I never loved anyone like I loved Cujo.

Cujo never loved anyone like he loved me.

When they took Cujo from me, they ripped me off.

Cujo and I were always talking of important things.

I hate my parents, and love Cujo, by the way.

Cujo gave me something to share—and I keep it.

Her boilerplate devotions to the other members of the dead army sound earnest enough, as if she were trying to shut them inside a group of little boxes that have been neatly hammered together by Teko and Yolanda. When she talks about Cujo, Guy gets the feeling that she is trying to praise him back to life. Guy thinks, Love without a soul to receive it is like a ghost. It's an odd thought for him, but there is such a haunting, searching quality to her voice. It is the inconsolable living who haunt the memory of the dead. Though that first blush, the idyllic inseparability, has long ago faded from his affair with Randi, Guy still tries to imagine what it would be like to know that she had died, to watch it from a distance as smoke signals hoisting the whole weight of their lives together into the air. The desolation.

Suddenly Guy is eighteen and on that dappled plaza, watching a girl walk into the morning fresh.

ONE LAST THING:

Canary pads. A child's delight. Her father brought them home for her and her sisters in his briefcase, along with ballpoint pens, paper clips, typewriter erasers, reams of twenty-pound bond. The agreeable fact that they came from Daddy's office, not from a store. Though that would have been all right too. Tania feels that if history has tossed her and this yellow pad together in this place at this moment, it is her own history. It's an oddly comfy feeling, if false, the one this urban guerrilla has in the rear kitchen, piebald with sun and shadow, of the apartment on Euclid Avenue.

She works diligently, in shifting natural light. Though the others are waiting, she loses track of the time it takes. It seems a long time since she's worked on a composition. From the other room comes Teko's murmuring voice. There is an oddly familiar quality to the murmuring. Tania realizes, with only the mildest surprise, that Teko is imitating the tone and cadence of Cinque's voice. He is recording his part of their collective eulogy to their fallen comrades, her own contribution to which she is now composing. She hears Yolanda loudly and contemptuously correct his pronunciation of W.E.B. DuBois's surname. "Shit!" says Teko.

She bends to the work, her hand pleasantly cramped. Occasionally she massages it in the softening light. She reflects that sometimes dusk can seem later and more urgent than any part of the night, courting as each day does the petty grief over its own loss on the blushed horizon. It is too late. Tania feels that the last fading plumes of her trust in the world evaporated in the sky above Los Angeles, along with her old measure of herself. The true self is here at this table, transformed and annealed, and she takes care to make plain that her tribute is intended not merely to lay the dead to rest but as an annunciation.

"Greetings to the People. This is Tania. Now that the fascists have assassinated our six brothers and sisters the pig media waddles up to the trough to feast upon their brutalized remains. The lies and falsehoods they are spreading about our comrades are beyond even what we had thought them capable of. Cujo was the gentlest, most beautiful man I've ever known. In the short amount of time we had together he sought only to teach me the truth that had been kept from me throughout my life among the pigs. In the end he gave his own life for the People willingly and without hesitation. Some pig probably got a medal for shooting him down, but beware, pig: the name Cujo means 'unconquerable.' You may have destroyed his body but his spirit lives in the hearts and minds of the People. I never loved another individual the way I loved Cujo. I don't mean the bourgeois love that seeks houses and fancy cars. I mean a mutual love based on the struggle for the People. They can't take that from me. When the pigs stole Cujo from me I understood at last how it felt for thousands of beautiful sisters and brothers in Amerikkka when they were ripped off by the pigs of their loved ones. We mourn together! Let our guns sing our grief!

"Gelina said it all with her beautiful words but she was burning inside with a fire to destroy the fascist insect. She came a long way to become the guerrilla warrior who died fighting the pigs. She taught me how to forget the past, to wash the blood off my hands, and make a fresh start as a revolutionary. How we laughed together, cried together, loved together, hated together. She loved the People as much as any of us.

"Gabi embraced all, she will be remembered as one of the true mothers of the Revolution. She was patient and gentle—but also a merciless killer whose shotgun barked pure death from its maw. She was murdered trying to wring justice from the fascists using the only method pigs can understand.

"Zoya died on her birthday. It is the sort of death that gives a fierce and passionate life like hers meaning. She was pure death, icy and meticulous, unflinchingly delivering vengeance upon those who would deny the People their freedom. She taught me how to kill—now she's taught me how to die.

"Fahizah understood the importance of her own righteous example. She understood the timidity of the middle-class, cringing, hamburger-eating pig and how that fear could paralyze. Her solution was to refuse to hesitate: shoot to kill, and ask questions later. She loved the People, and freedom, and she always will be loved.

"Cinque saw the future as a beacon up ahead and he steered us there tirelessly, his strong Black hand upon the tiller of freedom. He gave us the gift of himself, when he could have been with his beautiful sisters and brothers. He taught everyone that Black people and whites could be comrades, that the fight for freedom is color-blind. He was hard on us, a strict teacher and a stern leader, but he always let us see that it was his love for the People that drove him. He always told us that it wasn't how long you live that matters: it's how you live. When he was assassinated by the cowardly pigs he proved that in dying for the People's freedom his life had the highest meaning imaginable. On February 4, Cinque Mtume saved my life.

"The SLA goes on under the leadership of General Field Marshal Teko. As a fully functioning cell of the Malcolm X Combat unit of the SLA we are prepared to function autonomously. The pigs articulate no more than their own fear and alarm when they report that we are leaderless and broken.

"In the end, a small fire team of committed urban guerrillas faced down an army of cowering pigs, who could find only one way to defeat them: by setting fire to them with incendiary grenades. Perhaps in underestimating the commitment and bravery of the fallen SLA soldiers they had only their own cowardice to guide them. Now they call them suicidal: what a joke. Only the corrupt fascist insect would mistake courage for suicide. There was no surrender then, nor will there be now. Be forewarned, pig!

"Gabi's father understands and it gives us solace. To hear him speak so plainly and understandingly of our purpose even through his personal grief, you can see where she got her courage and strength. Likewise General Teko's mother. Cujo's father. What a difference between them all and the pig Galtons! One day, just before . . . uh . . . Cujo was talking to me about how my parents fucked me over. I was jealous, but happy for him, when he told me that his parents were still his parents because they'd never betray him or try to make him into who he wasn't. He said that my parents were really Malcolm X and Assata Shakur: my true parents will never betray me either.

"The pigs probably have the little Olmec monkey that Cujo wore around his neck. He gave me the little stone face one night.

"So, pigs. You've killed another brave Black leader. But in tearing that one hair out of your pig head another thousand will bloom in its place! Cinque lives! The People will unite and when they do the pigs will never be able to burn them out the way they could a handful of revolutionaries.

"I died in that fire on Fifty-fourth Street, but out of the ashes, I was reborn. Our comrades did not die in vain. They did not die in vain. I turned my back on the pig I was when Cin and Cujo gave me the name Tania. I have no death wish, but I do not fear death either. I would rather die than spend my life surrounded by pigs like the uber-Pig Galtons.

"Patria o muerte, venceremos! Death to the fascist insect that preys upon the life of the People!"

INTERLUDE 2

Lionel Congreaves Explains
the Current Situation

"**H**ELLO, THIS IS Lionel Congreaves speaking. I am not dead yet, but I still remain high on the SLA hit list. If the caller is a terrorist, please include your affiliation, so the credit for my demise can be properly awarded."

This recorded message greeted all callers to the home telephone of Lionel Congreaves, a man of carefully cultivated negritude, an East Bay resident of several years' duration, the erstwhile outside coordinator of the Afro-American Cultural Exchange at Vacaville Prison, and a more vilified and calumniated individual than you could ever hope to find.

As a matter of strictly personal interest, Lionel Congreaves maintained a collection of rumors, coincidences, and other allegations, baseless or otherwise, concerning the Symbionese Liberation Army and those murky areas in which its activities and his own gave the appearance of intersection.

And what was it that would constitute an allegation that had some basis? An excellent and thought-provoking question, indeed.

Now, Lionel Congreaves was prepared to admit to some embellishment of his personal résumé. Everyone fudged a little, here and there, and he was no exception to this general rule, which went straight to the heart of human nature (a consistently interesting area). But in his own case, he found that the problem was not with the actual claims he had made but with the implications that sprang, unbidden, from them. He meant, you put a bunch of guys in a cage and their imaginations ran wild. Because it was from prison, you see, that the "snitch jacket," so called, for which he had so carefully been fitted, was coming. All of the porcine, so to speak, activities that had been attributed to him derived from the febrile brains of a bunch of jailbirds he'd only been trying his best to help. So much for gratitude.

All right, he had made different claims to different people at different times. But the bare facts were the same, immutable: He spoke several languages, including French, Italian, Japanese, Korean, and Spanish. He had served seven years in two different branches of the armed forces and later had spent time in Indochina, in Vietnam and Cambodia, working for an American construction firm. And then he had obtained a post as a language instructor at UCB and become the outside coordinator of the Afro-American Cultural Exchange, a prisoners' group formed to provide education and foster self-esteem. A little change of pace, for Lionel Congreaves. He had been attracted to the groves of academe, to the steep green hills rising above the bay, and he'd wanted to give something back to the community. Nothing strange about that at all.

Here was a baker's dozen, some of the rumors that Lionel Congreaves took a certain bleak pleasure in cataloging:

Rumor No. 1 was that his employer while in Indochina, West Coast Construction and Engineering, Inc. of Los Angeles, was in fact a subsidiary of the Pacific Corporation, an alleged CIA front head-quartered in Delaware—a "stone's throw," as the news media would have it, from Langley. A very long toss, Lionel Congreaves had of-tentimes remarked.

Rumor No. 2 was that West Coast Construction and Engineering, Inc. had provided "tactical support" to the Phoenix Program, the CIA's scheme to eliminate Vietcong sympathizers in South Vietnam via infiltration by covert agents. Specifically, it was alleged that West Coast Construction and Engineering constructed state-of-the-art torture chambers, interrogation centers, and other places of detainment.

Rumor No. 3 was that the Afro-American Cultural Exchange had been a "behavioral modification program," an element of a new CIA program, CHAOS, whose purported aim was to recruit individuals "without existing dissident affiliation" to infiltrate leftist groups. In other words, a domestication of the alleged Phoenix agenda. These unaffiliated individuals would be those like, say, Donald David DeFreeze.

Rumor No. 4 was that the AACE encouraged prisoner participation by allowing itself to become known as a place where you could obtain "white snatch."

Rumor No. 5 was that Drew and Diane Shepard as well as Angela Atwood had been CIA, working with Lionel Congreaves to indoctrinate candidates within the AACE, the latter two individuals providing enticement as described in Rumor No. 4, above.

Rumor No. 6 was that Lionel Congreaves had been DeFreeze's control officer; that DeFreeze had come to the AACE when, after having enjoyed a string of surprisingly light punishments for repeated felony offenses and violations of probation (to say the least; Lionel Congreaves was in fact shocked by the leniency afforded the man in his chronic encounters with the law), he had finally run out of luck and been incarcerated at Vacaville; that DeFreeze had been highly recommended as a potential agent because of his many years' experience as an informant for the LAPD's Public Disorder Intelligence Unit.

Rumor No. 7 was that the SLA had been devised—by Lionel Congreaves, personally, himself (to the extent that it was claimed that he'd designed the seven-headed Naga figure)—to operate like a cancer within the Left.

Rumor No. 8 was that the future Tania had visited Vacaville under the auspices of the AACE, using the ID of one Mary Alice Siem, a lumber heiress, and that in the course of doing so she had become romantically involved with DeFreeze.

Rumor No. 9 was that after DeFreeze had himself been sufficiently programmed (according to some, via electrodes implanted directly in his brain—probably by none other than Lionel Congreaves, who could now look forward to listing neurosurgery among his many skills) and the central SLA cadre identified and primed, DeFreeze had been allowed to spin off a separate group from the AACE, Unisight, in which the members of the nascent SLA could finalize their plans. This accomplished, DeFreeze was shipped to Soledad, where arrangements were made for him to effect an "escape," after which he returned to the Bay Area and awaited the green light to begin SLA operations.

Rumor No. 10 was that with respect to the plans mentioned in Rumor No. 9, above, Lionel Congreaves had himself identified Marcus Foster as the SLA's first target, both because of Foster's capitulation to Black Panther and community demands vis-à-vis the whole student ID thing (*oy vey*, was Lionel Congreaves's personal opinion of that particular brouhaha), and because his murder would cost the Left dearly in terms of credibility if attributed to a putative leftist group, such as the SLA.

Rumor No. 11 was that Tania had participated in the plotting of her own abduction, in part to avoid marrying Eric Stump. Alternatively, that Tania had plotted to kidnap one of her sisters, Vivian or Helene, and been double-crossed. The victim's conspiring in her own abduction was supposedly proved by the fact that later the SLA was able to submit documents from the girl's wallet as proof of its possession of her, despite the well-reported, perhaps obsessively reported, fact that she had been removed from the house "half naked." The reasoning went, Where did the girl carry her wallet?

Rumor No. 12 was that DeFreeze in effect became Cinque Mtume, the name Lionel Congreaves was supposed to have chosen for him, and, having effectively evaded the control of his CIA handler (again, Lionel Congreaves) and set the SLA on a renegade course, was marked for termination "with extreme prejudice."

Rumor No. 13 was that because of the concatenation of all the alleged circumstances enumerated above, and spurred by a well-attended (by *The New York Times*, among others) press conference called by investigator Lake Headley just days before the L.A. "barbecue" (as it was being called) in which Headley had divulged DeFreeze's past as a police informer and his present intelligence connections, CIA operatives Teko and Yolanda had been instructed by their Los Angeles control agent, operating under the code name Prophet Jones, to remove Tania from the safe house at 833 West Eighty-fourth Street on May 16, 1974. The incident at Mel's

Sporting Goods was staged to alert the authorities to begin the termination op.

Lionel Congreaves had put that message on his answering machine to demonstrate a sense of humor. A sense of humor was sometimes the only thing you had left. Also, he thought it broke the tension. Because the fact of the matter was there were a lot of people calling up just to see if he'd been offed yet—most of them pro–Lionel Congreaves, incidentally—and he thought the message was considerate in a humorous sort of way, while also being a bit of a thumb in the eye of those who were less than well-wishers.

There were some other totally baseless reports too, plenty of them. But after having put them side by side in their endless permutations and studied them for a while, Lionel Congreaves had decided that this particular arrangement formed a nice, coherent chronology of innuendo. And he generally liked to take a break right about here to review some of the contradictory aspects of the above-mentioned insinuations, after which all the rest could be presented as the humorous miscellany of ridiculousness that it so plainly was. The fact of the matter was that he had done his best to help Don DeFreeze, as he had with all the worthless losers in the AACE, not to mention their exceedingly immature white friends on the outside, such as Willie Wolfe. What Lionel Congreaves had tried to do was develop a selection of courses in art, black history, literature, math, and political science (though basically his whole thrust was necessarily remediation). And in the spirit of free inquiry Lionel Congreaves was happy to admit Marx and Lenin into the curriculum; they were dandy as far as they went, which was pretty damn far in prison with its compulsory work rules and poor conditions and the natural solidarities that tended to form among the various constituencies thereat. But to urge a bunch of convicts to think of themselves as "soldiers" was just asking for trouble. The fact of the matter was that as soon as Chairman Mao entered the room where the AACE participants met, channeled by skinny upper-middle-class white kids like Willie Wolfe, Lionel Congreaves had scooted out double quick.

Now, Lionel Congreaves could certainly understand why, for example, a loser who had never managed to get a single thing right in his life might become transfixed by a vision of himself as a righteous soldier, a "prisoner of war" in a "fascist concentration camp," with a noble African heritage that had been hijacked from him. This was easier than admitting that he was an illiterate rapist or a pimp or the strong-arm thug for some pusher. But half these guys couldn't get through *The Cat in the Hat*, and here comes Willie Wolfe with "Political power grows out of the barrel of a gun." It was frankly humorous.

But the other big contradiction was: If Lionel Congreaves was such a key figure in the CIA, in the notoriously anti-Communist Phoenix program, why would he be teaching incarcerated felons about Karl Marx? Puffing up their self-righteousness for the next time they felt like aiming a pistol at a liquor store clerk?

Lionel Congreaves brewed a pot of tea, for himself and his visitor: orange pekoe with its excellent blend of choice Ceylon teas. A plate of English biscuits, just on the sweet side of savory. The afternoon sun was fading, slipping mellow through the big windows.

Another thing was, Lionel Congreaves wanted to be shown a *single slip of paper* that demonstrated that his years with West Coast Construction had ever been anything other than a matter of administering personnel. It was pretty humorous when you looked at it. The company had been incorporated in Delaware for tax purposes, as were many legal American enterprises. Otherwise, he knew little about its structure. Could he state with categorical certainty that it was *not* a CIA front? No, but that was precisely the point. He was a personnel administrator and stuck to his particular field of expertise. Was there a tape of him interrogating a prisoner? Was there a photograph of him standing outside one of these famous torture chambers that to hear people tell it, he practically had built himself, brick by brick? Oh, yes, and he had been in two branches of the armed forces as well, the marines for three years and the air force for four. That was supposed to prove something too. Very shady business. Right. One thing Lionel Congreaves could state with Cartesian certainty was that he didn't know the first thing about the Phoenix program. He certainly couldn't speak to allegations that it had led to the indiscriminate killing of thousands of South Vietnamese. Was there eyewitness testimony to the extent that "Lionel Congreaves worked for the CIA"? He was not *that* kind of "spook."

Speaking of which. Just some more happenstance that Lionel Congreaves had collected for his own edification and for that of those who were willing to look with their eyes, there was a novel by Sam Greenlee, *The Spook Who Sat by the Door*. The book deals with a spook, that was to say a black person, who works as a double agent, that was to say a spook, for the CIA. But he evades his control officer to recruit a multiracial, coed guerrilla army—which he characterizes using the neologism *symbiology*—the idea being to incite a race war. In the end, the brother and his group are cornered in a small tract house in South Central L.A., surrounded by overwhelming police fire power. Published when? 1968. Funny, huh? Coincidence was always *funny*. Wouldn't be coincidence if it wasn't *funny*.

You wanted to hear *funny*, now here was something so *funny* it might curl your hair. Book called *Black Abductor*. By a man named Harrison James, who nobody ever heard of. Published by Regency Press, which never before or again published another book so far as anyone knows. A PO Box address. Deals with the heiress of a famous California conservative family. She is kidnapped from the off-campus apartment she shares with her boyfriend by a multiracial band of revolutionaries. After indoctrination and many freewheeling sexual experiences with her captors, she is converted to their revolutionary cause and opts to join them. And oh, the name of the heiress is *Alice*. Year published: 1972.

But anyway. Lionel Congreaves was getting a little ahead of himself. Now, how—if the Shepards were the ones coordinating the assault on the SLA from inside—did the rumormongers get Don DeFreeze and company all the way from the house on West Eighty-fourth Street over to the house on East Fifty-fourth where they got cremated? The Shepards and the rest of the SLA were incommunicado after the machine-gunning at Mel's, so how did the Shepards "coordinate" DeFreeze all the way to a specific house in a totally different part of town? ESP? It's humorous; it's laughable in the extreme.

And DeFreeze. Supposedly he was the agent provocateur nonpareil, yet his single distinguishing qualification was that he had been a *police informer*? So a man who obviously *couldn't* keep secrets was expected to keep the lid on something like this? Assuming, for the sake of argument, the truth of the allegations regarding Lionel Congreaves's intelligence affiliations, his immanent pigginess, would he have selected or acceded to the selection of an individual whose instability was so luminously apparent?

Lionel Congreaves found the accusations concerning that poor kidnapped girl to be revolting. Personally, and only on the basis of what he'd read in the papers plus his own schoolmarmish knowledge of the inner lives of his AACE charges, he believed the girl had been snatched for real. Mary Alice Siem he remembered very well; she was what in an earlier time might have been called an "adventuress." She certainly was not the missing girl whose smiling face he'd been looking at in the papers for months. And it hardly seemed likely, at least to Lionel Congreaves, that the girl would dream up her own kidnapping to get out from under an unhappy engagement. He meant, first you wanted to try less drastic measures. A series of long and candid talks, therapy, a weekend in Sonoma, even a trial separation. He knew the drill.

Lionel Congreaves was always very happy to be asked what he thought instead of being forced to react to a bunch of Mickey Mouse charges with him at their center.

Now, and who hired Lake Headley to conduct this so-called investigation? Lionel Congreaves would surely like to know the basis for Headley's assertions that he, Lionel Congreaves, had himself worked with the LAPD's Criminal Conspiracy Section, particularly since this alleged partnership allegedly occurred during the period for which he was *already* being shellacked for allegedly building alleged CIA torture chambers in Laos, Cambodia, and Vietnam. He meant, Which was it? He wasn't prepared to offer up any confessions in either event, but it didn't quite strike him as cricket to be forced into a position where he had to play one baseless allegation off against another.

The fact of the matter was that anyone's life had a series of unknowable holes in it that, if you were resourceful and persistent and could get *The New York Times* to show up at your press conferences, you could pack with allegations and lies. See, the truly funny thing was, people were so eager to believe this stuff that they couldn't see the real consequences that stemmed from asserting the pseudoconfluence of all these pseudoevents. He meant, Where was the documentation? Everybody left a trail, the *Pentagon Papers* were a famous trail, and now the president of the United States of America couldn't erase the trail he'd made, and so how was Lionel Congreaves supposed to?

And here were the real consequences. The real consequences were, Lionel Congreaves was an educated and well-spoken black man who didn't spout the I-am-a-victim pieties of Movement theology, and the next thing you know he was putting masking tape on his windows so that the broken glass didn't fall onto the rug when the rocks started sailing. A man who looked old enough to know better just walked up to him while he was standing there outside a store and told him to "eat shit." White guy, middle-aged, with a shopping bag in his hand from Macy's. Eat shit.

And what a festival for the reporters. The reporters would set him up like the proverbial straw man: First they'd outline the so-called accounts of his overseas activities, then suggest that someone had insinuated that it was plausible that he might have possible connections in the intelligence community. None of which Lionel Congreaves was willing to deny outright because any man working at even the most innocent of jobs in a locale like that—a hotbed, as the term had it, of intrigue—was likely to make "connections" with God knew what. But they'd set him up. Then what fun they had, the reporters. Lionel Congreaves was "fat." Lionel Congreaves was "sulky." Lionel Congreaves was like a "nightclub comic." Lionel Congreaves wore "weird goggles." And Lionel Congreaves didn't have enough fingers to count the number of pieces that mentioned his knit cap. He meant, Your *cap* impeached your credibility? This was journalistic objectivity?

But Lionel Congreaves didn't have time to worry about his own personal *feelings* when it was his own personal *safety* that was most compromised by all this. Which was one reason why he was making himself abundantly available to the ladies and gentlemen of the press, and decidedly *not* because he was a "publicity hound," as some had labeled him. To set the record straight.

This was as good a time as any to bring up everybody's favorite party girl, Mae Brussell, the conspiracy queen. Lionel Congreaves rated a flattering *thirty-three* references in her seminal, so to speak, document covering the kidnapping, the SLA, and the proverbial kitchen sink. Forty-five thousand words by the I. Magnin princess, explaining it all to you.

Everyone made fun of Mae, yet for some reason they all repeated her crap as if it were gospel. "CIA agent Lionel Congreaves." Lionel Congreaves, "trained in the psychological warfare unit of the CIA." Lionel Congreaves "headed an experimental behavior modification unit, called the Afro-American Cultural Exchange." Lionel Congreaves "ran the AACE classes and decided who would be in the program." Lionel Congreaves "aroused the anger of black inmates against Foster." Mae Brussell, who thought Charles Manson was a patsy, thought that Charles Manson "might have interesting stories to tell." Thus spake Mae, cueing the heavy organ chord that should have accompanied most of her corny proclamations.

Manson. A *patsy*. So now the CIA (Lionel Congreaves's employer, remember) maintained a sinister interest in blood-drinking rituals on the beaches and in the deserts of California. To Lionel Congreaves, that kind of claim took a lot of chutzpah.

And any and all accusations concerning himself and the Marc Foster murder, in particular, gave Lionel Congreaves acid stomach. He grieved for the brother, he really did. Speaking of which. Lionel Congreaves was reminded of some more or less widespread rumors to the effect that Marc Foster and his deputy, Robert Blackburn, were CIA officers. As was, purportedly, Lionel Congreaves. Ergo what? Internecine war within the CIA?

Now, did it ever occur to anyone lofting these irresponsible propositions into the air that their sacred sources, the jailbirds of the California Medical Facility at Vacaville, were mentally disordered? That Vacaville was not merely a prison but a *loony bin*? That maybe that was the reason for the head-scratching anomaly of Donald David DeFreeze's mysterious transformation into the mighty Cinque Mtume, the Fifth Prophet? Unstable minds were notorious for their refusal to treat potent ideas strictly academically. He meant, What did they expect a man being pumped full of militant notions to do? Aspire to work in a car wash? He meant, You go with what you know. The guy was a career criminal, so he sort of tinseled it up, trimmed it with the bright baubles of revolutionary rhetoric. Didn't need any "control agent" for that. A few of the cons he'd taught were actually working their way toward college degrees, but did you ever hear about *that*? No, you heard about the CIA and blond pussy in miniskirts and electrodes in your brain and the Symbionese Liberation Army. If Lionel Congreaves had offered up a program in fry cookery and janitorial science, they would have scalded him as a Tom. But instead he'd opted, like a damned fool, for the high-minded approach, and so he'd become a "control agent," a useful label to stanch the flow of unintended consequences.

Lionel Congreaves moved heavily toward a desk piled with folders, accordion files, and loose papers. He set down his mug on a colorful ceramic tile he'd salvaged from some place or another. Actually he knew exactly where he'd salvaged it from, the leaky john in a French colonial mansion housing a brothel on the outskirts of Saigon. A little conversation piece that, for one reason or another, he didn't feel like talking about right then. Savoring the irony.

Now. Lionel Congreaves had in his hand a copy of a letter written in 1970 by Donald David DeFreeze to a Los Angeles Superior Court judge, one William Ritzi, in an attempt to preserve his probation. Lionel Congreaves was not sure what, exactly, he intended to demonstrate with the introduction of this pathetic document. A coda to this most recent long and curiously unsatisfying interview? A glimpse of what had lain within the popped kernel of the SLA, the desperation of its leader, the sheer scarcity of character, that had perhaps seen its best chance in an appropriate setting, a fantasy revolution, where only the charisma of the radical insurgent could obtain? It rambled on and on, the unformed script revealing and concealing in equal measure.

> . . . I am going to talk to you truthfully and like I am talking to
> God. I will tell you things that no one has ever before know . . . I
> had Just gotten out of a boys school in New York after doing 2½
> years for braking into a Parking Meter and for stealing a car . . . I
> was sixteen at the time and didn't have home, life in the little
> prison as we called it, was nothing but fear and hate, day in and
> day out, the hate was mading, the only safe place was your cell that
> you went to at the end of the day. I had only two frights, if you can
> call them frights. I never did win. It was funny but the frights were
> over the fact that I would not be part of any of the gangs, black or
> white. I wanted to be friends with everyone, this the other inmates

would not allow, they would try to make me fright . . . they even tried to make a homosexual out of me . . . After 2½ years I found myself hated by many of the boys there. When I got out of jail, people just could not believe I had ever been to Jail. I worked hard, I didn't drink or any pills nor did I curse . . . I had a few girld friends but as soon as there mother found out I had been to Jail, that was the end . . . Then one day I met my wife Glory, she was nice and lovely, I fell in love with her I think . . . I asked Glory to marry me and she said Yes. We had just met one month before we were married. My wife had three kids already when I met her. We were married and things were lovely all the way up to a few months. Then seven months later I came home sooner than I do most of the time for work and she and a old boy friend had just had relationships. I was very mad and very hurt . . . I really put faith in her, but somehow, little stories kept coming to me, one was that my boss had come to my home looking from me and that my wife had come to the door in the nude. I thought that if we had kids or a baby we would be closer, but as soon as the baby was born it was the same thing . . . I was trying to put up with her and hope she would change. But as the years went by she never did and she told me . . . she wanted a divorce because I was not taking care of her and the kids good enough, I was never so mad in my life . . . I through her out of the house and I got a saw and a hammer and completely destroyed everything I ever bought her and I mean everything! For months later she begged me to take her back and she said she had made a mistake and that she really loved me . . . I took her back but I couldn't face anyone any more . . . I started playing with guns and firer works and dogs and cars . . . I finely got into trouble with the Police for shoting off a rifle in my base-ment and for a bomb I had made out of about 30 firer works from forth of July. After I went to court and got Probation I was really ashamed of myself. I had not been in trouble with the police for years and now I had even lost that pride . . . All of my friends and family knew of my wife's ways and of my foolishness in believing her and forgiving her, it was just too much to face, I had to get out. I moved all over New Jersey but everywhere I went someone knew me or my wife or about my kids, I just couldn't take it anymore, I was slowly becoming a Nothing. I decided to move to California for a new start . . . I put my age up so no one would think about me having so many kids. I hoped it would be a new start for both of us, no one would know me or her or anything about my family. But more and more I was unhappy with everything. I started playing with guns, drinking, pills but this time more than I had ever before did. I was arrested again and again . . . I don't really understand what I was doing. She wanted nice things and I was working and I was buying and selling guns and the next thing I know I had become a thief. You sent me to Chino . . . They think I am nuts. I thought you would really send me to jail and Glory would go to New jersey . . . I started to tell you to send me to jail and that I didn't want to go home. But you should not have never sent me back to her. The day after I got home she told me she had had Six relations with some man she meant on the street when I was in Chino.

Sir Don't send me to prison again, I am not a crook or a thief nor am I crazy. I hope you will believe me . . .

Yours truly,
Donald DeFreeze

A portrait of the Field Marshal as a young man.

PART THREE

Revolutionary Pastoral

We had all simply wandered into a situation unthinkingly, trying to protect ourselves from what we saw as a political problem. Now, suddenly, it was like a Rorschach inkblot: others, looking at our actions, pointed out a pattern that we ourselves had not seen.

—RICHARD M. NIXON

T ANIA STANDS TRANSFIXED BEFORE the three-card monte hustler working on Broadway near the 103rd Street station. The cards are folded in the middle the long way, and he flips them with easy fluid motions of the wrists so that they dance across the top of the up-ended cardboard box he's using as a surface. His patter is meaning-less and as precisely rhythmic as the movement of the cards, "what you got you see, where you see it, here and here, what you see, where, here and there you got you see, where it at, here? or here? or where it at? come on and tell me here or here or where?" Players carelessly drop money in the hustler's direction as if they knew ahead of time they were never going to see it again. Tania's com-panion, Joan Shimada, stands with her back to the scene, taking in Broadway, until Tania is finished watching.

Whatever this city may have been it has now turned a corner to greet the spoor of world destruction that has been drifting through the air, a placeless anger, for sixty years. It's Charles Bronson's city now. All the froth of the Lindsay years has condensed and gathered in the corners like the scum of a rabid foam. To every street corner its screaming prophet. To every bench its unemployed habitué. Moving walls of thunder, colored with savage petroglyphs, beneath the sidewalks. Smoke rising, rising from the Bronx, visible from the high old terraces cut from the Harlem bluffs, from downtown, from Brooklyn, from Staten Island and the ironwork expanses of North Jersey.

The tabloids speak! The *Post* says: Boys take sledgehammers to pound through the walls of tenement buildings, tearing through the crumbling plaster and splintered lathe with their delinquent fingers to murder crippled grandmas, to snatch their meager purses, to toss babies from rooftops scarred with flashing cement. The *News* says: Girls are having sex at fourteen, at thirteen, at twelve and eleven; with their brothers, their fathers, with anyone; and for money. The

Post says: Saturday night specials are turning the streets into a bloodbath of horror. The *News* says: Rats crawled into a baby's crib in Bed-Stuy and stripped him to the bone in the time it took his mother to make herself a cup of instant. The *Post* says: Feral dogs are roaming the streets in packs, scaring away even the rats. And both agree on the subways: Hold tight to your tokens. Boys wait behind you to suck them right back up out of the slot. Then they snatch your chain off your neck. Cut your finger off for your high school ring. Take your keys and break into your apartment to rape and strangle you in the comfort of your own living room. Abandon all hope.

So they're all a little edgy here, out of their element. Tania's own knowledge of New York begins around Thirty-fourth Street and ends at Central Park South. So this bankrupt city is something of a revelation. The place is locked down, yet everyone seems to be outside, both in and of the tumult. It's like going to a sporting event where you root for yourself. Yet when she turns off Broadway, she's struck by the muffled quiet, the solid old apartment buildings, their floors rumored to be packed with dirt from the excavation of Central Park, reaching back from the corners to bracket rows of brownstones in various states of cheerless dilapidation. Men settle on the stoops, working at brown-bagged beers and flat pints of blackberry brandy, wearing the burden of their involuntary leisure lightly, scanning her with a sharply sexual interest informed more by boozy fraudulent nostalgia than by predatory intent. When she dares to look into their faces, she recognizes poverty's gray-scaled nuance, which her revolutionary reading, not to mention her life, has been scant preparation for. These are the People: starving, hysterical, naked. The cataloging of their pettiest transgressions could atomize the sensibilities of a nice girl like her. But there are always hints of the city's larger elegance just a few years, or blocks, away. She recognizes it. A girl like her can smell it.

Joan is really pretty, and self-possessed in a way that successfully combines artsy-fartsy la-di-da with poised confidence and a genuine delicacy that seems difficult to place outside the stale context of the Mysterious Orient. Tania wonders how Joan pulls it off; at this point she is conditioned to see nearly any manifestation of personality as a kind of pose. Whatever, she feels more comfortable around Joan than she has around anyone since Cujo and Gelina died.

Men drift toward them, their approach taking the form of a sort of gliding sidestep. They remind her of the pigeons at Trafalgar Square in their wary, insistent aggression. They talk and burble, muttering low and unintelligibly or projecting like the authorized sales representatives of some unspeakable act. Joan tells them all, in her peculiar accent, "Fuck off!" They droop and fade back or windmill themselves away in a flurry of arms. One man follows them for more than a block, hollering at their backs from a distance of maybe thirty feet. Tania wishes she were packing her revolver in her purse, but Guy has been pretty firm about the No Guns. "Especially in New York," he says. Which is pretty weird because from what she's heard half the city is armed and ready to kill.

Joan takes them on a roundabout route, walking north on Amsterdam a couple of extra blocks before circling, at 106th, to head back downtown on Manhattan Avenue. This maneuver is to avoid a couple of housing projects that stand between them and their destination. Tania wonders why they bothered: When they get there, the place has an appearance of such chronic destitution, with its gutted cars and scorched, boarded-up apartment buildings, that it makes the worst slums of East Oakland look inviting. In the middle of the block is a narrow storefront below a rusted sign that between two faded Pepsi-Cola crests reads STATIONERY CIGARS CANDY NEWSPAPERS. The lattice of a security gate is drawn across the plate glass window.

"Variety store," says Joan.

The two of them stand at the threshold and try the door, which is locked. Joan finds a brass bell push, which has been inexpertly installed near a flaking decal for Camel cigarettes. Tania can hear the rasping buzz deep inside the store. There is no answering buzz, just a soft click as the latch is released from somewhere within. They enter.

In the wall at the end of the narrow, dim space inside is a small window of thick Plexiglas with a slot at the bottom. To the left of the window is a steel door with three locks. The only sign of merchandise in the store is a soda cooler containing a few bottles of Tab and with a handwritten sign taped to one of its sliding glass doors, DON'T TOUCH—NO TOQUE. Joan approaches the window.

"Hi there," she says.

Tania can get only a vague impression of whatever it is that dwells behind the Plexiglas.

"Yoo-hoo," says Joan. "Customer." The voice is affectless, the perfect accompaniment to what seems to be Joan's persistent, depthless patience. Tania wants to say inscrutable. Finally there is a flurry back there, and what appears to be a face of some kind appears in the window.

"Good morning," says Joan, without evident sarcasm although it's after two in the afternoon. "Two dimes, please." She passes a twenty-dollar bill through the slot.

"Should we be holding that much?" asks Tania, anxiously.

"Give me a break," says Joan, like that's the least of their worries. Two fat alligator Baggies appear on their side of the window. "Thank you," says Joan. She puts the Baggies in her purse.

Outside she says, "That place gets on my nerve."

They walk and talk, taking the same meandering route back to Guy and Randi's apartment. Since Guy returned to the Bay Area to get Teko, it's just the girls, and it's been fun. Tania hasn't spent this much time hanging out with women since she was about sixteen, just before Eric Stump entered her life and she set up housekeeping with him like an imitation adult.

Despite the agreeable atmosphere, Tania understands that she's learning to live as a fugitive. So far it's a curiously unstructured life, with the four of them—Randi, Yolanda, Joan, and herself—awakening late and lingering over coffee, the TV blaring.

Tania personally can't get enough TV. The repeats on the local stations, punctuated by endless commercials for technical training schools, seem more in sync with the life of the great waning city outside the windows than what she sees on the news. They track the tale of being at home during the workday, which is a secret sort of life, scandalous in a pint-size way to remain at the edges while everybody else makes for the bustling center. Ricky tells Lucy he's heading to the club, and the next thing you know a frizzy-headed Puerto Rican–looking guy is turning from an oscilloscope to ask, in an accented English that both recalls and skewers Ricky Ricardo's, "How did I get this great career?" Technical Career Institute, is the answer. Offering certificate and degree programs in the rapidly expanding fields of Electronics; Computer Technology; Air Conditioning, Heating, and Refrigeration; Building Maintenance; Computerized Accounting Systems; and Office Technology. Free set of tools when you graduate. Then Lucy's back, getting Mrs. Trumbull to watch Little Ricky while she tries to work her way into the act, again. Waaaahh. That sexy single strand of pearls around her neck. They sit and talk, drag slices of toast through slicks of yolk remaining on their breakfast plates, as the credits crawl over the gray iridescent swollen heart that floats in the middle of the screen, suspended there by love supreme and the blasts of hot air rising from the rhumba beat of the theme song.

Back at the apartment, Joan lays the bags of pot on the kitchen table.

"Any trouble?" asks Yolanda.

"No trouble," says Joan.

"Pearl?" Yolanda uses Tania's new code name.

"No," says Tania.

"Are you sure no one saw you?"

"We said no."

"I just need to know, Joan. While we're waiting for Teko, I'm ranking officer."

"So next time you should go yourself."

"As the one in command it would be irresponsible of me to expose myself that way."

Joan repeats, "Expose yourself?" Tania snorts.

"Oh, very mature. But that's not even the point. The point is I don't think a debriefing is uncalled for after an operation."

Joan rolls her eyes. "Operation. We're buying some grass, for Christ sake."

"I really don't see why you have to like challenge my authority," complains Yolanda.

With a slight shift of her body, Joan shuts her out.

Yolanda says, "Pearl."

Yolanda says, "Pearl," considering the name.

"That name," says Yolanda thoughtfully, "doesn't suit you."

"Well, leave it to Teko to pick out a bunch of crappy names," says Yolanda.

She turns to study Joan.

"I think it would go much better with *your* personality, Joan. It's a very Oriental-sounding sort of name anyway."

"Joan goes OK by me with my personality," says Joan.

"Oh," says Yolanda, "I practically almost think of that as your *real* name."

"That's because you don't know me," says Joan. "At all."

Randi comes into the tiny kitchen. All four of them share the space with the appliances and the sound of a siren coming through the airshaft. The wall is of exposed brick and there is a little gap in the wall over the stove where a box of kitchen matches stays.

"I had a call from Guy today," says Randi. "He says he should be here tomorrow."

"Check," says Yolanda. "With the *package*."

"You mean that package with the wittle tiny wegs," says Joan, an innocent expression on her face. She knows Teko only through the descriptions she's heard, mainly from Tania.

"And the fuzzy wuzzy wustache," adds Tania. She and Joan begin to giggle.

"De wittle wevowutionary weader."

"De wascawy wabbit." Tania sags, putting her hands on her knees. She gasps for breath. She is laughing so hard that she hopes that she and Joan stay together forever. Randi hefts one of the bags of pot. "Have you two been into this stuff *already*?" Yolanda has a face of stone.

Tania hates the new names. They have no proud provenance, unlike their guerrilla names. They're just these ugly old *names*. She is Pearl, Teko is Frank, and Yolanda is Eva. And anyways they always forget to use them.

They can smoke pot in the apartment, but Randi puts her foot down about cigarettes. Verboten, nyet, no good. So Tania steps outside into a night street, heavy still air and the hum of air conditioners all around. She carries a pack of Tareytons and a disposable Cricket lighter. A very exciting invention. She lights it repeatedly, studying the adjustable flame, imagining what if she were from Vietnam or Russia or someplace and were handed this single object from which to make sense of America.

There are plenty of people on the street, despite the town's fearful reputation. Talking, always talking, and with an abandon to the talk, a rude candor that indiscriminately lashes all within earshot. Underlying it all, this supreme self-absorption. They either don't care that you're not interested or they assume that you have to be interested. And she *does* want to join in.

She considers it kind of funny that when they arrived in New York, practically at the instant they'd crossed the George Washington Bridge, any residual sense she had that maybe she ought to keep herself out of sight, to hide in the closet, vanished. There was no question of it, in spite of Yolanda's persistent bossiness. You've come a long way, baby. And you don't travel this far to crouch in fear. She allows herself some absurdly impossible ideas: She'd love to find an apartment like Guy and Randi's. The rents up here seem reasonable. She and Joan could fill it with Salvation Army furniture. She has to admit that she's basically a homebody. Fantastically, she sees herself working, getting a job at an ad agency or a publishing house (maybe Guy could help with that), keeping the SLA business confined to the weekend. The revolution appears far enough removed from New York to allow ROTC-type training. Anyway, here it seems as if the People already have the upper hand, or maybe it's that their poverty is so much more up front and aggressive that it itself is the establishment here.

A succinct breeze, more like the push of a ghostly hand, brings with it the explicit stink of rotting garbage and then disappears. Tania lights another Tareyton. She feels more stupid and noticeable standing outside for the purpose of smoking a cigarette than she does for being on the FBI's most wanted list. A man clad only in a hospital gown approaches her. The gown's got a dense small-figured paisley print, Tania can see, with the name of the hospital stenciled near the bottom. Pedestrian traffic subtly alters course, pointedly avoiding the unlikely pair while equally pointedly pretending to take absolutely no notice of her or of the half-naked man. She looks directly into his eyes. It seems like a smarter thing to do than to avoid his gaze. And ignoring him is out of the question; he's basically right on top of her.

"You have one of those?"

She hands him a cigarette. She asks, "Do you want a light?" He considers this for a moment and then tucks the cigarette behind his ear.

"You have another?" She gives him a second cigarette, and this one he puts between his lips, and Tania is glad to have the opportunity to use the magical Cricket once again. They silently stand and smoke for a minute or more, altogether too close to each other for Tania's taste, while he watches the people who pretend not to see him. He puts a hand to his throat, touches it softly, Tania notices. It seems like a pose.

"Can I come in for some water?"

"No, sorry," says Tania.

"No water?" asks the man.

Tania looks around, and her gaze lights on a bodega on the corner. "You could get some there," she tells him. He turns to look, then faces her again.

"For *free*?" One eyebrow raised.

"No, probably not."

He discharges something, less than an obscenity, more like the wordless expectoration of disenchantment: She has totally let him down. He steps back and wheels on one calloused heel, then steps carefully with his naked feet, continuing on his bare-assed way down the street. With his departure the spell is broken, and not only do the other pedestrians resume noticing her, but one addresses her as well.

"Bet someone's looking for *him*," says the woman, who walks a German shepherd.

"Bet you're right," says Tania, gazing at the police dog.

Inside, the living room is now dark, and as Tania tiptoes to the kitchen, where Joan and Randi still sit at the table, Yolanda raises her head from where she lies on the sofa.

"Quiet," she says, irritably.

"Sorry," says Tania.

Joan and Randi are laughing at something.

"Lately," says Joan, "I been having troubles with my vocabulary."

"It's OK." Randi laughs.

"It's like, the word's under here someplace but when I go to go after it, it's gone already."

"You do so well, considering." says Randi. "I mean, no offense. Anyway, you draw from inward for meaning. It's a matter of self-actualization. If you know what you mean to say, other people will too. It's a natural process."

"Yeah," says Joan. "But mostly people like to know the names of things. Heliotrope. Jack-o'-lantern. Deadly nightshade."

· · ·

Teko comes in, dressed like Al Green and clean-shaven under butterscotch-tinted aviators and hair that has been bleached blond. You walk into a room looking like that you take a second to let everybody get used to the glare. But Teko goes straight into his inspector general routine, like you're waiting for him to put on the white glove and swipe a finger across the lintel in a quest for fugitive dust. The point is, why bother even hoping for a change? Tania sits quietly on the wicker Queen Anne sofa, her hair damp from the shower and spilling over the white terry cloth robe she wears, she guesses it's Guy's, watching as Teko takes in the apartment. His canvas knapsack dangles from his hand. There are knickknacks and other useless creature comforts that Tania suddenly is seeing through Teko's eyes. She feels embarrassed by her own ease.

"Quite a bed of roses," says Teko. Teko wears that strange and insincere smile he has. It displays the peculiar concave camber of his upper teeth. Actually, it's quite an ordinary apartment. Aside from the wicker sofa, there are in this room two undistinguished armchairs, a footlocker pressed into service as a coffee table, a low bookshelf of unfinished pine, and in an alcove the "offices" of the Institute for the Study of Sport and Society: two file cabinets, a desk made from a hollow-core door, and a set of shelves extending from the wall on brackets.

"And here's the new recruit," he says to Joan.

"No," answers Joan.

"No? I thought you were joining us," says Teko. His voice is mild and laden with malice.

"Just a fellow traveler," says Joan.

"Well I don't understand the point of that."

"The point of I'm not joining you?"

"I mean what are you doing here then?"

"Joan and you all have a lot in common," says Guy. "We've *been* through all this."

"A babysitter's what you're saying."

"This isn't the term I personally would use."

"But you're saying if the shoe fits."

"I'm saying Joan's been living underground for more than two years."

"We have some potato salad and cold cuts," says Randi.

"Why would we start, I wonder," wonders Guy, "arguing about this the minute we come through the door? You knew what was on the other side of that door. We had three thousand miles to talk about what and I might add who was on the other side of that door."

"Cheese, orange kind and white kind, and coleslaw," says Randi.

"It's not, believe me," Guy says to the others, displaying his open palms, "it's not like we had this fun see-the-USA-in-your-Chevrolet trip, forget all our troubles, sit back and relax." He addresses Teko. "You were bugged about *everything*, the whole way. The waitress at the Big Boy is looking at you. The clerk at the store puts his hand on your brand of cigarettes before you tell him what you want. Your eye's glued to the speedometer in the desolate nether stretches of no place, where two deputies patrol a million square miles. You're unscrewing the mouthpiece on the motel telephones to check for listening devices. And all that time you knew who and what was waiting on the other side of that door in this apartment in this city, and you didn't say thing one."

"Ever wonder who came up with three-bean salad? I sure do."

"So tell me why now we're instigating some sort of dialogue about the basically settled issue of Joan."

"I just wanted to hear it from the horse's mouth," says Teko. He slurs it enough to make it sound like *whore's*. An additional tension takes hold of the room. The gratuitous insult has a presence, a weight, that is unignorable.

Tania thinks that there's something very Hollywood about borrowing and wearing a man's bathrobe in his apartment. Hollywood and sexily Goldilocks-ish.

"So now you heard it," says Joan, ignoring the insult. "I don't know who do you think you're giving orders to, but it's not me. I don't know who it's going to be." She looks at Yolanda, but Yolanda's eyes are downcast.

"I don't 'give orders,'" says Teko. He picks up a highball glass that sits on the footlocker and sniffs it.

"On the other hand," says Randi, "we could always do Jade Mountain."

"Just No-Cal," says Tania. Her hair whispers against the terry cloth as she turns her head toward him.

"Frankly, I could kill for some Chinese after a thousand hamburgers," says Guy. "Has Randi taken you girls to Jade Mountain yet? It's the best."

"Oh, have we been out on the town?" Teko shakes his head in disgust.

Guy says to Yolanda, "He's all yours."

"Guy, I just, shit," says Teko. "We're traveling undercover, and they're sampling the local cuisine."

"They're undercover too. But they've got to eat. An army travels on its stomach, says Mao."

In a concession to Teko's security concerns, Guy and Randi go to Jade Mountain to bring back takeout. They push the footlocker to the side, making room to form a circle on the living room floor, the white takeout containers clustered at its center. They eat hungrily, without talking. Guy eats scrupulously with chopsticks. Joan does not. The meal seems to mellow Teko out somewhat, and Tania watches him eat, fascinated: He reaches with his fork for the food on his plate and then hovers with it at chest level, waiting while his jaw works metrically at the previous forkload, revealing none of the epicure's contentedness or satisfaction, his eyes uninhabited behind the candy-colored sunglasses, a device, refueling, on standby.

There are five fortune cookies for the six of them. Don't ask how it happened but Joan and Tania, dawdling over their lo mein, are the ones who get stuck. Tania saw Guy's open hand shoot out to enclose one of them even before he was done eating. Guy's eyes take in the weight and measure of everything, calculating his best potential share. But the other one just disappeared. Joan doesn't care much, but the others insist they go halvesies. They insist! Come on! Laughter and camaraderie. Tania cracks open the brittle shell and grabs the end of the paper strip. It's a feeling so familiar it seems as if it dated back to the ocean's saline womb, as if mankind were created to tug paper slips from sugar wafers baked in a shaped crumple. She pulls and the paper is freed.

"Tear it in two," orders Yolanda.

"Now, how does that work?"

"Tear it and like see what it says."

Tania tears the strip down the middle and hands one half to Joan. "This is silly."

Joan glances at hers and shrugs. "It says, 'ning for Success.'"

Tania looks down and gasps. On the torn slip, plain as day, it reads, "You have a Year."

Laugh that one off.

A big hale fire department lieutenant named Lafferty drops by the apartment to deliver the summer lease to his Pennsylvania farmhouse and get the rent check, and beforehand there is this unbelievable scene, with Teko lofting himself into orbit because they're renting the place from a "pig."

Guy has become thoroughly weary of this word. Joan, wide-eyed after one single day with Teko 'n' Yolanda, confides: "These are some fucked-up son of a bitches."

Guy had harbored hopes that he'd be able to swing a meeting or two with publishers during his New York stay, but it's becoming pretty clear that he'll be lucky just to ferry Joan and the SLA three to their remote hideaway before they kill one another in his apartment.

Two grand, incidentally, for this summer rental—as Randi would doubtless point out, two *more* grand—and still not so much as a thank-you. A *simple* thank-you, as his mother might say. And Guy does feel a little like his mother, killing you with chips, crudités, pigs in blankets, drinks, ice, clean ashtrays, coffee, fresh baked cookies, German chocolate cakes, whatever hospitality program fitted onto the spindle of her faithful and discontented brain, waiting uselessly all the while for a sign of gratitude from the louts in her life.

Guy likes the ring of the phrase, *isolated farmhouse*. Rather than connote the *In Cold Blood* quality of total menace Guy would ordinarily associate with the countryside (with the horizontal threat of the Midwest still fresh in his mind), it sounds, at this hectic juncture, charmingly withdrawn from the hurlyburly of everyday life. The cover story the others will use, if asked, is that they're research assistants working for a New York writer—nominally him. And he can see himself in the midday quiet of the place, working away in a back bedroom overlooking a lawn screened by gnarled old shade trees.

For Guy, the bitch of life is that clear view the brain permits of inaccessible alternatives.

The day's work done, you remove the sheet from the typewriter platen and then go off to the swimming hole, or whatever it is you're supposed to do in rural Pennsylvania. But now he just wants to drop his argumentative little payload and head back to the Bay Area.

It's too bad, he was ready to meet anyone, anytime, anywhere. Carries his copy of *The Athletic Revolution* to say, I am real. My reputation precedes me. On the back cover his eyes glare out from under the dome of his skull. On the front, a big caramel-colored fist makes the black power salute.

(He holds the paperback up to the bathroom mirror. Joking/not joking: *My most recent book. Free Press. Division of Macmillan?* Seated at a plush red banquette.)

He leafs through the book, stopping here and there to read passages of varying length. Transformed—by politics, by violence, by notoriety—the sports issues he engages in the book continue to resonate. If, as they so love to claim, sport is a mirror of real life, then revolt in sport is a mirror of revolt in real life, gaining in popularity and meeting heavy resistance from those who have every reason to resist change. What he's really done is toss the phony paradigm back into their faces. In dealing with revolution explicitly, the SLA book project just extends these ideas. That's what makes the project so attractive. That plus the Tania factor makes for what Guy feels is instantly accessible material.

Still, the tautological justifications offered up by the SLA for the Foster murder, the shootings, the kidnappings continue to piss Guy off because he is, at root, an academic who prides himself on his critical thinking. Not an easy hop from plain Guy to Dr. Guy V. Mock. Heavy-duty, baby. Adorno. Barzun. Frankl. Spend enough time with those dudes, and you begin to develop a sensitivity to the slightest whiff of bullshit. And for all the captive hours he'd spent with Teko and Tania, the suggestible front seat intimacy of engine drone and wind murmur as they pushed on toward the horizon, there wasn't a single moment when either of them truly let their hair down, when he didn't feel as if he were dealing with the surviving tape loop of SLA dogma, a disembodied part that whirred and buzzed indiscriminately now. He does not want to become the SLA minister of propaganda. And as the events since he arrived in New York have amply demonstrated, these are some difficult people, emotionally speaking. As human beings they are selfish, prideful, envious, lazy, nearly all the seven deadlies. Fucked-up sons of bitches, indeed.

Here's how it began with the psychics. Imagine a middle-aged man you've just met standing in your living room, removing his clothing avidly, though without any sexual heat—the way, say, an insurance salesman might unpack his briefcase at your kitchen table, moving the cup of coffee you've offered to one side to lay out brochures and folders. Hank had an inkling something like this might happen. Lydia's face was frozen as the man stripped down to his Fruit of the Looms, until finally, faced with the greater part of his pale, flabby body, she covered her eyes with one hand and then slid quietly from her sitting position on the sofa to hide her face in a throw pillow. Hank gathered her up, buried his arms nearly up to the elbow in her armpits and raised her to her feet, then guided her through the doorway and to the foot of the stairs. He stood watching as she started up. Then he went back into the living room.

"So," he said, putting his hands together.

A minute later Hank was calling Hernando in from the garage. He introduced him to the man in his underpants.

"Would you please lift this gentleman and carry him to the car outside," Hank began.

Hernando listened and then hefted the man and carried him out to a car waiting in the driveway.

"Call me 'bitch,'" said the man.

Hernando threw him into the open trunk and slammed the lid down. The car then sped off, and Hank thanked Hernando.

Later the phone rang. "If you're willing," the middle-aged man said, "I'd like to recommend that we try again. I really didn't obtain a clear picture."

One man fondled her shoes. One pored over her photographs. One lay in her bed, pulling the pastel duvet up to his chin.

"But she hasn't slept here in years," Hank said. He switched on the light beside the door.

The man sat up, blinking irritably. He was a dour little man, with dark crescents under his eyes and finely etched lines framing his mouth. He spoke quietly, in a distinct midwestern accent, from amid the rumpled bedclothes.

"Alpha waves leave some of the most lingering impressions," he said. "I'm definitely getting something. If you'll excuse me." Hank left the room. Returning a few minutes later, he found the man snoring quietly.

A woman laid out a seven-card Solomon's seal and offered obscure answers to Lydia's anxious questions. Hank looked at the lurid and disturbing pictures illustrating the Rider Waite tarot deck as the woman's soft voice murmured on.

What hadn't he done right the day that she was taken? What ritual had he overlooked? He got in the car, he drove the car. To work. Downtown. Dinner, at the homes of friends, his wife silent at his side. There's something he was supposed to have done, to have been doing, something that had worked quietly day after day, all the years of his daughter's life, and one day it hadn't happened, had gone haywire like some humble cell inside the body that sets you up for disaster. Whatever the hell it was it had nothing to do with writing checks to favorite charities or bundling up old suits and putting them in the tall, heavy Goodwill bag. It was deeper and more integral, something beneath the surface of goodnight kisses and checking to see that the door was locked, something along the lines of an unspoken prayer or petition he hadn't even been aware of making. Something as real as the first bite of a juicy pear that you'd never remember again.

From whose life could trouble have been more distant? Well, he accepted the presence of the psychics because he accepted now that there were forces in the universe with which, unbeknownst to him, he always has been at odds, and he wanted to become acquainted with their ways and means.

She laid out the cards, and he heard their slap over the soft murmur of her words, Lydia leaning forward, looking drawn, for a change.

Affixed to the handrail on the second-story balcony above the screened porch, wrought-iron letters spell out P A I X. The house is on a slight rise, set fifty yards from a red barn, with a garage and two other small outbuildings in between at the head of the wide dirt driveway, halfheartedly scattered with gravel, that climbs from the road below. The barn and other outbuildings a deep red against the blue of the sky and the green of the tall grasses swaying in fields long relinquished to nature.

"You'll see the falling stars here at night, I bet," says Guy. He has on his face the look of a man who is backing away, figuratively. He and Randi will be spending the night, and then they're off. A mission to torrid Cuba, so Guy says. Guy pronounces it "coobah."

Inside is an American farmhouse. Tania is charmed. She has never seen the like. A mudroom filled with Wellingtons, faded buffalo check mackinaws, raincoats, flashlights, and the disused vacation things of the Laffertys: Louisville Sluggers and volleyballs and cross-country skis and a deflated float in the blue-gray shape of Disney's Eeyore. An enormous kitchen, with attached pantry, overlooking the kitchen garden and the barn beyond. Tiny bedrooms upstairs, three of them, each like van Gogh's room at Arles. Half a mile away a tiny town center forms at a crossroads. There's a country store. Tania is charmed, just charmed.

They explore the barn. Damp-smelling, loft still full of moldering hay. On its walls hang a bridle of rotten leather, which causes Tania to note the empty stalls, and rusty objects of faint menace, sickles, saws, and a pitchfork. Teko finds three abandoned toy guns, which he expropriates for training purposes. One is a revolver in filigreed Wild West style, with white plastic handgrips, and this he adopts as his own. He extends its barrel at the horizon. "Pow," he says.

Behind the house hills rise and fall softly, alive with the same swaying grass that covers the fields. A quarter mile away survives a stand of pines some pioneering farmer planted across the ridge of the tallest hill as a windbreak. Here in the faint daylight that penetrates these trees Tania picks her way over gray trunks felled by age and lightning. She carries the little plastic pistol she is supposed to be sharing with Joan, though Joan has told her that as far as she is concerned this whole pistol routine is a fucking joke. Teko has said that because they have gone so long without their weapons they need to refamiliarize themselves. So Tania is tramping through the woods, her finger resting on the trigger guard of this goofy toy gat, which is stamped "Tracer Gun" and which fires little colored perforated plastic disks, if she remembers correctly.

It's very nice to be walking alone in the woods. The millions of brown needles yield softly beneath her feet. Technically she is supposed to be familiarizing herself with the terrain, like a good freedom fighter. "The urban guerrilla never goes anywhere absent-mindedly and without revolutionary precaution, always on the lookout lest something occur. Eyes and ears open, senses alert, his memory engraved with everything necessary, now or in the future, to the uninterrupted activity of the fighter."

She does remember correctly because good old Ainley Hembrough III, her first love, had a pistol exactly like this. You pulled the trigger and this disk flitted out, wobbling klutzily in the air and invariably going off line well before reaching the target.

Ainley was a doofus, pimples and comic books. On Friday nights he always cut their assignations short, so that he could get back by ten to watch *Star Trek*. She'd chosen him simply because of proximity. She'd been going to Santa Catalina in Monterey, and he'd been at Robert Louis Stevenson in Pebble Beach, and she could look out and say, Round this craggy promontory dwells my True Love. She would send him notes to that effect, cutting the ironic melodrama of her faintly Victorian yearning with ridicule, so he wouldn't think she was taking it all that seriously. Though he actually was the sort of boy she liked: tall, wiry, quiet.

The pines there came right down to the white sand, a dark fringe. Sitting in the moonlight on the luminous, fine sand, you could look up at that lighted ball with its ancient scuffs and wounds, shining down on the world with all the mysteries of the night, and you could imagine that you actually were up there. Ainley said if he had a good enough telescope he bet he could probably see the lunar module.

But what the nuns did when they caught you out! Tania scrubbed more than her share of toilets. It ended up she liked the job, liked keeping things shining and clean, the porcelain white and antiseptic and the brightwork gleaming. It was their own dirty sensibilities that bestowed an axiomatic unpleasantness upon the chore. But she enjoyed seeing those big tiled rooms come clean to her own satisfaction.

Ainley smoked pot and then lied about it to her. It took her a while to figure out how she felt about it, exactly, but when she finally did, that was the end. She received, from here and there, sad little reports about this waning boy, pining away for her. She imagined him standing beneath her window, like poor dead Michael Furey. By then, though, she'd successfully petitioned her parents to get her away from those crazy Dominicans, and on her first day at Crystal Springs School for Girls, she had gotten her maiden eyeful of Eric Stump.

Nice to be alone in the woods. Tania hasn't had any time to herself in ages. The birdsong here is intermittent and plaintive. Now she touches the Olmec monkey on its thong around her neck.

He gave me the little stone face one night.

She slips her finger inside the trigger guard and takes aim at a bough high overhead. On second thought, might as well do it right. She mimes: Rack the slide, watch the round coming up the ramp and into the chamber. Feet apart, relaxed, raise the gun to find the target with your dominant eye. That tweety little bird, all innocence, chirping away up there. Align the sights (actually, only one on this toy) and squeeze the trigger.

"Move the gun to your head, not the other way around. And stop breathing."

Teko has come up behind her and stands, leaning against a tree. He is wearing shorts and a T-shirt that is dark with his sweat. Around his ankles are weights he had Yolanda make, sand sewn into heavy cotton socks.

"How'd you manage to let me sneak up on you anyway? Crashing through these woods, you should have had the drop on me. Lost in the stars, rich girl."

Suddenly he draws the toy revolver from his waistband. Tania flinches.

"Pow. Pow. Pow. Pow. See, you're dead. I killed you. You fail the test."

A ridiculous moment, the two of them in the trees, playing with toys. Tania abruptly remembers firing the submachine gun at Mel's, people flattening themselves against the asphalt, the gun bucking, fighting her as it emptied itself. Teko, meanwhile, had allowed himself to be disarmed. Teko had blown everything. RIP Cin, Zoya, Gabi, Fahizah, Gelina, and Cujo, Cujo, Cujo. Who'd "failed" when it mattered?

"Are those the socks you took from Mel's?" she asks.

"There are going to be some changes," he says.

"Yeah."

"Big changes around here. No more sitting around watching fucking brainrot TV. No more fucking takeout. No more fucking girl talk and giggles like a fucking slumber fucking party."

"Yeah, I bet."

"You watch that attitude, bitch. I got my eye on you."

Tania looks up from a paperback copy of *The Exorcist* to watch from the screened porch Yolanda and Joan walking together in the tall grass behind the barn. They walk slowly, contemplatively. Joan has her hands behind her back, the fingers of one gripping the opposite wrist. Yolanda gestures deliberately, sculpting a sort of compact box in the air, illustrating the solidity and unassailability of her thoughts, gestures that say, Let's Be Reasonable. Tania wonders idly what Yolanda is trying to con Joan into doing. A brief wind thrills the surface of the grass, momentarily drowning out the insect drone. Bugs all around here: grasshoppers and praying mantises and endless flies plus cicadas in the trees shrieking out the swan song of their long lives. Why they screened the porch in, probably. Nice in here, cool and with that summer-place smell of dust and must.

Off in the distance she sees Yolanda stoop and pick up a weather-faded tennis ball. Awkwardly she pitches it into the sea of waving grass, where it disappears. Then she and Joan continue their slow walk. Tania returns to her book, not looking up again until she hears someone climbing the porch steps. Joan opens the screen door and sits on a chaise, sinking slowly into its cushion, which audibly exhales.

"You wouldn't believe this," she says. "But what they want me to is dress up like a white. For to go to town."

Guy Mock's big idea was that Joan would be available to run errands and such this summer, keeping the lid on the red-hot fugitives. This was a way for her to return the favor he and Randi had done her by smuggling her out of California in 1972, when she herself had been red hot. Randi helped wipe down her apartment, and then Guy drove her to L.A., where together they boarded a New York flight, Joan carrying a huge stuffed rabbit and an Easter basket by way of disguise. Joan sometimes feels as if she's been continuously returning this favor for two years.

Here it's been tough duty. An Oriental girl sashaying into the general store, yeah sure, to buy Oscar Mayer baloney and Wonder bread. "Who you think you're fooling with that stuff, chink?" the clerk had finally asked her. One day she'd gone into the Goodwill just for a look at the paperbacks when she'd sensed another presence in the quiet nook where the books and old *National Geographic*s were piled, and she'd looked up to meet the disapproving gaze of the clerk, who'd come out from behind the counter to follow her.

She said, "We're *closed*."

"Oh, I'm sorry."

Leaving, Joan thought, stupidly, "That's funny, the sign says open till four, the lights are on, no one else seems to be leaving." The dawning that the woman had sought to protect her foxed old copies of national best sellers from Joan's gook depredations came upon her slowly and humiliatingly.

"She says, like, I'm just a little obvious."

"Duh," says Tania. "Why don't they just go themselves?"

"And blow the covers."

"Their famous cover. Research assistants don't buy groceries too? And what are you supposed to be, the Oriental houseboy?"

Joan snickers.

"Shit, I'll go down there myself."

"Someone is feeling frisky."

"Just bored around here all the time."

"Well, whatever else, they heard of you, star chick. Your face is the famous face."

Tania laughs, softly, and throws down the book, which she finds pretty boring, actually. Girl locked in a room with a bunch of authority figures trying to change her personality? That's entertainment? Plus every time Father Karras lights up a smoke, she wants one, and she's trying to cut down.

Tania never smoked at all before she was taken. Now she just can't stop. At the apartment on Golden Gate, where she first came out of the closet to join the others at their eating, training, schmoozing, fucking, standing guard, and all the other pursuits the nine of them had crammed into those two rooms, she took up the habit in earnest. Everybody smoking away in two sealed rooms with the heavy surveillance drapes over the locked windows. Actually, she began in the closet, accepting cigarettes just to be polite. She remembers Cinque advising her that smoking was like killing pigs. "Baby," he said, "once you start you just want to do it all the time." She tilted her head back as subtly as she could manage, trying to peer at her captor from beneath the blindfold she wore.

The depths of arcane knowledge she explored in that closet. The subject of blindfolds, for example. She came to know more about blindfolds than any human not similarly situated might ever have suspected there was to know. The different materials they were made from, the different methods of fastening them, their different purposes: concealment of the world or inducement to terror. Blindfolds made of bed sheets were most comfortable, but their tendency to loosen and slip down filled her with panic. Panic in the dark was not good. It was as limitless as the blackness and totally irresistible. When she could discern that the blindfold was no longer functioning, she would attempt to position herself in a way that she thought would indicate total noncomplicity in its failure. There she would cower. Blame was always a matter of who happened to discover her in there, concealing her wily capacity to examine the timeless dark. Cin would curse her, Zoya would roughly retie the blindfold, sometimes making it impossible to breathe through her nose, Teko would hit her, Cujo would rarely notice, and Gelina would cluck sympathetically. They put a pillowcase over her head and wound cord or twine around her neck to hold it on, but for some reason that didn't last. Someone came up with the idea of taping cotton to her eyes, wads of surgical cotton pulled from a blue box with a big red cross on it and then taped to her face. When she wept, the cotton efficiently absorbed the tears, holding them there, a soggy memento to her despair. Plus she got a kind of diaper rash on her face. Any decent blindfold design needs to take tears into account. People who are left tied up and blindfolded in little closets tend to cry, frequently. They talked about pinning newborn-size Pampers to her face, but the Pampers were too expensive. They tried sanitary napkins instead, but they just fell off, leaving her blinking in the dark, wondering whether she was going to get killed, socked in the face, hauled over the coals, or commiserated with. Finally they just fastened sponges to her eyes with thick elastic bands. That worked all right. Everybody achieved a satisfactory middle ground with that one. It seemed to fulfill the requisite need for grotesquerie; it blinded her; it was uncomfortable but not distractingly so. Thus successfully disabled, she continued to wait. She kept expecting to cross the threshold beyond which she would take a stand, of some kind, but she surprised herself, with her ability to go farther and farther, without protest, eating when she was told, waking up when she was told, bathing when she was told, having sex when she was told, speaking the words she was told to speak. It did not strike her as weakness, not in the least. Strength, rather. Strength that she could eat such food, in the dark. Strength that she could pull herself fully awake at a moment's notice, ready to agree with Cinque, to denounce the world. Strength that she could plod blindfolded and naked through the crowded apartment and then sink her bones into the grimy tub. Strength that she could endure the unwanted groping and gasping on the floor of her closet. Strength that she could learn to be another person, that she could empty the reliquary of herself, part with so much secret knowledge without once asking, "Is this really me? Then where do I think I'm going?" without even a moment's nostalgia. If it was nostalgia she was after then it was a nostalgic attachment to the functions of her medulla oblongata that she developed; to her old pals respiration, circulation, and kinesthesia; to the feel of the beaten-down carpet under her skinny butt.

"So are you going to do it or what?" she asks Joan.

"I said forget about it. And not just because it is a stupid idea or because I am offended, though it is and I am. But because bright ideas like this should have come like a month ago already, while we're still on Ninetieth Street. But they just don't think these things through, do they?"

"Well, Mel's is the total case in point."

"How horrible that must have been. Well, see. It happened how? Someone got a bright idea all of the sudden. There's a time to improvise, when you can just go off, and other time when you stick to your script."

"There was no script," says Tania. "That was the problem."

"I have my own script. The pigs come out here, get us surrounded, I go out the door with my arms up in the air. That's my script. Take me, I'm all yours. What's jail next to a million years in a hole in the ground? I can get along in prison. I can get along in any place."

Joan Shimada was from anyplace. She was sansei; her parents had been born in the United States, but did that mean dick all as the

Christmas season approached California in 1941? No, by then all eyes were on the coastal skies, looking out for treacherous, crafty, devious, scheming, wily, perfidious Japs in their "Zekes," "Kates," and "Bettys," zooming in for another cowardly sneak attack. None seemed to show up, so by and by Californians had to look closer to home, finding what they sought in the merchants and tradesmen of Japanese descent who'd settled in the state, sometimes several generations previously. FBI men came into the shops and groceries, going through vegetable bins and slitting open sealed cartons, tossing the back offices, looking for transmitters and secret communiqués from the Land of the Rising Sun.

President Roosevelt's Executive Order 9066 had the putative purpose of directing the secretary of war to "prescribe military areas . . . from which any or all persons may be excluded." In practice, this was understood to mean excluding people of Japanese ancestry from the West Coast. Usefully, Governor Chase Clark of Idaho suggested before a congressional committee at around this time that Japanese would be welcome in his state if they were confined to guarded concentration camps, thereby helping solve the problem of what, exactly, to do with all those "excluded."

Thus in March the first of those so excluded began to arrive at "relocation centers," such as the one at Manzanar, where Joan's mother and father found themselves one morning after a long and uncomfortable bus ride. Dust flew at them, waves of sandy grit that stung the eyes and coated the baggage that had been dumped from the trucks that had been loaded with belongings of the evacuees (as they were called) at the embarkation points. Joan's parents were assigned with two other childless couples to share a 320-square-foot compartment in a large barracks. So the first thing to do was to further partition this small space, hanging blankets and improvising with flattened cardboard boxes and the scrap wood remaining from the camp's construction. Even so, as Joan's mother later made clear despite her permeative reserve, it had been something of a surprise that they found the opportunity to conceive her.

Born a prisoner. Such was the weight she and her parents were required to pull, for the USA. The loyalty questionnaire asked:

27. Are you willing to serve in the armed forces of the United States on combat duty, wherever ordered?

28. Will you swear unqualified allegiance to the United States of America and faithfully defend the United States from any or all attack by foreign or domestic forces, and forswear any form of allegiance or obedience to the Japanese emperor, or any other foreign government, power, or organization?

The answers were yes, yes. They had always been yes, yes. Joan's father had tried to join the army after Pearl Harbor and been rejected. The Japanese emperor was typical royalty, the sort of mute and bloodless enigma both set above and emblematic of his nation that either fascinates or bores the hell out of Americans. Japan itself was a sentimental memory, at best an occasional dreamy riposte to the piston force of American life, which was the only kind of life either of Joan's parents had any familiarity with. But there they were, in suspense, yoked to this old strange multitude across the ocean. Meanwhile Joan began to grow into the memories her parents tucked away and treasured for her. Inoculated in infancy against the sorts of diseases that flourished in overcrowded conditions, she developed a terrible case of the "Manzanar Runs," nearly perishing from dehydration. That was one of the indistinct memories she was advised to hang on to: *She had nearly died; nearly died living in an American concentration camp.* It was the sort of unimpeachable, irreducible, immutable fact that some would turn into a lifetime free pass. But to Joan it didn't represent some perversion of normal life; it actually was her normal life. "Nearly" died; close, but no cigar. In other words, keep on moving. She had faint memories of her own: the Sierras peaking in the distance, the total lack of privacy, the toilets in the latrine lined up in a row of six back-to-back pairs, the carefully raked rock gardens ornamented by stones the men carried in from the desert, the absurd noise of the mess halls, the carnival-like events regularly held in the firebreak set between the rows of barracks. The soothing regularity of camp life. She was very young indeed.

The camp closed, but there was no returning to the other California. The two Americans packed up their American daughter and went to Japan. Her father got a job working as a translator for the British Commonwealth Occupation Force, and the family settled on Eta Jima, off the coast of Hiroshima, former home of the Imperial Naval Academy. Here cadets had meditated upon the Five Reflections each evening:

1. *Hast thou not gone against sincerity?*
2. *Hast thou not felt ashamed of thy words and deeds?*
3. *Hast thou not lacked vigor?*
4. *Hast thou exerted all possible efforts?*
5. *Hast thou not become slothful?*

As a matter of policy, the BCOF encouraged the wives and families of servicemen to settle in Japan. Special schools and shops as well as separate housing were constructed for the occupiers. To sort of suggest that the feeling was mutual, Joan's parents avoided occupation personnel outside work. Joan's father took a dim view of the BCOF's stated aim to enable the Japanese "to witness at first hand Western family life." Most of the units were Australian, and he did not like the Australians: the condescension of the officers, the yahoo bigotry of the rank and file. The cloddish Perth housewives in their housedresses trying to turn everything into a knotted back alley they could holler across, snapping their fingers at him and yelling in his face. To them all he spoke in the clearest English, chiming with the open tones of the native Californian, and got back a guttural mess, totally untransformed by tongue, teeth, or palate in its journey from the throat. They would demonstrate to him "the democratic way of life"?

After BCOF headquarters was moved from Eta Jima to Kure, Joan's father endured a brutal commute, taking a bus, a ferry, and another bus to get to work. This itself made him irritable, even as the work became less congenial; mostly he had been translating documents, but now that he found himself working often with the military police in Kure he regularly was called upon to interpret in the type of face-to-face situation that he found, in a word, embarrassing. Their pet Jap, pulling usable English sentences into shape for the Australians. What a job. One night the MPs picked up a man, a civilian, for possession of stolen goods. He'd been arrested near one of the many "roads, wharves, railway yards, local markets, villages, stores, or camp perimeters" that had been declared off-limits to civilians and servicemen alike. Your mere presence there got you a mandatory escort back to headquarters for a little chat. Fraternization was strictly out-of-bounds for servicemen, and the locals had to be watched to keep the booming black market under control. This guy was carrying sixty pounds of sugar in a pair of old Samsonite Streamlite suitcases.

Joan's father spoke to the prisoner for an hour or more, attempting to urge forth helpful information. Helpful to them all, he suggested. The man called him an *inu* and mocked his accent. Glancing at the clock, Joan's father could see that he would miss the last ferry to Eta Jima. The MPs shared their headquarters with the Japanese police, so when the MP sergeant grew tired of waiting, he simply walked the prisoner down the corridor to his good Nip buddies and had Joan's father explain the situation to them. The cops, who had been playing cards and drinking whiskey, were delighted with the diversion presented by the prisoner. They all headed for the motor pool, which was empty at that hour. Near the edge of the enclosure, by the chain-link fence, there was a concrete stanchion that had two eyebolts driven into it on opposite sides. The purpose of these became clear when one of the police, a plainclothesman, fed the chains manacling the prisoner's hands through the bolts, securing him to the stanchion. He then took a gasoline can and, carefully pouring out its contents, circled the post. Done, the plainclothesman lit a Lucky Strike and assumed a posture that you might call thoughtful or reflective, standing back from the bound man as if evaluating at a distance, taking in the whole of a thing. Joan's father noticed that the plainclothesman's suit was soaked through with sweat between the shoulder blades. The cop took his hat off and then reseated it on his head, gripping the crown of the fedora where it was crimped and tilting his head back into the gesture so that the lank strands of hair falling across his forehead were swept under the crown. He then reached for his handkerchief, but what unfurled when he removed it from his breast pocket was a clean white sock. There was a still moment as everyone measured the extent of the plainclothesman's discomfiture over the exposure of this improvisation. Rather artful, really. Everything everywhere was running short, why not a sock? The cop balled it up and put it in his trousers pocket. Until then Joan's father had thought that the tying up, the circle of splashed gasoline were merely features of a type of performance. But the sock incident had put the plainclothesman on edge, tensed him up, and the balletic series of slow relaxed gestures came to an end, and after pulling the Lucky from his mouth and taking a last look at it, he tossed it without warning at the prisoner's feet, where the immediate flames erupted so high that for an instant it was all Joan's father could do to see the terrified shape within them.

· · ·

Eta Jima itself was a beautiful place. Joan became Japanese there, something her parents felt pretty ambivalent about. She got friendly with a girl whose family had lived in Hiroshima. Akiko had a good story. She had been a baby when she was sent away to NijiMura a day or two before the bombing. Then the bombing had taken place, and that basically was the end of the story. The story did have clarifying footnotes, like: This cousin was never seen again, that sibling died of radiation sickness two months later, this uncle had no face, really. Akiko talked about it to Joan in a lively voice, passing on with great authoritativeness the secondhand information that had been instilled in her with the mesmerizing force of ritual. The story's appeal came from its balancing unities, the simple serendipity of the girl's having been sent away just before the singular holocaust and the horror-science fascination of all the human burn and spatter that was its yield. It was the first time that Eta Jima's proximity to the wrecked city on the other shore became central to Joan's perception of the world.

The A-bombed city. The place did not seem as if it were quite there. There was the ghost of itself that stood just behind it. Tourists moved in search of the ghost. They strolled through the neat grid of streets taking pictures and more pictures of the blandly pleasant city that was there in the place of nothing. Beneath it all, seared like a pitiless brand, the trilobites of human indecency. The city had wholeheartedly embraced the industry of its own devastation—as if the 350 years of its history preceding the bombing had been consequential only insofar as they had led up to the incandescent moment—while rigorously reconstructing itself in a manner that exhibited an aloofness from the experience. Municipally, the legacy of total war became a mandate to celebrate and aspire to peace. It was all strangely flaccid, curiously devoid of rage, though this Joan was too young to notice. She picnicked in a Peace Park. After the city had been burned to a crisp, the official ambition of Hiroshima, according to an English-language pamphlet, was "to keep advocating to the world people that 'Peace' is more than the absence of war, and it signifies a state in which the world people live together without prejudice in a safe and amicable environment, where each person can live a dignified and worthy human life every where in the world, seeking to resolve the various problems confronting humanity . . . by cooperation and collaboration on a global scale aiming at the realization of everlasting world peace and prosperity of humankind."

That, plus world-known Mazda passenger cars were produced there and distributed the world over.

Joan forgot her English. This was pretty hard to believe. The language was all over the place. But her parents had dropped the use of it at home, mostly for her benefit; Joan had her hands full just trying to be Japanese. Some schoolgirls told her that she had a wave in her hair; she must be part white. There was a certain impertinence to her that her teachers claimed to discern, chalking it up to some residual Americanness. But after a while she stopped being exotic, and to others she became just another kid with a funny way of talking who kept to herself. She got good at art. A light touch she had, delicate.

The language left her gradually, until what remained was her knowledge of the letters of the alphabet, the sort of simple expertise with which children flatter themselves. She was a Japanese girl. A Japanese girl. A Japanese girl.

She was basically happy. She had a few friends. She kept to herself. She had a cat named, in English, Bunny. A light touch that pleased her art teacher in school. Unusually precocious ability with watercolors. Basically happy.

The usual mixture of excitement and dismay when they moved. Her friends gave her a sendoff. She spent time recording the green peaks of Eta Jima in a sketchbook. They were going to a place called Fresno, which was supposed to be very flat, and she wanted to get these mountains down, these mountains that just came right up and joined you for breakfast. Trunks and suitcases were taken out of storage. Her parents made gifts of household goods to friends and neighbors, as mementos. Nothing too big or too practical, lest they be insulted. They just happened to be some of Joan's favorite things. Joan came home one day to find that Bunny was gone. It was a big rush. Their home filled with boxes. The rooms echoed strangely. Her parents began speaking to each other in English again. They tried it out on Joan, but who knew what they were saying? Then the family was gone. It had been such a slow process, cumulative, but ultimately they reached the threshold, crossed it, and no longer were there. The difference was one inch, one door shut and locked for the last time, but it was all the difference that was needed. Joan's equanimity crumbled. She sat on the bed her last night in Japan and cried. They were in a hotel near the airport, no place at all. Early the next morning they would begin their long journey to San Francisco. She cried.

It was, finally, the no-place of where they'd come to rest at the end of that final day, the random placement of all the familiar shapes that she could see out the window, the streetlights and white lines and the grassy rises, leading nowhere, packed behind retaining walls, the feeling that no one really belonged there or could possibly miss it once they had gone, that this, at the end, was what she was left with to say goodbye to: That's what got to her, and she cried. These were the shapes people invented so they would never forget loneliness, so that it could greet you anywhere, vast and numbing and repetitive, one anonymous landmark succeeding another, each standing alone. Her father stood over her. "You stop that. I don't need this. Just stop it right now."

Dear Mr. and Mrs. Shimada,

We have evaluated your child, Joan, for English language competency. This evaluation was performed by Mrs. E. Darer and Mr. J. Shemalian. For the purposes of this evaluation, the student has been tested in English both orally and in writing.

The scope of this standard test has been devised so as to determine a student's abilities in reading, writing, and comprehension, as well as in necessary auxiliary skills. Specifically, the test requires a student to:

- Recognize, state, read, and write statements and questions.
- Listen to short conversations and answer questions orally.
- Read and comprehend silently and aloud and answer questions.
- Determine the main idea in a simple paragraph.
- Demonstrate sequential ordering of events.
- Use a dictionary and other essential reference books.
- Demonstrate a basic knowledge of punctuation.
- Write legibly upper- and lowercase letters and properly use capitalization.

Our finding is that the student is unable at this time to meet the minimum standard of competency that would enable placement in

Grade <u>8</u>, the level at which a child of this age ordinarily is placed. The student will be required to demonstrate increased proficiency in all areas prior to placement at this level. In the interim, the student has been placed in Grade <u>2</u>, which will provide a better opportunity to learn at a more unhurried pace.

Should you have any questions concerning this matter, please do not hesitate to contact my office.

My very best wishes,

Louis F. Longcrier
Principal

Just the briefest portrayal of those Fresno Years, which began so inauspiciously. When Joan finally did get to high school at seventeen, the big deal of the thing evaded her. The Choklit Shoppe ethos reigned supreme, fifties swan song ringing out from the angular Seeburg jukes all the stiffs swayed to. Who'dja rather be, Betty or Veronica? Bro-ther! Joan rolled her eyes. The Little Jap in Black hung out with the strange ones, all the oddballs, misfits, loners, eccentrics, screwballs, nonconformists, and cranks. She smoked pot in someone's dad's pickup truck in a field outside Porterville. The smell of manure all around. For a minute she believed that what she was smoking actually was cow shit. She read a copy of *The Subterraneans* someone had lent her. Filled her head up with ideas; it seemed easier than she might have expected to wholly identify with, to imagine herself as, a Negro woman. What it filled her up with was the idea of leaving.

Throughout all this she'd kept winning prizes for her artwork. People were very reassured by this Japanese girl and her delicate touch. A dedication to the old traditional values of the Orient, all the gentle ceremony that seemed to be getting pushed out of the way in this startling new era of entrenched, highly motivated East Asian enemies. She enrolled at Fresno State——

"Well, I'll say one thing for the Japs," a grocer said one morning, as Joan entered his store. "I'll say one thing for them."

"What's that?" asked the man he was waiting on.

"At least they ain't Communists. They understand this system good. They make it work for them. They got it fixed so they got

224

quotas there in all the state colleges. They steal all our inventions to send on back home and then the Japs there send them right back to us, in cheaper versions. They ain't Communists."

——She enrolled at Fresno State but soon knew that it was time to be moving on. For one thing, the fine arts department was desolate, an orphaned entity on a third-rate campus. But she didn't need excuses. She just needed to get out of there. It can be said with some degree of certainty that her parents understood and supported her decision. She applied to CCAC up in Oakland, got in, and left. Exit Fresno.

It was possible, even in the late 1960s, for a person in the Bay Area, in Berkeley, to sustain an apolitical outlook. This was in itself a sort of political posture—albeit a crouch—particularly for someone like Joan, a person for whom politics had never had any point, who had always seen clearly that the divisiveness of political discourse ultimately and inevitably split people into those who were free and those who were "relocated." That at least was a kind of brutal commitment. True, the camps had preempted discourse, but there in the depraved fact of them lay the resolution of whatever dialectic may have ensued, then or now. In the paper she read of the army's "strategic hamlets" in South Vietnam, accompanied by a photograph of the peasants, baffled and defiant, behind the barbed wire that was to preserve them from the wrong ideas. There was a Nazi propaganda film she'd seen at the Art Institute; it announced, "Hitler has built a city for the Jews!" She remembered Manzanar, the mountains cut clean against the horizon, the white of the peaks against the white of the sky, from which they could be distinguished only by the glare at their summits. For a few years she went about her business, ignoring the political poseurs and the hippies alike, especially the hippies, who all seemed about two weeks removed from their crew cuts and prom tuxes.

It was three credits that brought Joan into alignment with her political kismet in 1969. She was lacking three humanities credits that she needed to get her diploma and move on to whatever the next thing was going to be for her, and she enrolled in a night philosophy course at Merritt, a JuCo in Oakland. There she met a man, Ralph, who very gradually introduced her to politics. That her newfound engagement was at the beginning inextricably linked to the powerful, explosive orgasms—her very first—that Ralph provided her seemed both just and honorable. By the time the course ended the affair was about over, but the aspirant beatnik from the Central Valley via Hiroshima via Manzanar had already developed a certain taste, for which the peculiar circumstances of her life had prepared her, for the exhausting encounters, the minuteman keenness, the leery reexamination of the old pieties, required of the political radical.

Joan met Willie Clay at one of the People's Park demonstrations in May 1969. By now, a week or two after the first riot, the National Guard, the police, and the demonstrators appeared to have worked out the blocking of the scene. It was the first time that Joan had actually been to the park site, and she hung back on Telegraph, keeping an extra half block between her and the center of things down Haste Street. Something about the whole setting that day, under the unseasonable lowering sky, gave her the creeps. It was the sort of weather that piss offed the bees, made the dogs bark and run across their yard at you. She was really just trying this People's Park business on for size anyway. It was all anybody was talking about, there were all those National Guard guys all over the place freaking everybody out (though Joan herself was familiar with the sight of uniformed, armed men), so why not? Now she was kind of sorry that she'd come, and it occurred to her all at once, as she was caught up in the crowd, the small, churning eddy of people below the steady current flowing through the Sather Gate and down Telegraph, that the affirming solidarity others found in the midst of a swarming, loud assembly was nothing that she needed, at all.

She was a stealthy, secret person, with a delicate touch.

What she had to offer was more than the pinprick presence of her body smack dabbed in the middle of a jam. It was something more, an individual voice that inspired, an individual vision that revealed.

OK, so this bared some lingering fucked-up values, some ego-type issues she still had to deal with. But right now she had to like get out of there. She'd reached the corner and could see that the demo had begun to disintegrate, that a sequence of discrete clashes had built into a rush toward the park itself, vacant in its ruin behind a defensive line of helmeted guardsmen who stood in impassive anticipation of the encounter. The hollowed voice, its pulsing monotone, coming through the police bullhorn, seemed to counterpoint the surging crowd and its own steady noise, like an ostinato playing against the surf:

"CLEARraaaaaTHEaaaaaaAREAaaaaaaDISPERSEaaaaaaNOW aaaaaaCLEARaaaaaaTHEaaaaaaAREAaaaaaaDISPERSEaaaaaa NOWaaaaaa."

Others at the edges now saw the swelling, and the confrontation waiting for it where it would break, and turned to run, pushing into the milling group that was on Telegraph and forcing it into two sections, angry where they had divided and coming together again, like reverse mitosis. Behind her Joan heard the sound of glass breaking and turned her head to see a heavy bearded man rolling through the jagged center of a broken plate glass storefront, just rolling slowly and as easy as you please. As she was pushed back, she felt with her heel for the curb, fearful that she would fall beneath all those feet, and she stumbled up onto the sidewalk just as the first heavy drops of rain began to fall. More people were coming onto Telegraph from Haste now, the bullhorn had quit, and she heard the sounds of combat, those intent on fighting sandwiched between police and national guardsmen, and the rest in flight. She saw a wispy trailing plume climb away from the police line, describe an arc, then vanish into the crowd nearby, where a pale haze gathered and expanded in the humid air, repelling people.

"Gas!" someone shouted. "The fucking pigs are gassing us!"

A man made for the canister. "I wouldn't grab that," another man said. With lucid calm Joan studied his T-shirt, which depicted a friendly-looking young man evolving in several stages into a ferocious pig clad in army fatigues and bearing a rifle, over the legend DON'T LET THIS HAPPEN TO YOU. "It's fucking hot," he added.

The first man removed his hat and, using that, gingerly picked up the canister. Again the plume rose, tracing its path back in the direction it had come, as he returned the canister to the police. Joan caught some of the fumes and instinctively brought her hands to her face, astonished by the speed with which the reaction arrived, bringing convulsive retching and elastic strings of saliva that swung from her mouth. She tried to keep her eyes open, but they fluttered spasmodically. Tears and snot rolled down her face. She lurched for the building behind her, figuring to grope and fight her way out of there. Her outstretched fingers jammed against something both hard and soft, and something seized her by the wrist and swung her back into the crowd.

"Watch where you're going, you dumb bitch," a voice said, aggrieved.

She tried again, but now her disorientation was complete. Light appeared between her eyelids, which thankfully had stopped flapping, but now they just sagged, sleepily half shut, so that she really couldn't see. She placed her hands in front of her face, palms out, and pushed forward. She decided not to panic. She felt panic approaching because she was caught in the crowd and she was feeling sick to her stomach and her eyes and her nose and her lips were burning and she was having tremendous trouble catching her breath and she couldn't see a damn thing. Panic was hanging back, but just waiting to sprint in and unhinge her completely. So she deliberately considered her case. OK, Joan, she said to herself, you're going to just walk until you run into something solid. Then you're going to hang on to it. This rule outs people, who move and fall. This rule outs cars, that someone can move or that can turn over. This rule outs the sidewalk, for there's nothing to hang on to, plus you might get walked all over. Her manner with herself kept her calm enough that she was able to keep going through the crowd, which, fortunately for her, had not yet discovered its direction. She was almost amused, and she kept it up. Well, Joan. You have really gotten into a good mess here. What in the earth were you thinking about? Joan, you are just not a crowd person. Then her palms were up against something flat and smooth. It was not a wall, and it was not a door, nor was it a truck or a bus, and panic finally turned up when she realized that she had worked herself face up to a big plate glass window like the one she had just seen the fat man fall through. The crowd heaved slightly behind her, pushing her a little, and involuntarily she let escape a cry. The moderating, mildly reproving voice inside had abandoned her, and she was left with a growing conviction that she would be pushed through the glass and cut to pieces. Then she felt a hand on her.

"You got gassed?" a voice asked.

She nodded.

"Can you breathe? Take deep, slow breaths. Don't take panic breaths. You're OK. You got bronchitis? Asthma? Tuberculosis? Lung cancer? No? You're probably OK. You might react, bronchospasms or something, but you haven't so far, so again, you're probably OK. Hold on and come with me."

She reached out, and her hand partly encircled a forearm—not a particularly hairy one, she noticed right off. They walked this way for a bit, forearm to forearm, and soon had turned off Telegraph and onto a quieter side street.

"Good thing it's raining," the voice said. It was a man's voice. "Tilt your head up. Did you rub your eyes?"

"A little," said Joan.

"That makes it worse. Here, now let the rain wash some out. I have a canteen here too. I always carry one to these demos. You never know when the pigs are going to start firing that stuff. You're not wearing contact lenses, are you?"

No, Joan shook her head.

"Good. Boy, they're murder. People wear them, though. Ego. Got to look your best. I guess you never know when you're going to meet that special someone. But listen, now I'm going to pour some water out of the canteen directly into your eyes. Just blink it out. How's your breathing?"

"Good. Better."

"Blink. Blink. Here, hold out your hands. You rubbed your eyes, you got it on your hands. How's your eyes?"

"Good."

"Can you see?"

What she could see was Willie Clay, nice-looking guy, trim, good face, a little short. Younger than she was, it looked like. What she said was, "A little better."

"What you really need to do is take a shower. You live nearby?"

Joan shook her head no. He blushed. Definitely younger.

"Do you think you might want," he suggested, his eyes widening as if he were astonishing himself, "to come back to my place?"

If Joan didn't want to deal with the crowds, she'd met up with Willie Clay at just about the right time, because to his way of thinking the demos were now entropically inclined. It was as if a buzzer had gone off and suddenly the idea was done. First off, people had started to show up looking for the hippies: the dancing naked girls with henna tattoos, the burnout freaks with flowers in their hair. This was *bad*. This made Willie feel useless, impotent, helpless, feeble, and shabby.

But then the dancing naked girls had started showing up too, and this Willie could not abide. Also to his way of thinking, even the most serious-minded group of demonstrators tended to find itself at loggerheads over the single central issue of intent. To wit: in the case of, say, an antiwar demonstration, most of the people who showed up, well, they just wanted the war to stop. OK, Willie would say to them, so we stop the war. Then what? Then we go back to drinking jug wine and eating table grapes? because so what about the farm workers? Then we go back to living in communities where the basic job of the pigs is to keep the blacks confined in their ghettos? Then we go back to our credo that every American has the God-given right to walk around his house in a T-shirt in the middle of winter and drive his Cadillac two and a half blocks to the grocery store? Then we go back to smoking dope with towels stuffed under the doors because they'll bust your ass and lock it up for years? Then we just go back to Nixon? Richard M. Nixon? Excuse me, but you mean we just go back to waiting patiently while Nixon serves out, *presides for*, eight years? Huh? And so they would look at you like, What the *fuck* is up your ass, man? We just want the damn war to stop. Or they'd go, It's the first domino, with the self-satisfied affect that only complete mastery of evocative but basically empty jargon brings. *Domino!* Willie repeated, fairly heaving with disgust. This is the image McNamara and Co. (he pronounced it, and Joan envisioned, "coe") came up with to sell the war here at home. To his way of thinking, these people, the purist war enders, would eventually form a new class: financially comfortable, tasteful, smugly proud of its impeccable progressive credentials, entrepreneurial, and totally, emetically bourgeois. Raising false consciousness to unheard-of levels of falsity. Just stand by until around 1984, and you'd see. To his way of thinking, when the government finally got around to ending the war—which wasn't likely to happen real soon if the opposition principally spent its time marching around on college campuses, which had about as much to do with the daily life of the average American as bathing rituals along the Ubangi—these poseurs would probably take the credit for it. Shameless! Here was Willie's opinion: To his way of thinking, you wanted to end the war by bringing the society that waged it, that developed and continually refined its rationale, to an end. You wanted total revolution. Of course, if you had that, you couldn't open a food co-op somewhere or buy yourself a nice piece of land in Bolinas. You'd have to *commit*; you'd have to *fight* and *struggle*. His right fist hitting his left palm for emphasis.

Willie could work himself into a real lather. He was the sort of intense, wiry little guy that Joan had been noticing at the fringes of things for years, since she'd returned to America and kept her eyes and ears open behind the humiliating primary school readers she was obliged to master before joining children her own age in school. In high school she'd hung out with several of this type, but the light had already started failing in them; mostly what they were fighting and struggling against was following their fathers into the produce business. Joan figured that this was Willie's way of beating a similar rap. And as she was drawn further into Willie's circle, her foremost impression of these young radicals was that despite themselves, they felt that they were getting away with something, beating the rap, that the makeup of the thing was 50 percent revolution and 50 percent defying expectations.

So it was just big talk. Not that Joan didn't love to hear Willie talk. To have him sitting there, all five feet seven of him, taking up revolution's case in his polished and unconscious American idiom, was like listening to a Little Leaguer talk dirty to you. Innocent, exciting, and erotically charged. Willie was unconscious of it, and there was nothing he could have done about it had he tried; he couldn't halt his big American self-confidence even in his stylized oppression, couldn't stop it any more than he could stop himself from rooting for the Cubs or preferring the micronite filter of Kent cigarettes. Willie was politically very aware, but he was also a bright, interesting, sexy fantasist, and Joan fell in love with him.

Then he asked her to rent the bomb factory.

It was a vacant, detached garage in Berkeley that was renting for twenty-eight dollars a month. Joan called the number Willie had copied from the hand-lettered sign taped to the roll-down door and, identifying herself as "Anne Wong," agreed to meet the landlord to inspect the place. She showed up at the designated time, did whatever she thought would indicate her sincere interest in a sheltered, secure parking space for her car—pulled down the door a couple of times, tried the switch that turned on the overhead light—and then rented it on the spot, sealing the deal with a month's security and the first month's rent in advance. The way Willie had said "bomb factory," eyes alight and with a goofy smile, aided Joan in her belief that he didn't actually mean it, that he had been interested in renting the garage for some other purpose, though what that purpose might be Joan couldn't guess. Willie's friends didn't exactly seem poised to begin blowing things up, no matter what they might say around the kitchen table. But then Willie began to produce certain items, some of them from hiding places within the apartment—where, it became clear to her, Joan had been living in a state of willed benighted-ness—produced them and started to move them, in stages, to the garage, from placid objects, like notes and communiqués attributed to "The Revolutionary Army" to such terrifying materials as ammonium nitrate, ammunition, blasting caps, fuses, gunpowder, guns, and pipe bombs.

From the first, through self-interest alone, Joan found secrecy an easy burden. Then, gradually, trust eliminated the weight entirely. Born a suspect, she was happy to become a coconspirator with whoever would bank on her. Sometimes the Revolutionary Army was Willie alone. Sometimes members of Venceremos joined in. Occasionally the odd Weatherman or two. Always Joan's participation was unquestioned; her race, prized.

Willie's original objective was armed propaganda. After-hours bomb blasts would be visited upon banks, brokerage houses, and other temples of capital in deserted financial district streets and suburban office parks. Small blows, systematically delivered, would damage the system while sparing the comparatively innocent, was the idea. This rule did not apply on the day in 1971 when Joan drove with Willie to O'Connor's, a cop bar across the street from the Hall of Justice in San Francisco. It was about 4:30 when they pulled up, just around the time when cops, bailiffs, marshals, and deputies began filling the saloon. Willie sat in the passenger seat with a Styrofoam cooler on his lap. In it was a six-pack of Olympia beer, only five of whose cans contained the brew. The sixth held gunpowder, nails, and carpet tacks. For this Willie had devised a fuse by scraping the substance from Fourth of July sparklers and crushing it, mixing the resulting powder with water, and then dipping string into the mixture. Once fuses of varying lengths had dried Joan had tested several, timing each as it sparkled and popped itself into a length of gray ash. She had done it in the alley outside the garage, squatting on the cracked slab of concrete angling into the space, whose door she had discreetly lowered. Two boys zipping up the alley on banana bikes had come to a stop so that they could watch. Eventually, after a period of reverential silence, one had been moved to ask, "What're those for?"

Joan had given him a tight smile. "Chinese New Year," she said.

Ten seconds was what she had figured. Enough time for Willie to light it, toss it in, get back to the car, and get away. She had cut several fuses to the proper length and placed them in a plastic bag that previously had held sticks of incense. Now, as Willie took the bomb from the cooler, she reached for the bag of fuses. In her nervousness she dropped one as she withdrew it from the bag.

"Come on, c'mon," said Willie.

The musky incense smell filled the car. Hare Krishna, thought Joan, Krishna Hare. She didn't know why. She put her hand to her mouth to stifle a laugh.

"This is the exact frame of mind I had hoped you would avoid like the plague," said Willie. "You either think this is funny or you're panicking and in either case you're scaring the shit out of me."

Joan snorted. She couldn't stop; she definitely had the giggles. Willie took the bag of fuses from her, pulled one out, and fitted it to the beer can grenade.

"Now. I'm going to go. I'm going to do it. Be ready to get out of here." He threw open the door and was out of the car. Joan bit the insides of her cheeks and prepared to drive off. Then Willie was back. The beer can still in his hand.

"A light?" he asked, gesturing with his free hand at the bomb.

Joan scanned the car. She reached out and pushed in the dashboard cigarette lighter.

"That's it? That's the light we brought?"

Joan started giggling again.

"Oh, for Christ's sake." He waited, jiggling his leg, the beer can held gingerly by his fingertips, until the lighter popped out, and then grabbed it.

"Better hurry up," said Joan. "It colds down real fast."

He dashed to the entrance, sheltering the glowing end of the lighter, the bomb cradled against his chest. Joan ticked off: Light fuse, open door, toss in grenade, dash back to car.

"Go, go, go go go!" he said, though Joan had the car moving before he had closed his door. "That ought to get them. That ought to take care of them."

"Did you mail the communiqué?" asked Joan.

"I figured I'd wait until the action was over."

"It won't get picked up until tomorrow, you know. Unless we take it right to the post office."

"It'll keep," he said. "What do you say we go to Flint's? We can eat in the car and listen to the news."

But there wasn't any news. Whether the grenade had been stomped out by a vigilant off-duty cop or had simply been a dud, the thing didn't go off, and there was only a small item in the local section of the *Chronicle* the next morning. No radio or TV coverage at all. Disappointed, Willie began to plot out more ambitious actions. His visits to the garage became lengthier and more frequent.

On March 30, 1972, two policemen on patrol were hailed by a Berkeley housewife who told them that she was smelling gas "out back." After advising dispatch to notify PG&E, the cops went into the alley that ran behind the street, where they made a cursory examination of the area, just sticking around until the utility guys arrived. The alley was lined with freestanding garages on one side, with the backs of bungalows and apartment houses on the other. Coming from one of the garages was a keen, chemical odor that aroused the curiosity of the cops, not the odor of gas, but it was a faintly familiar smell, and it was a slow morning, and they had a valid pretext, so what the hell. The cops picked the garage door lock easily and rolled it up, extending daylight into the small space. There they discovered the appurtenances and raw materials that constituted what the newspapers, with typical color, soon described as a "massive" bomb factory. Although, coming almost exactly two years after members of the Weather Underground had blown up a Greenwich Village town house by accidentally touching off thirty sticks of dynamite, such hyperbole was perhaps understandable.

Joan typically woke to a clock radio, a device that enchanted her and drove Willie nuts. She woke up to the news, to even-toned voices telling of faraway things! It was a lovely idea, to lie there in her bed, next to Willie, allowing her consciousness to absorb the world events of the last twenty-four hours. On the morning of Good

Friday 1972, the top news was local: Three men had been arrested and charged with operating a "massive bomb factory," right there in Berkeley. This had Joan sitting bolt upright. The men apparently had been on their way to bomb the UC Naval Architecture Building when the police had taken them into custody.

Joan had only just typed out the communiqué: "Any stage in the production of the Empire's death machines is a legitimate target of revolutionary war, including the training school for the technicians of Death."

Also discovered in the suspects' possession were notes plotting the kidnap of Robert S. McNamara and a detailed plan for the bombing of the UC Berkeley space sciences laboratory. Two of the suspects were identified as Paul Rubenstein, twenty-two, and Michael Bortin, twenty-three, both of Berkeley. A third man remained unidentified. That was Willie! Holy shits! No wonder the pigs weren't knocking down her door! He'd given her a chance to get out of there. But to go where?

Of all Willie's friends, the one who in his raffish self-confidence had most appealed was Guy Mock, whose every word seemed to insinuate a supreme ability to compartmentalize, a detachment from the moment at hand, that just as one project was beginning to cool off another was simmering and about to bubble; that no matter where he was or what he was doing there was always a different place where he would soon need to go or to be. If connections were the most important thing, whether in business, bureaucracy, or revolution, Guy stressed his connections *everywhere*, dropping names into conversations like depth charges. If anyone could help her out in a quick jiffy it would be Guy. And Guy loved to acquire people; she'd felt it herself from time to time when he'd cozy up to her, weird big eyes glowing, with this sort of Hey Sexy Exotic Little Jap Bomber Girl Pound for Pound You are a Pearl of Great Price, covetous but not in a strictly sexual way. She knew he would kill to have her owe him a favor.

She took a pair of clean panties and her toothbrush and put them into her purse. She left the apartment then, heading for Guy and Randi Mock's place on Fifty-eighth Street. As she had guessed, Guy was delighted to help. Two days later she was flying out of LAX, seated in first class, with Guy beside her and an enormous stuffed bunny on her lap.

The questions of who is to run into town to perform errands, and in what guise, remain unanswered, forgotten, and gradually it becomes plain to Tania that what Teko and Yolanda put forward to Joan as issues concerning the well-being of the entire group, matters of crucial importance, are actually excuses to manipulate her, to boss her around. Joan remains stubbornly resistant to this sort of handling. She bluntly declares that the SLA's concerns and her concerns are two different things. She will not take part in the drills—in the biceps curls, shoulder shrugs, paratroop push-ups, sit-ups, knee bends, leg lifts, and jumping jacks that Teko, Yolanda, and Tania practice every day, though she enjoys the regular morning and afternoon runs. She will not participate in the study sessions, which bore her, or the political discussions, which she refers to derisively as "fantasyland." She declines to be comradely with either Teko or Yolanda. She reads the Sunday newspaper, works the crossword. She carries a lipstick and occasionally applies it. What's especially infuriating, from Teko and Yolanda's perspective, is that Joan's insubordination is accomplished with that unruffled equanimity that comes as naturally to her as breathing. She is not rude or unpleasant about it, simply dismissive in a very forthright way, in the manner of a gracious child rejecting what is offered. What remains is the assurance of a young woman whom it is impossible to intimidate or coerce.

Later, at trial, this same resistance to intimidation will bag her five contempt of court citations.

Tania is duly impressed. Nor is this impression lost on either Teko or Yolanda. So the summer's design works out to something like: Take a crack at Joan every day, see what the yield is (Teko persuades Joan to pour him a glass of orange juice when she pours one for herself = major victory); take turns trying to destroy her growing influence on Tania.

Early one morning Teko gathers rocks, about thirty-five pounds of them, and loads them into an old canvas knapsack. Hoisting it, he guides Tania's arms through the straps.

"Now run," he says, pointing at Yolanda, who waits before a group of birch trees by one of the property's three ponds, a hundred yards distant. She waves back at the two of them, less a friendly gesture than as if she were trying to hail a cab in the rain. "Run!"

Tania begins to trot. The pack weighs more than a third of what she does, the stones dig into her spine and rib cage like a dozen elbows. Teko jogs beside her. "Run all out, or I'll be right behind you, kicking your ass." To illustrate, he drops back and dispenses a kick to her left buttock. Tania gasps.

"Come on, Tania!" Yolanda hollers, waving with both arms now. Mist hangs low, in gnarled puffs, over the pond.

"You want another one?"

"No!" pants Tania. "Please!"

He kicks her anyway.

"Get down there! Move! Christ!"

"Come on, Tania!"

She plods along toward Yolanda, the pack chafing her shoulders, the rocks jabbing her, the sound of Teko's breathing behind her. Finally, she reaches Yolanda. She halts and bends at the waist, getting the weight of the knapsack off her shoulders while she catches her breath.

"Well, what are you stopping for?"

"You heard her, keep going!"

Tania looks blankly ahead of her. They stand at the edge of the pond, which drops away from the shore to a total depth of around eight feet.

"Get in there!"

Tania begins to slip out of the pack.

"With the pack, come on!"

"With this pack?" says Tania. "I'll drown. It's too heavy."

"What if," poses Yolanda, "you were being pursued by the enemy and you were carrying essential supplies? Would you just stop at the edge of the water? Or would you go on, like a true guerrilla?"

"You'd get in there," says Teko.

"No, but I'd leave the pack behind," says Tania. "No way I'd get in there with it." To her this is still a situation to which she can apply reason. In spite of everything that has happened to her, she believes this.

"We're not saying this is a choice-type scenario. This is you're being hunted down by a fascist death squad."

"I'm not. It wouldn't happen. And I'd totally leave the pack."

"Not everything's a damn choice you get to make," says Teko.

"This is a dangerous mode of thinking, Tania. It's almost counterrevolutionary. I have to wonder where these ideas of yours are coming from."

"Oh, we all know where they're from. We don't even have to mention where they're from. If you want to be like Joan, just lying around with the fucking Sunday funnies, waiting for the pigs to burst in on you, then be my guest. Just don't waste me and Yolanda's time. You want to be like *her*, go ahead. But you saw—you *saw* what the pigs will do to you. You saw it in L.A."

"How about we just pretend I'm carrying the pack?"

"Not listening!" says Teko, and shoves her in. She splashes forward a few steps, arms flailing, then pitches forward, landing on her knees in about two feet of water. The bottom of the pond is putrescent mud, totally gross. Plus, in falling, one of the rocks, slung forward within the pack by inertia, has smacked her in the occiput. Dazed, angry, she remains motionless in the water.

"Now get on your feet and wade in. Do you think in 'Nam we didn't carry full packs into the paddies?"

Tania knows, from remarks Yolanda has made during her arguments with him, that Teko spent six months in the rear echelons in Vietnam, then was stationed for the remainder of his East Asian tour on Okinawa, manning an officers' club. Probably this is something it would be wiser not to bring up just now. She gets to her feet and begins to wade.

"You need to remember your duty. You need to remember this isn't any damned vacation. I know that god damned bitch has filled your head up with ideas. We lost six comrades, Tania! The pigs smoked them like they were nothing. They smoked Cujo!"

The mention of Cujo's name has the desired effect. She doesn't cry, but she feels an intense physical thrill that begins somewhere behind her breastbone and surges into her lower abdomen, where it blossoms with a kind of viral sapience. She lumbers forward in the murky water, her body's knowledge undeniable. It knows, for example, that at this moment she is possessed by the spirit of Cujo (a kindergarten daydream, like the one she sometimes has of Cujo gazing down on her from a cotton ball heaven, standing at the side of Jesus, Ché, Lou Gehrig, Anne Frank, George Jackson, John F. Kennedy, Pope John, and a benevolent white-bearded God); it knows again the days and nights of their short time together. How *could* Joan understand? Joan thinks that she is helping, but she couldn't possibly grasp how close, how very much her family Teko and Yolanda are. She marches out into the middle of the pond, the water rising above her hips, her waist, the good soldier; praying to live, praying to die.

Drown.
   Drown.
   Live.
   Drown.
   Live, drown.
   Drown.
   Live, live!

When Tania enters the house in her sodden, mud-caked clothes, followed by an unusually buoyant Teko, Joan says nothing, just studies her for a moment and then drops her head, bending to the tablet on which she daily writes letters to Willie or diaristic notes. Cold, hungry, and by now thoroughly abandoned by the spirit of Cujo, Tania thinks that what Joan is writing has to be some contemptuous observation about her, and for a moment she flashes with the anger that Teko and Yolanda exhibit at the sight of Joan writing away. She climbs the stairs to her tiny bedroom and strips off her clothes, tossing them to the floor. She actually liked those clothes, too, is the thing. The mud, pervasive, streaks the folds and interstices of her body, the spaces between her toes and the flesh beneath the slight droop of her breasts.

The clock on the wall has stopped at three minutes past nine. Tell the truth, they could throw all the clocks into the pond for all it mattered. Time enough to bathe later. Time enough for everything. She looks at herself in the mirror atop the bureau, at the stone monkey on the lanyard knotted around her neck.

"Bastard," she says. It is unclear whom she is addressing. She pulls on some slacks and a T-shirt and goes back downstairs, heading into the sunny parlor, where Joan sits between two windows in a Morris chair, her leg tucked underneath her.

"I was just writing Willie about you," says Joan. Joan's letters, which contain coded names, places, and events, are forwarded and retranscribed by a series of intermediaries before ending up in Willie Clay's lonesome hands in Soledad. Her admission comes as a surprise to Tania.

Joan says, "I tell Willie you're getting stronger all the time. Every day there's a little bit more of you. Amazing." She points at the tablet with her pen. "But I was just saying that you know who and you know who must have put serious pressure today. It's a long time between a day like this."

Tania feels the muscles in her mouth jerk downward, as if pulling the tears from the ducts in her eyes.

"I thought to be honest you're like a fruit or a vegetable when I first met you. Then a little better, back on Ninetieth Street. Then *he*"— she jerks a thumb Teko-wise—"shows up, and it's bad all over, worse than before. Sheesh, I say, this girl's fucked up. Nothing really happening up there." She taps her forehead. "Don't cry, honey," she adds, closing the tablet to indicate that it's time to concentrate on making Tania stop crying.

"It was really *terrible* today," she says.

"People can really screw around with you. Some people, it's like their *job*."

Tania nods, sniffling.

"But you know, I know you've been through lots; every time you turn around it looks like you're starting all over someplace; you are kidnapped, your boyfriend is killed, you're here, you're there, wow. So I am bare in mind from the minute I meet you that you're together at all, like shampooing hair and eating. I know just from watching that there's hope. And"—a brief pause; Joan flings open her hands, fingers spread wide, to indicate the radiance of what she's saying—"there is."

"Your boyfriend and mine have the same name," says Tania.

"I know, honey," says Joan.

"Isn't that like the funniest coincidence?"

"It's funny. And either of us don't see them anymore. But it gets better. I'm telling you you're here to get better and you are."

LYDIA STOOD IN HALF-LIGHT. She was in the doorway leading to the lighted hallway, and he was standing on the other side of the doorway in the living room, a newspaper in one hand, just about to turn on a lamp, in fact. Her face was in shadow.

"You're going to meet with him, then?" she said. This is a conversation that they'd been having off and on. "No matter what I think of it."

"I think it's important to keep the lines of communication open."

"This is not the sort of person from whom I would have thought." She didn't finish. Then she said, "Lines of communication?"

Hank was going to meet with Popeye Jackson, paroled leader of a group called the United Prisoners Union. Jackson had earlier been named by the SLA as one of the people they wanted to oversee the food distribution program, and he gave off the impression of having multiple contacts and connections in the underground. When his parole was nearly revoked after a tainted bust for possession, Hank had printed an editorial supporting him.

Talk to the man. Find out what he has to say. Lydia's problem was that she was still awaiting a white knight who would ride to the rescue of an untainted daughter. Untainted being a crucial conceit. Hank had the impression when he spoke to his wife that she would prefer a dead child to the return of a living one who would shame her. White being a crucial conceit as well. The interpolation of a man like Jackson as a kind of medium suggested that the gap between the Galtons and their child was greater than that between the Galtons and Jackson, not to mention between Jackson and their child. Well, what an idea; Hank didn't find it any more palatable than Lydia did. But there she was. To a willfully ignorant observer, like Lydia, it appeared that Alice had simply vanished into a rabbit hole, equidistant, in the mystery of that other dimension, from every normal thing on the planet. But it was becoming clearer to Hank, from conversations with his reporters, with Stump, from the necessity of conversations with people like Jackson, that she was close, close enough for a Jackson to say credibly that he could find a way to get in touch. Seams of mistrust divided them, and at every level Hank would have to overcome these, mining further into the black earth of her disappearance.

Later he sat watching *Swing Time* on channel 20. Deadeye Fred Astaire, late for his own wedding. How easily the man could have played a gangster, the cold-blooded city boss from a Hammett novel. Hat cocked low and over one eye, he speaks, he sings, he pretends he can't dance. How well he lies, only to reveal the lie in the moment when he begins to move his body. And yet there is some complicity in the person lied to—for who wouldn't know Fred Astaire just from watching him walk across a room? But there is a definite, defining distance to him, as if in some unfeeling being a sublime gift had been vested, a gift that made everything easy, that made him pitiless. Astaire dances into the middle of a storm in the hostile nightclub, and all is well. All is well, Astaire says, legs, arms, and easy, deadly smile. All is well.

Guy is silent and fretful throughout the drive, gnawing his nails; the car has become a familiar enough space to them that Randi believes they have divined a way, sitting side by side for hours and days on end, to be apart from each other. And so they sometimes ride, hushed and remote, as if in separate rooms. Guy is a garrulous man, but prone to fits of cavernous brooding, and the indecipherable silences he enters without warning come when you might expect him to be at his chatty best: in cars, in elevators, in bed. Usually it's fine with her because there's always a lot of reading to get caught up with in a life. But today Randi happens to feel like talking, and Guy, what is the right way, he *parries* her every comment or cheery observation. She is feeling kind of put upon, to tell the truth. She hasn't breathed a word of protest about zipping back and forth across the country, not one complaint, and so she feels it's not unreasonable that Guy should give her a smile of acknowledgment when she points out the hawk wheeling overhead, or the horse peeking its nose out the back of its trailer, or the water tower painted red so that it looks like a giant tomato on stilts. Instead he grunts or shrugs or says ah with an exquisitely nuanced lilt to indicate a total lack of interest. She feels he ought to stop without hesitation at the roadside stands selling cherries and peaches, but he doesn't. Lunch, she wanted to try a place they'd been driving right by for years now. Homemade pizza. Homemade ice cream. Homemade pie. *Sounds good, doesn't it?* But Guy shoots by as if there were a hydrogen bomb inside.

They have not been back to the farm since dropping off the four fugitives. While not explicitly promising anything, Guy had suggested to Randi that their visits would be more frequent. Randi doesn't want to be a harpy about the whole thing, but she feels her central point is well taken: They ought to get some kind of enjoyment out of the two thousand dollars. Concerning money, Guy has all the sense of a drunken sailor; in her mind this old phrase of her mother's calls up the image of Guy, reeling through the streets, tossing handfuls of cash to his left and to his right. But she senses that what is operating here is a sudden wizening sense of prudence, not to say paranoia. The Cuba trip is suddenly off; they are "too hot." No sooner are Guy's parents back in Vegas than Guy is badgering them, trying to get information from those poor old people about his brother, Ernest: his whereabouts, his recent activities, any comments he may have made or questions he may have put to them about Guy ("No matter how innocent-sounding!"). Guy makes cheerily innocuous telephone calls from the apartment and then descends to the street to call the same people from a booth.

But what if the people he's calling's phones are tapped? Randi wonders.

"That's *their* problem," says Guy.

Until "the critical issues," as he puts it, are resolved, Guy apparently intends to spend most of his time sitting in the living room on Ninetieth, drinking Dr. Brown's Cel-Ray, watching the Mets on channel 9, and complaining bitterly about Tom Seaver's sciatica.

Drops the hand he's been tearing at back on the wheel and lifts the other to his lips. He worries and gnaws at the nails, shearing them far back from his fingertips. Occasional utterances from out of nowhere, but why bother. Totally incoherent. Here are the subjects of her husband and helpmeet's fragmentary conversation:

• *The daily Tom Seaver update.* They pitch him despite the pain Guy knows he's feeling in his hip and lower back. "Excruciating," Guy says. Excruciating.
• *The Bicentennial Minute gets everything wrong.* "It's a total opportunistic misread of history. You'd think for one lousy minute a night they could pick something where they weren't afraid to tell it straight. Typical Paley. Tiffany network, my ass."
• *Some newscaster in Florida blew her head off on TV and you can buy a copy of a film of her doing it for five grand.* "It's like porn, but not. You hear about that South American porn where they kill the chicks after they're done fucking them? Down in the slums of Rio they film these

guys doing these women, and then bam, they're sawing off fingers and disemboweling them right on camera. Guys, *couples*, the cream of society, lining up with sackfuls of dough to get into these secret screenings, glitzier than Graumann's Chinese. She's not fucking, the news chick, though, is the thing. So is it worth five thou? I think yeah, because she's a semicelebrity. Celebrities don't have to fuck. Yet."

• *Nixon, Nixon, Nixon.*

It's not until the afternoon that Guy announces "the plan." Guy chooses to deliver the offhand announcement immediately after they blow by the restaurant over her objections, and this move so compounds his naked unconcern for her feelings that Randi chooses to view it as a kind of touching testament to the utter sincerity of Guy's monomania. "The plan" involves, guess what, the expenditure of additional cash. "The plan" is that Guy will stay on at the farm for a couple of days, playing the part of the industrious writer checking in with his research assistants, while Randi drives north, across the New York state border, to rent yet *another* house. Why? Joan has called collect from a pay phone to let Guy know that Teko is freaking the fucking hell out: The propane man showed up and spent a good five minutes flirting with Tania. And plus *then* Tania met a little girl in the hills picking blueberries. So Teko belted her one in the face, which did not, Joan dryly suggested, mitigate the risk that they might be identified, though Teko now is making them all paint freckles on their bodies and Yolanda is in a trance of ascetic preparation, chomping on half sticks of gum to discipline her body and chanting seventeen-syllable terrorist haikus while running backward up the hills. This is how Guy puts it, anyway, tearing at his cuticles. It sounds terrible to him, suspicion and mistrust on the rise and the four of them out there in the sticks getting ready to kill one another. On top of all this, there is the general nervous tempestuousness of being a Guy Mock–type person in troubled times, and this is too much for Guy.

On the other hand, Randi has a far closer relationship than Guy with the statements that arrive each month from the bank and has been monitoring the erosion of their balance with something resembling, in the fine old phrase, mounting horror. To Guy this is a nonissue; money is never an object. She considers which has the greater palliative effect: her own frugal habits or Guy's spendthrift ways. On the basis of close observation, she would say that however terrific it might feel to her to save half a dollar here and there, it doesn't approach the deep fulfillment Guy evinces after he's dumped a nice fat wad of cash. In her opinion, the reason he has been being anxious and nudgy and weird is that the money is still there, burning a hole in his pocket.

Guy nearly overshoots the driveway, and in jerking the wheel to avoid missing it, he sends the old Bug's suspension into a sort of tailpipe-banging seizure. After this grand entrance, Randi notices that the place seems quiet. They enter the house and discover it in a state of fetid disarray: days' worth of dirty dishes in the sink and on the counters, garbage overflowing, dirt and mud all over the floors.

So much for the deposit.

"Well, they've been eating at least," Guy says. He holds up a chicken bone between thumb and forefinger.

"Thanks to Uncle Guy and Aunt Randi," says Randi.

Guy removes his cap and runs his hand through the hair thinning at the crest of his scalp. "Let us not measure the extent of our commitment," he says, affecting a round, oratorical tone. "Let us only measure its depth."

Yeah, yeah.

Guy roots around in the refrigerator, which, owing to a strange habit of Yolanda's, is full of uncovered plates containing half-finished meals. He pulls out a couple of bottles of Schmidt's. He opens the squat brown bottles and carries them out to the porch, where together they sit on a faded love seat to wait for the others. Side by side, again, though without all the business of shifting and signaling and checking mirrors. Randi remembers that when she and Guy were first together, he always joined her on the same side of a restaurant booth. Waitresses frequently acted put out by this, as if to serve them in this manner would fall foul of an honored eatery tradition. Not that new lovers, their whole world shrunk to two hearts' desire, concern themselves with mere mortals and their sense of trespass. And now here they were, still together, but long ago having entered the time and motion world in which those waitresses subsisted, everything a matter of mechanics.

"Where could they be? Aren't they supposed to be, you know?"

"Laying low? To say the least. Especially given the panic over the propane guy and the blueberry kid. You'd think they'd be under the beds or something."

"Oh, come on. They're not that paranoid, are they?"

Guy shrugs. "Maybe they are. We didn't look. Hey, if it were me, and I were here, I might have just killed us, waltzing in like this."

"Aren't they expecting us, Guy?"

"I wouldn't exactly say *not* expecting."

"But you think they might have killed us." Randi is not shocked, not ever, but what is the word, nonplussed.

"No, I think *I* might have killed us. What I think is it's a good thing *I* wasn't here to get the drop on us." Guy laughs.

"The drop on us. You're not the killer type."

"History's populated with the nonkiller types who kill in the clutch."

"Name me one."

"Ah, Alan Ladd in *The Deep Six*."

"Name another."

"Anthony Perkins in *The Tin Star*."

"One more."

"James Stewart in *The Man Who Shot Liberty Valance*."

"Nice try, but that was really John Wayne if I recall."

"Secret sharer."

Movie characters as history, certainly the memory of lanky Jimmy Stewart and little Alan Ladd coheres into something realer, more authoritative, far more satisfying than the frail group that Randi and Guy have arrived in Pennsylvania to gather up and replant. Except of course that one of their number *is* a star. Again Randi wonders what exactly it is that they have here in this particular revolution. Whenever she tries to envision what the future holds, it's never anything she can imagine having had its origin inside Teko's skull. You know? Guy advised her to forget about idealism.

" 'History is made by men, but they do not make it in their heads.' Speaking of Mr. Conrad. He daid."

Yeah, and does Guy think the SLA is going to make history?

"They already made it. It's made. I know, they're a highly suspect organization, politically speaking. Nonsensical. But the politics have to take a backseat to the show. Maybe they say they want to over-throw the government. Maybe they even believe it. But if anything, these guys' relationship to power is parasitic. Symbiotic, if you will, heh. What they really excel at is preempting the regularly scheduled programming. These guys are running with an idea that's been sort of sitting there unexplored at the margins of every single thing go-ing on since the Free Speech Movement. How do these nice kids from these nice families turn out this way? Before, it was always somebody else's kid, and the press is dutifully pasting together this blurry picture of bearded, long-haired filthoids who you could never in a million years imagine they belonged to Four-H or toasted s'mores over a campfire or had a catch with Dad, and the SLA ze-roes in on the story of one particularly nice girl and how she be-comes a little fanatic waving a gun around. It's the fucking movie of the week."

But it isn't a story, Guy. It's her real life.

"You should've seen her in that car riding across country, Randi. Anytime we saw a highway worker, a tollbooth clerk, she'd want to blast him for being a pig. She'd sit and X out the faces of executives in the financial pages of the paper. This nice kid sitting there with her Brearley accent rattling on about rich fascists. It could happen to her, it could happen to anybody's kid, is what the SLA is saying. And you bet it's history. Posterity's going to look back, and it'll be one thing if she dies out there in the wilderness, the terrorist princess. But it'll be a whole 'nother thing if she cops a plea, says "just kidding" and turns state's evidence and then after a couple of years in minimum goes back to the name and the millions and the uptight boyfriend with the mustache. If she's some Hillsborough matron in twenty-five years, remembering on Dick Cavett her crazy days as a revolutionary, then *that'll* be the story of the sixties, so called. That'll be the whole and only story."

And enfolded in events, are we simply awaiting our *interpretation*? To Randi it is looking less and less like an ordinary American after-noon, with wind bending the tops of the pines along the ridge and gently rustling the birches closer to the house. Now it is the doom-scape of history. She drove to Pennsylvania today, but Guy obvi-ously has been making a journey into history with a capital *H*. She stretches and then slowly, almost hesitantly, lays her head on Guy's shoulder. He switches his beer to his left hand and then, carefully, as if he's worried he'll scare her away, shifts so that his right arm is around her. They sit and wait for the revolutionary castaways.

The others arrive near dusk. They have been "on maneuvers" in the woods and fields. Teko is bursting with a steroidal energy, at the border of a jolly hostility familiar to Guy from the halftime locker room, an inflammatory and self-renewing aggressive confidence. He moves around the kitchen while dinner is prepared, joyous, plates and glasses clanking angrily together in his hands. Yolanda talks blandly with Randi about the kitchen garden, which is overgrown and neglected but still producing "fantastic" tomatoes, according to Yolanda. Joan has disappeared into the parlor. Guy listens to Teko recount the day's martial triumphs while keeping an eye on Tania, who sits silently at the kitchen table, her shadowed face further darkened by a large eggplant-colored bruise blooming on her left cheekbone.

Teko is feeling *so damned good* that Guy knows he'll have a tricky time selling the idea of moving to him and Yolanda. He's not shying away from a confrontation, exactly; this is the kind of conversation he's handled before, expertly. Usually the key, when delivering bad news is to appeal to their pride in their own self-possession. To say, you have to either bargain for this stuff, take it with equanimity, or you might as well go in for managing the produce department at the Alpha Beta. Hey, yeah—day in and day out with the vegetables; stacking them in neat pyramids, checking for rot, setting the misty spray mechanism to go off at designated intervals; remembering names, prices, varieties, growing seasons. Sell organics even; go to work at Rainbow or the Berkeley Bowl and turn the whole dreary enterprise into the politics of self-congratulatory smiles. Why not? Everybody loves a greengrocer. None of the stain, the flesh stink, of a butcher in his bloody white coat, and the hard hat to remind you that meat is a heavy industry manufacturing its product from the inert flanks of huge corpses. Now there's a challenge, to work amid the fury, the chain saw din, of the meatpackers! So usually that's the key. That's what the key is, to these type conversations. Guy indulges in his reverie as Teko paces and talks. He'll wind down, Guy thinks, and then I'll tell him. But Guy has the impression that Teko has been overcranked for a few days now.

"Joan's a natural," Teko is saying, flinging his arms out before him. "We're dealing with a question of motivation."

"Motivation," repeats Guy.

"She doesn't *want* to lead. I say, what about your responsibility to minorities? The SLA was conceived and recruited with minority leadership in mind. I want to assure you that my position as General Field Marshal is strictly an interim thing. I don't deserve to lead the revolution against white fascist corporate Amerikkka. Maybe if I was a homosexual. I only deserve whatever small role I'm assigned."

"They have these bugs," Yolanda tells Randi.

"She could take over right now if she showed only the slightest iota of interest. But as it is, she's a barely functioning guerrilla."

"I think she thinks her time with you is an interim kind of thing too," says Guy.

"Well, I wish you'd talk to her about getting with the program . . . I think if she just gave it a real try . . . She could be *dynamite*." Guy notices a shit-eating grin creep onto Teko's face.

"Everybody loves Joan," says Guy. This is true. Joan exercises a gravitational pull, the tasty mystery of good-looking people with dark secrets they hold close. Nobody is quite sure of Joan's history, including Guy. He knows about Manzanar, sat up straight at the mere mention of the magical name Hiroshima. OK, the chronology is a little screwed up, might be something as trivial and vain as Joan's lying about her age. The Big Three-Oh, or something. But this is something he believes she's entitled to, as a person displaced by events, a displaced person. He thinks of Negro cemeteries he's been to, the cockeyed stones lacking birthdates, lacking surnames, free of all the administrative litter that joined a life to its lineage. And now Teko's developed a little sheepish crush on her. Odd too, considering that from everything Guy's seen, and everything Joan has reported, Teko seems to resent everything about her. Well, maybe not so odd. If Guy's ever met a man with an angry little hard-on quivering at the center of his antagonism, General Teko is it. Well, he certainly wouldn't "talk to her." It's difficult enough to keep Joan functioning in this limited capacity without Guy's pushing her over the edge by blatantly pimping on behalf of the SLA and the concupiscent longing of its interim chief. He changes the subject.

"How about Tania?" He looks directly at her, to will her into the conversation. She doesn't return his gaze, continues to look so intently into the kitchen depths that Guy half turns his head in the direction of her stare, sees only the hutch with its smudged glass doors.

"Hopeless," sneers Teko. "Never going to be a guerrilla. Nev-ver."

"Well, you know, she might have value in another role." Guy says this offhandedly, without a trace of sarcasm, though the minute the words are out he's wondering if Teko really sees Tania's fulfilling no greater function than that of a foot soldier, if he's so intent on replenishing the ranks of his depleted army that he'll put Tania on the front lines, wherever *they* are. Guy never had a chance to meet Field Marshal Cinque, and in fact he's always taken a slightly patronizing view of the man, but it abruptly strikes him that whatever else you might say about the guy, the SLA's dead founder possessed a markedly more subtle sense of the uses to which the Missing Heiress could be put than Teko does. The famous photo of Tania hefting the carbine from her hip and training it on whatever her vacant stare encountered beyond the edge of the frame was infinitely more useful, more suggestive, more pregnant with violent potential than actually having her splatter a fucking sporting goods store with .30-caliber slugs in the middle of some petty shoplifting incident. For, what, sweat socks?

"What kind of role?" Teko is all suspicion now.

"The public face," Guy says, "of the SLA."

Teko drops his chin, shaking his head as if he were embarrassed, holding a closed-mouth smile. Then his hand comes up, a single argumentative finger raised and waggling, as he takes two strides toward Guy, to whom this collection of movements seems familiar, but unplaceable. Suddenly he flashes: Ralph Kramden.

O, the Great One: admonishing, reproving, cautioning, scolding, clarifying, elaborating, *expanding upon*; the farcical delusions of grandeur; the ideas and schemes, the preposterous crescendoing plotting, all from out of the Spartan home he returned to each day from the bus comp'ny, that room as bare as Beckett, that perfection of obscurity, with the wife who never, never once, let him forget that he was all impotence and frustrated ambition. Teko as Gleason! Guy would surely laugh out loud if he dared. How sweet it is!

Teko is saying, "See, I think what you're thinking is this is about her. When actually what it is, is it's about the revolution."

Guy edges away from where Teko has cornered him, pinned him

with his back to the counter, advancing with those two bullish strides. "*See, Norton, what it is,*" says Ralph Kramden, "*is it's about the revolution.*" Caramba! He joins Randi and Yolanda by the sink. Randi slices tomatoes, their skins creviced and blackened where rot has gotten to them but still shining and beaded with water droplets.

"Well, it's funny but that's what, well, I've been wanting to talk to you."

"Yeah?"

"We need to get working on this book."

"Yeah, yeah."

"And frankly I think we all know that, unfair as it may seem, the focus isn't exclusively going to be from the Symbionese perspective. I mean, 'Let the voice of their guns express the words of freedom.' It's a good point. In fact, an *excellent* point. There's your political program in a nutshell and you articulate it in the amount of time it takes a bullet to reach its mark. 'Say it with guns.' Madison Avenue would give its eyeteeth to come up with that one. But."

"But what? So what's your idea?"

"Well, first, everybody's heard that. And second, book-wise, you're going to have to lead with your strength. In a book people are actually going to want to pick up and read, the emphasis falls naturally on her."

He gestures at Tania. Teko is silent.

"I told you it was fucking bullshit, Teko," says Yolanda. "He's just trying to exploit us. To get to *her.*" She's been standing beside Randi, maintaining a posture of such chummy intimacy that Guy has been wondering whether she was even listening. She was. She strikes. Snakelike person. Yolanda has to crane her neck, looking beyond Randi and Guy, to address this to Teko, enhancing Guy's impression of a cobra, rearing.

"I'm not trying to exploit you. I'm trying to encourage you to develop and fully utilize your notoriety. And she's your best argument on your own behalf. She's living testimony to the power, the persuasiveness of the SLA viewpoint!"

The public face of the SLA massages her left wrist, her face expressionless.

"It's always about *her,*" says Teko, bitterly. "She's just *accidental.*" He shakes his head adamantly.

"Six figures is what they tell me. Knowledgeable people. Six figures for a story that accentuates the Tania. Not an exclusive focus, mind you, a *highlighting*. Six figures. And this is before serial rights, paperback rights, foreign rights, movie rights, the whole schmear."

"Don't believe it, Teko," says Yolanda. "They don't want to pay us. They want to *kill* us. They don't pay revolutionaries for their stories in this country. They silence them. Look at what happened in L.A."

"That was L.A.," says Guy. "They don't know from publishing there. They move in with their newsreel cameras, get their shaky blurry footage, and, you know, that's good enough for them. But in New York they know a story isn't really whole, isn't done justice, until a topnotch writer publishes a twenty-thousand-word think piece and later expands it into a book."

He decides to push it a little.

"What if I were to tell you that I heard **Norman Mailer** was on his way to JFK to grab the first flight to the Coast the minute he heard about the shoot-out? **Tom Wolfe** was desperate for a piece of it. **Hunter Thompson** expressed a strong interest. **John Lennon** wanted to hang out with you guys. These are top-quality writers and in **Lennon's** case I guess a top-quality cultural raconteur–type star person."

"John Lennon!" Teko seems impressed.

"I mean, there is a definite clamor for this. The story is wanted. People definitely want it. But people also have certain understandable priorities. To a firm doing business in a high-rise building on the island of Manhattan you have to grant the right to determine its own priorities based on a mixture of experience and common sense and an altogether acceptable amount of mercantile trepidation. They want to be able to position a book so it can compete to its best advantage against what are frankly some really schlocky titles that have come out, paperbacky supermarket rack kind of junk."

"And just where does that leave you?" asks Yolanda, a shrewdness flickering across her features. "Where does that leave you if Mailer or whoever does the book?"

Guy draws himself up, swelling with an approximation of dignity. "Everything I've done, I've done with your best interests in mind. I have an interest in the book, yeah, but that's not a secret thing. We discussed it day one, back in Berkeley. If Mailer's the guy you feel you want to go with, then I'm Mailer's lackey. If you and Lennon

decide to go ahead with the revolutionary opera that Johnny"—
Johnny!—"seems so fired up about, I'll tune his guitar if that's where
there's a place for me. Or I can pull out right now. I'm a role player."

There is silence for a moment as Teko considers this information.

"What I propose," says Guy, "is that we withdraw to another location and get down to work."

"Another location?" says Yolanda. "Where?"

"In my opinion, the less you know, the better." Here Guy shifts
ever so slightly so that he can peer out the window over the sink, as
if scanning the kitchen garden for intruders.

"Why?"

"Well," says Guy, "those security breaches, for one thing."

"Security breaches?"

"The propane guy, the blueberry kid."

"Do you think it's that serious?"

Guy pauses, for effect, privately savoring the puzzle piece, its
thorny shape, he is about to drop just so into its place.

"There are other concerns."

"Like what?"

"Better for you not to know. But the choice is yours. You have this
place through October first. Or you can come to the new location.
In either case, your whereabouts are safe with us, but with us having
rented the place under our own name and all, sooner or later things
will be traced back to us. But don't dwell on it. Talk it over. Make up
your minds. And for courage, think about the book. Picture it between covers, full buckram, with a dust jacket, with blurbs on the
back. That's what always does it for me."

"It would be like *Prairie Fire*," says Teko.

"Yeah, but with a little extra oomph," says Guy.

On a saucer before her, Tania is absently arranging sardines she
takes from an open tin. The oily fish ring the dish along its rim, and
in the center she has arranged a column of three, their heads facing
in alternating directions.

"Farrar, Straus and Giroux," says Guy. "Good. You're thinking
ahead."

With that, Guy walks out of the kitchen, assuming a stately gait
and maintaining the upright posture that together help subordinate
his anxiety, his lack of will, his basic pointlessness to levels of near
imperceptibility. What is perceptible—what is in fact plain as fuck-

ing day—is that he is a person of *substance* whose pronouncements carry some *gravity*, and he notes with satisfaction that as a measure of that *substance* and *gravity*, dinner seems all but forgotten about. Behind him the kitchen already sounds—how should he put it?—emotionally evacuated. No prep sounds, no water running, no eating sounds, no chairs scraping across the floor, no conversation. A lunatic thrill accompanies the exercise of this sort of power, as insignificant as it may be. He's a ballsy guy who takes his recklessness to the brink and teeters . . .

On some level, Guy has been dishonest—good, frank word—with Randi about the reasons for the move's necessity. With Guy Mock there is always an additional level.

Randi, though, has long ago realized that she is accustomed to Guy's tendency toward vagueness. It's almost as if she would rather *not* know. What had her awareness of Erica Dyson netted her? Shit, what had it done for Guy, other than to provide him with a pirate's scar slanting rakishly over one eye? At this point all she wants is to sleep in the same bed for one month straight. If they're not going to be able to pull that off, then she doesn't necessarily need to know the true and correct reasons why. Perhaps, in the fullness of time—a phrase that delights Guy because it makes delay and procrastination sound so right, so just, so principled—he will come clean with her. Perhaps on his deathbed, Randi thinks.

The reason that Guy has to send Randi out to rent another house in the middle of the season is an inapt admission Guy made to his older brother, Ernest, in Las Vegas, Nevada, earlier in the summer.

Happily subsidizing the excesses of the Organization of Petroleum Exporting Countries, Guy had zipped cross-country yet again, this time to visit his parents, to reassure himself of their silent complicity in his activities and incidentally to have a dip in their pool and slip into their Jacuzzi to submit his genitals to the constant warm caress of its jets. There he'd come face-to-face with Ernest.

"Oh, it's you," his mother said. She was dressed, just a little before noon, like a woman who intended to forcefully communicate her eternally thwarted desire to eat lunch at a nice restaurant. Guy leaned to kiss her but before the lying gesture had a chance to fully take shape she turned from him at the threshold and walked into the unit. He followed her, swinging the olive drab canvas poke that held his clothes and toiletries.

"Oho! The prodigal returns." There Ernest sat in the living room, nice and settled, looking very Vegasy in crisp new khakis, loafers, and a sport shirt. At his feet were shopping bags from Penney's and a couple of other stores, filled with shirt cardboard and tissue paper and other packaging. Ensconced, is how he looked. The shopping trip had probably happened in the morning. That was Ernest's great time, a smile for everybody and a slap on the back. Their parents fried his eggs and poured his coffee for him, that son of a fucking bitch. It was appalling. The guy was a bullshitter who honed his bullshit to its brightest burnish in the a.m., and Guy sometimes felt that of all the effortful attempts he'd made to get his parents to recognize one kind of truth or another, the most effortful of these attempts occurred whenever he was trying to convince them of the mendacious dissemblance that charged the nucleus of Ernest's character. The Breakfastime Ernest remained embedded in their consciousness as a sort of Norman Rockwell son, paper opened to the sports page and propped up against the sugar bowl.

Now Ernest held a tall glass filled with ice and club soda colored with what looked to be a splash of bourbon. Guy knew these as Ernest's visiting-Mom-and-Dad highballs. He would sit around the house the entire day, pacing himself, a subtle drunk, steadily emptying and refilling these junior prom drinks. Around five he'd go and lie down, pulling an electric blanket over himself in the frigid cold of their parents' bedroom, and sleep off the muzzy edges of the drunk until he awoke an hour or so later, sharp and mean enough to make their mother cry over dinner. Then he'd take the car and head out to the bars, where he'd drink until he fell off his stool.

"Hello, Ernest."

"I like the look. You look real natural, Guy-Guy. Like a guy who crashes the Haight-Ashbury Free Clinic for the atmosphere."

"Does he get a hello? He walks in, he's driving since the crack of dawn, and the long-lost brother is all over him."

"I greeted you when you came in. Guess you want me to try again. Hi, there, little brother. And now we resume our broadcast day."

Ernest paused to drink. Ice chimed.

"That is some mop. It looks like dune grass on that bald head of yours. C'mere, Guy-Guy. I want to pull your hair, see if it's real. Like Santa's beard."

"Still hung up on Santa, Ernest? Explains the back-to-school clothes. Did you get some galoshes too? A nice pencil case?"

Mrs. Mock explained. "We took Ernest to the shopping center this morning. Because there was a sale."

"My desert ensemble."

"You look more like a Wilkes-Barre golf pro."

"Ah, ha. Ha."

"He needed some clothes. You boys *need* clothes."

Ernest sipped his drink. "I'm sure Mom can drive you over to the Goodwill after lunch."

"Oh, lunch," said Mrs. Mock.

"Lunch sounds good," said Guy.

"I don't see any sign of your father. And where is your lady friend, Guy?"

"*Randi? Randi*, you mean?"

"Of course that's who I mean. Why, Guy, you didn't bring that other young lady friend of yours back here, did you?"

" 'Other young lady friend'?" Ernest smiled at him over the drink. "What sort of friend?" Guy felt sudden, atrocious pain in the vicinity of several small, little-known organs.

He smiled back. "I have lots of friends. Friends are good, Ernest. Friends are our friends. Only you would consider the having of a friend to be an inherently suspicious thing."

"I don't think we can count on your father right now. He said something about cleaning out the rain gutters," said Mrs. Mock.

"My guess is he's a no-show," ventured Ernest.

"They have rain gutters in Las Vegas?"

"Form's sake," said Ernest.

"What gets in them that you have to clean them?"

"Fallout?"

"*Is* she coming? Should we hold lunch for her?"

"Who? *Randi? Randi* is not here."

"Who really is?" Ernest emptied the glass and rose from his chair. Guy watched. He seemed steady on his feet. He figured he could chalk the belligerence up to his unexpected arrival. Was it belligerence even? Guy had discovered that as often as not, a provocation from Ernest was intended as an invitation to a special, dangerous genre of fellowship. Ernest conversed best, most fluently and easily, with strangers seated twenty feet down the bar, via digs he delivered in the direction of the mirror directly opposite, while occasionally reading in the eyes of a wary bartender the telemetry gauging the reaction to his comments. Declining an invitation to share in the interests of a man who enjoyed being punched in the face required a certain amount of tact and discretion, neither of which was Guy's strong suit.

Surprisingly, maybe, lunch was uneventful. Mrs. Mock devoted herself to preparing and serving the meal, Ernest read the newspaper, explosively clearing his throat from time to time, and Guy stared through the sliding glass doors at the blanching sun that threw itself over the shadowless day. Afterward Guy put on his trunks and went out to the pool, where he swam laps. He paused in the middle of the pool after a while and, treading water, spotted his father behind the cabins. Mr. Mock moved forward, but erratically, pausing every couple of steps to do something that looked as if he were trying to get dog shit off his shoe. As he approached, Guy realized that he was smoothing with his foot the gravel that lined the walkway on one side. He was wearing a faded dress shirt and a pair of jeans that he had cut the legs off unevenly. Guy waved, but the old man took no notice of him.

"We're in Libya," Ernest said later, sitting with Guy at the bar of the Golden Charm Casino, which consisted of the bar and four slot machines. "A 'hot spot,' as they say."

"Who's in Libya?" said Guy. It was around one in the morning and they were very drunk. Guy felt himself leaning forward with the eagerness of a child, listening to Ernest. He sipped his beer and stuffed a handful of dry roasted peanuts into his mouth.

After dinner Ernest had grabbed Guy by the hair, rapped hard on his forehead with a pair of knuckles, and invited him out for a drink. Here they were. Ernest was feeling chatty.

"A CQA op, it was. I'd been doing blunt and edge work, very comfortable with it, but I wanted to branch out. They had a triple S op—safe, simple, and secret—and I wanted to give it a shot."

"Who had?"

"They said, can you do falls?"

"Who said?"

"I said, you give me a clear seventy-five feet of vertical passage and a hard surface and I'm your man."

"Whose man?"

"I arrange with the subject to meet. It's different. Blunt and edge, you have either a simple or a chase situation. Blunt, usually simple. The guy turns his back, you clock him in the temple with a hammer. Edge, you are frequently teaching a lesson."

"Teaching who a lesson?"

"Edge, there's severing involved, and mess. Gory stuff. Subtlety is not an issue. As a technique, it's inherently terroristic. So you are in a chase or guarded situation. An unhappy, resistant subject, running, begging, bleeding. You get used to it, and you don't—this was always a big plus for me—you don't have to hone your interpersonal skills. But in this case, like I say, it's simple and secret. And I am not used to setting up meetings. So I am, you know, a little tentative."

Here Ernest called the bartender over. Like all bartenders seemed to for Ernest, this guy immediately dropped everything—in this instance a lengthy and highly vivid, yet still suspiciously adumbrated description of his personal collection of intaglio prints, delivered to an off-duty chorine, half in the bag and so statuesque Guy would have sworn she was a transvestite—to rush right over and take Ernest's order. Guy couldn't figure it. Ernest wasn't an overgenerous tipper. In his new J. C. Penney clothes, he was dressed about as well as he ever was. He did not feign camaraderie with bartenders or sympathy for their ontological condition. Something about Ernest made bartenders come running, though.

"Wild Turkey 101 on the rocks," he said, "and another Shirley Temple for the kid. They said, Ernest, the subject drinks. This is a perfect cover: case your height, get him loaded, take him up there, and drop him. Sounds easy, right? But you know how hard it is to get a drunk drunk in Libya? Hard is how hard."

"*Who* said?"

"But I figure I'll manage. They fly me in on Shitheel Air, sitting with the goats and the chickens, just like everybody else. I got a seersucker suit and a Canadian passport and I'm carrying an old Pentax for a prop. I got an envelope full of cash. Bad news is, every place you go, you're hemorrhaging dinars. To get an entry visa. To get a cab. To get a table. To get a menu. To get a room. Good news is, with enough dinars you can get anybody to get anything for you. Get it? Makes that envelope skinny as a mermaid's pussy, but in the end I get my booze. See?"

Guy raised his glass of beer and moved it from side to side, a gesture meant to indicate comprehension, a concentration of attention, an eagerness to hear the story unfold.

"Now, my powers of persuasion are, OK, they leave a little to be desired under the very best of circumstances, but it is not real difficult to finesse a drunk into ascending to a great height with you. I told him I had a business proposition to discuss. I'm a Western stranger in a seersucker suit and a fedora, a universally familiar type, and it sort of follows that I would have a business proposition to discuss. Now, my great height. For my great height I had picked out an old converted villa with thick walls and a marble staircase and an old-fashioned elevator in a cage that we could ride in the pretty predictable event of drunken fatigue." He built the place with his hands as he spoke. "Among other things the place housed the Tripoli bureau of the Associated Press, for a steady and inconspicuous influx of pushy Westerners like myself, and an outfit called Mustafa Importing, which supposedly is the firm I'm supposedly doing business through and which I happen to know is closed on that day. Oh, what a shame. They appear to have stepped out. Would you care to come up to the roof with me, have a cigarette? I believe there is an excellent harbor view. Whatever bullshit. The building rises six fucking stories above a street made of opportunely solid cobblestones. It has a parapet about yea high."

His hand hovered about three feet above the ground. Guy looked down the bar. The bartender was back with the chorus girl, who had been joined at the bar by a man wearing a black leather vest and a sort of sombrero with fringed balls dangling from the brim.

"I am *nervous*. The guy's drunk, I don't think he's at all leery, but all I can think is: can't pull this off I'll have to go back to blunt and edge. Which is fine when you're first breaking in, but after a while you realize that for all the anatomical knowledge involved there is just not a whole lot of prestige in cracking someone in their temple or severing their spinal cord in the cervical region. People don't respect it, they don't see the nuance, they don't understand how improvisational in nature it can be. Rightly or wrongly, as a specialty it has zero cachet."

Guy crossed his arms and laid his head on top of them. Soon the bartender was over, rapping sharply on the bar with a shot glass near Guy's ear.

"No sleeping in here, buddy."

"He's all right," said Ernest. "He's listening."

"Listen sitting up."

Guy raised himself. He felt unusually tired. He wanted to go home and fall asleep on the couch. He felt the beginnings of a hemorrhoid massing sinisterly on his anus, like a rehearsal for cancer. Ernest's story kept moving forward, but it had grown impossibly ponderous, like a glider made of scrap iron. Ernest had been giving him the foreign intrigue routine for hours. The formal rigor of a haiku—

> Soldier in mufti
> arrives on a decrepit
> (airplane, ferry, bus).
>
> A mission of death,
> the locale's meanest season,
> grim job to do well
>
> Soldier: a brother,
> a good son, a brave comrade;
> kills out of duty.
>
> Blade of bright sunlight,
> now red, as a sunset!
> night covers all.

—with none of the brevity and lightfootedness, Ernest's voice steady and unwavering as he unpacked the stories like merchandise from a sample case. Guy found that who he was sitting tiredly next to was a drunken braggart, not the bold raconteur of memory.

"He sits on the parapet, smoking," Ernest was saying. "My chance is come. I bend down like to tie my shoe. Then I grab his ankles. I lift them up, get them above the level of the parapet, where his whole center of gravity shifts, he's leaning back, the fear just caught in his throat, terrible, nothing's coming out, he's just seized up. I look him in the eye. The souls meet for a sweet adios! Then I give him a shove and he's gone, goodbye."

"Wow," said Guy, without enthusiasm, watching his beer going flat.

"So." Ernest elevated his chin to stare down at Guy. "How's the Institute of Soviet Socialist Sports?"

"We're just fine."

"You, the Olivetti, and the file cabinet."

"A Smith-Corona, actually."

"Very patriotic. I approve."

"Yeah, well, you can laugh, but personally I think we're doing some important work. I think we're ready to start to branch out a little. I think we've set forth our ideas pretty clearly and I think they lend themselves to extrapolation so that they can be applied to society as a whole. I think we've built a solid foundation to work on—"

"Oh, ho." Ernest waved out a match, dismissing Guy. "Nobody needs help latching onto these parlor pink *ideas* of yours, Guy-Guy. Everybody knows these *ideas*. The whole fucking world has picked up on these *ideas*; these *ideas* are what Leonard Bernstein is talking about with Teddy Kennedy over dinner at Kay Graham's house. These *ideas* are what Mr. and Mrs. Front Porch are paying to send their kids to Columbia and Ann Arbor to learn. *Ideas*, he says. You got a little niche, and you're working it, man. Don't bullshit me."

"I'm not," said Guy. "We see things differently, is all." Guy felt as if the effort to defend himself, to strain clarity from the murky impressions filling his head, was too much to ask of himself. That plus this same hardy argument had reappeared, ghostlike, so many times, and its materialization here had outpaced any memory of it that might have emerged to warn him.

"Your *ideas* are all about having more *ideas*. I mean, what are you actually doing?"

Guy noted: *He had only had to say the word* ideas *exactly once to provoke this sarcastic ricocheting.* (So relax, let it go.)

Guy noted: *Such a reaction was the one predictable general effect of having had* ideas. (So let it go already.)

Guy noted: *Whether from the right or the left, the* ideas *always take it on the chin.* (No problem, then, just letting it go.)

Guy noted: *This is not the time, the place, or the person for his candor.* (Drop it, veer off, let it go!)

What he said was, "You want to know what I'm 'actually doing,' secret agent man?" Then he told him, rewinding the tape back to the day in June when he'd first offered his assistance and providing details on the cross-country trips, the Manhattan stay, the Pennsylvania farmhouse not far from where the two of them had grown up.

"Ah," said Ernest.

"Really," said Ernest.

"How interesting," said Ernest.

It was later, as the desert dawn began to light up the living room and Guy huddled under his blankets on the couch, that it came to him: Ernest had copped that whole Tripoli rooftop scene from *A Kiss Before Dying*. The chutzpah: they'd seen it together at the Ritz, in Scranton, back in 1956. With Robert Wagner, a young Joanne Woodward, and an old Mary Astor. Also Virginia Leith, who later was to achieve a certain renown portraying a chatty severed head in a bathing cap in *The Brain That Wouldn't Die*. The son of a bitch, Guy thought, that son of a fucking bitch.

So in effect it is no more than the shape and will of his own big mouth that Guy is seeking to evade here as July comes to its close. The next couple of days are a dumb rush as the company prepares to depart, waiting to learn the location of whatever place Randi manages to find for them. Now he encounters for the first time the SLA's disturbing propensity to rapidly accumulate and then leave behind vast amounts of evidence—papers, mostly, notable for their blazing, suicidally self-incriminating contents. And so dreary. In a marbled-cover composition book he finds Teko's "Revolutionary Diary."

Wed., July 24

Day clear and mild. Added approx. 5 lbs. sand to supplement dumb-bell weight. I was only one who tried: T. made typical complaints. J. absent at fall out, must speak to her again. Y. claims wrist injury. Ran 3 miles, w/ankle weights.

Inventoried provisions: need corn flakes. (Kellogs!)

After lunch found T. and J. in living room. T. reading "Fear of Flying", J. bourgie book on Quebec separatism movement. Unsatisfactory reaction to my vocal disapproval. Then advised them that it was time for Criticism/Self Criticism session. Very disrespectful, undisiplined response overall (esp. J.)

Dinner: rice & beans. T's wash: burned rice not off bottom of pot. Must speak to her again. Too much "relaxing" as usual after dinner:

	BEER	CIGARETS
self:	I	III
Y:	I	IIII
T:	II	IIIIII (!)
J:	II	IIIII

(Objection: expense, physical readiness, usual disipline.)

Clear night, many stars.

What do we want from such documents? Guy wonders. What do you think you may one day need to remember about your life? Major Scobie keeping the record of his fifteen years in Sierra Leone in the tin box beneath his bed. What good did all that minutiae do him? Guy chucks the notebook back onto the mound of papers on the floor in Teko and Yolanda's bedroom, sending the stuff near the top sliding down around his ankles. Joan comes to the doorway and stops short; she won't come in here.

"Basically we're all set," she says.

"I knew you'd be."

"Will you look at all this shit?"

"How come you're so tidy?"

"You haven't heard? I'm a bourgeois."

"Oh, yeah," Guy says vaguely. He sits down on the edge of the rumpled bed, starts, reaches under the blanket, and pulls out a dirty athletic supporter.

"For *what*?" asks Joan.

Guy drops the jockstrap. "Where's your protégée?"

"Tania's out. She goes over to the trees. Try to be alone out there."

"And she's doing how?"

"Don't blame me responsible."

263

"I'm not holding you responsible. Though you are a responsible person. The only one around including me I might add."

"Oh, shut up. I cheer her up. There's a real person inside there someplace. But, you know, the thing, though, is, like, I'm thinking it probably isn't the person who it was before."

"Before Cujo died?"

"Before she got snatched."

"No shit." Guy says this sincerely. He trolls his eyes like a pair of searchlights over the small, pretty woman in the doorway.

"She's figuring it out. Who she's got to be. When she isn't sure, she just switches off. Drives them"—she nods at the pile of Teko and Yolanda's papers, their metonymic essence—"nutter-butters. They make her do things. Run! Carry! Jump! Then she's turned back on, starts up talking—they get even madder. Smack her in the face, which I tell her she hasn't got to take."

"They don't hit you, do they?"

"I told that little shrimp you ever touch me I'll kill you in your sleep."

Guy returns to Tania. "So, figuring it out, hmm."

"Not everybody gets to grow this big strong tree of a personality like you, Guy. Some people are always having a new one they work on."

"You a tree? Or a whadayacall, a sapling?"

Joan has correctly intuited that Guy has never, for a moment, doubted who he is. A touch of fatalism in that. Why, ultimately, his career as an athlete topped off at the level it did. He could never articulate the physical striver's questioning of his own identity, his measurement of his own worth on a scale of millimeters, or hundredths of a second; he'd never needed to see if the difference between winning and losing would embody itself in him, make him, by the breadth of a hair, a new man nothing like the one who'd touched his feet to the floorboards that morning. He hadn't been interested, an attitude that could piss coaches off in record time. Now here you have a Joan. Life is a whole bunch of forks in a whole bunch of roads for her. Who to be next? How strong? How brave? In the younger woman she would have to have seen something of her own self, in the constant adaptation, the knack for living.

The rattle of the Bug comes to them from the road below and grows louder as the little car turns into the driveway and climbs the rise toward the house. Soon they'll find out what they're about. Soon they'll be safe.

Sᴀʀᴀ ᴊᴀɴᴇ ᴍᴏᴏʀᴇ ɪs seated in the Learning Center at the Palo Alto headquarters of the California Society of Certified Public Accountants, where she is enrolled in a CPE course in estate taxation. Other accountants surround her in the fluorescent gloom of the windowless basement room. There is something wrong with the air conditioning down here in the Pit, as she has heard its subterranean denizens, the mailboys and shipping clerks and pressmen, refer to it, and the door is propped open to allow air to circulate. A mail clerk, a tall, good-looking boy wearing a T-shirt that says ᴄᴀᴍᴘ ᴛᴀʟᴄᴏᴛᴛ, has brought in a standing fan and set it up in a corner where it blows stale air across the room, ruffling the edges of their papers as it oscillates, describing a forty-five-degree arc. The boy's colleague calls out to him down the corridor, and his response is clear but incomprehensible: "Sir Jade, Sir Jade."

The issues concerning the field of estate planning and taxation that the sole practitioner faces today are. Who gives a shit. She hears the sharp *crack-crack-crack-crack* of the equipment through the wall as it cuts freshly printed brochures and stacks them. There is a smell of ink and oiled machinery. She just wants to get this crap over with, get her four hours in so that she can maintain her certification. Already the State Board of Accountancy has sent her a semithreatening piece of official correspondence, claiming that she has not kept up with her Continuing Professional Education requirements. And of course it's the CPA society that offers the courses. All in cahoots. You can bet that if she were with Touche Ross or Coopers & Lybrand she would not be sitting in some stifling basement room with a bunch of nose-picking dimwits. And she has a busy day. After she signs out, she has to head up to the city to meet with Popeye Jackson about People in Need, ask him a few disingenuous questions about the location of certain fugitives from justice, call the *Examiner* to leave a message for Hank Galton, and then drop by the FBI office to be debriefed by Tommy Polhaus. And then there's the dry cleaning.

At lunch Sara Jane first follows some of her colleagues, who wander down the corridor to the break room. She catches a glimpse of the inside of the shipping room, where the walls are festooned with cutout pictures from *Playboy, Oui, Penthouse,* you name it. One of the moron clerks inside, operating a curious device that shoots out measured lengths of prewetted packing tape at the touch of a button, gazes at her without interest. She opens the door to enter the break room but finds nothing there but her awkward-looking classmates and two vending machines.

Instead she goes upstairs to have a smoke in the fresh air. The building is on Welch Road, right across from Stanford University Hospital, and on the second floor several doctors have their offices, according to the directory mounted on the lobby wall. A woman, her head and face swathed in bandages, with glossy dark contusions under both eyes, is helped out of the elevator by a woman in scrubs and guided toward a waiting car. Curious. As she smokes, Sara Jane watches a Cadillac pull into the lot and park, and a middle-aged man steps from it to help another woman, similarly bandaged and bruised, out of the passenger seat. She emerges gingerly, grabbing hold of the man's proffered arm with two hands, and together the two of them walk slowly from the large gleaming auto toward the entrance of the building. As they pass her, the man gives Sara Jane a slightly suspicious once-over. These dames are in serious discomfort with their busted-up faces. All at once Sara Jane remembers some *Reader's Digest* article she once read describing the aftermath of certain types of plastic surgery. Blackened eyes from shattered noses. Stitched-up faces, the raw flesh employed as a sling against gravity. How foolish and pathetic. Going to a doctor to let him break your nose with a mallet. How very Palo Alto.

She tries to sign out forty minutes early, during the open book test, and the instructor nails her. Total cahoots; no doubt he gets a piece of the action too, of course. The discussion gets a little heated, and he asks her out into the hallway. What is the difference? She has finished her test and is a grown person with responsibilities. She could tick them off, just to see his eyes go wide, this dumb bunny from Bakersfield. Estate planning, how presumptuous, blechh.

Sara Jane double-parks her car on Twenty-fourth Street and charges into the dry cleaner's, her ticket held at the ready. The pinheaded man behind the counter looks up without even a vestige of a smile on his sour puss. Only something like $250 a year she spends here. She decides to check carefully for stains because she knows she pointed them all out.

Oh here's one.

She leaves a muumuu behind because sometimes you have to make the point that you won't just take it from them all the time. There are other dry cleaners in this city. There are synthetic fabrics that require only a brush or a sponging down and need never be ironed and so the dry cleaner man needs to get it into his head that he should be thankful for her repeat business and for an old-fashioned girl's taste in old-fashioned textiles. He takes the garment back from her and hangs it up and then patiently copies her driver's license number onto her check. What is that going to tell you? How does a driver's license number protect you from a bum check? It is all part of control. The numbers are gathered here at the very bottom of things and circulate upward to the heights of power. Driver's license information. Social Security numbers. Telephone exchanges. She signs the check "Alice Galton." Just to see if he notices.

"Sally, you are overwrought."

"I go into the dry cleaner's for two minutes. One, there's a stain on an item. Two, he requests my personal driver's license information. Height and weight and date of birth? What does this have to do with accepting personal checks?"

"Sally."

"Three. I come out with my bundle and there is a man in a little pizza delivery cart putting a ticket on my windshield. I think you could say I am on police business."

"I don't know if I could agree with that."

"You could agree with it but you won't. I do not see why you can't secure me with a placard or a sign. They give these to teachers. They give these to handicapped persons in wheelchairs. They give these to roving reporters."

"That would be the police. The FBI has to go to the local police to get their parking permits as well."

"What are they called? Those pizza carts?"

"It's called a Cushman."

"If I go to the man in the Cushman and tell him I am on FBI business, will I get a placard?"

"I sincerely doubt it and I hope you'll consider how inadvisable it would be for you to do such a thing."

"I think I'm entitled to some recompense."

Thomas Polhaus reaches behind him to take his suit jacket off the back of his chair and gets his billfold from the inside pocket. The ticket Sara Jane Moore has thrown onto the surface of the desk before him is for ten dollars, and he removes a five and five singles from the billfold.

"I would think the FBI would have a more formal way of disbursing petty cash."

"We probably do. Would you like to wait the usual two to four weeks?"

"I have just had a bad day. You don't have to make fun of me."

Polhaus says, "I'm not making fun of you. I'm trying to get you to relax and see things in perspective. Everybody gets a ticket now and then. No one's ever happy about it. And while I'm always delighted to see you, you know that the reason for your coming here today wasn't to appeal your parking citations or to air your grievances concerning the shoddy practices of Noe Valley dry cleaning establishments. Come on, Sally. I'm counting on you."

"It is a lot of pressure on me. And then there are these aggravations, which I just want you to know about because it goes right to the matter of difficulty." She looks as if she might be about to cry. That wouldn't be unusual.

"Nobody ever said that doing the right thing is easy."

"But does the State Board of Accountancy have to weigh in with its two cents right at this juncture?"

"Sally, what are we talking about?"

"I am taking supposedly required courses at this advanced age of my career in a Palo Alto basement where they perform disfiguring surgeries. That's what. What kind of a day is that?"

"Maybe this can be the best part of the day."

And it can. Polhaus knows he can lay a hand on her wobbly instability, restore purpose, direction, and meaning to a sorry and disconnected existence. It's a bad moment when an ordinary person suddenly has to confront the way that the everyday evades significance. How unaccompanied, how unheralded, an ordinary life can be. Sometimes all that a person deciding whether to become an informant needs to push her over the line is the belief that life won't always be able to disregard everything she says or does. Life doesn't always have to be so infuriating; one doesn't have to suffer unaccompanied. There is actually a written record, kept in a big building, guarded by men with guns. To these armed men, this record is important, and that is the ultimate rebuttal to habit and its dissatisfactions. Half the "informants" he deals with are lonely zanies, dialing from remote phone booths out on the Great Highway or the basements of faded hotels on Bush Street—grandmothers and secretaries, he imagines them, dockworkers and retired animal control officers, old men from the Avenues who see menace in the odd parcel someone sets out on the sidewalk with the trash. They call the Bureau to let them know. They report seditious conversations they overhear in Justin Herman Plaza or Union Square. If it's mysterious and baffling and doesn't quite seem to fit the definition of a crime as set forth by that Webster's of the everyday, prime-time TV, call the FBI. Call early, call often, and don't forget to ask for your case number. We like making them up on the spot.

But Sally Moore is exceptional. The nutburger who through a serendipitous series of accidents manages to find herself in precisely the right place to serve the Bureau's purposes. There were plenty of middle-aged folks whose heads had been screwed up by the last ten years. Drugs. Politics. Vietnam. Civil rights. Long hair. You name it, there were a thousand causes, ideas, and substances into which an American human could disappear. But when, as inevitably happened, they finally became angry with their exciting new lives and, eager to turn in some coconspirator in their frustration, picked up the phone, the Bureau usually found itself with a misdemeanor drug case on its hands, which it routinely referred to local authorities. But now Sally is interesting. She has all the screwy hallmarks of the sort of person who'll call up to report a few pot plants in the next backyard, or even an imaginary nuke in a suitcase, but instead of bailing out of the Telegraph Avenue scene and heading for a commune in Mendocino or a master's program back East, this oddball manages to get herself a job keeping the books for the People in Need program and, moreover, manages to ingratiate herself not only with both Henry Galton and Lud Kramer, the program's administrator, but with Popeye Jackson and other radicals, jailbirds, and bad hats the SLA had stipulated to oversee the distribution. All this Thomas Polhaus learned in the course of the routine sub rosa check he'd ordered on the PIN operation and its key workers and volunteers. It piqued his interest, but then what really got him was when he learned that Hank Galton quietly had sought out Sally Moore on his own, to serve as a liaison between himself and Jackson. Hank old pal, Polhaus had thought, how could you? Thought we were going to share and share alike. Of course the Bureau's (subordinate, minor, marginal) role in the L.A. firefight had somewhat dulled the Galton family's keenness to cooperate with it and then there had been Saxbe's asinine comment about Alice's being a common criminal.

But Polhaus thinks that he's noticed something changing in Hank, something he might have missed if it hadn't been for the tensions now evident between the Galtons. Lydia is one tough cookie. He'd become aware of that when she accepted another term as a UC regent in contravention of an SLA directive. If the kid ever comes home, Lydia is ready and willing, even eager, to do what she can to send her to jail. Polhaus thinks that he detects in Lydia a certain dislike for her missing daughter. It's almost as if the distaste she evinced at the idea of Alice's having joined the SLA were a masquerade emotion, designed to throw pursuers of her inner life off the trail. Lydia feigns—Polhaus's pretty sure—angry confusion over Alice's statements and actions, but the true and palpable sentiment is the fuming self-satisfaction you feel when someone fulfills the low expectations you had for them. Hank, on the other hand, seems truly lost and upset. He seems more the jilted and deserted lover than Stump (to Polhaus's eye, Stump generates as much amorous heat as a night-light). In fact, Thomas Polhaus thinks that Hank will do anything to restore contact with his daughter, even aiding and abetting her fugitive life. And so he was pleased with his intuition when he learned that Hank was making overtures to Popeye Jackson and doubly pleased when he discovered that their go-between was Sara Jane Moore, who would become as tractable and willing an informant as one could wish for. All Sally has to do is tell him where the girl is first, before she takes it to Hank, and Operation GALT-NAP is all sewed up, right here at home where it belongs.

But not today. Today's news is more bullshit from Popeye pertaining to some issues clinging to his messy parole situation. He seems to have mistaken Hank Galton for his parole officer. Well, Hank asked for that particular headache.

"I am really not feeling so well," says Sally. "Do you mind if I just sit for a few minutes?"

"No, Sally. Can I get you some more water? Some coffee?"

"Can't you open that window?"

"No."

"I don't see the point."

"Me neither," says Polhaus cheerfully. "Sure is a pretty evening, though." He lifts the telephone receiver, puts it down.

"I don't know what to do with myself right now," she says.

"Go home. Make a drink. Watch the news. Have a bite."

"Is that what your evenings are like?"

"Just a suggestion."

"Not a very exciting one."

Is she flirting with him? Polhaus is pretty sure she's giving some to Popeye; does she want to compare equipment?

"I'm afraid I don't have much excitement on my mind. I have to prepare for a court appearance tomorrow. In Sacramento."

That ought to keep her out of the office.

"Oh," she says, "well." She closes her pocketbook. Then she stands. "Have a good day in court tomorrow. Do you have to testify? Or are you just going to lend moral support?"

Thomas Polhaus has to smile. It's one of the funniest things he's heard lately.

TANIA AND JOAN CREEP through the woods, dense mixed stands of birch and willow on the flats, pine on the slopes. They are on point/ slack maneuvers, searching for the "enemy" team of Teko and Yolanda. Though today Teko has designated Tania and Joan as the pursuers in his new game, he and Yolanda are naturally disinclined to behave like prey for long. From far ahead they usually lay an ambush for the other two.

Joan takes a dim view of all this. She's really just keeping Tania company. Tania is particularly terrified of Teko and Yolanda's surprise attacks, Teko crashing out of the trees, screaming, tackling her and pretending to draw a knife across her throat or cutting her and Joan down with simulated gunfire. Frequently, when these assaults occur, she wets her pants.

"He always goes for *me*," she says.

"He knows what I'd do if he laid his hand on me."

"He's worse here."

"Honey, he's worse everywhere."

"Here" is Jeffersonville, New York, where Randi has found them a place, another nowhere, except this time more so. Up a private drive hewn out of the pinewoods that line the road, their house sits adjacent to an old forsaken creamery, surrounded by acres of wooded land. If their isolation from the outside world seems more complete than before, inside the house there's a near-total lack of privacy; it's one big room, with a sleeping loft. It's a dusty place, void of character and charm, nothing like the Lafferty place. Tania finds dead spiders in the corners. She finds old newspapers on a shelf. She watches moths batter the overhead light. That's the local color.

And it's true that here Teko apparently has found much to nourish his authoritarian spirit. These military exercises he undertakes with great seriousness of purpose. Compulsory political study group every evening. The usual running, weight lifting, and calisthenics. He calls Guy repeatedly from town, urging him to supply the SLA with weapons for training, until Guy, ragged with worry about the steady stream of calls to his number from the remote upstate hamlet of Jeffersonville (as he pictures it being phrased in the papers), capitulates, bringing with him on his next visit two old Daisy Red Ryder air rifles, which Teko holds in his hands as if they had been sculpted from shit. Still, he sets up one end of the creamery for use as a rifle range. Guess who gets to pick up the BBs for reuse when practice is over. He plots and schemes toward the day when the group returns to California, the day the Revolution begins, anew.

A breathless day, overcast with occasional zags of lightning crossing the sky followed by the low rolling rumble of thunder, but no rain to relieve things, just the fraught light that passes through the storm suspended above them.

The two pupils sit side by side on upturned milk crates in the old creamery. Teko faces them, arms folded across his chest, Yolanda at his side. It's the People's elocution class.

Teko says, "You had this bunch of rules impounded into you. They told you what to do and when to do it. And of course you didn't notice, but they even told you how to speak. You"—Teko here indicates Tania—"so that you could take your place among the ruling elite. And you"—Teko thrusts a forefinger in Joan's direction—"because you were at their mercy. A member of a defeated people, you had to learn the language of the imperial oppressor."

There are plenty of rules here too. According to Teko and Yolanda, the People's vernacular is the same as Amos 'n' Andy's. Nonrhotic. Dropping of the final *g* in the present participle and gerundial forms. Lack of definition of final sound in word-ending consonantal clusters. Multiple negation. Omission of word final *s* and *ed*. Substitution of word final *f* for *th*. Substitution of word initial *d* for *th*. Substitution of auxiliary *be* for first-, second-, and third-person singular and plural present and past indicatives of that verb. Not in so many words.

It is much too uncomfortable to call it a lazy day. Tania moves constantly, freeing herself of her clothes where they adhere to her. She crosses one leg over the other, sits for a moment, and then switches. Though the creamery's huge door has been left open to allow air to circulate, it does no good. The sounds from outside are muzzy, without definition, except for the thunder, which rolls, enveloping them but bringing no rain.

As usual, Joan is giving Teko and Yolanda shit. Tania wishes that just this once she would go along with these two maniacs. It is so hot. They sit side by side on the upturned crates. If they touch accidentally, the impulse to move is both simultaneous and immediate, and as they peel apart, Tania feels their two skins, every centimeter of the way.

"You're laughing, Joan, but take the accent, for example. They trained you to retain it, to mark you as an outsider."

Joan giggles.

"Well, they did!" Yolanda is adamant.

"A lack of consciousness of the purpose of these differences is built into their design," confirms Teko, somewhat obscurely.

Tania watches Teko prepare for his afternoon jog. Every afternoon the same thing: the same purposeful stretching, the eyeglasses left at the same spot on the porch rail, the same huffing breaths as he strides to the point at which he begins, every day, to run at the same leisurely pace. She checks the kitchen clock: 5:03 today. Teko and Yolanda are creatures of habit, rapidly falling into a pattern anywhere they find themselves, any situation. Naturally, Tania is obliged to share these shifts in behavior.

Ordinarily Tania is a person who takes comfort in the familiarity of habits and routines. Forms them quickly, adapts to those of others. Those of her parents. Those of the church. Those of her schools. Even those, God knows, of Eric Stump. She'd felt, with him, in that apartment on Bienvenue, as if the steadiness of their lives together would either stave off the death of love or slow its approach. Their habits hardened them into their apartness from each other, though the change was barely perceptible, evolutionary and profound, so that eventually they became two different creatures, divergent but both superbly adapted to the conditions of their common environment, who might chance to look up and gaze at each other with passing interest. All she'd wanted to do was to sit opposite the man: two laps, two books open in them, two glasses of wine on the coffee table. She might have made a life out of that. She could have. Even in its most difficult aspects it would have been the easiest thing to do.

But then came the habit of the closet. A routine that was irresistible, a cocooning, and when her chance to exit first arrived, on the day when she had sat in the VW van, sweating just like this and waiting for Teko and Yolanda to return from Mel's, she realized that she couldn't because for the first time in her life she had achieved the habit of novelty, every day, with Cujo—with all of them, really. So she'd picked up the machine gun and fired, pow!, to maintain unobstructed the steady flow of the untried. Of course, if the theft of the socks/bandolier hadn't been enough in itself, that act had sealed Cujo's fate. But even the grief was new, as transfiguring as anything she'd ever endured. And *was* it her fault? She'd spent a lot of time working on that one, idly, picking the problem apart and studying it.

It was Teko who'd left the van illegally parked so that it was ticketed,

Teko who'd gotten caught stealing,

Who'd dropped the gun Yolanda had registered in her real name,

Yea, and it was Teko who'd left the parking ticket in the van when they ditched it.

She'd decided finally that wherever the blame lay, she didn't regret firing that gun. Pow!, into the new; pow!, into the forefront of things; pow!, into the unknown.

. . .

They huddle, is the only word for it, around the radio, draw close to one another from opposite ends of the big room and then stand gaping at the device. Twelve days after the House Judiciary Committee votes to adopt the First Article of Impeachment, three days after the president (another self-incriminating packrat) releases the transcripts of what will become known as the smoking gun tape, inducing eleven Republican members of the committee who voted against impeachment to announce that they will change their votes, the **[expletive deleted]** himself is on the air to offer up a farewell to the nation.

"To continue to fight through the months ahead for my personal vindication would almost totally absorb the time and attention of both the President and the Congress in a period when our entire focus should be on the great issues of peace abroad and prosperity without inflation at home," he says, "Therefore."

There is a lengthy pause, and each of them leans forward, straining to hear. When the voice resumes, falteringly, it doesn't even attempt to conceal its bitterness and unfocused loathing: "I shall resign the Presidency effective at noon tomorrow. Vice President Ford will—"

They whoop, leap into the air.

Teko hugs Yolanda.

Yolanda hugs Tania.

Tania hugs Joan.

"Ding dong," cries Teko, "the witch is dead!"

Now what?

The group has taken to traveling to the nearby town of Youngsville for occasional recreation, usually ending up at the One-Step, a tavern where they drink cheap pitchers of draft beer and play shuffleboard and pool at coin-op tables. On one outing Teko is standing at the bar waiting for the bartender to pull his beer when he eavesdrops on a nearby conversation.

"I find it completely unacceptable," says the man.

"So you'll call the agency when we get back to the city." The woman tends to her two small children, who sit dangle-legged on barstools, drinking Shirley Temples. "You want your cherry? Mommy wants your cherry if you don't."

"I could make an issue of this. Damages are involved."

"What, damages? The car broke down. It happens. Don't blow bubbles, Richard."

"We didn't put down a deposit?"

"So we'll get there a little later."

"What if we lose the room?"

"He says the Grossinger's bus leaves in a half an hour."

"I still can't believe there isn't a taxi in this town. What else do they have? Party lines? Outhouses?"

"Shhh."

"I expect any minute now to hear the theme from *Deliverance*."

"Shhhhh!"

"This is why, you ask me why I never want to leave the city. This is why I never want to leave the city."

"It's ten miles. Don't kick, Sylvie hon."

Teko pays for the pitcher of beer and carries it into the back room. He puts it on the table.

"Ever hear of Grossinger's?"

"What's *that*?" asks Tania.

"Big Jewish resort. Lots of rich doctors and whatnot, coming up from the city. It's just down the road, it turns out."

"So?" asks Yolanda.

"So? So, purses and wallets left by the pool. Room keys. We could clean up in one afternoon."

Cash is an issue, again.

"There's a bus," Teko continues. "I'll take it up and see what there is to see."

"Funny," says Joan, "you don't look Jewish."

"We can work around that. I'll bring Tania with me. We'll blend in."

"Aww," says Yolanda.

"I don't think it's a good idea for the two commanders to accompany each other on a dangerous mission," he explains.

"Don't be an idiot," says Yolanda. Turns out she's not objecting, just giving him necessary advice.

The bus is nearly empty, with Teko, Tania, and the aggrieved householder and his family from New York the only passengers. They disembark at the Ferndale depot, where several cabs await to take passengers on the last leg of the trip to the famous resort. Teko is digging in his pocket to count his change when they are approached by a middle-aged man who seizes Teko by the wrist.

"Joshua."

"Excuse me?"

"Joshua. As in, Joshua and Beth, the new staff. Right? Your mother called to tell me that you would be taking the later bus. I had just about given up on you but for your mother's sake I decided to wait, and here you are. Well, come on. We are very shorthanded and there's no time to waste. If we hurry you can start helping get the Pink Elephant ready for the first dinner service."

"The Pink Elephant?"

"You're a restaurant critic? The ambience falls short in your opinion? Look, the way business is, we'd serve dinner in the parking lot if that's what the customers wanted. People want to drink, eat, and see a show all at once."

"OK."

"So what are you waiting for?" He pulls a little, and Teko takes a step forward. The man keeps his grip on Teko's arm until they arrive at a big Chrysler. He turns. "Beth, what are you waiting for?" Well, cheaper than a cab. The man unlocks the door, and they get in. On the backseat are cardboard boxes full of grass skirts, garlands of paper flowers, plastic tiki figurines, and paper umbrellas.

"Don't ask. All right, go ahead. What it is, we've discovered that our target customer is on account of lowered airfares and more frequent departures heading for Hawaii. I don't see the big thing, personally, but the place has a certain charisma right now that you can't deny. We keep hearing about clean beaches, pleasant weather, warm buoyant water, half-naked women, and breathtaking natural scenery. It has all the earmarks of a total fad, but as a trend it is bleeding us dry. So we thought we'd institute a Hawaiian Night. Kosher luaus and fruity drinks out of fishbowls. I know a girl who's half Puerto Rican and half Chinese and does exotic dancing who I figure she can give a few hula lessons to interested parties. Worth a shot, right?"

The car enters the grounds of the resort, rolling up a long wooded drive toward the main cluster of buildings.

"Now, Joshua, we'll start you in the kitchen. You've done prep work—chopping, peeling? No? There's nothing to it. But Beth, honey." He grabs her knee. "You, *you* I'm putting out on the floor."

He gives a little squeeze. "Now," he says briskly, "we got to get some uniforms on you. There's not a minute to waste. You can just leave your bags in my car for now." Tania casts a sidelong glance at Teko. Apparently their host hasn't noticed that they carry nothing with them.

The man steers them up a gravel pathway that leads to the kitchen door, which is propped open with a battered old hubcap. Two young people, dressed in whites, drop cigarettes and grind them underfoot into the gravel.

"Come inside, everybody," says the man cheerfully. "Show Josh and Beth how hard we work around here." They step into the enormous kitchen. "Here's Josh and Beth. They've come to save the day."

A desultory cheer goes up in the kitchen.

"Attaboy. Now let's get some uniforms on you."

They stand before a group of lockers in a brightly lit passageway linking the kitchen to several dining rooms.

"Take any locker you want. If you don't have a lock it doesn't matter because you kids can always sort it out amongst yourselves in the unlikely event of a misplaced personal belonging. That is to say it happens rarely if at all around here. Now get dressed, go see the captain, and give your mother my very kindest regards when you call her first thing tomorrow."

For the next two hours neither Teko nor Tania sees anything resembling a purse, a wallet, or a room key. She sets tables, hand washes spotty glasses, rolls silverware, folds napkins, fills cruet sets, fills monkey bowls with Parkay pats and single-serving creamers, vacuums, polishes chrome and brass, evens stacks of coasters, straightens barstools. He fillets chicken and fish, peels and chops vegetables, washes lettuce, prepares trays of desserts and salads, schleps beer kegs up from the storeroom, sterilizes and stacks dishes. For the first time since the Marines he is doing the work of the People, though in this case the People mostly are boys and girls speaking of Columbia Law or the dentistry program at NYU.

By the time the diners begin to enter the room Tania is exhausted, and she stands with Sarah Horowitz, a psych major at Sarah Lawrence and a veteran of five weeks at Grossinger's, on the gravel path outside the kitchen door, smoking and drinking black coffee.

"You look sort of familiar. Where you from anyway?" asks Sarah. She looks her up and down. "The Upper West Side, or something?"

"California," Tania answers promptly. She drags hard on the cigarette.

"California!" exclaims Sarah. "Westwood or the Valley?"

"Bay Area, actually."

"Didn't know they had Jewish people in the Bay Area."

"What about Levi Strauss?" They laugh a little.

"You better hope he's funny, Beth."

"What? Who?"

"The comic tonight."

"OK, I hope he's funny."

"Ha. Seriously. He's not funny, they don't tip."

"Really?"

"You kidding? Everything's our fault."

"What's funny up here?"

"Take a look at the house." She shrugs. "Strictly Geritol." She tosses the cigarette. "We better get inside. It's about to go bananas."

They duck inside, Tania kicking the hubcap and allowing the kitchen door to slam behind them.

"Get out there, twatlick," explains the chef. "I'm not taking shit because your section's orphaned."

Tania steps into the dining room in time to see their driver from this afternoon, wearing evening clothes, stride out onto the stage. Apparently he is the show's compere as well, his right hand placed strategically over a small gravy stain on his left lapel so that he assumes a pious or patriotic mien.

"Ladies and gentlemen, we are so happy to have each of you here with us as our guests tonight, to see you having such a good time. And so you should. Many of us work too much, too hard, too often. We are terribly pressured every day and often can't find any time for ourselves, for contemplation, for recreation, for some peace from the rat race and the endless demands. Some do this—they go to the shul or synagogue or temple of their choice on Shabbat. They sing, they read Torah, they listen to a sermon. Some talk to their friends. Some visit with their grandchildren to play and dote and incidentally to strike a lasting family bond with their son- or daughter-in-law as the case may be. And some come up here to our beautiful Catskill region, for a weekend or with our special family rates for a stay of a week or of even longer duration, circumstances permitting. Not anymore the most fashionable destination maybe but still a place for family togetherness and the company of like-minded people getting away from it all like yourselves. Forget the daily grindstone for a while and cut yourself off from the everyday tsuris that besets us all. Relax, forget the stock market, the clients, the customers, the patients, the students, the office politics, and all the other concerns that nag at a person. It's better than golf, though here we have a quality golf course that visitors with a professional involvement in the game have showered with the highest praise. It's better than canasta, though here a willing partner is always to be found. It's better than watching your favorite television programs, though here each of our comfortable rooms is equipped with a famous maker seventeen-inch color set. So live a little. As they say in the antacid commercials, try it, you'll like it. And that reminds me, incidentally, the chef has asked me to mention that our specials tonight, the baked halibut and the apricot-glazed chicken, are very fresh and still in plentiful supply. These each come with a lovely cauliflower kugel in fresh tomato sauce, as well as your choice of tossed salad or the soup of the day, of which we happen tonight to have two, which are cream of asparagus or a delightful gazpacho."

"So what's this gazpacho?" asks a man.

"I've had it; it's a mechaya. It's *Spanish*. Like from *Spain*."

"Nu?"

"I tell you, you'll love it. Young lady, could you or could you not plotz from it?"

"I think so," says Tania, uncertainly.

"Pfeh," says the man, waving dismissively. "Give me the cream of asparagus."

"Fine. Suit yourself. *I'll* take the gazpacho. Then you can sit here with a face on you that you could drag across the carpet until I offer to switch. And," she adds, "I *hate* cream of asparagus."

"Pfeh," says the man.

"Now tonight," continues the compere, "in addition to the contemporary sounds of David Lubash and his Love Rush, we have some really prime entertainment. Direct from some very well-received engagements in the tristate area, we're happy to bring you without any further ado the very funny *Jules Farber*."

Here the small band strikes up a jaunty, snare-driven theme, to which the compere sings words in a vaguely cantorial tenor:

With the closing *brrr* the compere jokily wraps his arms around himself as if to indicate enclosure in a walk-in freezer and then, perhaps realizing the ambiguity of this gesture, begins to applaud while backing off the stage. Farber enters the small circle of light that surrounds the microphone stand and stands there for a moment, looking blearily into the audience. He is about forty and wears a rumpled business suit and has the general mien of a man searching the carousel for his checked baggage after the worst commuter flight in the history of commercial aviation. He waits with visible impatience for the house to settle down. He then begins, appropriately enough given his appearance, with a story about airports and air travel. Glamour of the jet age. Well, there's the pilot with his Captain America voice. The buxom stewardess demonstrating the life jacket, wink. The turbulence moment. The in-flight movie, the meals and snacks. Barf bags and "occupied." Fear of hijacking. A Cuba joke. A Cuban cigar story. The uncle who rolled cigars. His Aunt Malka, who lives in Florida. A Collins Avenue story. The audience is polite and attentive, though the waiters are just beginning to serve dinner and each crash and tinkle seems to send a frisson of nervous energy through Farber's body. He wipes his palm on his jacket, examines it, essays a look into the audience.

"So I have to ask," he says. "Didn't this week just wring you out? A new president, wow. Anticlimactic, a little. The thing of it is the show's over. Ford's like your high school guidance counselor taking over from the Wicked Witch of the West. A little quiet, kind of a stiff, actually, always trying to get you to apply yourself, get your marks up. Question is, am I relieved, nauseous, bored, or all three? I mean, we're all glad Nixon's out of there. Across the political spectrum, as they say. Whatever our individual reasons. It's too late to do any good, but for form's sake. So they'll look back at us kindly in the future and say, 'How well they preserved our democracy for us!' This is some shortsighted posterity, no? An honest historical appraisal of Richard M. Nixon and his times would approach the subject like a documentary about typhoid or bubonic plague. 'What conditions allowed him to germinate, to thrive?' Those are the good questions. But who wants to imagine a posterity that'll be critical of us? How deflating. We want from the future what we want from our kids: Sit up straight and listen. 'Oh, we are the greatest generation! We defeated Hitler, we made the desert bloom, we moved to South Orange, and last but not least we got Nixon the hell out of there. So, love, honor, obey, cherish, venerate, adore, and—please—call once, make it twice, a week.'"

This draws a smattering of applause, mostly from among the older women in the audience.

"But what explanation is there for Nixon's ascent, his ascendancy, his political longevity? Remember this is the oracle of the past getting quizzed by an unfortunately skeptical future, its answers coming out of some smoky void, a deep voice, Lincolnesque, theatrical, like God in *The Ten Commandments*, though what I'm actually picturing in my head is a columnist for a major metropolitan newspaper in a drip-dry suit. 'No, sir, you have the question backwards. It is not a matter of Nixon's being unsuited to high office. It is not a matter of a small-minded opportunist taking the expedited route to ultimate success in his chosen field of endeavor. It is not a matter of a man who at every crucial moment made himself over to reflect whatever generosity or meanness of spirit moved the times. It's not a matter of how did he *make it* at all. What it's a matter of is how did he *fail*.' Yeah, the old tragic flaw. The great man, done in by hubris. The old op-ed shuffle."

Stiffly, Farber thrusts his arms into the air, forming the familiar V signs with the fingers of either hand. "'Peace,'" he says, in a Nixon voice. Then, thoughtfully: "'That ought to look good on my résumé.'" There is some laughter, and the audience settles down for an impression, for some of the traditional comedy trademarks. You can see them leaning back, settling in after the jagged beginning, relaxing after that edgy way an audience partakes of failure. But Farber waves the conceit away, dispelling it like smoke in the hazy air, and then drops his arms and shrugs to resettle the creased jacket on his shoulders, like a bird ruffling its feathers.

"You want to find at least a trace of something to admire about this Nixon, though. Sift the ashes a little, you should pardon the expression. What you have to is you have to admire Nixon sticking it out as long as he did. What is the word, tenacious. Forget the shifty eyes, the concentration camp guard posture, the black sandy jowls. Forget these things, file them someplace dark and inaccessible, beside maybe the Instamatic snaps of your second cousin Rebecca's bat mitzvah which they held at the Village Temple. In the on deck circle, Sheldon and Bruce, awaiting the celebration of their union. A lovely reception to follow at Marc Ballroom. So forget these things. Certainly Becca you should forget. She's just your average nice Jewish girl from the West Village—going to Elisabeth Irwin, living on salted popcorn, and dreaming of rhinoplasty. Likewise forget the eyes, the Treblinka mien, the hairy face. And what you have is you have a bulldog, nah, a doberman, hanging on for dear life. Does a Jew know an attack dog when he sees one? Growling, ropes of gamy-looking spit looping out from between the jaws, swinging there, those powerful yellow teeth pressing down into their quarry, the front paws paddling with excitement at the empty air."

"Tell a joke!" someone shouts.

"Jokes, you want. Question: How many Hasidic rebbes does it take to change a lightbulb? Answer: What is a lightbulb?"

Silence.

"OK, so you didn't like the dog, the image of the dog? This is a unique, strange face, Nixon's. Let alone the brain doing its crazy gavotte behind it. Gavotte! The words smart Jews make their very own! Aggravation. Tumult. Excellent words. Unimpeachable goyish pedigrees, like nice shiksa girls named Mary and Betty; they went to Smith, Radcliffe, and Barnard, and now they're in the hairy hands of these Jewish boys from Ocean Parkway, these nonmatric students at Brooklyn College, ogled and defiled like the pictures in the old stroke books. But a strange face. The mind gropes for comparisons. Only America makes a face like this. Healthy, but sick. Well fed, but malnourished. Intelligent, but lit by instinct. You look at your old Action Comics, Whiz Comics, Star Spangled Comics. The archvillains, well, you're talking typecast. I mean, villains they were conceived, and villains they shall come off the drafting table, ever more. But if you look, schlepping around in the background of one of those comics you'll always see the shoe clerk, the guy selling train tickets behind the barred window, the guy running the elevator, the guy who blends in and pledges his allegiance to the front runner— and *that's* the face of Nixon."

"Tell a joke!" shouts somebody.

"What, you want jokes, tonight? All right already. How many Lubavitchers does it take to change a lightbulb? Hmm? None; it'll never die. OK? But listen, with that face, on Monday it's 'Floor, please,' and Tuesday he's hanging from your trouser leg, growling and snapping. The dog within. I like that, I can see it on the checkout rack at the A&P, Bantam, right next to *The Sensuous Woman* and *The Strange Case of Alice Galton*, which might actually be the same book. *The Dog Within*. By Kate Millett. It's all about keeping that dog tied up in there, out of sight. You take a Nixon and you reduce him to the sum of his ad campaign. Nasty, Brutish, Short, Nixon's the One, and then it's just a matter of time until, oh yeah, they're playing 'Hail to the Chief' while your guy's waving his way down the gangplank of Air Force One, stomach all abubble over the prospect of tearing some ass, Pat with her Valium stare grafted to his side. So far so good, right? And then the product just, like, *implodes*. Like if the pilot of every plane in Pan Am's fleet decided to nosedive into the ground the same day. The horror. The betrayal. The sense of having been taken. The thing is, Nixon did it to himself. Can't you see them, the ad men, sitting in a room where the walls are covered with beautifully framed tampon ads, the window has a million dollar view of Birdshit Plaza, 'Nu, Dick? Why? We had it all. China, détente, peace with honor, law and order. What a package. The only thing we didn't deliver was good water pressure and a Sunday *Times* with no missing sections.' McGovern was *finished*. A zero. Half of America thought he was a pinko. The other half thought he was Gene McCarthy in drag. And the third half thought they were both the same thing. Eagleton was the last nail in that coffin. Yeah, a VP fanning his lower lip with his index finger, making with the buh-buh noises? Little too close to the bone for comfort. This is the age of the VP ascendant. Ford, Nixon, Johnson, Truman. All of them succeeding men who'd basically died in office. Nixon had it all sewed up. But I always knew he'd screw things up in the end. The guy's like Charlie Brown. It's so long to the White House, the big valedictory speech, the ultimate Norma Desmond moment, and what comes naturally are the applause lines that used to wow those Chamber of Commerce luncheons back in Whittier. 'This country needs good farmers, good businessmen, good plumbers, good carpenters.' Genetically designed to run an employment agency on Fourteenth Street. What a brain, he always belonged behind that Steelcase desk, brown-bagging it or fried chicken from the five-and-ten lunch counter, real treyf, a blackboard behind him listing steam table jobs, housepainting work. 'You got a chauffeur's license, Mr. Kissinger? No? How about shoe sales? You think you could handle it? Fast-paced environment? See Mr. Dugatkin at Brunell's.' Later Dugatkin calls up. 'Nixon, what's with this Kissinger you're sending me? He insults Mrs. Weinapple and her daughter Caitlin who shows such a talent for the folk guitar. He says Caitlin's feet are like two lake bottom canoes. Since she's this big I'm fitting this girl for her Keds and I'll grant you she's needing a little extra support in the arches, but size is not an issue. And after lunch—a seventy-minute lunch, but who counts?—he takes fifty-six cents from the March of Dimes box.' Nixon's mad, but in a prefab sort of way. He knows Dugatkin's just kvetching, that the guy has every foot in Stuyvesant Town locked up. He wonders what the fuck is up with Kissinger, though. He had such an excellent presence. Very commanding. And that sexy accent. Who would have expected this? So he feels a gesture is incumbent upon him. So you want to know what he does, what he does is he sends Kissinger the next day to work for Shimmy Pressman, whose own Gala Shoe is just a few blocks up First Avenue from Brunell's. Shimmy's got the same stranglehold on Peter Cooper Village that Dugatkin's got on Stuy Town. Same turnover problem too. I mean neither of these guys is a breeze to deal with, let's face it; Dugatkin's son ran away from dentistry school to dig clams out of Portsmouth Bay, Pressman's daughter is a large animal veterinarian who communicates via ham radio from remote locations out west only during the High Holy Days. The kids grew up together, know each other from Camp Emanu-El, were on the same side in the yearly campwide maccabead. Team Masada. *Ya gotta! Ya gotta! Root for Masada!* Great, suicide cults of the ancient world."

A hand reaches out for Tania, clutches her sleeve.

"What type Jell-O? What type Jell-O have you got tonight?" It's an old man, his eyes rheumy behind the unbelievably thick lenses of his eyeglasses. The words come out of a soft mouth that seems to be lacking many teeth. But his grip is like iron.

"He wants to know," says a woman at his table, helpfully, "what the kind of Jell-O is that you've got here tonight."

"Pressman's on the phone even *before* the noon break: 'Nixon! I'm sympathetic, the man is down on his luck. He shows initiative and he takes an interest. But then he tells Mrs. Glassman she'd have a better shot at getting a good fit if she went to the rowboat concession in Central Park.' So Nixon, you know, he feels he's accomplished something. A balance. Shuttle discourtesy. Plus, you know, it keeps Henry away from the office. He sits in that straight chair on the other side of Nixon's desk, eyeing Nixon's Woolworth chicken, kibitzing when Nixon has to take a phone call, erasing things on Nixon's chalkboard when his back is turned.

"But that's all finished now. Nixon's back in San Clemente. Guys in suits out on the lawn, behind the flower beds, talking into their lapels. Neighbors complaining about the noise, the lights, the traffic; it's their own personal Götterdämmerung. Nixon's picking up the Trimline phone in the living room to call Pat in the kitchen to ask her to bring him in some sunflower seeds, please. Sure he has things to do: *Match Game*'s on at ten-thirty. He likes all those game shows where the secrets are concealed under sliding panels, behind rotating sections of a big lit-up board. So much friendlier than the hearings. If it had been Gene Rayburn instead of Peter Rodino doing the questioning, we all would have been out of there in nothing flat, goes his way of thinking.

"All finished. The laws of physics have won; this is a body at rest. But since he wasn't ever interested in laws, why should now be any different? The tenacity, while it lasted, back from the dead, back again and again, it's like a picture Roger Corman said the hell with. Because you want to show everybody. Hanging in there, sticking to those rusty old six guns. You want to show *everybody*. I got rachmones, standing up here, believe it. His what they call political base is gone, man. He may have been the one climbing onto that helicopter waving bye-bye, but the people are the ones who left *him*. They're wiping the dust off their ColorTrak TVs with lemon Pledge, prepping the tube so it's fit to receive its first images of the new top man. President Whatshisface. Well, far as they're concerned, anybody's better. Polls show people hate Nixon worse than they hate Hitler, Jack the Ripper, Count Dracula, and Idi Amin, in that order. They'll all come back, though. *He'll* come back. After all, it was just a third-rate burglary. For *that* he gets *this*? What about all those old report cards he sweated out? He participated, he got along well, he showed respect, he obeyed rules, he showed self-control, he followed directions, he worked neatly, he had excellent penmanship. He scored a four-hole outhouse for the annual bonfire at Whittier. Only president to visit all fifty states. His own mother said he was the best potato masher, to die for. He's got one more act coming, and he knows it."

Someone hollers, "Say something funny!"

"Something funny, he says. OK. How many congregants does it take to change a lightbulb in a synagogue? '*Change*? You're wanting we should *change* the lightbulb? My grandmother donated that lightbulb!'"

Diffuse laughter.

"For now, though, it's all over. We're all going to have to spend some time healing, recuperating from this long national nightmare. I see myself in a hospital bed, being spoon-fed Junket and kneaded with VapoRub by a round-the-clock team of nurses who look like Yvonne DeCarlo, Virginia Mayo, and Jane Greer, though all votes for Gloria Grahame will be counted. Thank God for major medical."

"Young lady," says an older man holding a menu, who then, having gotten Tania's attention, turns to a young woman seated beside him. "You eat what you want. Get whatever pleases you, not a word I'm saying. It's your stomach. But stop trying to have an influence." The young woman rolls her eyes.

"Young lady," he says again. "You got a nice piece of boneless chicken breast? It's fresh? It's not just sitting there in the kitchen under lights? All right, bring me a piece of boneless chicken. And make sure it's all the way cooked." He turns again to his companion. "You want to eat chazerai, go ahead. Be my guest. Not one word from me. You're big. It's your stomach."

"Chicken. God, Daddy."

"The whole time, though, I'll be waiting for him to come back. I'll be waiting, you'll be waiting, he himself will be waiting. In the meantime, what? A little notecard to Rose Mary Woods? Rose

Mary, she put in her time, God knows. She just wants to do her linoleum cuts of woodland scenes and have a second piece of coffee cake, for Christ's sake. A little paint by numbers. She's got nothing but time. She knows she'll get a call in a couple of years and she's willing to wait."

Farber looks slightly distracted as he slowly walks to the lip of the stage. He thrusts his arms stiffly into the air to form the familiar V signs. Then he turns abruptly and walks off. Though a few have applauded automatically, most of the audience is astir with unease. They feel cheated. "Comedy Tonight," it had said outside, and this guy got up, and just what did he do, exactly? A woman summons Tania. She appears furious. *Everything's our fault.*

"What's wrong with that man?" she says.

FIFTY THOUSAND TIPS. THIS is a measure of something Thomas Polhaus has never encountered in a lifetime of investigative work. He expects the public to take well-known cases to heart, he expects civilians to follow developments as reported in the press and to form commensurately ill-informed opinions concerning the Bureau's work. He expects an above-average level of interest in the cases that set the screen aglow on the six o'clock news. He expects the people who want to get into the act: search here, dig there, check this out. Fields full of sheep shit in Petaluma, swampy lowlands, eerily lit by will-o'-the-wisp, near Modesto; places so lonely it ached to know that you were there looking for nothing. He expects that, always. He expects the delicately private reaction that the wider social phenomena in which the Bureau has become involved—the civil rights movement, the Left as a whole—can engender in a certain type of person. But this protean case is different. GALTNAP tosses away all the usual assumptions. It isn't only a question of having an opinion about the case or the Bureau's handling of it (of course there was more of that than usual). It isn't simply that people either like the girl and sympathize with her family or despise her and her entire clan and want her shot on sight. There is also a feeling that people are calling, in effect, to ask the Bureau to investigate *them*, to understand *them*, to explain them to themselves, that at the kernel of each call, each letter, each message tied to a brick, is a secret, some concealed thing illustrious and profound to the sender but unutterable. This held true for both the patently frivolous leads and the ones Polhaus felt obliged to take seriously. Polhaus feels for them, understands that in every case the Bureau, and he himself, have disappointed, by failing to immediately decipher the secret, to recognize what is concealed.

The fifty thousand tips were the usual mishmash. After sorting through the mention of lost husbands and second wives, through noise complaints involving neighbors and neighbor dogs and neighbor stereos, through references to Madison Avenue and to the Pope; after hearing of the man who'd fucked his mother-in-law's Thanksgiving turkey, coming in the chestnut and sausage dressing, of the woman who overheard her doctors discussing murdering her; of the man whose mother constantly projected psychic pain waves into his head from the back bedroom in which she sat smoking, pretending to watch her soaps, of my street was ripped up four separate times in the last year—once phone, once gas, once electricity, once water—and this is a known fact, and no one does anything. Sort through all that, and the tips found the missing girl sitting on a bench on Whipple Avenue, reading a paperback *Peanuts* book. They placed her on El Camino Real, passing out religious tracts. She was at shopping malls and weddings, serving kosher meals at Grossinger's, and blending in with the crowd at ethnic festivals and Uriah Heep concerts.

The ones to which Polhaus pays close attention are the tantalizingly reasonable ones, which place a thin girl with a mole on her face at a gas station on I-5, filling up a dusty Nova or a Maverick. She got gas. She bought American cheese and Campbell's soup. She drank coffee and paid with a twenty. Because if these are not genuine sightings, they are at the very least duplications of actual events in which she was involved. The agents' reports on their interviews with the service station attendants and waitresses and checkout clerks are his own personal pornography; with vague hostility he can imagine her right into the rhythm of these dull events. So this is what it's like without the protection of the dazzling name, without the allowance checks and the trust fund income. How do you like it now? The kid had held one job. One god damned job, working the stationery counter at Capwell's. Probably sounds pretty good around now.

GARY KEARSE ARRIVES AT the farmhouse out of the blue one after-noon. Though Yolanda's account of their cross-country trip had been imbued with a careful affectlessness, it's clear that she is excited to see him. The sudden infusion of raw sexual hunger into the usual SLA routine of gaudy self-abnegation has a turbulent effect. All Kearse and Yolanda have to do is smile at each other across the table. Not since before Mel's has sex been acknowledged as a part of life, though mostly this has had to do with everyone's habitual re-luctance to have sex with Teko, who has handled the subject by re-casting sex as simply another component of the cadre's overall requirements, like ammunition and sacks of rice.

Drew and Diane Shepard married for more or less typical reasons at a more or less typical age. Still, it was a good little wedding, fun, unpretentious, the sort of wedding lots of people might be happy to have had. It was held at Drew's mother's house in Indianapolis. Most of the guests had driven up from Bloomington. A local judge officiated. After being forced indoors by a sudden storm that had thundered across the pancake expanses at the heart of the state, everybody crashed all over the living room where the ceremony had been held. Nobody had to dress up. Drew's mom was cool that way.

And later, after Diane's parents, slightly shaken and not quite sure what to make of this hairy little man their daughter had married, had been driven to the motel where they would be spending the night, after Drew's mother had received a sustained ovation from her young guests for testily shooing away the two patrolmen who'd driven their cruiser *up onto her lawn* to shut down the noisy, cheerful party, after Drew had spent an hour in the backyard discussing the MC5 with a biker he knew vaguely, after all that, the groom and his bride retired at last to their bedroom (up the stairs, first door on the left, right next to the bathroom). The sky had cleared, and the soft light of the moon, its cool glow, fell into the room; Diane moved, became naked in the moonlight, became liquid metal flowing there at the head of the bed. Drew and Diane had been living together for months, but Drew felt a momentousness at this instant, watching his bride disrobe. Her having married him, her disrobing for him as his wife: these things struck him as unique gifts to him, as if he were being allowed to probe a virgin orifice. Because in fact it was true, that by virtue of the transformative power of the ceremony, their renovation into husband and wife, she was again new, she was again something that she would never be for anyone else.

He knelt on the bed in the dark, throbbing with lust, awaiting her approach. This was long before he had thrown off the shackles of bourgeois propriety, and he was completely unconflicted in his fierce desire to *fuck* this woman who was now *his wife*. And it was a desire that had stayed with him. Through it all, General Teko wanted nothing more than he wanted that Indiana bride, lustrous in the Indiana moonlight, with the sound of water running through the pipes inside the wall.

Nobody else, however, has any way of knowing about any of this, least of all Yolanda, who has always taken at face value Teko's oft-professed conviction that the sexually monogamous relationship is an unforgivable impingement on individual rights. She certainly has never seen herself as liquid metal, as virginal again, as uniquely Teko's. She smiles at Kearse across the table. He smiles back over the rim of his mug of Red Zinger, crossing his left leg over his right knee and fingering the three diagonal stripes embroidered onto the side of his sneakers. Teko slams plates and glasses into the cupboard while Tania washes up at the sink.

"Looks like *rain* again," he says.

Yolanda stretches, languorously. "I'd like to get a walk in before it starts to pour." Back arched, arms coiled behind her head, her eyes are on Kearse.

"I'd sure like to stretch my legs after that drive."

Teko slams a glass into the cupboard. It breaks against an earthenware bowl, a jagged edge slicing into his fingertip.

"Ouch," he says. "Shit."

"What a klutz," says Yolanda, slackening into her normal posture. "We're not going to have any glasses left by the end of the summer."

"You want to run some cold water on that," says Kearse. "Before you wash it."

Teko grunts in answer. Giotto-perfect circles of blood form an ellipsis across the countertop as he carries his injured finger delicately to the sink, holding it above his heart and squeezing it at its base with the fingers of his other hand.

"May I?" he says, gently shouldering Tania out of his way. In the sink he tenderly washes his hand with Octagon. Tania marvels: The guy's so calm. She wishes he'd hurt himself every day. But of course she knows, she *knows*, knowing the two of them as well as she does, she just *knows* that this is yet another episode of the Teko and Yolanda saga, just as she knows that although the moment idles, free of any sense of danger, Teko is transmitting a clear signal to his wife, who is ignoring him, who couldn't be less concerned with the man at the sink wincing and sighing, who at present is very suggestively cutting into a Sara Lee pound cake.

"Delicious," Yolanda says, putting the tip of the blunt knife into her mouth and licking off buttery residue. "Mmmmmm." She stares at Kearse. She says, "So good."

"How about a Band-Aid?" says Teko.

"Teko. They're all the way in the bathroom," says Yolanda.

"I'll get you one," says Tania.

"Oh," says Teko, "that's all right." He wraps his clean wound in a dish towel and goes to the bathroom.

"Acts like he's going to bleed to death," says Yolanda, before filling her mouth with cake.

When he gets back, his finger is rather showily dressed in gauze and surgical tape, tinged merthiolate red beneath. He wiggles the finger, as if to satisfy himself that it still works.

"Well, we're on our way," says Yolanda. She and Kearse stand.

"Jeez, well, what about the rest of us? I think we all want to take a nice walk."

"You'll just have to catch up," answers Yolanda. "You take way too long."

"But my finger!"

"If you'd cut the damn thing off, that'd be one thing. See you!"

Kearse and Yolanda go out. Tania watches as Teko silently cleans the pieces of the broken glass from the inside of the cupboard and throws them away. She goes outside and sits on the lawn before the house.

Joan's voice comes from behind Tania and from way down in her diaphragm: "Mmmmm, delicious."

"How *about* that?" says Tania, without turning around.

"Suck . . . my . . . *knife*, Yolanda." Joan utters this in a baritone.

"Oh, God," says Tania.

"Oh, Gary," says Joan, coming around and throwing herself on the fragrant grass, arching her back, moaning. "You make my labia tremble!" She and Tania burst out giggling. Then the front door opens, and Teko emerges in his jogging clothes. Tania turns her wrist to glance down at a watch that hasn't been there since February. But she knows without checking that it's nowhere near five o'clock.

"They're right," he says, "it's a great day for a walk in the woods."

It's a lousy day, overcast again and humid.

"We're OK here," says Joan.

The usual stretching. Eyeglasses in their usual spot on the porch rail.

"Well, I'm off for a jog," he says. He takes the usual brisk steps, huffing and puffing, and then launches into his usual canter. His feet pound in their usual way against the ground as he runs up the path he has worn into the grass and then turns into the woods. Everything as usual, except that it is too early and the day feels too different, as if they had somehow misused it. Though Tania and Joan hug their knees and laugh, sitting like any two girls on a square of lawn anywhere in America, the tone is dark with premonitory shadows. Though Tania knows that Teko would probably behave exactly the same if Yolanda were planning to cuckold him with a genuine urban guerrilla—especially if the act were to leave him with nothing more than a bum finger to keep him company—she feels that Kearse is an intruder, a tourist lazily dipping into their revolutionary ways and conventions. Why'd he have to show up?

They talk and read and doze as the misshapen afternoon crawls by. Once an enormous burst of lightning lashes across the sky, bridging the clouds, yielding an enormous and instantaneous crack of thunder, and as the still air begins to move, cool now and reeking of ozone, they gaze upward, seeking the rain that seems sure to come. Tania sees Teko's figure come out of the woods and make for the creamery.

"I'm head inside now," says Joan. "I'm like a cat about getting soaked in your clothes."

"OK." Tania lifts a hand in a lazy farewell, her eyes on Teko's back as he muscles the creamery door, sliding it open a few feet on its stubborn track and then vanishing inside.

She studies for a moment the dark gash the open door forms in the face of the creamery. After getting to her feet, she begins walking that way, not quite sure why. The first drops of rain splat on her back, and she feels them, warm through her T-shirt. She thinks of the circles of Teko's blood on the countertop. The rain comes down steadily. She can hear it now, falling softly through the trees and, as she approaches, hammering on the corrugated tin roof of the creamery. Hiding behind the broad door, she creeps along the apron of concrete laid outside the creamery entrance and peeks into the opening. Teko has drawn a tall silhouette on the wall, comical, unmistakably Kearse's, and he is firing at this target with one of the air rifles. She steps inside.

It's deafening in the creamery, a steady pounding on the tin roof that echoes throughout the unfilled spaces of the building. Shafts of gray light fall through the noise from window slits overhead. Teko stands in the shadows, engrossed in his shooting, firing, cocking the rifle, and firing again. The sounds of the gun and of the pellets striking the wall are lost in the battering noise of the rain. Tania reaches up to smooth her hair, gathering the wet locks at the back of her head and squeezing them, wringing out the rainwater onto the soaked fabric of her shirt. She shivers now. She's cold. It was funny, and now it's not so funny. She has never really thought of him as a man before and now she's struck by her curiously mingled feelings of empathy and schadenfreude. When Teko turns and looks at her, he seems unsurprised at her presence.

She asks, "Did you catch up with them?" She has to shout.

"I caught up," he shouts back.

"How far did they get?"

Teko inclines his head vaguely.

"Oh."

Teko turns, raises the gun to his shoulder, and fires again.

"New target?"

"Yup."

"Tall."

"It is that."

"So. Are they heading back to the house?"

He asks, "Who?" Then: "Oh."

He says, "I don't know what they're doing."

He says, "I don't know what they're doing right now." He turns, raises the gun to his shoulder, and fires again.

"They'll get pretty soaked."

"Pour cold water on them. That's what they do, right?" He laughs curtly, but to Tania it's just a smile and a shake of the head, silent in the drumming noise. She looks at the silhouette, gangly and absurd, its head perforated with tiny punctures, its torso. Tania notices the crudely drawn sneakers on the silhouette's feet, with three diagonal stripes running down the sides.

"Go ahead and keep shooting," she shouts. "Don't let me bother you."

"I don't want to. These guns stink." He throws the rifle. It lands without a sound in the clattering din. They stare at the spot where it lies for a moment. Teko asks, "You want to know where I found them?"

"OK?"

Teko advances on her, two big steps toward the little girl shivering in her wet T-shirt. "I found them in the woods. Under a tree. Fucking. Like a pair of animals. Like *hippies*."

Tania says, softly, "I'm sorry, Teko."

"What?"

"I said I'm sorry!"

"Sorry about what?"

"I just am."

"Don't be sorry!" And then he turns his head, the voice is lost again, there is only an outraged animation amid the noise. Tania can't quite believe it, but what she thinks she hears, the voice moving in and out of intelligibility, of audibility itself, are the words *security breach*. Teko shrugs and pulls at himself, his mouth moving.

Security breach.

Security breach?

"—security breach—"

"OK," says Tania.

"'OK.' Don't patronize me."

"OK."

"You think you're clever. You think you know something. You don't know shit. I've been telling you that all along."

"OK. I don't know anything."

"*You don't know shit!*"

"I don't know shit!" They are screaming at each other through the racket of the buffeting rain.

"I'm sick of this," Teko says. He reaches out and grabs her by the upper arms with freezing hands.

"You try to work democratically and all you get is disrespect.

. . . a total lack of discipline.

. . . you all act like you're at sleepaway camp.

. . . from now on I just take what I want. No more asking.

. . . or something."

He seems to be airing a couple or more different grievances. Tania feels dizzy. His icy fingers still clutching her right arm, he reaches down and unsnaps her jeans, poking her in the crotch as he gropes for the zipper.

"Come on," he says.

The wind rattles the big door in its frame and the hammering intensifies, panning now across the roof in slow strafing surges. Cataracts of water fall inside through the window slits and into the darkness below. Teko unzips her jeans and tries to yank them down, "Come on now," he says, "help me." The breath he chants into her face is sweet, putrid, cigarettey.

"No, Teko, I don't want this."

"It's going to happen."

"No, Teko."

"Help me now," he insists, pulling, his fingernails raking her.

"No, Teko."

"You have to."

He has her hand now and is jabbing at himself with it; she keeps it as dumb and stiff as a mannequin's but can't mistake the hot, jouncing erection for anything other than what it is. The sheer intimacy of this assault is all needful rage; the thing Teko is trying to wrap her hand around demands a satisfactory answer; that other, usual, anger of Teko's—the comic, blustering ire—is nothing compared with this thrusting, jockeying, earnest vehemence. In the days of the closet, when Cinque, Teko, and, god damn it, yes, Cujo had taken turns with her, it was all compounded talk and cajolery and appeals to what was portrayed as her born culpability that led to her humiliated surrender. But this is spiked with a greater violence, plain and awful.

He tries forcing her down, getting his leg behind her knees to fold her there so that she crumples partway and then dropping her. She lands, lightly and solidly, on her back, breathing in the old smell of sweet hay and manure gone stale. Teko stands over her for a moment, and she brings her foot up, kicking him in the balls. As Teko doubles up, grunting and panting over the reverberant drumming of the rain, she sees in a corner near the yawning door the two upturned milk crates where she had sat, studious and compliant, learning the People's tongue.

Teko straightens up, puts his small, shriveled penis away. Then he falls upon her, a collision that expels the reek of his stale sweat. He grips her jaw in his hand and shakes it.

"Do that again and you're dead. Dead." He shakes her jaw roughly, then pops her hard in the chin with the heel of his hand. "Dead."

Finally Teko rises. On his face is all the dull satisfaction of having definitively uttered the last word. After a moment she moves, lifting her ass off the floor and removing a BB that has embedded itself in her soft flesh. She holds it between her thumb and forefinger and lifts it so that she can examine it.

Teko looks as if he were about to speak, and she knows that what he is going to do is he is going to raise the issue of the unswept-up BBs. For the first time since she entered the creamery she experiences true anger, anger undiluted by fear or confusion. She glares at him, angry now beyond the assault: at the daily harassment, at the man's inability ever to quit while he's ahead, at the last three months she's spent enduring him and his bitchy hag of a wife.

Her limited concept of him has been—well, it hasn't been broadened. Say infected with foreign impurities. The perception of him as a man frail with unhappiness and self-doubt, a man capable of these emotions, gained brief admission to her consciousness, drew her to the creamery in curiosity and wonderment and baffled sympathy— and he's made her pay. There's a new complexity to her hatred; that's what's broadened. Perhaps reading some sign of this in her face, angry and pale against the broad boards of the floor, Teko backs off, stands in the doorway under the shelter of the roof that shakes and pings in the siege of the rain before he leaves without having uttered another word.

. . .

Joan sees Teko's face, flat and expressionless as an aluminum pie plate, through the kitchen door. They are gathered around the table again: Kearse with his arm draped over the back of Yolanda's chair; Yolanda in turn inclined toward Kearse, one hand resting on his thigh. Joan sits across from them, smoking. The conversation simply expires as the door swings open and Teko walks through it, drying his eyeglasses on his shirt, into a room he fills with his own spent hostility. Not that the abrupt quiet has everything to do with Teko; the same silence fell when Joan entered, the first to pop the insulating bubble of Kearse and Yolanda's complacent lust.

"H'lo," says Teko.

"Evening, General Field Marshal," says Kearse. "Good run?"

"You looked like maybe you lost your way when we saw you," says Yolanda. Kearse starts, jolted with a quick, silent laugh.

All that moves in the kitchen then is the smoke rising from Joan's cigarette in the ashtray. The sight of it curling dumbly up from the burning cylinder annoys her all at once and she reaches to stab the cigarette out. Like Tania, she feels Kearse's presence as the unbalancing of an equation. She experiences nothing like sympathy for the little man, who now goes to wash his hands in the kitchen sink, the stream of warm water loosening and washing away the soiled bandage that covers his forgotten injury, only disgust with Yolanda and her resolution to test, now, the strength of this one particular "revolutionary conviction" and with Kearse for assisting her, for casually coming in here and planting his lackadaisical sneakers all over their painstaking equilibrium. And with Guy too, while she's at it. What the fuck's he thinking? Sending them guests like this is Martha's Vineyard. What trouble it all is.

She asks, "Where's Tania?"

"I left her in the creamery," says Teko.

"Ahhh, the creamery." Yolanda giggles. Kearse starts again, rocked by his silent gestural laugh. Funny stuff. Lots of fun sitting around with these comedians all afternoon. Lots of fun today with Gary and Yolanda, and lots more to come, Joan can just tell. Everybody in the whole wide world is full of shit, Joan thinks sourly.

"Think I'll go see her," she says. None of the others, each of whom has an idea about who does and who does not belong in the kitchen, objects.

· · ·

She finds Tania sitting cross-legged on the creamery floor, massaging her jaw. Some ugly dishevelment might have signaled the entire story to Joan, flashed it neon-bright into her brain, illuminated a whole territory she's sometimes seen when she and a man's anger have overlapped. But she sees only her friend sitting in an odd place on a dark wet afternoon. When Tania's eyes roll around to focus on Joan, though, she sees something's going on.

"Are you OK?" she asks.

"I'm actually pretty good, I think," says Tania.

Joan comes closer. "What happened to your jaw?"

"Teko did it." A shrug. Then she laughs, a little. "I kicked him in the balls."

"Good girl," says Joan. "Next time kick him once for me."

Guy and a young man sit at the table and chairs Guy has dragged from inside the house and set on the grass. The young man is the journalist Guy has recruited to help write the book, an overweight guy sweating in the dwindling heat of the August evening, carefully dressed, as if for a job interview, in tweed jacket and gray slacks. Guy is in a particularly jovial mood, Tania sees, trading on his neuroses, exaggerating them for comic effect, charming their guest. She wonders: Does he have to?

"Fortune tellers?" Guy is saying. "I love 'em. Tarot, psychics, palmystics, crystal ballbusters. They're a diversion and they're a habit and they're surprisingly rare, a comment incidentally on the prejudices lurking behind local zoning laws. Let me tell you about the all-time number one fortune-telling experience of my life. I go to a chick who's got this tiny closet of a stall on Church Street in San Francisco. Looks and sounds just like Maria Ouspenskaya, a schmata on her head, earrings the size of hula hoops. Minute I sit—bang!, she starts telling me all about myself. Where I was born, what happened to me when I was a kid, all that jazz. Great, I mean, really on the ball, but what do I need to know all this for? Tell me the things I *don't* already know. So she says, 'This you don't want to know? About what you want to know? Who it is has it in for you? Who your true love is gonna be? What's that pain going a boom-a-boom in your side right about here? What it is will become of you?' And I say *shit*, no. I say I've been eating all this crappy food for like two weeks straight, and what I really want to know about, the issue pushing itself to the forefront of my thoughts is, *What kind of things have I unknowingly been eating all these years?* I read this thing in the *Bay Guardian* about what the FDA allows in prepared foods. They have special Filth Labs that analyze foods for what they call defects. What's in Fig Newtons alone is enough to put you off your feed for a couple of days. So, I just want a sampler—so I know what I'm up against. You know? All you have to do is read the papers to know that these are bad times, dark times, nutritionally speaking. So she takes a deep breath. Passes a gnarled old hand over the crystal ball. 'You are certain?' she says. Of course I'm certain. Think I'm walking in here just for the good news? Save it for the tourists, baby. You're the real thing; well, I'm the real thing too: a haunted man. Desperate, or curious at any rate. So she passes the hand over the crystal ball again and then hunkers down over it.

" 'There have been at the least one hundred and twenty-seven incidents in the last three years when you have consumed veterinary drugs, in particular antibiotics, along with meat,' she says. 'Enough?' Go on, I say.

" 'At least twice you have eaten food that was contaminated with measurable amounts of radioactivity,' she says. 'Enough?' Keep going.

" 'The Korean barbecue, the taqueria, the dim sum, the Jack-inside-of-the-Box, these are all fine and likely places where to encounter certain uncommon and exotic livestocks in cooked form,' she says. 'Enough?' Don't stop now.

" 'Soft-serve ice cream from all purveyors is a virtual poison to human beings because of certain diminutive parts in the apparatus used to make this confection which are requiring but never getting virtually constant disinfection,' she says. 'Enough?' More, more.

" 'The number of times you have devoured insect parts, larvae, and waste are far too copious to enumerate,' she says. 'Enough?' Onward!

" 'Once you consumed pretzels and other gratuitous comestibles in a saloon in San Bruno, and these were tainted with human urinary and fecal residue,' she says. 'Enough?' Not by a long shot.

" 'A tubercular waiter who did not like you did an expectoration in your soup in a restaurant last month,' she says. 'Enough?'

"And finally I say, OK, enough. That is just *dandy*."

The young man is laughing; the table is rocking on the uneven surface of the lawn. Guy tells the story with his usual animation, his hands periodically moving to reshape the crystal ball he has formed in the air before him.

"Guy, how do you suppose she knew about that pain in your side?" the young man asks.

Guy's face falls.

In the kitchen Yolanda is cursing and throwing empty bottles into the trash.

"Norman *Mailer*, he said, god damn it! Hunter fucking *Thompson*!"

The young man is Adam K. Trout, an instructor at a junior college over the Canadian border. Ph.D. from Brown and—more important, for the purposes of revolutionary accreditation—an expellee from the London School of Economics. "I took a shit on a picture of the queen," he says, proudly, by way of explanation. Trout gazes at Tania over his bottle of Genesee cream ale and her face slips into a practiced glazed dullness: Trout has that now-familiar starstruck look.

Guy leaves them again, climbing into the indefatigable Bug and taking to the road, leaving behind the writer, a tape recorder, and miscellaneous stationery supplies.

Teko talks about a dog he had, Rex. Who taught him the value of selflessness. Of loyalty.

Yolanda talks about the injustice she saw working as a waitress in Illinois. It was a form of awakening.

Trout's face, impassive and still, gazes steadily at each of his interlocutors from over the tape recorder sitting between them.

Later they listen to the playbacks, Teko and Yolanda do, while Tania, Joan, and Trout play gin rummy in the kitchen. Their own voices unspooling, monotonous and strange, from the tape. The afternoon's session has captured them sounding banal, clichéd, incoherent, naive, rambling, tongue-tied, and unaware, to list things alphabetically. Not to mention the sounds, embarrassing to the point of faint nausea, of the quotidian goings-on the tape has arrested. At one point in the recording, Yolanda whines, "Gimme couple more, some more of that ice. Will you, sweet pea?" Really, is that how she sounds? In the background is Teko's unintelligible response and the tinkling of the extra cubes he drops into a glass.

Why is it so embarrassing on tape?

Because it reveals to you as naked and obvious the open fact of your own preposterousness, a fact that normally is concealed only from you?

"What I saw was like I saw maybe there was something more than what I like thought there was. I mean like a different world, society or whatever?"

Tomorrow they will do things differently.

Here is the way Teko decides that they will do things differently: They will work out questions ahead of time, with as little assistance from Trout as possible, and then fabricate appropriate answers to them on paper. These scripts will be recorded, then retranscribed, and then the transcripts scrutinized to identify and correct any inconsistencies between the statements provided by the SLA three (Joan has declined to participate), to firm up and clarify matters of political dogma and philosophy, and to begin to shape the interviews toward the desired end, a finished book. In short, an assembly line approach, precise and controlled.

Trout's reaction is diffident but unenthusiastic.

Tania works on a mattress in the sleeping loft, lying on her side to write. So many choices. Was she kidnapped, rescued, liberated, or saved? Was she converted, rehabilitated, reeducated, or transformed? Is she a freedom fighter, a revolutionary, an insurgent, an urban guerrilla? So many decisions. Well, definitely not saved, she thinks. Or converted. Too evangelical-sounding.

She rolls over onto her stomach and continues to write. Soon it'll be time for her session with Trout. They'll sit outside on the grass, if it's pleasant, or in the creamery. Someplace informal, Trout says.

So many questions. They proffer themselves to Tania, though most are far outside the parameters of the "Tania Interview" as established by Teko and Yolanda.

Did she love her family? Does she see herself as different from the person she was when she lived with them? Did she see herself as different from the others at the time?

On the tape, she says, "The media knowingly spreads propaganda lies regarding how close my family is."

She says, "An upbringing like mine, coming from my class position, was all about bringing me in line with my parents' and their friends' values and ideas. In high school everyone I knew was from a background like mine. Though I was embarrassesd by and ashamed of my parents' wealth, I had no support, no one to help me understand why I felt the way I did. Everyone was too like me."

Does that make sense?

Who is she now? Is the SLA her family? Is a family something it is possible to choose? Did she choose the SLA? Did Cinque actually offer her a "choice" per se? Hadn't she already, in effect, chosen—left her birth family; surrendered some of the burdens and privileges of that "class position" and its "values and ideas"—by choosing to live, out of wedlock, in genteel though hardly luxurious circumstances with Eric Stump?

On the tape, she says, "I wanted Eric to take me away and change my name. I felt very safe with Eric. I thought that I would be able to escape my ruling class upbringing with him."

She says, "I cooked dinner and cleaned the toilet. I let my mother plan my wedding. I posed and smiled for the engagement pictures. But soon I was wishing to escape from this relationship that I'd begun to hate."

Does that make sense?

Does she remember making love to Eric for the first time in his Menlo Park apartment, then driving to Draeger's for thirty dollars' worth of gourmet specialties that would please him? That would please them both? Was there anything that she hated on that day, anything that she felt other than the most delicious sense of triumph watching Eric's face tighten as he convulsed with his orgasm?

When, at Draeger's, she tore the personal check out of her checkbook and passed it over to the checkout clerk, did she thrill a little as she saw the clerk's face brighten with useless comprehension at the sight of the famous name?

Hadn't she wanted to be engaged? Hadn't she dreamed of a station wagon, with a big dog hanging its stupid head out the window?

And hadn't she always really liked to cook? Wasn't it actually the fact that Stump was ready and willing to eat just about any old slop that was around that had provided her with her most acute marital, as it were, dejection?

303

Who is she now? Who in the end had changed her name?

On the tape, she says, "It only took me a week or two at most to begin to feel sympathetic with the SLA."

She says, "I was given a choice: join the unit or go back to my parents and Eric Stump. I was worried I wouldn't measure up, but my new comrades were enthusiastic about helping me acquire the military and political skills I needed, as long as I was willing to truly struggle."

Does that make sense?

Did she choose the SLA? *Did* Cinque actually offer her a "choice"? Has she forgotten the daily death threats? Has she forgotten having been locked in a closet for six weeks?

On the tape, she says, "Well, it was pretty cramped in there."

She says, "What is meant by 'brainwashing'? To me, now, it seems mostly to refer to what the fascists refer to as 'mandatory education.' School begins the process and the pig media ensures its continuance."

She says, "How could I disagree with the goals of the SLA? How dishonest would I have to be with myself to disagree with the idea of wanting hungry children to have enough to eat?"

And, "Starvation, hunger, ghettos, poverty. This is the real tragedy, not that one rich bitch has been kidnapped and might get killed."

Does that make sense?

Is it really self-honesty that causes a person to seek common ground with the people who threaten to kill her?

Does she actually not understand that she was the "rich bitch" who might get killed? Has her conversion in any real way relieved the plight of the poor? Would her death have relieved it?

Who is she now? Does it matter, really, to anyone except her?

On the tape, she says, "Most of us in the struggle are like millions of other young people. We have overcome our conditioning to see Amerikkka for what it really is."

She says, "That is what scares the pigs. They would like to portray us as freaks and outcasts, but we are in every town, on every street, in every house. We could be anyone's child, spouse, sibling, neighbor, or friend."

She says, "My parents used their grip on the media to rouse public sympathy. My family exploited their plight to sell newspapers."

And, "It was the fascist nightmare of a little white girl carried off by strong black men. They used my baby pictures to stoke fear."

Does that make sense?

Is it not clear to her that she is not just anyone's child? How effortful could it have been to "rouse public sympathy" for suffering parents?

Does she really believe her kidnapping to have been her *family's* plight?

On the tape, she says, "My parents left our care to others, to nannies and governesses. They didn't want to dirty their hands. We were their little trophies."

She says, "My mother was on drugs too often to be a real mother to me. Even as a child I found it to be very unappealing."

She says, "Both my mother and father had problems with booze and pills."

And, "Only now does my mother deign to talk to me. She cries crocodile tears in front of reporters and advises me to trust in God. But she dresses in black which tells me that as far as she's concerned I'm already dead. Well, bitch, the feeling is mutual."

Does she really hate her parents? Or do these answers serve the purpose of exposing her parents' "values and ideas" and by extension those of their class?

Who is she now? Who changed her name?

What might have brought about the change, other than some form of coercion?

On the tape, she says, "The geniuses of the pig media suggest that during the early weeks with my comrades I was falling in love with some member of the group. How bourgeois that they could not recognize that it was the People with whom I was falling in love."

She says, "Cujo sat outside the closet, before I got a light in there to study by, and read aloud to me from Stalin's *Dialectical and Historical Materialism* and other essays."

She says, "He was very patient with me. He answered all my ignorant questions, knowing that I was growing and changing under his attention."

And, "I had a lot of positive and strong feelings for him before my acceptance as a member of the cell."

And, "Cujo was patient, loving, devoted, enthusiastic, and passionate."

And, "Cujo was beautiful, gentle, kind, and tender."

And, "Cujo was strong, brave, resolute, and unhesitant."

And, "Cujo and I grew stronger and more purposeful because of the reinforcement and encouragement we provided each other."

And, "Cujo and I were assigned to different teams because our skills and talents complemented those of different people. It was definitely *not* because we were in love and the others wanted to separate us."

Hmmmm.

J. V. Stalin: "Hence, the practical activity of the party of the proletariat must not be based on the good wishes of 'outstanding individuals' . . . Hence, the party of the proletariat should not guide itself in its practical activity by casual motives."

Must she deny him even now? Or is it simply easier? What would it cost her to attempt to describe the intricacy of her feelings concerning this brief and intense affair? To reveal the stubborn, continuing effort to camouflage the political infelicity of love as another form of radical camaraderie?

Oh, Cujo. 6'4" freckles stupid peaked cap the mustache that wouldn't grow Stump he said Stump had a mustache dumb-dumb jealous of Stump! that smile of his gone belt buckle in the newspaper photo pigs standing over that crushed pile of ashes and bone "beyond recognition" with his belt buckle there she spotted it and who got the monkey?——

How frequently does she reach up to touch that stone monkey nestled in the hollow of her throat?

——and what about her other feelings? Cujo on her in the closet, having "asked" for the opportunity to be "comradely." Wasn't forgiveness accelerated by death, that one wedge between them knocked aside only once he'd vanished into oblivion?

Does she begin to lose her enthusiasm for the interview process at this point? Do the neatly written questions and answers, and the various interlinear and marginal interpolations and emendations, suddenly appear meaningless, trite, remote from her real preoccupations? Does Trout's face, opposite hers, eager behind the impassive mask he wears, begin to betray his impatience as he waits for her to speak?

Who is she now? Is she more articulate now? More aware now? More brave now? More critical now? More experienced now? More fit now? More happy now? More lonely now? More mature now? More moral now? More practical now? More ruthless now? More smart now? More strong now? More sympathetic now? More tired now?

Is she less dependent now? Less elitist now? Less frightened now? Less helpless now? Less ignorant now? Less naive now? Less pliant now? Less sentimental now? Less silly now? Less spoiled now? Less squeamish now? Less tongue-tied now?

So many questions. They proffer themselves. Though most go unanswered, like prayers.

A ROAR AND A glow in the air, both faint, both coming from Candlestick Park off to the southwest. Extra innings coming to their clammy finale in the fog and the swirling, stymieing outfield winds. The rolled-up windows of Popeye Jackson's car are all fogged up from the hot breaths of its occupants. Popeye sitting with Deandra Booker, a sweet little sister up from East Menlo. She seems somewhat nonplussed by the proposition he is making. I mean like not what she expected.

"Popeye, I got *work* down there. In a office? You know?"

"What work? You type?"

"Learned in school."

"So you say you can't go to this *office*, type up these letters and shit, just as well from right here?"

"What I'm suppose to take, the SamTrans? That's a hour. And I have to get downtown to the bus stop first."

"Get another job. Here in the city. Sunday paper's full of them."

"Uh-huh."

"It's just for a while."

"Popeye. Besides. What's my landlord going to say he sees you at my house?"

" 'Sir.' "

"Ha-ha. Really."

"Why you always have to think about some *contingency*? Why, Jesus?"

"I have to think about getting to work when the clock says eight-thirty."

"Eight fucking thirty? I thought *nine* to *five* is the general rule."

"Maybe someplace. Not at DFW Corporation."

"What's that? Dumb Fucking Whitey?"

"Popeye. You bad."

"You know it."

"But why?"

"Why what?"

"Why you want to stay at my house?"

Because . . . Popeye shakes a cigarette out of the pack on the dash and lights it with one of these here Cricket lighters. Flick, flick, flick, small flame briefly illuminating the interior of Popeye's car, the small woman gazing at him from the passenger seat, like bursts of light from the muzzle of a gun. The story. A woman. Old gray-haired lady Sara Jane Moore. Woman was a strange damn woman. Worked as a bookkeeper for that People in Need. While all the time she's also working for the FBI, informing on the Left. Like what could *she* know? They pouring whole milk on cornflakes instead of skim? Sneaking they garbage into the neighbor's cans? The FBI probably could learn more just reading the *San Francisco Bay Guardian* every week, but whatever. FBI never know nothing, just like to make up they files. Anyway, Sara Jane begins bringing Popeye glad tidings from Henry Billionaire Galton who has got it into his head that Popeye maybe can put in a word with his daughter Alice. Who Popeye never laid a eye on or said a word to but so what. Anyways, they fuck up his parole with that fucked-up smack bust, and what does Popeye sit down with his a.m. Postum to read? A *Examiner* editorial extolling the United Prisoners Union and singing his praises as if he was Martin Luther King. So basically Popeye will be putting his ass in the driver's seat of a little mother-fucking airplane and skywrite a motherfucking valentine from Daddy to his daughter if that's what Henry Galton want. Back and forth they go, Popeye paying out his line, getting his hook into the man.

He knew the SLA, sure.

Donald DeFreeze was this kind of man, see. Not smart, but not too dumb, either. Not crazy, but the dude was not all there, know what I'm saying.

The rest, they just followed along.

They all dead now, though.

Alice is someplace nearby.

This was all conjecture, see, but the Parole Board reinstated his parole.

Play him long enough Galton could get Popeye elected to Congress.

Then Sara Jane Moore came one lonely day into the sweet-smelling room where Popeye had just vipered down a joint and something about her desolate earnestness so impetuously stirred Popeye that he thought he'd itch her gibs just for the fuck of it, and it fucked her up good. Coming around all the time practically saying ahh. Sorry, bitch. One taste is enough.

Turn it to the left. Turn it to the right. Sara Jane now's officially a revolutionary. The FBI are the bad men, get caught holding the bag with a bunch of bullshit files full of *bull*shit courtesy Sara Jane about whether Venceremos is adding Downy to its laundry suds. But guess the fuck what? Guess who is a "informer" against the "Movement" now? Guess who's "betraying" the "revolution" by "getting too close" to Henry Galton?

Suddenly it's all alarms and Fourth of July and shit. Nobody give a rat's ass that Sara Jane is walking down the corner phone booth to ring the pigs that Huey Newton poured his used motherfucking motor oil down into the motherfucking storm drain but if old Popeye tries to work out a accommodation to keep his ass out of stir it's time for a turkey shoot.

He's getting death threats. Signs indicate that they are for real. Like, he left this shirt laying on the bed and when he got home it's not there. Like they took it away and shit. Get a sample of his cellular structure do some weird shit to him. And some glass on the table still filled with ice cubes. How they're not going to melt while he be out? Someone in there, waiting. He felt the shadow of a murderous presence. Good thing they got bored.

Which is why Popeye is sitting in his car on a cold San Francisco night trying to convince the beautiful Deandra Booker to swap apartments with him.

The glow in the southwestern sky is suddenly diminished; the lights ringing the parapet atop Candlestick have been doused. Popeye leans forward and rubs some of the condensation off the windshield in front of him, peering out into the murky gloom. "Well, look at it here," he says.

"What?"

"Fog. Gets into my bones, makes 'em achy. Big mildew crawling up the shower curtain. Bottom of my shoes turning green in the closet." This is true. Pulled some dress shoes out for another bullshit hearing and found a delicate mold, the color of lichen, spreading across the soles. "My age, that ain't good. Turn into a asprin junkie."

"What do I want with green shoes?"

"Maybe some Irish in you."

"Ha-ha."

"We going to do it?"

"Let me think about it."

"Don't be thinking too long. I'll get someone else. Lose this exclusive opportunity." Popeye is joking, but he is sweating, nervous. He would like to be on the Bayshore right now, heading down to Menlo Park. "Popeye Jackson, police informer." How tight that snitch jacket is once they get it on you. And here comes somebody, fuzzy and indistinct in the light pooled around one of the lampposts up near the corner. Popeye watches the figure approach, vague and misty, through the little clean patch of windshield just in front of him.

"I don't know if I'm buying what you're selling." She reaches out and takes the pack off the dash, shakes a smoke out, and lights it. "Too smoky in here," she says, cranking down her window a few inches. "Open yours too."

"No," says Popeye.

"Popeye, open it!" Deandra leans across him and begins to turn the crank.

"I fucking said no!" Popeye grabs her by the shoulders and throws her back into the passenger seat, where she sits staring coldly at the foggy windshield, cigarette snapped in two like a Benson & Hedges ad. "Fucking said no, bitch," Popeye adds, quietly.

Footsteps are audible as the figure passes the car. Popeye sits perfectly still, quiet, tense. Then Deandra says, "Popeye, what?" The footsteps stop. Popeye is in the act of raising his index finger to his pursed lips when the first shot shatters his window, catching him in the left shoulder. The second shot hits him in the back, ricochets inside his chest, where it severs his aorta, and then exits under his left nipple, lodging in the upholstery of Deandra's seat. The third shot enters the back of his skull and tears through his brain. For the fourth shot the killer rounds leisurely to the other side of the car and shoots Deandra in the right eye through her open window.

Just to prove that some people take things seriously. Popeye's last thoughts? Righteous righteous self-righteous pain.

On the morning of the seventh day, Trout's suitcase lies open on the coffee table, his clothes piled haphazardly inside. Trout sits on the couch in his T-shirt and undershorts, meditatively dipping a piece of toast into the yolk of a soft-boiled egg whose shell balances in an eggcup improvised from a shot glass. He is alone in the big room below the sleeping loft, having already bid goodbye to Tania and Joan, who've left early to go to town and run some errands. Before him is a stack of cassette tapes. Seven of them bear numbered labels reading "T." Others, also numbered, read "Y." or "Tk."

This has been an uncommon week for Trout. By now he's just about completely lost interest in the project Guy had made sound so exciting. Conned him into, really. It took him maybe two hours after his arrival to realize that Teko and Yolanda were completely indifferent to literary matters, to questions of style, flavor, pacing, wit, and spontaneity. Chiefly, they were concerned with compulsively controlling all aspects of the making of the book. First the questions. Then the answers. Well, to be honest, at first Trout had thought the scriptwriting thing might help, if only because he figured it would disabuse them of the notion that the book was just waiting out there—free, ambient, ready to be harvested. Writing one was a bitch of a job and he was happy to have them know it. But it only encouraged their obsessiveness. Even after they'd begun working from the scripts—Trout rattling off the inane prompts he'd been supplied and fidgeting through the even more inane answers, like David Susskind in Hell—he'd watched them resisting their own words, suspicious of what they themselves had composed only hours before. They'd stop the tape to go back and examine some abandoned draft, make sure it didn't contain the precise turn of phrase they felt was required. During playback Teko and Yolanda would express their great disapproval with the tone of voice in which certain of the questions had been asked or their answers provided.

As if it mattered, any of it; each of them spoke in the voice of the revolutionary automaton. The committee of three would withdraw into its little floating ministry of truth—the creamery, the woods, the funky-smelling sleeping loft—to shape and vet these anodyne dialogues. Trout had begun taking long walks alone in the woods after the sessions to avoid whichever of the three might attempt to take him aside to privately rebut the lies of another. Or it might be Joan, blowing off steam of her own.

It's become clear to him that his function is first to humor them, second to offer a shoulder to cry on, and third to serve as a buffer between them and Guy. Guy, who, when Trout phoned him from town the other evening to kvetch, had grievances of his own to air. Worked his ass off and not a word of gratitude, etc. Did he have any idea how much all this was running him? Etc. Poor Trout. He'd had to rummage through his pockets for change to feed the pay phone at the operator's command, while Guy rambled on.

Eventually they decided that Guy would drive out today to pick him up. Trout's had enough, and now he's ready to head back to Canada, transcribe the tapes, and await further instructions. He does not anticipate receiving his share of the six-figure advance Guy had talked about so, ah, rashly. Not exactly Book-of-the-Month Club material they have to work with here. Guy had thought that by some osmotic process he could turn these dogmatic wackos into a group of impassioned moderates bearing a message of uplift, ha-ha. A summer in the country, juicy berries and sweet corn on the cob: It would be like the Fresh Air Fund, right. Big, big mistake Guy had made, appealing to their vanity while dangling big bucks over their heads. They had amped up, not toned down. These tapes couldn't possibly depict the adoption of a temperate way of thinking.

What they hadn't quite gotten was that the fascist insect was interested only in Tania.

He finishes the last scrap of toast and wipes his mouth on the back of his hand. Then he notices Yolanda gazing steadily at him from the top of the ladder leading to the sleeping loft.

"Good morning," he says. He reaches to lift yesterday's shirt from on top of the clothes piled in the open suitcase, patting the breast pocket for his cigarettes. When he raises his head again, Teko has replaced her up there.

"So today you're leaving."

"I spoke to Guy. He thinks we have enough for a start."

"And how's it going selling the book?"

"I couldn't say. Guy's department."

Teko nods. It's a rhythmic nodding, a bobbing, really. There's silence. Trout feels the cellophany semicrumple of the cigarette pack in his hand.

"And so you're going off to do what, exactly?"

"Well, as I said, Guy thinks we have enough to begin. I'm going back up north, and, you know—" He puts down the pack and mimes the act of typing, fingers flailing away. Then he picks it up again, lightly squeezing the butts through plastic, paper and foil.

"Huh," says Teko. He expels the sound with a rank sourness, like some gaseous discontent. He lowers first one leg and then the other and begins climbing down the ladder.

"I don't know, man," he says.

"I'm sorry?"

"Just. I don't know. Never mind." Teko waves a hand and heads for the kitchen.

Trout feels his release as surely as if he'd been held there on the lumpy, sprung couch by force. He looks and finds the pack of Larks still in his hand. The suitcase still open. The tapes still there, beside the shot glass glazed with yolk.

What Trout doesn't know is that Teko and Yolanda have arrived at a sour, exquisitely paranoid consensus: The reason that Guy Mock wants all the material taped and in his possession is so that he alone can reap the financial benefits from the sale of the book when, having removed the tapes, he calls in the police death squads, which will then kill the occupants of the farm. To demonstrate the authenticity of his material, he will have the tapes of their voices. To facilitate their murder at the hands of the cops, Guy has relocated them to this particular isolated and indefensible property in Jeffersonville.

This fever dream quickly becomes the only possible scenario.

What Trout also doesn't know is that Teko and Yolanda have come up with a counterplan. Today, after Guy and Randi arrive, Teko and Yolanda intend to kill them, along with Trout, and bury the bodies in the woods.

What about Tania and Joan?

Good question.

At the last minute, early in the morning, Yolanda decides to send them to town to buy some groceries.

Trout's in his tweed jacket and gray flannels again. Traveling clothes, as he thinks of them. His watch tells him that it's a little early to expect Guy, so he's taking the air, waiting. He strolls toward the dark boundary of the trees, grasshoppers leaping out of the tall weeds ahead of his every footfall, his hands jammed into his pockets, shoes glistening and pants darkening from the heavy dew. He climbs a gentle incline at the edge of the woods and pauses. Turning, he sees the house, the lawn, the shaded entry to the road, the creamery, all laid out in the near distance below him. He also sees Teko, striding across the lawn, carrying an air rifle in one hand. Spotting him, Teko stops, then raises the rifle. Its barrel gleams as it catches the sun. A greeting? Or? Before Teko continues on his way toward the creamery, Trout notices that he awkwardly cradles something against his chest with his other hand. Trout peeks at his watch again. Then descends, quickly.

Inside the house, Trout can see that the cassettes are no longer on the coffee table.

"You're wondering about your tapes." Yolanda smiles at him serenely, but her body is taut, her arms crossed over her chest.

"Yes."

"We'll be holding on to those."

Trout's mouth falls open to form a question, though he's not quite sure what it will be; his mouth is just following his upper body's lead: head jutting forward, shoulders hunching—a pantomime of skeptical incredulity. He shrugs and juts his head, mouth agape, as if an insect has suddenly stung him on the back of the neck.

His question turns out to be: "Why can't I have my tapes?"

"It's a question of we have to safeguard our security. So they'll be staying here with us."

"I really don't see why. It's counterproductive. Guy will be very unhappy when he finds out."

"Oh, fuck Guy!" Yolanda's voice lilts pleasantly, as though she were talking to a child. And Trout is aware that his own voice sounds small, boyish, petulant, overcome. One fissure, and he has revealed everything.

"You almost," she continues, "have me believing he's fooled you too."

"Fooled?"

"Please."

Teko comes in. He still carries the BB gun.

"Beautiful morning," he says. "Beautiful, beautiful morning." Thrusting his hand into an open box of cereal on the kitchen table, he draws up a handful and proceeds to eat it. Mouth full, he says, "Hemingway figure it out yet?"

"He's getting there."

"I'm sorry," Trout says, "I'm very confused right now. I've spent a week of my time out here, and I really don't understand this at all."

"Like you need an explanation," says Teko.

"Please do explain," Trout says.

"Lays it on thick, doesn't he?"

"All I can say is, we are so disappointed," says Yolanda.

"Disappointed?" says Teko. "Does Guy Mock think we're an idiot? We've got Tania! Right here in her own words! Tania! Tania!"

"I really have no idea what you're talking about. Guy's loyal to you. He's dedicated to this book."

"Oh, yeah?" says Yolanda. "Then how come you're not Norman Mailer?"

Trout is rendered speechless. After all, there are so many reasons.

Now here's an unexpected development. Trout appears indirectly to have become the casualty of Guy's self-assured persuasiveness. What Trout does know is that the editors Guy has approached have expressed an enthusiastic, though guarded, shall we say, attitude toward an SLA book. Certain conditions apply. The tenor of their stipulations being along the lines of: Bring us a lock of Tania's hair, a fresh fingerprint, a Polaroid featuring the renegade heiress posed with the headlines of the day. And signed releases, too, would be a big plus. "Shit," Guy had said. "You think an agent would help?"

Still, Trout is hesitant to reveal this intelligence. First of all, he doesn't think that he can make as strong a case for the truth as Guy can for pie in the sky. Second, he knows the money situation here is dire, too dire, really, to abruptly withdraw the promise of "six figures" that's infected everyone's imaginations, induced a type of febrile, depraved expectancy that seems tremendously unrevolutionary, to say the least. And third, there's the air rifle, which Teko cocks, slipping his finger inside the trigger guard.

"Are you going to shoot me with that BB gun?"

Teko must interpret this comment as an insult, an attack on the dignity of his weapon. Smiling his strange smile, he raises the gun to his shoulder and takes aim at Trout. Plainly, Trout reflects, he has in this case erroneously deployed a modifier.

"Teko!" Yolanda's shout makes both Trout and Teko jump, and the gun discharges, shooting Trout in the hand. He and Teko both look slightly confounded by the blood trickling down his wrist, the back of his hand, between his fingers, by the meaty reality of the wound.

"Don't get excited," Yolanda says to Trout. "We'll have a full discussion. What time's Guy coming?"

The familiar clatter of the Bug. And warm greetings for good old Guy from Teko and Yolanda. Guy, wired and loopy and irritable, unfolding from behind the wheel of the VW for like the 863rd time in the last eight weeks, extending himself into country sunlight and a veritable chorus of hail-fellow-well-met salutations and good cheer. Guy, Guy, here's Guy! What happened to Eat Shit? he wonders numbly. Oh, he's tired of these people. He folds the front seat forward so he can remove the paper bag containing the spread he's brought, a celebration lunch of cold cuts, cheese, bread, potato salad, slaw, and cold beer. Not every day you finish the first preliminary stage of a potential project that may eventually turn into the draft manuscript of a book somebody somewhere might want to buy sometime! It's about as lame as that sounds, but Guy wants his revolutionaries optimistic and upbeat. The better to evict them from his life.

We're so glad to see you! Where's Randi?

Randi coming?

Where is she, Guy?

All this concern over Randi. So odd, so new. Refreshing, even. They'd always treated her before as a sort of appendage. Guy lifts the bag out of the backseat and turns, notices for the first time Trout's ashen face, the bandage around his hand.

"What happened to you?"

"Just an accident," says Yolanda. "Will Randi be coming later?"

"No," Guy says. "Randi took a pass today, I'm afraid. She's feeling sort of traveled out. Frayed was one word she used. It's known to happen; take a nice young person and run them ragged and there you go, a disinclination to take trips of this sort. And then there's always the problem of the not-so-spacious backseat and who has to sit in it on the way back. Should I just go ahead and say, she has a hemorrhoid?"

"But she knows you're out here?" Teko asks.

"Of course she knows," Guy says, suddenly alert to the ulterior. There's a kind of calm—physical, impenetrable, and stifling—that lies over things the way a woolen blanket covers up a bloody sheet. "Of course. What kind of accident?"

"Well," says Teko, "I shot him. Can you believe it?"

Trout remains silent. He has a sullen, dazed look on his face.

"A mistake, Guy," says Teko.

"Of course it was," says Guy. He shifts the paper bag from one hand to the other. Teko and especially Yolanda stare at him fixedly. "And where are the others?" Guy asks.

"Tania and Joan? We sent them into town to run a couple errands."

"I could've—" Guy begins to speak but stops. "Well. Done is done. Hope I don't miss them. A nice lunch, and then your intrepid reporters are off." And running. Guy has a very, very bad feeling.

On the kitchen table is wound litter: a bottle of antiseptic, some scraps of cotton and tape. The air rifle lies on the floor. The house smells of sweat and stale smoke. Guy sets the bag on the counter and rapidly begins to unpack the food, laying it out. Buffet style, as his mother would say. Eat it and beat it. They'll take the tapes back to Ninetieth Street and see what's there. Through all of it, all the difficulties—the thousands of miles, the thousands of dollars, the occasional sardonic report from Joan, the near-tears phone calls from Trout, the bulging suspicion that this was not, after all, going to be the book the educated middle class would turn to at bedtime to knock itself out—the project has persisted in Guy's brain, burning there, just out of reach in his cranium, the apparition of its own perfect embodiment. Eventually he'll grab hold of it, with or without the help of the SLA.

He's appeared alone here today because of Randi's refusal this morning, flat out, to get out of bed if the purpose of her rising was to travel to Jeffersonville. Just overflowing with hostility these days. Hot to get back to those brown California foothills, the tinderbox calm of late summer. There's been scene upon scene over the last week or so. Tiresome and, irritatingly enough, ultimately persuasive. Randi began by pulling out the last few months' bank statements, charting for him the oceans of cash that had flowed out of their hands. This never bothered Guy, but he understood that for Randi money was always a suitable way to frame an issue that had moral dimensions. He was like, OK, develop your thesis. Moving right along, Randi pointed out that if anything, he had less sympathy for the SLA's tactics and objectives today than he'd had when he first heard of the group. That Teko, Yolanda, and Tania did not hesitate to demand money, food, shelter, transportation, supplies, and weapons but viciously rebuked the Mocks for their politics, values, and way of life. That Joan, too, now not only seemed to take their largesse as her due but appeared also almost to resent their ability to provide it. She suggested to him that it was only a matter of time before the feds linked the personal check Guy had written to Fire Lieutenant Lafferty to the place in South Canaan and were all over it and them.

Uh, Guy still hasn't gotten around to mentioning his little indiscretion with Ernest to Randi.

But these are suddenly the problems of the past. There are more immediate problems to be dealt with, Guy can see that. He can be blind to many things, God knows, but the data rolling in here are hard to overlook. Missing parties. Wounds. Suspicious questions. He's moving quickly, finding a bread knife, a bottle opener; fishing condiments out from around the uncovered plates of congealed food Yolanda has stocked the fridge with, yuck, getting things together in a hurry. He drops a saucer removing it from the cupboard and watches it fall, wheeling itself gracelessly toward the linoleum, absurdly slow. It bounces on impact, lucky break. He reaches for it, thinking of the traditions encased in a single life, secret and rich and headed for oblivion. The way, for example, he turns a loaf of Italian bread on its side, to easily slice it lengthwise. The way, say, he rings a plate with overlapping slices of cheese. The way he wipes his ass and then examines the toilet paper. The various stylistic distinctions of superficially indistinct men. Oh, how he does not want to die. Not ever, really, but certainly not here and now. Could be he's just being paranoid. Could be that. But there is a dread feeling here, an alarm, a ghost vibe drilling its way right through his skin.

He turns from the counter, holding plates of food in both hands. Still no Tania, no Joan. Could it be that they're already occupying the hole that waits for him and Trout? The modern way to go, standing at the edge of an open pit, at the head of the final queue.

"Here's the food," he says.

They eat hurriedly, without conversation. Trout remains sullen, wordless, making short, stabbing gestures at the food on his plate. Teko eats in his robotic fashion until he empties his plate, and then he immediately pushes it away. Yolanda lingers over her food. Guy notices that she makes faint humming noises as she eats. When he looks into her eyes, he discerns a sort of patient hostility there, latent and coiled. She's been sitting on it since day one, but she studies him now with an anticipation that sends a chill down his spine. Does he imagine her pupils dilate at the contemplation of him?

Tania says, offhand, while they stand waiting for the clerk to finish slicing liverwurst for another customer, "They're taking Adam's tapes before he goes, you know. Guy'll be pissed off."

"Who?" asks Joan.

"Who else? I heard them talking up in the loft."

"All that work."

"Funny, huh? What a waste of time."

"Why, I wonder."

"Oh, I know why," says Tania. "They think Guy wants to rip them off for the book. I'm like, *what* book?"

"Guy? Steal the book?"

"For the money, I guess. They're totally paranoid."

"Why? What else they said?"

"They said he was setting us up, that the whole Jeffersonville move was a setup."

"A setup, God. I'm sure Guy has a secret reason for being us up here, but that's not what it is. Must have been tough for you not to bust up laughing."

"Oh, my God, it was. They said they had to get the tapes and shut Guy up before we got out of here. I'm like, where are we going *now*?" She yawns, glances at the wall clock.

"What do you mean shut Guy up?"

Tania offers a noncommittal shrug.

Joan's reaction is delayed for a moment, but then she takes Tania by the elbow and leads her out of the store.

"Joan, we left the groceries."

"Come on, honey."

Whatever grievances she may have against Guy Mock, however much evidence she has gathered proving that his every move is informed by self-interest, however much of a pain in the ass he may be, however much better off she personally would be with him out of the picture, Joan is skeptical of Teko and Yolanda's view of things, and she most assuredly does not want to see Guy Mock die at their hands because of some wacky misapprehension. Stiff them out of some of their advance, maybe, but sell them out to the pigs?

"What's going on? Why are we rushing back?"

They hurry along the side of the road. A dog dashes across the yard before a house and stops at the edge of the lawn, circling, pawing the mown grass and barking at them as they walk past.

"Good dog," says Joan.

It's all been heading here, Joan realizes. Talk all that talk about guns and death, call people *pigs* and *insects* until they stop being people, until they're nothing, *vermin*, just a *problem*, and suddenly it's easy: You press a button; they die. Why not? She remembers with Willie, when his beliefs, the gale force of his righteousness, weren't close to being enough anymore. That stupid bomb factory! First they blow up IBM Selectrics, Xerox machines, and acres of indoor/outdoor carpeting, all the things that make today's modern offices so distinctive, so interesting. Then one day they're trying to off a saloon full of cops. She's glad he got caught, she's *glad*. If he were to have tried something like this, she would have rushed to stop him. Is it prescience that moves her now?

After the meal Yolanda invites Guy and Trout on a little stroll.

"OK," says Guy. "I think we have time. Have to hit the road with those tapes soon, though."

"Oh," says Yolanda, "couldn't you just call Randi, tell her you're spending the night? And for God's sake, ask her to come."

That's it.

Still, Guy has to step back and admire himself a little; his impulse is to try to wheedle the tapes out of her, just so he can hold them, possess them. Despite the approach of death—his certainty that even as he and Yolanda chat pleasantly, Teko is sneaking up behind him, ready to stove in his braincase—he talks right on through, trying to gain the tapes even as he awaits the deathblow.

And then, from under the dark awning of the trees covering the road, Tania and Joan appear. Joan runs to Guy. She hugs him. She hugs him!

"What the—what are you doing back so soon?" asks Yolanda.

This is the moment when Guy realizes that he will live, will remain alive for the foreseeable future, overwhelming emotion flooding his system: deep relief—not happiness, but a grateful sense of reinstatement. Grateful for: the little birds. Grateful for: the blades of grass.

Prescience:

Guy is destined to leave behind his pride, a stack of cassette tapes, and about eight dollars' worth of delicatessen food and to take with him both his life and Adam K. Trout.

Whose wounded hand will begin bleeding again near Port Jervis, New York.

Who will devote much nervous talk to gangrene, sepsis, and blood poisoning, none of which he is fated to suffer.

It is predestined that Guy will prevail upon Trout to seek treatment for his wound at home in Canada, with its superior system of socialized medicine.

His confidence restored, Guy redoubles his effort to get the tapes. Teko stammers something about transcribing the tapes himself. Too incriminating, too risky to let them out of his possession. Plus, Yolanda adds, Tania sounds like a fucking zombie on them: bad PR. Guy smiles and agrees, his counterarguments falling away, growing small and faint. He will live. For the foreseeable future. Whatever that means.

Grateful for: the ceaseless insects. Grateful for: the gentle breeze.

Guy will use his dwindling funds to purchase a Greyhound bus ticket to that nation for Trout; on the bus Trout will sit next to a recently released ex-convict who will suffer four petit mal seizures during the trip, further rattling the academic cum freelance writer's nerves.

After leaving Trout at the Port Authority Bus Terminal, Guy is fated to enter a Blarney Stone tavern on Fortieth Street, where he will sit moodily drinking draft Schaefer and eating pretzels while watching the Mets beat the Atlanta Braves 6–5.

It shall come to pass that Guy will return to Ninetieth Street to find

Randi all packed up and ready to announce that she has unilaterally accepted an offer from a friend, an offer Guy long sat on, to move the operations of the ISSS to his spacious house in Portland, Oregon.

Yolanda barks at Tania to get inside the house and put the groceries away, then notices that neither Joan nor she carries any. Tania and Joan break up, and Yolanda flushes a deep red.

"Get inside anyway," she says.

Tania flips her a quick finger but turns and goes in.

Yolanda draws Joan aside. "What brought you back so soon? Forget something?"

"I thought you might need me," Joan says.

Guy consciously cedes control. It is part of the mechanism of his gratitude, that he should give up that which he most desires, other than his own life. He watches it all float away. Everything, drifting high into the blue, penetrating in the course of its lazy flight the cotton puff clouds that hang above. For which, too, he is so grateful.

They need to get across the country, Teko says. Guy feels— redundancy intended—drained, exhausted, spent. Not enough synonyms to sum up this feeling of toilworn fatigue. But grateful. And all he wants, really, is to help them get across the fucking country. A rare confluential moment, unanimity of opinion. Let him, if living is to be his compensation, undo everything he has done, restore things exactly to what they had been at the beginning of the summer. Let him, if he is to survive to see another day—or, OK, say at minimum another twenty, twenty-five years—return these people, these comrades, these trusted friends, to their fatherland (so to speak), to their familiar folkways, to their lares and penates.

But Randi will kill him if he spends another dime.

CORRECTION: Guy will emerge from the tavern to discover that his car is "missing," though he will not report the apparent theft for a week.

After the car is discovered, wrecked and vandalized, near Seelyville, Pennsylvania, Guy and Randi are destined to realize $1,160 in insurance proceeds.

"Coincidentally," Seelyville is only a few miles from the South Canaan farmhouse.

In the glove compartment police will find a sheet of paper seeming to detail a cross-country route.

Teko has a plan in mind. His hand is on Guy's arm, fingertip-light, as he explains the revolution's progress. The revolution already shows signs of going well in California. He sounds like an entrepreneur dealing in subversion, speaking of bombs going off the way he might of new franchises opening: happening all over the state. He has people in place, in key positions, doing advance work, opening up the territory. He's been in touch with Susan Rorvik; she's been laying the groundwork, establishing a "second team." Teko is relaxed, enthused, happy at the prospect of returning to the West Coast. This was all it took. Just like Randi, Guy thinks. People just get hooked on the damn place. Is it the weather, the earthquakes, or the blood-drinking beach cults, or are they all basically the same thing? But he's grateful. Grateful for: the warmth of the summer sun. Grateful for: unfettered access to a revolving charge account.

The $1,160 will turn out to be just enough money to cover the rental of a Ryder truck and the cost of separately transporting Teko, Yolanda, Joan, and Tania to the West Coast.

Once again Guy will squire Tania, to Las Vegas, where Guy will install Tania in a vacant room in his parents' motel (Thinking: Touch of Evil. *Thinking:* Psycho*) until Jeff Wolfritz arrives to transport her to the new safe house, the origin spot for the New SLA, in Sacramento.*

Everybody's happy! Skoal! Cheers! To health, prosperity, and long life, and let Guy's generosity flow and flow.

At the outset of his journey, Guy is destined to order a hamburger at an A&W stand. Opening the burger to administer salt and pepper, he will discover a foreign object, a small, jagged piece of plastic amid the pickle relish and ketchup.

Dateline:
Hillsborough

All the signs point to a breakthrough!
A breakthrough in the case!
Here is Thomas Polhaus, agent in charge,
    special agent, ah, in charge,
San Francisco office. Of the FBI.
With no comment at the present time.
He has no comment.
He is playing it close to the vest.
Tight-lipped.
Whatever the feds have, they aren't
spilling it.
He is entering the Galton home. The Galton
mansion.
Special Agent in Charge Thomas Polhaus, a
veteran of many investigations, is entering
stately Galton Mansion here in exclusive
Hillsborough, with few words for the the
members of the press assembled outside.
Tommy to his friends, his many friends.
Could it be that there's been a break-
through?
The Galton case has baffled law enforcement
authorities for just about a year now.
There's been speculation
    some speculation. That the trail is grow-
ing cold.

The arrival here, today of Thomas Polhaus,
in charge of the investigation from the beginning, raises speculation that there may
have been a breakthrough.

The press is here, outside stately Galton Mansion in the exclusive enclave of
Hillsborough, California.

It's hard to imagine tragedy touching a
town such as this. But

it has.

The press has been here every day. The
Galtons

the gracious Galtons

have been very accommodating of the needs
of the press.

They understand as perhaps few others can
that the press has a job to do. Just as they

just as the FBI

has its job.

The first family of journalism. Henry Galton
is publisher of the *San Francisco Examiner*.
Handsome, amiable fellow.

Under strain, though   under visible strain

visibly under strain. This ordeal. The
ordeal of his daughter, kidnapped just a
little under a year ago, by the radical

the radical left-wing

Symbionese Liberation Army.

And there is Thomas Polhaus, entering
this well-appointed home. Under the eyes of
the press.

Also visibly under strain. Though not as much

not as much, of course, as the heartbro-
ken parents of the young heiress, who now
calls them pigs.
Just gotten engaged to be married when
tragedy struck.
Full-faced, beautiful girl. Calls herself
Tania and is photographed carrying a gun,

a machine gun, wearing the baggy combat
clothing of the left-wing revolutionary.
Could this mean a breakthrough?
The press has been waiting patiently.

Keeping a vigil. Doing their best not to
disturb the family.

Eating doughnuts, over nine thousand
doughnuts. About two dozen a day, I'd say.
From the look

from the looks of things. And drinking
coffee. The Galtons have been kind enough
to set up an urn

the urn you see before me here. This silver urn has been kept filled with coffee. Day
in and day out. Rain or shine. Inge and
Maria have kept that urn filled with hot,
fresh coffee for the members of the press
keeping their grim vigil

the grim yet hopeful vigil outside
stately Galton Manor.
They are members of the staff here. Inge and
Maria.

Both as hardworking and friendly a pair of
   of servants as you'd ever hope to meet.
Impossible to estimate how much coffee
   just how much coffee has been consumed by
the press. Tens of thousands of cups. Or
more. Also, neighbors
   concerned and sympathetic neighbors have
donated food. Not so much lately but at first
   there was quite an outpouring of support
from neighbors, all understandably sympathetic. And it came in the form of food.
They supplied fried chicken and macaroni
salads, all of which were devoured
   all of which were much appreciated by the
members of the press. Though lately the
press has sent out for sandwiches, now that
the outpouring has subsided. Though you may
be assured that the sympathy has not.
Letters and cards arrive daily
   sacks of correspondence expressing con-
dolences
   wishing the family well.
The girl who one year ago on February 4 was
taken violently from her home
   the home she shared with her fiancé.
Now she stands accused
   she has been accused of participating in
numerous unlawful activities with these
same captors
   the same people who violently wrenched
her from her home she shared with her fiancé.
Who would have predicted these

this turn of events a year

a long year ago.

She was to have been married in June.

And we can only speculate as to the reason
why Mr. Thomas Polhaus has arrived here
in the beautiful town of Hillsborough, at
Galton Manor, as he has countless times before, since this tragedy began to unfold, a
little under a year ago, special agent of
the Federal Bureau of Investigation, which
has devoted countless man-hours to investi-
gating this one single case. Special Agent
Polhaus heading up this case, the investigation of this case, he himself has put in
countless hours sifting through leads and
whatever this breaking news is that he may
be bringing he is keeping to himself, now
entering the elegant home that few of

few members of the press have seen the
inside of, despite our grim vigil here on
the lawn

the green lawn, so well groomed it would
seem nigh impossible that such a lawn, not
to mention the elegant manor house it
surrounds, could be touched by terrible
tragedy, tragedy that goes to the heart of
the fears of the parents of every youngster
in these confusing times, keeping the news
to himself at this time, until he shares it
with the anxious parents, Mr. and Mrs.
Galton

Lydia Galton quite a beauty in her day,
but now under visible
visibly under strain.
Gracious folks, very gracious, tolerating
the presence of the members of the press
here on the great lawn before Galton
Castle, as they keep
we keep our vigil
a job to do and we do it as Mr. and Mrs.
Galton well understand what with
given their historic connection to the
newspaper business among other
among vast
among many other holdings, including
television and radio stations, magazines,
mines, real estate including working farms
and ranches, and stock in many of our nation's largest corporations. One of the
wealthiest families
among the wealthiest
one of the first families of the United
States. And Mr. and Mrs. Galton will as they
always have share whatever news Mr. Thomas
Polhaus brings in their own
at whatever time they deem appropriate
which is the least
which is the most
which is all we can ask of them at this
difficult and tragic time.

PART FOUR

Phantoms of the Coming Emptiness

Somewhere between the Yolo causeway and Vallejo it occurred to me that during the course of any given week I met too many people who spoke favorably about bombing power stations.   —JOAN DIDION

A CHILLY GRAY MORNING, not much sunlight at all, and the young woman fumbles as she affixes a flashbar to the bulky Polaroid camera she holds in her left hand. She is here, alone, outside a coffee shop at the Arden Plaza shopping center, in an unincorporated area of North Sacramento, preparing to photograph the Guild Savings and Loan Association, which sits bland and blameless across a painted grid of empty parking spaces. A sheriff's department cruiser glides slowly through the lot. A good time to put the camera away and study the newspaper headlines framed in the vending machines lined up outside the coffee shop.

Lies come to her, arrive smoothly and without delay, and she selects one about waiting to meet a girlfriend here, about not wanting to go inside and start eating without her. It strikes her as the most unverifiably credible. But the cruiser, one of a total of five on patrol at any given time, exits the shopping center without stopping and drives away. She pulls a memo pad and pen out of her shoulder bag and notes the time.

Several newspapers mention her name in their headlines. It seems it's been a year to the day since she was kidnapped. She gazes at a picture of herself in blank astonishment. Like, she can't relate. In it, she is captured midstride as she approaches the photographer, feathered hair bouncing and haloed bright in the sun. She wears a clingy knit wraparound dress—the sort of thing her mother would have bought her—that hangs funny on her and makes her look fat, she thinks. Her full face is creased in a phony smile that makes her cringe now. The picture has been cropped so that her left arm extends, unseen, beyond its right margin, and she remembers that in the vanished portion of the photograph Eric Stump had walked at her side, gripping her hand, looking goofy and uncomfortable in blazer and loud patterned tie. The newspaper has apparently decided that he is of no importance; on that point she and it are in agreement.

That was the day they'd had their engagement photos taken, suffering through eight or ten rolls of film as the photographer, a fussy little man who'd driven up the hill from Burlingame, bitchily exhorted her to stop slumping and hunching. Their dead eyes above those castor-oil smiles. Eric laid his hands on her tentatively, and even now she could feel herself pulling away, caving into herself at his unsure touch. In the library she posed sitting on a straight chair while he stood behind her, his crotch, unfamiliarly sleek in pressed gray flannels, pushing hotly into her upper arm. But his hand gripped her shoulder as if it were a dirty diaper. And his face, don't even ask. Sit up straight, honey. And smile.

Her dad holding the toothbrush to his upper lip. Her mother peering up from the books of silverware patterns she studied at the dining table. "Knock it off, Hank. You're not a bit funny." As far as her mother was concerned, she literally could not be bothered. If this unfortunate union had any chance of being transformed into something plausible, it would require her fullest attention to these crucial details.

Through the plate glass window, she sees the same cropped photo repeated inside the coffee shop, where several patrons gaze at copies of the paper as they eat breakfast, but she feels little concern that she will be recognized. She is well disguised today, in a red wig and blue-framed eyeglasses, with freckles dotted carefully on her nose and cheeks. In her purse is a valid driver's license in the name of Sue Louise Gold and a Sacramento City College ID in the name of Sue Louise Hendricks, her "married name," though Teko had urged her to select the name Anderson. For the initials, ha. Also, there's a Colt Python, a weapon she disfavors because of its uncomfortably flared wooden grips. She feels loose-limbed, springy, ready for work. She moves out from under the overhang that shelters the shopping center walkway, standing beneath a decorative Tudor arch of tan stucco as she removes the Polaroid from the shoulder bag and lifts it to her face to snap photos of the bank, GUILD SAVINGS / G/S / INSURED SAVINGS, can't miss it. Then she strolls over to have a look through the windows. It's dark inside, a little over an hour to go before the place opens.

In the dimness, she sees the usual long wooden counter with several open tellers' stations, the usual freestanding metal posts, velour ropes suspended between them, set at intervals on the carpet, the usual desks off to the side, and the usual carrels, or whatever you call them, with chained ballpoints and pigeonholes for deposit and withdrawal slips and a little placard indicating the date, which she notices has already been set to February 4, 1975. In the memo pad she makes a rough sketch of the bank's interior: a rectangle, three circles, and a squiggly line.

Also, there's an arrowed sign in the rear, softly glowing red in the darkness high up on the wall. Somewhere back thataway is the exit Yolanda spoke of, the "perfect" exit letting out into an alley behind the shopping center, from which a pedestrian walkway doglegs over to Venus Drive. She notes the location of the sign on her crude floor plan and the direction in which the arrow points. She walks around the periphery of the center, taking her time, trying to look as if she were just the sort of person who might want to take pictures of the ass end of a shopping center, for artistic purposes.

The alley curves in a series of stair steps around the rear of the center, with its back entrances and loading docks. Yellowjackets hover irritably near sealed Dumpsters. A chain-link fence runs along the other side of the alley, beyond which she can see glimpses of houses between closely spaced trees and thick undergrowth.

The back door of the bank is marked with the number, 4375, and the bank's name. She stands before the back door, noting the terrain. Exiting, you'd bear left down the alley and then take the sharp right onto the walkway. She walks the route. The bank's neighbor, the Arden Plaza Dry Cleaners, has its back door propped open with a cinder block, and she catches a whiff of the heavy fumes. The man inside, busy before a pile of clothes, ignores her.

About fifteen seconds, she figures, from the bank to the walkway, which is itself shielded from view by high stockade fencing on either side. She pays careful attention to these details, mindful of Marighella's reflections on the prepared urban guerrilla: "Because he knows the terrain the guerrilla can go through it on foot, on bicycle, in automobile, jeep, truck, and never be trapped. Acting in small groups with only a few people, the guerrillas can reunite at an hour and place determined beforehand, following up the attack with new guerrilla operations, or evading the police circle and disorientating the enemy with their unprecedented audacity." That's the idea. Plus they're low on cash right now.

She moves along the walkway toward its outlet at the intersection of Vulcan and Venus. The sun is just beginning to burn through the morning overcast. An old blue Chevy is parked at the curb nearby, and a young man sitting on its hood looks up from the newspaper he is reading.

"You know, you look just like her," he says, holding out the paper and slapping it with the back of his hand.

"Oh, shut up," she says, pulling open the passenger door.

"Cuter, though."

He comes down off the hood and climbs into the car on the driver's side, tossing the paper into the backseat.

"So how's it look?"

"Yolanda wasn't bullshitting. Far as I can see, it looks pretty easy." She removes her eyeglasses, folds them, and places them in her purse.

He bends to her then, catching her slightly off guard. He can hear her feet shifting on the rubber mat. With impatience? He lifts out of the kiss, hoisting himself up with one hand on the steering wheel and feeling, as ever, importunate. As usual there is something she will not yield, some kernel of herself that remains inviolate, despite the complex emotional message he means for his kisses to impart, the response he intends for them to elicit. Fresh taste of her, like sweet corn on the cob, her lips satiny where he'd had his mouth, relaxed and leaning back into the seat, breathing evenly—but still absent, her eyes elsewhere. He gently puts his hand on her thigh, and she turns it over, examining the yellow knobs of callus that ridge the fold of his palm. She spreads the fingers apart, palpates each, slides a loose-fitting ring halfway up his index finger and then down again. His hand remains still, relaxed, throughout her inspection. Then she pats it: all done now.

"Anyway, like I say. Pretty easy." She rattles off some of her observations, counting them on her fingers, while he starts the car and puts it in gear.

"Easy for you, maybe," he says. "You're not on the assault team."

"I god damn well should be. I'm the only one who's ever robbed a fucking bank around here."

Those ghost images from inside the Hibernia Bank, Mack Sennett armed figures running, jumping, standing still.

"So the appropriate term for what this is is robbery, or expropriation?"

"This," she says, "is a stickup." She forms a gun with her thumb and forefinger and places it to Roger's head. "Drive."

"Where are you *taking* me?" he gasps in mock fright.

"Do as I say and you won't get hurt." She giggles.

A tidy city, Sacramento, laid out in its alphanumeric grid in that same year, 1848, when greed seized and validated the newly American territory. That tidy plan, delineating the extent of the upheaval, the overthrow of the old alcaldes; a tidy plan refuting that chaotic, revolutionary greed while facilitating its very ends: California's First City Welcomes You. But Roger Rorvik thinks very little about the history of a place. He likes the tidiness. He approves. It's a fairly easy drive from the East Bay. He finds his way around. It seems manageable and sensible. Manageable, sensible: not words he'd use, but they tag the comforting sense this burg gives him.

Plus it's here that he first fell under her spell, making the place itself somehow magical, absolving it of its shortcomings, as such coincidences will. She'd arrived in California first, before Teko and Yolanda had returned from their travels with their flinty yen to whip everybody into shape and their nostalgic urgency to pick up the revolution where they'd left off. General Field Marshal Teko's sweet autocratic logic had dictated that they situate the recrudescent cell in Sacramento, and obediently Roger's cousin Susan had rented the apartment at 1721 W Street. It had been agreed that the new members of the group, who so far included only Susan and Jeff Wolfritz, would try to maintain their aboveground lives and contacts for as long as possible, but making that round-trip commute two, three, four times a week was just wearing them thin, so Roger had been tapped to help babysit their famous comrade.

He was game. All he'd had going was a semiregular housepainting gig with Jeff. It was a living, though the job had triggered a program of regular calls and letters from his aunt, all centering on the theme of *What was he going to do with his life*. This was a question she'd taken an interest in ever since Roger's mother had died and he'd come to live with his aunt, uncle, and cousin twelve years ago.

Now she'd lost a daughter, a nephew, and a potential son-in-law to the sinister magnetism of the Bay Area and was in dire need of some reassurance. Roger could see her standing at the kitchen extension back in Palmdale, with stupid fuzzy slippers on her feet and a cigarette burning in her hand, that look of wounded incomprehension crossing her face as they spoke. It was all distance between them, razz and buzz. Berkeley! Three years you've been there, and you're painting houses. This is a summer job for a teenager, not an occupation for a grown man. And now. Now your cousin. Now your cousin Susan goes on television blithering all about those crazy radicals. Berkeley! Berkeley! His aunt uttered the name in a clipped, parrotlike intonation, and Roger pictured the prissy, contemptuous face she formed in order to enunciate it. "She didn't 'go on TV,' Aunt Rose. The stations covered it, like *news*, you know?" As if this were the sort of news a mother dreamed of her daughter's making. But it didn't matter. Nothing mattered. That the "children" had drifted there separately, in a phased process, freaked her out, as if that were proof enough that the whole thing of Berkeley was a depraved program, instead of being whatever it was, which anyway he wasn't so sure about, so he never did feel as if he could effectively defend the place to her.

So it was good to be able to report that he had a job waiting in Sacramento ("Property management," he'd announced), as clean and nice a town as there was to be found, home of Ronald and Nancy Reagan, for Christ's sake; secure from the hippies and the Hare Krishnas and the malevolent leftist influence of the East Bay. And frankly, it was good to get out for a number of other reasons. For numerous reasons. A plethora of them. He'd been getting forgetful, a sign of creeping boredom he knew all too well. Losing words, trains of thought vanishing. The monotony of the long summer and the several dozen student apartments he painted. Lay the dropcloth over the cheap shag and slap it on, one shabby and fucked-up room at a time. Hot-boxing it in his car at lunchtime, a thin David Dubinsky rolled of Humboldt County's finest, insulting his short-term memory. Found himself before the kitchen sink, holding a glass in one hand with the other frozen above the tap. Righty-tighty. Lefty-loosey.

He brakes, descending to the surface road and turning onto W Street. Roger always experiences a vague sadness driving up these mopey blocks, every single time; dispiriting is the word for the place. The duplex is strictly a dump, a sagging box in the middle of the block, three nothing rooms a stone's throw from the overpass, with freeway thrum twenty-four hours a day. The bungalows they pass have settled into their decrepitude, plywood weathered under the torn tar paper, crumbled cinder blocks holding up the porches. A hand-lettered sign leaning in one front window promises BEAUTY—NAILS. A tarp draped over an old sedan flaps stiffly in a sudden gust of wind. He pulls up before the duplex.

"Better kiss me now," she says, grabbing a handful of his hair. "You won't get another chance until later."

He'd met her before, following the Los Angeles massacre. His impression then had been of a small person, underfed rather than delicate, seething and wordless, mostly wordless. He'd shied away from any encounter beyond a simple hello; he'd gotten something about the dead boyfriend and was intimidated by the idea of confronting naked and angry grief. In fact he'd stayed in the background, literally; leaned up against the wall of the little apartment on Euclid Avenue with his arms folded while Susan worked out some arrangements with Teko and Yolanda concerning the trip East. Not that he didn't study her, seeking to reconcile this slight figure, her hair slashed and badly dyed, her little feet crossed primly at the ankles, with the divergent published likenesses of the chilly deb and the sexy, gunslinging insurgent. It was a third person who was present, neither a combination of the other two nor entirely distinct from them.

And mostly wordless. That much she shared with her photographs. Ah, well, what else could she be? The terrible fire drawn up into the sky, the wind its bellows and chimney; the armed, uniformed men; the businesslike wrath of authority: It was a spectacle belonging to television, familiar to all of them, but its meaning, you dodged its true meaning, recognized maybe the half of it, until the day you were able to say, had to say, having seen it, "all gone," and then maybe you just didn't speak again, for a while.

He hadn't talked to her. Zero chemistry. Then the SLA three were gone, and he'd put them out of his mind. The long summer stretched ahead. Lay the dropcloth and slap it on, over thumbtack holes and the dark stains left by oily heads. The little car filling with the sweet and pungent smoke. His head emptying. To tell the truth, his aunt had a point.

She arrived in Sacramento about three months later on the overnight Greyhound from Vegas. Susan sent Roger to the depot to meet the bus, and he felt an unexpected anticipation. The pneumatic door hissed open to release the Americruiser's consignment of hard-up traveling souls, and she walked into his life, accompanied by Jeff Wolfritz, revolutionary chaperon. They both looked like total shit. Still, there was, for Roger, the sense of an auspicious beginning.

That fall, the getting-to-know-you period, they'd spent a lot of time driving around. Just lazy cruising. He'd taken her down 80 to where there was a stretch of cropland, bearded a deep green late in the season, over which you could sometimes see a cropduster, drifting, turning sharply at the end of the furrowed rows, dipping low and then soaring away, leaving behind cloudy trails of the poison it dumped, a kind of improvisational aviation that tightened his throat and nearly made him want to cry. Though he knew that he also was waiting for the pilot to misjudge the angle of his cavalier descent, to nip a telephone line, to stall too near the ground to drop the nose and recover; waiting to see the thing crash, explode, and burn. And had he taken her there, pulled over onto the dirt shoulder as traffic zinged by, so that she could see that too?

All those apple-picking colors burning through late autumn and on into winter. There might actually even have been apples in the backseat once or twice, a paper bag of fruit, ripe and lustrous, from the U-Pick. Who knows? They say there's two trees in Sacramento for each man, woman, and child.

W ITHOUT KNOWING QUITE why, Teko reaches above his head to where items, suspended from hooks, dangle brightly over the bins of merchandise at waist level. Just needs to touch. The gleam attracts him, and to feel these things—the HOLES studding the circumference of the COLANDER, the bat-eared PROTRUSIONS on a STRAINER, the artichokelike LEAVES of the STEAMER BASKET, the barbed HELIX of a CORKSCREW—is both exquisite and exquisitely unsatisfying. Yet his awareness of this, too, is strangely occulted, concealed from himself behind the jangling static at the forefront of his mind, which seeks to work the word *panther* into the sentence of a budding communiqué:

—the beating heart of a (black?) panther

—all the grace and power of a (black?) panther

—as the (black?) panther does not suffer those who would deny its freedom

—our beautiful brother of the wild, the (black?) panther

Teko sees this as a rhetorical step forward. First, in the purely literary sense. As he'd noted in his Revolutionary Diary, "Metaphor=OK?" Second, he thinks of it as appealingly inclusive. Plenty of animal lovers out there who may be ready to take up arms against the government at any moment. Third is the subtle homage to the Black Panthers. Because you never know.

Overhead he spots a paring knife, secured to its cardboard backing by two thick staples, a two-inch blade sprouting from a handle of drab green plastic. Sixty-nine cents. He removes it quietly from the backing, popping the staples to free it, and then slips the knife into his jacket pocket. He looks up to meet the gaze of an older woman, who promptly averts her eyes.

"Shhhhh," he advises, mildly, bending to lift the basket. He strolls toward the front of the store, just another householder, for the items in his basket are truly quotidian: ball of twine, roll of tape, 7¾" x 5" notebook, pack of Bic pens, Prell shampoo for dyed hair, box of Tide, package of sixty-watt lightbulbs, and three cans of cat food for the ungrateful strays that make the backyard stink of piss and that Yolanda has unaccountably taken to feeding. They ought to keep a tighter grip on their money or soon they'll be eating the shit themselves. Not that it's an issue today: Susan had come through again, delivering, via Roger, four freshly purloined MasterCharge cards. The one he offers to the cashier is imprinted with the name Harland Funderbunk, no doubt some hapless sojourner at the Sir Francis Drake, and he watches edgily as she fingers the thick monthly circular, its every page covered with fine-print columns listing stolen credit card numbers, sitting near the credit card blanks. But she is only moving it out of the way.

Soon he's headed out to the car, stopping to examine the newspaper headlines. *Hey, hey, SLA, made page one again today.* The anniversary of the kidnapping, and the general drift of the coverage appears to be that the pigs have absolutely no fucking idea what they're doing. Not that Operation GALTNAP, as the FBI has dubbed it, has anything to do anymore with solving a kidnapping or rescuing a hostage. "Miss Galton will face a number of state and federal charges, including attempted murder, bank robbery, and kidnapping."

Yeah, right. Teko accepts it as an article of faith that the pigs will simply blow them all away. Originally the marked-for-death belief had seemed a suitably fiery fantasy of Cin's, the idea that they were the *meanest*, the *baddest*, the most extreme revolutionary army of them all, killing Uncle Toms with phony liberal agendas and their CIA handlers, firing on elderly bank depositors whose creaky joints couldn't deliver them to the prone position quickly enough to suit, swooping down like angels of death upon the children of the ruling elite, so bad and so mean, so camped out on the raggedy edges of the lunatic fringe that the only choice the fascist insect would have would be to annihilate them.

Then, of course, the pigs *had* annihilated them, and what Teko had noted well was his own sense that some safety circuit that should have tripped before things had gone too far had malfunctioned or been entirely absent to begin with. What he couldn't shake was what no one else could shake either, in the aftermath: the index of juvenile achievements attributed to his dead comrades, the glowing faces and carefully styled hairdos of their yearbook photos, the fact that it wasn't their commitment to revolution or justice or even their having had their hearts in the correct place that he, personally, would have submitted as corroboration of their right to continue living, but the penumbra of utter conventional ordinariness that fell upon them to veil and contradict all that they insisted they were. All he insisted he was. It was the good people, from the comfortable houses and safe neighborhoods, turning out to bring those tortured bodies home and pass through those same leafy streets, a sad suburban cortege, to bury them in mahogany coffins with polished brass handles. It agitated him to realize that he had thought this marked them as different, exempt, that because their bail would have been made, because they had college degrees, because albums were filled with faded snaps of their birthday parties they would, at the critical moment, be allowed to avail themselves of privileges never before denied them. It agitated him to realize that despite all that had drawn him to Cin, filled him with near veneration, he had accepted Cin's subfusc forecast as tongue-in-cheek rhetoric.

His belief in Cin's prescience now is in fact the most prominent of the differences marking Teko from the new group of Susan, Roger, and Jeff Wolfritz. Overall, a bookish and chatty bunch, which is one reason why he's chosen to involve them all in the Bakery Operation, so called. Get them out there, pointing guns at people and making elemental demands. Give me, give me, I want. The pure playground logic of it, get the superego the hell out of the picture for a change. It might even help if they actually were to shoot someone, to scorch the cost of commitment in their minds. Simple as yes/no, on/off, with us/against us, alive/dead; strictly zero sum, the reality from which they hide behind books and talk. That was the mistake he made last summer, allowing Guy Mock to talk him into disarming and laying low and then allowing the bitch, Shimada, to set a lackadaisical and insubordinate tone. If he'd been smart, they would have shaken up one of those hick towns, but good. It would have bound them together, made them stronger, announced to the world that the revolution had arrived on the East Coast. Instead they whiled the time away, drinking draft beer and playing shuffleboard in local taverns, loading change into the jukebox.

Another reason, then, to involve the others in the Bakery Op is to make them criminally complicit in the revolutionary activities of the SLA and end any conflict between their divided, their treasonously bifurcated loyalties. Which of course gives rise to a third reason (which he admits to himself only cautiously): He has to get these people serious because their casual attitude presents an obvious and attractive alternative to his own martial approach.

The wind stirs briefly, ruffling his collar and kicking up trash that has gathered at the curb. The barest threat of sun at the corner of the somber sky. Winter in Sacramento. He gets into the car beside his wife, putting the bag of supplies between his feet.

"Why didn't you just buy it?"

"Buy what?" His hand moves to the pocket where he has concealed the knife.

"The paper."

"Oh, God. And deal with the bitch preening all day? The *star*?"

Yolanda reaches over to pat his hand mockingly. Then she asks, "Oh. Did you remember the cat food?"

She backs carefully out of the diagonal slot. Too slowly to suit the guy behind her, mug in a pickup who hits the horn with the heel of his hand, once, twice, three times as she straightens out the wheels and then begins rolling forward, arriving at the intersection and bringing the car to a stop as the yellow light turns red. The guy edges forward, annoyed, until the pickup's grille fills Yolanda's rearview. Then he revs the engine, vehement bursts of noise as he toes the accelerator. The moment the light turns green his horn begins to sound.

"What a creep." She turns around to see if she can get a glimpse of the guy, sees only the grille.

"Well, don't make a scene," says Teko.

Yolanda heaves a sigh. There are many questions she might ask, rhetorical questions, concerning the man beside her, concerning their marriage, that cry out for the intuitive second sight of a Dear Abby. Would the astute Abigail Van Buren, whose cornerstone opinion seems to hold that all problems are universal and that the practical solutions to them may thus be universally applied, agree with Yolanda's unhappy conclusion that the only hope the marriage has is (deep breath) separation?

Ask yourself. Are you better off with him or without him? I suggest that both of you attend counseling. If he won't go, go alone.

Though even Miss Van Buren might find herself stumped by Teko himself, if not by the reasons for Yolanda's most recent bout of alienation from her husband. For the first time in more than a year, for the first time since she and Teko abandoned their neat, white-painted, plant-filled apartment to go underground with Cin and the SLA, Yolanda yearns for the unrestricted sanctuary of normal life, open, free, and sunny. It was while she and Teko were sightseeing in her hometown, Chicago, as they traveled leisurely westward, that these feelings had first intruded. They went to the Art Institute. They went to the zoo. They sat at the edge of the sand, the elegant facades of Lakeshore Drive to their backs, the first hint of winter in the wind that traveled to them across the choppy surface of the lake. All the rigors and trials of the long summer, all the objectives they'd held fast to melted away when she sank her strong teeth into a Vienna Beef hot dog. When they walked on Addison in the shadow of Wrigley Field, quiet now that the season had drawn to another unsuccessful conclusion, Cubs buried in the cellar twenty-two games out, Yolanda realized that she would be happy to perpetuate all this, that coming home and behaving like a tourist made her feel as if all the pleasures of the city had been arranged for her comfort and delight. When Teko suggested that they take a little trip to the West Side—he had a list of public housing projects he wanted to inspect—she'd resisted, oh so slightly, just enough to put him off until it was time to head to the Greyhound terminal. The tired sign there, yellow with cigarette smoke, still said LEAVE THE DRIVING TO US, but beneath it a man wearing a vinyl jacket and jeans dirtied to a shiny greenish brown nodded, his chin bouncing on his naked chest. This was the sort of found wit that had always delighted roving photographers for the *Sun-Times*. Yolanda watched him offhandedly, marveling at the spindly prison tattoos that blossomed on his neck, clutching protectively in her hand the paper bag of goodies she'd bought at the five-and-ten. She felt as distant from the man, from that victim of society, as she possibly could. She felt, even, a spark of indignation that he'd allowed himself to fall into that condition.

Then they'd arrived in Sacramento, and there were Susan and Jeff and Roger and Tania, all cozied up in the tatty little W Street apartment. Yolanda couldn't help noticing how tidy and clean things were, how sweetly Tania kissed her hello, how thoughtful and amiable Jeff and Roger were. And then Susan had performed for them, for an evening of safe house recreation, a dramatic reading from *Telephone*, a San Francisco Mime Troupe skit, raising the paperbound anthology, *Guerrilla Theater*, to proudly declaim the piece's final triumphant line:

. . . In Cuba the phones are free!

pausing ever so slightly before emphasizing, with the slightest throaty soupçon of Latin inflection, "*All of them!*" Yolanda was charmed, thrilled, delighted—but Teko had reverted to form and started issuing ukases the moment he walked through the door. He'd worn her out at last.

Yolanda proposed, casually, to Teko that they rent a second safe house. She explained that she had come to see that it would be very **difficult** to continue, **politically** or **militarily**, **without** first **sorting out gender and authority issues**. After all, **no black people** had turned up at their door to **assume leadership** of the group, and Joan, who'd refused to play follow the leader to Sacramento and was living in San Francisco, **refused** to formally join them; so by default it was the **women** of the SLA who comprised its most **inherently oppressed** members—not a **minority class** per se, she knew, but as a **potential revolutionary class** the most promising. **Experientially**, the **women were leaders**, deserving of a spot **at the vanguard of revolutionary change**. She thought it would be a good idea to establish a separate **women's collective** within the SLA to address the **pertinent issues**.

Teko mimed turning his pockets out.

So the Bakery. Yolanda has thrown herself into the job, typing up notes, making sketches, reconnoitering the area, staying focused on the little Sacramento hideaway she imagines. Can it be that revolution has become a means, an excuse, for her to further herself? If the goal of achieving revolution, and *its* goals, justify and affirm her sacrifices, then it follows that her own personal fulfillment can serve the revolution. She's convinced herself of that much.

"I won't," replies Yolanda. She moves as slowly as she can through the intersection, the pickup behind, honking furiously, swerving in successive vain attempts to find a path around the smaller vehicle. The guy just blows and blows his horn.

Startled pedestrians raise their heads, hunting for the commotion. Their general look says, This doesn't happen on the quiet, well-tended streets of Sacramento.

Ernest spread his hands wide, palms up. Below them, on the bar, and centered between them was the twenty-dollar bill he had placed there, a good-faith gesture, a fresh bill distinct from the small pile of change from which the bartender had been drawing to replenish Ernest's bourbon and water, all of which, implicitly, was now the bartender's personal property.

No soap. "You've had enough, bud. You're not going to give me a hard time now, are you?"

Slowly Ernest picked up the twenty and put it back in his wallet. He rose carefully to go to the men's room, trying to look dignified and poised as he sauntered to the rear of the saloon. They thought this was drunk? This wasn't drunk. This was nothing. He could show them drunk.

Heated by a stout riser, the tiny WC was warm after the drafty barroom. Ernest settled on the toilet and all at once felt sleepy. Next thing he knew, someone was rapping on the door.

"Don't pass out in my men's room, bud. Come on now, I don't want to have to come in there after you."

Ernest knew this didn't require a verbal response. He reached above him and pulled the chain dangling from the tank, felt the breeze on his ass, and then stood, wet his hands, rubbed the sleepers out of his eyes, and emerged. The bartender was back behind the bar. Two of six patrons who'd been scattered throughout the place had departed. His cigarettes and Zippo were where he'd left them. The pile of change remained untouched. Ernest took his coat from the rack near the door and shrugged himself into it, eyes on the high ceiling, the elegant woodwork climbing toward it, the stained glass over the archway that led into what had once been a rear dining room. Gilded Age refinement, on a miniature scale. Plenty of places like this remaining in Scranton, abandoned to their ruin once all the money had taken a powder. Ghosts. The bartender wore a flannel shirt and drew Pabst and Schmidt's from the taps, working-class beers for his working-class clientele. Ernest imagined that not all that long ago the man walking the duckboards would have been in an evening jacket, with bow tie. Not that this was a bad guy. He had a feeling for bartenders. He decided to give it one more shot.

"Hear the one about the drunk sleeping with his head on the bar? Bartender comes up, goes, 'Buddy, you gotta get lost. You can't sleep here, and you've had enough to drink.' So the drunk sits up, thinks for a minute, then says, 'Well, how about a haircut?'"

The bartender laughed, polishing the space in front of him with a rag.

"Come on, one for the road? It's cold as a witch's tit."

"Not that cold."

Ernest winked at him. "You don't help me out, I'll be sober when I see my wife."

The bartender took a shot glass and filled it to the line with bourbon. "Champ, drink this up and then go home. OK?" He rapped twice on the bar with his knuckles. "Good luck. But then that's it. Gabeesh?"

Ernest's eyes filled with tears. A guinea bartender felt bad for him. A guinea bartender bought him a drink. A guinea bartender laughed at the expense of his nonexistent wife. For a moment he felt the familiarity of competing impulses, an admixture in this case of sentimental gratitude and murderous violence toward someone who dared condescend to him. For a moment he felt confusion. He hefted the shot glass, unsure whether he was going to throw the whiskey at the man or drink it down. In the end he drank it. No need to prove anything to this wop. He'd been cut off by better bartenders in better bars. He walked out. In a gesture of cavalier magnanimity, he left the change, three or four dollars, on the bar.

He thought maybe he ought to go see Lily. She would be up now, washing her hair to get the smoke out of it, listening to music or watching the late late show. The thought of her, of her little apartment with coffee perking in an old Silex maker on the kitchen table, made him happy. But when he pulled up across from Lily's apartment building, no lights showed in her windows. He sat in the car for a few minutes, waiting, and then got out, taking a scrap of rag with him. In the front door was centered a small window of scuffed and scratched Plexiglas. Ernest wrapped the rag around his fist, double, and then punched out the little square of plastic, which clattered on the tiled vestibule floor. He reached through and let himself inside. The postman had tossed the day's mail on the floor, and Ernest stooped and went through it. Nothing of note. He walked into the hallway and up two flights of stairs and then approached the door of her rear apartment, pausing there. The building was silent, except for the buzz of the overhead fluorescent and the hiss of steam pipes. He leaned his face against the door and pressed his ear to it, listening intently. Nothing. He knocked softly, then louder, then pressed his ear to the door again. No noise escaped the apartment. He wished he'd thought of phoning, but a surprise seemed like such a nice idea. So who got a surprise?

Live alone. Die alone. And, incidentally, wait around for a broad alone.

He went and sat at the head of the stairs and lit a cigarette. Who the fuck was this bitch anyway? He considered this lucidly. He knew he ought to feel tired, but instead he felt buoyant. He felt like talking. He felt like fucking Lily. He felt like drinking some more and driving around and then sitting in some brightly lit place eating his eggs at four in the a.m. He felt like going out to the cemetery and lying across the graves, pretending to be dead. He felt like throwing rocks through the windows of an abandoned warehouse. He felt like emptying a few clips at the range. He felt like going to a playground and flipping the swings, so that they wound themselves on their chains around the top of the swing set. He felt like standing on a rooftop, sailing 45 rpm singles away into the night, one after another. His knuckles began to ache. He reached between the banister rails and dropped the cigarette, hearing the infinitesimal sound it made as it landed in the ground-floor hallway. Then he lit another one.

It was murder being between jobs.

Suddenly he was in his car, his lights carving a tunnel into the darkness surrounding him. The impulse to leave, to stop waiting had come so abruptly that he'd nearly lost his balance lurching downstairs. His knee hurt from banging it on the door frame on the way out, and he squeezed it with his aching knuckles. Eventually everything starts to hurt. But the thing was that in the course of his solitary meditation on loneliness and rejection at the top of the stairwell, back when only his knuckles had been killing him, he'd suddenly drawn up an archetypal memory: of himself, at ten, sitting alone, forgotten, in the backseat of the car, driving home from some excursion, while Guy snuggled between his parents in front. As they entered the outskirts of Scranton, his mother had had the nerve, the horse-faced old bitch, to turn around and *compliment* him on his behavior during the ride, praise with which his pussy-whipped father murmured his agreement. And then Baby Guy had raised his head to gaze back at him, a look of arrogant self-satisfaction on his tiny buglike face. Ernest acted swiftly and decisively. Before him there'd been a jumbo ashtray, filled to the brim with butts and ashes. He pulled it out of its housing and shook it, emptying its contents, over the occupants in front. In the slipstream of air coursing through the car from the cracked wing window, the ashes scattered and flew, a blizzard of rank gray fallout that made his father swerve and nearly lose control of the car and his mother sputter with rage and confusion. And Guy? He'd cried and cried, his precious little eyes full of the gritty stuff. Ha-ha—bug-faced son of a bitch! His mother had waited patiently until they arrived home, then had removed Ernest from the car and taken him by the hand, leading him upstairs to his parents' bedroom, where she laid him across the flowered spread and hammered his bare ass, beating him hard and with single-minded dedication, while he inhaled all the perfumy smells of her side of the bed. It was like fucking her.

Now, as periodically came to pass, it was time for Guy to get his. It seemed to Ernest that whenever he bothered to look up, not that he did all that often anymore, there was Guy, still nestled between their parents, still drawing far more than his due. Little bastard! Dragging them into this stupid plot of his, *exposing* them. And they ate it up, as usual. Whatever little Guy-Guy wanted. Well, enough of that. He happened to know a captain on the Scranton PD, Earl Fry. Always meant to look him up when he was in town, and what better time than this, when the security of the nation was at stake.

Police HQ was a forbidding old building, part citadel, part prison, part bankrupt public institution. Ernest responded to its looming presence uneasily, on some hindbrain level. A ramp led down from a gated archway beyond which the motor pool lay, but public parking was found in the court out front, deserted now except for a sheriff's vehicle, probably there to transfer a prisoner to the county jail. He pulled up behind the sheriff's car and got out, looked the place over. He felt good about the idea. It felt right. Bring the whole thing home where it belonged. Earl Fry. Old high school pal. Knew Ernest, and he knew Guy too. Ernest could imagine Fry rising from his desk to greet him, What a surprise, and then his jaw dropping as Ernest dumped the gift-wrapped news in his lap.

All there was, though, was a cop, with corporal's stripes, behind a desk, leaning toward a sheet of paper half rolled out of the typewriter in front of him and daubing at it with Liquid Paper. The cop did a really professional job of ignoring Ernest until he'd finished his daubing, blown on the page to dry it, and then rolled it back into the platen.

"Help you?"

"Let me speak to Captain Fry. Please."

"Off duty."

"Who's on duty?"

"There's me. There's Sergeant Durkin. There's Lieutenant Bricca." He did not say this in a friendly way, but as if he were reviewing an obvious set of data for the benefit of an idiot.

"Let me talk to Bricca."

"He's Code Seven."

"What's that? On the shitter?"

The cop studied him for a moment. "Dinner," he said, finally.

"When's he back?"

"What do you have?"

"I'll tell him."

"Suit yourself," said the cop, indicating a bench.

"When did you say he was back?"

"I didn't," said the cop. "He's the lieutenant. You know?"

Ernest sat. He watched the cop type and file some papers for a while. Two patrolmen came in with a drunk who smelled like puke and led him around the front desk and down a corridor for processing, quickstepping him, as if they were tired of dealing with him. Back where the holding cells must have been someone started singing:

> *Hoya polski naga polka*
> *Meenzata lavuso*
> *Hoya polska gnocchi polka*
> *Mordenchoo leverno*
> *Polka chevy qualum cherchez*
> *Lavooie hardehar*
> *Return to me and always be*
> *My melody of love!*

It echoed down the corridor and into the lobby, and the cop on duty rose and slammed a door, cutting off the sound.

"I'm Polish, you know," he said. "I hate that fucking Bobby Vinton."

Ernest bestirred himself. "Shoot the bastard."

"Shit no. Slow death. Death of a thousand cuts. Chinese water torture."

"You want to shoot him in the throat. Never sing another note." Ernest spoke authoritatively.

"That'd be nice. I hear the motherfucker's getting a show on CBS next fall. Just what I need. The fuck." He gestured, as if the man in the cell were Vinton himself.

A man in plainclothes came in holding a Styrofoam cup of coffee. "Anything up, Casimir?"

"Yeah, no, Lieutenant. This man's waiting for you."

"Yeah?"

"He wanted Captain Fry."

"Fry works human being hours."

"So I told him."

"He misses all the good stuff."

"That's what we all say."

"Goes home and has his supper at six and watches prime-time TV like a regular taxpayer."

"We were just talking about TV."

"It's no good for you. This is what's good for you."

"Sure it is."

"Work work work for the dawn is coming."

Bricca turned toward Ernest and lifted his cup to his lips, blowing on the coffee as he gave Ernest the once-over. Ernest bared his teeth in a smile.

"What in Captain Fry's absence can I do for you?"

"You're Lieutenant Bricca."

"Twenty-four hours a day."

"Just about, huh?" Ernest looked around him, as if the late hour resided in the corners of the room.

"You want to see me about what?"

"You have someplace we can talk?"

"People talk in my office sometimes."

They sat on opposite sides of Bricca's desk.

"I have to admit that I'm sitting here with you because I'm a wee bit intrigued that a man claiming to be a friend of St. Earl's wanders in here at fucking whatever it is in the a.m. looking like a boozer at the tail end of a long unhappy binge. You're a *personal* friend, are you?" The lieutenant's face and voice were full of unveiled hope.

Ernest sort of sized up the way things stood between Fry and Bricca.

"What's the problem, Bricca? His office prettier than yours?"

Actually, Bricca's office was pleasant, looking more like a college professor's than a cop's with its embrasured windows set in the thick stone walls and the row of bookcases and the framed diploma identifying Bricca as the possessor of a bachelor's in criminal justice from Shippensburg University. The room was softly lit by a green-shaded banker's lamp on the desk.

"In about thirty seconds I'm going to make a determination that you're publicly intoxicated. Class A misdemeanor."

"Determine away. I'll sleep it off and talk to Earl in the morning."

"Sleep? That's what you think. I guess you didn't hear the fucking Polack nightingale in there." He paused. "So," he said finally, "is there something you wanted to tell me?"

Ernest hadn't been anticipating this kind of hard time, and he was just nonplussed enough to dig in his heels a little. But he'd begun to feel profoundly tired sitting here, and the prospect of a night in the drunk tank held no appeal for him.

"I have information."

"What kind of information?"

"Information concerning the whereabouts of a certain missing person. Very high profile."

"Who would this person be?"

"The Galton girl."

"Uh-huh."

"You don't believe me?"

"Let me just say that my training and experience have led me to be skeptical of such claims."

Ernest's eye flitted to the diploma. The elenchus of Shippensburg. "You know," said Ernest. "I've got some pretty high-level government contacts from covert operations I've been involved with, and I could have taken this information directly to them." He raised a finger and wagged it at the policeman.

Bricca rolled his eyes. "Oh, dear sweet bleeding Jesus. Not one of these people. Why is it everybody with the high-level contacts somehow ends up sitting in my office three sheets to the wind in the dead of night wearing a dirty shirt? Please, the suspense is killing me, this is something you found out about from a fortune cookie? Spacemen transmitting radio waves into your morning glass of Tang? God talking to your internal organs? I should just leave you for St. Earl to deal with."

Ernest tried staring him down.

Oddly, Bricca slackened, with a high, soughing exhalation, as if all the tension had left his body.

"Where's she supposed to be?"

"South Canaan."

"Well, I suppose that's not too farfetched. You could hide the fucking Statue of Liberty in South Canaan if you wanted to, though so far nobody has. Where exactly in South Canaan?"

"A farm. I don't know the address. But I could find it."

"And how did you happen to see the young lady?"

"I never did."

"Ah. You never saw her at a place you don't exactly know where it is."

"My brother put her up there. He told me."

"And who is your brother?"

"A god damned Communist."

"That's a tough way to make a buck. I was just reading about the Red Chinese in *Time*. Their standard of living isn't due to approach ours until the year 2000. But I meant who, not what."

"Guy Mock."

"Well, Brother Mock, what's his connection to all this?"

"I said already, he's a radical. Lives out there in Berkeley, all that. He knows these type of people. Gets all buddy-buddy with them." Suddenly he sounded ridiculous to himself. He should have just gone for the 4 a.m. eggs. "Look, it's not just her. It's the other two too. The Shepards."

"And they're all up there right now?"

"No, they left about three months ago. But I'm telling you you can find them. You can track them down. Somebody's seen them. You can question my brother. He's got to know where they are. He's trying to write a god damned book about them."

Bricca thrust out his right arm dramatically, addressing his appeal to the diploma on the wall. "Do I take this sfatcheem seriously? Or do I just go out the back door and keep going until I wander into a hobo jungle somewhere and allow myself to be murdered for my Thom McAn's?"

"I'm the one, smart-ass. I could walk now."

"No, you couldn't. You could've. But like a good three-in-the-morning lush you had to speak right up. So now you have to sit. See, usually I get to go home soon to my empty little apartment and un-wind sitting on my empty little couch waiting for the empty little test pattern to go away. But you just had to come in here and bend someone's ear with this fucking story of yours. I only wish it had been your good pal Captain America. But he'll be here soon enough, bright and early and shaven clean and happy-happy to be awake in the daylight like a normal citizen. Until he sees you. And then of course"—Bricca consulted a list of telephone numbers trapped beneath the rectangle of glass on his desk—"he'll have the FBI up his ass too. Because if you really want to talk about this, you're going to talk about it with the FBI."

"Yeah, I want to talk."

"Here's the number right here. Scranton Resident Agency of the FBI. If you're fucking around, now's the time to quit. Say, count of three?"

"He tried to involve my parents."

"One, two, two and a half, two and three-quarters. OK, three. Here we go."

"I already look like a fucking idiot."

"Yeah, well, you won't get any argument from me there." Bricca picked up the phone and dialed, squinting at the number under the glass on his desk.

Roger drives to the Bay Area, listening to a special radio broadcast, *The Kidnapping of Alice Galton: A Year Passes*.

"Where is Alice?" the announcer intones. "The FBI doesn't know but believes you may be the person who will telephone them someday and say the young woman with the mole on the right side of her face below her mouth is Alice—your neighbor or a salesperson at a neighborhood store."

Even at this hour there is a slight slowing, the sense of a queue forming, as he approaches the Carquinez Bridge. Bridges make him consider all the things we take on faith. That this old relic won't simply fall into the strait below, for instance. An earthquake measuring exactly what point what on the Richter scale would shake this thing to pieces? He glances over at the bridge's twin, tries to remember which of the two is newer, is touted as being stronger, safer, more soundly constructed.

"Parents in well-to-do suburbs are asking themselves: 'Are my children too sheltered? Have I given them too much and made their lives too easy?'"

His tires whine on the roadway grid high above the dark and

churning water. The car drifts slightly to the right, and he corrects generously, overcorrects, recorrects. A series of corrections, brain handling these NASA-like calculations with dazzling speed, and all in the service of an old Chevy with crappy alignment, shimmying the vehicle back into the center of its lane. High above dark water.

The car dips suddenly, and he has crossed over onto solid ground, safe for another day. Cheers! Just ahead, another car's blinker pulses once, twice, before it slips into his lane, and he drops back, calm and unruffled, happy to be over the span. A new program begins on the radio.

"The caveman was all right in his day. He squatted beside the fire, snatched his lump of meat, pulled it apart with his hands and teeth. If he saw anything he wanted, he grabbed it. If someone was in his way, he knocked him down."

Right on. Kind of the way he feels. The evening ended with the four of them—he and Tania, Teko and Yolanda—sprawled on the front room floor around a pot of rice Yolanda had (grudgingly) made. The pot was scorched on its sides and bottom and missing one of its two Bakelite handles, and it looked forlorn and out of place on the shivered floorboards, a photo from a *Life* exposé of urban poverty. They ate in sullen silence. Well, look at the time. Got to head back down to Oakland.

She walked him outside, stood on the porch with him in the cold evening air. Trucks rattled by on the overpass. He hugged her, drawing her slight body close, surprised by how exhausted he suddenly felt. But he resisted the dubious appeal of his customary bivouac on the front room floor. It'd been a difficult day; there was bickering, a splintered atmosphere from the moment Teko and Yolanda walked in. Tania seemed to shrug it off easily enough; she was used to it, and soon there would be a second safe house, paid for with the money obtained from the "bakery," their coded term for the bank.

Roger isn't quite sure yet how he feels about the whole thing of the bakery. The necessity of the second safe house is tautologically self-justifying, apparently: an additional safe house is required because one isn't sufficient. This doesn't strike Roger as a particularly revolutionary reason, really. Though so far the revolution hasn't threatened to interrupt his idyll here; it's been kept at a distance, postponed by cash infusions and stolen credit cards regularly provided by Susan, still toiling away at the Plate of Brasse. But a second safe house is beyond the means of a waitress pulling shitty shifts and her housepainter boyfriend.

Maybe they're not telling him everything. But he doesn't want to be, has never wanted to be, a wet blanket. Always a good egg. Always game. He allows himself to entertain only slight misgivings about what he's committing himself to. Frankly, he's more concerned about whether Susan will be displeased with the smallishness of her assignment, which is to involve sitting in the coffee shop adjacent to the bank and timing the sheriff's department's response. He's hoping she won't be. It's right up her alley, really, an incognito moment, a camouflaging of purpose. Lingering over toast and coffee and feigning curiosity when the pigs tear into the lot, one eye on the sweepsecond hand of her watch.

"Who wants a caveman around today? Along with houses, tables, knives, and forks, we have developed standards of friendship and courtesy that make life a lot more enjoyable."

Susan sits at her kitchen table, wearing an old terry cloth bathrobe of her father's, all dangling threads, a comfortable ruin stolen from the back of his clothes closet on her last trip home. She looks at her cousin, sitting opposite her.

"Teko called me a semiretard," Roger complains. He holds a cup of tea in both hands, his fingers interlaced. To Susan he looks amused rather than insulted.

"Nothing semi about it," she says. "Reminds me. I made your excuses for you to Mom, as usual. But I think she still expects a call now and again."

"I'm in no mood."

"And I come off shift just raring to hear the latest dispatch from the lonely desert outpost of Palmdale."

He laughs through his nose, an exhalation coupled with a short hum, as if he were clearing his sinuses.

"I'm serious, Roger, somebody needs to help me out with this woman."

"She should take a class. Adult ed."

"Perish the thought."

"A creative writing workshop."

"That I should suggest to Mom, with her clippings and her used paperback books of famous psychology cases and the history of England that she brings home in a shopping bag."

"Art appreciation."

"I'm going to suggest to her that she is an uneducated person."

He shrugs, smiling: You win.

"Well, so what's the latest dispatch?"

"They had a streaker last week outside the Civic Center."

"There's a Civic Center?" Roger raises his eyebrows in mock surprise.

Susan glances at the electric clock hanging over the stove. Greasy yellowish dust on its face. Two in the a.m. Tomorrow—today—she has lunch and the first dinner service at the Plate of Brasse.

The businessmen work you, but it's the tourists who run you off your feet and then stiff you. Party of six on Tuesday ran up a check of more than a hundred bucks and then left her a *deuce*. After she did everything but compliment their ugly sweatshirts.

"And so what did you tell her for me?"

"I said a girl," says Susan, "what else?"

Her cousin smiles secretly. "Next time, actually, you could tell her a brain tumor."

"Oh, you *are* nuts."

"I'm sort of serious."

"I'm sure you can imagine for yourself, the blizzard. The blizzard of clippings. If you were even to hint."

"Just a feeling I have. I'm making a mental picture of something growing on my brain. It looks like a walnut."

"Your brain? The size is right."

"Please."

"You know she's equal to the job. Maybe she still calls it the Big C, but she can handle the research. Remember Grandma?"

"Oh, God."

"Mom could only whisper the word, *leukemia*. But she found out *everything*."

She had too. Doled out what her daughter and nephew had dubbed the "Platelet Report" every morning. Returned home from the ReSale Oasis with shopping bags full of books about the disease. Living with it. Dying from it. Cures derived from apricot pits. Meditation therapy. Recipe books for chemo patients. A book about a young man with leukemia who fell in love with his young nurse.

"And then she just went, Grandma. Went downhill real fast."

"But Mom didn't," whispers Susan. "It was more words to whisper. *Multiple myeloma.* You want her whispering at you?"

"No," he whispers back.

Americans talk about getting sick the way she imagines Europeans talk about sex or food: with real gusto and a connoisseur's recognition of the quality, value, rarity, significance, and magnitude of a given malady. I am sick, I must die. Lord have mercy on us. And a cuckoo, jug-jug, pu-we, to-witta-woo.

Sick or healthy, they hit the hay. Susan wants some shuteye. But she finds herself crawling out of bed early, to sit at the table in the sunlit kitchen, the schematic of a felony flickering in her brain.

She shakes a cigarette out of the pack before her, places it in her mouth, and lights it. The smoke curls in the sunlight, winds toward the ceiling in ghostly bluish plaits, though of enough substance to cast a shadow.

The thing will happen. They will storm onto private property and forcibly take money. It will be planned to the last detail and timed to the last second, an operation of military precision. And soon. Turns out she does like her part, imagines herself dressing for it. Imagines herself picking something good and American off the diner menu, something above suspicion. Crucial role. Timekeeper. Observer. How many cops? Lights and sirens or silent approach? Guns drawn or holstered? Will the media appear? The intelligence she gathers will be used to refine their technique for the next action.

Politically the value of the action is questionable, since they don't intend to exploit the propaganda opportunity presented by the assault. What they do intend is to melt into the earth, carrying undisclosed amounts of cash, traveler's checks, and money orders. She means, in other words it might be interpreted, not altogether incorrectly, as just another bank holdup.

She appreciates the idea of the second safe house. And the idea of a women's collective is near and dear to her. What bothers her, though, is her skulking impression that as a justification for armed robbery it is pure needy childishness, driven by a kind of bored nihilism. But she's not about to examine things too closely. Oh, how she's been waiting for this. They came to her—to *her*! And then like an idiot, she handed them off to Guy Mock. She should have learned her lesson about him during those early days in Oakland.

They came to *her*, and there was room for nothing but compassion, what with all the SLA dead, and the empathy aroused by the idea of their being survivors on the run, an overflowing of good and generous and openhanded spirits, and Berkeley felt righter and better than it had in years, with expressions of condolence and solidarity from the Movement, with memorial graffiti on the walls that made them all cry; and they fed them cookies and soup, and brought them changes of clothes, and saved the newspapers for them to read, and delivered their revolutionary communiqués, and then she gave them away to Guy fucking Mock.

Stupid idiot! Once the prick saw that he'd cornered the SLA market, he cut her off. All summer she felt sick at heart, frustrated, unfulfilled, empty. They disappeared into their adventure, distant and mysterious, while she spent her days fetching extra dressing and replacing unsatisfactory flatware and sending perfectly good food back to the kitchen because it wasn't cooked silly. She and Jeff argued over whether her support and concern for the SLA were counterrevolutionary, since (in Jeff's opinion) it stemmed from her "personal feeling" (he made it sound obscene) for Angela, which (according to him) had the "unmistakable aroma" of "the personality cult." Susan fumed. Jeff was still annoyed, Susan knew, by the notoriety she achieved addressing the crowd at Ho Chi Minh Park; he had work that day. Now he was giving her shit, telling her how "concerned" he was about her "preoccupation," which he "felt morally obliged to say" he thought was "not politically based." She told him to just stick to painting apartments.

But then, midsummer, the calls began. Teko and Yolanda, calling separately, calling together, from public phones. We need you, Susan. Don't forget us, Susan. She was thrilled. Jeff would conk out after a day painting down in Castro Valley or Hayward, a copy of *Grundrisse* open across his chest, and she'd be dragging the extension into the bathroom to have the kind of intense, whispered conversation she'd been missing since Angela had gone. They planned for the future, schemed and plotted. She sent money, packets of cash wrapped in dark paper and sealed in manila envelopes addressed to general delivery. She set aside more money to rent the W Street place. They worked the arrangements out, speaking frequently, fervidly; it was intimate and seductive, communication beyond words, she felt. She tried to project soulful desire into every phrase she uttered into the mouthpiece. She *missed* them. She *wanted* them.

But it was as a revolutionary that she signed on, even as she formed this emotional bond, and as a revolutionary recruit she expected a more formal sense of belonging, she expected a clear channel to the truth through the many, many shades of gray that she was certain they'd consider, she expected a studious solidarity, the cell hunched over its synoptic texts. It's beginning to dawn on her that what she has is a small and argumentative group cohering around its mutual discontent, assigning it a name ("fascism"), and using it as a pretext for every kind of dim-witted excess.

Jeff comes into the kitchen, dressed for another day of life-affirming manual labor. She stubs out the cigarette in an ashtray that says GREAT ELECTRIC UNDERGROUND and seizes the soft lapels of her old robe in her hands, draws them together over her breasts. No, this isn't the time for analysis. She's always had her doubts. She had them when she found out that Angela was involved with them. She thought it was stupid and fruitless to assassinate Marcus Foster. Viscerally alarming that they invaded the home of Alice Galton and carried her off into the night. Ostentatiously self-seeking when they robbed the Hibernia Bank and shot two depositors. Boneheadedly dense to have risked shoplifting—what was it, socks?—when they were supposed to be laying low in L.A. But she's caught up in something now, committed, successfully outpacing her boredom, for once. She will be drawn in and implicated, move beyond the everyday, into a kind of history, a legend amid the outlaw annals, larger than ideology.

LYDIA GALTON SAT AT her desk, waiting for Thomas Polhaus to arrive, alternately composing anagrams on a sheet of paper and gazing out the window at the ladies and gentlemen of the press who clustered below, seeking shelter from a cold drizzle beneath the wind-whipped canopy pitched on the lawn. There were more reporters than usual this morning, the reason being the occasion of her daughter's twenty-first birthday, she supposed.

A good anagram for *diazepam* was "zap media."

Though everything seemed to have a reason nowadays. She was always being presented with reasons for appearing before television cameras, for permitting reporters into her home, for providing emotional responses to "the situation" on demand, for traveling to places she had no wish to visit, for speaking, all the time, to policemen with their roving eyes.

p a i d   m a z e

She understood perfectly well that the reasons had been made up. If you were told why you had to do something, there was a greater chance you'd shut up and do it. Damned simple. In the end, of course, if you had any sense, you shut up and did it just to shut up the people intent upon providing you with all those good reasons they cooked up. It was why she'd married Hank, for God's sake. She'd become so tired of hearing about him that she'd guessed it would be simpler just to live with him. Eighteen years old, and all she knew for certain in this world was that she'd rather hear anyone's voice every day than her mother's when she was mounting a campaign. The campaign to turn Lydia Daniels into Mrs. Henry Hubbard Galton, into an entirely different person, had been the last Lydia endured at her hands. And now here it was thirty-seven years later, and Lydia was an old lady, and her mother was dead and buried, and now all the good reasons that were presented to her each day as solid, practical, and virtually self-evident were to explain things, situations, that hadn't existed even as possibilities back then. She imagined that hers was a shared perception, a fairly common take on the times: *Where had the world gone?*

Hence the remark that had made it into the papers, that had become notorious, scandalous, that had begun the process of turning her into a dotty joke. She'd suggested to Eric Stump—in passing, so she'd thought, a mere observation—that if *Clark Gable* had been in the house with Alice, those hoodlums couldn't have taken her. "Where are all the real men?" she'd asked rhetorically. If Stump were a "real man," he would have taken it in good part and laughed with her. If he'd been capable of understanding who Clark Gable had been, what he had meant, then the implication of the remark would have been obvious. But to Stump, to all these ignorant young people, Gable was merely something obsolescent, a superseded precursor of some contemporary creature like Jack Nicholson holding food between his legs. If she could begin to explain why a Jack

Nicholson, or a Dustin Hoffman clouting wedding guests over the head with a crucifix, was not a patch on Clark Gable's ass, for all their easy gestures of defiant contempt, she would be a professor of movies (something she was always astonished to note actually existed). It was a nostalgic remark: that's all. A man who is jealous of movie stars is no man at all; he is a nitwit. If Stump had possessed the good sense to realize that she was not directly comparing him with Gable, that Gable was incomparable and that that was precisely the point, she might have forgiven him everything (though she doubted it). But instead Stump had scuttled off, looking all *wounded*, straight to the reporters, who naturally distorted the remark. When it appeared, the story had become Can you believe what the silly old bat had to say? Clark Gable, imagine that. Direct from the days of the wind-up Victrola!

Her nostalgia was not only out of place but out of style as well. The young people had their own synthetic nostalgia: a television show, *Happy Days*; a Broadway musical, *Grease*; and a movie, *American Graffiti*, all of which concerned a sentimental 1950s past. Men, women, and children alike seemed to accept these spectacles as the truth of the era, its absolute limit. Lydia sometimes watched the television program in the kitchen with the cook (it was Tuesday night, it was eight o'clock, it was Hank hiding from her in his study, so why the hell not sit watching the kitchen portable beside a woman with the last name of Núñez?). The lettered cardigans and pomaded hair, the snickering references to backseat sex that all of the nation, in the year 1975, seemed to find titillating. This was the first time Lydia could remember when there seemed to be a strong communal will to reverse the clock, an attempt beyond nostalgia actually to construct a living imitation of the past from the shinier and more durable pieces of its debris and then to dwell in it. There was of course the inconvenience of people her own age, not to mention the thousands still walking the earth who could vividly recall something as distant as the last century. While the conventional take on the ascendancy of *Happy Days* etc. was that these diversions provided an "escape" from the "perplexing" "reality" of a "turbulent" era, Lydia had little doubt that around the 1990s there would be a television comedy all about the trigger-happy days of the seventies. All this would be funny in the distant future!

Though to Lydia the fifties didn't really seem all that distant. Just yesterday, really. Certainly nothing much had changed in Hills-borough. And what else? Walter Winchell was gone, but Herb Caen was still writing. *Gunsmoke* was still on the air. Mutual funds were very popular now. Willie Mays had joined the Country Club. Paperback books were respectable. So were California wines. Ann Landers suggested divorce occasionally now. The United States lost Vietnam, but who'd really wanted it? People drove little toy cars from Japan and had machines that answered their telephones. The people who called to talk to them talked to these machines instead. They still stocked Mallomars in cooler weather only. Israel was still there, and people seemed just as angry about it as they ever had.

Well, the anger. That was the difference. She couldn't remember the anger, from back then. She was certain that it had been *out there*, somewhere, but it hadn't been *right here*. There had been boredom and fear, there had been some terrible photographs in *Life*, there had been plenty of boorish people, most of whom seemed to end up in the United States Congress, who arrived with their wives for din-ner or cocktails and who'd had strong notions about Negroes, Communists, taxes, labor unions, and young men who played the guitar. And then they left and you didn't think anymore about Negroes or guitars or what have you. But now you couldn't buy a house big enough or build it on a hill high enough to get away from the anger. It was an angry age. Restraint had been swept out of fash-ion. People working in the grocery store and the filling station were angry. The man skimming the pool. They were angry about their jobs, or about not having jobs, or about having jobs when other people didn't seem to need to have jobs. They were angry about preservatives in food, about air pollution, about miniskirts, about college tuition, about property taxes, about there not being enough left-handed scissors in the world. They were angry about things people never even used to talk about. Had they *always* been angry?

The people who'd taken her daughter were angry with her, and she had no bloody idea even who they were. She could imagine perhaps kidnapping the daughter of someone who had, say, run over one's dog. *That* she could imagine. A dog was, in many ways, more valuable and satisfying than a daughter. But to kidnap your daughter simply because you lived in a nice house and belonged to a prominent fam-ily? It was difficult to understand. There were certainly plenty of people in the neighborhood with more money than they had. Yet *their* daughters were dressing nicely and keeping up with their studies and preparing to become leading citizens. If these revolutionaries were such marvelous democrats, they damned well should have driven to Woodside and Atherton and Portola Valley and Los Altos Hills and kidnapped *everyone's* daughters. Let *everyone* open the *Chronicle* in the morning and have to read about himself, "Mrs. Galton briefly appeared in the luxuriant front garden before her impressive home. She waved to reporters but declined to answer their polite questions. At ten in the morning, she sported a costly-looking string of pearls around her neck and a large diamond glittered from one finger." In the end it came down to anger. They were angry with *her*. Take a number. Certainly Hank was angry with her, and she was beginning to think she had no idea who he was either. Alice was angry with her, and she'd never quite known what to make of her. Lydia was pretty convinced that the reporters below were angry with her.

I d z a p m e
i z m a d a p e
i z m a d
    m a d

The other thing about *reasons* was that when she failed to provide a reason for something she had done, even when it was something she'd done without a thought, without, as it were, having had any reason at all, there was trouble. If she dressed in black, they wondered if she was mourning prematurely. If she dressed in a colorful print, they wondered if she'd put her daughter out of her mind. Why are you crying? Why aren't you crying? Are you on tranquilizers? Pep pills? Have you been drinking? She was obliged to fabricate reasons for the way she dressed, for the jewelry she wore, for the hairstyle she preferred. No wonder that in the midst of this flurry of improvisational rationalizing she had to perform she sometimes got it wrong. There were the professional explainers, like Henry Kissinger, and then there were private citizens. And of course the newspapers, those mandarins of cause and effect, were all over her. Rainstorms and scarce parking spaces and the profusion of sex in today's motion pictures, they had an explanation for everything. Nobody wanted only news; they wanted reasons as well. If you didn't give them a good reason, they just made up a bad one for you. Here was a good example: Dutch Reagan had offered her, simply as a formality, her own seat on the Board of Regents of the University of California, a seat she'd occupied since 1956, those happy days. Of course she accepted the reappointment. It was a responsibility, it was a privilege, it was an honor. What it had never before been was news. But were those good enough reasons? Why, no. The reason, Lydia was startled to read, was that she was *arrogant*. It was *arrogant* not to allow herself to be pushed around by the gangsters demanding that she leave the board. It was *arrogant* to have done so without wringing her hands over it in front of the TV cameras.

Outside, a young man from KRON dashed out from under the canopy and began to sing a few lyrics from "Singin' in the Rain." There were a few laughs, a general murmur of appreciation. A little something to break up the routine of another boring day spent standing outside the Galton house. It was a practical form insanity could take. Or anger. Probably anger. Lydia remembered going to pay someone a call at the Huntington Hotel once upon a time and spending a perfectly awful afternoon, drinking tea and dodging catty remarks. It had been one of those visits. Afterward, stepping off the automatic elevator on the lobby floor, she'd paused on the threshold and then ducked back inside to press each of the buttons, from B all the way up to PH. She had no idea why other than that she'd been angry. "Singin' in the Rain" was about the least angry song she could think of; it made "Happy Birthday to You" sound like "Ride of the Valkyries," but why wouldn't they be angry, standing under a canopy in the rain all day like a bunch of damned fools?

The doorbell rang, and there she was getting up, rising from her perfectly comfortable seat. She could greet Agent Polhaus or she could take cover in the bathroom. Probably she would go downstairs and meet her visitor. Hear him out. And then see him out. She had begun to suspect that Polhaus's motivation for calling on them to deliver his status reports derived more from his interest in the twelve-year-old Laphroaig they kept behind the bar than from any sense of decorum or professional courtesy. She felt as if she ought to say, No daughter, no scotch. But then she'd be in hot water again. Well, whatever his "reasons," there he was, and if Hank wasn't going to hide from him, she was damned if she would.

T RAINING AND PLANNING. Tania scouts the area, working from Yolanda's painstakingly detailed notes, typed up on the Royal portable (§VI.A.2., *knowledge of main access routes, natural barriers, defiles, parks, schools, dead-end streets, stop signs, stoplights, shopping centers, parking lots*).

Teko picks Jeff to lead the Bakery Operation, but Jeff greets the suggestion with naked panic. Teko persists; they conduct drills under the assumption that Jeff will be in command. Quickly it becomes clear that Jeff can't even rehearse the job without fucking up; so huge is his nervousness that the hand in which he holds his unloaded pistol shakes disconcertingly; he stammers and falters when demanding money from Susan or Tania. Teko agrees to take over. Jeff will cover the bank with a shotgun and keep time. Three minutes in and out.

She and Roger drive all the routes, for the hell of it, to have it down, to get out of the safe house: W Street to Arden Plaza; Arden Plaza to the switch point; switch point to the McKinley Park rendezvous; back to W Street. Yolanda's list is all heads and subheads and sub-subheads (§VI.A.4.d., *final dry run with all drivers*), multiple indents. It's a thing of beauty, they agree. A glimpse of the inside of her head.

Tania's not at all sure why Teko feels confident about handing a nervous man a shotgun inside a confined space. Just say she's glad she won't be anywhere nearby. Still, she diligently instructs Jeff in the weapon's use, shows him how to hold it, how to swing it in an arc. She teaches him the zone system, though she knows the gun's sawed-off barrel makes the knowledge useless. Still, maybe her expertise and confidence will rub off. The shotgun was her first firearm; she learned it by feel in the closet. This particular gun dry fires awfully easily, though. A hair trigger, she and Jeff agree.

On the way back to W Street they pull over near Southside Park, deserted at this hour, or rather two figures are on the lakeshore, practicing tai chi with complete absorption, remote beyond the physical distance. Across the street, the freeway structure and beyond that a windswept softball field. She turns to Roger.

"OK, wheelman. Fuck me, now."

They do it in the car. Under the trees in the park. Roger is reluctant to fuck in the house ever since awakening one night in the liv-

369

ing room to find Teko sitting in the sagging chair opposite him and Tania, holding a submachine gun in his hands, a sign of a growing craziness he could feel but couldn't put a name to.

One afternoon Jeff lets the muzzle cross her as he moves with the weapon. She is about to tell him, again, "Be muzzle aware," when she hears the click. For a moment they freeze.

"Sorry," he says, finally.

"Keep the safety on," she advises him.

"In the bank?" he asks.

"Especially there," she says.

Three minutes in and out. That's all.

A FEW CARS HAVE already parked at Arden Plaza. Susan watches the Chevy turn into the lot, bouncing on its ruined shocks. Some depositors stand waiting outside Guild Savings, their hands buried in their pockets against the early-morning chill. Inside, a man in a suit bows deeply, unlocking the front door. His necktie slips out of his jacket and swings free for a moment as he works the key in the lock at the base of the door. Standing upright, he carefully straightens the tie and places it back where it belongs before opening up, waving the customers in, holding the door as they pass.

Susan has the *Bee* open before her, and she pretends to read it while spreading grape jelly on a buttered English. 9:01: The Chevy pulls away from the front of the bank. She smiles up at the waitress and accepts more coffee. 9:07: She hears distant sirens. 9:09: A sheriff's cruiser enters the lot. Uniformed deputies leap from the car, leaving the doors open, and run into the bank, guns drawn. She turns over the check and puts a couple of dollars on the table, then ambles over to join the gathering of curious shoppers and store clerks assembled outside the bank. A deputy stands blocking the door, telling everyone that the bank is closed. He still holds his .38 in his hand. Susan can hear another siren's faraway howling.

Beside the pond in McKinley Park, Tania and Yolanda sit on a bench, sharing a cigarette and watching the approach of the switch car, a green and white Plymouth. Tania holds a Styrofoam cup of tea that she sips through a small hole she's torn in the plastic lid. The car pulls to the curb, and Jeff and Teko get out. Roger, waving, attempts to catch her eye from behind the wheel. She lifts a single finger—not now. Actually, she feels like ignoring him. In fact, she feels a mild distaste for all three of them: for their fear, excitement, and affected bravado. She can tell immediately that everything went smoothly inside the bank, that the entire incident will assume an epic contour as it is told and retold and retold still again. As Jeff and Teko begin to relate their adventure, she cuts them off sharply. Yolanda allows herself a slight smile. Chastened, the men get back into the Plymouth and continue on their way, leaving behind a hemp bag containing the weapons and disguises and a green duffel holding the money for Tania and Yolanda to carry to the bus stop. Yolanda hugs the duffel tight as they ride back to W Street with kids playing hooky and two Mexican cleaning ladies carrying their supplies in a stained plastic caddy.

GUNMEN ROB NORTH SACTO BANK

(February 25) Two men robbed the Guild Savings branch on Arden Way shortly after the bank opened on Tuesday morning. The men entered the branch, located at the Arden Plaza Shopping Center, and immediately announced the robbery, displaying guns and ordering customers and staff to the floor. One suspect acted as a lookout while the other forced a teller to fill a bag with cash and money orders. Both suspects then fled through the bank's rear exit with an undisclosed amount. No one was injured. The suspects are described as Caucasian males in their mid-20s. At the time of the robbery both were wearing long raincoats and hats, and one covered his face with a scarf or bandanna. Eyewitnesses told sheriff's deputies that the suspects were dropped at the bank in an older blue sedan.

This particular bakery yields an oven-fresh $3,729. They sit in a circle while Yolanda removes a small blue duffel bag from the larger green one that camouflages it and then counts up the cash, separating the folding money into neat piles of twenties, tens, fives, and ones, a skill derived from many games of Monopoly on the screened-in porch back in Clarendon Hills. Yolanda always liked to be the banker, an irony that does not occur to her now.

"Pakes," says one of the technicians. He is looking at the wrought-iron lettering, spelling out P A I X, affixed to the balcony handrail. He lights a cigarette and leans against the car. "That who owns this dump?"

"No, it's some fireman in New York. Lafferty." An FBI supervisor from Scranton, Silliman, is outside talking to the technician because neither of them has much to do. The technician is up from Philly to look for trace evidence, but the place is turning out to be clean. Shoe prints? No. Tire impressions? Not even theirs. No semen, saliva, sweat, vomit, or blood in drops, pools, spatters, splashes, or stains. No slugs or shells. Plenty of hair and fibers. Some of the hairs appear to be synthetic, but there's nothing in particular that looks foreign to the scene. Fragments of broken glass here and there, chips of paint. This and that. They bag the stuff and tag it. Each day for a frigid week they've returned to the farm.

"You talk to him?"

"We talked to him. He rented it out to Guy Mock all right. Summer thing. He said Mock claimed to be an author who needed a nice quiet place to work."

"Ain't that pretty."

"He sure got it. Christ, go nuts out here." Viewed from the house, the pines stand plain and lonely atop the bare gray hills. Silliman slaps his gloved hands together and rubs them briskly. The air feels cold enough to slice the skin.

They've talked to everybody. Storekeepers, neighbors, mail carriers, the propane delivery man. Silliman's certain that they have the right place. Everyone who's gotten a look at it remembers Guy Mock's face, everyone speaks of a nondescript couple, a pretty Oriental girl. Or gook, depending on who you talk to. Silliman has an inkling of who this person might be.

"How's the garbage?"

"They burned it in a pit back of the house. The usual cans and bottles and bones. They're trying to lift prints from them."

"They're animal bones?"

"Oh, shit yeah. Pork chops and chicken."

The propane man recalls seeing an additional woman, who lay on a cot with a blanket over her head for the entire time he was there. In July heat. Silliman elects not to show him the photo of the famous fugitive. No sense inviting every crank in the county to put their two cents in. He waits for the dogs to arrive on their chartered flight from California. They go apeshit when they get a whiff of the cot.

Chartered flight. He likes that.

"Let's go in. I'm freezing my ass off."

Inside the house, furniture is draped with dropcloths while dusting for prints goes on nearby. No visibles. No plastic impressions. No latents so far, though there are plenty of indications the place has been wiped, not least of which is that there are no prints. But this is not evidence, this is not admissible, this is merely suspicious, something that gives cops a reason for rising each morning and banging their heads against the wall. Dusting continues. Elsewhere, where dusting and evidence gathering and photographing have already happened, the government men have tossed the place. Silliman knows the fugitives were here. Because there's no sign they were here.

Silliman goes through pockets in the mudroom. He finds receipts from local vendors dating back to the mid-sixties. He finds a shopping list that mentions "Tricks Cereal for Brian and Tim" and concludes that this is the work of Mrs. Lafferty, whoever she is or was. He finds thirty-seven cents in change, including a dime and a penny minted in 1974. He bags the coins. He bags a Bic pen that has bled half its ink into the pocket of an old field jacket. Screaming Eagles patch on the shoulder. He finds a book of matches advertising the U.S. Auto School and bags that too. In a Lee Riders jacket that looks as if it would fit someone about sixteen years old, he finds a beat-up copy of *Penthouse Forum*. It falls open to a certain page.

Dear Penthouse Forum:

I want to write about the greatest oral sex I have ever had. Now let me say that due to my above-average (ten inches) endowment I have never had satisfactory oral pleasure from any woman. I have long wanted someone who would eat me—all of me—whenever I so desired, swallowing all of the frothing sperm cocktail I pumped into her soft willing mouth, while asking nothing more in return than to be regularly walked, fed, and watered, the ultimate lover and soul mate. Well, in my four-year-old collie Donna I have found mine. Donna is gorgeous, with a long, silky coat and expressive brown eyes. One day when she was a puppy I awoke to find her licking dried sperm from my abdomen (I'd fallen asleep after jerking off). Well, one thing led to another and before I knew it I'd trained her to pleasure me orally. Now, let me tell you about the beautiful blow jobs I receive from Donna. Not once in four years has she bitten me, not even a nip. Well,

Silliman closes the magazine. It does get lonely out here, he guesses. Brian? Tim? Lieutenant Lafferty himself, dreaming of the firehouse Dalmatian? He bags it.

He went to bed one night a spectator and awoke—was awoken, actually—the next morning, engulfed. A weird feeling. He's followed the whole thing in the papers and on the news. It's the Bureau's case, but it seemed to have little to do with anything he knows. Scranton Resident does some organized crime. It works with Treasury on bootleg cigarette sales and such. There are bank robberies; some laid-off mine worker will wander into a local branch with a peremptory note and wander out with a paper bag full of a thousand dollars in bait bills. It is not, in short, a glamour assignment. Now here comes this case, straight from California, filtered through the gaunt sunlight of a Pennsylvania winter. California's not big enough for all the craziness it engenders? Silliman has twenty years in the Bureau. Silliman understands criminal pathology. He understands the easy money mentality of some moron who drives across state lines in a truck loaded with butts missing their revenue stamps. He understands the miner whose wife closes the fridge and says there's no food and there isn't going to be any. He understands a lot of things, but he has trouble understanding these boys and girls who seem to want a different sort of government. What for? He *is* the government, and he can assure these kids that any conceivable alternative would have men just like him, doing just what he does, at its heart. Of course they wouldn't believe this. He tries to imagine what they do believe but can envision only a buzzing rush of static in his head: a void, chaotic. It scares the living shit out of him. It has nothing to do with Pennsylvania. What do these sturdy old farmhouses have to do with revolution?

374

His wife always wants to go out to California. She thinks it's one big beach, full of movie stars.

Silliman feels that he occupies the quietest zone in the case. Every day he enters a house that in its placid inscrutability tells him little yet offers the most reliable view into the missing girl's daily life. She stood here, she sat there. Washed her dishes in this sink. When she came out and stood on the top step, this is what she would have seen. He drives down the road and walks the same three aisles she would have walked at the country store. Pork chops and chicken.

The furious storm, and he's at its eye. The papers have been full of it lately: no breaks, no news, the case already a year old. So quiet here: you could go nuts. But for now he wants to hold the isolation close. The press doesn't yet know about this place. After interrogating him, Silliman recommended that the Bureau immediately ship Ernest Mock overseas on an all-expenses-paid trip to Europe. He didn't think Mock would be able to keep his mouth shut for a second.

Just as Silliman is about to wrap it up for the day, an investigator comes into the room holding a bag containing a folded, crumpled section of newspaper, six months old. *The New York Times*, perfect. It has been discovered stuffed into a hole in the underside of one of the mattresses upstairs. That's a good find. That looks promising. Silliman tells the investigator so; he likes his men to feel as if they're not totally wasting their time.

Back in Scranton the next afternoon, Silliman gets a call from the fingerprint examiner at the lab in Philly. He has managed to lift a latent partial print from one of the fragments recovered from the garbage pit, a piece of a shattered drinking glass. In the expert opinion of the fingerprint examiner, the print matches one on file with the United States Marine Corps listed as belonging to Andrew Carlyle Shepard, aka Richard Frank Dennis, aka William Kinder, aka Jonathan Maris, aka Jonathan Mark Salamone, aka General Teko of the Symbionese Liberation Army, currently wanted by the United States of America for violation of the National Firearms Act. The examiner also mentions that using ninhydrin spray, they managed to develop prints on the section of newspaper discovered in the mattress. No match as yet, but the examiner notes casually that the prints display the frequent whorls characteristically found on persons of Oriental origin.

· · ·

G<small>UY WANDERS INTO A</small> strip club, a workingman's place off the high-way: a perfect place to sit, think, and throw away a little more money. The girls onstage are dancing, if dancing is the word; mostly they sway off beat to contemporary hits, swinging from smudgy chrome poles.

There's not much to strip. Girls taking the stage wear a bra, heels, and a G-string, with maybe a boa or a cowboy hat, tops. "Midnight at the Oasis" is fading out as Guy takes his seat at the bar, and by the time his beer arrives Marvin Hamlisch's version of "The Entertainer" is forlornly playing out. Guy figures he is witnessing an unusual confluence of indigenous American imaginative artifacts. A song written around the turn of the century to be performed in the genteel parlors of bordellos—scandalous then but currently popular as a nostalgic evocation, albeit a jarringly anachronistic one, of the 1930s—is serving as the accompaniment to a contemporary and aggressively vulgar display that falsely promises the sex the whore-houses delivered but hid from public view.

In a hundred years, when vending machine sex-robots fuck us for quarters, they'll probably play disco.

The girls don't know quite how to respond to this tune. One humps the pole, sliding up and down its length, her tongue hanging out in a caricature of rapture; another walks up and down the narrow stage, looking oddly reminiscent of a stewardess patrolling the aisle of a 707. The patrons, too, seem confused, confused and riled; these scoured westerners didn't come here to listen to Scott Joplin tell them how damned sad everything is. It makes Guy nervous. He probably should have just taken a six-pack into one of the vacant cabins at his parents' place, but he half expects to be arrested any day now, and that's the first place they're likely to look.

Even the mindless serenity of the strip club is adulterated by the clanging and flashing of the slots parked in every corner. He is sick, sick, sick of Vegas. Sick of the heat, sick of the sun, sick of the recycled air, sick of the dry, rasping cough he rises with each morning, sick of tourists, sick of natives, sick of loud, dumb radio ads for the shows at the casinos, sick of getting the thermonuclear shakes from underground testing.

"You Ain't Seen Nothin' Yet" comes on, and everyone seems relieved.

The phone rang one fine morning up in Oregon, and it was his mother on the line. Just wanted to let him know that Ernest had called to say that he would be visiting Europe for a while and that he'd informed on the whole family to the FBI. Agents would probably be paying them a visit once they'd confirmed the details of Ernest's story. She spoke with a sort of polar calm.

"What do you think I should tell them, Guy?"

"Mom, don't tell them anything."

"Well, if they are going to take the trouble of coming all the way out here, I feel bad just turning them away."

"They're probably just coming from the Federal Building downtown, Mom."

"Still and all, they have a right to the truth."

"No," said Guy, "they don't. You need to call a lawyer. And in the meantime keep your mouth shut. Do you understand me?"

"Guy, do you really think an attorney is going to be necessary?"

"Yes, I do, Mom. This is serious business as your beloved son Ernest well knows. No wonder he's—"

"Maybe Dick Taranutz can recommend a good attorney."

"Taranutz? That guy across the street?"

"He's very well set up in business. I'm sure he'd know of a good one."

"Don't you say word one to Taranutz about any of this."

"But he and Minnie are *such* good friends."

"Don't say a word."

But three days later, after Guy and a more or less totally disgruntled Randi had decamped from Portland—Randi traveling to visit friends in San Diego while Guy flew to Las Vegas to head off an unsupervised encounter between federal agents and his parents—Guy arrived to find his mother riven and dispirited, gazing sadly at the huge stucco eyesore across the road with the Cadillac gleaming in its driveway. Apparently the Taranutzes had taken a dim view of the Mocks' unlawful activities. The wonderful friendship was at an end. No lawyer had been retained.

For two days Guy sat in his parents' apartment watching his mother slice fruit—for fruit salad, for pies, for banana bread, for breakfast cereal. The woman handled a paring knife as if she were the skilled practitioner of some ancient and vaguely theatrical craft, like weaving or crocheting. On the whole it was pretty useless, Guy thought, because you couldn't send the grandkids bowls of sliced fruit the way you could a sweater or a scarf. In fact, you couldn't even eat it all, not in the quantities that she was cutting up. His father, sitting on the couch watching television as she desperately sliced apples and grapes and mandarin oranges, put forth the proposition that Dick Taranutz was a jerk and that he always had been. Neither of them would hear of Guy's calling a lawyer.

"I am ready to come clean," his mother declared.

"Bunch of thieves," his father said.

On the morning of the third day Guy was in the living room executing a headstand and watching *The Electric Company* when there came a knock at the front door. His father groaned experimentally, rising from his seat, but Mrs. Mock failed to appear, so he went to the door and answered it himself. Two men stood outside in the fierce sun. They didn't want a cabin.

"Guy Mock, Senior?" said one.

"Yes," said the old man.

The man handed him a folded document. "You're served."

"What is it?"

"That is a subpoena directing you to appear before the Grand Jury of the U.S. District Court for the Middle District of Pennsylvania for questioning."

"Questioning?"

"The subpoena provides details," said the other man.

In the living room Guy remained very still. In his shoulder he began to feel a piercing pain.

"And who are you? Police?"

"Federal Bureau of Investigation. Special Agents Vanaken and Oakes." Out with the stupid badges.

"Have you spoken with your son, Mr. Mock?"

"Ernest's in Europe. But I guess you knew that."

"Never mind what we know," said Oakes.

"I meant Guy, Junior."

"Guy? Sure, I've talked to him. He's up in Oregon."

"Actually he isn't," said Vanaken crisply. "We were wondering if you could tell us where he might be."

"Oh, a lot of places. Guy has lots of friends."

"Friends," said Oakes, raising his chin.

"Oh, sure. What do you want with Guy?"

"We'd just like to talk with him about a few things."

"What sorts of things?"

"The subpoena will tell you everything you need to know."

Mr. Mock slapped one open palm with the subpoena held in the other hand. "I guess I have to read that subpoena."

"May we come in and ask you some questions?"

"I'm afraid I'm awful busy right now."

"Busy," said Oakes.

"All right. Is Mrs. Mock at home now?"

"Oh, she's not feeling well."

"Would Mrs. Mock be able to tell us where we might find Guy?"

In the living room, Guy could bear it no longer and dropped out of his headstand, silent upon the thick carpet. He crunched into a little ball and rolled toward the nearest corner. "And what about Naomi?" the TV said.

"Someone learning to read?" asked Vanaken, craning his neck. "My little girl watches that show."

"Oh, well. I like to keep it on. You know. Makes it feel like someone's here."

"Isn't Mrs. Mock at home?"

"I couldn't possibly disturb her."

"Her son could be in a lot of trouble."

Mr. Mock shrugged. "He's big."

"We'll be back, Mr. Mock."

"Goodbye, then." He shut the door.

Guy said, "Thanks, Dad."

"Oh, shut the hell up," said Mr. Mock.

Now Guy's stuffing dollar bills into the G-string of a young lady with dyed red hair cut short. He's called PSA to find out about flights to Los Angeles. At the last possible minute he'll call Randi and ask her to meet him at LAX. He can just imagine: Sick unto death. Had it up to here. Et cetera. He would love to be able to assert to her that he can explain all of this. The explanation thing is at least mildly entertaining for him. But they've moved beyond his rationalizations and into the realm of necessity. Until now, today, this moment, it's never seemed as if actual trouble for him and Randi were anywhere in the vicinity. They are still *justifiable* sort of people, only peripherally involved with all this craziness; he is first and fore-most an academic, an activist, an advocate, an apostate, an author, not necessarily in that order but still, a person to be taken seriously and accorded respect, not one of the insane citizens with whom life is constantly bringing him into alignment. Savor it, he's being hunted by the FBI because of something *Ernest* has told them. OK, maybe what Ernest spilled concerned things he, Guy, could be said to have done, but you have to consider the source, don't you? This is what he'll tell the FBI if it turns out he has to tell them anything at all: Consider the source.

And where do we go from here?

Which is the way that's clear?

The redhead grips the pole. It's an interesting gesture because Guy sees all the fingers working, each seeking purchase on the sweaty shaft of metal, gripping and regripping like the fingers of someone operating a sewing machine, or throwing a pot, *this is really work*, Guy thinks, his fourth beer half empty before him, she grips and bends low and in one of the lulls in David Essex's spare piece of pop poetry he hears her grunt, an earthy sound, allied with exertion and weariness and digestion and excretion and other functions that would seem to have absolutely nothing to do with this tits 'n' ass phantasm set down in the middle of this derelict land, and as she sways to the left her hand gently sweeps across the top of his head, knocking his cap off, and as she sways to the right her fingers softly caress his scalp and the high border of his dwindling hair, and his own hand rises with a five-dollar bill in it. Why not? This is *work*. Nothing else could possibly look like work next to this. She takes the bill, folds it in half lengthwise, and strokes her labia with it, then tucks it in the teeny-weeny waistband of her G-string. Then she strides off; her work here is done. It's enough to make him want to cry. He wants to be up there. He wants to feel it all for himself. He actually does begin to tear up. In the end that's the only thing they could really accuse him of, the only thing they could ever really find him guilty of. He just wants to know for himself what it all feels like.

Randi has two large red American Tourister suitcases that she would never have dreamed of bringing to San Diego if she'd had the slight-est notion that she would be staying for only three days. Her whole life these days seems to consist of dealing with the consequences of errors in judgment. So, having finally checked these millstones, she's trying to live it up a little, drinking a martini out of a plastic cup in the departure lounge and flirting with the tall graying business type who "lent" her a cigarette. They sit and smoke, gazing at the huge machines rolling down the taxiways, aware of having little to say to each other and equally aware that each is trying to keep up the conversation. Sexy, in an awkward way. She has no idea why she is attracted to this very straight-looking fellow. He's not exactly Republican straight, more like former Young Democrat straight, which, to her mind, is better. Room for hope. Though Guy would certainly, and loudly, disagree (her lip curls into a slight sneer at the thought of Guy). Would it be a terrible thing if she and this gentleman were to find a quiet corner of the terminal in which to fuck? It's the fantasy lingering here and in every such place on earth. The regional planners put their sagacious heads together, they obtain the zoning, they condemn the land, they build the airport, they install the Gay Nineties saloons, the gift shops and newsstands, they bring in the fleets of shiny jets—in short, they alter the landscape, the cadence of an entire region, life itself, and all around are these boxes in which you can deposit, for a dollar and a half, a completed, preapproved application for life insurance. Everything made clean and shipshape and trimmed with smiles and bright lights, *fixed*, and still, they have these depositories to remind you of the statistical presence of death. The payoff, if your flight explodes in midair or corkscrews into some subdivision, is scads of dough. Not for you, though. And what if she were to write across the face of the insurance policy, "Inform my husband that three hours before my fiery death I gave a hand job to a very nice man in a Hathaway shirt and a rep tie in return for a Vantage. See if he doesn't take the money. Tell him that I whacked off a hundred men, all of whom had questionable class sympathies, in a dozen airports; tell him that I never cared, never shared his obsessions, so my death isn't a loss, it's nothing he'll suffer—and just see if he doesn't take the god damn money and never thinks twice about me again."

The Young Democrat has never, ever, ever forgotten his wife's birthday.

Never cut her vacation short.

Never made her spend a single moment, much less weeks at a time, in a VW Bug.

Never sat across from her and discussed his digestion, his bowel movements, his reflux, his prostate, his hematospermia, his unjustly weak orgasms, his desire to wear women's undergarments, his bunions, his ingrown toenails, or his personal sense of what Hegel would have had to say about the day's headlines.

Never gotten drunk around the kitchen table with stupid undergrads or even more stupid ex-football players and erected tall towers of empty beer cans.

Never had an affair with a hypochondriacal little twat like Erica Dyson.

A flight is announced over the PA, and the Young Democrat picks up his briefcase and raincoat and rises. He tells Randi to enjoy her flight and then he's gone, heading toward the cluster of people forming near one of the gates. Randi opens her pocketbook and checks her wallet to make sure (again) that she has enough money to buy a ticket aboard the flight. Sixty-four dollars and she is only now vaguely realizing that she could have driven. She could have rented some nice roomy American car that doesn't sound like a heart attack heading down the road and just driven up to L.A. without hassling with taxis and skycaps and Hare Krishnas and Young Democrats before climbing aboard some skinny tube that's likely enough to plummet to the earth that they think it's levelheaded to install special boxes where you can lay a bet in favor of your own death. As long as we're throwing away money anyway. As long as sixty-four dollars here, there, and everywhere doesn't mean diddly-squat compared with the thrill of being a fugitive from the law.

Her plane is a tiny prop with two rows, each ten seats deep, extending to the rear of the plane. A curtain separates the cockpit from the passenger cabin. A uniformed man wearing a change apron comes aboard just before the pilot seals the hatch to collect fares from passengers buying tickets. Randi gives her name as Eileen Rimer. A cousin. The plane takes off and an hour later it's Welcome to Los Angeles County International Airport. Two seconds in the terminal and she's already seen three women, hair out to here, wearing these Suzy Creamcheese outfits that are designed not so much to make the women wearing them look terrific as to make women like herself feel dowdy. Works like a charm. And here's Guy, walking through the place looking like the sixth Marx Brother. Oglo. Staro. Gawpo. He spots her and heads over.

"For God's sake," he says, "it took you long enough."

She just sat in the damn thing and they pulled the throttle back, or something, and it went. What does he want from her?

"Don't be so sensitive. This is no time for you to be sensitive. They're looking for us right now."

"Who?"

"Who do you think? The federales. Bearing grand jury subpoenas. They already served Dad."

"What does that mean?"

"It means they can compel testimony."

"In connection with what?"

"A certain house in Pennsylvania, for one thing."

"We never tried to hide the fact that we rented it."

"It's who was there."

"We went over the place. What could they have?"

"Who the hell knows what they have?"

"They shouldn't have anything."

"Well, apparently they do."

"Who would have told them?"

"Ernest, apparently."

"Ernest? How could Ernest possibly know anything?"

"I didn't mention this in Portland?"

Randi stops dead as they are approaching the baggage claim area.

"You mentioned nothing. Nothing specific."

Guy scratches his nose thoughtfully. "I can't believe I didn't say something before we left up in Portland about it. Well, my oversight. The thing is, I may have spoken out of turn. I may have mentioned something I shouldn't."

"To *Ernest.*"

"Well, yuh, um."

Amazing, Guy is at a loss for words. They stare at each other for a moment before he recovers. "He hasn't said anything, not a word, for all these months."

"*Months?* Ernest's known about this for months?"

"Look, we have another flight to catch."

"And then you can tell the stewardess. Keep up the good work."

"Sarcasm isn't useful right now, particularly."

She thought she was moving in with a sportswriter. That was the thing. She knew about sportswriting: you got good seats to everything. Even her father had thought it was a great idea. Things had just gotten weirder and weirder and weirder.

According to a lighted sign blinking over the carousel, the luggage from Randi's flight has been mixed together with that of several other small commuter flights, but evidently the baggage handlers are sending up each flight's luggage separately. As the large group of people standing around the carousel watches quietly, a single flowered suitcase moves in a slow circle, alone on the conveyor belt.

"Looks like something they'd give a prestigious award to and then put on permanent exhibition at the Whitney," says Guy.

She thought sarcasm wasn't useful right now.

"Call it 'Jet Lag.' 'Position Closed.' 'Carry On.' 'No Show.' 'Round-Trip.' Hmm?"

She just glares at him. Other bags begin to appear. Eventually the American Touristers nose out of the opening in the center of the carousel and tumble down onto the belt.

"Jesus, Randi," says Guy, "why'd you bring all that?"

AGENTS LANGMO AND NIETFELDT are seated in the front seat of a light blue sedan outside the bungalow on Fifty-eighth Street. People go in. People come out. They check out the people's faces. They're G-men.

"I'm still thinking of that person starting with *M*," says Nietfeldt, who sits behind the wheel.

"That *male* person," says Langmo.

"Affirmative."

"Are you the author of that local bestseller *The Ethics of Revolution?*"

The two agents snicker.

"No, I am not Herbert Marcuse."

"Fuck. That one was a total giveaway. Are you a Canadian writer who believes that the media through which communication takes place are more influential over people than the information contained in the communication?"

"No, I am not Marshall McLuhan."

"Are you the nobleman of humble origins who commanded the English and Dutch forces during the War of the Spanish Succession?"

"Uh, negative."

"Are you a real person?"

"Affirmative."

"Are you a German film director who depicted subjective states of mind using a moving camera?"

"Using a movie camera?"

"A *moving* camera."

"Name one of his pictures."

"What the fuck? German, director, moving camera. Begins with M."

"Come on, name a picture."

"*The Last Laugh.*"

"No, I am not F. W. Murnau."

"Bastard. Are you the French author of comic plays that expose human folly by embodying it in caricatured universal types?"

"No, I am not Molière."

Across the street, a Chevy with a Trans Rent-a-Car sticker on the rear bumper pulls to the curb and parks. Nietfeldt and Langmo watch with mild interest. The driver opens the door and places one foot on the road. Langmo lights a cigarette.

"Gimme one," says Nietfeldt.

"Rental car," says Langmo, shaking one out of the pack.

"That's a new wrinkle."

The driver wears jeans, a western-style shirt, a denim jacket, and a floppy cap. He steps completely from the car and heads for the bungalow. A figure remains in the passenger seat.

"Hmmm," says Langmo.

"Let me take another look at this bug-eyed motherfuck," says Nietfeldt. He puts the cigarette between his lips and, tilting his head back to keep the smoke out of his eyes, removes from his jacket pocket a strip of oak tag to which three pictures of Guy Mock are stapled: his driver's license photo, a news photograph, and the photo from the back cover of *The Athletic Revolution*. "I think we got him," he says.

Langmo leans over, examines the pictures, then watches the figure retreat up the driveway and into the building.

"I believe you're right." He shakes his head. "Coming back here. Imagine that."

"Numb nuts."

Whatever Mock carries with him out of the building a few moments later, it is small enough to fit in his pockets. This makes Nietfeldt and Langmo slightly nervous, but Guy Mock is not known to be a gun-toting man. Most likely he has picked up something more practical, like passports. He gets back into the rental car and starts it up, drives off immediately.

They follow at a distance, a nondescript blue shape in anyone's rearview.

"He wouldn't go anywhere near them," says Nietfeldt.

"You never know. He came back to the apartment."

"If he even knows where they are anymore."

Up ahead, the Chevy runs a stop sign, accelerating sharply.

"That's peculiar," says Langmo.

Nietfeldt touches the brake and stops at the intersection.

"Now," he says. "Nice, slow, legal." They begin again. They pick up the Chevy at San Pablo, where it sits, waiting to turn right. Nietfeldt brings the sedan to a stop behind a VW bus, pilgrims with Kansas plates. Following their bliss right into Emeryville, it looks like. Bummer. The Chevy makes its turn. Nietfeldt waits for a moment and then moves out from behind the VW, noses up to the intersection, and turns quickly.

"Watch it," says Langmo. The Chevy comes to a stop at a red light at Alcatraz. Nietfeldt pulls to the side of the road, blocking the driveway of an auto body shop. A worker carrying a tire iron approaches to tell them to move it. Langmo flips open his bi-fold and displays his shield, averting his gaze in a practiced way. Nietfeldt doesn't take his eyes off the Chevy. The light changes. An AC Transit bus pulls away from a stop, cutting them off. To the left they are blocked by a truck.

"Shit," says Nietfeldt. "I can't see shit." He steers the sedan into opposing traffic, which brakes, swerves, sounds horns. Wheee. Nietfeldt shoots through a gap in the traffic back into the northbound lane. Now there's nothing between them and the Chevy. The Chevy accelerates again, heading toward a dense pocket of traffic nearing Ashby, veering into the left-turn lane at the intersection. Nietfeldt brings the sedan up behind a pickup that separates them from the Chevy, but on a yellow light the Chevy darts straight through the intersection, crossing Ashby and leaving the two agents stuck in the left-turn lane and behind the traffic massing at the red light.

Spring Chronicle

Yolanda goes out one morning and returns that afternoon wearing a nurse's uniform, from the cap down to the white support hose. She's rented an apartment over a grocery on Capitol Avenue, just another RN looking for a place to rest her tired toes.

"Great," Teko says. He opens the newspaper, shakes it to get the pages to lie the way he wants.

They pack up W Street. The entire thing has the feeling of a divorce to it. In fact, the running theme seems to be "Does Tania want to stay and live with Daddy or does she want to go and live with Mommy?"

Of course she will be joining the women's collective, won't she? Yolanda, in an attempt to establish "sisterhood" with Tania, daily conducts her beloved criticism/self-criticism sessions—just the two of them, one on one. Do we feel as if our commitment to the doctrine of direct revolutionary action has come at the expense of our work toward a new feminism? Check.

Teko has stopped bathing, Tania notices. This seems to be his way of rebuking Yolanda.

They pack up. Papers, guns, and clothing go into cardboard boxes Tania scrounges from the Lucky supermarket. Flat old pillows and threadbare blankets that regular people would put out on the sidewalk for the garbageman. While the others box these sorry possessions, Teko lectures on the Vietcong; how a guerrilla would head into the jungle for months at a time carrying only ammunition, a sack of rice, and minimal personal belongings in his pack. A quart bottle of Colt .45, Teko's latest affectation, sits empty on the kitchen counter.

One night there is an argument in the bedroom, fierce and whispered. Tania and Roger lie in the darkness, frozen with embarrassment.

Teko throws things, picks them up over his head and hurls them, into the boxes. He yells. But Yolanda will not be drawn in. The mailbox outside has a label that reads "Mr. and Mrs. Carroll Simmons," the name Susan selected when she found and leased the dump. It's an alias never referred to, as if Teko's shame at having to accept the gift of this neutered name had rendered it taboo. Now Tania sees that the "& Mrs." has been crossed out. She is unsure who is rebuking whom.

Yolanda feeds the strays in the backyard. She stands amid the debris back there, holding an open can of cat food in one hand and a soup spoon in the other, calling to the animals in an unnatural high-pitched voice.

Roger tells it again, to Susan, to Jeff, to Tania, who was right there beside him: He woke up, and there was Teko, cradling the submachine gun.

Before dawn one morning, just before the move, the three are awakened by flashing lights shining through the windows and the sounds of the police, surrounding them. They immediately take up their positions in the house, prepared to shoot it out. Squatting by the window, Tania crams shells into the loading port of a shotgun. But the police activity ebbs. Two of three patrol cars drive off, leaving a pair of cops to offer vague and blasé answers to the queries of sleepy residents dressed in robes and pajamas. One citizen carries an alarm clock in his hand, as if to prove that the hour is inappropriate for such goings-on. An ambulance rolls up, slowly, without lights or siren, and the cops stand by as the attendants remove equipment and a gurney from it. By first light the street is quiet again. Then around midmorning a young policeman appears at their door to question them about what they may have seen or heard. He wears a department-issue windbreaker that is stiff with newness and a hat that is too small. Turns out a man was robbed and beaten to death next door, in the overgrown lot separating the duplex from the neighboring bungalow. Yolanda clucks her tongue and gasps at the policeman's narrative, standing at the partly open door and blocking the cop's view into the apartment. He touches two fingers to the brim of his little hat as he turns to leave.

The smell of something dead pervades the Capitol Avenue apartment. It begins with a faint smell in the kitchen, the slightest whiff of something putrid, and Yolanda and Susan pace across the linoleum, sniffing, talking lightly of it, their voices echoing throughout the empty rooms. But soon the stench has taken over the apartment. Tania walks in one afternoon to find Yolanda seated on two cardboard cartons, holding a paper napkin to her nose. A little exploration reveals that a mouse has died within the wall just behind an electrical outlet, and after removing the fuse and unscrewing the faceplate, Tania squats, a bandanna covering her nose and mouth, working at the stupid rodent with a tweezers, trying to remove it from the tangle of cable and wire where it managed to lodge itself before it died. Breathing through her gritted teeth behind the bandanna, Tania grabs hold of the mouse by the ear, birthing it slowly out of the hole in the wall, the stink really blossoming now, and the mouse keeps coming, it is the longest mouse in recorded history, until finally she has the enormous reeking corpse.

Joan isn't happy that she's walking out on her life again carrying a toothbrush in her purse and that's it. When the pigs find her, they find her, but what she truly hates is the idea of all those guys going through her underpants.

This is not a way of life she would recommend to everyone. Though things have been going OK up into now. She left the East Coast separate from the others. She met up with a restless friend in New Jersey, Meg Speice, and they drove to San Francisco together. No way was she going to Sacramento. She'd had it with these hick towns, she never wanted to lay eyes on Teko or Yolanda again, and she considered her so-called debt to Guy Mock paid in full. She and Meg moved into a flat on Clayton. She kept tabs on Tania through Susan Rorvik, who also got Meg a job at the hotel restaurant where she worked.

So for the past few months she has been indistinguishable from a hundred thousand other girls: young, single, maybe with a problem relationship or two under their belt, living in a roommate situation at the edge of a total shit neighborhood, trying to apply all the fucked-up shit they'd learned to the world around them.

Then one morning she walks out the door and guess who's on

page one of the *Chronicle*. People live for this? She ducks back inside and makes Meg go buy her the papers.

"What happened?" Meg asks, dropping the *Chron* on the table. The two of them stand over it, hands on their hips.

"I don't know how they could have found the farm if Guy didn't tell them, but I can't believe he would. My guess is he opened his big mouth up in the neighborhood of the wrong ears."

Meg puts her index finger on one of the columns of type, taps it, and then moves it in a circle around a group of words. "They found your fingerprint."

"What the fuck? We went over that place with a fine tooth combed."

The dummy rented the place in his own name. Guy has an ego he can't help but see his own name printed on all the blank spaces of the world.

Roger picks her up before noon, and they drive north.

"We have a lot of space now," he says.

Joan doesn't respond.

"It's kind of nice up there," he offers.

"You're the one getting laid."

His right ear, the one facing her, colors. The back of his neck. She folds her arms and stares straight ahead through the windshield.

MAN SOUGHT IN SLA CASE SURFACES, DENIES RUMORS

by N. Palmer Hockley

SPECIAL TO THE NEW YORK TIMES

SAN FRANCISCO, CALIFORNIA, April 9. A man sought by Federal authorities for questioning in connection with the militant Symbionese Liberation Army emerged from the shadowy world of the radical underground less than twenty-four hours after televised news reports that he and his wife had left the country. Accompanied by their attorney, Guy Mock, 32, and his wife, Randy, held a press conference this morning here to "offer living proof" that they had not fled to North Africa and to issue a statement concerning their activities over the past year.

The F.B.I. has sought the Mocks since February in connection with their suspected activities on behalf of the S.L.A., whose surviving elements went into hiding following a deadly confrontation with police and federal agents in Los Angeles last May that left six members of the radical left-wing group dead. According to a source close to the investigation, the Mocks are suspected of having aided fugitive members of the group, possibly including Alice Galton, by maintaining a "safe house" in rural Pennsylvania for their use last summer. The Mocks dropped out of sight after a federal grand jury subpoena was issued in February.

The Mocks resurfaced after several Bay Area newscasts carried reports Tuesday night that the couple was en route to Algeria. At a hastily called press conference the next day, the pair's attorney, Francis Cahalan of San Francisco, stated that he wished to give his clients "the opportunity to counter potentially detrimental rumors and to begin to take control of their portrayal in the press." He also suggested that the F.B.I. was "harassing" the Mocks in order to "deflect attention from their own lackluster and ineffectual investigation."

Thomas Polhaus, who heads the F.B.I.'s investigation of the S.L.A. case, later responded, denying the harassment charge and adding, "To the extent that Mr. and Mrs. Mock can provide us with information concerning the whereabouts and activities of the S.L.A. and Miss Galton, we are very interested in discussing these matters with them. At the present time the Mocks do not face criminal charges." He added that the grand jury would have to complete its investigation before deciding whether to bring indictments.

At the press conference, Mock, a sportswriter long associated with left-wing causes, did not deny outright that he had helped the group, but took exception to the couple's depiction by the "news media," claiming, "Our actions over the past year are completely defensible." Mock presented a rather disjointed list of grievances against the federal government which he claimed "have stripped it of moral legitimacy." Mock added, "We want to make clear that we find the tragic and senseless killing of Marcus Foster to be morally and politically intolerable."

The Symbionese Liberation Army first gained attention with the murder of Foster, the Negro superintendent of Oakland schools, in November 1973. Some three months later they burst into the national consciousness when they forced their way into the Berkeley apartment of 20-year-old Alice Galton and her fiancé, Eric Stump. The heavily armed group beat Stump to the ground and carried a screaming, half-naked Miss Galton from the apartment.

The Mocks refused to divulge where they had spent the last few weeks and vigorously disputed that they had been in hiding. "We were visiting friends," Mock claimed.

GALTON PRAISES SLA ALLY, URGES
GOV'T RESTRAINT
by Dorsey Nebarez

EXAMINER STAFF WRITER

(April 11) Examiner Publisher Henry Galton today lent his personal support to a man the F.B.I. says may have aided the radical left-wing Symbionese Liberation Army in its efforts to remain in hiding. The same radical left-wing group on February 4 last year burst into the quiet apartment of Galton's 20-year-old daughter, Alice, carrying away the struggling co-ed.

Speaking today of Guy Mock and his wife, Randi, who have been sought by the F.B.I. in connection with their activities on behalf of the revolutionary sect, Galton said, "While I do not necessarily agree with Mr. and Mrs. Mock's political philosophy, I have no reason to believe them to be other than non-violent sincere people. I believe that if they have offered their assistance to members of the S.L.A., it has been for humanitarian reasons." Referring to a deadly confrontation with law enforcement officials last May 17 in which six of the group's members were killed in a Southern California ghetto following a botched holdup attempt, Galton added, "After what happened in Los Angeles last year, I think the Mocks were following through on an impulse that many people felt, ourselves included; that it was necessary to safeguard these young people from overzealous police action." Mock, who holds a Ph.D. from UC-Berkeley, is suspected with his wife of subsequently having aided the surviving members of the S.L.A. by obtaining a "safe house" for the group's use last year. Sources close to the investigation say that the group may have spent most of the summer at this hideout, located in rural Pennsylvania.

The Mocks, who are not alleged to have participated in any of the S.L.A.'s criminal activities, went into seclusion in February following the issuance of a subpoena seeking their testimony before a federal grand jury, re-emerging on Wednesday to refute news reports that they had fled the country and to justify their involvement with the S.L.A., which Mock described as "completely defensible." The Mocks and their lawyer, well-known San Francisco attorney Frank Cahalan, have not denied aiding the group but have publicly distanced themselves from the S.L.A.'s violent activities.

Galton also said today that he had urged the government to take under consideration what he called the "special circumstances" of the Mocks when deciding whether to bring charges against the couple. "As one deeply affected by this case, I have contacted both Thomas Polhaus and Taggart Wilde and made a personal appeal to each of them to approach the Mocks with sensitivity to their unique position." He did not elaborate. Polhaus, the F.B.I. agent in charge of the investigation, has said that the Mocks presently face no criminal charges. Wilde, U.S. Attorney for the Northern District of California, declined to comment.

"You did what?" said Lydia.

Hank sat with his feet in a plastic tub filled with fizzy blue liquid that he'd created by dissolving powder from a packet into hot water. He was sitting in the easy chair in his study, with newspapers spread on the floor under and around the tub to protect the carpet.

"I said that I got in touch with Guy Mock through Frank Cahalan."

"Is that the reason for that ridiculous endorsement you gave him on the front page? I couldn't believe my eyes."

"The man can tell us something about our daughter."

"The man is looking for a soft touch, and he's found one. Just like your good friend. Popeye."

This actually startled Hank. *De mortuis nil nisi bonum.* He remained silent for a moment, watching his wife. She stood angled forward on her pelvis, her shoulders hunched and her arms folded and pressed into her abdomen as if she were fighting off stomach cramps. Which perhaps she was. "Popeye died for having helped us out," he said, finally.

"He died the way those people always have. Ever since I was a child. The papers never even bothered with printing stories about shootings on the colored side of town, there were so many."

"We won't argue."

"Oh, the great friend of the Negro people."

"Please, you had something you wanted to say about Guy Mock?" Hank lifted his left foot from the tub and examined it. It was glistening with a light blue film, an anklet of blue froth encircling it. The foot itself was wrinkled from its immersion in the hot water. He dropped it back into the tub.

"So convenient that you could just plant something like that on the front page, masquerading as news. And those references to Alice's being carried off into the night! That's not how the *Chronicle* talks about it. The *Chronicle* calls a spade a spade. They refer to her as what she is: a criminal. I want to know, did you actually utter that execrable nonsense or did you write it down and give it to the reporter?"

"As a matter of fact, Guy Mock wrote it." Hank lifted his right foot. The water in the tub was begining to grow cold.

"Oh, did he?"

"Yes, he did. He typed out a statement and had it delivered to me and said that if I were sincere about wanting to deal with him then I'd print it on the front page as my own. And I did."

"Now we let them tell us what to put on the front page."

"I'll tell you. I would let Drew and Diane Shepard edit the whole damned paper if it meant I could talk to her myself, see her, make sure she's all right."

"I'm sure that's what they're counting on. They see you coming. They all see you coming a mile away. Who better to tell them all about what a pushover you are than Daddy's little girl?"

Hank took the towel he'd draped over one arm of the easy chair and lifted his feet one at a time from the tub and dried them.

"And why are you soaking your feet, you old woman? It makes me sick. You've become like an invalid. You're ridiculous, driving around in a station wagon and soaking your feet like a bartender or a policeman. What happened to the man I married? He lets himself be taken in by little nobodies, and then he comes home and soaks his feet. What's next, Hank? Dry toast for dinner? You used to be a steak man. I married a steak man, god damn it."

"I had Chinese food for supper," said Hank, extending his hands, palms up.

"Well, that, that is not *food*, Hank. That is exactly what I'm talking about."

"I really don't know what you're talking about." He stood, put on his slippers, and then bent to lift the plastic tub to carry it out to the kitchen.

"This is what I'm talking about," said Lydia, suddenly animated, her limbs unspooling from the taut center of her body. "*This*. What are you doing *carrying* this? Who do you think we are?" Her arm shot out, and she slapped the tub out of Hank's hands. A cataract of blue liquid arced from the falling vessel, splashing the carpet, the easy chair, and a coffee table covered with books and magazines.

"Bull's-eye," he said mildly.

Lydia sank to the floor and began to sob.

"I'm sorry," she said. "I'm really sorry. I don't know why I said those things."

Hank had been reaching for the empty tub but he stopped and reached for the crying woman instead. He got down on his aching knees (though his feet felt terrific) and put his hands on her shoulders and when she didn't snap and growl he put his arms around her.

"It's all right," he said.

"I really don't know. I really don't know why I said those things. I'm so upset all the time. I just want these people out of our lives and I feel like you're always bringing more of them in."

"I probably am."

"I don't mean it. I never mean it."

"It's all right. I understand. I know this isn't you talking."

"You shouldn't have to understand."

"It's all right," he said.

"It's *not*." She pulled back from him. "For God's sake, Hank. Do you have to be such a weakling?"

Tania goes to the movies, leaving Yolanda like any coupon-clipping suburban parent, sitting at the kitchen table on Capitol Avenue and searching through *Standard & Poor's Register* and the *Bee*'s financial pages, researching potential terror targets.

"Have fun," says Yolanda.

Tonight she goes with Joan and Susan to the 49er Drive-In. There are a few station wagons holding families, a couple of pick-ups, their beds crammed with noisy, dateless teenage boys. No throngs this Thursday night, just lots of empty space and the meditative evensong of crickets at the weedy fringes and in the dark trees beyond. Susan steers the car across the cracked pitch to a remote spot and parks. The two fugitives send her to the snack bar to buy food.

Awaiting the movie, Tania is eager to see what signs and omens will paint the night, forty feet high on a rust-stained screen.

When she'd first started coming, with Roger, she sat smack up against him on the front seat. Not snuggling, exactly. More like huddling. She'd fidget with him—with the rivets on his jeans, his watchband, examining him with her fingers, reaching up occasionally to touch the stone ape hanging from its moldy cord around her neck. She hadn't been to a drive-in since that terrible night in May. Roger lightly rested his arm on her, petted her hair, while eating french fries from a cardboard tray. He never pushed her away or said he was uncomfortable. If he knew what she was thinking about, he never said a word. After a while she'd settle down and watch.

The movies tell us we can communicate with the dead; the movies *are* the dead communicating with us, shining out of the darkness with the smiles and intimacies of all our beloved. She can still feel the hole, the absence where Willie had been in her life. Anytime she wants. In one hour of one afternoon of one day it had all gone away.

One of the teenagers throws a beer can at the screen.

But once she began watching the movies, she noticed a curious thing: They all seemed to be about her. Not in their particulars, but in their design, their narrative pattern—it was too eccentric and too consistent to be a fluke. At first, it had driven her to burrow more deeply into Roger. She studied him, while he watched the screen blandly, sipping from a Coke. Could he *not* see it?

Eventually she had to learn to relax. Identifying and tracking themes: It's straight out of Sister Marie Dominic's ninth-grade English curriculum. Sister Motif, they called her. So she'll say to herself, There's something in the air. Or: It's not *exactly* a coincidence, but these are the sort of things people are thinking about. Her own name is tossed out as a sort of laugh line during one movie (a reporter, on the trail of a big story, is dressed down by his editor, who reminds him that he had once claimed to know her whereabouts. A light ripple of mirth passes through the audience: Oh, yes, her), and she realizes exactly how notorious she has become, a cultural touchstone, a catchphrase whose meaning hasn't yet been worn down through repetitive use.

She sees *Thieves Like Us* (three bank robbers gradually feel themselves seduced by the newspaper coverage of their exploits).

She sees *Big Bad Mama* (Angie Dickinson plays a bad-ass bank-robbing mother).

She sees *The Wind and the Lion* (kidnapped woman falls for her captor and the nobility of his cause).

She sees *Sleeper* (bored, shallow member of the ruling class first is kidnapped by and then joins the rebel army fighting the police state that holds power).

She sees *Dog Day Afternoon* (hostages begin to identify with their captors as the incident in which they're all ensnared becomes the cynosure of the media's attention).

She sees *Going Places* (outlaw drifters abduct a girl and work to bring around a sexual response on her part).

She sees *The Sugarland Express* (fugitive outlaw steals a car and kidnaps its owner to further a quixotic, doomed mission, attracting the relentless interest of a bored, story-hungry media).

"We want the movie, we want the movie," chant the teenagers.

The drive-in is showing a double feature tonight, *Night Moves* (missing girl is traced at the request of the mother who hates and envies her) and something called *Savaged*.

"What's playing first?" asks Susan.

"The stiff," says Joan. "Elsewise everybody splits after the first picture and they don't sell the popcorn."

"Which one's that?"

"The one they show first." Joan bites into an onion ring.

The movie starts. The print is in such bad shape it seems as if it must have been touring these second-run theaters for years, but the copyright says MCMLXXIV. SAVAGED, the screen says.

Savaged opens in an apartment furnished with plaid couches and Naugahyde beanbag chairs, a shag carpet on the floor, and Day-Glo posters hung beside an incongruous framed diploma on the wall. A young man wearing long hair, eyeglasses, a paisley shirt, and an ascot sits reading a book whose cover reveals its title as *Eastern Philosophy*. A young woman in skintight hot pants and a tube top enters the frame, holding a textbook.

"Hey, babe," he says, "dig some grass?"

"You know I have a big exam tomorrow," she says, flipping her feathered blond hair.

"Well," he says, undaunted, "as an assistant professor of philosophy [*note* BOOK *and* DIPLOMA] at this institution of higher learning, I hereby authorize you to expand your mind." He raises and lowers his eyebrows as he withdraws from his shirt pocket and flourishes a joint roughly the size of a small cigar.

"Oh all right." She gives in.

Now there is some crosscutting between the two, hysterical giggling in SSTTEERREEOO RREEVVEERRBB [*note* JOINT, *which billows smoke like a room fumigator*], meaningless reaction shots.

Here's an abrupt cut. The couple are suddenly a foot or two closer to each other. The stock is grainier.

"It's the next day," says Tania.

"It's the next movie," says Joan.

The boom drops into the frame.

"Testing, one two three," says Susan.

The couple is embracing and muttering sweet endearments at each other. In a burst of wit the man tells the girl to address him as Professor, then abruptly reaches to pull off the girl's tube top. He has some trouble extricating her from it. There's another stutter cut. The Professor's shirt is now unbuttoned partway as the couple continues to clinch. Suddenly, there is the sound off camera of glass breaking.

"Must be another grade grubber," says Susan.

The Professor tells her to Wait Here, but before he gets very far, he is confronted by two Black Men with Guns, both wearing combat fatigues.

"What is it you want?" whines the effete intellectual.

"Sitchassdown," says the Black with the Authoritative Baritone, "muhfucka."

The second Black mugs and speaks with a high-pitched, crazy voice. Soon the obliging Professor provides the two Black Men with a pretext to pistol-whip him, which the Crazy Black accomplishes with a maniacal grin on his face. An uncomfortably edited montage: the girl's expression of horror, the grinning face of the Crazy Black, the implacable face of the Authoritative Black, the Professor, his eyeglasses slipping from his bloody face, and the book of *Eastern Philosophy*, lying open and abandoned on the floor.

"Now hep me wit de bitch," says the Authoritative Black. The Crazy Black puts his Black Hands all over the White Girl's White Torso as he helps the Authoritative Black restrain her so that she can be carried out the door, whitely Half Naked.

Tania gasps, folds her arms across her chest. "I can't believe this."

"What?"

"That. Up there." She points. "Can't you see? That's not what happened!" Tania's indignant. She's never before mentioned to anyone the confluence of her peculiar life and the cinema's honed insight about what might be possible, or timely, or desired, or just, or true. So far the point of juncture has been achieved through synchronicity or—OK—coincidence. But this is so clearly *her*, up there. "Jesus."

"What, you're saying that's suppose to be you?" Joan looks at her.

"Totally obviously."

"It's a movie, honey."

"Shitty movie," adds Susan.

"That totally happened to me. That's exactly what happened."

"You just said it wasn't what happened."

"But that's not what I meant. I meant, it is what happened, but they got it wrong."

On the screen the two Black Men toss the girl into the trunk of their car.

"Help me," she screams. "Help me, somebody, please!"

Down goes the lid.

"*That* happened," Tania says.

"Well, where else are you going to put somebody?"

"I've done it before," says Tania. "You don't have to throw someone in the trunk. It's really *mean*."

"I'm sorry," says Joan. "I think maybe we're talking about two different things."

"I don't think you're sorry at all."

"We're talking about the movie or what happened to you?"

"They're stealing my life, is all."

"No," says Joan, with infuriating calm, "the people who threw you in the trunk stole your life. Get that right."

Tania's face is burning. For a moment she wants to hit Joan. She considers demanding to be taken home. But she watches the screen in deep-breathing silence. Shortly, the movie's plot sharply diverges from her own; it was just another abduction-by-the-light-of-a-big-white-bra after all. She feels acute embarrassment for having said anything at all—for allowing her comrades, her friends, to see that she associated herself with some shrieking celluloid nitwit, for having allowed Joan the chance to cast doubt on her life, to remind her that they scared the shit out of her, beat her, fucked her, called her names; that she sat blindfolded in a cramped closet for weeks. What had she later called it for Adam K. Trout? "An environment of love," in which she learned how to live. Fuck that shit.

The atmosphere is uncomfortable inside the car, and Joan suggests leaving after the first feature. On the way home, Susan says, "Maybe they did borrow from it a little."

"What," says Tania.

"I mean, it was familiar from the news. The basic facts. Eww, was that supposed to be Eric Stump?"

"They got him right."

"But not you, is that it?" Joan turns to look at her.

"No, that wasn't me at all. I was scared."

"I bet, honey."

"No but wait. I was ready. Just like you. I was ready to join. I didn't know it then but I was."

"If mama won't come to the mountain," says Joan.

"Take the mountain to you," says Susan.

"Take the mountain to me."

"Hallelujah," says Joan. "But next time maybe they should ask."

Pacific heights. this part of town strikes Guy as being just a little freaky. Quiet houses, too big, too wealthy, with a sort of haughty though listless grandeur that somehow always reminds Guy of how foreign he still feels in California, even after all these years. These houses spot strangeness in the cut of a jacket, the lay of a haircut, the burnish of a shoeshine. Uneasy fools like him wander in and immediately start seeking an exit as they might from the scariest slum.

Five blocks and he's encountered exactly one other human pedestrian, a stocky man in livery with a face, as his mother might say, stamped with the map of Ireland. The man paused on the steps of a large Queen Anne house and brazenly followed Guy with his eyes until he was certain Guy was continuing on his way. Ex-cop? Who knows. Much of the capital flowing through the state bottlenecks here in these icily pleasant streets with nary a sign of the gated doorways and barred windows just down the hill in the Fillmore. It isn't class intimidation that keeps all these rich folks safe at home in their beds.

Then again, how safe are they? He's heading to his lawyer's house to meet with the father of a girl who'd relied one day too many on the assumptions of a privileged life. If she'd simply said, "Who is it?" when destiny had banged on her door that evening, who could say that she wouldn't have gone to bed and awoken the next morning with nothing more to concern her than the dirty dishes she'd left soaking in the sink the night before? He's always wanted to ask her just why she'd opened up her house to her abductors. Had she thought she was charmed? Though Stump of course had done the actual opening. But same difference. The press acts as if Stump had blown into the Galtons' orbit like a stink from the other side of the tracks, but come on: Palo Alto upbringing, Princeton man. He was a variation on a theme. So was Willie Wolfe, a doctor's son, the nth-generation Eli. The Galtons didn't really know from the wrong side of the tracks until they heard catty rumors that their daughter had been knocked up by Cinque.

Funny, but this is the first subject Hank Galton wants to broach when they finally get around to talking turkey.

Well but first they had cocktails, and then claret with dinner, and port with dessert, and now they settle in the parlor with the vodka again, whereupon Frank Cahalan discreetly withdraws and Guy realizes that he's drunk. He's pretty certain Hank is shitfaced too; he keeps adding little half-ounce tipples to his own glass, topping it with soda from a chrome siphon. When the glass gets down to a certain level, Hank fills it up again. They talk sports. Can the A's do it again? Guy thinks not. Catfish Hunter has become the Three Million Dollar Man and is pitching in a Yankees uniform. No doubt the rest of the team will soon follow him into the lucrative new territory of free agency. Hank notes that Guy sounds almost as if he disapproved. Surely a man like Guy would favor free agency. Guy favors it for the sake of the players but is unsure whether he wants to pay five bucks to sit in the bleachers. They clink glasses. There's a certain self-congratulatory air to Galton's bonhomie that his agreement with Guy on this throwaway point underscores. Probably Hank sat in the bleachers once. Probably thought it was the best time he ever had. Probably can't even remember who was playing.

Tentatively, the subject is raised at last. Guy is careful to limit what he says to avoid self-incrimination.

```
     There's a certain  individual.  An indi-
vidual I believe  we have in common.
     We're talking about the same person I
think  I think I can find ways to  get in
touch if if
     With this person. If the person you're
talking about is the person I'm talking
about well I'm very interested Guy⅂ in
making contact.
     Well through an intermediary⅂ mind you
Hank  I'm  I think this can be arranged
and but with  other  parties who'd have to
approve.
     Of course I would accept any  restric-
tions these parties decided to impose⅂ Guy.
I always have.
     Yeah but basically I'm just saying this
individual probably would not  it would not
be possible to make personal contact⅂ Hank.
     Well   I mainly want to know
```

```
Hank?

I want to know about her  health.

You mean is the person in good health?
The person I'm talking about is perfectly
healthy, Hank.

And the last time that you saw the per-
son, Guy, was ...?

Some yuh a few months ago.

I wonder  what you might know about the
current state of the person's health?

The person's in good health as far as I
know. I mean I  I would have heard any
news to the contrary.

I guess I don't mean  health  per se.


I'm  I'm not  getting you.
```

"Was she pregnant? Was she pregnant by Cinque?"

"Oh," says Guy, surprised, and then he understands. "Ah, no. She had a pregnant belly they made. She wore it as a disguise sometimes."

"Oh, thank God," says Hank. "It would have been. I just can't imagine how much harder it all would be if she'd had a child. Especially his child."

"They're actually pretty careful about that stuff." Guy's guessing, but he figures he's got to be right. The Manson Family screwed their brains out too, but those women were dropping kids left and right.

They're silent for a minute, Hank perhaps taking solace of a kind in the thought that his daughter has been diligently practicing family planning.

He asks, "Is she all right?"

"She's fine."

"Is she happy?"

"Well, you know. I don't know what it was like before L.A. From what I've heard it sounds like it was weirder, more violent, more squalid, more doctrinaire, and more, I don't know, incestuous if you get my drift. But since then they've found some different ways of looking at things, met up with some new people."

"Like yourself, for example."

"I suppose. We weren't really day to day with them, Randi and me. Just kind of checking in. But the point is I don't think we would even have been allowed to help them back in the Age of Cinque. That guy really had them marooned on that psycho island of his. The world was exactly what he said it was. I think Drew Shepard still has a little of that in him. But it's a matter of time. Let me just say that I doubt they believe they're going to overthrow the system anymore. Maybe Drew and Diane do. Probably definitely Drew Shepard. He's sort of a hopeless case."

"A romantic," says Hank dryly.

"What I think is she's surrounded now by a bunch of more or less ordinary people who have the sort of ideas about things that even a man like yourself, no offense, is bound to have encountered over the past few years without once giving them a second thought. Believe me, these people don't want to shoot the president. They want to do yoga. Basically they're back to where they started out from, more or less, you know? They're people you might actually *like*. Is she happy? Who can say. It's OK. I think she has a pretty regular life. It's acceptable to her. You'll think this is nuts, but."

"What?"

"A mutual friend put me in touch with them after L.A. And you want to know the truth, I had serious reservations about helping them out at all. It wasn't just the Marc Foster murder, though that whole thing was so stupid it made me want to cry. It wasn't the total dumbness factor, the idiot hyperbole, all that fascist insect crap, which everybody on the Left just loved to point to, but I was always like, hey—glass houses, OK? It was the kidnapping. I just hated it. It was like something out of some shit-ass midnight movie that gives you the willies. Maybe if it was *you* they'd kidnapped I'd say all right. But even then. But this is the crazy part. This is the part where you'll think I'm crazy."

"Yes?"

"You know, it wasn't the worst thing for her. She's a strong person, you know that? I don't know if anybody ever would've found that out. She had to come through a lot of shit. She was a basket case when I met her. Out of the closet, what? Five, six weeks? Her boyfriend had just gotten barbecued by the pigs."

"They were together?"

"You heard that tape. Can't fake that shit, Hank."

"What about the mind control, the brainwashing?"

"Well, she wasn't brainwashed in the Laurence Harvey sense. But she wasn't thinking for herself either. She said what they said. She did what they told her to do. But"—Guy laughs—"no more."

"Really?" Hank smiles. Not a bad smile, Guy thinks. Happy for his kid, like she's coming out of her shell at school.

"But these people," Hank says, "you're telling me they're all through with violence?"

"Um," says Guy, "notionally, yes."

"Notionally?"

"Maybe some armed propaganda here and there."

"You'd said more or less ordinary people?"

"Well. 'More or less' meaning 'relatively,' in this context."

"Damn it, relative to what?"

"Don't kill the messenger, Hank."

"But?"

"Relative to, say, Cinque. Relative even to Drew Shepard, for Christ's sake."

That seems to make an impression. Dump it all on Teko. The two-faced little bastard deserves it.

"Does she ever talk about us?"

"She liked *you*," says Guy.

A carriage clock tucked into a bookcase in the gap between symmetrically shelved volumes softly bongs the hour. Only one chime, and surprised, Guy looks at his watch to confirm the time. Hank is stretching, suppressing a yawn, and Guy can see that their meeting is about to come to an end. He's done a good job of fooling himself into believing that he came here tonight out of the goodness of his heart. But while he will be delighted to facilitate communications, if not an actual meeting, between parent and child, he needs to secure some sort of quid pro quo.

"Well," Hank says, "I've kept you long enough."

"De nada. I was happy to help you out. You know. People just need to, you know, help each other out. When they need help."

"Of course."

"That's the way I do things. That's the way we did it for Alice."

"I appreciate that. And if there's ever anything I can do for you, be sure and let me know."

Will he ever, baby. For the modern Samaritan there are scores and scores of hazards waiting on that ancient road between Jerusalem and Jericho.

POLHAUS PACES THE FLOOR in his office. He's been feeling jumpy lately. A pushy young woman holding a microphone caught him outside the building after lunch, stuck the mike right in his face. Startled the hell out of him. For a long long time, since RFK, since *Ruby*, he's carried around a mental image of an individual emerging from a crowd, separating from it, breaking from the communion of its focus to carry forward its secret longing, to consume and destroy the object of that focus. The usual deadbeats were outside trying to get a quote from him in time to make their deadlines, and suddenly, "out of nowhere," here comes this girl in a pantsuit. He jumped—then gave her the quote. They're working hard every day to fulfill the hopes, dreams and aspirations of the world. Whatever. A dream is a wish your heart makes. He patted her ass; sue him. Why should he have to put up with this shit all the time?

He has Nietfeldt's memo reporting a meeting between Hank Galton and Guy Mock. Nietfeldt: a few bricks short but good, perceptive, and he believes Galton's trying to contact Alice independent of the Bureau's efforts. Polhaus can just imagine how it'll play if he has to arrest Hank as a material witness. Nietfeldt compares Galton's front-page advocacy on Mock's behalf with the *Examiner*'s earlier support of Popeye Jackson. See what that got him. Mock'd be wise to watch his step.

Mention of Jackson makes him think of Sara Jane Moore, who hasn't haunted his office in a while. He sits behind his desk, pulls out her file; since just before Popeye's death, word's been that she's gone back over to the other side.

    Subj. Moore observed leaving residence of known Black Panther
    Subj. Moore in altercation with merchant
    Subj. Moore evaded Agent known to her

Subj. Moore observed distributing left wing handbills on Memorial Glade
Subj. Moore obtained Post Office Box using forged documents

The boundary's always permeable for someone like Sally. She needs only to be able to say that all that screwball concentration, that single-mindedness, *belongs* to something, is on a *side*, supports a *cause*. Doesn't matter what.

He glances at the memo. Nietfeldt's saying, Keep watching Mock. That's dandy, but if someone fucks up, the guy's perfectly capable of vanishing. Then they'd have zip. An empty farmhouse. There has to be something beyond Mock and Shimada, though. There has to be another link.

T EKO IS LIVING IN a state of bachelor squalor in the dumpy apartment on W Street, a condition that mirrors his mood. Only Jeff is willing to stay with him there, and only occasionally, and only for a night or two at a time, tops, so while Capitol Avenue is always noisy and cheerful, W Street is sullen, made more so by the shrill cheer that emanates from the black-and-white portable that seems constantly to be on, the liveliness of miracle deodorants and mouthwashes.

"Two!—two!—two mints in one!"

The money goes fast. Seven people, two safe houses, some spendthrift overindulgence, and abruptly they're needy again. No one questions the revolutionary impetus behind the next bakery scheme; it's all but irrelevant. They need the money, and that's simply that. Tania sees this very clearly. She's happy to have Joan nearby, but Joan's stories of the last several months in San Francisco, her naked contempt for Sacramento, for Teko and Yolanda, make Tania impatient to leave. They drive over to W Street one day to receive their marching orders.

Teko has been scouting large banks in regional centers, looking for a bigger score. As well be hanged for a sheep as a lamb, goes the thinking. Tania herself has been dispatched to Citrus Heights, Davis, and Auburn to check out branches there, returning to read aloud the found poetry of her notes: *5 women + two men/ One is young*

+ nervous/ Manager is fat + Black/ Guard/ Camera/ Peds + traffic. She drives around, from B of A to Wells Fargo, dropping her ashes into a beanbag ashtray on the dashboard. The beanbag has a tendency to slide from one end of the dashboard to the other, depending on whether she's turning left or right.

Teko announces that their target is a Crocker Bank branch in Carmichael, another unincorporated area. It has no guards or cameras, and the place abuts a vacant lot on one side and has no windows facing the street. Yolanda has observed employees from nearby businesses showing up to cash their paychecks, probably drawn on Crocker payroll accounts, so the branch likely keeps a decent amount of money on hand. Teko also informs them that Yolanda will lead the assault team. Going in with her will be Jeff, Susan, and Roger. Tania and Joan will drive the two switch cars, taking assault team members back to the two safe houses. Teko will observe the operation from across the street, timing the response and providing backup.

After the meeting Teko asks Joan to stay behind. He goes into the bedroom, and warily, Joan follows. She finds him rooting through a footlocker, from which he extracts a stack of familiar-looking cassette tapes and a file folder full of notes. It's the old SLA book. Teko tells Joan that he wants to revive the book project, as a hedge. So it all comes to money, Joan thinks. Due to Guy Mock's "very favorable deportment" lately, Teko would like to offer Guy the opportunity to sell the book. Deportment is like a word from your report card if memory serves.

How well Joan remembers the Summer of the Book, the big spiel from Guy about how publishers would be hammering on his door with fistfuls of thousand-dollar bills, how John and Yoko wanted to write and star in a musical about them, all the razzle-dazzle horseshit that made her realize that there isn't one single radical in the USA who hasn't spent a minute or two wondering who'd play him in the movie.

"We have to get in touch with Guy," Teko says.

"I'll try," says Joan.

It turns out that Guy is the only revolutionary fugitive in recorded history who files a change of address with the PO when he goes underground. It takes Joan about a day to find him. She thinks

Teko is disappointed, like he wanted mail drops, coded messages, smoke signals for all she knows. Guy is raring to go. Tells her that he's all ready to fly to New York and set up meetings, though he's bugged that he hasn't got a copy of the manuscript.

"Count your blessings," she tells him.

They begin the grim work of rehearsal, pretending daily to rob, threaten, and assault one another. It goes poorly from the beginning. Jeff Wolfritz shakily levels a revolver at Tania that has bullets in the cylinder. Working with an automatic, Susan similarly chambers a live round and points the gun at Joan's head. Yolanda insists on using the same fluky Remington 870 that Jeff carried into Guild Savings. It keeps dry-firing accidentally. The rasping click stops them all dead, every time.

"That's getting worse," says Jeff.

"I know how to handle a gun," she insists.

Curious doings, according to the lights of any respectable California homeowner. A certain Janet White rents a garage to store her mother's car, so she says. And then asks if the place has an electrical outlet. Well, it does. That is what is known as a modern convenience. But how curious that Miss Janet White should make such an inquiry. What else is a California homeowner to do but to contact his acquaintances in law enforcement?

Acquaintances in law enforcement agree with a California homeowner: It is a curious inquiry. Curious and suspicious (if those aren't really and truly the same thing). Acquaintances in law enforcement affirm that such an inquiry suggests the *possibility* that the garage will be used for some nefarious purpose. The stripping of stolen cars, for example. The setting up of a buzz saw to divide innocent damsels in twain. Not that a California homeowner should get his hopes up or anything.

Still, a California homeowner does tend to get his hopes up. That's a portion of what leads him to enter the fraternal bonds of homeownership to begin with: optimism, of a kind. Fortunately a homeowner's suspicions are substantiated when the woman turns up five days later, accompanied by a long-haired male friend (!), who drives a second vehicle, to park "Mother's" car. And how many kind, patient, apple-cheeked mothers drive Pontiac Firebirds? a California homeowner might ask, rhetorically, though appositely, from behind the curtains where he watches. Where he has been watching—a California homeowner has kept his eyes open since the day Janet White first appeared, April 9. A California homeowner who is on top of things writes down license numbers. Time to make another call.

Acquaintances in law enforcement are apologetic, but there is very little to be done at the moment, even if it does turn out that the license number matches that of a Firebird stolen recently while its owner attended a party in Berkeley (!). A California homeowner should himself do nothing. Acquaintances in law enforcement are discouragingly firm on this point. The thing to do is to wait for law enforcement to handle it. Law enforcement, due to problems of resource allocation, can only put the location involved in the Strange Case of the Stolen Firebird under what is termed periodic, or loose, surveillance. This is indeed disappointing, but fortunately a California homeowner can see to it himself that the garage is under constant, fixed surveillance! A California homeowner has a thermos full of coffee, some salty snacks, a book of crossword puzzles, a transistor radio, a working telephone. All the necessary tools.

And yet. Even a California homeowner is obliged, at times, to leave his post. Salty snacks and plenty of coffee can do that to you. That such an event is foreseeable does not make it any less necessary when it occurs. And in that necessary and foreseeable event, a California homeowner may happen to miss a suspicious person or persons entering the garage and driving away in the Firebird, removing the suspicious vehicle to another, unknown location. This is precisely what occurs on April 20.

Now a California homeowner's thoughts turn to the next act in this drama. A California homeowner may wish to inquire of acquaintances in law enforcement as to whether a California homeowner should preserve the scene for any investigation law enforcement chooses to conduct. A California homeowner is always more than happy to see to it that nothing is disturbed. A California homeowner may also choose to poll friends and neighbors who are members of the real estate or legal communities: Does a California homeowner have an obligation to assume that there exists a binding contract with Janet White, or can the garage be made available for rent again? A California homeowner doesn't rent out a garage for fun, you know.

FEW CLUES TO BANK ROBBER I.D.'S
by Dylan Mantini
BEE STAFF WRITER

(April 22) Sheriff's deputies are no closer to identifying the members of a gang which killed a female customer during yesterday's $15,000 robbery of a Crocker Bank branch in suburban Carmichael.

Mrs. Myrna Lee Opsahl, 42, was fatally wounded by a blast from a shotgun wielded by one of the robbers. Witnesses stated that Mrs. Opsahl, who had come to the bank with two other women to deposit collection receipts from the Carmichael Seventh Day Adventist Church, had provided her assailant with no provocation. She died later at American River Hospital. Her husband, Dr. Trygve Opsahl, a physician there, was at her side. In addition to Dr. Opsahl, Mrs. Opsahl is survived by four children ages 13 to 19.

The robbery began shortly after the bank opened its doors at 9:00 a.m. Three heavily armed men and a woman, wearing winter clothing and ski masks, entered and announced the robbery, ordering patrons and employees to the floor. It was at this point that Mrs. Opsahl was shot, and investigators speculate that she may have moved too slowly when ordered to lie down. The robbery then continued while Mrs. Opsahl lay dying. Witnesses reported that the female robber monitored her wristwatch throughout the operation, calling out the time to the others as they removed money from the teller's drawers. After approximately five minutes she announced that it was time to flee, and the robbers exited through a rear door, escaping through a fence to a Pontiac Firebird parked behind the bank.

A spokesman for Crocker Bank, Darren Cumberbatch, described the bank's losses as slightly over $15,000. He added, "Our financial losses, of course, are inconsequential compared with the loss of life suffered in this tragic situation. Our heart goes out to the family of Mrs. Opsahl during this difficult time, and we are co-operating fully with law enforcement authorities in their efforts to apprehend and bring these killers to justice."

Myrna has about thirty-eight seconds before someone's clock radio goes off, and then there they'll all be, standing around the kitchen together, a spill of containers and packages, dirty knives and smears of butter, spread across the countertops, the happy clamor of up and at 'em. This is all well and good; ordinarily she is pleased to help her husband and her four children get into the swing of things, feeding them and such, handing them multivitamins and clean socks, until they are of a mind to consider for themselves the day gathering around them. Today, though, she has to lend a hand with the collection receipts from Saturday services. Usually this takes place on Sunday; she and Rochelle and Mary gather in the low-ceilinged church office to prepare the weekly deposit. But yesterday Rochelle visited her mother, and Mary said that since she is finally seeing *something* of her husband with tax season over and done with, she'd like to take advantage of it, if that's OK with everybody, so they postponed it until today.

It probably is not a three-person job, but they have a good time. They spend an hour or two working, with coffee cake or strudel. Only Mary actually drinks coffee, though not in the church office. They talk: husbands and children, television and radio. Who is trying to grow rockrose and wild lilac because they can withstand drought. What is the name of, can anyone remember what that chicken casserole is called, the one with cream of mushroom soup and green chiles?

It is always interesting. They add up the cash and checks. They roll the coins. Some people leave postage stamps in the plate, despite Pastor Robert's veiled entreaties against the practice, and for this what they do is they take money out of petty cash and swap it for the stamps. Probably an auditor would raise issues, but Mary's Jim is a CPA, and she generally just shrugs. One time Myrna found an old Liberty Head dime among the coins, and they spent a little while discussing do they simply deposit it or hold it back and find out how much it was worth. And in that event, should they try to find out who contributed it? Finally they called Larry Darling, who is something of a numismatist, which is a coin collector, and asked him did he think it was worth anything. Without missing a beat, he said, "About seven cents." Then he'd laughed. Another time she found an old ten-dollar silver certificate. This Myrna just went ahead and replaced with a regular ten-dollar bill from her pocketbook. She figured it had educational value.

Myrna opens the front door and steps over the threshold. This is the time-tested way of assessing the weather. The weathermen get it wrong a lot, but the front step is right every time: a warm and cloudy day, absolutely. She goes back inside the house, heads for her bedroom at the end of the hall, listening for stirrings within the children's rooms as she passes them. She selects a light blouse, off white with a red and black check, perfect for the warm day.

"It was funny the way the girl didn't do it in a nasty way. She says, 'The ones with the frosting? What you mean is the *Cream Supreme*.'" Mary chuckles, reaching into a white pastry box to cut a pair of bloated doughnuts in two. One actually seems to burst when it is punctured by the knife, sighing and settling as it deflates, bleeding custard-colored filling. Around the two wounded doughnuts sits a selection of crullers and old-fashioneds. "I mean I didn't know they had names, even. And I'll tell you, it is so bad there on a Monday morning. Everybody in a hurry. Line going back to here. It has got to be easier for them if you refer to the pastries by their proper name rather than just pointing, this and this and one of this."

"How was your Sunday with Jim?" asks Myrna. She is unwinding the cord from around her adding machine, which she prefers to Pastor Robert's calculator. She likes to be able to consult the paper tape.

"He has all these *extensions*," Mary says, her hand hovering over the box. She selects a glazed chocolate old-fashioned, a doughnut with some heft to it.

Rochelle is writing the church's account number on the paper sleeves they roll the coins in. In about twelve seconds she will say, as she always does, that they should put in the account number ahead of time. Then she will empty out the cloth bag that contains the fif-

413

teen or twenty dollars in change the church received this week and begin to separate the coins.

"And how is your mother, Rochelle?" asks Myrna.

"She is OK," says Rochelle, pausing. "I wanted to take her outside to feed the ducks after lunch but she wouldn't eat lunch. I brought her a Quarter Pounder with cheese and she didn't touch it."

"How's her mood?"

"She cried. All she does is cry and try to breathe." Then Rochelle begins to cry herself. Myrna puts the adding machine down on the long folding table where she likes to work on collection deposit days. She walks over and puts both hands on Rochelle's shoulders.

"It's all right," she says. "There, there."

"I'm all right," says Rochelle. "It's just so sad." She looks at the flattened paper sleeves before her and inhales deeply. "We ought to just put in these account numbers ahead of time. Save all this work."

"Maybe," says Myrna, happy to recite her part in the weekly litany, "you should just go ahead and write it in on some extra ones today."

They go about their business. Mary, discomfited by Rochelle's display, chatters nervously, forcing Myrna to add the receipts a fourth time. She likes the soft sound her fingertips make striking the keys of the machine. But she steals a glimpse at her wristwatch and sees that it is about twenty to nine. She can imagine the line at the bank first thing on a Monday, and she wants to arrive early. She asks Rochelle a question about her children's doctor. This will quiet Mary down plus help to bring Rochelle back to the everyday, away from the awful place she inhabits alone with thoughts of her failing mother. Kill two birds with one stone. But especially quiet Mary down. As Myrna knows she will, Rochelle answers the question carefully. The doctor is a colleague, after all, of Trygve's.

Mary finishes rolling the coins, and Myrna removes from the church secretary's desk a canvas money pouch. The pouch says LOOMIS and has a zipper with a broken lock at one end. Myrna enjoys placing the money in this pouch so much. It makes the whole procedure extra significant somehow.

The three women leave the church building and walk to the parking lot under the broad eaves extending from the steeply gabled roof.

"Is it just me or—" says Rochelle, dabbing at her face with a

Kleenex. She shouts over the noise as another jet from McClellan AFB rumbles into the sky overhead. She tries again.

"Is it just me, or is it hot? You certainly dressed right for the weather, Myrna."

Myrna is pleased with this remark.

"I was saying to Jim just this morning that the temperature was starting to feel tolerable, but this is *too much*. Something is *not right*." Mary sounds particularly adamant, as if she won't be fooled.

Rochelle needs a lift home after the bank, so Mary says that if it's OK with everybody can they just take one car to the bank and then she'll just drop Myrna off back here? Of course they can. Mary just wants everyone to ride in her new Cutlass. However, Myrna is less than thrilled when in climbing into the back, she places the adding machine on the seat before sitting down herself and Mary says, "Please, dear, mind the upholstery." She reminds herself not to be spiteful, to be a charitable adult who is aware of the many, many ways in which Mary fights her many, many weaknesses. But she can't help herself, for she just has to say, as Mary is pulling out, "A new car somehow smells *cheaper* than it did when Trygve and I bought one two years ago. Or maybe it's just the Oldsmobile, do you think?" and she is ashamed, especially when Mary lapses into a wounded silence that she sustains throughout the five-minute drive to Crocker Bank.

Mary turns into the bank's driveway. The low structure is oriented lengthwise on its lot, and the building presents only its blankly decorative concrete walls to the street, its windows and entrances invisible to anyone passing on Marconi Avenue. Mary steers around the building's pointed outcropping to park in one of the painted spaces near the bank's entrance, joining several other cars there. Myrna checks her watch: 9:02.

"Look at them," says Rochelle.

A small cluster of people are on the other side of the cyclone fence that surrounds the lot. One pushes his way through a large gap in the fence where its links have been cut and then holds aside the section of fence to allow the others through. In all, four figures climb into the bank lot. They wear heavy jackets and woolen watch caps.

"I thought I was hot," Rochelle says, fanning herself.

"Maybe they were out hunting this morning," says Mary. None of the women knows much about such things. The group of four begins advancing toward the entrance as the women get out of the Oldsmobile. Myrna carries her adding machine with her.

"You *can* leave that in the car," says Mary.

"It's all right," says Myrna.

"I'm sorry," says Mary. "I didn't mean to be a so-and-so about it. A new car can make you into the nastiest so-and-so. I almost can't wait until I put the first dent in it."

"Or one of your kids does it for you," says Rochelle.

"Amen to that," says Myrna. Carl and Sonja both drive. Jon's just learning. Her heart is in her mouth all the time now.

"Please don't feel you have to carry it," Mary says.

"I don't mind. I'm already out."

Mary reaches for Myrna and squeezes her wrist. Then the women head for the door, but here are the hunters—they're young people, seemingly a little awkward in the presence of actual grown-ups, shuffling and avoiding eye contact, and Myrna is surprised when one of them reaches for the door and holds it open for the older women, making a stiff after-you gesture with his free hand. She smiles up at him and says, "Thank you."

Inside a short line winds around the floor before the teller's stations. Three butchers wearing yellow hard hats and long white bloodstained coats stand in line together, one leaning in toward the others confidentially, making compact motions with his hands as he tells a story. The three laugh quietly and then, the joke told, direct their attention toward the long counter and the tellers working behind it. A man stands filling out a deposit slip, and Myrna sees him pause, raising his right leg to scratch his left calf with the toe of his shoe. Rochelle fusses with the pouch for a moment, flipping through its contents with the fingers of one hand, checking.

"I'll go ahead and get in line," says Myrna. She takes a step forward.

"All right, everybody put your noses to the carpet!"

She turns around, and there are the hunters, and strangely enough they've brought their guns into the bank with them. There is a moment, a clear moment devoid of anything for Myrna but innocent curiosity, when she wonders if people really hunt with .45 automatics. She remembers her father's telling her that you couldn't hit the broad side of a barn with one of those, and she imagines it must make it tough to shoot game. Then she realizes what's going on.

"Get down!" says one of the hunters. "Get the fuck down!"

Myrna winces at the language. She does not understand why, she has never seen the sense of using such language to make a point. She is scared now, abruptly. Such language scares her, but mainly it's the guns, here in this bright light. She has the general impression that people are carefully beginning to kneel all around her.

She turns to put the adding machine on the counter. There is a flash of light, and she is lifted.

boys want to eat at six there is a   casserole in the refrigerator they should put
in the
            oven at five-thirty.
  baking soda
           three fifty
mac and cheese
      de grees
            Sonja needs
brow nie mix

     what Son ja needs is help with the
enc enc y c lopedia
brea a d
cok e
a prescription, in Trygve's name, for T a g
T a g a m e t that she needs to f i l l
    at Long's. In her
on ions
          purse
potatatoes

                                    She h a s

    yogurt
    ce e ereal

                              all
                              her old m a g a z i n e s
    cheddar ch e eese
    bananannananan a n a n a a a a
                        she p r o m i s e d
                                    Lacey before she do n a t
                                    e s them
    milk
    tomato sa u c e
                        s h e   promised her a
                              c h a n c e to go through
                        them, the ol d m a g a z i n
                                    e s
                        before she   d   d
                                    d   dies
                                                      ?
                                    NO

    str   aw b e r r i e sssss
    the zip per on her pleated skirt fixed.
    enchilada sauce

                        Sonja! Skirt!
                  Mom and Father
                              and who
                                    who is th e r
                              e for t h e m?
    Who o o o wi l l   t e l l   t h e m?
                  w ho wi l l
                  she n e e d s to send   picu
                              pc pictuj school

                                    418

"For the living know that they shall die: but the dead know not any thing, neither have they any more a reward; for the memory of them is forgotten.

"Also their love, and their hatred, and their envy, is now perished; neither have they any more a portion for ever in any thing that is done under the sun . . . Whatsoever thy hand findeth to do, do it with thy might; for there is no work, nor device, nor knowledge, nor wisdom, in the grave, whither thou goest."

Enter the long sleep of the soul, and rest thee, Myrna.

THE RADIO PLAYS ON Capitol Avenue, noise and life, excited voices cast across the territory, calling out the tragic news between Top 40 triumphs. A woman, a mother of four, has been struck down this day. And now, "Philadelphia Freedom." Where the hits never stop coming.

They sit quietly in the kitchen. They haven't counted the money, just shoved it in the closet. Doesn't matter. The news tells them that they got away with fifteen grand. The news also tells them that numerous people took note of Teko's stolen car's stolen license plate: 916 LBJ. 916 being the local area code. LBJ being the memorable monogram of the late president. The car was ditched in Fair Oaks, though, so perhaps this is academic.

So what happened? You can always count on a few hairy moments, a few deviations from plan, a few chance encounters. These are normal operational risks. Try to minimize them, but there's never an occasion you can call textbook. In this case everything went as planned except that Yolanda's shotgun "just went off," as anyone might have predicted.

Yolanda is pale and shaking. She appears to have been crying. But she manages to repeat, "She was just a bourgeois pig."

"Shine a light through the eyes of the ones left behind."

Tania smokes and smokes, lighting one from another, smoking right down to the filter. She thinks she feels awful about the woman. Definitely she feels fearful, and not of abstract retribution; for the first time she recognizes her likely punishment will be years in a cell. And for what? This is stage one of abandoning the revolutionary project. Tania is certain of this, at least. Nobody here knows what to think about it yet, but there's a sack of cash in the hall closet: the primary objective of, the principle underlying, their action, and its useful consequence as well. The other consequence is lying on a slab. A woman is dead. A mother, if you want to privilege her that way, though why bother? What's the difference? We freed no one today. Fed no one. We damaged no fascist enterprises, stopped nothing, disrupted nothing. What we did, we killed someone for a little chump change and then ran like thieves.

Teko takes a split and blistered shotgun shell hull from his pants pocket and holds it in the palm of his hand.

"The murder round," he says. Only he seems to be in good spirits.

"Put it away, please," says Susan.

"I'm going to put it where no one can find it," he says, putting on his jacket. When no one presses him for details, he adds, "I'm going to bury it beneath a tree in McKinley Park."

After he leaves, Susan says, "For God's sake. There's a Dumpster right out back. Collection day is tomorrow unless I'm sadly mistaken."

"Maybe he wants to grow a shotgun tree," says Joan.

Yolanda sobs without warning, with the rasping sound of a chair scraping across the floor.

"Are you OK?"

"She was just a bourgeois pig, a bourgeois pig!"

"Till the whip-poor-will of freedom zapped me right between the eyes."

A little later Teko returns. "All done," he announces. He hangs his jacket up, whistling.

Yolanda looks up at him with red-rimmed eyes. "I want to get out of this town," she says. "I want to go back to the Bay Area. I'm going to really start the women's collective down there."

"Oh ho, not that again."

"I'm taking my share of the money and moving back down there."

"What brings this on? Just because you killed some bitch today?"

Yolanda doesn't answer.

"Well, like let's put it to a vote," Teko says. "I think we've been doing real well here, considering."

"You stay," she says. "I'm getting out of here." She gets up from where she's sitting on the floor as if she were going to leave immediately.

"*I'm* certainly not to blame for what went on today." Teko jabs himself in the chest with his thumb, lets his arm flop down at his side. He stands awkwardly for a moment. "Where'll we live?"

"I don't know where you're going to live," says Yolanda. "Look in the paper. That's what I'm going to do."

They all wanted to move down there anyway. The whole point is now's their chance. The whole point is now there's money available, to leave with. Fifteen grand in that sack in the closet, according to the Action News team. A daring early-morning bank robbery that's left one woman dead and a grieving family asking why.

Adventures in Wonderland

TWO DAYS AFTER GUY arrives in New York, he stands at the counter eating strawberries from a lattice basket of green plastic. A sunny morning, the bright time in his kitchen. With a paring knife, he cuts soft spots out of the berries before popping them into his mouth. He grabs a sponge and is about to work a pink spot out of the Formica when the phone rings.

"Is that Guy Mock, then?"

"Yes."

"Difficult one to pin down, aren't you? I'm going round, all thorough like, but it seems you've left each of your last-known addresses unattended. I says to meself, he's a crafty, peripatetic sort, this Mock is. Leaves with a secret face and a quiet mouth. Stops the papers and the mail. The milkman's wholesome shadow does not darken his doorstep. Long holiday? I think not."

"Who is this?"

"Me name's Roy Hume. I represent the *National Eye and Ear.*"

Guy hears "iron ear," pictures some nightmare prosthesis.

"It's a journalistic enterprise of exceedingly poor reputation, it is. I shall save you the bother of asking and, standing in your own inquisitive place, rhetorically put the question of 'How come?' In keeping with newspaper tradition I shall now provide me own answer. There are three elegantly simple reasons. Number one is that as a national publication we feel no bleeding obligation to cover the news from a local angle. Sod that. A local angle would bore our readers silly, it would. We've discovered via scientific inquiry that our sort of reader doesn't seem to come from anyplace at all, actually. He simply appears in the foul hollows of the country, equipped with a modicum of literacy and an insatiable gullibility. This journalistic approach is in fact an innovation originating in the mother country, which for the sake of convenience we shall identify as Britain, although morally and ancestrally speaking, I consider meself a Scot. The second reason is that we have the sensibility of a bricoleur, as the poofs like to say. We have a few stock bits we keep round that time and still another scientific inquiry have amply demonstrated are evergreens of reportage, stimulating constant reader interest. Contrary to popular opinion, the average end user of news and information tends to rally round the familiar bits of disaster, plague, and salacious ruin. Contrary to popular opinion, novelty's not what he's after. Not a bit of it. He wants the familiar bits. They provide comfort, they do, in all the vague specificity of their permutations. He wants the water levels to rise and submerge Manhattan. He wants mass murders in the remotest points of South America. He wants a joint Soviet-American project to develop an invisibility spray in an aerosol can. He wants the devil to rule the earth from 1975 to 1978. He wants the seat of world government to be switched to caverns under Wichita."

"So," says Guy, holding the sponge aloft and examining it, "what can I do for you?"

"Don't forget there's a third reason, mate."

"OK."

"The third reason is that our undisguised motivation is profit. We actually make money on the bleeding newsstands. No Pulitzers for us. We have the space aliens and we have Satan. For all their glistening Pulitzers, has the bloody *New York Times* ever had space aliens and Satan? I think not."

Guy hangs up the phone.

Adventure No. 1

After waiting in a glum chamber filled with books from the prestigious house's current list and decorated with a bronze wall relief depicting the publisher's famed Irish setter mascot, Red, Guy is ushered into a meeting at Stumpf requested by Borden Cratty, a managing editor still riding high from his stewardship onto the national bestseller lists of *Party Games** (**for adults only*), a book that, according to insider gossip, single-handedly rescued the marshmallow and whipped topping sectors of the processed food market from unprofitability in the third and fourth quarters of 1972. Cratty, an apparent dwarf, wears hand-painted ties and smokes cheroots and grabs Guy's hand in both of his, drawing him into his office and seating him across from a man he introduces as Standolph "Libby" Tinsby. "Libby" is Stumpf's "longsuffrin corprate counsel," and he's "got a lil ol Q 'n' A for yall." Guy settles into his chair.

"In light of the recent Clifford Irving hoax that turned out so unfortunately for our colleagues at McGraw-Hill, we would like to make absolutely certain that you are indeed in authorized possession of, or, alternatively, soon to be in authorized possession of, a legitimate manuscript written or cowritten in substantial measure by actual representatives of the apparent breakaway state of Symbionia."

"I actually don't believe it's a nationalistic-type sobriquet—"

"Well praps they alld *like* that."

"Accordingly, we have taken the liberty of drafting a set of affidavits, a representative sample of which I hold in my right hand, that in pertinent part affirm that each individual signing thereto is a citizen or denizen of Symbionia maintaining an active role in the events described in the proposed Narrative."

"Aint this just the silliest damn thang but you know we gotta cross the tees and dot th ahs—"

"In addition, there is one supplementary affidavit, to be executed by the individual presently d/b/a Tania, affirming that indeed she is, or at any rate was, Miss Alice Daniels Galton."

"Yall can understan that. I know it."

"Incidentally, these affidavits and any other legally binding documents that set forth terms or an understanding of any nature between Stumpf and the Symbionese are understood to be governed by the laws of the United States of America. That is, such documents do not recognize Symbionese authority, such as it is. Ha-ha."

"Oh, Libby. Haw."

"Naturally, the signatures that the Symbionese attach to these affidavits will need to be witnessed by a notary public certified by the state or commonwealth in which each Symbionese currently maintains his or her principal domicile."

"Jest a precautionry measure. A mere formaldehyde, as they say befoe any undahtakin."

"Then and only then can Edgar E. Stumpf & Co., in consultation with its parent company, Gulf & Western, take under consideration the possibility of contracting to put into published form the proposed Narrative authored by Guy Mock, Junior, and the Symbionese."

Guy simply rises and walks out of this one, bringing Cratty scurrying at his heels.

"Guy! What can I say? They are havin evry one of us fo breakfiss since Irvin fucked it up for evrybody with that fuck-ass Howd Hughes book. Fake it! I don care. You are goin to have a Irish settah rampant across your spine! The spine of your book, that is! I swear it!"

"We seem to be experiencing a bugger of a connectivity problem," says Hume. "Occurs each and every time I ring you up, it does."

"Maybe you should talk to the transatlantic operator."

"Ho!" says Hume, delighted. "I'm in South Florida, I am. Let me relate a thing or two about me life in this earthly paradise. At this very moment I'm watching a bloke wrestling this absolutely smashing marlin onto the dock of the marina whilst seated in a plastic chaise longue. He's seated, that is. I'm on me feet, riveted, steaming up one of the floor-to-ceiling glass windows here in me bleeding breakfast nook, a glass of fresh-squeezed Florida orange juice from concentrate in me hand. The brute must weigh twenty stone. He's a real brute, he is. Soon I'll step out onto the deck to rub coconut oil on me pale British flesh, submit it to the blandishments of the tropical sun. This is far in excess of what I dared imagine for meself, for me future, as a small lad growing up in a gloomy scheme, it is. Far, far indeed."

"Try the operator," says Guy. He hangs up.

Adventure No. 2

Small & Grey asks for the book. But there is no book. "I have got to have something to give to sales," says the editorial director, Jane Pancake. "If I don't have something to give to sales, they'll laugh me out of their tiny, windowless offices. Loud eruptions of braying laughter accompanied by derogatory comments about the way my legs look in sheer hose, which really is nothing I can control. When I was at Wellesley, we weren't even allowed to *say* 'hose' except during Punt Hill Week. There's nothing to be done about these men.

So, no, gaga as I may be over the concept, I simply can't go to the salespeople on this one empty-handed. Though I think it's got all the makings of a sure winner."

The next day the phone rings. "I was caught between floors in the elevator with a large, lupine specimen of our sales staff, and he smacked his lips with loathsome satisfaction as he advised me that he'd heard that I'd rejected what promised to be one of the Blockbuster Books of '76. I'm not sure which book he meant. Perhaps it was yours. 'Pack up your desk, piano legs.' That's what he said, nice as you please. So do you think you could dash off something that I could cringingly tender to the sales oafs and messenger it over here? One colorfully descriptive page, single-spaced, ought to do the trick." Phone rings. "Try as I might, I simply can't *see* those chattering rifles, that flaming tumbledown bungalow, those writhing wounded, those oppressed masses—though surely I would like to. Really, how can you ask me to put myself on the line with those storm troopers in the dimly lit realm of sales? They call me 'Chain Pantsuit,' did you know? Everyone knows. I've devoted my adult life to the kind of quality literature that possesses a strong potential for a mass-market paperback sale, but *they* don't care. Look up *scumbag* in the dictionary and there's a group photo of our crack sales staff. A bunch of chauvinists who can't stand the fact that a young woman from Larchmont with big feet and several small but nonetheless persistent obstacles in her path has managed to rise very near if not actually to the top in a man's game. According to them, I should have gone into educational television programming, if you can believe it."

A letter arrives the next day telling Guy to meet Pancake at her office off Union Square. "Look out the window. See those junkies down there in the park? One of them is actually Ed Sforenza, 'our' sales manager. How does a man like this come to represent the interests of the old buttoned-down gentlemanly house of Small & Grey? A house with its origins in the decorous wards of Boston's Back Bay? If I dared to show my face wearing a soiled overcoat like that I'd never be invited to another book party again. These men don't care about book parties. They loosen their ties and drink canned beer out of paper bags right on the sidewalk. This is what I'm up against. This is a fact many people are aware of. Even if they are afraid to say a single word. What have you got for me?"

She sits on the edge of her desk and pulls the typewritten proposal from the envelope, breathing, "Onionskin," disenchantedly, before settling in to read, fidgeting and slapping the empty envelope against her thigh. She looks up abruptly.

"I'm afraid I'm going to have to ask you to hurry out of my office and down the stairs if you please. If anyone spots you, tell them that you work in maintenance or that you're simply a mugger lying in wait for a slow-moving elderly person ironically taking the stairs for his health. Don't mention my name under any circumstances. Honestly, if you haven't yet come up with something that I can deliver to the sales staff without ducking, I don't think we'll be playing music together, that's the phrase?"

Guy shrugs.

"They'll be Xeroxing dirty pictures of my private parts on interoffice memo paper again. Drawings, I mean; highly exaggerated and inaccurate drawings. Hurry now. Get out."

That afternoon the telephone rings. "I don't know why you stormed out the way you did. Can you resubmit? Give me back that glorious and promising proposal, and I promise we'll have a competitive offer on the table by tomorrow afternoon."

The next afternoon the receptionist at Small & Grey advises him that Jane Pancake has left the company to become a literary agent.

Guy picks up the ringing phone.

"Mock, mate."

"Can I help you?"

"It's the other way round, mate. It's I who can be helping you if the rabbit and pork is on the up and up. You get me?"

"What?"

"Talk, mate. Talk. Rabbit and pork is talk. Ach, how I yearn to get back to that sodden land where the women are women and the men are named Nigel."

"What's the talk?"

"Can't say explicit like. Ah, bollocks. Who'm I fooling? No wiretaps on little old Roy Hume's telephone. It's not like I represent the bloody *New York Times* and their shining phalanx of bleeding Pulitzer Prizes. It's not like I'm a revered national correspondent with the soi-disant Paper of Record, now is it then?"

Guy looks out the window. The bricks on the other side of the airshaft face him, textured in the morning sunlight. He sees a curtain move in the window above him and to his left, and then a woman's arm, heavy and pale, emerges from the open window to overturn a full ashtray into the alley below, sending up a cloud of ash and cinders.

"Right," says Hume. "What I want to know is whether there's any truth to what I've been told about you and a certain young lady from the Coast who's gone missing. That you are involved."

Guy hangs up.

Adventure No. 3

BACCHUS

A DIVISION OF SEGAL & SOWER
12th Floor
30 Rockefeller Center
New York, NY 10020

Richard Detective
Senior Editor

Dear Guy,

We're more than merely interested in your proposal—we're ready to clear the decks right now. Your project is poised to join the group of exciting books we currently have planned. We've acquired a California novel, *Radical Desire*, that has its thumb right on the frantically beating pulse of that bellwether state, and this dovetails ingeniously with our forthcoming *The Black Panther Sex Manual*, which—like the sort of long black Christmas stocking it's intended to stuff—is packed with one sensuous surprise after another. A book exploring the lives, loves and unusual lifestyles of some of our most famous revolutionaries seems the perfect complement to these two arousing titles.

I wonder if you'd submit to a few probing questions, first. My thrust is, your proposal was a little on the dry side, a trifle too focused on politics, revolution, etc. Of course those of us who've paid close attention have been interested in those aspects of the story, yet one area of the case that demands to be deeply penetrated deals with the private lives of those who would assassinate our leaders, bring down our institutions, destroy our way of life, and so on: How, in short, do such people "get it on"? You promise to deliver a "candid account" of the underground life of the S.L.A., but I think it would be much better if we were all clear on this: Of what, exactly, does such candor consist?

So if it's all right with you, I'd like a few explicit lines on the extent to which your project intends to directly address the erotic life underground. I think readers would like to know who is "doing" whom, and how often, and by what means. Are there S.L.A. orgies? Is there much "forbidden" sex involving mixing of the races? Is it true that some members of the S.L.A. are or were or will be lesbians? Do photographs exist? These are the sort of questions that we would need to find the answers to in a book we chose to publish concerning the S.L.A., or anyone else for that matter.

Anticipating your rapid response.

All good wishes,
Dick

"What we have here, is *failure* to *communicate*," says Hume, in a fair approximation of an American accent. He continues, "I have to admit I had been looking forward to the prospect of working with you. I can't say I'm seeking full reciprocity. In me profession that's a dangerous, dangerous folly. We maintain strict boundaries with all, be he source, informant, or stooge as the case may be. On Fleet Street we lived by a saying. Me first boss, Pobjoy, liked to drill it into me, he did. In a manner of speaking."

"What's the saying?"

"Oh. 'Y'haven't got any friends.' Some such. Years ago, it was. I've toiled many a day since, under the glowing tan and worldly manner still just an ink-stained wretch in a naff suit of clothes, I am. Still haven't a friend in this slithery world either, I'm quite happy to say. Now. We were about to speak of your involvement with a certain Miss X."

"What sort of involvement?"

"I would be lying, mate, if I didn't admit that it would be to me advantage if the involvement were romantic in nature. The betrothed heiress in the arms of the bolshie jock. However, we do not invent the news. We create it when necessary, but we do not invent what isn't there. I'm fully prepared to take what I can get, I am. Toward that end I have been authorized to extend a very generous offer in your direction. That's right, checkbook journalism. A dirty word to the bloody *New York Times*, but not to the humble *Eye and Ear*, moiling away to serve the needs of the silent majority. Sometimes you have to put aside your high-mindedness and get down in it. And there's a certain beauty to it, there is. What I have in mind requires absolutely no face-to-face meetings, no divulging of confidences. All I require is a token from the young lady in question. Say a soiled pair of knickers, a chicken bone from her dinner plate, or a used shell casing."

"What for?"

"We secure the item in a bank vault, an event to which our solicitor, a chartered accountant, and meself bear eyewitness. Then we poll our far-ranging network of paranormal adepts: What exactly is this highly personal memento? What state of mind does it bespeak? Have at it, fork benders! Their correct answers shall make for a very nice spread and of course enhance the value of our offer to you."

"So what if they don't identify it correctly?"

"Well then of course it wouldn't be worth quite as much, now would it then?"

Guy very gently puts down the telephone. He leans on his hands on the windowsill, peering down the airshaft at the dark alley below. Directly beneath the window across the way there is a small mound of ash and butts that has accumulated over many a day.

Adventure No. 4

Guy takes the subway downtown and climbs out at Twenty-third Street, leaving the deep, long rolling rumble of the train behind him. He strolls past the residence for the blind, who feel their way into the noontime traffic on the avenues, tap tap. Guy knows how they feel. Twenty-five thousand miles on the road, and here's where he ends up, still chasing a decent advance.

Well, not quite here. The restaurant is near Madison Square. (Next time a cab.) Outside, workers from nearby insurance companies walk the streets carefully, conscious of the grim actuarial promises latent in every sight and sound. Haverford Dodd meets Guy at the bar, though "his" table is unoccupied and awaits him. At Dodd's signal, the head-waiter moves forward to seat the two himself, moving the table aside so that they can settle into a plush banquette of deep red and then handing them menus in leather covers. The staff moves silently, with darting grace, like a school of rare tropical fish.

Guy has gotten Dodd's name from a friend, a journalist whose two books had been edited by Dodd, one of which had done rather well on the basis of an ultimately empty and insubstantial rumor that it was to be well reviewed in the *Times*. The rumor alone had lent a kind of strength and momentum to the book, and Dodd had presided over it all as the book went into a second printing and sold to paperback even before its pub date, as if shoppers wanted posses-sion of the book prior to its event, wanted themselves to be at the nexus of that event, a celebration of prescient consumerism that val-idated its standing as our primary avant-garde.

How depressing. No wonder Dodd would be interested in a book that discusses how much its authors wish to destroy him: it'll never happen. This restaurant, these waiters, the chef will not permit the revolution to come to pass. The waiters wear fucking brocaded jack-ets. He'll bet that no one in the SLA could make a decent basic white sauce if their lives depended on it. It's all a joke. Guy feels a wave of cynical ennui, familiar from the last several days, wash over him.

Guy notes that Dodd appears cultivatedly weary, as if he were making a slow but spirited recovery from devastating intestinal ill-ness. Guy can't decide whether Dodd would look more at home on a horse or bundled up in an Adirondack chair on the porch of some puritan sanatorium. He has graying blond hair, watery blue eyes, and a deeply cleft chin. Guy can't tell if he's thirty-five or sixty.

"So," he says, "are you enjoying spring in the city?"

"Oh, nice," says Guy.

"I was out on the Island again this weekend. The solace of the off-season: no guests. Just a little time alone with the muse. You and your wife will have to come out sometime. The beach is fringed by magnificently precarious houses and token stands of the woods destroyed toward their fabrication. One such house is my mother's, weathered and rotting in a prosperous seaside way, like a rich old woman."

Dodd laughs into his handkerchief at his own joke. He has a rasping, dry laugh; it makes his shoulders shake and his chest rattle. Waiters break their stride, carefully arranging expressions of concern on their faces, until they realize that what Dodd is doing is laughing.

"Of seven estates, which together formed an elongated ellipsis of faded gingerbread, rickety widow's walks for the vigilant Dutch wives of popular antiquity, and pale erosive land, ours is the last remaining. Now, beyond the dunes and the wayward pickets demarcating their perilous swollen rises, there are evenly laid-out cottages, newly made, of aluminum and plastic. Built, I imagine, to capitalize on the attractions the place holds for the newly affluent, which I would characterize as a perception of stolid 'authenticity' and 'character' on the part of its year-round people—qualities which I can assure you are entirely mythical—and a desire to passively partake of the xenophobia historically to be found in such a place."

The waiter arrives with two fresh martinis and a steaming appetizer. Dodd laughs as he sets them down.

"Now, on my part of the Island the sights are magnificently decrepit, void of utility, void of any trace of this century, white hot and peeling in the sun: the church, the jetty, the seawall, the lighthouse. These places exist solely as monuments to averted catastrophe, offerings to the angry gods of the elements, and they now creep with the most primitive of organisms. Jellyfish, the wives of Jewish businessmen, and so on."

Dodd seems nearly about to shake himself apart with the cannonade of laughter this provokes, and the restaurant's din hushes for a moment as he comes to himself. Guy is still and very quiet.

"You said something about the muse?"

"Oh, *yes*. I work when I can, indeed I do. Oh yes yes yes. Not as often as I'd like; the editorial work is so demanding. Nothing terribly elaborate, mind you. Good old-fashioned stuff. A beginning, an end. A man, a woman. A conflict, a resolution. It seems to me that so much contemporary writing resembles the sort of undertaking that dark intent little persons should be working on in laboratories in Massachusetts and California even as we speak. Thoughtful little intent dark persons doing thoughtful things, with the aid of blackboards and slide rules. And yet I see myself as a writer who happens to pass the time as an editor. The thing is, I enjoy helping people. I enjoy it a great deal. I love to wrest rough, promising work from the hands of an arrogant young writer and mold it into a sleek piece of salable work. It just isn't any fun otherwise."

An unnerving clatter issues from Dodd, and the table shakes lightly. He focuses on Guy.

"Now. Your proposal. The most exciting thing to cross my desk in three or four months. A very exciting-sounding project. Oh yes yes yes. But I'm assuming you're looking for top price. And Dearstyne, Harbottle has never let anything like money stand in the way of its reputation as the most prestigious literary publisher on the block. That is, we don't pay out much of it."

Dodd laughs into his handkerchief.

"And even if we *were* to do so in this case—saying so, mind you, merely for the sake of argument. Well. As captivated as I am by the story you propose to tell, I am beholden to superiors, sales staff, and shareholders; to Mr. Dearstyne, who, though he lies abed in a state of enfeebled senility, still ratifies each acquisition so that this clubby little world we all live in knows that the list under the imprimatur of his name is still decisively reflective of his singular vision; and to CBS, which is looking to acquire us for tax purposes, though it's safe to assume that they are interested in losing only so much money if you get my drift."

"Do you think you're going to lose money on this book?"

Here they pause for a moment as Dodd laughs.

"But of course! It would be—oh, too tedious to explain the arithmetic, the accounting involved, but I think I can state categorically that we lose money on *every* book Dearstyne, Harbottle and Company publishes."

"How do you stay in business?"

"Well, it's a matter of prestige. We have it; the other fellows don't. Nordic used to, but their list's far too big now. Oh, yes yes yes. Rommel, Mays and Croix likes to pretend. But in reality, there's only us. And so they settle for vulgar profitability. Though, truth to tell, the others all are losing money as well. Schlock or not, it is a tough market out there. Tough, tough market. Yes yes yes. I know, I

know: it seems healthy, robust. Every time you turn around someone has sold a million copies of this book or that. But it's tough, believe me. Just keeping abreast of the trends must be difficult. If
you're the sort of publisher who feels he has to do that. Last year it
was dolphins. This year it's sharks."

Dodd hacks his mirth into his handkerchief.

"So, really, I don't think I can make an offer. Or, rather, any offer
I'd make would be insultingly small."

"Try me," says Guy.

"Oh, no. No no no. I couldn't. I wouldn't. You deserve a publisher who can get behind this project both emotionally *and* financially."

Guy leaves him laughing into his handkerchief, unfolded and
spread to cover the lower part of his face, as if he were afraid of in-
fecting the world with his rueful self-deprecation.

PART FIVE

Nice, Normal
Revolutionaries

"It seems very pretty," she said when she had finished it; "but it's *rather* hard to understand!" (You see she didn't like to confess, even to herself, that she couldn't make it out at all.) "Somehow it seems to fill my head with ideas—only I don't exactly know what they are! However, *somebody* killed *something;* that's clear, at any rate—"   —*THROUGH THE LOOKING GLASS*

T HE PRESS WAITED EXPECTANTLY under its canopy. The strange
lingering season of waiting was about to expire, and there was nothing to do except continue to wait until the end. Tomorrow each'd
turn up at work and be assigned to the Hall of Justice or to a super-
visors' meeting or to hang around plaguing tourists at the turn-
around on Powell and Market.

Two long moving vans ("One just for the paintings and sculp-
ture," went the rumor) came up the driveway. It was hard for the
press to believe that this was that very last thing they'd been waiting
for: two trucks slowly filling with cartons and furniture. It messed
with their sense of narrative. It was supposed to be hugs, kisses, John
Wayne framed in the narrowing space of a closing door, isolated and
cast off as Natalie Wood returns home from her prolonged sojourn
among the savages.

Instead, Hank and Lydia had put their spread up for sale and were
moving to a deluxe apartment on Nob Hill. Their public statements
concerning the move were elliptical—irritatingly so. Clearly the
couple was attempting to say goodbye, to break things off.

But the press had its questions. The public had its needs. How big
was the new place? Did it have superb views? Did they look forward
to having all the amenities of the world's greatest city right outside
their front door? Would the family keep the same staff? Would
some of those faithful retainers have to go? Would the couple miss
the home in which they'd raised a family? How did the children feel
about the move? Were they supportive, or had they raised objections? (And) did this move suggest that they had given up on Alice?
That was the big question, the one they wanted to shoehorn in.
There was no one to ask it of, however. No sign of Lydia or Hank
(They were staying "in a six-room luxury suite at the Fairmont,"
went the rumor).

Turned out one of the trucks was taking extra furnishings directly to a storage facility in San Mateo. The new apartment on Nob Hill couldn't hold what the house had.

The canopy was faded and weather-beaten, torn and repaired in places. The grass beneath it had died. Some had been there under it almost every day. Theirs was the subtle side of the story. A family in shock. A family coming to terms. A family moving on. They stood, they ate sandwiches. After Lydia had complained about the drive-way's being full each day, they'd parked their cars and vans at the side of the road below, at the slight risk of bodily injury, not to mention parking tickets. Their ranks thinned over time, but some stayed. When the daily buffet stopped appearing, they formed groups and began breaking for lunch. After Inge and Maria stopped setting out the urn, they took turns riding down the hill to Burlingame for coffee each afternoon. Under the canopy an etiquette evolved. A pecking order. They dropped their cigarette butts into a standing ashtray Hernando provided that looked as if it had been looted from an office building in Mesopotamia ("Probably priceless," went the rumor). Someone began remembering to save the brown paper bags the delicatessen packed their sandwiches and coleslaw in, and they used them to collect trash. They were scrupulous about such practices. They wanted to be good guests. They wanted so much to be the one gleaming, exemplary facet of the whole sad story.

By late afternoon it was clear that the trucks would not be loaded by the end of the workday, that despite having spent more than a year under the canopy, the press was to be deprived of the privilege of closing the door on the story. The last truck would leave, and there'd be no witness to write, "The last truckload of furniture and the accumulation of decades of privilege rolled slowly down the driveway leading from Galton Mansion today, leaving behind an empty house with more than its share of ghosts." The day took on a elegiac cast. People said their goodbyes. Tomorrow the assignment would be over, and the greater world would once again take its measure of them.

Tania awakens on the sofa in the middle of the night. Light enters the apartment through the big windows overlooking the street. She gets up, feels around on the table with her fingers, finds cigarettes, though her throat is raw and the first drag tastes like yarn.

The place is on Geneva Avenue, charitably described as the ass end of town, an apartment over a dry cleaner's with dropped ceilings, guttering fluorescent lights, and Armstrong tile covering the floors. When they moved in, they sat around groping for comparisons. Like a Lion's Club in an ebbing industrial city? Like an abortionist's office? It was a perfect spot for them, transient, impersonal, a place to sit in a folding chair and eat out of a Styrofoam tray, your mind somewhere else.

This is the home of the women's collective, that perplexing splinter. Men Welcome, kind of. On the table are piled yellow pads, covered with writing, a dog-eared and marginally notated copy of *The Dialectic of Sex*, and pamphlets with titles like *Mother Right: A New Feminist Theory*, *The Bitch Manifesto*, and *What Is the Revolutionary Potential of Women's Liberation?* All this literature, all these pamphlets coming from places like New York, Cambridge, Chicago, Pittsburgh (Pittsburgh?). Typed, Xeroxed, stapled, illustrated with rough line drawings, each booklet is sufficiently crude to lend it power and a labored gravity. Yea, sister! A space has been cleared away for the Royal portable with its jumpy ribbon and sticky keys.

An uncharacteristic late-spring rain drums on the windows. Tania goes to study the street below. She sees a woman walking briskly, bare-headed, staring straight ahead. She's trailed by a man in a slicker who stops and shouts after her, then trots to get up ahead, where he turns to face her, walking backward, gesturing placatively with his hands and looking over his shoulder to avoid running into anyone. The woman keeps walking, eyes front, stepping nimbly out of the man's way. They follow this pattern, continuing on toward the corner, where two men stand under a pool hall awning, sipping from drinks in brown paper bags. They are loudly amused, and the man in the slicker responds angrily. The woman keeps going, crosses Mission and heads up the hill on Geneva. The man in the slicker knocks the brown-bagged drink out of the hand of one of the men standing under the awning. Fists come up, the circling, the shouts, foamy liquid from the spilled container pooling on the shiny sidewalk. The other man under the awning serenely sips from his drink. The woman keeps right on going up the hill. Rainy midnight at the edge of San Francisco.

. . .

Yolanda wanted to segregate them here, get them working on something that would define them categorically and undeniably, edge them away from random destruction. But as an analysis gradually emerges, Tania finds herself unconvinced by the latest Truth. She lifts the limp sheet of paper rolled into the machine and reads the passage typed on it:

> Middle class women are most positively situated, due to their education and sophistication, to see the inherent contradiction between the promises of society and what is actually offered to women, to see the extent and placement of the fault lines in our "democratic" Amerikkka beyond simple questions of racism and imperialism. Moreover, as Marcuse explains, the "prosperity" of a given society DOES NOT DIMINISH THE NECESSITY OF LIBERATING ONE'S SELF FROM IT.
>
> In this sense FEMINISM IS THE MOST COMPLEX AND VALID ISSUE OF THE DAY for you have ONE HALF OF THE POPULATION HELD IN SUBJUGATION BY THE OTHER HALF. Though we are conscious of women's oppression per se, we must not lack in our consciousness of most women's class oppression!!! We CAN discuss the oppression of the black man, but NOT without addressing the shocking sexual exploitation of black women. To us, the primary issue remains male supremacy. Once this has been overcome, we can truly and comprehensively address the problems of an unjust society.

Her time in the closet, this hot air is its ultimate lesson? Everything she's experienced over the past year stems from such social and historical "circumstances"? All the reading, the talking, the takeout; the stolen cars, the graffiti, the threats; the calisthenics, target practice, and drills; the shit-stained toilets and scummy shower stalls, the inflammatory rhetoric, the guns and bombs, the robberies, the cold-blooded homicide? This is their penance for Myrna Opsahl's murder? Does it make her feel better about Myrna Opsahl and her motherless children to conclude that what happened was necessary in order to free them all? The passage is from an essay provisionally entitled "Women in the Vanguard: Toward a Revolutionary Theory," but it might as well be "Why We Need to Move into Our

Own Place." In their eagerness to get out from under Teko, they have talked themselves into a new reality.

She's been having these dreams that make her eyes snap open hours before sunup. Tonight she's dreamed that she was standing in a kitchen talking to a Chinese man. The kitchen appeared to be that of a restaurant, with lots of pots and pans hanging overhead, chrome racks, tall worktables, etc. She and the man spoke while he cleaned and gutted fish, reaching for them and then slicing them up the length of their bellies and removing the entrails. Finally, he reached, and instead of a fish he picked up a cat. Tania protested—That's not a fish, you can't do that, and so forth—but the man simply held the limp and passive cat in position, looking amused. Tania averted her eyes. But when she looked again, she found that the man had been waiting for her. He slit the cat open.

Sometimes when they're sitting here, halfheartedly hacking out an "analysis," Tania asks the others what they think of such dreams. They readily set aside their work.

Yolanda opens a beer. "Once I dreamed that a robot was walking down the street. So I jump onto his back and try to tear his nose off. I'm screaming how I want it for myself. Then suddenly I'm like not on his back, so I break into this building to get away. The robot tries to come in after me, and I look and now there's this old lady hanging on, a grandma really, and I run up the stairs and there's this girl, she's really high, and she's carrying a silver tray of grapes."

"I dreamed I was walking in the rain," says Susan. "I meet a nun, and I ask her why I can't forget my ex-boyfriend. She says I have to be more romantic. Then she's like *gone*. So I keep going and I hear this whimpering sound. And there's this duckling crying, trying to get out of the mud. It's black with soot and soaking wet. I pick it up, and I'm carrying it home, and when I get there it's turned into a golden retriever puppy."

Joan says, "I'm taking a bath with a strange lady. I see a oven. There's a strange feeling. The lady goes, 'Dissatisfaction is the partner of loss.'"

"That's just goofy," says Tania.

"I'm in a church with a doctor. He says, 'Serenity is the partner of confusion.' I see a washing machine. I feel ashamed."

"Don't make fun."

"Who's making fun?" Joan is making notes on a sheet of paper headed "OUR BODIES: WE'VE NEVER REALLY OWNED THEM." She wears a slight smirk.

Joan's been edgy lately, moody. Tania often senses that she's bull-shitting them, playing up the Far Eastern angle, toying with whatever stereotypifying residue may linger here. It has to be boring. At each stage in the discussion, as they struggle toward their feminist critique, they literally turn to her, as if she were the natural arbiter of how oppressed they are.

But it isn't just that. Everything changed after Myrna. Joan's ragged patience finally wore out, and she announced that she was ready to take her chances, to return to the East Coast, free of them all. Tania begged her to come to San Francisco.

"Aren't you cured *yet*?" Joan had asked, with annoyance. But in the end she came.

Actually, Tania feels as restless as Joan: bored with the SLA, eager to leave, troubled by Myrna Opsahl's murder, anxious about getting caught. The standard gamut. But she doesn't have a lot of options. The SLA's talent for getting attention is coming back to haunt them. Each month brings a new opportunity for the press to resuscitate the story of her celebrated absence, brings renewed calls for the FBI to solve the case, and she has to lay low.

Everything changed. She wants to say, if only she'd known—but the guns had always been there; they'd fetishized them, carried them, fired them, spoken of their mystical, liberating power. You aim one at somebody, you better intend to fire it at him. What other possible use could a gun have? Teko and Yolanda didn't see it that way. Actually, they didn't see it any way at all. At first, Teko had exulted in the murder, but he soon realized that his wife was not in an exultant mood. It became a closed subject, occulted, taboo. They moved to San Francisco *to form the women's collective*. That's the official reason. The money that funded this undertaking might as well have materialized out of thin air.

Also, *to commence a bombing campaign*. Teko insists. No more fucking around! They must have action! Let Yolanda, Tania, Susan, and Joan puzzle out the solution to anatomical supremacy, build their little ship in a bottle, but Teko's still General Field Marshal.

. . .

Though some things have changed. The feminism thing may be total bullshit in theory, but in practice Teko hasn't tried to hurt Tania in months.

She'd taken a leaf from Joan's book: pointed a .38 at his head one day when he raised a fist to her and threatened to pop him in the skull. They were alone together, and she bore the full weight of his pedantry. It had been the usual argument. Tania why did you leave the dishes in the sink. Tania what is this mess here. Tania didn't I tell you to. Her response—insolent contempt—was well within the boundaries they'd established for dealing with each other after the incident in the creamery, but for some reason she managed that day to infuriate him and he'd grabbed a belt from where it was hanging over the back of a chair and made for her. And automatically, without a single moment's deliberation that she could trace afterward, she lifted her revolver out of her purse and aimed it at his head. He froze, an astonished expression on his face, the belt in his hand swinging limply.

"Better put that down now," he said.

She just smiled at him.

"I mean it, Tania. That's an order."

"Kiss my cunt, Adolf."

"You couldn't kill me. What'll you tell the others?"

"You'll never know, will you?"

He breathed heavily, looked irate—then backed off. It felt good.

She thinks she'd like to try Boston. Joan's mentioned it, repeatedly, as the place she's most likely to go, and Tania would be happy to accompany her.

She talks to Roger; she holds his hand. She wants to plant a seed, put him where he can see the change that's coming. She's familiar enough with the routine; she's always been pretty direct when it comes to breaking up with a boy. But she feels a little guilty in this case: She wants to get rid of him, but she wants to keep him in reserve too. He's getting all funny over her though. Brings her little gifts, arrives bearing flowers or whatever wearing his paint-spattered overalls. Flecks of paint in his hair, his eyelashes. In Sacramento it was sweet; he was the bright spot to her days in that lonely burg. Here, home, he's just another person looking to her to heat up the soup.

Boston. She has a stash of two thousand dollars wrapped in aluminum foil in the freezer. She has a stolen BankAmericard and a valid California driver's license. Anywhere she wants, she can go. For now, that's enough.

WHEN YOUR BROTHER CONTACTS *law enforcement authorities and suggests to them that you have been involved in the commission of a federal crime, elect to smoke a joint.*

When your father, in a near-apopleptic rage, begins breaking the camera equipment of hardworking members of the press, though not enough of it to prevent the nationally syndicated appearance of a photograph of the old man, wearing a torn pair of cutoff shorts and an old oxford shirt with holes in the armpits, attacking a tiny woman reporter, combine the over-the-counter analgesic of your choice with the sort of opiate informally offered for sale on a nearby street corner.

*When your mother's blood pressure consistently rises to levels at which her physician feels it prudent to utter diagnoses like "You really should be dead," prior to placing her on a medication that has hair sprouting from her chest and has her darting through her home at 11 p.m. vacuuming, washing, and waxing the floors, drink a bottle of fortified wine and gently rest your head on a curbstone. (*What's the word? *Thunderbird!* How's it sold? *Good and cold!* What's the jive? *Bird's alive!* What's the price? *Thirty twice!)*

When your wife refuses to have intercourse with you, to touch your penis, to let you stroke her breasts, to kiss you on the mouth, to put her arms around you, to meet your eyes when she speaks to you, to speak to you at all unless absolutely necessary, to be in the same room with you except when socially requisite, to spend time in the same state with you, the oft-feared occasion has arrived for you to publish a depraved novena to St. Jayne Mansfield in the back pages of a magazine and then hire a scantily clad woman found walking in the vicinity of Taylor and Pine streets to serve as a "surrogate."

When your funds have diminished to nearly nothing, *when your friends refuse your phone calls and slam the door at the sight of your face on the doorstep, when you are rejected, rebuffed, and snubbed at every turn,*

consider eating peyote and then walking, backward, with your eyes closed,
on a busy freeway . . .

Guy sits at a table in Señor Pico's, waiting for the Galtons to show, keenly aware that this is his last shot. He finally talked to Susan Rorvik after spending weeks chewing his nails down to the quick, and she explained that they needed to meet, to talk. He half expected her to stipulate someplace picturesquely subterranean, a cafeteria on lower Mission maybe, packed with bleak souls, fruitless lives, and botulism. He was pleasantly surprised when she suggested that they meet the next day at Aquatic Park.

By then all the hopeful rhetoric he'd peddled a year ago had turned into a psalm of maltreatment and neglect, the money I spent, the time I wasted, the risks I took.

He told her about his deeply disillusioning experiences with publishers.

He told her that *The Athletic Revolution* was going out of print and that he'd arranged to buy three thousand extant copies before they were pulped and have them shipped from a New Jersey warehouse to his place on the Upper West Side.

He told her how his landlord there wanted to evict him because he was running a business out of his apartment.

He told her that his mother was on the verge of a nervous breakdown and his father was reeling. Reeling.

He told her Randi was about to leave him.

He told her about the legroom problem on the flight from New York.

He told her that the Portland weather was causing a fungus to grow on his private parts.

Great talking to her, and he'd see her tomorrow.

The next day he waited for her at the edge of Fisherman's Wharf, eating clam chowder from a hollowed-out loaf of sourdough, wearing a Mets cap and a creased corduroy sports jacket with a folded newspaper stuffed into one of the pockets. He looked thin, tired, unshaven, grimy, travel-weary, like a man awakening from uneasy dreams at a YMCA or aboard a Trailways bus. He saw her approaching from the direction of the Wharf, cutely dressed in her waitress costume.

He'd done it. It had been fucking hard to get a decent hearing for a book proposal in the present environment; apparently the field of Symbionese Studies was rapidly growing very crowded. Quite an existing library had sprung up in the last year or so, and firsthand reflections didn't necessarily mean you'd cornered the market. They might have missed their moment. But he'd done it. He showed up, he sat down, he talked. He ate a lunch that required four separate forks. He pretended he'd read *Steal This Book*. He shared a cab with a man who rejected *Gravity's Rainbow*. There was interest. They'd definitely showed an interest.

They were walking through Fort Mason along a footpath on an embankment overlooking the enormous vacant docks and empty warehouse streets below when Susan had advised him that Teko had changed his mind about the book, again. Just a breezy whim that first blew him to one side of the issue and then back to the other? *The money I spent, the time I wasted.*

"What does he want to do then?"

"I sometimes think the only thing he really believes in is the revolution."

Oh, Jesus, please. Teko? Revolution? Come on. Had he sent Guy to Havana? Hanoi? The jungles of Central America? Is that where he'd wanted to make contact, establish relations? No, Guy had been dispatched to Rockefeller Center. Teko wanted what every kid snug under the blankets with his secret wishes wanted, the cover of *Rolling Stone*. If Guy lifted up that serving wench skirt, would he find Susan's head stuck up her ass? He actually reached for it, grabbed the material between thumb and forefinger. She snatched it away angrily.

He underhanded the hollow crust of bread down the embankment. It bounced and rolled. For whatever reason, he'd gotten hooked on the SLA: couldn't stop helping them, flaunting them, bragging about them, denying them, scolding them; trying to manipulate them, reform them, fold them into his peculiar reality. They'd seen it; they'd conned him, gotten more and more and just a little bit more out of him.

Susan kept the meeting short and sweet, wouldn't explain a thing. She said goodbye on the Marina Green, surrounded by people with Frisbees, dogs, and wicker picnic baskets. Overhead, a seaplane climbed, ungainly on its fat pontoons, astonishing as always.

Drove them himself. Laid out all that dough. Smashed up his

own car with a sledgehammer to get Allstate to pay for their trip home. Now they were jerking the last post out. He felt the vertigo of his sudden plunge.

Now he waits. While he does, he drinks two frozen margaritas. Actually, what he orders each time is a margarita and a shot of Cuervo, taking a head-throbbing slug from the frozen drink and then dumping the shot in to strengthen it. Well, so, this is how he's been feeling lately. A person is entitled. He has a drumming headache, he's extremely photosensitive these days, one of his kidneys is making him feel as if someone's hit him in the side with a baseball bat, his anterior cruciate ligament is on the cusp of saying "*¡adios!*" and his nose seems to be rotting from the inside out. In addition to which he's noticed that the angle at which his erection hangs from his naked body has increased markedly, from a taut twenty-five degrees to a droopy forty-five degrees.

In other words, Guy is exhausted. Again. Knowing what he knew, no sensible person would have touched the SLA again with a ten-foot pole, but Guy just couldn't lay off. Saw himself signing his name to a contract, saw fame, saw respect, saw another popeyed portrait leering out from the dust jacket of a book. Saw commercial potential harmoniously wedded to radical credibility. Saw six (*!*) figures (*!!*)—winged, already aloft, and heading out the window in the manner familiar to all readers of the funnies, though how the hell could he have known that? He himself flew hither, he flew yon, and when all was said and done, the undertaking was worthwhile even if it had come to naught. Because what is life if not an adventure? What is achieved if nothing is risked? Huh? Now all he has to do is convince himself of that, but first and foremost he is exhausted.

He sees them moving toward him through the dark and he rises, slightly unsteady on his feet. All he's had to eat are a couple of bowls of tortilla chips. Not a problem. The menu at Señor Pico's is so heavy with cheese, beans, and ground beef he'll have sopped up all the booze by the time they take the troughs away. This is his first eyeful of Lydia, and he sizes her up as she walks over. Sees the mom who'd give you a pretzel stick and a glass of tap water when you came over after school. The lady who knows the levels of all the bottles in the liquor cabinet, who knows offhand exactly how many crescent rolls are in the bread basket, who's been keeping an eye on things no less vigilantly than any old Amsterdam Avenue housewife leaning on a dirty pillow set up on a front room windowsill.

"Hello!" He waves.

Hank comes across as the same old hail-fellow-well-met type, but Lydia fixes Guy with her eyes and extends a hand in his direction as if there were a loaded .45 in it. So naturally he grabs it and gives it an eager yank like the slick little bastard she already thinks he is. (Of course, he and Tania had some pretty good chats about old Mom. Tania had used adjectives like suspicious, bigoted, selfish, rude, intolerant, self-righteous, narrow-minded, rigid, hidebound, authoritarian, punitive, and unforgiving. Sounded to Guy like a malignant version of the Scout Law.)

"Well, I have some good news," Guy begins. What's the good news? The usual hearsay, secondhand rumors, and idle gossip, combined with raw conjecture on his part. From what he has managed to learn, he infers that their daughter is feeling homesick and nostalgic. That the group is fragmenting. That its personal conflicts have started to become overwhelming. That ideologically the group makes less sense than ever. That a philosophical split has devolved into a dualism as simple as NO GURLS ALLOWED / BOYS KEEP OUT, so he's pretty certain that he'll be able to restore to the Galtons a young lady who is a feminist but not a Maoist.

Even to someone like Lydia, this has got to be a big distinction. Take your choice: You want a daughter who sticks a gun in a utility executive's face, or her pussy? "Eat me now, bourgeois man-pig!" It has a nice ring to it, no? Better than "Death to the Fascist Insect." You recuperate from cunnilingus. You definitely pull through. Though Guy has a feeling Lydia may disagree with him on this. But this is really all good news. She wants to see them. She misses them. OK, she hates everything they stand for, but as sentiments go, this is pretty standard issue nowadays. They can probably work around it.

But Guy doesn't articulate a word of this. His sense is that were he to utter a word such as *pussy* within the hearing of Lydia Galton, he would instantly transform into a wizened piece of rock, some pre-Cambrian formation, ancient and eternally silent. Plus, in the instant that he takes to gather his thoughts before plunging into his spiel, Lydia leans forward and addresses him.

"I want you to know that my husband places a great deal of faith in you. He is a very gullible man. I haven't seen anything to indicate that his faith is justified other than your assurances that you're in touch with our daughter and that she's all right. That would be the sum of it."

"I haven't got any reason to lie, Mrs. Galton."

"Oh, yes, you have. That's why I've come along to this event. Hank never will out and ask what it is that you want. But I won't hesitate. I've had a bellyful of you people over the last year and a half. You've each wanted something. You lecture us about how corrupt we are, and then you hold out your palm for our money. Now we haven't heard from you in three months, and suddenly you're in touch. Clearly you have something in mind."

"I just. More information has come to light."

"And what would you like in exchange for this information?"

"Lydia. Guy freely offered information to us last time."

"Isn't that how pushers work? The first time's always free?"

"Apparently you know more about that than I."

Guy gazes wistfully at the icy dregs in the bottom of his glass.

Lydia says, "Oh, don't pretend to be embarrassed. You don't have to put on a phony display of discomfiture."

"If he's embarrassed, it's because you've done your best to embarrass him."

"I think he's shameless."

"You've made that very clear. Why have you come?"

"Because you have always been the type to pick up strays, Hank. It's not enough that you give them a job or money, whatever it is they want. You have to offer them a share of our lives. That girl. Alice's friend from Crystal Springs."

"Oh, God, no. Not Betty Azizi again."

"Yes. That little Arab girl. Always at the house. Always picking things up. 'Oh, this is so beautiful.' Picking things up and turning them over in her hands. Searching for the price tag perhaps? Had nothing and wanted everything. Eyes lit up every time she came through the door."

"If I remember correctly, her father was a lawyer who worked for the Iranian consulate. Big house in the San Carlos hills."

"When they're that close, they want it even more. Especially an Arab."

"Um," says Guy. "Iranians aren't Arabs." The couple ignores him.

"Even Eric Stump," says Lydia. "You practically *adopted* him."

"No, I did not. I tried to make him feel at home. It's my nature to be friendly. How was I to know he would turn out to be such a cold mackerel?"

"Exactly." And Lydia raises that .45-caliber hand again and points directly at Guy's head. Nice well-bred lady like her, pointing.

"Look," says Guy, "I helped your daughter when she was in need. I'm still helping her."

"You call that helping her? If you'd wanted to help, you might have told her it was time to come home and face the music rather than arrange a summer retreat," says Lydia.

Guy experiences the strange lighted calm he used to feel just before a meet against an opponent he feared. He continues. "She thought the cops were going to off her. Not too farfetched at that point."

"As ye sow," says Lydia.

"That summer retreat cost me about eight grand, incidentally. I've spent a lot of money."

"Here it comes."

"I don't expect to see that dough again. But I could use a little help. I've got lawyer bills. I've got doctor bills. I've got phone bills like you wouldn't believe. I've got bills from auto mechanics. Bartenders." He essays a faint smile. He was going to say drug dealers. Joke falls flat anyway.

"Tsk, tsk. You may have heard that we made our own modest contribution to our daughter's Wanderjahr."

"Your daughter. Not my daughter. Listen. Hank here told me, and I quote, if there's ever anything I can do for you, be sure and let me know. I need a hand. Not a payoff. A job as a sportswriter for the *Examiner* maybe. A columnist working for a paycheck every week."

Lydia bursts out laughing, an awful, high-pitched laugh. Hank cringes.

Well, time for the chimichangas! Lydia has the taco salad, which she "picks at" in time-honored fashion. A pitcher of dark beer sits untouched before the couple. Guy orders another margarita, though he skips the Cuervo on the side. Lydia really fucked him, bringing up his motivations straightaway like that. Now he has to wade back in, deeper and deeper, reclaiming his position. What was it Hemingway said? Fly-fishing in the swamp is a tragic adventure? Lydia has his number, all right. Guy knows that Hank does too; the guy just doesn't give a damn. Not going to nickel-and-dime his kid's life at this point. Guy figures the best thing to do is to talk. He has nothing to lose giving up information. Or he does, but the thought of quantifying that loss makes his skull throb within the generous, taco-shaped space behind his forehead. So he goes ahead and says that Alice is thinking about leaving the group. That while it may not be practical for her to come aboveground, she'd like to be in touch with her family. That her urban guerrilla days are probably more or less over, that she and some of the others, the more normal others, have been talking in terms of a "small-scale revolution," and no, he doesn't really know what that means either, but he's heard snatches about local activism, community gardens, the Equal Rights Amendment, and food co-ops; about boycotts of table grapes, lettuce, tree fruit, and other agricultural products; about marijuana decriminalization, mandatory recycling, antinuclear protests, nonpartisan elections, handicapped parking spots, and other such issues. Lydia's expression is carved onto her face, and her ramrod posture does not slacken, but he can see Hank relax; who *wouldn't* want to hear that these are the keynote issues of the armed opposition? It's like being told that the editorial page staff of the *Village Voice* is massed outside the walls of the keep.

And, as Guy speaks, he considers how things have changed. War over, Nixon out, and all the wind basically went out of the sails of the Movement. Stands to reason that a zany little twerp like Drew Shepard would be the last man on deck.

Not to mention that every young grease monkey, factory worker, and warehouseman now was as hirsute as, now was taking the same drugs as, now was listening to the same sort of music as every hippie, radical, and hanger-on from Bloomfield Hills, Brentwood, and Great Neck. Even the cops had mustaches and long hair. The sixties had finally arrived in the prefab dells and factory barrens and methedrine parishes of hamburger America; the People had been won over after all. Suddenly the Left felt the fear, seized up with those old class prejudices; it was all well and good to *feel bad* for the snaggle-toothed trailer kid, the guy who mixed the paint at the hardware store, the jokester squeegeeing your windshield at the Union 76, but it was something else to share your blanket and weed with them at the festival, to have them sticking their big uncircumcised pricks into your women, to suffer their ineducability, their ignorance, their dinner conversation. These were *the People*? No, no, no, no, no: the People were black and brown and red and yellow, a beautiful smeary rainbow with a pot of moral indignation at its end. The People were beautiful. They wore cardboard shoes and ate cakes made of newspapers when they hungered. They migrated from one oppressive job to another. They were raised in shacks or in cinder-block slums. They were subdued by heroin and malt liquor. They were incarcerated unjustly in Amerikkkan concentration camps, where they painstakingly taught themselves to read, to write, to study. They weren't these louts from Kalamazoo and Pomona and Queens, with their muscle cars and their Bachman-Turner Overdrive eight-tracks. What had failed to transcend race and age had managed, to an extent, to transcend class, and the Left was uninterested. The Left had gone to the disco.

I See Phantoms of Hatred and of the Heart's Fullness and of the Coming Emptiness.

And here, thinks Guy, comes the end point of the Movement. For all the talk—about the minority this, about the false that, about the bourgeois this, about the Marx's that, for *all* the endless talk—the only thing that had been successfully accomplished was the carving out of another bourgeois role. And to play that part, you needed money. He acknowledges. Sadly. He's laying it on thick for Mr. and Mrs. Mom and Dad here at the Mexican restaurant, making a play for his grubstake. Does Tania really want to be dealt out of the game? He thinks maybe she does. Running gets you down. Tires out your eyes, your neck, your jaw. Uses up cash. Depletes your body of B vitamins. Shrinks your dick. Had she really wanted to cause the downfall of the U.S. government? Hadn't that already happened without her? Happened in committee rooms while they were playing popgun in the woods? Now it's business as usual, with the blandest of all possible alternatives in charge. If she wants out, it's either boredom, fear, or a complete understanding of the magnitude of the task they face, if they're really serious about the whole thing. But who really is "serious"? Everyone admires the Vietcong, loves those courageous little bastards to death, but who the fuck is prepared to spend a thousand years fighting, waging war against an army that brings Coke machines and cases of cigarettes and whiskey into the field with it? Around you everywhere you look are things you wouldn't dream of doing without, not for a month, not for a *day*, notwithstanding the premeditated squalor demanded by Cinque

Mtume, the Fifth Prophet. It's the psychos, the Tekos and Yolandas, who set the example of austere self-denial. Guy grimaces, sticks a fork into the friable surface of his chimichanga. Suddenly all he can smell is fat, fat and old cooking oil.

"I'd need," he says, "to be able to go to her and say that you were willing to make a significant good-faith gesture."

"More significant than picking up the tab for every deadbeat in the state with a brood of kids to feed?"

"Shhh," says Hank.

"I'm not talking about money."

"I keep hearing you say that, but I'll believe it when you walk away with nothing for your troubles."

"Please don't change the subject," says Hank.

"I mean more like go to her with a political good-faith gesture."

"More political than giving up control of our front page?"

"Shhh," says Hank.

"Like you quitting the UC Board of Regents," Guy says calmly to Lydia.

"What?"

"It couldn't hurt," says Hank.

"I won't. I won't be bullied. We've been over this."

"OK," says Guy. "It's your decision. Let me just say that your being on the board is an irritant. I mean, it doesn't help. I won't even go into your actions as a member."

Someone once fired a rifle bullet into the limousine Lydia was riding in. Tore through the rear fender just behind her and flattened out like a ball of clay dropped from a height. Designed to separate her body into a variety of unexpected segments. The woman had remained undaunted.

"Go right ahead."

"No, I'm literally not arguing. It's your call. Let me just say that it's important to your daughter that if she comes out, she does it without compromising her political viability. She needs to be able to maneuver in the Left. It's important to her and to everyone." Especially Guy. Because without Tania's viability, what would become of his own? He doesn't want any dumdums heading his way.

"Oh, so that she can continue with her asinine politics I have to abandon my own?"

"That's a good way of putting it."

Guy feels pretty good. Nice recovery. It's no skin off his nose whether Tania visits her parents at Thanksgiving or not. Sits under the gleaming tree, tearing open presents. Whatever the sacred daydream is. They talk for a while longer. He senses that some sort of accommodation is going to be made. Sweet, sweet relief. In a grand gesture, he takes a paper napkin and writes a number on it. He doesn't know it's going to say twenty thousand dollars until he begins writing. Does some rapacious Ouija spirit guide his hand to form the figure? He pushes the napkin over to Hank.

"Look, I'm not *asking* for anything. But this is just so you know. That is all out of pocket."

Guy goes to the men's room, where he lays the most gigantic log he believes he's ever produced. It does not have a healthy look to it, or a healthy feel coming out, either. He struggles, briefly and distressingly unsuccessfully, to remember what he ate for dinner the night before. When Guy was growing up, there was a kid, Carl Harrigan, who would call you into the bathroom to look at his turds. Gigantic shits were his specialty, his contribution to neighborhood lore. It was both fascinating and deeply embarrassing. Kids would rush in—everybody was always at everybody else's house—to group around the toilet, gazing down at the monstrosity, coiled around the inside of the bowl or half concealed in the hole, like a sullen and dangerous animal in its burrow. Carl would linger over it, babbling praise, reluctant to flush his impressive creation. The things you think of.

After Mock and the Galtons leave, Nietfeldt remains at his table at Señor Pico, working away at a seafood burrito. File it under Seemed like a Good Idea at the Time. After each bite he pauses to consider the thing, until it becomes a gelid mass on his plate, inedible. He pays the check and heads back downtown.

He can't quite figure it. As near as he can make out, Hank and Lydia are very close to establishing contact with their daughter through Mock, but there doesn't appear to be any happy accord. Hank's looking out for his daughter, but for reasons that aren't clear, Lydia is ready to put the kid through the wringer. Who knows why? It occurs to him that it might be a good idea to talk to the Galtons, separately, to remind them of the penalties they face if they attempt to shield their daughter from justice. Hank will brush them off, but

Lydia is likely to be considerably more forthcoming. She's not interested in shielding Alice from shit, doesn't care whether the kid's in custody the next time she sees her.

That's an approach he knows Polhaus will go for, but the sixty-four-dollar question is, Does Lydia actually have any useful information to provide? Nothing Nietfeldt's seen so far has led him to conclude that Mock is in any kind of regular contact with the fugitives. Could be he's stringing the Galtons along. Might be a nice chunk of change for the man who steers things to a storybook conclusion. But all Mock's been seen doing is talking to the Rorvik girl and that's about it. Flew to New York to try to pitch an SLA book at some publishers, but that was a fairly predictable development, boring if not incriminating.

Curiously, Polhaus hasn't ordered any kind of surveillance at all on the Rorviks or Jeff Wolfritz. An FBI camera crew was dispatched to the thing at Ho Chi Minh Park, and that was that. Rounding out the file. It was just kind of assumed after Susan's speech had been broadcast all over the country that they were too hot, too obvious, for the SLA to come near them. It strikes him that in overlooking the obvious, they may have fucked up royally. Rorvik makes for a nice link in the chain: SLA to Atwood, Atwood to Rorvik, Rorvik to Mock, Mock to SLA. He examines the photographs taken that day last June. The girl from Palmdale, latitude 34.5523°N, longitude 118.0709°W, elevation 2780. Yearbook editor, pep chairman, Girl Scout counselor. Another nice girl who didn't know what she was talking about, pointing fingers, making a fuss. He makes a mental note to begin a background check tomorrow.

OF COURSE I DID, Hank. You are holding a newspaper in my face, shaking it and asking whether I really said those things, and you know that I did. For how long did you think that I would allow you to humiliate us? To sneak around like somebody with something to hide? To lie to the Federal Bureau of Investigation? You never could dance; years ago you were smart enough not to try. Drove your custard-colored Fiat and put a flower in your lapel and swept every girl off her feet, but you knew you couldn't do much with your own. And *now* you're trying, and it is just pathetic.

You always used to know your limitations.

Every day that this continues I feel another part of myself die. You have been laughing at me for years, saying that my propriety is old-fashioned and disproportionate. But for me there's never been anything else. Your family always got its neon charge from its taste for notoriety. Didn't matter what your name was actually worth or where the celebrity had come from. But *we* had nothing but our good name. Our good name and an old house. My mother taught me that I had to hold tight to anything I had that was worth anything. When we married, I thought I could do something for you. Poor fellow whose father disgraces his entire family, taking up with an actress. Entertaining Hollywood fools on the high seas. Building a castle and filling it with gaudy junk, like a Jew. I thought I could do something for you! You said I was your angel. That was what we both wanted.

But it all caught up with us. Your daughter makes your father look like a Benedictine. Bad to worse. I should have known back when the nuns said they couldn't do anything with her. I should have told them: Then do nothing, and both of you endure it. Because that is the business they're in. Cast the spirit, inhibit the flesh. Teach each its place. But I listened to you. You listened to her, and I listened to you. Let her go to day school. Let her pick where. If I had only looked, I would have seen where it was all leading. So would you. Maybe you did. Now you think you can do what you've always done. Accommodate the circumstances, find "another situation" for her. Not this time. There is no other situation.

She stopped belonging to us long ago. That's no surprise. We've both known it. I knew all about the boys. You think I am rigid and severe, but I have made my concessions to the times. I don't brag, or complain. I listen to the others at the country club, and that is their response to their lives. They valorize the concessions they make or they protest them publicly. But I never have. Even when Stump appeared, I said this is how things are done now. Thinking, How unhappy do I have to become in order to be contemporary? Because it seems to me that in order to accept the contemporary, one has to spend a lot of time pretending, and what one mostly pretends is that one is numbly satisfied with every idiotic alternative that society proffers. So I know that she no longer belongs to us.

But now she belongs to everyone. People *draw* her, did you know that? I mean they *draw pictures*, like kindergarten children. They just have to draw their favorite photographs of her! I was down at Stanford last week, and there they were, all over White Plaza and the Old Quad. Stanford! Some very poor draftsman had put ink to paper and copied that photo of her with the gun, in those baggy, ugly coveralls. What could that be about, when you actually have the photograph and you need to draw it anyway, to work its contours under your hand? What I think is, I think they are trying to take some of her for themselves or to put something of themselves in her. Some of them are *our* photographs, you know. They came right out of our album. I gave them up with misgivings. You thought it would help. They belong to them now. She belongs to them now.

Day after day in the newspapers, on the television. You lose something. You become a reflection, all detail and very little depth. It's as if she's in a trance, the glowing replica of every living soul's fears and wishes, mute and impenetrable. In tracing those pictures, they trace her, like forming the sign of the cross. She is exactly what they say she is. When her presence no longer is required on the television and in the papers, the day she stops, perhaps she will have come to herself. But I know that the girl she comes to won't be the one we knew. And you want her back. Believe me, I understand you. But what I believe is that if you were to think clearly about it all for a minute, you'd see that she'll never come back. She can sit on this sofa beside us, she can sleep on the bed in the spare room, she can scrape her plate into the garbage pail, and to me it won't be her here. People think I can't be hurt, but I am. I am hurt down to the marrow. And I am not letting you give her another out.

Take that newspaper, Hank, and put it down. Yes, I talked to the FBI. They came to me, and I told them exactly what I knew about Guy Mock, what he'd proposed. And then I told the *Los Angeles Times*. And they printed it, on a bright Sunday morning. For once *she* can hear through the press what *I* have to say. About her and her friends. She can try to guess what we know and how close we are. She can wonder which of the people she has to deal with are trustworthy and which are trying to take advantage of her. Guy Mock is hopping mad? Well, I hope so. I hope that this ends it with Guy Mock. You don't even notice it anymore, Hank, how it is to have to contend with slippery little nobodys like Guy Mock. I know how she felt in that closet, the world reduced to the little rectangle of light that occurred whenever someone opened the door. Guy Mock, the psychics, the radicals, the FBI: They all come around to present their magic lantern show. Each of them shows up to give us his particular version of the rectangle. And now they're just part of your life. But they're not supposed to be part of our lives. Well, Guy Mock won't be. He promised you something that you know deep down he couldn't deliver. That girl is in trouble. There is no avoiding it. You can't save her from what she's brought upon herself. He thought we would be his meal ticket, but I've cut him off. And they—she and the rest of them—they'll never let him get close to them again.

I'm sorry if that spoils the reunion. No, I'm not sorry. Talk about divorce if you really like, if you think that these are sufficient grounds. But I truly believe that we do not have to pay for what she's done. She has to pay. You can't save her. And now I've proven it. Our negotiations with Mock are over? You've missed the point all the way through. It's the negotiations with our daughter that are over. If you'd use the good sense God gave you, you'd see that's what she's doing. Playing games because she can. That's the whole point of this revolution of hers. Send a nobody to try to collect twenty thousand dollars in exchange for a telephone call or quick visit. Well, I'm on to them. Guy Mock overplayed his hand.

And I'm not quitting the damned Board of Regents either.

SARA JANE MOORE HAS a grilled cheese sandwich, coleslaw, and a 7-Up arrayed in front of her on a flattened brown paper bag. See, the problem is that white bread grills faster than wheat. There are added sugars in the white bread, reason enough to avoid it, and so it causes the bread to brown quickly. It's a fact of nature, a process named caramelization that she learned about during one of the many desultory and unfocused stretches she's served, this one at an institution called the Western States Culinary Academy. So the cheese is barely melted when they remove it from the grill, see? She phoned in the order, stipulating wheat. Made the man read it back to her: wheat. The sandwich is delivered to the office where she's temping as a general ledger accountant. White.

She's looking at a copy of *Silver Screen* that the girl she's replacing for two weeks left behind. On Sara Jane's first day, the girl had sort of shown her around the desk. "Training her," as she put it. She'd introduced her to her collection of stuffed animals perched and roosted here and there on her desk and in the empty spaces of her bookshelf, making the introductions with solemn formality. "This is Sir Jenkins," she'd said, "this here is Daisy."

She's reading about The Tragic Truth Behind Peter Duel's Suicide. "He was an actor on the way up, with money in the bank and his clean-cut cowboy image in just about every young girl's heart." Sara Jane doesn't really remember the young man's show, *Alias Smith and Jones*. Happy western buddy-buddy stuff, men patting the hindquarters of horses?

Lois Kane of *Silver Screen* just doesn't understand what could lead such a young man to shoot himself. The roots of his mad act simply are not visible. To Sara Jane this is hardly a matter of mystery of the week. It is so easy to feel hemmed in, unappreciated, underutilized, taken for granted.

The young man was crazy about ecology and hated pollution. "He would not use plastic cups on the set—only glass ones. He would not use anything that would not dissolve and go back into the earth."

Sara Jane tosses the sandwich into the wastepaper basket. She speculates that the young man probably felt that he'd thrown in his lot with the wrong people. It can be a very difficult situation. Someone seems to want you, to need you, and it is natural for a warm and friendly person to respond to that in kind. And then you find out it was all a put-on.

Speaking of guns, Sara Jane has one right here. She's been carrying it in her purse lately. She hasn't needed it so far but you never know. People are still mad about Popeye. But he had put her on. Thomas Polhaus had put her on. But you needed protection.

Five minutes later she's on the street, getting into her car. Mrs. McCarthy had sneaked up behind her, Do you need something to do, Are you looking for something to do. If you need something to do just speak right up. Whatever she'd said. Office manager drivel.

Speak right up. "Train" her. Like she is a spaniel or hound, begging for dinner table scraps.

Just looking at that gun gave her the courage, the nerve, to tell that McCarthy bitch off and walk out, past all the dumb faces of those drones working there. She forgot to get her time card signed, but that's OK. The gun makes her feel better about that too. Money becomes so abstract, the nitpicky refuge of the chickenhearted, at the uplifting sight of a gun, its pure power to convert whatever you need or desire into something you actually have.

NIETFELDT HAS A ONE-BEDROOM apartment on Lupine, a little spur off Geary. The building is built into the side of a hill, so that his third-floor apartment is reached by entering the building's lobby and walking down a flight. The whole building is low ceilings, long corridors, right angles, dark corners, and the thin institutional smell of ammonia. Utterly claustrophobic.

Gradually he's turned into one of those men with great bundles of dirty laundry piled in the corners, leftover pizza in the refrigerator, old newspapers on top of the stove. For someone else the rooms would be a rebuke, the embodiment of his seclusion, the measure of his digression from the norm, but for him this is the norm. So his wives had discovered. Anything else would be cosmetic, a disguise. Still, he avoids the apartment as much as he can. Checks in long enough to get the mail, put it on the table.

Tonight he takes the time to open a beer and have another look at Joan Shimada's file. Here's a new wrinkle. Susan Rorvik's logged eight trips to Soledad over the last three years for the purpose of visiting William Clay, Joan Shimada's former lover and comrade-in-arms. He finds that in the Shimada file, right in front of his face all this time. If that were the only connection between Susan and Joan, Nietfeldt wouldn't be all that impressed; a steady stream of pilgrims from the East Bay have gone to call on Willie Clay. What has impressed him is the discovery that working side by side at the Plate of Brasse with "Susan Anger" is a certain Meg Speice. Speice is a Jersey girl who was a dead end in the Shimada investigation three years ago. She admitted then that she and Joan were friends but that Joan had long since gone on her way and she hadn't seen or heard from her. No reason to think Speice was lying in 1972. But now she pops up here in San Francisco right around when the summer hidey-hole had to have been abandoned, working side by side with a known SLA sympathizer with links to Guy Mock. His chain is looking longer and stronger.

He has the vague feeling that he'll regret it, but what he needs is to have an agent in Southern California head out to Palmdale to pay the Rorviks a visit. He could go himself, but Gary Haff was extrasensitive about getting his toes stepped on. Brilliant work he'd done on the case last May. Just brilliant.

Summer Chronicle

The women's collective meets, possibly for the last time as such. The members have decided to set aside their work for the time being to pursue more absolutely the goal of revolution, in keeping with Teko's intense desire to begin blowing things up.

On the agenda is the matter of prostitution. They are attempting to decide if sexual entrepreneurialism is liberating, oppressive, or simply retrograde. Tania, "troop scribe," as Joan has dubbed her, jots down the minutes.

Susan suggests that a woman who is in business for herself, who controls the means of production, is more correct, politically, than one who's been turned out by a pimp. Cf. her own experience as an actress v. her experience waiting tables; oh there are some quite long reminiscences.

Joan speculates that in the socialist or barter economy that might exist in an emerging postrevolutionary state, such "entrepreneurs" might then be politically obliged to stop seeking payment for their services and thus be placed in a position of slavery all over again, trading sexual favors for subsistence. She seems to enjoy lobbing such near paradoxes into their midst.

Yolanda says that all sex workers will receive training in the manual art of their choice, be it auto repair, locksmithing, air conditioning and refrigeration, or computer programming.

At some point they agree that all men are pimps. In theory. Meeting adjourned.

Tania sits on the floor in her panties, topless. She leans against the couch, her legs extended under the scarred coffee table. Her paint-spattered clothes are piled on the floor. She feels grimy, bone tired:

465

two units today, at a complex up in Diamond Heights, a mixed neighborhood as they say, with black families trudging home from the Safeway, laden with grocery bags, beneath clean modern houses built into the bluffs overlooking the city. She'd felt safe enough venturing out, but the landlord, a friendly old guy with a limp, someone's good grampa, had brought them lunch and then stuck around to argue good-naturedly with Roger, Giants versus Dodgers stuff, so she'd withdrawn from sight, actually putting in a day's work, finishing off the first unit in the hot bare sun streaming through the western windows and then doing the hated bathroom of the second. In a daze of ennui and fatigue, she sits holding an unlit cigarette in one hand and a paperback book in the other, staring blankly at one smudge among many on the wall.

The book is *The Collective Family: A Handbook for Russian Parents*. Teko found it while prowling around Moe's—a stupid move, his going there; Tania doesn't even want to know if he pocketed it—and he presented it to her casually one day, almost like a joke, after Tania had mentioned offhandedly that she wanted children eventually.

"This here's like the Soviet Dr. Spock," he said.

As she might have known, whereas someone normal might expect a thank-you note, what Teko requires is a full report on A. S. Makarenko's tome, and she has barely cracked its spine.

Makarenko says, "Such parents never command discipline. Their children are simply afraid of them and try to live out of range of their authority and power."

Fuck Teko. She gets up and walks into the dark kitchen to drink cold milk out of the container, standing in the light of the fridge.

She returns to the living room and flips on the Philco, stands watching, right hip jutting out and her weight resting on her left leg, as the old set warms and the image spreads gradually across the surface of the picture tube. And here's the Miss Universe pageant. The girls strut their stuff down the runway in the ballroom of the National Gymnasium in San Salvador, each of these hardworking beauty queens appearing in what Tania gathers is traditional native garb. Misses Sri Lanka, Sweden, Switzerland, Thailand, Trinidad and Tobago, Turkey, Uruguay. Bob Barker's narration of the procession skillfully combines both veiled lecherousness and false reverence for the honored customs each elaborate outfit represents. "Miss USA," he announces casually. But wait. The pretty brunette sauntering across the screen appears to be wearing combat fatigues, a beret, and an automatic rifle. She arrives at the edge of the stage, like all the milkmaids, priestesses, and native dancers going before her, and, flashing a gorgeous smile to acknowledge the sustained applause that has greeted her appearance, lifts the weapon to her hip, and trains it on the members of the audience, swinging slowly to the right and then to the left, as she might if she were to clear the room, firing full auto.

Tania watches the pageant until the end. Miss USA ends up coming in third, behind the first runner-up, Miss Haiti, and the winner, Miss Finland. She is named Miss Photogenic, having tied with Martha Echeverry of Colombia for the honor.

They're sitting in traffic one day, Teko and Jeff up front, Tania and Susan in back, the car like an oven, when Jeff and Teko begin to argue, then fight. They slap and shove each other across the sticky front seat, breathing hard, pausing for a moment so that Teko can throw the car into park. They struggle, aiming shots carefully across the short distance separating them, covering up, panting in the swelter, in the blare of horns.

More movies:

She sees *Dark Star* (isolated outer space explorers become bored, cynical, and out of touch with the original purpose of their mission, living only to wreak violence while arguing endlessly among themselves).

She sees *The Stepford Wives* (women who resist the stifling conformity demanded by their small town and the patriarchal group that runs it are replaced with compliant replicas).

Jeff Wolfritz brings an old friend around, a white man doing grad work in Afro-American Studies at Berkeley, the idea being for them to submit themselves to the guy's scrutiny, become the subject of his fieldwork. But the man is perplexed and piqued. *Where are my black people?* he demands. The answer is, Hang on, any minute now. We're doing the best we can.*

. . .

---

*Ultimately the man's dissertation is published under the title *Revolutionary Minstrels: White Appropriation of Black Oratory in Postwar American Radical Rhetoric.*

After going early one morning to firebomb the house of the day's fascist, a construction company executive (the bombs, which explode at dawn, destroy a small greenhouse and kill a cat), Tania and Roger take a drive down Highway 1. It's a brilliant day, the ocean sparkling below them, and they stop at Montara, sit on rocks overlooking the tidal pools, hold hands. Sweet Roger. A group of children, bundled up in sweatshirts and windbreakers, plays on the beach. Their parents, huddled on wind-ruffled blankets, watch benignly as the children pretend to shoot one another and to be shot, rolling on the sand in extravagantly enacted death throes. One of the kids, fresh out of murder victims, rushes up to them.

"Pougghhhh!" he says, pointing a reasonable facsimile of a snubnose revolver at them.

"Pow!" says Roger, who carries an automatic concealed in a camera case.

"You're dead," says the boy. There's no heat to the remark, only a simple statement of fact. He stares at Roger, the snubnose held at his side, and Roger obliges him by toppling over into the sand.

"You killed him!" says Tania. She kneels and turns Roger over. He doesn't move a muscle, doesn't crack a smile. A thin dusting of sand coats his cheek and lips. "You've killed my husband!" She takes a crack at keening.

The boy, alert to the wit involved, cautious about becoming the butt of the joke, takes a wary step forward to examine Roger's immobile form up close. This is something you want to check out. Tania recalls the childish thrill of playing so hard, pretending something so intensely, that you just about believe it if all the cards fall right, if everybody cooperates, your stupid friends don't mess it up, call time, screw you out of the climax that is your due. Here comes the kid's mom, looking halfway curious, halfway concerned.

"What's going on here? Michael?"

She's about thirty-two, wears black toreador pants greenish with age, a San Jose State sweatshirt, and sunglasses. Her hair is tied back in a scarf. She sips something from a Styrofoam cup.

"Don't bother this man and lady," she says.

Roger opens his eyes and sits up, brushing sand from his face. "It's OK. We were just—"

"He was dead!" the boy screams, outraged at Roger's resurrection. "You're dead! I killed you!"

He runs to join the other kids in his group.

"I'm sorry," the mother says. "I don't want him to play with guns, but he wouldn't let up. The others. Look at them all! I'm so sorry." She seems as distressed as if Roger really had been shot.

"It's OK," says Roger.

"It really isn't," she says.

"I didn't mind."

"It's *not* OK." She says it sharply this time and leaves.

Blowing things up becomes just another job. A routine is established. A workaday mood prevails. Owing to her past experience with Willie Clay's Revolutionary Army, Joan is drafted as explosives expert. She's a little rusty. Some of her bombs blow up; some don't.

The actions are incoherent, like punctuating their rambling argument against the system with inarticulate screeches. A partial catalog of them is gnomic, imperspicuous:

> GMC, San Jose
> Pillar Point Air Force Radar Station
> Vulcan Foundry, Oakland
> KRON-TV, San Francisco
> PG&E transmission towers, Oakland
> PG&E substation, San Jose
> PG&E installation, Sacramento
> California DOC parole office, Sacramento
> PG&E office building, Berkeley
> Prison Guards' Rifle Range, San Quentin
> Bureau of Indian Affairs, Alameda
> SFPD Mission Station
> SFPD Taraval Station
> Emeryville Police Station
> Marin County Civic Center

They cram the bombings in amid continuing quarrels over strategy, philosophy, politics, over ever-keener edges of extremism that need to be explored, rejected, studied. The most persistent arguments have to do with revolutionary violence—i.e., "armed propaganda" versus murder, assassination, etc.—and black leadership, that enduring problem. Teko insists that they are mere stewards of the Black Revolution.

"And you're the stewardess, right?" Joan asks Yolanda.

Yolanda lectures her. "You need to take this more seriously, Joan. You're the one who's refusing the moral responsibility of assuming minority leadership. You."

The new development in the evolution of Teko's revolutionary thought? He's decided that only the members of a certain enlightened class of white—such as, say, himself—may participate in the class struggle. Other whites are worse than useless. Teko would simply put them up against the courtyard wall. Anyone exhibiting counterrevolutionary tendencies at any time would be eligible for such therapy.

"These aren't terms you can present," says Susan.

"I just presented them."

"You can't win this way. Nothing'll change."

"It's got to be this way."

"Teko, you're not black."

"I feel like, in many respects, I am black."

" 'Woman is the nigger of the world,' " adds Yolanda.

Joan takes Tania aside. "Now's the time, hon."

Tania's eyes widen; a smile spreads across her face. "Boston?"

"One step at a time. Out of here, for sure. This is final craziness. This is some sort of political puritism, not revolution."

"I didn't think you cared about revolution," says Tania.

Joan gestures dismissively. "It's all crap. The point is if Teko's only interested in offing white people, then what's left but dying? I mean serious martyr stuff. Even on the farm I was like screw that. But we're here now, not out in some boondock. Pigs all around. Now I can understand what happened in L.A. That Cin-Q must have been some sweet talker, because I really think they died on his say-so. It dawns on me now that this fight to the death idea is the *plan*. No revolution, only suicide."

"THE GIRL HAS SHOULDER-LENGTH blond hair."

"Yes?" Rose Rorvik held a plastic laundry basket under her left arm and drew on the cigarette in her right hand.

"Lives in the Bay Area, with her boyfriend. Works as a waitress."

"Ah?"

"Tell me if this sounds familiar: 'Brings to the cloistered Nell a sort of irascible verve, making of her senile ramblings at Nagg lucid poetic sense.'"

That, she had no idea what he was talking about.

"Does any of this remind you of anyone you know?"

The two men stood on the porch, sweating beneath their suits in the August heat.

"Yes."

"How about this? Does this sound like something you might have heard before? 'Keep fighting! I'm with you! We're with you!'" The man tried to restrain a malicious smile as he raised his right fist, a decidedly stunted little flourish, like a Nixon wave. His jacket was dark with sweat at the armpit.

"Yes, it does."

"Tell me, has anyone told you not to talk to Agent Toomes or myself?"

"Who would've told me that?"

"This person we're discussing."

Rose drew on the cigarette and flicked the ash before it got too long and fell into her clean wash. She'd been going to hang it up outside when these two men drove up. She liked the smell of clothes that had dried on a line.

"You'd better wait for my husband."

"Oh, your husband knows the story."

"*She* doesn't know the story."

"The husband knows."

"A girl who talks to her father, Manhardt. But not her mother."

"Very, very odd, Toomes."

"In my experience the girls talk to their mothers."

"Not in mine," said Rose, as breezily as she could manage.

Howard's car pulled into the driveway then and Rose set the basket of laundry on the porch and went down the steps and up the

walk to meet him. He looked curiously at the men but seemed un-
perturbed as he went around to open the trunk and remove a bag of
golf clubs from it. It didn't help that he was dressed like an idiot, in
a lemon chiffon shirt, buff and orange plaid slacks, and white patent
leather shoes.

"They're from the FBI," she told him.

His face just hung there, drained of anything but its own blank
astonishment, like the moon in a play for children.

"They're asking about Susan," she said in a low tone. "But they
won't *say* anything."

"OK." He hoisted the bag of clubs onto his shoulder and began
down the walk. "Howard Rorvik." He extended a hand toward the
nearest man, Toomes. Toomes glanced briefly at Manhardt, then
took it.

"We'd like to talk to you, Mr. Rorvik."

"About my daughter, yes. Come inside."

"That's the subject, is it?"

"So my wife tells me, yes."

"Is that right?" Toomes smiled.

It was cool and dim inside the house. Rose offered the FBI men
something to drink and was thankful when they declined.

"I'll get to the point, Mr. Rorvik. We're looking for your daughter. In fact, we're trying to find both your daughter and your
nephew."

"How can that be? They're right there."

"Right where, Mr. Rorvik?"

"Why, living together. They all live together along with Susan's
boyfriend and God knows who else up in San Francisco. You know
how things are these days."

"If you say so. And exactly where would that be?"

"Someplace downtown. Let me double-check." He got up and
went into the den, where in one of the cubbies of an old secretary he
found a letter. He came out wagging it.

"Let me guess," said Manhardt. "Six Two Five Post Street."

"So you do know where she is."

"I know where Industrial Photo Products, Inc. is. That's what's at
Six Two Five Post."

"I don't understand."

"No one lives at Six Two Five Post. Here's something else I'll bet you didn't know. Your daughter has been working under an assumed name. Susan Anger."

"Fiery!" said Toomes, smirking.

"Now tell me," continued Manhardt. "Why would perfectly nice, law-abiding kids start lying to their folks, assuming fake names, using mail drops, and suddenly disappearing?"

"I don't know."

"They must be the only people in town," said Toomes.

"They must be the only people in the entire state. You didn't hear out here in Palmdale about your daughter's little rally for the Symbionese Liberation Army?"

"Oh, that. She and Angela Atwood were very close friends. I think she was just hurting after Angela died."

"Ever heard of the Bay Area Research Collective?"

"Can't say I have."

"It's your daughter and a group of other very close friends. Dedicated to publishing and disseminating left-wing revolutionary propaganda. You didn't know about that, did you?"

"No. No, I didn't."

"Not your sort of reading material." Manhardt glanced at the coffee table. *Life, Time, TV Guide, Shōgun.*

"No."

"So you'd agree there are some things about your children that you don't know?"

"Apparently so."

Manhardt said, "We'd like to talk to your daughter about a friend of hers. Has she ever mentioned a Guy Mock?"

"Jeff's sportswriter friend," said Rose.

"That's right. Very good." Manhardt said this in a nasty way that made Rose want to spit in his eye. He continued. "How about Joan Shimada? Your daughter ever mention her?"

"Joan . . . ?"

"Shimada. An Oriental girl. Japanese."

"I think maybe."

"She would have stood out, wouldn't she?" asked Toomes. "You were a fighter pilot, weren't you, Mr. Rorvik? Which theater?"

"Pacific," said Howard.

"Ahhh so," said Toomes.

"Didn't I read about her in connection with Alice Galton? And Mock too?"

"You might have seen their names," said Manhardt.

"Joan Shimada spent last summer with Alice Galton, we think," said Toomes. "Shortly after your daughter Susan was pledging allegiance to the SLA in Ho Chi Minh Park, so called. Shimada spent her time in a house in Pennsylvania that was rented by your daughter's friend Guy Mock. After that we lose her trail. Turns out she has a friend in San Francisco."

"Not just any friend," added Manhardt.

"No. *This* friend arrived from the East Coast right around when Joan Shimada's trail vanishes. Her name is Meg Speice. And guess what? Meg Speice and Susan Anger happen to work the very same shift at the Plate of Brasse. Isn't that an interesting coincidence?"

"What else do you expect me to make of it?" said Howard.

Rose said, "We're not even sure Susan knows this girl, Shimada."

"We are," said Toomes, brightly.

"Do you want to hear something even more interesting? Your daughter's paid a few visits to a friend in Soledad."

"Soledad," echoed Toomes.

"There's a state penitentiary there," said Manhardt. "The man she's been to visit lives in it. He's named Willie Clay."

"Your daughter ever mention this man?"

Howard and Rose both shook their heads.

"Clay got busted a few years ago for running a bomb factory out of a Berkeley garage," continued Manhardt. "He was head of a group called the Revolutionary Army."

"Catchy," said Toomes.

"Your daughter ever mention this outfit?"

Howard and Rose both shook their heads.

"Thing is, Clay was working with a few associates. Two were caught. The other is at large."

"That would be Joan Shimada," said Toomes.

"Your daughter's friend Guy Mock's friend. Your daughter's colleague Meg Speice's friend. A woman who spent two months last year with the fugitives your daughter publicly swore allegiance to. See? There's a pattern."

"You want to talk to your daughter and nephew, Mr. Rorvik.

474

You want to fly up to Frisco and try and talk some sense into them."

"How would I do that if this address is a fake?"

"Oh, someone there's passing on the letters. A friend."

"A fellow traveler."

"A dupe. Who knows? Would we bumble in there with a bunch of stupid questions and scare them off? Send a note today and tell them you'll be there on, say, Friday."

"Look at that face," said Toomes.

"The Bureau will *pay* your expenses, Mr. Rorvik."

"You want me to pump the kids for information. Find them for you so you can follow them."

"They'll thank you for it later," said Toomes.

"We'll put you up at the Hilton. You'll buy some sourdough bread, ride the cable cars, toss some change at a mime. Take the whole weekend. A working vacation."

"Everybody loves Frisco."

"Write the note today and we'll be back tomorrow with your plane ticket. All right?"

"All right," said Howard.

Howard couldn't get over the dog manure. Everywhere you looked on Post Street it was Dog Dropping Heaven. Somehow he'd managed to avoid stepping in all but one ripe turd, but that was a beaut. He had to hang on to a lamppost while he scraped the sole of his shoe against the curb. He did this delicately, a little tentatively, as though in ridding himself of this ordure he might offend some sense of propriety that existed among the natives here, a blighted pride in their specific metropolitan disfigurement that they might assert, defending it against the judgmental gaze of an outsider. But they just ignored Howard, wobbled by. Definitely high on something. Howard had taught high school long enough to recognize intoxicated kids, though these weren't kids and this clearly was not a matter of Testor's glue in a paper bag or a few beers. This drug usage was not recreational; it was a matter of life and death. The possibility that it wasn't dog crap underfoot briefly occurred to him.

How could the kids live like this? Susan had always been the most fastidious of children, and Roger was always so damned grateful for everything he had. Though Howard consoled himself with the thought that they weren't really living like this at all—just picking up their mail here to avoid being located by the authorities. Swell.

He found 625 Post, a shabby storefront (what else?) under a sign that read INDUSTRIAL PHOTO PRODUCTS, INC. A smaller sign, in the window, said POST RENT-A-BOX. No products were on display in the window. Inside, the simple-looking clerk barely seemed to comprehend Howard's request to leave a message "for some of your postal clients." Maybe it was just indifference. Howard had written a note on hotel stationery and stuck it in a hotel envelope, and now he addressed it. He hoped to see the clerk put it in a P.O. box, a cubbyhole, some evidence of actual delivery, but the envelope remained on the counter next to the clerk as he read from a creased issue of *Archie's Pals 'n' Gals*, lips muttering silently.

Back into the dog poop. Amazing quantities of the stuff, considering that the streets were not populated with dog walker types, exactly. In fact he'd seen no dogs since he'd strolled past Union Square. Maybe they roamed in packs, after dark?

Not until late afternoon did the phone in his room ring. It was Susan, who sounded thrilled to have heard from him and then smoothly lied about the need for the mail drop. He hadn't even asked. It wasn't encouraging. He arranged to meet the kids near Federal Plaza. Then he called the agent Toomes had referred him to, a man named Nietfeldt.

Hugs and handshakes. They stood in the shadow of FBI headquarters, discussing where to have dinner. He took them to a bar for a couple of beers. He stopped at a little place and bought some postcards and an ashtray with a picture of a crab in it while the kids laughed at him, the tourist, good-naturedly. The Oriental lady who sold him the things was practically an American, I mean zero accent, none at all; she was joking along with him and the kids, and it set him to thinking about this Joan Shimada, and Guy Mock, and the overcast reason for his visit here, and he carried his stuff out in a little white paper bag, feeling sorry for himself and, in the chill damp of the evening, slightly drunk. Supposedly he was up here "on business," though this would have been plenty vague even if he weren't a schoolteacher whose only business trips were to L.A. for occasional training. Didn't matter anyway; they ended up at a steak house and what's practically the first thing he does once everybody's slid into the banquette? He tells them the FBI's looking around for them.

"Look, they just want to talk, and they're not bad guys, so maybe you should just do it," he finished.

Roger looked as if he were going to puke. Susan said, "Not bad guys? I can't believe they fooled you. The FBI are a bunch of liars." She had a baked potato in front of her and waved around a piece of it on the end of her fork.

This was his daughter, flourishing a hunk of spud and hissing at him in a restaurant full of people. Well, they hadn't agreed on everything these past few years, but Howard had always been able to lump it all, these disagreements, into a pile of minor wrangles: you know, like painting her room a funny color or wearing something that came up to here. Kicking-over-the-traces stuff. Even getting on the TV and hollering about the SLA seemed isolated, a passing thing. Until now he hadn't realized that she was heading in the direction of being a totally different person.

Susan said, "They're liars."

Susan said, "You can't trust anything they say."

Susan said, "We're using the PO box 'cause someone was stealing the mail off our front steps."

Susan said, "I was upset about Angela. That's all. It's better now."

Susan said, "I've never used *any* name but Rorvik."

Susan said, "I did visit a prisoner for a while, some guy I don't remember his name, part of this volunteer program I signed up for. It was a drag getting there so I quit."

Susan said, "I've never even heard of Joan Shimada. I do work with a Meg, but I don't know her last name."

Susan said, "I haven't even talked to Guy Mock since he left for Oberlin maybe two years ago."

She was so good, the complete actress. It struck Howard as a shame that she'd missed her calling. He knew she was fibbing, though he couldn't really believe that she'd had a hand in any of the bomb throwing, but what he wondered was why she'd chucked this golden talent of hers to do . . . what? Wait tables and publish propaganda? At least with acting you got your big break one day. Did that happen with left-wing pamphleteers? He doubted it. Maybe her whole life was an act now, a matter of slipping fluidly from one invented personality to another. Susan Anger, what a name. He hoped someone else was writing her material if that was the stuff she was coming up with.

The restaurant was emptying out. Two waitresses sat at a table in the corner, eating dinner salads. One had kicked her shoes off and was kneading the ball of her left foot, tucked under her thigh, with her right hand. Some men at the bar watched a ballgame, Phillies leading the Giants in the eighth. Nobody wanted any dessert.

It was chilly outside now, and Howard was wearing only a polo shirt. Hugging himself, he asked Susan: "Look, where are you living now? Are you together?"

"We're sort of in between spaces right now. We're staying at different friends' houses. Dad, it happens all the time. People just don't settle into one place like they used to."

He must have gaped at her. It was true; even this was difficult for him to understand. *Why* don't they?

"It's nothing *serious*. Dad, you look so tragic."

He reached out for her. The bar at the steak house had a separate door, and just then it flew open, expelling a sour odor of stale beer and crushed cigarettes. Three men exited.

"Fucking Tug McGraw," said one.

"Fucking *Halicki*," corrected another.

The third cast a glance at Howard and Susan. "Too fucking young for you, pops."

"Fuck you," said Roger.

"Bet you'd like it, faggot. Get back to Castro Street."

The men disappeared, jaunty, bustling down the street as if they'd approached them to ask the time of day. That the entire encounter had generated so little heat, had been hostile for the sake of hostility alone, bowled Howard over. This was the city of peace and love? Maybe he was just in the wrong neighborhood.

"God," he said suddenly. "Is this any way to live? What are you doing here? Why don't we all fly back together? Look, you've got no place to live, and you're what? Waiting tables? And you're painting houses? Let's get the hell out of here. Come back home. Breathe clean desert air, instead of—" He hadn't been planning on this, but suddenly he wanted to gather them up, be a family under one roof again. What had happened was that things had fallen apart little by little. Decisions he hadn't approved of but kept his mouth shut about had built up, it was clear, into something huge, uncontrollable, something he would never have kept quiet about if he'd seen it coming. Did every father, at some point, urge his children to just quit it, come home, they weren't fooling anyone? On the whole, he thought he was being reasonable. He could accept a certain amount of foolishness up to a certain level. When you had a houseful of kids, it was normal to expect a certain number of matters that would have you tearing your hair out by the handful. But none of this was normal: the FBI at your door with a dossier about your own kid? Time to come in now. They'd made their point, but listen, things are getting serious. The FBI is not horsing around. But all he could think of to say was: "Dog shit. How can you live here? This whole god damn place is Dog Shit Heaven. You can't walk. You can't breathe."

It ended up being exhausting. Like a dope, instead of taking them to task for doing whatever it was they'd done to arouse the interest of the FBI, he'd broadly censured their adult lives. He should have just let Rose write them another letter. They argued for two hours, wandering the downtown streets until, bushed, he allowed them to steer him back to the Hilton. Susan, the official spokesperson, cried.

"Dad, there's nothing to worry about. We can come down in a few weeks and spend some time with you and Mom."

"I can't urge you enough. Call these men. Tell them what you told me." At least he'd gotten back to the point, but he felt useless, old, contemptible, traitorous. And now he'd have to go back upstairs and tell Nietfeldt that he'd told his kids that the FBI was on to them. If he could only get them all home again, he'd take the old patterned sheets out of the linen closet, cowboys and Raggedy Anns, make the beds himself. Read to them, the forgotten books on the low shelves, until they were asleep, get back to some time when he was supposed to be having an influence.

Thomas Polhaus takes Nietfeldt's memo and folds it in half. What he wants to do is fold it into fourths, place stiff cardboard covers on both sides, drill a three-quarter-inch hole in the center, and then drive a bolt through the thing and straight into his forehead because if he's going to walk around looking like a fucking asshole he might as well go whole hog.

"Nietfeldt, what happened?"

"You wouldn't believe it."

"I believe it all. I'm doting, overcredulous, and naive."

"You wouldn't believe this."

"Go ahead and test my faith. I'm sitting here on a Sunday."

"The guy said he wouldn't meet with the kids if we tailed him. So we didn't break surveillance, but we hid it a little. I mean, no one in the restaurant. Which is a shame. I hear the fish is very fresh, locally caught. Anyway, they moved around a lot. A bar, the restaurant, then just walked around. The thing is, L.A. gives him this cover; he's supposed to say he's up on business. He's a high school teacher out in the desert, it's summer vacation. I mean, what kind of business? Good deals on number two pencils? How's he supposed to not blow it when you give him a cover like that?"

Polhaus let his mouth fall open and allowed the phonemes to escape, two breathy sounds carried on the still air: "L.A."

"It was L.A.'s idea. I'm sorry. I had a bad feeling."

"It's L.A., the whole bright idea for this brilliant family reunion."

"Should I even mention that we were about a half an hour from Herself? That if the conversation between Rorvik and the kids had gone as planned—to the extent that the conversation was necessary, was a semi-intelligent idea and not something an ape swinging through the jungle would have rejected out of hand—we would have found her and had her right now?"

"Maybe you shouldn't mention it. So what else happened?"

"Rorvik said that he asked them what they were doing these days, and they said working. Susan's at Plate of Brasse."

"Until Friday she was."

"Roger's still painting houses."

"You think this is true, or you think it's more bullshit they're feeding the old man?"

"Roger shows up with paint on his clothes, anyway."

"Why does L.A. do this? Why?"

"My suggestion is check out small jobs in the area. Small nonunion painting jobs. I would think the Peninsula. All those complexes in Belmont and such. Probably a lot of work getting bid out. Labor Day's coming up. Big moving day."

"So check them out." He dismisses Nietfeldt.

Eventually you realize that L.A. exists just to be at fault. Not the Bureau office, the whole fucking city. It has an infinite capacity to absorb blame. Whatever goes wrong in the country, there's always L.A.

Used to be New York, but L.A. took over. The cognoscenti understand this. Jew haters still blame New York. Right-wingers blame Berkeley. The unobservant blame Polhaus's beautiful golden San Francisco. But you want to trace everything that's wrong in the world, from tits in the movies to niggers in the streets, you look to L.A.

Small nonunion jobs. Maybe they'd get lucky, but things aren't looking up. The single useful lead that they have in the whole thing of the case, 625 Post, is blown. They could send them electric trains and a salami, they could send a carton of Milky Ways and an ounce of grass—they'd never go near the place again.

Rose hung up the receiver, then stared at the kitchen phone. A beige wall unit, set in the center of a dark corkboard in the shape of a flower, to whose petals were pinned a shopping list, a business card, a prescription, a mechanic's estimate, something in a slit window envelope. And oh yeah the postcard from her sister, who'd visited Porterville. She wasn't sure if her sister had been joking around or not. These things said Life Goes On. And how.

She was a woman with a grown child. Two, for all intents and purposes. She was waiting for her husband to return from an out-of-town trip. She would have liked to say that the house felt empty. She would have liked to say that now she could get to all the things she'd been meaning to do. She would have liked to say that she had converted Susan's bedroom into a sewing room. She would have liked to say that there were Kodachrome snaps arriving in the mail each month, accompanying lengthy, chatty letters of the kind she had always been in the habit of writing. She would have liked to say that she and Howard were going to take a couple of months and visit sunny Italy, a second honeymoon. She would have liked to, but basically it was just quiet around there.

She knew Howard was on his way home because he'd checked out of the Hilton. She knew that because the kids had just called her to say that they'd missed him there but to let him know that they weren't involved in any kind of trouble. Oh, and hi. Not in any trouble, but don't be too upset if she doesn't hear from them for a while. But things should straighten themselves out soon. Then, fire up the barbecue! They'd be home for a nice long visit.

It was when they assured her of the imminent visit home that it occurred to her that her entire life as a mother had been a failure.

Because this was a lie as transparent as the lies they were telling about their lack of intimate involvement with armed revolutionary groups, state prisoners, and fugitives from justice. The whole known past had been abruptly dethroned by a hidden counterpart that was monstrous in its secret and unknowable details; that so thoroughly excluded her that it might as well have happened to people she didn't know. Worse, it worked in only one direction. *Her* life remained as open to them, as accessible, as it always had been, while they denied her basic knowledge about such things as where they happened to be laying their heads, the hair on which she'd cut herself right here in this kitchen, with newspapers spread over the linoleum. But a mother couldn't afford to be willfully enigmatic. She'd had her secrets—secret garments, secret devices in the medicine chest and hanging from the showerhead, secret silences—but they were not deceitful secrets. Not even Jocasta deliberately deceived her children. And there weren't many of them, her secrets. They were things that had happened before they were born. They were things she concealed on and inside her person. They were things she carried alone, in her head, without speaking of them or acting them out, without even dreaming of speaking of them or acting them out. Everything else, her whole life, belonged to her children, or at any rate was there for them to take. But the things her children were supposed to have been up to! Whatever she thought she'd been teaching them all these years, all she'd really taught them was that it wasn't advisable to tell their own mother the truth. Who did they tell the truth to? They told each other the truth. They told their friends, unfamiliar to her. Probably they thought they were telling the truth whenever a bomb exploded or a gun went off. And she'd given them everything. It wasn't fair.

She realized that her number one tactic, the jeremiad, didn't work, hadn't ever worked. She'd employed it all these years in the belief that by putting across her point of view she could impose the reality it urged. But all those letters had carried no weight. Now that she thought of it she recognized that all she'd ever obtained was some token deference. Then the kids went ahead and did whatever they pleased. As carefully as she wrote, as lucidly as she framed her arguments, as diplomatically as she lodged her objections, as skillfully as she obscured her appeals to the children's fears and guilt feelings, as astutely as she expressed her familiarity with them as individuals, it was all only words, capable of changing nothing, remote from any existence other than its own as words on a page, reflecting nothing but her own sense of the way things stood, or ought to stand.

Normal sounds. A sprinkler, darkening the desert earth and bringing forth flowers and grass in the unwavering sunlight. Motorcars, back and forth, and one in particular that pulled into the driveway and stopped. The monster she loved was home again.

The door. "I'm home," said Howard. He put down his overnight bag.

"Well," she said.

He paused by the door to go through the mail stacked on the table near the entryway. She knew he had to do this when he walked through the door, and she waited, reaching for the embroidered clasp purse in which she nested the pack of cigarettes she was working on. Soon he would walk into the kitchen and have a glass of tap water, using the ridiculous plastic cup (picturing Donald, Huey, Dewey, and Louie) that he kept beside the sink for this purpose.

"The kids look good," he said. "They seem all right."

"They just called," she told him.

"They did?" he said.

"They wanted to say goodbye."

"What?" He had crossed the threshold of the kitchen and stood before the sink, letting the water run to clear the pipes of lead traces, germs, and insalubrious residue. "What do you mean, goodbye?"

"They called to say we wouldn't see them anymore. They're in trouble, Howard."

"Now wait just a minute. That's not what they told me. They told me this was all a mixup. Maybe you misunderstood." He took the cup and filled it, then stood drinking it down. Rose watched his Adam's apple bobbing as he swallowed.

"No," she said. "You misunderstood them."

"The FBI only wants to talk to them, I told them I thought it would be a good idea, and end of subject. We finished dinner and had a walk and talked about this and that."

So it was him too. It would have to be to complete the chain. The FBI lied to him, he lied to the children, and then together he and the children lied to her. They made telephone calls for the express purpose of lying. They drove out to the desert. They boarded jets and flew hundreds of miles, just to tell lies to each other and to her.

And as the one who didn't get a chance to lie she'd only now gotten the chance to figure it all out. And when she had—oh, how ugly that he should come home and reward her perception by pretending not to know what she was talking about.

All these years only to realize that her family had been a conspiracy against her.

"I don't know what I did to deserve any of this," she said.

"What are you crying for? It'll all be over soon."

"That's what they told me too."

"That's because it's true. It'll all be straightened out. It'll be over."

"No, it already is. We won't see them anymore."

It was never too late to start lying. It was easier when you meant it. That was the thing about the untruth, the part she'd never before understood: The lie was easiest when you knew that you yourself fought against disbelieving it. It hurt her to see Howard's face fall, his shoulders go slack. But they never would come back. It was not what they'd said, but she knew it to be true. All she was doing was, what do they call it, fabricating a quotation. If she were only to pass on the children's lie it would simply echo his own, and keep her forever excluded.

GENEVA AVENUE IS ABANDONED in frantic haste once the Rorviks deliver the troubling news that Susan's old man dropped in to take them out to a steak dinner and then told them that the FBI was picking up the check.

It is bluntly and definitively made clear that the rationale for any new living arrangements will be to quarantine the Teko and Yolanda Show in a theater of its very own. Yolanda finds a place for herself and Teko in Bernal Heights, on Precita. Susan and Jeff move into a place in Daly City right away, but Roger, Tania, and Joan are obliged to stay with Teko and Yolanda while they search for quarters. Teko takes heart at this, makes a last great flailing effort to bring them all into line. Joan especially gets a lot of shit, is brought up-to-date on the status of the continually evolving verdict against her handed down by the People's Court of Teko: She is a tricky, renitent, untrustworthy, untruthful, divisive, frigid parasite. So much for the last vestiges of fellowship remaining from the watershed Summer of '74. Teko speaks expansively about future actions (all kill plots) and describes the ongoing search for black leadership (the latest candidate, a convicted murderer named Doc Holiday, has just been released from San Quentin).

They have to make their move soon, get out of town. None of them wants to be involved with another killing. There's still cash, that Carmichael blood money, and when Roger and Jeff wrap up their current project, a contract to paint most of a big complex on the Peninsula, that should put them over the top.

After a week at the field marshals' home, they find a place in the outer Mission, on Morse Street. A two-bedroom flat, though they'd move in if it were half the size.

LANGMO AND NIETFELDT EAT sandwiches and drink coffee in the front seat of their blue sedan. It's twelve-thirty, and they're parked at a housing complex in San Bruno hard by 280. Langmo opens a copy of *Time*. The cover has a picture of Lynette "Squeaky" Fromme and reads, "The Girl Who Almost Killed Ford." Nietfeldt glances at it and smiles.

"Who'd've thought the Manson Family was for Rockefeller?"

They'd showed the manager a sheaf of photographs: pictures of the Rorviks, Jeff Wolfritz, all the unfamous faces that wouldn't cause a stir. Without hesitation, he'd picked out Wolfritz's picture.

"He in trouble?"

"Well, you know," said Langmo. "His contractor's license expired."

"Oh, really? Tell you, if I'd known, I wouldn't've hired them."

"Oh, we know you wouldn't have done anything like that," said Nietfeldt.

The apartments are clustered in groups of twelve in low buildings with dark wooden exteriors. The manager pointed out one particular cluster at the northwestern edge of the complex looking directly upon the freeway, where the apartments, currently vacant, are being painted and recarpeted. Y'should see what they do to these places. Sneak cats in and get nail polish on the carpeting. Flush objects down the john. And y'find the weirdest things left behind. They parked in view of the old dark Ford that the manager said belonged to the painters. There they wait. It's Monday, and the lot is mostly empty. The sun moves. Nietfeldt finishes his *Chronicle* and tosses it in the backseat. Langmo flips the pages of *Time*. A boy walks by the car and peers in at the two men.

"It's a school day, son," says Langmo. "Why aren't you there?" The boy moves on.

"Isn't it Columbus Day, or something?" asks Nietfeldt.

"Who?"

The G-men are laughing when a young woman, her clothes covered with white paint, comes out of one of the front apartments. Leaning against the Ford, she lights a cigarette. Her hair is drawn back in a ponytail and her clear, close-set eyes seem to be looking directly at the blue sedan.

"There's Lazy S.," says Nietfeldt. His eyes are wide with excitement and his voice is unusually high. He reaches out and grasps his partner's forearm and gives it a light squeeze. "There's Susan."

"Holy shit," says Langmo. "Finally a break. You think she's alone in there?"

"Doubt it. Manager says they're painting two apartments a day. There's got to be at least a couple of them."

The young woman tosses her cigarette to the ground and returns to the apartment, closing the door behind her.

"Better call it in."

"Fucking A." Nietfeldt picks up the radio.

At 5:30 Susan and a young man leave the apartment. Langmo flips through the bundle of photos the agents carry.

"Who you think? Jeff?"

"He'd be the logical one."

The man climbs into the driver's seat and starts up the Ford. Revolutionaries or not, men like to do the driving. Nietfeldt allows the Ford to leave the lot before he follows. He noses out into traffic and watches as it heads toward the on-ramp for 280 North, then follows the car onto the freeway, tailing it at a distance.

"They're staying in the right lane," observes Langmo.

"Probably getting onto three-eighty."

The interchange comes up but the Ford keeps heading north on 280. Nietfeldt steers the sedan into the lane that will channel them onto 380, a spur that cuts across the Peninsula, linking 280 with the airport and the Bayshore Freeway to the east. Polhaus has positioned several cars along likely routes to be able to pick up the Ford at any point on its journey.

"Well, we're out of it," Nietfeldt says.

They approach the raw brown hills just below the city, on one of which letters spell out the announcement:

SOUTH

SAN FRANCISCO

THE INDUSTRIAL CITY

Nietfeldt remembers when the letters were whitewashed onto the hill, surrounded by colorful wildflowers. The idea was to give the sign the look of a sampler that had been embroidered by some old industrial granny, patient in her industrial rocker. He remembers it aloud, as usual. Langmo looks out the passenger side window and surreptitiously rolls his eyes. Now the letters are of poured concrete, concludes Nietfeldt. As usual. Five feet high.

They round a curve and suddenly the manufacturing and warehouse topography on their right drops away and the bay is brilliant there. Up ahead is Candlestick, not so brilliant. Hereabouts the radio burbles, and Langmo grabs it. Turns out they're back in it. Code Three call. Exit 101 at Army and wait at Army and South Van Ness.

They ease to the curb at a bus stop before a low-rise housing project. An old armchair with one broken leg sits propped up on the sidewalk, and a man in faded fatigues sleeps in it, a near-empty bottle of Cisco ("Takes You by Surprise") cradled in his arms. Langmo radios in their position.

Soon they see the Ford rolling down the hill toward them, stopping for the light at Mission, signaling a right turn. Nietfeldt pulls into traffic, turns left onto Mission, and eases up to the curb outside Cesar's Palace, a nightclub. Langmo begins to drum softly, a Latin-type beat, on the dashboard.

"Ever been here?" he asks. Nietfeldt just looks at him.

The Ford draws abreast of them and comes to a stop. Nietfeldt feels the hair prickle up on the back of his neck. The last thing he wants is to be shot sitting in his car outside a Mexican dance hall. He hazards a quick look out his window. Susan Rorvik is talking and sipping from a straw stuck in a big paper cup. The cup says "COLD

Drink," and icicles have formed on the letters of the word *COLD*. Brrrr. Abruptly the car turns left onto a narrow side street. Precita.

"Jesus," says Langmo, "that's a one-way street."

"Once a cop," says Nietfeldt. Langmo was an Oakland patrolman for three years before joining the Bureau.

"After them!" says Langmo, affecting a theatrical baritone.

They radio in the Ford's position and proceed cautiously up Precita. Shortly they arrive at a narrow wedge of park that effectively forks the road, but they can see the Ford, still pointed in the wrong direction, parked up ahead and to the left on Precita.

"Dumb-ass," says Nietfeldt. He takes the right fork, intending to turn around so that he's traveling with the traffic, but this turns out to be a mistake, and they wind through the hilly streets of Bernal Heights for a few minutes, looking to pick up Precita again, turning left onto it just in time to see the Ford finish executing a broken U-turn and head back the way it had come. The unidentified man still drives, but he's alone now.

"She lives here," says Nietfeldt confidently. 200 block. He picks up the radio; let someone else chase the Ford for a while. Lazy S. is here. Herself: right here.

10 p.m.

"Ever figure out your secret name?" asks Nietfeldt. He holds a burrito in both hands, its lower half wrapped in a thin sheet of aluminum foil. A strawberry drink sits before him on the dash.

"What's that?"

"Take your middle name and the street you lived on last. That's your secret name." He takes a bite and chews, nodding. "Or it can be your confirmation name plus the street you grew up on. But I like it the other way. It changes more often."

"What the hell do you do it for?" Langmo eats like a ravening beast, and his supper is long gone, the aluminum sheet stuffed into the empty paper cup on the floor. Nietfeldt eats slowly, partly from habit, partly to irritate his partner.

"For fun, you dummy."

"OK. What's yours?"

"Charles Lisbon. I'm actually cheating. The very last place I lived was out on Twenty-fifth Avenue."

"That is cheating." Langmo is irritable.

"Never even heard of it two minutes ago and now he's telling me the rules."

"If that's what it is, that's what it is."

"The expert."

"Anyway, I don't get what the problem you have with it is. Charles the Twenty-fifth. Sounds positively royal."

"There were only two Charleses. So what's yours then?"

Langmo drags furiously on his cigarette and stubs it out in the packed ashtray. "Xavier Moraga," he says, finally.

Polhaus has a San Francisco map tacked to the wall and he stands before it, a ruler and a pack of felt-tip pens in his hands. Holding the ruler in place against the map, he carefully draws a yellow line around the San Bruno complex. Then he draws a red line along the 200 block of Precita. Finally, he places an orange line along the 600 block of Morse Street. This last is way the hell out there, far from Postcard San Francisco, the Outer Mission or the Ingleside or something. Not a neighborhood he knows. Agents Bockenkamp and Protzman followed the Ford from Precita to this location. Its driver went into the house at number 625, entering through the door leading to the upstairs flat. Lights were already on up there. Tentatively, they made the man as Roger Rorvik. They waited until after the lights had gone out upstairs and then called it in.

The agents wander in, looking red-eyed, vaguely unkempt, but ready for his spiel. It's muted, but Polhaus senses anticipatory zeal in the room. They're days away, maybe hours. It isn't just the Rorviks trundling around. Sooner or later whoever else it is will show themselves. Nobody comes to San Francisco just to stay indoors. If they're here, it's because they were dying to get back into circulation. Sooner or later they'll come out. He's willing to bet that they've been biding time in one shitheel town after another, all downhill from South Canaan. His guess is that the Precita place is the central location. Hence his candy red mark on the map. He is certain. He is so certain that his plans include round-the-clock surveillance at Precita, but no check of the job site in San Bruno and only occasional drive-bys at Morse Street.

"I suggest that we at least put a team on at Morse," says Nietfeldt.

"Somebody was already there when Roger drove up," says Bockenkamp.

"Maybe he leaves the lights on when he goes out," says Polhaus.

"My mom used to do that," says Langmo. "To scare away burglars."

"Did it work?" asks Holderness.

Polhaus ignores them. "Precita is where we need to concentrate our attention."

"What about San Bruno?"

"We already found them. We aren't going to lose them again." If his logic strikes Polhaus's subordinates as flawed, they say nothing. "Anyway, we need all the firepower we can spare. Remember what happened the last time they were cornered in a house."

"You planning on doing that in Bernal Heights, sir?" Nietfeldt raises his eyebrows. "The whole district'll go up."

"Personally I would have to mark my ballot against burning down the city," says Langmo.

"This isn't a democracy," says Polhaus.

"Death to the fascist insect." Nietfeldt leans in close to Langmo and whispers this.

The surveillance takes shape, establishes its cadence. A panel truck with curtained rear windows takes up a space on Precita right near the park, earning two parking tickets. Two other cars cruise the neighborhood. Men with pushcarts selling paletas, churros. The smell of fried dough in the air. The whole scene is very agreeable to Nietfeldt. An old city boy, used to catch the J-Church not too far from here and ride it to Mission High. His father would take them to Speckmann's for sauerbraten and stuffed cabbage rolls. Stole his first kiss in a dark doorway on Liberty Street. How ironic, how literary, is that?

Another variant: your middle name and the place you first made out. Charlie Liberty.

That girl's lips tasted like fresh sweet corn.

Day one. Roger Rorvik appears in the Ford around 10 in the morning, once again headed up the street the wrong way. Susan emerges from number 288 and gets into the waiting car. In the van, Bockenkamp and Protzman take pictures with a telephoto lens. Girl walking, girl waiting, girl with finger up nose. Langmo gets out of the sedan a block away and walks past the house, holding a rolled-up magazine in his hand. He and Nietfeldt rendezvous around the corner. Nothing to be seen from the street. Curtains pulled. A dreary day. McQuirter gets shit on by a bird and makes a big deal out of his new checked sports jacket. Somebody's lunch order gets screwed up.

Day two. Rorvik shows around 10:30, headed in the right direction this time. Inside the van there is a spontaneous round of applause. Susan comes out and the cousins drive off. Another ticket is placed with the others under the van's wiper blade. Failure to properly block wheels on grade.

"Hey, get over here and tell me if you think I'm parked at an angle," radios Protzman.

"An angle to what?" asks Langmo.

"Don't be a juvenile. I'm serious."

Nietfeldt, driving for the hell of it with one finger on the wheel just to demonstrate the delicious responsiveness of GM power steering, rounds the corner onto Precita to comply with Protzman's request when the door opens at 288 and who should come outside but a short bearded bespectacled fellow with dyed black hair. He walks down the steps leading to the sidewalk.

"You guys fucking see that?" Protzman's overwrought voice crackles over the radio. Nietfeldt passes the house slowly, and both men take a sidelong look.

"Shepard?"

Langmo is studying their collection of Drew Shepard headshots, laid out in a strip. None shows him wearing a beard. None shows him in prescription eyeglasses. "Can't tell for sure."

The man stands with his hands on his hips, looking first one way and then the other, up and down the block. Then he turns and trots back up the steps.

At 11:30 Nietfeldt is about to say something about lunch when the call comes in.

"Two subjects, double-timing it. Heading your way."

Nietfeldt sees two figures jogging toward them. The man from the stoop and, to his right, a woman. Shorts, T-shirts, sneakers.

"You know," says Langmo, "I doubt they're armed right now."

"That's definitely something to bear in mind," says Nietfeldt. "You think they do this every day?"

The joggers pass them. The man seems to be straining to keep up with the woman. Neither pays the car or its occupants any mind.

"What about her then?" asks Langmo.

"Well, it isn't Herself. And it isn't Shimada, that's for sure."

"Diane." Langmo is looking at his photos.

"That's my guess."

"Drew and Diane. Tell me why am I not that excited?"

"We're all here for the same person."

"I feel as if, I don't know."

"You have a goal. You don't have a partial goal."

"The thing is, I'd rather have Herself and leave them."

"Then you're just too complex a lawman for me."

Langmo looks at Nietfeldt, ready to needle him back, but realizes that he is speaking perfectly sincerely.

"This is the one," says Stepnowski, poking one picture of a smiling Shepard with his index finger, "the one I was talking about before."

The agents sit crammed around a table in a Mission Street taqueria.

"Oh, you'll like it here," says Nietfeldt.

"I missed this," says Langmo. "What were you saying?"

"Check out his teeth." Stepnowski jabs the picture.

"I fail to see what's so great about this place." Holderness picks up a bottle of green sauce from the table and gives it a sniff.

Nietfeldt leans forward as if he's about to lay a hot stock tip on Holderness. "*No rice.*"

Stepnowski says, "Those upper front teeth don't come down as far as the ones on either side of them."

"Guy looks like a fucking vampire," says Protzman.

"Smaller burritos, but they don't fill them up with rice. Meat, cheese, beans. That's it." Nietfeldt is whispering.

"Maybe he just has little front teeth is all," says Langmo.

"It's good without the rice," says Protzman. "Not as filling."

"We need a good look at him."

"I favor the carnitas," says Nietfeldt.

"NO rice?" says Holderness, suddenly, as if the import of what he is being told has just sunk in. "You mean, NO rice at ALL?"

"The fuck you shouting for?"

. . .

Mystery Man goes into a laundromat two blocks down, carrying a white canvas bag marked US MAIL.

"Isn't that a federal crime?" asks Langmo.

"Get in there and check out the teeth."

"What business do I have in a laundromat?"

"Ask directions. What do I know?"

When Langmo enters, he heads for a phone booth in the corner, keeping an eye on the man across the two rows of Speed Queens. He lifts the receiver and speaks into it. He says, "The boy stood on the burning deck. Yup. Whence all but he had fled. The flame that lit the battle's wreck shone round him. O'er the dead. Right. Yet beautiful and bright—bright, yeah, uh-huh—beautiful and bright he stood. OK? G'bye."

Mystery Man sorts laundry. Two piles, whites and colored. His mother would be pleased. So would the KKK. He opens the lid of one of the top loaders and is obscured from view. Langmo steps out of the booth and walks to the attendant, who sits on a high stool reading the *Sporting Green*, jingling his change apron.

"Change of a dollar," says Langmo.

"Where's your clothes?" asks the attendant.

"Oh, I just. Parking meter, you know."

"Change for customers only." The green sheet comes up again.

Langmo drops it. He turns, folding his dollar bill lengthwise, and here's Mystery Man, ready to get his own change, lips pursed. Their eyes meet. Langmo breaks into a big smile and a shrug, meaningless but friendly. Mystery Man stares holes through him. Needless to say, he doesn't smile back. Langmo gives him a last once-over; notes a scar on the man's left knee.

6 p.m. Nietfeldt follows the Mystery Couple inside a bodega. The pair moves up and down the store's two aisles. He heads for the cooler and gets a bottle of Coke, a bag of chips. Just another paunchy citizen who can't make it till dinnertime. He takes his booty to the counter. The couple lingers in one of the aisles. The clerk rings him up; he asks for a pack of Larks. Pays, asks for matches. A man comes in and buys an *Examiner*.

"Good idea," says Nietfeldt, to no one special. He grabs a paper and eyes the pair. While he fishes his change out of his pocket he notices a coffeepot behind the counter, and he asks the clerk to fix him a cup. But when the coffee has joined the paper before him on the counter, he remains lamentably alone up there. He opens the freezer case and takes out an It's-It.

"Maybe next time you should make a list," says the clerk.

"I thought it was the impulse buys that paid the freight in a joint like this."

At last they come up. Rice, dried beans. The simple life. Of course they could have had meat for the same price if they'd just walked to the Safeway three blocks away. Maybe on top of everything else they're fucking vegetarians.

Nietfeldt takes his groceries and his coffee and steps aside to make room. He smiles. The woman gives him a polar stare. The man does not return the smile, turning to ask for a pint bottle of plum wine. Nietfeldt tries to recall the timber and cadence of General Teko's voice on the "eulogy" tape, but that was a guy pretending to be black, and this is just another overeducated Caucasian who happens to be asking for sweet wine.

Field Marshal Cinque's favorite drink, Nietfeldt suddenly recalls.

Later they get the news over the wire: LCpl. Andrew C. Shepard, USMC, received an operation on his left knee during his hitch.

Polhaus is ready to go upon hearing this. Far as he's concerned, tomorrow's the first day of the rest of his life. No more explaining to asshole reporters why he can't pick up the trail of the SLA. No more providing daily briefings to Director Kelley. No more Lydia Galton wincing whenever Hank pours him out a couple of fingers of scotch.

He's actually been asked if he'll miss working on the case once it's been closed. As if he were some sort of artist laboring over his magnum opus, stringing it along, afraid to move on to the next project. Well, federal agents don't suffer from completion anxiety. And unlike an artist, he hasn't imbued the final product with his own likeness, flattered himself so much that he wants to keep gazing at it. His labors on the case have left no impression on its specific set of facts at all. Find, interpret, conclude. Plus soothe and placate. Wheedle and cringe. Rage and fawn.

Nineteen months—suddenly this is it. He knows that where the Shepards are, Galton is. Has to be. He'll take his chances with a(nother) false arrest. (The way these longhairs piss and moan.

Sworn enemies of the State Apparatus but invariably shocked, outraged, and happy to avail themselves of the civil courts when wrongfully arrested.) If he loses her this time, that's simply that. Not that he's a pessimist, but he's already planned his resignation from the Bureau in that event, put out discreet feelers in the field of corporate security. He's seen the pastures out to which they put you.

And if he catches her? Director of the Bureau? Governor of California? Surely the case has prepared him for a career in politics, but he's acquired a love of anonymity over the years, working under Hoover's showboat directorate. Something satisfying about wielding power incognito. Polhaus never wanted to be a cop, because he hadn't wanted to wear a uniform while he waited to get into plainclothes. Perhaps politics wasn't for him. In addition to which, all that COINTELPRO stuff might come back to haunt him.

So maybe just the old routine, tossing his jacket over the back of his chair, eating his danish and drinking his coffee, bringing his newspaper into the bathroom with him. That'd be fine. Face the reporters one last time, their faces too familiar for him not to notice that they'd newly been stamped with bogus respect, tell them I told you so, and then throw them out into the street: The one who'd written that he looked "like a none-too-bright bloodhound whose quarry has just slipped out of reach." The woman who'd called him "one of the last of the old breed" in a distinctly pejorative manner. The columnist who'd said that his "methods must be questioned and his motives, distrusted." Gone at last!

Day three. For the first time agents have been positioned in the area around the clock. Nietfeldt and Langmo play chess through the night by the light of the dashboard, using a magnetic travel set. They're both lousy players and spend most of their playing time either warning each other of lurking danger on the board or apologizing for taking each other's pieces. Roger arrives for Susan at 10 today.

"Talk about banker's hours. Wouldn't harvest much cane for Fidel if they showed up in the fields after ten."

Nietfeldt yawns.

11:30. A covered pickup stops outside 288 and turns on its flashers. A young Negro male exits the cab and climbs the stoop. He wears a white jalabiyya and matching kufi. That's a new wrinkle. Out comes Mystery Man.

"Who's the sheikh?" says Langmo.

Mystery Man takes cash from his pocket and together the two walk down the steps and to the truck, where the young man drops the gate and hauls a white joint compound bucket toward him. He removes the cover and takes from the bucket a fish, holding it by the tail. Mystery Man hands over some money and the young man wraps the fish in a couple of sheets of newspaper.

"He'd be better off selling that on Friday around here."

"Right after Vatican Two my father started making hamburgers on Friday," Langmo says. "Every Friday it was burgers: with cheese, with bacon, with Lipton onion soup mix mixed in, whatever, as long as they were dripping blood. Threw them on the grill. Liked to eat them on a kaiser roll. Enough of this fish shit, he said."

"Hated fish."

"He hated fish. Loved the Latin mass, but he hated fish."

"I'm kind of attached to the old ways, myself."

"Really?"

"I don't kill myself or anything, you understand."

The young man drives off as Mystery Man carries his fish and yesterday's news up the steps.

At ten to one the door opens again and the Mystery Couple comes out. They're dressed for a jog, in shorts and T-shirts.

Bockenkamp radios. "Anyplace they could hide a weapon under there?"

"Search me," says Nietfeldt.

"Ho-ho. I mean, this is it. Now's when we take them."

Langmo's bouncing in the passenger seat.

"Let them do their jogging. Wear them out a little. I'm sure as fucking hell not chasing them up and down these hills," says Nietfeldt.

The couple starts trotting in the direction of the park.

Subjects rounding Alabama. South on Alabam. You copy?

Ten-four. Car one, you got a print kit ready? ID this guy right away. Nip it in the bud if we're wrong.

Progress, car two?

Still on Alabama. They usually, the routine is, down Alabama to Ripley.

Copy that, two.

Um, stand by. Stand by.

What's up, two?

Subject male is stopping. Stone in his shoe or something, looks like. Subject female is continuing.

Shit. They're not together, you mean?

Negative. You copy?

Car one, Base. Take up position on Folsom. They don't join up we'll take her fast so he doesn't see.

Copy.

Here he comes. Shit, he's going flat out. Gonna have a heart attack.

Stay in position, one.

Ten-four.

Two here. Subjects together.

He caught up.

Subjects turning north onto Folsom. You copy?

Ten-four, two.

One here. Visual contact.

Base here. Move in, three. Take up position at Two Eight Eight.

Approaching 288, the couple, sheened with perspiration, slows to a walk. McQuirter, Stepnowski, and Holderness emerge from their sedan to surround them.

"FBI," says McQuirter.

Mystery Man looks blankly at the three agents, but his companion screams: "You sons of bitches!" Then she turns to run. And there's Nietfeldt, hustling up from the corner, covering her with a shotgun. Covering all five of them, actually, at this distance—but who has time to consider the petty details? She freezes, and Holderness grabs her, and then Langmo is rushing past Nietfeldt to assist Holderness, and Nietfeldt can put up the gun.

"Get the fuck off me, you motherfuckers! Let me go!" She thrashes, kicks, and spits.

"Get her in the fucking car and get her out of here," says Nietfeldt. "We don't want Herself hearing the ruckus."

"Where's that kit?" says McQuirter. Mystery Man is still standing quietly beside him, Stepnowski's .38 aimed at his head, holding his uncuffed hands away from his body slightly, fingers spread, as if he were air-drying freshly painted nails.

497

"Like we need it," says Nietfeldt. But he takes a stamp pad and a five-by-eight out of his jacket pocket. He'll feel a lot better when all the guns are put away.

Polhaus walks through the apartment: cluttered, but not quite like the packrat middens they'd discovered in Clayton and Daly City and on Golden Gate. The usual guns and bombs (including, Polhaus notices, a Red Ryder BB gun), dozens of linear feet of papers, but all neatly stored in one of the two bedrooms. The rest of the place looks as ordinary as can be.

Polhaus contemplates the middle-class comforts the apartment encloses and perceives the terminus of the adventure. The apartment foretells this afternoon, his own presence here, more acutely than anything else could. Running exhausts people. Hiding bores them silly. The last fantasy of the SLA, even more implausible than that of leading a revolution, was that they could revert to this. Neighbors say that they were a nice couple. Even had a few of them up for tea. Coffee and cake. Plants on the windowsills. Scented candles in the bath. Even upon them, Polhaus thinks, the normal exerted its pull. At the furthest point of their renegade orbit it may have looked as if they'd broken free, soared, but to the end they remained natural satellites of the culture; it hauled them back every time; and whenever it did, they were complicit.

Their final alias was Carswell, Christopher and Nanette. It's there on the mailing label for the *TV Guide*.

THEY GET UP LATE on Morse. The fugitive's privilege. No work, no worries, and Teko and Yolanda all the way up in Bernal Heights. They have a routine of making coffee and then sitting around drinking it and talking and smoking until it's time to make tea. Ridiculous. Drifts of dirty laundry covering the floor, dirty dishes hidden under the beds. Roger does most of the cleaning up.

Another lazy day. They move around one another in the kitchen, each familiar with the other's way of doing things, her sense of space. Joan pours hot water into the mugs to allow them to warm before she serves the coffee. This is an elegant and fine-featured act, a small marvel each morning. Never would have occurred to Tania. Once again Tania is stumped to characterize it without recourse to the Exotic East.

One waits to occupy the other's space. Tania pauses, holding a container of orange juice, waiting for Joan to vacate the patch of countertop next to the refrigerator, where she pokes a fork into the side of her English muffin, separating the two halves. Crumbs and smears of jam on the tile surface of the counter. They step around each other, pause and wait their turn, like the oldest of old couples. The hot water is emptied from the warmed cups and the coffee is poured at last.

This is almost what Tania wants. Endless days, without ever exhausting the subject, whatever it happens to be. It's all ahead of them. They're all set to go to Boston.

She has a new name all picked out. Amy Ralston. She'll never have to deal with a dumb nickname. Goes with the tony accent Teko was never able to get her to shake. She has the birth certificate: died in infancy.

She hears a lot of good things about Boston.

Today Joan has a letter to share, and Tania sits with one leg tucked under the other, waiting patiently while Joan introduces the letter: She sat up last night and wrote to her Willie, a long postmortem on the dissolution of the Symbionese army, nation, and people.

"I had to get this off my chest," says Joan, shaking the pages before she hands them over. Soon she'll entrust the letter to the system of retranscription and coded paraphrase that has allowed her to correspond with her lover for three years. Joan is silent about the mechanism of this system. Always that reticence to her, a holding back, the promise of a subjacent stage richer than one might imagine. The mysterious Orient.

"The group," Tania reads, "has ceased to be a group."

A week ago Roger met Teko at a Mission bar to kiss off the SLA for good. Only two other men drank in the afternoon quiet, letter carriers from the post office around the corner, their satchel carts brazenly parked outside. Teko had been expecting Tania and was disappointed when Roger walked in alone. He wanted the opportunity to say goodbye to his protégée. They'd been through so much struggling together. So Roger had quoted him. Bullshit. The final argument, a few days prior, had been a deafening marathon. She and Joan had toted over to Precita a lengthy letter they'd written criticizing SLA leadership past and present, grounding the appraisal in the feminist arguments that had been useful enough to boost them out of backwater Sacramento. Dug out the opus, "Women in the Vanguard: Toward a Revolutionary Theory," and worked those old changes one more time.

They handed him the "divorce letter," so called, and he stood in the parlor at Precita, reading, tossing the pages on the floor as he was done with them. Yolanda bent to pick up the discarded sheets as they fell, and they stood beside each other, heads bent, reading the familiarly phrased counterclaims.

"This isn't political criticism," said Yolanda. "This is a personal attack." Well, whatever she was, she wasn't dumb. Nor was she, of all people, blind to the private uses to which "politics" could be put. Compared with what it already had been used to justify, this was nothing. To liberate yourself from Petaluma or Goleta, assassinate a school official. To shake off the fetters of dusty afternoons in Clarendon Hills, kidnap an heiress. To turn your back on the stifling hush of Hillsborough, tape a harangue, type up a screed, author "Articles of War," swear out a death warrant against your favorite corporate criminal, blow up a power station. Cut down a churchgoing homemaker in pursuit of cold cash.

They argued until two in the morning, until all four of them noticed that the rhythmic pounding they'd felt was actually the neighbor, hammering on the wall. Some people have to get up for work in the morning. She and Joan caught a bus on Mission, and that was the last she saw of her field marshal.

They'll go to Boston, work as community activists. She'll garden in a backyard plot, assemble a collection of recipes on three-by-five cards, walk the dog, eventually have a child. All the old imaginings cohere around the new authenticity she's made.

Amy Ralston is the name.

Joan writes *long* letters. She writes of the "fucked-up interpersonal dynamics" within the cadre. She writes, "We, those of us who decided to go our own way, discussed the matter and it became obvious to us what the problems were. On the surface it seems as though we all agree and believe in the same thing, but after working with them, we've come to the realization that we do in fact disagree politically very drastically." She writes, "And to add to this is the personal aspect of these people. They are two individuals with weak egos lacking very much in sense of themselves." She writes, "They are doctrinaire Marighelaists. These people are totally unable to check out the objective situation and deal with it. They simply do not know how to take a theory and apply it to the reality that exists."

Tania thinks, Is this the sort of letter an imprisoned man awaits in his lonely cell? But she reads on, though the coffee goes right through her and she has to pee. She stands. Too bad. She never gets to read Joan's penultimate paragraph:

> I wish that I could talk to you and tell you in every detail about everything. Some day I will. I tell you this is an experience I'll never forget! It was horrendous but at the same time I've learned a hell of a lot. Now I understand more clearly my political views and, oh, the sense of myself I've gotten out of this ordeal— I wouldn't exchange it for anything! I think most of us came out of this ahead. I hope you'll have the chance to meet A.G. She is incredible! She amazes me! I swear only the toughest could have come out of it as she did. What an ordeal she went through!! What an ordeal all of us went through!! I can write a book about it.

No, there's a man in the apartment with a gun and he says FBI and this is it. All along, the one indelible gift the SLA had imparted to her was a belief that the authorities were coming to kill her. This, the cornerstone of the mysterious "conversion" that perplexed the world, seemed unshakable. Everything Cinque said had come true: When they couldn't rescue her, they relabeled her. Made her a common criminal. Such was the phrase used by the attorney general of the USA. Simple as switching a tag. Named her a criminal and then came gunning for her, burned her lover and her friends. All it took was the potency of a new classification.

Isn't your life supposed to flash before your eyes or something? Amy Ralston.

The guns are in the bedroom and she takes mincing backward steps, heading for her trusty carbine.

"Freeze or I'll blow her head off," says the man. Joan is pressed up against the kitchen counter, and she swivels her head, reflexively avoiding the gun, her eyes finding Tania's, and it seems that Joan's face suddenly bears the weight of every single day of her thirty-odd years, as if all the petty retributions the world demanded of her throughout her effortful life had suddenly come due all at once.

Now here's another man. Another man, another gun. That appears to be the scheme of things. He calls out her name and involuntarily she moves forward. So much for Amy Ralston.

The second man spins her around and handcuffs her. Asks her where the guns are. Already she feels the lure of another master viewpoint, the influence of another eager and unrelenting authority, the inauguration of another phase during which she will have to earn and defend everything she has, everything she does, everything she says. The closet, again. Can all of life, at its essence, finally be reduced to the span of the chain that joins the cuffs? One freedom left. She was going to pee, and so she does, right in her pants; it keeps coming and coming, fear, doubt, nervous blood, coffee, whatever, all exit. It's a decision she makes, no more and no less. God knows when she'll see a toilet bowl.

WHEN IT BECAME OBVIOUS that Herself was not hiding among the knickknacks, papers, and sawed-off shotguns at Precita, Polhaus took steps to secure the apartment and preserve the scene. Neighbors milled about. SFPD started arriving. The local parochial school would let out soon. If a fire truck turned onto the street, he wouldn't have been surprised. It was like the stateroom scene in *Night at the Opera*.

Polhaus had a few addresses left to check. Nietfeldt could split hairs on whether he should have had them covered to begin with, but now wasn't the time. The adrenaline was still coursing through him; his body still thrummed and tingled as if with fever; his arms felt the phantom weight of the fearsome shotgun he'd aimed at that angry, crazed woman. Months of mocking her, and he had to admit that coming face-to-face with her scared the hell out of him. Polhaus told him and Langmo to check the Morse Street address, and Nietfeldt was eager to head down there. It was the next best thing to a stiff drink.

On their way to the sedan he spotted two San Francisco cops,

Fleischer and Sparks, who'd worked the Hibernia Bank case. Want to come along? They led the way, taking obscure byways that steered clear of both traffic and well-paved roads.

A man works in the garage beneath the parlor floor apartment at 625, spray painting kitchen cabinets that sit on sheets of newspaper. He's inspecting the job, absently shaking the spray can he holds in his hand, when he notices the four men standing in the open doorway of the garage. He reaches for a rag, to wipe his hands with.

Now Nietfeldt creeps up the back stairs, followed by Fleischer. Man in the garage saw nothing, knew nothing, recognized no one, but he did say that "the two girls" were in the upstairs apartment *now*. Then asked them not to mess the place up.

Nietfeldt feels improbably serene, given his agitation earlier. His heart thuds in his chest at its normal rate. He holds his .38 in steady hands. The sound of his feet on the steps, the feel of the wood's slight give beneath them, reminds him faintly of summer, the beach, of steps climbing toward a boardwalk. At the landing between floors he pauses to look and listen. There's the sound of water running through pipes. He continues upward. As he approaches the back door of the apartment, it occurs to him, gazing at it from the extremely foreshortened perspective his position affords him, that there is something peculiar about the way the window in the door emits light. That is, it seems as if the door *actually were made of light*. These thoughts do not occur to him in words, and by the time he is ready to articulate them to himself, before he has a chance to dismiss them as mild hallucinations arising from lack of sleep, he has reached the upstairs landing and rapidly is assimilating the fact that the door *is* made of light. That is, the door is open. That is, he is staring directly into the eyes of a pretty Oriental woman who stands before a kitchen table. There's a writing tablet and a teacup on the table, and there's a lumpy purse there too. Who knows what could be in that. Nietfeldt brings the gun up. "Freeze!" he says. "FBI!" He moves into the apartment—and there *she* is, rising from the table, falling away, falling into the dark hallway, leaving him behind, leaving all of them behind again, and Nietfeldt feels a destitution, watching her disappear, like that of the world's most bereft lover. Suddenly he's filled with sadness, and a tremendous fatigue. His arms, holding out the pistol before him, feel as if they weighed a hundred pounds apiece.

"Freeze," he says. The word comes out like a dreamword. Icicles have formed on the letters of the word *freeze*.

Can he really be falling into the abyss of sleep, standing right here?

"Freeze," he says again, finding himself, "or I'll blow her fucking head off." He sights on the Oriental girl, who flinches, turning her eyes from him. Never shot anybody. Never liked guns. But the threat brings *her* back into view. Now Nietfeldt feels Fleischer moving behind him, past him, shouldering his way into the hall where she is. Does he hear her giggle? Then he hears the cuffs. The Oriental girl is still as a statue.

"Hands behind your head," says Nietfeldt, reaching for his own cuffs.

In the lumpy purse there's a loaded Colt Python. A Detective Special is in a pocketbook hanging from the back of a chair. The women lead them to more guns concealed throughout the apartment. When Nietfeldt and Fleischer begin to escort the two women down the stairs, *she* turns around and looks him in the eye.

"Could I please change my clothes, please?" she asks. "I wet in my pants when you guys came in."

THE SEDAN ARRIVES AT the Federal Building, slowing to a crawl as it proceeds into the delirium of light and noise that awaits it, then stopping. The expectant crowd turns at its appearance, and the sky is lit a thousand times, the sedan and its occupants baked flat in the cold light, the contours of things at the margins leaping in shadow; everything beyond the ardent focus of the uproar languishing in the negated colors of natural light and everyday darkness. At first Tania is frightened by the photographers, and Joan reaches for her with her manacled hands, soothing. The crowd engulfs the sedan, reporters hammering on its roof and fenders, hollering through the windows, and the photographers press up close, capturing the brilliant shadowless figures in the backseat, making fast those dazed faces that will exhibit the confirmation of any sin or virtue the picture editor chooses to assign to them, vivid and so beautifully *there*, aloof no longer.

It's all for her. The revelation comes gradually; she knows that she's become famous, but this? The car begins slowly to move forward, gently prodding the coruscating figures who gradually open up a narrow lane leading to the mouth of a dark tunnel that will take her to the future, and the parking garage. All for her—her own monumental meaning, whatever it is, shining brighter than the moon and stars. And so she smiles, receiving her public, instinctively fulfilling them, and as the famous face widens, opening to their scrutiny, there is hungry stirring outside, as though the true extent of the yearning for this particular smile, these particular teeth, had only now become clear, and when she raises her shackled hands, her right formed unmistakably into a fist, she is bathed in light again, waves of it that rise and fall, drenching the sedan and causing it to halt once more, polishing her bright with her own blank renown.

Let My Gun Sing
for the People

SARA JANE MOORE HOLDS the telephone receiver absently, cocked over her right shoulder, as if she were about to throw it. So Thomas Polhaus won't take her phone calls any longer. Mr. Big Shot.

She can tell when she is beginning to be considered a burden. This is the hard-won intuition of five deceased marriages. Here you are, trying your best, and sooner or later someone gets around to telling you that you won't do. Then all you can do is point an angry finger. At his full to bursting refrigerator that contained exactly one stick of margarine, a pound of spoiled bacon, and half a bottle of apple juice the first time you opened it. At the shiny floor and glistening toilet. At the savings passbook with its regular deposits earning 5 percent. Each a noticeable improvement but looks like someone got bored.

He doesn't take her calls and the Gal Friday type who answers is the kind who puts you on hold without asking. So you wait fruitlessly on the other end of a rude gesture. What it all adds up to is a bad taste in her mouth.

Some people change when they get their names in the paper.

Meanwhile over on Telegraph Avenue the other day she receives the total deep freeze from any acquaintance she happens to encounter. This is an exceptional first-time thing. She made it plain to Thomas Polhaus that their conversations, which as an informant she is perfectly entitled to, are confidential between the two of them alone. And Thomas Polhaus seems to agree; he nods or gestures in the commonly accepted affirmative manner, because what good is she to them if her credibility is damaged? No good at all. Naturally this comes before she is cut loose by the FBI. What they did was pump her, then cut her loose, then set her up. Sara Jane realizes that it serves their purposes to have her killed or silenced.

Wherever she goes they can find her. They set it up way back, collecting the information. Telephone number. Social Security number. Mother's maiden name. She sees at the bank the other day, that adorable little Filipina teller goes, "Now you can have your personal driver's license number printed directly on your checks." She laughed all the way out onto the street.

Good thing she has a gun.

Speaking of guns, she is flipping through some magazines today and there on the cover of *Newsweek* is a story about Lynette "Squeaky" Fromme, a devotee of Charles Manson's, who in Sacramento had wandered into the crowd engulfing President Ford with a high-caliber handgun and murderous intent and advised onlookers that "the country is in a mess. This man is not your president," before taking aim at the chief executive. The attempt was thwarted by a Secret Service man who astutely inserted the webbing between his thumb and forefinger in front of the hammer of the pistol as it fell, preventing the gun from firing. That must have smarted. Fromme later explained that she had "wanted to get some attention for Charlie and the girls."

Besides, here is an ad, for this package of frozen waffles, across which a banner runs, pledging "Improved Waffle Taste!" This is the sort of embedded, subliminal stupidity that colors everyone's book of days. You don't need to go any further if you're looking for a reason to overthrow the established order. Here it is. Waffles with improved waffle taste. Do they even hear what they're saying.

The *Newsweek* article is written by someone named Dan Russell. This is a name that rings a bell from the case of the Famous Fugitive. How could it, how can it be? She checks the date on the magazine: September 15. This is a clear message, planted in the magazine three days before the capture. It is for her, tentacular, linking the two cases, *directing* her.

What tends to happen when you no longer see people you've gotten used to seeing is you miss them. This is a fact of physical and cultural anthropology both.

She's talked to exactly one agent exactly one time since she's been trying to get ahold of Thomas Polhaus. An impatient type named Von Isenbarger. She has it written in a notebook. Whether this is a first and last name both, or just some lengthy last name, she isn't sure.

Funny she should have picked this particular magazine up today. The president is swinging through San Francisco tomorrow. She believes presidential assassination is a federal crime and the FBI would have jurisdiction.

She will see Thomas.

She will restore her reputation amid her friends and comrades.

She will draw a line, unmistakable, connecting the case, demarcating the old from the new. Fromme being the former and herself being the latter.

She will kill that bastard Ford.

Or maybe it's the Secret Service whose jurisdiction it is?

Sara Jane writes a poem to celebrate the event before it even happens. It just comes out of her, this must be what they mean by inspiration. Besides, somehow she doesn't think she'll have much time afterward.

> *Hold-Hold, still my hand.*
> *Steady my eye, chill my heart,*
> *And let my gun sing for the people.*
> *Scream their anger, cleanse with their hate,*
> *And kill this monster.*

Sounds like the beginning of something.

Why don't you go to the prison beauty shop?

—CATHERINE HEARST TO HER DAUGHTER PATRICIA,
AFTER THE LATTER'S ARREST,
CONCERNING THE CONDITION OF HER HAIR

My greatest trouble *is the present and the past, and I guess the future too.*

—PATRICIA HEARST,
RESPONDING TO A SENTENCE COMPLETION TEST,
CA. THE SAME PERIOD

AUTHOR'S NOTE

Fiction based on real events always risks appearing to be coy about its proximity to the actual, whether or not its author hews closely to the facts. Still, I thought in this case it might be of use to affirm that while many of the situations this novel depicts, and the people it portrays, are drawn from a well-documented episode in recent American history, I have disregarded the record whenever it's served my purpose to do so. Among many adulterations, I have, strictly according to my own lights, emphasized, diminished, conflated, and omitted incidents and individuals; I have frequently invented characters and incidents altogether; and I have occasionally changed the chronology of events and consciously indulged in anachronisms. I have freely included invented documents, newspaper articles, and the like alongside genuine ones. I have, through my characters and narrators, offered opinions or hypotheses that are entirely spurious when placed outside the invented context of the novel. In short, I exercised the novelist's right to avoid those things that did not interest me and to take imaginative liberties with those that did.

Accordingly, readers should note that while many of the characters in this book have counterparts in real life, their actions, thoughts, beliefs, personalities, and, certainly, legal and moral culpability as depicted here are, finally, the product of an author's imagination.

A note on sources: Many, if not most, of the sources dealing directly with the SLA that I reviewed were written while the case was ongoing in one sense or another and attempt to present factual accounts from a journalistic perspective. While these accounts provided a vivid glimpse of the mid-1970s to aid my own shaky memory, they've suffered from the passage of time in all the usual ways. Facts have been superseded by newer and more influential facts. The authors frequently bring to their material oddly insistent personal agendas, at once both tangential to and entangled with the larger subject, that persuasively demonstrated to me the narcotic allure of the SLA/Tania story and the ways in which people relate certain public events to their private lives. Finally, it should perhaps go without saying that both the relevancy of such matters and our way of thinking about them have drastically changed since I started writing in the fall of 2000.

One book that I found indispensable was Vin McLellan and Paul Avery's *The Voices of Guns* (New York: G. P. Putnam's Sons, 1977). Equally valuable were the lengthy articles by David Kohn and Howard Weir that appeared in *Rolling Stone* in 1975–76. Shana Alexander's *Anyone's Daughter* (New York: Viking, 1979), though it often careens into the personal in the manner described above, provides a thoughtful and candidly bemused look at the "establishment" take on home-grown radicalism and its consequences. Robert Brainard Pearsall's annotated compilation *The Symbionese Liberation Army: Documents and Communications* (Amsterdam: Rodolpi N.V., 1974) both collects those things and places them in welcome context. Patricia Campbell Hearst's memoir, *Every Secret Thing* (Garden City, N.Y.: Doubleday, 1982), and the LAPD's official report "The Symbionese Liberation Army in Los Angeles," while both somewhat self-serving, offer information unavailable elsewhere. Another book that was of particular help was Jeanne Wakatsuki Houston and James D. Houston's *Farewell to Manzanar* (New York: Bantam Books, 1974), an impressionistic look at the Japanese-American experience during and after World War II. Still other sources are acknowledged in passing within the novel.

As is my habit as a fiction writer, I conducted no fieldwork, archival research, or interviews toward the completion of this book. Seekers of documentary truth are gently encouraged to look elsewhere.

Among those on whose help, encouragement, advice, and support I relied I must acknowledge Ira Silverberg, Lorin Stein, Cary Goldstein, Bradford Morrow, Leon Friedman, Richard Wong, Gilbert Sorrentino, Sam Lipsyte, and especially my old friend and tutelary saint, Jonathan Lethem.

Of course many others provided aid and comfort to me during the writing of this book, and I hope I've managed to reciprocate when I could.